Lies & Hearts

A Lies, Secrets & Betrayal Romance Collection

Alison Reid

Lies & Hearts – A Lies, Secrets & Betrayal Romance Collection

by Alison Reid

ISBN: 978-1-7645079-2-9

First edition

Independently published

Introduction to...

Lies & Hearts

A Lies, Secrets & Betrayal Romance Collection

Welcome to **Lies & Hearts**—a collection of emotionally charged romances where secrets, misunderstandings, and betrayals threaten to keep true love out of reach.

In these standalone stories, strong-willed women collide with men who challenge their hearts in ways they never expected. From shocking revelations to forbidden desires, every tale explores the delicate balance between trust and temptation, heartbreak and hope, deception and redemption.

Each novel in this collection is a complete standalone romance, previously published individually, written in the spirit of classic Mills & Boon with a modern edge. Expect slow-burning passion, high emotional stakes, misunderstandings that push love to the limit, and alpha heroes whose hearts are as vulnerable as the women they fight to protect.

Inside these pages are stories of second chances, secret passions, and truths that can't stay hidden. There is no cheating, and every story delivers a guaranteed happily-ever-after.

Whether you're discovering these characters for the first time or returning to familiar favourites, **Lies & Hearts** invites you to sink into a binge-worthy collection where love survives even the deepest lies.

Enjoy the journey.

Table of Contents

A Billionaire for Christmas

Alison Reid

A complete standalone romance

Previously published individually

Chapter One

Christian Harrington adjusted the sharp cuff of his tailored tuxedo, the platinum link catching the ballroom lights like a sudden spark of lightning. His smile, flawless and practiced, slid into place—polished enough to satisfy the crowd, yet hollow at the edges. Flashbulbs erupted in a relentless storm, immortalising what was meant to be a triumphant moment: the Harrington heir, centre stage, announcing his engagement to society's most celebrated darling.

To the glittering crowd assembled in the Mayfair Hotel ballroom, the scene looked like a fairy tale. Champagne glasses chimed in silvery harmony, jewels scattered shards of light beneath the grand chandeliers, and every guest leaned forward with eager admiration. At Christian's side, Clarissa Ashford sparkled in a diamond-studded gown that shimmered like frozen water. Her manicured hand rested on his arm with deliberate possession, her beauty precise, her composure unshakable. Clarissa looked as though she had been groomed for this very moment: poised, commanding, untouchable—the kind of woman who knew the cost of everything, but the value of very little.

Inside, Christian's stomach tightened with every cheer, every toast, each subtle reminder that this performance was no longer an act—it was his future.

His grandfather's lawyer's voice echoed in his head with merciless clarity:

Marry before New Year's Eve. Remain married for five years. No infidelity. Shared household. Only then will you inherit Harrington & Co.

Billions. More than Harrods. An empire his grandfather had built with ruthless brilliance, guarded like a fortress, and handed down as both gift and punishment. And now all of it was chained to a woman who seemed to breathe applause as naturally as air.

Clarissa leaned toward him, her ruby mouth curving into a smile sharpened by calculation. "Smile, darling," she murmured, velvet over steel. "You wouldn't want the shareholders thinking you've been dragged to the altar."

Dragged? Christian's jaw flexed. Shackled was closer to the truth.

"Of course not," he replied smoothly, brushing a polite kiss against her cheek. Cameras erupted, devouring the image of Britain's most eligible bachelor—captured, claimed, and engaged.

Clarissa turned back to the crowd, her eyes sweeping the room like a general surveying her army. "They'll adore this," she whispered, triumphant. "The markets love stability. And once we're married, the Ashford and Harrington names together will be untouchable. Think of it—a dynasty. London will never stop talking about us."

Christian's gaze flicked to her profile, coldly perfect as sculpted marble. Not once had she spoken of love. This was not a marriage—it was a merger, a contract, a throne she intended to occupy.

A darker thought gnawed at him: his grandfather hadn't trusted him to grow up, to lead, to choose wisely. And now here he stood, hand in hand with a woman he didn't love, bartering his heart for an empire.

Yes, Christian had been wealthy long before this arrangement—tall, commanding, with the kind of presence that turned heads. Private jets, penthouse views, priceless art—he could buy almost anything. But Harrington & Co. was not just wealth. It was bloodline, legacy, the empire built by men whose ambition left no room for compromise. Letting it slip was unthinkable. And yet, as his eyes lingered on Clarissa—glittering, hollow, consuming—he wondered if the cost might not be measured in billions at all, but in something far greater: his freedom. Perhaps even his heart.

Henry Holloway's face surfaced in his mind. Henry, his closest friend since Eton, who had found the one thing Christian had never known—love that was fierce, messy, unpolished, and entirely real. Henry's wife, Mary, wanted no titles, no fortune. She wanted only Henry. And now, expecting their first child, they radiated a joy Christian could not counterfeit.

Whenever he visited, he saw it in the way Henry's shoulders eased when Mary entered a room, in how her laughter softened every sharp edge of his day. Their love was not a performance—it lived, it breathed, it consumed. And Christian knew, with an ache that clawed through him, that he would trade every boardroom, every title, every diamond—if he could only have that.

Clarissa drifted across the ballroom, flaunting the enormous engagement ring she had demanded, her hand raised at the perfect angle for the chandeliers to worship. A jewel, yes, but more press release than promise.

"Required," she had called it.

Required for whom? For investors? For the gossip pages? For herself—proof to admire in every mirror?

The answer was as bitter as the champagne on his tongue.

His gaze cut through the glamour, the glitter, the endless music. Clarissa shone like a star, radiant, untouchable—and Christian felt like the condemned man at his own execution.

"Christian."

He turned, and for the first time that evening, warmth cracked through his mask. "Henry. Mary."

He embraced Henry like a brother, pressed a kiss to Mary's cheek, his smile softening at the sight of her hand resting protectively over her rounded belly. She glowed—not from diamonds, but from something far rarer.

"You look well," Henry said, though his eyes searched deeper. After a pause, he glanced toward Clarissa, then back. "Well… perhaps not entirely well. You look like a man walking to the gallows."

Christian gave a dry laugh. "You don't mince words."

"Never did," Henry replied, his gaze steady. "Tell me I'm wrong. Because from where I stand, she's already wearing the crown, and you—you look like you're bracing for execution."

Mary's touch was gentle on Henry's arm, her expression tender. "We only want you to be happy."

Christian's throat tightened. His eyes caught on Henry's hand sliding protectively over Mary's waist, a gesture as natural as breathing. Love, simple and unshakable.

Henry leaned close, lowering his voice. "Don't do it. Not for the company, not for the billions. It isn't worth it. She isn't worth it. If you marry for the wrong reasons, it will eat you alive."

Christian swallowed hard, forcing a smile that didn't reach his eyes. "I don't have a choice."

"There's always a choice," Henry countered, his voice firm. His eyes flicked toward Clarissa—laughing too brightly at something she hadn't even heard. "You deserve better than this. Better than to chain yourself to ice. Better than to sell your heart for gold."

Christian said nothing. He couldn't. Clarissa, radiant and ruthless, beckoned him with a triumphant smile, already tugging invisible strings.

And for the first time, he admitted it: *Henry was right.*

A familiar wave of expensive perfume swept over him before he could answer. Clarissa materialised at his side, glittering with the full arsenal of diamonds, beads, and practiced charm, as though the very ballroom revolved around her.

"There you are, darling," she cooed, sliding her hand possessively through his arm. Her dazzling smile never touched her eyes. She turned to Henry and Mary, her tone syrupy with disdain. "Henry. Mary. How... quaint to see you both here."

Mary, gracious as ever, offered a gentle smile. "Congratulations, Clarissa. The ring is beautiful."

"Isn't it?" Clarissa lifted her hand, angling the enormous stone toward the chandelier light until it fractured into a thousand blinding shards. "Christian insisted only flawless would do. Appearances matter, after all. A woman in your... condition"—her gaze dipped to Mary's belly, her brow arching ever so slightly— "might not have much use for jewels, but in society, they're indispensable."

The muscle in Christian's jaw twitched. Mary's smile faltered only for a moment before she straightened, her dignity intact. Henry's arm curled protectively around his wife's waist, his eyes darkening.

"Some women," Henry said, his voice pointed, "don't need jewels to prove their worth."

Clarissa's laugh was airy, dismissive. "Of course. Of course. But still—people talk. They always do. Fortunately, Christian and I understand what's required to maintain appearances."

Her words were daggers wrapped in silk. Christian caught the flicker of discomfort in Mary's eyes, the heat simmering in Henry's, and a wave of shame coiled in his chest.

Clarissa tugged lightly on his arm, her diamond brushing his sleeve like a brand. "Come, darling. The investors are waiting, and we can't afford to seem neglectful."

She didn't wait for his reply. She never did. With a radiant smile, she led him back into the sea of admirers.

Christian glanced over his shoulder. Henry's gaze followed him, steady and unyielding. It carried no judgment, only a plea: *don't do this.*

For the first time that evening, doubt crept in. The weight of the night, the charade of it all, pressed against his chest until he could barely breathe. Maybe he couldn't go through with it. Maybe it wasn't worth it.

Later, in the hush of the limousine, the night pressed in like a weight. The ballroom's laughter still echoed faintly in his ears, but already it felt like a hollow performance he'd been forced to endure. Clarissa leaned into him, her head brushing his shoulder. He allowed it, though the gesture stirred nothing but a faint irritation.

When they reached her apartment, she turned with a practiced pout. "I thought we were going to your penthouse."

Christian shook his head, exhaustion roughening his tone. "No. I'm too tired, Clarissa. It's been a long evening."

Her lips pursed, irritation flashing before she smoothed it into a sigh. "Fine. When will I see you? Don't forget we leave for St. Moritz in two weeks. I'll need to shop for the trip."

A dull throb of resentment flickered in his chest. He'd agreed months ago, before the funeral, before this engagement had become a noose. Now, the thought of being trapped with her in another gilded cage made his stomach turn.

They hadn't been intimate since his grandfather's funeral four weeks earlier. The last time had been mechanical, an obligation performed without desire. Since then, he hadn't even tried. Clarissa, of course, seemed unfazed. She was adept at navigating his moods, taking what she wanted, and surrendering nothing. If keeping him distant meant keeping him compliant, she was content with that arrangement.

"Well—goodnight, darling," Christian said, brushing a perfunctory kiss across her cheek. His lips barely grazed her skin, the gesture formal, detached.

The chauffeur opened her door. Christian waited, posture stiff, until she stepped out.

"I'll call you," she said lightly, as if their engagement were a business deal awaiting confirmation.

"Yes. Sleep well," he replied, already retreating into the shadows of the leather seat.

The door shut softly. The limousine slid into the blur of London's night, headlights scattering across wet pavement. Christian leaned back, closing his eyes against the city lights streaking past. Soon, he would no longer be able to drop her at her apartment and retreat into the solitude of his penthouse. Soon, they would share a home—her hand in his, her shadow in every room.

The wedding was set for December 28th, three days before the deadline. A grand society affair, dictated by Clarissa in every detail: flowers, photographers, the endless guest list. Each decision cost him money. Each demand cost him something far more precious.

Clarissa thrived on spectacle, on performance, on the admiration of strangers. And he—he was surrendering. Piece by piece, smile by smile, he was handing over his freedom, his peace, his very sense of self.

For all his wealth, for all his power, Christian Harrington had never felt more powerless.

And as the limousine carried him through the glittering city, one thought seared through the fog of duty and resentment:

He could endure the cage. He could endure the show. But what he was sacrificing—love, freedom, the quiet chance at happiness—he might never reclaim.

Chapter Two

Eliza Preston sat frozen in the small room just off the altar, the walls of the modest Queensland church seeming to press in around her. The morning sunlight slanted through the narrow windows, dust motes drifting lazily in its glow, but she barely saw them. Her bridesmaid, Sally, flitted nervously, fussing with loose strands of hair and tugging at the folds of Eliza's gown, but Eliza hardly noticed. Her gaze was fixed on the polished wooden floor, her hands trembling in her lap.

This was supposed to be her wedding day. By now, she should have been standing beside her fiancé, Brad Clarke, exchanging vows, smiling at him while the congregation looked on. But Brad wasn't there.

It had been Sally who received the message. With a trembling voice and eyes full of pity, she delivered it almost apologetically: "Eliza… he says he won't be coming."

The words fell like a hammer blow. Won't be coming. Not delayed. Not confused. Not even an excuse. Just a bald, merciless truth—he wasn't coming.

And then, as faint whispers of gossip drifted in from beyond the door, the full humiliation cut through her. Brad had left. Not just the wedding—but her. He had run back to his ex-girlfriend, Clair. The same Clair he had once dismissed as "just a friend," the woman he swore was firmly in his past. The man she trusted, the man she had built her future around, had chosen someone else.

Her stomach knotted, disbelief and rage crashing against heartbreak. How could he? After all the promises, the laughter, the carefully woven dreams. Memories once sweet now turned bitter, like ash on her tongue.

Sally hovered at her side, unsure whether to speak. "Eliza… maybe you should go out there," she whispered gently, almost pleading.

Eliza shook her head, breaths shallow, chest tight. "No… I can't," she murmured, her voice so faint it seemed fragile enough to splinter. Her knees threatened to give way. She wanted to scream, to run, to tear the satin dress from her body—but she couldn't move. Each heartbeat mocked her with the cruel reminder that Brad Clarke had chosen Clair over her.

In that small, sunlit room, surrounded by the remnants of a wedding that would never be, icy reality settled over her. "We're supposed to be married by now," she whispered, disbelief trembling through every syllable.

Sally's eyes softened with sympathy. "I know, honey," she murmured, squeezing Eliza's cold hand.

Eliza let out a hollow laugh, sharp and bitter. "This wedding cost me a small fortune." Modest by society's standards, yes, but she had paid for almost everything herself, convinced it was the first step into a life they would share. Brad had promised that once they married, everything would be theirs, joined and whole. She scoffed, the sound echoing emptily off the church walls. What a cruel joke.

Part of the money had come from her inheritance—the modest sum her parents had left after the car crash that stole them from her. She had saved it carefully, guarded it like something sacred. Now it was gone, swallowed up by flowers, linens, and a dress that would never walk her down an aisle. A bitter pill, coated in betrayal.

Her mind turned to Brad and Clair. She could almost picture them now: Brad grinning like a fool, Clair preening in some boutique hotel, playing the part of the triumphant lover. A dark smile twisted her lips. "Enjoy your little reunion, Brad," she muttered under her breath. "Tell Clair I said congratulations… on stealing my fiancé and my money."

Then, suddenly, anger surged. She pushed to her feet, wobbling slightly. "Get me out of here."

Sally slipped an arm around her shoulders, steadying her, guiding her to the waiting limousine. Sunlight glinted off its polished surface, cruelly bright, mirroring the storm in her chest.

Inside, Eliza traced her fingers along the smooth leather, her mind spinning. St. Moritz. That had been Brad's choice for their honeymoon. He loved skiing: the slopes, the chalets, the crisp mountain air. She had never skied in her life, but she agreed, imagining herself wrapped in wool and laughing as he caught her falls. His fantasy, not hers. And now he was gone, chasing Clair instead.

She pressed her forehead to the glass, watching the streets blur past. "Everything I own is already in England except for my honeymoon suitcase," she whispered.

Sally squeezed her hand. "I know, honey."

Eliza thought of the tickets, the crisp snow, the fear of standing on skis with no idea how to move. Brad should have been there—guiding, steadying, holding her. Instead, he was with Clair. Their future together crumbled like frost in the sun.

A fierce spark rose in her chest. Maybe St. Moritz could still be hers—a honeymoon gone rogue. Maybe she would take this holiday for herself alone, throw herself down the slopes, let the cold winds strip away the last of Brad's betrayal.

Eliza straightened, wiping her eyes. "At least I have the tickets. I'll go to St. Moritz, then on to England. I already have a job lined up."

Sally frowned. "Are you sure, Eliza? Going alone… it's a big step."

"What choice do I have?" Eliza's voice was firm now. "The lease is in my name. It's paid for two months. If I hate it, I'll come home when it ends."

By late morning, Sally had brought her back to her modest home, the quiet Queensland street oddly calm after the chaos of the church. Inside, her parents waited, worry etched into their faces.

"I'm so sorry, Eliza," Jenny Watkins said gently. "We didn't know what to do."

Her husband, Martin, nodded, his voice low. "We should have stopped him somehow…" His words faltered.

Eliza gave a dry, humourless laugh. "There was nothing anyone could have done. He made his choice." Her mind flicked to the envelope with her honeymoon tickets and spending money. If Brad had taken them… she pictured him whisking Clair away in her place, the image so vile it made her stomach turn.

Upstairs, Sally helped her out of the heavy dress. The satin felt like shackles now, every layer a reminder of betrayal. "What should I do with it?" Sally asked cautiously.

Eliza stared for a long moment, then shrugged, her mouth curving in a dark smile. "Burn it. I don't care."

Sally exhaled, relieved. She understood—the dress was no longer fabric, but a symbol of promises broken.

Later, Eliza sank into an armchair in the Watkins' cozy living room. The aroma of coffee wrapped around her, warm and steady. Sally perched beside her, her parent's opposite, watching with quiet concern.

Jenny hesitated, cup in hand. "Eliza, are you sure about Europe? England? Alone, it's… a lot."

Eliza lifted her cup, the warmth grounding her. A wry smile tugged at her lips, steel beneath the softness. "I'll be fine. If England doesn't work out, I'll come back when the lease ends. But I can't curl up and hide just because Brad decided I wasn't enough."

Jenny's worry lingered, but she nodded.

Eliza's smile grew, a touch defiant. "I can handle it. I won't let one man ruin everything I've worked for—or everything I still want."

Sally squeezed her hand. "That's the Eliza I know."

Martin raised his cup in a quiet toast. "To new adventures—and to making them yours."

Eliza took a long sip, the coffee rich and steady. For the first time all day, excitement sparked beneath the grief. St. Moritz awaited—snow, slopes, and a holiday entirely her own. And after that, England. A new chapter. Written her way.

Eliza clutched her passport and the neatly stacked flight tickets Sally had organised, staring down at the itinerary that looked both impossibly long and impossibly thrilling. Brisbane to Zurich. Twenty-four hours of airports, flights, and a layover in Dubai before she would finally set foot in Europe. Her stomach fluttered, part nerves, part excitement. It was her first time travelling internationally alone, and every anxious heartbeat reminded her of the disaster she had only just escaped.

For a fleeting moment, Brad crept into her mind—probably lounging somewhere with Clair, smug and careless. She tightened her grip on the tickets. No. This trip wasn't his. It was hers. Her suitcase held not only clothes for St. Moritz but the carefully counted spending money Brad had once promised to use to dazzle her—or more likely, squander on himself. The thought made her shiver. At least now, every cent was hers.

When she finally landed in Zurich, she stepped onto the crisp pavement with awe and trepidation. The train awaited—a winding, scenic journey through the Swiss Alps: Zurich to Chur, then onward on the Rhaetian Railway to St. Moritz. Three to four hours of snow-tipped mountains, glacial lakes, and forests dusted with ice. Each turn of the track carried her farther from the humiliation in Queensland and closer to a world of mountains, escape, and maybe—just maybe—freedom.

For the first time since the wedding debacle, a spark of anticipation stirred in her chest. She was alone, yes, but for once she was choosing herself. Avalanches, icy slopes, clumsy skis—let them come. St. Moritz would be her playground, her sanctuary, her "honeymoon gone rogue."

When the train pulled into St. Moritz, the peaks glittered in the late afternoon sun like cut crystal. Eliza stepped onto the platform, her boots crunching against the icy cobblestones. Cold air bit at her cheeks, sharp and exhilarating, carrying the scents of pine, wood smoke, and snow. She pulled her coat tighter and smiled. She had left her old life behind—if only for a while.

A short shuttle ride delivered her to the chalet. The reception glowed with polished wood and bowls of fresh flowers, the staff brisk yet friendly, their German- and Italian-accented English filling the air. Eliza approached the desk, fumbling with her passport and tickets, nerves prickling after the long journey.

"Good afternoon. Welcome to Chalet Edelweiss. Do you have a reservation?" the receptionist asked warmly.

"Yes… yes, I do," Eliza stammered, passing her documents across the desk. For a moment, she faltered. The booking had been made months ago, back when she had expected to arrive with Brad. Her heart twisted. Then she steadied herself. "Eliza Clarke," she said firmly, giving the name she was meant to take.

The receptionist typed, then smiled and slid a keycard across the counter. "Room 212, second floor. Enjoy your stay, Mrs. Clarke."

Eliza's fingers closed around the key, a shiver running through her—not from the cold, but from the surreal strangeness of checking into a room under a name she didn't yet own. Clarke. Not today. Today she was still Eliza Preston—but tomorrow, for appearances, she would be Clarke. A small part of her winced, but another, stronger part—the part Brad had underestimated—thrilled at the defiance.

Balancing her suitcase in one hand and her overnight bag in the other, she navigated the gleaming foyer toward the lifts. The scent of pine and firewood wrapped around her, grounding her, but all she could focus on was not dropping her bags—or herself. Then—a soft impact. Someone brushed against her, and she stumbled.

"Oh! I'm so sorry," she blurted, her Australian vowels sharp with panic. She looked up—and froze.

He was tall, impeccably dressed, dark hair falling across his forehead with effortless precision. His eyes met hers—calm, steady—and for a heartbeat, everything else disappeared.

Christian looked down—and froze. She was beautiful in a way that stole the air from him. Dark hair spilling to her waist, green eyes wide with embarrassment, a figure unpolished yet impossibly alive. Juggling a suitcase and overnight bag, she looked unsteady, and yet astonishingly composed.

"No, no. My fault entirely," he replied, calm, measured—but for a heartbeat, he forgot everything else—the slopes, Clarissa, the calculated perfection of his life.

They lingered, caught in a moment neither had expected. She noticed the faint curve of his lips, the quiet assurance in his stance, the way his gaze held hers without judgment. It was nothing—just an accident. And yet it felt like something. Her cheeks warmed. She tucked a stray strand of hair behind her ear, painfully aware of how flustered she must look.

"Th-thank you," she managed, tugging her suitcase forward, desperate to appear composed even as her pulse raced.

Eliza shook her head as she reached the lift. Foolish. She wasn't here to notice men. But deep down, she couldn't deny the faint spark of curiosity unfurling in her chest. Perhaps this "honeymoon gone rogue" held more surprises than she'd imagined.

By the time she reached the second floor, her arms ached from the bags, but she pushed on until she found Room 212. Sliding the card into the reader, she heard the beep and stepped inside.

The room was an alpine dream. Polished beams crossed the ceiling, honeyed wood panelled the walls. A thick wool rug softened the floor beneath her boots. To the left, a stone-framed fireplace waited to be lit, promising warmth on frosty nights. Fur throws draped across a deep sofa, and a small writing desk stood ready for plans and thoughts.

Floor-to-ceiling windows unveiled St. Moritz rooftops dusted in snow, jagged peaks gleaming beyond. Ski lifts in the distance creaked steadily toward the glowing summits.

She set her bags aside and inhaled deeply. The faint scent of pine and wood polish cleared her chest. Running her hand across the fur throw, she let out a small, incredulous laugh.

"This is really mine… even if just for a few days," she whispered.

The heartbreak and betrayal back in Queensland felt far away now, blurred by snow and silence. She catalogued the details—the antique lamp, folded towels, the coffee station with mugs stamped St. Moritz. Finally, she sank onto the bed, exhaling long and deep.

She had made it. Alone, yes. But free—at least for now.

Chapter Three

Christian had been distracted, thoughts split between the promise of the slopes above and the taut, unrelenting presence of Clarissa. Two days in the chalet, and all she had done was hold court at the bar—dazzling, distant, untouchable—while he lingered in the background, restless, quietly suffocating. He longed for solitude, even a sliver of it.

He watched the green-eyed beauty go, faintly smiling before he could stop himself. She was bright, fragile, alive—and for reasons he didn't yet understand, she lingered in his chest even as she moved toward the lifts.

For the first time in days, Clarissa seemed irrelevant. Someone—someone like this—might awaken something in him that wealth, duty, and perfection never could.

Desire? He understood. Attraction? He had been surrounded by beauty all his life. But this was different. Not lust, not the calculated assessment of worth. It was a spark—strange, inconvenient, rare—that burned quietly in his chest.

He didn't even know her name. A woman with dark hair and green eyes who had collided with him in the hotel foyer, who had looked at him without calculation, without hunger for recognition. Just flustered apology, a faint blush, and something disarmingly unguarded that left him unsettled.

It shouldn't have mattered. It shouldn't have lingered. Yet the echo of that brief encounter hummed beneath his skin long after she had gone.

Christian forced himself to focus, dragging his mind back to the reasons he was here—the slopes, the appearances, the endless game of managing Clarissa's moods. Clarissa, who at that very moment was almost certainly holding court at the bar, her diamond flashing, her laughter loud, her presence impossible to ignore. Clarissa, who demanded everything and gave nothing. Clarissa, who symbolised obligation, empire, legacy—all the shackles his grandfather's will had bound him with.

And yet… it wasn't Clarissa who was on his mind. It was the woman in the foyer. The one who blushed. Who looked at him as though she saw not a name, not a fortune, not an heir—but a man.

He shook his head sharply, tugging at the cuff of his sleeve as though the gesture could steady him, banish the absurd pull in his chest. She was no one. Just another guest. A fleeting encounter.

And still… she remained.

The next morning, Christian rose early, grateful for an excuse to escape the suffocating air of the chalet. The sky was washed in pale gold as he stepped into the gondola, the cable car lifting steadily above the glittering slopes. The town below shrank with every passing moment, chalets and pines reduced to toys scattered at the foot of the mountains. The higher he went, the freer his chest felt, the alpine air sweeping through him like a tonic.

Thank God Clarissa had refused to ski.

"I don't like how my nose goes all red," she had declared the day before, lounging like a queen on a velvet chair in the bar. She had smoothed her glossy hair, her diamond flashing firelight, and looked at him as though the matter required no argument.

Christian had stared, incredulous. "Then why organise this trip?"

Her laugh—light, brittle, rehearsed—still echoed in his ears. "Because it's expected Christian. You must know that. St. Moritz is the place. The paparazzi have already taken photos of us together. That's all that matters."

That had been the end of it. No mention of the slopes, the mountains, the freedom waiting beyond the chalet walls. For Clarissa, the trip was never about snow or adventure—it was about being seen.

So now, as the gondola rose into brilliance, Christian felt only relief. Clarissa was back at the bar, holding her court, and for a few blessed hours, he was free.

At the summit, he stepped into the blaze of morning. Snow stretched boundless, peaks carved sharp against an unbroken blue sky. Skiers darted down the slopes, laughter and shouts scattering on the wind. He adjusted his gloves, his body thrumming with anticipation.

On the mountain, there were no contracts. No obligations. No Clarissa. Only the hiss of skis, the rush of speed, the sting of cold against his face. For a man defined by control, the mountain was release.

Yet even as he tightened his bindings, memory intruded. A woman in the foyer—dark hair, green eyes, that blush. He shouldn't still be thinking of her. And yet he was. Absurdly, he even wondered if she, too, might be among those waiting at the top of the run.

He set his jaw, pushed off with his poles, and let gravity claim him. The snow hissed beneath him, the wind tore at him, and for the first time in months, he felt like himself. Not the Harrington heir. Not Clarissa's trophy. Not the man shackled by a legacy.

Just a man, carving down a mountain, chasing freedom.

On the other side of the resort, Eliza was having a very different morning.

She stood awkwardly at the base of the beginner slope, bundled in rented ski gear that felt both too tight and impossibly bulky. The boots pinched her toes, the skis dragged against the snow, and the poles kept slipping through her gloved hands. She must have looked ridiculous compared to the graceful figures gliding past her, carving arcs with effortless ease. But she reminded herself—it was her trip, her "honeymoon gone rogue," and she would not let a pair of sticks strapped to her feet defeat her. Not today.

"Just… stand up straight. Easy," she muttered under her breath, planting one ski, then the other, wobbling like a newborn calf. The icy wind bit her cheeks, the powdery snow crunched beneath her skis, and a humbling awareness of her utter inexperience settled over her. A group of children zipped past, their laughter tinkling in the crisp air as their instructor called encouragement. Eliza gritted her teeth, forcing herself to focus.

She pushed forward—and promptly toppled into the snow with an unceremonious thud. Snow sprayed her scarf, stung her cheeks, and left her blinking through a flurry of white. She groaned, then let out a choked laugh. "Brilliant, Eliza. Absolutely brilliant," she muttered, voice trembling with a mix of frustration and relief.

With effort, she hauled herself upright, brushing snow from her jacket, tucking rogue strands of hair beneath her beanie. She wasn't graceful, and she wasn't fast, but she was determined. Step by wobbling step, she began inching down the shallow slope, heart pounding with both terror and exhilaration.

Despite the cold biting at her nose, despite the humiliation of falling in front of a dozen strangers, Eliza felt something shift inside her. For the first time since Brad had abandoned her, she wasn't crying or raging, wasn't drowning in heartbreak—she was laughing. Clumsy, breathless laughter, carried away on the alpine air, leaving her chest strangely light.

It wasn't freedom yet. But maybe, just maybe, it was the first small step toward it.

She slid to a shaky but triumphant stop at the bottom of the beginner's run. Legs burning, breath short and frosty, hair escaping her beanie in wild strands— she had done it. One full run without falling. Laughter bubbled up, warm and unguarded. She felt lighter than she had since Brad's message had shattered her wedding day.

Eliza unclipped her skis, wobbling as she lifted them under one arm. Triumph quickly gave way to the ache in her legs and the awkward weight of her gear.

Balancing skis, poles, and her own unsteady body was harder than she'd anticipated—and then it happened.

She collided hard with someone coming from the opposite direction.

"Oh—sorry!" she blurted, skis tilting dangerously.

A strong hand caught her elbow before she could topple. She looked up—and froze.

Him. The man from the foyer.

Christian's dark eyes met hers, assessing, steady. A faint smile curved his lips—calm, effortless, confident. "Careful," he said smoothly, his voice low and cultured, yet edged with a warmth that softened it. "The slopes take enough victims without adding the walk back."

Her cheeks flushed, the cold forgotten for a moment. "I'm really sorry," she stammered, juggling skis and poles as though they had conspired against her.

His smile deepened—not mocking, but faintly amused. "It's fine. Honestly. Looks like you survived your battle out there."

For a heartbeat, neither moved. Snow swirled lazily around them, glinting in the sunlight. The world seemed to narrow—just the two of them standing in a quiet pocket of cold air and something unspoken. The faint spark from yesterday flared again, sharper now, tugging at something deep in both of them.

Eliza gave a nervous laugh, breaking the spell. "Barely," she admitted, adjusting her grip on her skis. "I should... before I drop these and cause an accident."

Christian stepped back, giving her space, though his gaze lingered as she moved past. He should have returned his attention to the slopes, to the rhythm and precision he usually demanded of himself, but his focus refused to shift. There was something about her—bright green eyes still wide with surprise, pink cheeks flushed from the cold, a few dark strands escaping her beanie to catch the light—that held him still.

He'd seen hundreds of women like Clarissa—perfect, polished, practiced. But this one... she was unguarded. Real. The kind of woman who blushed when she laughed and meant every apology. It shouldn't have mattered, yet it did.

Eliza could feel his eyes on her as she walked toward the ski racks, her pulse thrumming faster than it should. She told herself it was nothing—just politeness, just the rush of embarrassment—but something about him lingered. There had been a charge in that look, a spark that warmed her in a way no amount of ski gear could.

Christian adjusted his gloves, trying to shake it off. He had somewhere to be—Clarissa would be waiting at the chalet bar, impatient and exacting as ever—but the idea of leaving suddenly felt… wrong. For the first time in years, he found himself wishing for a delay, a reason to stay.

Eliza set her skis in the rack and glanced back once, unable to resist. He was still there—tall, self-assured, the wind stirring his hair as he looked down the slope. Their eyes met for half a second—brief, accidental, electric.

She smiled faintly and turned away, her heart fluttering.

And as Christian watched her disappear into the crowd of skiers, a tiny flicker of curiosity, intrigue, something unnameable, clung to him like a shadow at the edge of his mind, refusing to be ignored. For the first time in what felt like forever, Christian Harrington realised, with a mixture of surprise and something almost thrilling, that he might not want it to go away.

Chapter Four

It had been two days since Christian had seen her—the woman with dark hair and green eyes who had collided with him in the foyer, whose startled laugh and unguarded gaze had lodged itself in his chest. Two days. And every day since, he found himself scanning the chalet, the slopes, the cafés, the gondolas, half-expecting her to appear from the crowd—bundled in rented ski gear or brushing snow from her jacket. But she never did.

He told himself it was madness. A fleeting moment, a random collision, nothing more than a polite encounter. And yet, try as he might, he could not stop thinking about her. The memory of her nervous smile, the flush on her cheeks, the determined tilt of her shoulders—it haunted him. Every time he closed his eyes, he saw her standing there on the snow, juggling skis and poles, and impossibly, it made his chest tighten.

The night before, during dinner with Clarissa, the distraction had been painfully obvious. He barely touched his meal, his fork idly pushing food around his plate, his gaze constantly drifting—to the window, the slopes beyond, anywhere but the chandelier-lit bar and Clarissa's practiced charm. She noticed, of course. Women like her always did.

"Christian," she said sharply, leaning across the table, her diamond ring catching the candlelight like a warning beacon. "Are you even listening to me? You've been… distant. Distracted. Honestly, you must make more of an effort. This is St. Moritz, the press, the other guests—they're all watching. You can't just… drift away into space."

He offered a measured nod, murmured that he was fine, but every word rang hollow. She didn't understand—couldn't understand. The distraction wasn't her, and it wasn't the slopes, the luxury, or the impeccably orchestrated life around him. It was her. That woman. That fleeting, impossible, utterly unaccountable pull lodged in his chest and mind, invading every quiet moment, every thought.

He had even indulged in private fantasies, recalling the curve of her shoulders, the way her green eyes widened in surprise, the faint blush colouring her cheeks. He tried to dismiss it, telling himself it was nothing—after all, he hadn't had sex in nearly two months. And yet, the memory of her, so startlingly alive in his imagination, stirred him in ways he could not control, no matter how hard he tried.

Now, as he zipped his jacket, adjusted his gloves, and prepared for another morning on the slopes, the thought nagged at him like a pulse he could not silence. She was out there somewhere. Perhaps skiing, perhaps lost in her own thoughts. Perhaps unaware of the effect she had left behind. And yet, he could not shake the hope, however irrational, that their paths might cross again.

Madness. Obsession. Curiosity. He didn't care what it was called. All he knew was that Christian Harrington—a man who controlled empires and lives with the precision of a surgeon—had never been distracted like this before. Not by scandal, not by wealth, not by desire. It was her. And she had him completely, irreversibly off balance.

Eliza had spent the last two days navigating the beginner slopes, wobbling, falling, and laughing at herself in equal measure. Each tumble had been a lesson, each scrape of snow a small victory. Slowly, almost imperceptibly, she began to feel the skis obeying her rather than the other way around. Muscle memory was forming, balance improving, and for the first time, she felt a tentative confidence—enough to consider something she never would have imagined two days ago: the higher slopes.

The ski lift loomed ahead, its mechanical hum both intimidating and exhilarating. She adjusted her beanie, tugged at her gloves, and drew a deep breath, letting the crisp mountain air fill her lungs. The gondola would carry her far above the nursery slopes, where seasoned skiers swooped gracefully, carving arcs into untouched snow. Her stomach fluttered with a mixture of fear and excitement. She couldn't deny it—she was nervous. Very nervous. But beneath the nerves thrummed a quiet thrill, a pulse of anticipation that made her heart beat faster.

As she stepped into the lift, the cable groaned under her weight, lifting her steadily into the sky. The view unfolded beneath her: snow-blanketed peaks glittering in the morning sun; chalets clustered like tiny toys in the valley; ski runs winding like ribbons across the mountainside. The world below felt impossibly small—and impossibly far from the disaster she had escaped. The wedding, Brad, Clair—all of it shrank in comparison to the grandeur and beauty surrounding her.

For the first time in days, Eliza felt free. Free of heartbreak, free of expectation, free to stumble, to rise, to learn, to try. The wind whipped against her face, crisp and biting, carrying away the weight of the past week. She let herself savour a small, private thrill, a spark of joy that belonged entirely to her. Maybe, just maybe, this solo adventure—her "honeymoon gone rogue"—was exactly the escape she needed.

The ski lift groaned softly as it reached the top, depositing her onto the narrow ridge. Snow crunched beneath her rented boots. Eliza drew a deep breath, chest tightening with anticipation and something that felt a lot like fear. The slope stretched before her, smooth and glittering under the morning sun, glistening like a sheet of crystal. Her skis felt heavy and foreign, the poles unwieldy in her gloved hands.

She hesitated. Maybe this was a bad idea. Maybe she should have stayed on the beginner slope, taking it slow and safe. The lift could carry her back down at any time. But no—she squared her shoulders, forced herself to breathe steadily, and whispered, "I'm not scared."

Slowly, cautiously, she pushed off. Her skis bit into the snow with a tentative hiss, wobbling beneath her weight. Step by careful step, she began to descend, eyes darting to maintain balance, heart racing with terror and exhilaration alike. The crisp alpine air burned her lungs, and for the first few moments, she thought she might topple at any second.

Then it happened. A sudden gust of wind swept across the ridge, heavier than anything she had felt on the beginner slopes. Powdery snow erupted into the air, stinging her cheeks, coating her goggles, briefly blinding her. Her stomach lurched as her skis wobbled beneath her, threatening to cross, and she lost the rhythm she had been building. She tried to steady herself, planting her poles, but the wind pressed against her with relentless force, tipping her off balance.

Panic prickled along her spine. Her first confident descent—her moment of triumph—was slipping away. The slope suddenly felt impossibly steep, every movement uncertain. She fought to stay upright, but each turn sent a fresh spray of snow in her face, and the skis beneath her skidded dangerously. Her breaths came fast and shallow, ragged from exertion and fear, and for the first time, she questioned her decision to leave the beginner slope.

Eliza's heart hammered as she zigzagged, trying to regain control. Her muscles screamed with tension, every joint taut as she leaned forward and shifted her weight, desperate to keep her momentum. But the gusts weren't letting up, and the slope ahead seemed to stretch endlessly—a wall of white and cold.

For a brief, disorienting moment, she froze mid-turn, skis threatening to slide out from under her completely. She imagined herself tumbling, helpless, alone, swallowed by the mountain's raw power. Her small victory of freedom teetered on the edge of disaster.

And yet—even as adrenaline surged and fear tightened around her chest—a spark of exhilaration pulsed through her. She was testing herself, pushing against limits she hadn't known she could face. Terrified, yes—but alive. For the first time in days, her pulse raced not from heartbreak, not from betrayal, but from the unpredictable, thrilling challenge of standing on her own, teetering on the edge of mastery—and just barely holding on.

The wind tore across the mountains, a keening howl slicing through the frozen air and whipping snow into jagged, blinding swirls. Christian tightened his gloves, squinting against the powdery veil, scanning the slope for movement. He had been ready to descend like every other guest, chasing the crisp thrill of speed, when something caught his eye.

A figure. Struggling. Skis splayed, arms flailing, wobbling in an unsteady rhythm that made his chest tighten. He couldn't immediately place her, but the helplessness in her stance tugged at something deep inside him. Normally, protocol—and the urge to maintain control—would dictate he let her manage herself, that he skied on. But he couldn't. Not when she was so clearly out of her depth, battling both slope and wind.

Christian pushed off, carving down with practiced precision. Snow hissed beneath his skis, each turn sharpening his focus. Adrenaline pumped through his veins as the wind screamed in his ears. Then came the rumble—not distant, not harmless, but low and menacing, vibrating through the mountains like a living thing. Snow tore from a ridge above, a cascading wave of white powder spilling down the slope with frightening speed.

"Shit," he muttered, pivoting toward the struggling skier. The avalanche wasn't massive, but it was enough—enough to bury a novice, enough to turn a slope into a trap. Visibility collapsed, the swirling storm making every step treacherous.

"Watch out!" he shouted, skidding to a stop mere metres from her. She froze, eyes wide, skis flailing like twin planks. And then he saw her clearly—the woman from the foyer, the one lodged unbidden in his thoughts for days. "We have to move—quickly!"

Her face went pale beneath the flush of exertion and cold. "I… I can't—"

"Yes, you can," he said, voice firm but steady, gripping her arm to guide her. "Follow me. Keep close. Don't let go of your poles."

With deliberate, controlled movements, he led her down the slope, body angled to break the wind, skis carving a path through thickening powder. Snow lashed their faces, cold biting through every layer. The world narrowed to a hiss of white and the rhythm of their descent. Christian steadied her at several points, pressing a reassuring hand against her back, adjusting her posture, coaxing her to trust him—and the skis beneath her.

The avalanche powder roared behind them, a creeping wall of white, swallowing the slope they had just descended. Every second felt like a gamble, every misstep potentially catastrophic. Visibility dropped to mere meters; trees and rocks appeared as ghostly shapes. Christian's muscles burned as he skied, guiding and steadying her, forcing both of them to focus on the next movement, the next turn, the next breath.

Finally, the slope levelled, and through the swirling snow, a small wooden cabin appeared like a beacon—a safe haven rising from the frozen chaos.

"Come on," Christian urged, urgency sharp in his tone. "We need to get inside before it gets worse."

She nodded, shaking but obedient, following him across the remaining distance. Skis crunching in the fresh, blown snow, they reached the cabin, hearts hammering, breaths ragged—but alive.

Christian closed the heavy wooden door behind them, shutting out the howling wind and blinding snow. The cabin was small and rustic, built for emergency refuge rather than comfort. Timber beams ran across the low ceiling, walls lined with rough-hewn planks. A simple wooden table sat against one wall, flanked by two sturdy chairs. Fur rugs were scattered on the floor, and a modest bed—covered with a thick wool blanket and a few pillows—promised warmth. A tiny bathroom, just a sink, toilet, and shower, hinted at basic accommodation. Snow still clung to their clothing, and the cold radiated from the floor, pressing against them despite the shelter.

Christian set his skis carefully against the wall, then turned to Eliza, brushing snow from her jacket. She shivered, cheeks flushed, finally meeting his gaze, eyes wide and green, flickering with relief.

"Thank you," she said softly, voice nearly swallowed by the storm outside, carrying vulnerability and genuine gratitude.

Christian held her gaze a beat longer than necessary, aware of the tension, the unspoken connection. "You're welcome," he replied quietly, measured, yet edged with warmth.

The storm raged outside, snow lashing the cabin walls, wind rattling the shutters. Inside, the world shrank to the small timbered room—alone, suspended between chaos and the uncertain journey ahead.

Eliza set her skis aside, fumbling slightly with her poles, and glanced up. Christian watched her—not with judgment or amusement, but with captivated attention that made her stomach flutter. She flushed, acutely aware of his gaze, of how the firelight caught his dark hair, the sharp line of his jaw, the intensity of his eyes.

She cleared her throat, extending her hand awkwardly. "I'm Eliza… Eliza Preston," she said softly, words nearly lost to the storm's roar.

Christian took her hand. The moment their palms touched, something jolted through him—electric, sharp, alive. His chest tightened, pulse kicking against his ribs. "Christian Harrington," he returned, voice low, smooth, measured. But beneath the polish, something raw and unscripted startled even him.

He searched her eyes, expecting recognition, calculated charm, a quick appraisal that most women offered when they realised who he was. But there was none. Just Eliza. Genuine. Shy. Unshielded.

Her smile was small, unpolished, utterly sincere. And it disarmed him completely.

"It's nice to meet you, Christian."

"You too, Eliza."

He released her hand slowly, lingering a heartbeat longer than he should have, reluctant to sever the unexpected warmth. This wasn't a transaction. Not attention he had commanded, bought, or manipulated. It was something different. Something real. Something dangerously compelling.

For the first time in longer than he cared to admit, Christian Harrington felt curiosity—and desire—that had nothing to do with power, wealth, or perfection.

He stepped back, giving her space, though his gaze never fully left her. The cabin smelled faintly of pine and snow, tinged with damp clothing. He hung his jacket near the door, eyes flicking over their refuge: the low bed tucked in the corner, fur blankets inviting but rumpled; the plain table with two chairs; the tiny bathroom behind a narrow door; and the rustic touches lending intimacy to a space meant for shelter alone.

Crossing to the fireplace, Christian crouched and stacked wood into the grate. Sparks caught, the fire crackled, and a warm glow began to chase away the chill.

Eliza watched silently, tucking a damp strand of hair behind her ear. "So… our emergency lodging," she murmured, half-joking, half-nervous. Her gaze flicked toward the bed, then away, cheeks colouring. "At least we're not out there," she added, tone light but edged with truth, as the wind rattled the cabin walls.

Christian looked up, firelight catching his eyes. A faint, amused smile tugged at his mouth. "Yes. Comfortable enough for a storm like this." His voice was calm, even, but with an undercurrent that made her pulse quicken.

Eliza lowered her gaze, fumbling with her skis, snow clinging stubbornly to her boots and jacket. "I—uh—thank you," she said softly, almost vulnerable. The storm outside had stripped her defences, leaving her words bare.

Christian's expression softened, a flicker of protectiveness—and quiet amusement—passing over him. "For what?"

"For… saving my life," she admitted, blush deepening. She gestured vaguely toward the storm. "I don't think I would have made it here without you."

Christian's lips curved into a faint smile, warmer this time, touched with something deeper. "You would have," he said gently, though his eyes betrayed his own certainty.

Her laugh came then—soft, nervous, breathless—and struck him like an arrow. He leaned forward slightly, caught by the sound, drawn without realizing it.

"You should probably take a seat, warm up a little," he said, voice quieter now, roughened by something he didn't name. He nodded toward the bed. "The storm isn't letting up anytime soon."

Eliza hesitated, acutely aware of the closeness, of the quiet strength radiating from him, and of the subtle current charging the air between them. With a small, self-conscious smile, she crossed the room and lowered herself onto the bed, brushing the fur throw with nervous fingers, grateful for heat seeping into her chilled bones. The cabin was small, rustic, far from glamorous—but in this moment, it was enough. Enough to shield them from the storm… and, perhaps without her realizing it, from the world outside.

She let out a breathy laugh, shaking snow from her jacket. "I can't believe my first time skiing—and I end up here, alone, with… well, with you." Wonder threaded her voice, as if she still wasn't entirely sure this was real.

Christian leaned casually against the table, arms crossed, studying her with a focus that felt far too intense for such a simple confession. "First time?" he asked, eyebrow lifting. "You've never skied before?"

"No," she admitted, corners of her mouth curving into a rueful smile. "I probably should have stayed on the beginner slopes, but I felt brave. Not so much now," she added, glancing toward the rattling window, fingers toying with her jacket's edge.

Something in Christian's gaze softened. Amusement glimmered faintly in his dark eyes, tempered with warmth. "Brave can get you into trouble," he said lightly. After a pause, his tone deepened. "But sometimes it leads to… interesting situations."

Chapter Five

The words hung between them, heavy with an unspoken challenge.

Her eyes lifted to meet his—green locking with dark—and for a heartbeat, the storm outside seemed to fall away, leaving only the small, firelit cabin and the quiet tension crackling between them. Neither moved. Neither spoke. Yet something undeniable lingered, fragile, electric, insistent.

Eliza swallowed, pulse skipping. "Well… I suppose we'd better make the most of it," she said at last, her attempt at levity softened by nerves—and something else—that threaded through her voice.

Christian's lips curved slowly, deliberately, into a smile that hinted at more than amusement. "Agreed," he murmured. In that single word, in the way his gaze held hers, there was something dangerously close to a promise.

Privately, he felt relief, gratitude. She wasn't panicking. She wasn't frantic. She was steady—even in this storm. To Christian Harrington, that steadiness was more alluring than he could admit.

He moved to the small kitchenette, pulling down the modest kettle. "We should get something warm going," he said, voice steady, low, measured, as though the storm outside weren't enough to rattle him. He filled it with snowmelt water from a small spigot, the quiet trickle oddly soothing against the howling wind rattling the cabin walls.

Eliza perched on the edge of the bed, tugging off her damp gloves. "I didn't even think to bring tea," she murmured, eyes following him with a mix of awe and amusement. Everything about him—his quiet efficiency, the way he moved as though he belonged anywhere—made her forget, if only for a moment, the stress of her impulsive solo adventure.

"Don't worry," he said without looking up, a faint teasing smirk tugging at the corner of his lips. "This is survival, not a five-star hotel. We'll manage."

She laughed softly, delicate, and genuine, and the cabin already seemed cozier, though the fire had yet to be lit. Rising, she draped her damp jacket over the back of a chair. Her muscles ached—partly from skiing, partly from the tension that had clung to her since the mountain.

Christian glanced at her, taking in the way she shook snow from her hair, the faint blush on her cheeks. "You should take off your boots," he suggested, nodding toward the fur rug. "Feet first. Warmth radiates from the core."

"I…" She hesitated, aware of the subtle heat radiating from him, then shrugged and bent to unbuckle her ski boots. "Thank you," she whispered, quieter this time, almost to herself.

He busied himself with the kettle, rifling through the cupboard until he found two chipped enamel cups. The gesture was small, almost casual—but deliberate. He gave her space without withdrawing entirely, instinctively balancing presence and distance, reading her quiet cues without words.

The kettle whistled, a shrill, comforting note. Christian poured the steaming water into the cups, the rising heat mingling with the faint pine scent from the hearth. He handed her a mug. "Here. For the hands."

Eliza wrapped her fingers around it, letting the warmth seep into her frozen skin. She looked up at him, and for a suspended moment, neither spoke. The storm battered the cabin walls, the space close and intimate, yet it wasn't silence that filled it—it was awareness, subtle and charged.

Christian finally lowered himself into the chair across from her, leaning back just enough to relax while keeping his gaze steady, curious. She sipped the water—simple, unflavoured, yet comforting—and he allowed himself a flicker of satisfaction at the way she seemed to ease, even slightly, under his watchful presence.

For a long moment, they existed in that quiet bubble, the storm outside nothing more than a distant roar. The small cabin became a world entirely their own—fragile, suspended between the chaos of the mountains and the slow, undeniable pull growing between them.

Minutes passed with only the whistle of wind, the clink of mugs, and the faint drip of melting snow. Neither felt the need to fill the quiet. Somehow, the silence was enough—steady, grounding, yet charged, a subtle current humming between them.

At last, Eliza set her mug down, warmth blooming across her cheeks. "Well," she said softly, "I guess we wait it out. Nothing else to do."

Christian inclined his head, the corner of his mouth curving ever so slightly. "Yes," he murmured, low, private, intimate. "Nothing else to do."

Something delicate settled between them then, unspoken yet real—the first fragile thread of connection, taut with possibility.

He studied her for a long, deliberate moment before asking, "So, Eliza… are you from Australia?"

"Yes. A small town in Queensland," she said, smile faint but genuine. "You?"

"London. England."

There was no flicker of recognition, no pointed glance, no acknowledgment of who he was. Just her answer—simple, unaffected. For the first time in longer than he could remember, Christian Harrington found the absence of expectation refreshing. The weight he was so accustomed to—the endless assumptions, the greedy anticipation in a woman's eyes, the careful calculations—was gone. She looked at him as if he were just a man stranded in a storm, not the living embodiment of the Harrington empire.

"So," Eliza said after a pause, tilting her head slightly, "is there someone who's going to notice you're gone?" Her tone was casual, but her eyes searched his with honest curiosity.

Christian's mouth curved faintly, almost automatically, but he stopped the thought—her question pressing against him like the wind battering the cabin walls. He knew the truth. Clarissa would notice, of course. Furious—not with worry, but with outrage at the inconvenience. How dare he be late? How dare he exist outside her carefully controlled orbit? The image of her, pristine and perfect, stabbed at him like a shard of ice. Clarissa was every calculation, every rehearsed movement, every sharpened smile.

Eliza waited—patient, open, without judgment.

For a heartbeat, Christian almost spoke the truth. Almost let the words slip— that somewhere down the mountain, his fiancée waited with a diamond as cold as her heart, that his life, polished and gilded, had already been promised away. But something inside him rebelled. Here, in this cabin, with the storm raging outside and Eliza looking at him as if he were simply a man who had helped her down a slope… he didn't want that truth here. Not a single mention of Clarissa.

He cleared his throat softly, voice lower than before, roughened slightly by the storm outside and something unspoken within. "No. No one," he said at last— the lie smooth, deliberate, practiced, carrying an ease he didn't entirely feel. His gaze held hers steadily, measured, daring her to doubt it, though a small, restless part of him wondered if she could sense the tension lurking beneath his composed exterior.

"And what about you?" he asked, tilting his head slightly, curiosity threading his voice. "Husband or boyfriend waiting for you somewhere?"

"No," she said simply, shrugging just enough to show she was unbothered. "I'm here on my own."

Christian didn't know why it mattered so much, but a subtle warmth spread through his chest, undeniable yet quiet. He had to force himself not to smile too broadly, though a small, private thrill tickled the edges of his composure. There was something in the ease of her answer—her independence, her unaffected honesty—that struck a chord he hadn't realised still existed.

Eliza's lips curved into a small, genuine smile, unguarded and without guile. "Then I guess it's just us," she said softly, as if the thought held no fear at all, only quiet reassurance. Her words, simple and honest, made the cabin feel like a sanctuary amid the chaos outside.

And Christian felt it then—a tightening in his chest, a twist of feeling he hadn't experienced in years. For the first time in a long while, he wasn't entirely sure whether he was shielding her from the truth, sparing her the complication of who he really was… or whether he was protecting himself, afraid to let the world intrude into this rare, uncalculated moment.

The storm howled outside, battering the cabin walls, but inside—filled with the faint scent of pine and melting snow, with the hum of the fire and the warmth of her presence—everything else—the obligations, the engagement, the gilded life he'd been living for appearances—felt impossibly distant. For a fleeting moment, it was just them, two strangers suspended in the same space, and the rest of the world had vanished.

"Are you hungry?" Christian asked, voice low, casual, but threaded with a trace of genuine concern.

"A little," she admitted, a small laugh escaping her. "I skipped lunch… not such a good idea now." Her laughter was airy, effortless, something that made his chest tighten just slightly. Carefree in a way that drew him in without him realizing it.

Christian turned toward the kitchenette, scanning the cupboards with practiced efficiency. "There's a couple of tins of beans here," he said, holding one up. "I can heat them over the fire."

Eliza's eyes followed the tin, a wry smile tugging at her lips. "Maybe we should share a tin. We're not sure how long we'll be stuck here, after all."

"That's… a very sensible suggestion," he said, the faintest trace of amusement lifting the corners of his mouth. For a heartbeat, he let himself take in the cabin, the storm outside, and the quiet intensity of her presence—the snow clinging to her jacket, the curve of her smile, the steady honesty in her gaze. For just that moment, everything else—the Harrington name, the obligations, the expectations—fell away.

Before she could stop herself, the words tumbled out, shy and impulsive. "You have a nice smile."

Christian froze, the tin still in his hand, caught off guard. He met her gaze, dark eyes flickering with surprise—and something else he couldn't name—a quiet, unspoken acknowledgment that left him momentarily disarmed. Her honesty, her unguarded nature, struck him in a way few things ever had.

For a long moment, they simply regarded each other. The flickering firelight painted warm, dancing shadows across the small cabin, and the wind rattled the wooden walls. Yet inside, the air felt charged, intimate, impossibly close.

Eliza misread his hesitation and leaned back slightly, a small, nervous laugh escaping her. "Sorry… I didn't mean to make you feel uncomfortable."

Christian shook his head quickly, forcing a small smile. "You didn't. It's just… no one has ever said that to me before."

Her green eyes widened in disbelief, softening into amusement. "No one?" she laughed softly, tilting her head. "That can't be true."

"It is," he said, low, almost hesitant, voice carrying the weight of unexpected vulnerability. The corners of his mouth twitched into a faint, shy smile. For the first time in years, he didn't feel the need to hide behind charm or perfection.

He lowered the tin onto the small table beside them, suddenly aware of how close she sat on the edge of the bed. The warmth from the fire brushed over him, mingling with the faint scent of pine and snow clinging to her jacket. He noticed the way her hair fell in dark waves around her face, the subtle flush of her cheeks, the way her eyes lingered on him—not calculating, not expectant, simply observing.

Eliza felt her pulse quicken under his gaze. There was something magnetic about him, something that didn't demand attention or obedience—it simply existed, pulling at her curiosity. She shifted slightly, bringing her knees closer together, her hands wrapped around the warm enamel mug. The heat seeped through her fingers, grounding her in the moment, yet her heart fluttered at the unspoken possibility that this—this quiet, stolen moment—was more than mere coincidence.

Christian's lips curved into a soft, almost imperceptible smile as he settled into one of the chairs. He let himself watch her—study the gentle movements of her hands, the way her lips curved when she let herself laugh, the way her eyes darted up to meet his only to look away shyly. It was unintentional, uncalculated, yet it made him keenly aware of the pull he felt—a magnetic tug that had nothing to do with desire or conquest, nothing he could name.

"Well… I like your smile," Eliza said softly, her voice cutting through the quiet of the cabin. "It's… warm." There was a hint of curiosity in her tone, mixed with something tentative, as if she weren't sure she should say it aloud.

Christian's gaze flickered to hers. "Thank you," he murmured, low, private, intimate. "Tell me about yourself, Eliza."

She hesitated, fingers tightening slightly around her mug. "Not much to tell… I work in childcare. My parents…" She paused, swallowing. "My parents passed away in a car accident about a year ago."

Christian's expression softened, the flicker of vulnerability he rarely allowed anyone to see surfacing. "I'm… sorry," he said quietly, genuinely.

"Thank you," she replied, voice barely above the hum of the fire. "I don't have any brothers or sisters, and no uncles or aunties either."

"None?" he asked, eyebrows lifting.

"No… both my parents were only children." Her tone was matter-of-fact, yet a quiet loneliness threaded through it, fragile. After a moment, a small smile broke through. "When I eventually get married… I want to have more than one child."

Christian arched an eyebrow, a teasing glint in his eyes. "Oh? And when do you think that will be?"

For the briefest instant, a shadow crossed her face—pain, maybe regret—but it vanished as quickly as it appeared, replaced by a wry, self-deprecating smile. "Not anytime soon," she admitted, light but tinged with melancholy. "I can't imagine."

He studied her, noting the honesty in her voice, the way her words carried both hope and realism. Something about her openness, her lack of pretence, made the cabin feel smaller, warmer, more intimate. For the first time in years, Christian felt like he wasn't analysing, assessing, or performing—he was simply present.

He pulled a small pot from the cupboard, emptied the tin into it, and moved to the fire, letting the warmth and flickering light wash over him as he stirred the simple meal.

"I'm a CEO," he said simply, understated. He didn't tell her that he was the Harrington heir, the man whose name carried wealth, expectation, and influence beyond imagining. "I have no brothers or sisters, and my parents… have passed as well."

He added the last part softly, almost offhandedly, but the quiet weight behind it—the vulnerability he rarely revealed—hung in the air. Eliza's green eyes met his, and for a heartbeat, the space between them seemed to hum with unspoken understanding: two people who had lost much, caught together in a storm, discovering a fragile, unexpected connection.

Eliza leaned back slightly, letting the fur throw cushion her, the fire's warmth seeping into her chilled bones. "I… I guess we're not so different, then," she said softly, a trace of wistfulness threading her words. "Both of us on our own. Well… sort of on our own." She gave a small, wry shrug.

Christian's gaze lingered, noting the delicate curve of her lips, the way she held herself—open, unguarded, yet cautious. "No, I suppose not," he said, voice low, almost merging with the crackle of the fire. "I've been… used to handling things on my own for a long time. It becomes a habit. Sometimes a comfort… sometimes a cage."

She tilted her head, studying him. "A cage?"

He nodded, eyes dropping to the flames as if the fire gave him courage to speak. "Expectation. Image. Responsibility. Always having to be… everything to everyone. It leaves little room to just… be."

Eliza's expression softened, a quiet empathy in her gaze. "I know a little of that feeling too. After my parents… it's like you're left carrying everything alone. Decisions, grief, responsibilities. No one to fall back on, no one to guide you. You just… keep moving, even when it's hard."

He lifted his gaze to hers, and for the first time, the intensity in his dark eyes didn't feel imposing—it felt honest, open. "Exactly."

She laughed softly, part humility, part self-mockery, entirely disarming. "It's either resilience… or stubbornness. I'm not always sure which."

Christian's lips curved into a faint, genuine smile. "There's a fine line between the two," he said, leaning back slightly, relaxing into the cabin's warmth. "But I think you've got both. And that's… impressive."

Her cheeks warmed, not entirely from the fire. "Thank you," she murmured, quiet, hesitant. "It… it means a lot, hearing that from someone else. Someone who doesn't… have to say it."

He studied her, memorising the honest simplicity of her words. "Eliza," he murmured, almost to himself, "I have a feeling you make people see things differently… even without trying."

Her green eyes widened, caught off guard by the intensity in his words. She opened her mouth to respond, then paused, the heat of the fire and the storm outside making her acutely aware of the moment—of him, of the closeness, of how the world outside seemed to vanish for just this small, charged space.

The wind howled against the cabin walls, snow tapping against the windows, but inside, time seemed to slow. Two strangers, stranded together, sharing warmth, words, and a rare, unguarded connection. Neither knew what tomorrow would bring, how long the storm would last, or what would happen when the world outside intruded—but for now, they had this: small talk, shared glances, and the quiet thrill of discovery.

Christian stirred the warming pot, the soft clink of metal against enamel filling the cabin. His gaze flicked toward her, and Eliza caught him, pulse skipping. She tried to look away, pretending to study the fire, but the heat rising in her cheeks betrayed her.

He lifted the pot from the fire and carried it to the table, ladling its contents into two bowls. "Dinner is served," he said with a mock bow.

Eliza giggled. "Why, thank you, kind sir."

She slid into the chair opposite him. The table was small, and as she pulled her chair in, her knees brushed his. Both froze for a heartbeat, the contact light but electric. Christian's dark eyes met hers again, and she noticed the faint catch in his breath, the way his jaw flexed almost imperceptibly.

"Enjoy," he murmured softly, more to himself than to her, acknowledging the charged tension between them.

Eliza laughed nervously, brushing a strand of hair behind her ear, drawing them subtly closer. "I will," she said, voice softer than intended, lifting her spoon and beginning to eat slowly.

Christian tilted his head, studying her. "You don't seem afraid," he said, low, teasing but tinged with admiration. "Even with all this… chaos outside."

"I'm not afraid," she admitted, though her pulse betrayed her. "Just… aware."

The air thickened, charged, as if the storm had funnelled all its energy into the small cabin and the subtle gravity between them. Eliza's breath hitched, and Christian felt it too—the controlled composure he wore for the outside world slipping just enough to notice her fully: her laugh, her warmth, the quiet courage in her posture.

"You're… different," he said quietly, almost lost beneath the fire's crackle. "I mean… not like anyone I've… met before."

Eliza looked at him, startled. Lips parted, then closed. "I could say the same about you," she whispered.

Christian's gaze softened, dark eyes lingering on hers, and the cabin seemed to shrink around them, leaving just the two of them and the unspoken tension neither dared to name but both felt.

Chapter Six

They ate the simple meal, and the mundane act of sharing food became oddly intimate. When the bowls were empty, Christian rinsed them quickly and gestured toward the small bed. "You should probably rest. It's going to be a long night if the storm keeps up."

Eliza hesitated, aware of the warmth radiating from him. "I… I suppose so," she said softly, then, almost impulsively, brushed her lips against his cheek. "Thank you again for today."

He touched the spot lightly, voice quiet. "You're welcome."

She sank onto the bed, tucking the fur blanket around her legs, appreciating its simple comfort.

Christian tended the fire with careful, practiced movements. The flames crackled, sending waves of warmth through the cabin. Eliza watched him, noting the curve of his shoulders, the quiet intensity in his dark eyes. She tucked a loose strand of hair behind her ear, suddenly shy under his gaze.

"Sleep well," he said finally, nodding toward the bed. "I'll just be on the floor by the fire."

She blinked, taken aback, but there was a protective, unspoken respect in his tone. "Are you sure?" The bed was small, yet she found herself wishing he would lie beside her.

"I insist," he said simply, not meeting her eyes, as if no explanation were needed. "You've had a long day. You need rest."

She nodded, heart racing, feeling simultaneously reassured and keenly aware of the quiet intimacy of the arrangement. For the first time in days, she felt safe— protected by someone who didn't demand, judge, or expect her to know who he was.

Christian settled on the small rug near the fire, leaning back on his hands, keeping a steady watch without intruding. The cabin was silent except for the storm outside, the occasional pop from the fire, and their shared breathing.

Minutes passed, then she spoke, quiet, tentative. "I… thank you again, for today. For… everything."

Christian glanced at her, a faint, knowing smile tugging at his lips. "It wasn't anything extraordinary," he said softly, though his eyes conveyed more. "I just… couldn't leave you up there alone."

Eliza met his gaze, and for a fleeting moment, neither spoke. The storm outside raged, the world beyond the cabin suspended, and in that tiny, fragile space, a thread of connection—fragile, electrifying, entirely unspoken—settled between them.

Neither could predict the next hours. The storm might last another night—or two. They could be trapped together, navigating the small cabin, the roaring wind, and the treacherous slopes beyond. And for the first time since the wedding disaster, Eliza allowed herself to hope that being stranded with him… wasn't entirely unwelcome.

She closed her eyes and feigned sleep, though every nerve in her body was alert. The soft crackle of the fire mingled with the faint whistle of wind against the walls, creating a cocoon of sound that made the space feel even smaller, more intimate. Her heart thudded erratically, loud in the quiet room.

She had never felt such a pull toward a man before. Not just attraction, not just curiosity, but a deep, almost startling desire to be near him—close enough to feel the warmth radiating from his body, close enough to let the softness of his presence ease her guarded edges.

Her thoughts betrayed her: she wondered what it would be like to be in his arms, to let him hold her completely, no walls, no pretences. To feel the strength in his embrace, the calm assurance in his movements, the subtle rhythm of a heartbeat almost synchronised with her own.

She imagined his hand brushing a stray lock of hair from her face, the faint brush of lips against hers, and a shiver ran down her spine. Heat rose in her cheeks at the thought, warm and insistent, making her stomach twist in a way that was both thrilling and terrifying.

She tried to steady her breathing, to calm the fluttering excitement that threatened to betray her pretending, but the thought of him nearby, so achingly close, made it impossible. Every muscle hummed with anticipation, every glance she'd stolen at him replaying in her mind, magnified by longing.

Her imagination wandered further, daring herself to consider what it would be like to let go—to kiss him, to feel lips meet, tentative at first, then more insistent, more claiming. Her body betrayed her again, warmth blooming from her chest outward, a heat no blanket could contain.

And yet, she stayed frozen, feigning sleep, both wanting and fearing what might happen if she opened her eyes. If she dared, the magnetic pull between them might finally take over, and the safe, fragile cocoon of the cabin would no longer be a barrier—it would become a stage for a temptation she wasn't sure she could resist.

For a long moment, she lay still, listening to the fire, listening to him—whatever he was doing on the other side of the room. She let her imagination run wild, picturing the feel of his hand on her arm, the tilt of his head as he leaned closer, the low, private warmth in his voice murmuring something meant only for her.

And somewhere deep in her, a quiet, almost reckless hope stirred: that maybe, just maybe, he felt the same pull she did.

Christian shifted slightly on the rug by the fire, careful not to make a sound, every fibre of him alert. He had felt the subtle tension in her earlier movements, the way she hadn't quite relaxed, and something deep inside stirred—a quiet, insistent pull that made him acutely aware of her presence.

He studied her, the firelight illuminating the delicate planes of her face. There was something achingly fragile about her—vulnerable yet quietly brave—and he couldn't look away. Her beauty was understated, natural, unadorned. Those large, bright green eyes were like uncharted waters, and for a fleeting moment, he felt he could drown in them without ever wanting to surface.

Slowly, deliberately, he inched closer, just enough for the warmth radiating from him to brush the edge of the bed. He didn't touch her, didn't make a sudden move; that wasn't his way. Instead, he let his gaze linger, dark eyes softening, tracing the rise and fall of her hair as it caught the flickering firelight.

The silence stretched, heavy with unspoken tension. Sometimes the words left unsaid carried more weight than those spoken aloud. A small, careful movement brought him to adjust the fire, and the flames leapt and danced, casting shadows across her face. She looked impossibly close, impossibly fragile—and yet, there was a quiet strength about her, a resilience that drew him in like a tide he could not resist.

His mind wandered, imagining the softness of her hands, the warmth of her shoulder, the curve of her lips if she dared to open her eyes. He fought against the urge to close the distance, to test the magnetic pull humming between them. He had never met anyone like her—someone whose presence was at once grounding and incendiary, capable of undoing the careful composure he wore like armour.

Somewhere deep inside, he recognised that this night—this storm, this tiny cabin, this fragile tension—was a rare, unrepeatable pause in his life. A pause demanding attention, awareness, and restraint all at once. He let the fire's warmth wash over him, letting her even breaths and the storm outside dictate the rhythm of the room. Yet he did not move away. Not truly. He remained close enough that the air between them shimmered with possibility, desire unspoken, a promise neither had dared name.

His mind flickered involuntarily to Clarissa. Would she even notice his absence? Of course she would—he was still her prize, her meticulously curated possession. The thought left a bitter taste in his mouth. Then he thought of Henry and Mary, the way they loved each other openly, tenderly, without reservation.

And then his attention snapped back to Eliza. She would make a man very happy one day, he realised, and a slash of pain cut through him. The idea of another holding her, of her laughing, sleeping, or being touched by someone else, tightened his chest in ways he hadn't anticipated. Desire surged unbidden, raw, and urgent. His body reacted before his mind could fully process it, a hardening that made him acutely aware of every breath she took, every subtle movement in the small, firelit room.

Christian drew in a slow, controlled breath, forcing himself to focus—not on want, not on the impossible, but on simply being present. Even as he tried to temper the heat rising in his veins, he knew it would be a struggle. Eliza had unsettled him completely. For the first time in years, he didn't want to be in control.

He watched her sleep, the flickering fire casting warm, dancing shadows across her face. Every soft rise and fall of her chest, every delicate curve of her features, pulled at something deep inside him—an urge he hadn't felt in years. He wanted to reach out, brush a strand of hair from her face, feel the warmth of her skin beneath his fingertips. The thought made his pulse quicken, a low, insistent ache he struggled to ignore.

He didn't know how long the storm would last. Minutes stretched into hours, and with the snow piling higher outside, leaving the cabin unreachable, he realised they could be trapped here for days. Days in this small, firelit space with her so close, so achingly present—and he wasn't sure he could keep his hands to himself.

The thought both terrified and thrilled him. He knew the rules—restraint, boundaries, distance—but every instinct whispered otherwise. Her presence was magnetic, grounding, intoxicating. He had never met anyone who made the world shrink so completely, who made him feel simultaneously cautious and reckless.

He shifted slightly on the rug, careful not to wake her, forcing himself to focus on the fire, on the shadows dancing across the walls—but every glance in her direction reignited the tension in his chest. The temptation was almost unbearable, a quiet, simmering heat threatening to overtake the careful control he prided himself on.

And yet he remained, just watching, just feeling, silently marvelling at the way she existed so wholly—so unguarded—right there in front of him. The storm raged outside, but inside, it was only the two of them, caught in a fragile, electric moment that neither could deny nor control.

The first sharp bite of cold woke Eliza, pulling her from a light, restless sleep. Her blankets had shifted in the night, leaving her chilled. She shivered, hugging herself for warmth, and remembered the tiny bathroom tucked into the corner of the cabin. Quietly, so as not to disturb Christian, she swung her legs over the bed and rose on unsteady feet.

The room was dim, lit only by the flickering fire and a faint glow from the moon spilling through the window. Her boots, coat, and damp gloves still lay neatly in a corner—a silent reminder of the storm outside. She tiptoed to the bathroom, the cold wooden floor jarring her bare feet.

Inside, the cramped space felt almost comically small, the chill emphasizing her vulnerability. Once finished, she lingered a moment, adjusting the warmth of her sweater and wrapping her hair more securely around her shoulders. Then, carefully, she opened the door and stepped back into the main cabin, the firelight casting long, wavering shadows across the floor.

She tiptoed toward the bed, measuring each step, aware of him lying there in the shadows. Her pulse quickened—not from fear, but from the acute awareness of him so close, so still it almost felt as if he had merged with the firelight itself.

Just as she stepped around him, her foot caught something solid. Christian, sensing her movement—or perhaps shifting in his sleep—rolled slightly, and the edge of his leg brushed her ankle. She stumbled, a startled gasp escaping her lips, and gravity claimed her.

Eliza fell against him, landing softly on his chest. Christian's eyes shot open, dark, and wide, registering the unexpected weight. His arms went instinctively to her sides, steadying her. Heat radiated through her sweater, a delicious warmth igniting through her core.

"I—I'm sorry!" she whispered, heart hammering, her face brushing his shoulder. She froze, acutely aware of every inch of him beneath her, the firelight tracing the taut line of his jaw and the subtle catch in his breath.

Christian stayed still for a heartbeat, letting the tension curl between them like smoke. Then a low, almost inaudible chuckle escaped him, rich and warm. "Careful," he murmured, husky and teasing yet steady. "Or I might start thinking you planned that."

Eliza's cheeks burned crimson. She scrambled slightly, trying to regain balance, but he didn't release her. His hands lingered lightly on her waist, grounding her, anchoring the moment. The closeness, the warmth, and the soft firelight made her pulse race.

"I swear I didn't mean to—" she began, voice trembling with embarrassment and something unnamed, but he cut her off softly, eyes dark and unreadable.

"Relax," he murmured, barely above a whisper. "It's... okay. I was only teasing." His gaze met hers—intense yet gentle—and the way he held her made her heart thud against her ribs.

The cabin seemed smaller, warmer, charged. Outside, the storm raged, but inside, in that quiet, firelit space, everything else—the cold, the snow, the world beyond—faded to nothing. In that suspended moment, Eliza realised just how dangerously close they had become.

Her hands fumbled against his chest as she tried to pull back, warmth pressing into him more than intended. Christian's grip, gentle but insistent, didn't let her slip entirely. His dark eyes searched hers, calm yet smouldering, and for a heartbeat, she felt exposed—yet safe.

"I—I'm so sorry," she whispered again, cheeks flaming, trying to lift herself upright. The movement was awkward; the rug offered no purchase, and her fingers brushed his shoulder, sending a jolt through her that she tried—and failed—to suppress.

Christian chuckled softly, teasing. "You're apologizing too much. No harm done."

"I didn't mean to—"

"Shh," he interrupted, brushing a finger lightly against her wrist to still her frantic movements. "It's fine. You're... careful, that's all." His tone was measured, deliberate, but underneath it pulsed a warmth that made her shiver in more ways than one.

She hesitated, caught between moving away and staying too close. The small bed, the firelight, the quiet of the cabin, and the storm pressing against the walls created an intimacy she wasn't prepared for. Every nerve in her body hummed with awareness. She could feel the steady rise and fall of his chest, the subtle heat radiating from him, the dark, magnetic pull in his gaze that made it impossible to think clearly.

Christian tilted his head, observing her with careful intensity. "You're tense," he murmured softly, almost gently, his voice low enough for the fire to swallow the words. "Relax. There's nothing to worry about."

Her lips parted slightly, and she swallowed, aware of the tremor in her own voice. "I... I know," she said, almost incoherently. The words were true—and yet meaningless compared to the sensation of him so close, grounding her while making her heart race.

He eased slightly, giving her a fraction of space but didn't release her entirely. The shift was subtle, just enough for her to move without falling again, yet still close enough for their bodies to brush—his warmth seeping into her.

"You didn't hurt yourself?" he murmured, dark eyes flickering with something protective yet daring.

Eliza shook her head, biting her lip as she settled back onto the bed. The fur blanket had shifted in the commotion, and he tugged it gently over her legs, a touch that made her pulse thrum.

Christian sank back slightly onto the rug, close but not crowding her, letting her feel his presence without touching more than necessary. The storm roared outside, the wind rattling the cabin walls, but inside, time had slowed. Each heartbeat, each quiet inhalation, felt amplified—a shared rhythm neither could ignore.

Eliza closed her eyes again, body still buzzing from the collision of nerves and desire. She told herself it was the heat, the proximity, the fire—but deep down, she knew it was him. The man who had unsettled her completely, who made her ache with curiosity and longing, who was now just inches away—silent, steady, impossibly compelling.

Christian watched her settle under the fur blanket, but the tension between them remained taut, stretched tight like a drawn string. Every glance, every subtle shift of her body, every quiet breath she drew, was etched into his awareness. He had resolved—sworn, even—to remain in control, to respect the fragile boundaries of the moment. Yet the storm outside, the cramped intimacy of the cabin, and Eliza herself conspired against him in ways he hadn't anticipated.

The shock of her body landing against him when she stumbled had his pulse spiking, every nerve alive. He had instinctively gripped her hips, a light, protective touch—but the heat of her against him ignited something deeper, more urgent. Desire coiled tight in his chest, raw and insistent, and for a moment, reason seemed to fall away.

He wanted—more than he cared to admit—to roll them both over, to claim her lips, to kiss her until she was breathless, until the small space between them vanished entirely. His body reacted before his mind could catch up, hard and taut with need, yet he remained still, torn between control and the magnetic pull she exerted over him.

Christian's dark eyes lingered on her, tracing the curve of her shoulders, the gentle rise of her chest, the way her hair framed her face in the firelight. Every detail anchored him in the moment, feeding the tension that hummed between them—a promise unspoken but impossible to ignore.

He drew in a slow, steadying breath, forcing himself to focus, to cling to the restraint he had vowed. And yet the thought lingered, unbidden and undeniable: if he let himself, if he dared, the storm outside would pale in comparison to what they could create here, together, in the flickering firelight, tangled and breathless.

Chapter Seven

Morning crept into the cabin in muted shades of grey, filtered through the storm that still howled outside. The wind moaned against the roof beams, and snow tapped relentlessly at the frosted panes. Christian stood by the small window, hand braced against the frame, staring at the drift climbing higher and higher against the outer wall. The storm hadn't relented through the night; if anything, it had grown fiercer. The snow was already halfway up the cabin, swallowing them whole in its relentless grip.

They weren't going anywhere. Not today. Perhaps not for days.

His jaw tightened, but beneath the weight of responsibility, there was no panic. Instead, there was… stillness. A sense that the world outside had been muted so that this moment inside could stretch, linger, become something it otherwise never would have.

Behind him, the fire crackled low, embers glowing red. Eliza slept, curled beneath the heavy furs, her breath steady and soft. A loose strand of hair had fallen across her cheek, and Christian's chest tightened at the sight. In sleep, she looked impossibly serene, lips slightly parted, features unguarded—vulnerable, yet breathtaking.

For a long moment, he simply watched. The storm could rage and roar, the snow could bury the cabin, but in here, she was warmth, she was calm—and he felt himself drawn to her in a way he had never allowed before.

His body remembered the weight of her when she had stumbled into his arms in the night—the sudden softness against him, the press of her hips beneath his hands. He had sworn he would not cross the line, that he would protect her, that he would never take advantage of the fragile intimacy the storm had forced upon them. Yet as he watched her now, sleeping peacefully beneath the furs, desire surged low and sharp inside him all over again.

Drawn by something he could not reason away, Christian moved to the bed and lowered himself to sit at its edge. For a long moment, he simply looked at her, chest rising and falling with quiet restraint. Then his hand lifted of its own accord, brushing back the loose strand of hair that had fallen across her cheek.

God, she was beautiful.

The touch lingered longer than he'd intended, the back of his fingers ghosting along her skin, tracing the delicate curve of her face. She stirred at the contact, a soft sound escaping her throat—sharp, immediate—and his body reacted before his mind could intervene.

Her lashes fluttered, green eyes blinking open, still hazy with sleep. "Christian…?" she whispered, fragile, uncertain.

"Morning," he said softly, voice rougher than intended. He didn't pull away. Instead, his hand slid slowly, reverently, down her cheek, as if committing the feel of her to memory.

And then it happened—something that stole the air from his lungs.

Eliza moved, sudden and certain, her small hands clutching the front of his shirt, tugging him toward her. He caught the flash of determination in her eyes just before her lips met his.

The kiss wasn't tentative. It wasn't careful. It was raw, immediate, tasting of longing and something deeper neither dared name. Christian froze for the barest heartbeat, shock crackling through him, before the control he had clung to so tightly fractured. His hands slid to her waist, gripping, pulling her closer, his mouth answering hers with a hunger that had been simmering for hours— maybe longer.

The storm outside raged on, snow piling higher against the walls, but inside that kiss, there was only heat, only fire, only them.

Christian had meant to stay in control, to resist the pull of her mouth, but the instant Eliza kissed him, everything inside him fractured. His lips moved over hers with a hunger that surprised even him—a deep, aching need that had been clawing at the edges of his restraint all night.

Eliza's hands tightened on his shirt, tugging him closer, as if she couldn't bear the space between them. Her lips were soft, warm, insistent, and kissed him with a desperate kind of honesty—unguarded, fearless. It undid him.

Christian groaned low, the sound vibrating between them as his hand slid from her waist to cradle her jaw, thumb brushing the delicate line of her cheek. He tilted her face, deepening the kiss, unable to stop himself. His other hand pressed lightly to her hip, fingers flexing as though testing how much he could hold before losing all reason.

The bed creaked beneath her shift, rising against him, matching his fervour. Every brush of her lips, every gasp of air between kisses, fanned the fire roaring through him. He had kissed women before—many, too many—but never like this. Never with this kind of raw urgency, the sense that if he let her go, something vital would be lost forever.

"Eliza…" he breathed against her lips, half warning, half plea.

She silenced him with another kiss, fiercer this time, and his control wavered dangerously. His body remembered the weight of hers from the night before, the way she had fallen against him—and now, with her warmth pressed willingly to him, that memory ignited again in his hands.

His lips trailed to her jaw, then lower, brushing the sensitive hollow beneath her ear. She shivered, a soft sound escaping that sent his blood surging. He pulled back just enough to look at her—really look at her—her flushed cheeks, parted lips, green eyes wide with something that mirrored his own need.

"God help me," he whispered, voice rough. "I want you."

And then he kissed her again—slower this time, deeper, a claiming kiss that spoke of everything he had tried not to want but could no longer deny.

Christian's hands moved with deliberate, careful urgency, sliding from her waist to her back, feeling the curve of her as she pressed against him. Every inch of contact was electrifying; every sigh, every shiver drove him further past restraint.

Eliza's hands tangled in his hair, tugging him closer, guiding him as if she had always known what she wanted. The kiss deepened, tongues brushing in a slow, searing dance that left them both gasping. His chest pressed to hers, the heat of her body searing into him, making him ache in ways he hadn't known he could.

He pulled back slightly, just enough to see her face—flushed and luminous in the firelight, eyes darkened with desire, a flicker of daring mischief. She was breathtaking, more than he could have imagined, and every careful barrier he had built around himself began to crumble.

"Eliza…" he whispered, lips hovering near hers, breath warm against her cheek. "I shouldn't… we shouldn't…"

The words cut through the haze like a cold rush of air. Her chest rose sharply, and in an instant the daze of desire shattered. Her eyes widened, the flush on her cheeks deepening into a fierce blush as realization struck.

"Oh, God," she breathed, pulling back just enough for his warmth to slip away. "I—I'm sorry." Her voice trembled, almost inaudible over the storm. She pressed a hand to her mouth, as if to hold back the memory of how close she had come to giving in completely.

Christian's hand lingered in the empty space between them, aching to reach for her, to pull her back—but he forced it still. He watched the rise of colour in her cheeks, the way her gaze darted away, shame and confusion mingling in her expression.

"Eliza…" His voice was low, rough with restraint. "Don't—don't apologise."

She shook her head, eyes lowering, unable to meet him. "I don't know what came over me. I wasn't thinking, I—" She broke off, breath shaky, as if even admitting it was too much.

The storm raged outside, snow pelting the windows, but inside the cabin it was another kind of storm—words unspoken, emotions too raw, too dangerous to name.

"I should not have done that... I..." She looked up at him shyly, voice trembling. "Forgive me."

"Eliza..." His voice was low, steady, carrying both restraint and something far more dangerous. "It's okay. You don't need to apologise."

She shook her head again, biting her lip, still flustered. But Christian reached out, brushing the back of her fingers where they twisted in the blanket. The simple contact made her breath catch.

"You think this was one-sided?" he asked softly, gaze holding hers. "That it was just you, caught up in the moment?" His thumb grazed her knuckles, slow, deliberate. "Eliza, I've wanted to kiss you since the day I bumped into you in the foyer."

Her lips parted, surprise flickering in her eyes.

"I tried to ignore it," he admitted, voice roughened with honesty. "Told myself it was nothing, that I had no right. But every time you look at me... every time you laugh... it's there. That pull. So don't ask for forgiveness—you've done nothing wrong."

For a heartbeat, silence stretched between them—thick, heated, fragile. The storm outside thundered against the cabin walls, but neither moved, caught in the raw truth he had finally spoken aloud.

"I've never done that before," Eliza whispered, cheeks still flushed. She searched his face, as though hoping he might make sense of it for her. "I can't explain it. It's like there's some sort of..." She trailed off, words failing her.

Christian leaned in slightly, dark gaze steady on hers. "I know," he said softly, voice a low rumble that seemed to reach right through her. "I feel it too."

Her confession hung in the air, fragile and electric, her wide eyes fixed on him, afraid of what she'd just admitted. Christian's chest tightened. He wanted her—God, he wanted her—but every instinct screamed to hold back.

He drew in a rough breath and abruptly pushed to his feet, turning away. The fire crackled in the silence as he raked a hand through his dark hair, pacing a few steps across the cabin. "This isn't..." he muttered under his breath, jaw tight. "...I can't."

But the truth was, he already felt undone. His body still remembered the softness of her lips, the trembling way she'd clutched his shirt, and the storm inside him refused to be contained.

He turned back. Eliza sat up, the fur blanket gathered around her, green eyes luminous in the firelight—vulnerable, uncertain, and yet impossibly brave. One look at her, and his restraint shattered.

Two strides closed the distance. He reached for her, hands sliding around her waist, drawing her up against him. For a heartbeat, he hovered, forehead nearly touching hers, as if giving her one last chance to pull away.

But she didn't.

"Eliza…" he whispered, her name rough, reverent. Then, surrendering to the pull he could no longer resist, he lowered his mouth to hers and kissed her— fiercely, hungrily, as though he had been waiting his entire life for this moment.

His lips claimed hers with a hunger he had fought too long to contain. Eliza melted into him, hands fisting in his shirt as if afraid he might pull away. The kiss was desperate, insistent, yet threaded with something tender—something that made her pulse race even faster.

He groaned low in his chest, the vibration travelling through her as his grip tightened at her waist, pulling her flush against him. The fire's glow painted her skin in warm gold as his hands slid higher, framing her face with reverence that contrasted the raw urgency of his mouth.

Eliza gasped softly, and he deepened the kiss, tongue brushing hers in slow, devastating strokes that left her dizzy. She clung to him, body pressed to the solid heat of his, every nerve ending alive, sparking.

The storm outside howled, wind battering the cabin walls, but she barely noticed. There was only Christian—his breath, his touch, the intoxicating way he kissed her as if she were the only woman in the world.

He pulled back just enough to meet her gaze, forehead resting lightly against hers, every line of his body taut with restrained desire. "I tried to resist, Eliza… God, please tell me you want me too," he whispered, voice rough, uneven with emotion.

Her breath hitched at the raw honesty, lips parting, a whisper escaping. "I do… I want you, Christian," she admitted, voice trembling with relief and longing.

A deep, low groan escaped him, vibrating through the space between them. Her words shattered the last of his restraint. He gathered her into his arms, the press of her body sending a shock of heat coursing through him. Slowly, reverently, he lowered her onto the bed, the fur blanket curling around them like a protective cocoon, shielding them from the cold outside—and from the world beyond.

His lips traced a line from hers down her jaw, along the delicate curve of her neck, each kiss feather-light yet electric, leaving her trembling beneath him. The soft scent of pine smoke and fire mingled with the subtle perfume of her skin, intoxicating and dizzying all at once.

"Eliza…" he murmured again, low, reverent, aching, as though her name itself were a prayer, a confession, a promise.

She arched into him, fingers tangling in the thick dark hair at the nape of his neck, holding him close as if she could anchor herself to him, to this moment. Her whispered gasps, muffled against his mouth, were both invitation and surrender.

Christian's hands traced the lines of her body with careful hunger, memorising, cherishing, never rushing. Each brush of his fingertips sent shivers cascading down her spine. Every small movement—the tilt of her head, the rise of her chest, the soft gasp of her lips—ignited him further, consuming him in the need he had restrained for far too long.

The firelight flickered over them, casting dancing shadows on their entwined forms, as if the cabin itself held its breath. Outside, the storm raged, snow lashing against the windows, but inside, the world had narrowed to just this—just them, caught in a tide of unspoken longing, finally letting go of every careful boundary.

Christian's lips found hers again, deeper, more insistent, and she responded with equal fervour, pressing into him as if she couldn't get close enough. Every brush of their bodies, every sigh and gasp, drew them tighter; the storm, the snow, the cold—all fell away until there was nothing but their heat, their closeness.

Her frantic fingers found the hem of his shirt, tugging it free from his pants with desperate need. Her hands roamed his bare chest, tracing the taut muscles beneath his skin. He groaned, low and guttural, vibrating against her lips, before pulling back just enough to catch his breath and then yanking the shirt fully over his head, tossing it aside.

Her hands travelled immediately higher, exploring his chest and shoulders with eager urgency, pulling him down to her again. Christian yielded, pressing his body against hers, rough heat sparking wherever their skin met. Every heartbeat, every shiver running along her arms and down her spine, drew him deeper into the storm of sensation between them.

The fire crackled, casting flickering light across their entwined forms. The cabin felt impossibly small, impossibly intimate, as if the walls themselves were holding them close, witnessing the slow, electric surrender that had been building since the first touch, the first brush of hands.

Christian's hands traced the curve of her back, the line of her waist, anchoring himself while letting her set the tempo, pulling him closer, demanding the closeness he had craved but restrained for so long. Her lips never left his, her breath ragged, and he groaned again, pressing into her, feeling the heat of her body radiate into his, a fire matched only by the flames in the hearth.

Every moment stretched, thick with sensation, a delicious tension neither wanted to end, the storm outside mirrored perfectly in the whirlwind of need consuming them within.

She pressed against him, lips barely brushing his, breath hitching as she whispered, urgent and raw, "Christian… touch me… please."

He didn't need another word. His hands moved with a certainty born of years of restraint finally breaking, sliding beneath her shirt, over the curve of her body. The shiver that ran through her wasn't from the chill of the cabin—it was him, the heat of his touch igniting something deep inside her.

His hands cupped her bra-clad breasts, thumbs brushing over the sensitive skin just enough to draw soft gasps from her lips. Her fingers tangled in his hair, pulling him closer, body arching instinctively toward him, craving more, needing more.

Chapter Eight

Christian's lips followed the path his hands traced, trailing kisses along her jaw and neck, each touch a silent confession of the longing he'd carried since the moment he first saw her. The cabin seemed to contract around them; every sound—the crackle of the fire, the wind thrashing outside—melded into the rhythm of their desire.

She moaned softly, breathy, and low, and he groaned in response, pressing her tighter against him. Their bodies moved together with a raw, unspoken urgency. Every brush of skin, every whispered gasp, deepened the magnetic pull between them, erasing boundaries until it was impossible to tell where one ended and the other began.

With a bold, fluid motion, she pulled her shirt over her head, tossing it aside to join his on the floor. Christian's dark eyes followed her every move, and when she reached behind to undo her bra, letting it drop carelessly beside her shirt, his breath hitched.

"God… you're so beautiful," he murmured, voice rough, almost reverent.

His hands roamed freely now, tracing the curves of her body with reverent hunger, memorising every line he had longed to touch. Every shiver she gave, every involuntary gasp, sent sparks through him, igniting a fire he could no longer resist.

Eliza's fingers tangled in his hair, tugging him closer, desperate for his heat, the certainty of his touch. Her body arched instinctively, pressing into him, skin to skin, the electric intimacy of their connection. The fur blanket beneath them cocooned their movements, shielding them from the world outside, sharpening every sensation, every shiver, every brush of lips and hands.

Time itself seemed to slow. The storm outside faded into insignificance as the heat between them consumed every thought. In that small, firelit cabin, they existed only for each other. Every gasp and moan a confession, every touch a silent promise. Christian's lips found hers again—slower, deeper, tasting, exploring, memorising. She responded immediately, hands roaming his back, sliding under his shirt, feeling the heat of him, the taut tension beneath his skin. Every movement was a conversation; every shiver and sigh a confession.

He cupped her face, thumbs brushing over her cheekbones as he deepened the kiss, and she arched into him, body pliant and warm. The fur blanket shifted and crinkled beneath them, soft and protective, yet it did nothing to dull the electricity crackling between them.

"Eliza…" he murmured against her lips, low and raw. "I've wanted this… since the moment I saw you in the foyer."

Her green eyes fluttered open, wide, luminous, locking on his. She parted her lips, breathless: "I… I feel it too."

The words sent a jolt through him. He had tried to resist, tried to hold back the storm building inside him, but now there was no pretence, no restraint. He shifted, gathering her fully into his arms, letting their heat fuse as he lowered her gently onto the bed.

Their lips met again, urgent, needy, yet threaded with reverence—an acknowledgment of trust, of the raw vulnerability between them. Every touch, every brush of skin, drew them deeper into a rhythm all their own.

Christian's hands traced her curves with deliberate reverence, memorising the softness, the warmth, the way her body responded. She shivered, fingers tangling in his hair, lips parting in soft, unguarded gasps. The cabin, the storm, the fur blanket—all faded away. There was only them, only tension, heat, and the undeniable pull that had grown since the moment their eyes first met.

Her hands trembled, not from hesitation but from sheer, overwhelming want. While his mouth devoured hers, hungry and unrestrained, she slipped her fingers to his waist, fumbling with the button of his pants until it gave way. The slow rasp of the zipper sounded deafening in the quiet cabin, louder even than the storm raging outside.

Her hand slid beneath the fabric, bold now, cupping him with tender certainty. Christian jolted in response, breaking from the kiss with a groan that rumbled from deep in his chest.

"God, Eliza…" His eyes squeezed shut, control hanging by a fragile thread.

But she whispered, voice shaky with need, lips brushing his jaw: "I want you, Christian… more than I've ever wanted anyone in my life. Please."

The plea undid him. His carefully built, fiercely guarded restraint crumbled in an instant. He opened his eyes, and the desire, vulnerability, and certainty in her face burned away the last of his hesitation.

"Eliza," he rasped, pressing his forehead to hers, breath ragged. "Do you know what you're asking me for? Because if I give in…" He swallowed hard, his thumb brushing her lips. "I won't be able to stop."

Her only answer was the way she tightened her hold on him, arching into his body, eyes bright with determination.

That was all he needed.

With a groan that was half surrender, half reverence, he claimed her mouth again—deeper, hotter—his hand sliding over her hip, pulling her flush against him, erasing the last of the space between them.

She gasped, answering his hunger with her own, pressing closer as if she'd been waiting her entire life for this moment. Her trembling fingers fumbled at his waistband, tugging at the fabric in desperate urgency. He stilled, then rose to his feet—eyes locking with hers in a single, searing heartbeat—before, with deliberate control, he pushed his pants down and stood bare before her. The firelight caught the taut lines of his body, casting shadows over sculpted muscle and the glint of heat in his gaze.

Eliza's breath hitched, the sound sharp in the stillness. Her hands moved to her own waistband, trembling as she unfastened it and let her pants fall in a soft heap at her feet. Now only her silk panties remained—a fragile barrier that whispered against flushed skin, teasing where the air met heat.

He stood at the side of the bed, tall, powerful, exposed; every line of his body radiated strength and desire. The sight of him—the curve of his muscles, the hard plane of his chest, the flush of heat along his skin—made her pulse race. Every nerve in her body screamed to close the distance, to melt into his heat and power.

The storm outside raged, the fire crackled and hissed, yet inside the cabin, the world had narrowed to just the two of them—raw, unguarded, poised on the precipice of something neither could turn back from.

Christian sank onto the edge of the bed, firelight gilding every line of his bare body. His hand moved with reverence, tracing the delicate curve of her cheek, gliding down the slope of her neck, pausing at her shoulder before cupping her breast. His thumb brushed over the taut peak, drawing a shiver from her, before sliding lower, past the gentle curve of her stomach to the silk still shielding her from him.

His voice was low, unsteady, almost reverent. "Eliza… are you sure? I want you more than I've ever wanted anyone, but only if you're certain."

Her breath came faster, shallow and trembling. Instead of answering with words, she took his hand and guided it beneath the silk, pressing him to the truth of her desire. His fingers met the heat and wetness waiting for him, the intimate contact stealing his breath and fracturing his control.

A soft gasp escaped her lips, eyes fluttering closed. "I want you, Christian. I've never felt like this with anyone."

The confession undid him. A low, guttural groan rumbled from his chest, raw and primal, as his fingers traced her curves with deliberate, reverent care. Every touch, every brush of skin against skin, made her arch instinctively into him, silently pleading for more, for everything he had been holding back.

The firelight flickered across their bodies, casting shadows that danced like the storm outside—but neither noticed. There was only her, only him, and the magnetic pull that had drawn them together with an urgency neither could deny.

Slowly, deliberately, his hands moved lower, teasing the delicate line of her hips before sliding the silk fabric of her panties down her legs, leaving her bare beneath his gaze. She shivered—not from the cold, but from the electricity of his attention, from the way he looked at her, as if she were everything he had ever wanted, and more.

"You're incredible," he murmured, voice rough, dark eyes drinking her in. "Absolutely… breathtaking."

He lowered himself along her body, every movement measured, attuned to her responses. His hand traced the curve of her thigh, sliding closer until he found the warmth that welcomed him. She gasped, arching instinctively, fingers threading through his hair as if grounding herself in him. Every touch, every teasing press of his fingers, made her pulse race, igniting a fire she hadn't known she carried.

Christian's lips claimed hers again, a mixture of hunger and reverence, stealing their breath and making the world outside the cabin vanish. The firelight danced across their skin, shadows flickering over the contours of their bodies, and for a suspended moment, nothing existed except the heat between them.

She parted instinctively, silently offering herself to his touch. His movements were careful yet urgent, attuned to her shivers, her gasps, the subtle arch of her back. Every brush, every stroke drew her closer to the edge until her body finally shuddered in release, and her voice called his name—raw, unrestrained.

Christian held her through it, lips brushing her hair, letting the intensity of the moment wash over them both. When the trembling subsided, their breaths mingled, heavy and uneven, the quiet aftermath of surrender settling around them like the lingering warmth of the fire.

Eliza shifted, hands pressing against his chest as she rose above him, straddling him with a slow, deliberate confidence. Christian's hands followed instinctively, cupping her breasts, thumbs brushing over the sensitive peaks, drawing a soft, involuntary gasp from her.

She paused for a heartbeat, their eyes locking, the storm outside fading into irrelevance. Firelight danced across their flushed skin, casting shadows that mirrored the heat crackling between them. She held him firmly, feeling the hard length pressing against her, and with steady, daring intent, guided him to her damp core. Then, with a slow, deliberate motion, she sank onto him, their bodies aligning perfectly.

A low, guttural groan escaped Christian, deep and raw, as every nerve ignited. The friction, the warmth, the heady heat around him sent shivers of pleasure coursing through his body. He gripped her hips, holding her close, sensing the balance of strength and surrender in her movements—the electric connection between them pulsing like the storm outside: wild, untamed, impossible to resist.

Eliza leaned forward, hands braced on his shoulders, rocking slowly, deliberately, feeling the solid strength beneath her, the way his hands cupped every curve. Christian's breath hitched, low groans escaping as he guided her, eyes dark with desire yet searching hers for every unspoken signal.

"You feel... incredible," he murmured, voice rough, ragged with need. "Eliza..."

Her hands tangled in his hair, pulling him closer, tilting her head as she pressed her lips to his in a desperate, hungry kiss. Every movement, every press of her body against his, sent sparks racing through them, setting every nerve ablaze.

Christian's hands slid down her back, over her hips, feeling the heat of her skin, the tension coiling in her muscles. "I've wanted you... since the moment I saw you," he admitted, voice low, reverent, each word igniting something deeper between them.

She froze for a fraction of a second, chest rising and falling rapidly, then whispered against his lips, "I've wanted you too... more than I ever thought I could."

That was all it took. Christian's restraint shattered completely. He thrust into her again and again, pressing her flush against him, hands and lips worshiping her as firelight danced across their entwined bodies. Her hands roamed over him in return, tracing the lines he had longed to feel, each gasp and moan binding them tighter together.

Time dissolved. Outside, the storm raged, but inside the cabin, nothing existed beyond the heat, the weight, the press of skin against skin, and the slow, intimate surrender of two bodies finally giving in to what they had both wanted from the first moment they met.

Every movement was deliberate—tender yet urgent—a dance of passion and trust. Her whispered pleas, the slick warmth of her skin beneath his fingers, the taut grip of her thighs around him: each sensation pulled them deeper into a world where nothing else mattered.

And in the quiet between gasps and kisses, in stolen glances and whispered names, something profound bloomed—a connection deeper than desire, a tether forged in longing, trust, and the undeniable truth that neither would ever be the same after this.

Eliza's movements grew more urgent, riding him with a rhythm born of desire and the heat between them. Christian's hands gripped her hips, guiding her, holding her steady as every press, every roll of her body against his, sent jolts of fire through them both.

"Christian… please…" she whispered, voice ragged, breathless, each word a thread pulling him closer to the edge.

He groaned in response, lips brushing her shoulder, then her neck, trailing kisses that made her arch instinctively into him. "Eliza… God, you feel… so perfect," he murmured, voice a mixture of reverence and raw hunger.

Her fingers threaded through his hair, tugging gently, urging him closer even as she pressed herself against him. Every movement, every gasp, every whispered name built the tension between them, coiling tighter and tighter until it became unbearable.

Christian's hands slipped along her back, down her sides, holding her flush against him, feeling the heat, the slickness, the desperate need that mirrored his own. "I'm so close… Eliza…" he rasped, dark eyes locked on hers, searching for the same fire reflected there.

"I'm… I'm with you," she gasped, lips trembling as waves of sensation rolled through her. "Don't stop… don't ever stop…"

The words were enough. The restraint he had tried to maintain dissolved completely. Christian's body surged into hers repeatedly, every movement precise yet frenzied with desire. Their bodies moved as one, the cabin shrinking around them until there was nothing but heat, friction, and the wild rhythm of two souls surrendered entirely to each other.

Her nails raked his chest, her breath hot against his ear, and Christian groaned deep in his throat as he followed her lead, matching her movements, giving, and taking in perfect, urgent harmony. The firelight danced across their skin, highlighting tense muscles, flushed cheeks, intertwined limbs, and the raw intimacy of the moment.

Then the tension coiled to its breaking point. Waves of sensation tore through them both, crashing in exquisite, shuddering release. Eliza cried his name, body trembling and arching against his, every muscle alive with the fire they had ignited together. Christian groaned, a deep, primal sound reverberating through the cabin, his entire being consumed by overwhelming pleasure and the undeniable truth of their union.

He surged into her one final time, their bodies moving in perfect, urgent harmony. The culmination of their desire shattered any remaining restraint, and with a low, guttural groan that seemed to echo through body and soul, he released himself deep within her, the heat of the moment vibrating through them in a shared, shuddering climax.

They clung to each other in the aftermath, breaths ragged, hearts still hammering, the storm outside mirrored only by the wild, lingering rhythm of their connection within the small, firelit cabin. Every tremor, every gasp, every lingering touch spoke of surrender, trust, and a closeness that would linger in their memories long after this day had passed.

When the storm of sensation finally subsided, they remained pressed together, chests heaving, foreheads resting against one another. The cabin was quiet now, save for their shared, uneven breaths and the soft crackle of the fire.

Christian's hand traced lazy circles along her spine, still trembling slightly from the intensity of their release. "You… you're incredible," he murmured, voice husky with emotion—more than just desire.

Eliza buried her face against his chest, wrapping her arms around him, and for the first time in a long time, she felt utterly safe, utterly wanted—not just for her body, but for everything she was. "I… I've never felt like this," she whispered, every word carrying awe and relief.

Christian pressed a gentle kiss to the crown of her head, inhaling her scent, feeling the steady warmth of her body against his. "Neither have I," he admitted softly. "Never like this… never anyone like you."

Outside, the storm raged on, relentless, snow lashing against the windows, wind rattling the cabin walls. Inside, however, the small space had become a world entirely their own—a sanctuary of surrender, trust, and raw intimacy neither had anticipated but both recognised would change everything. Every touch, every kiss, every shared breath had left its mark, leaving them tangled together in more ways than one.

The last thought that crossed Eliza's mind before she drifted into sleep was a quiet, astonishing truth: she had only ever shared herself fully with one other man, Brad, her runaway fiancé. Even then, she had waited months before truly letting herself go with him. With Christian, it had only been days—and yet there was no hesitation, no regret. It felt inevitable, natural, as if every nerve and instinct in her body had known it long before her mind had caught up.

She melted against him, the warmth of his body beneath her anchoring her, his steady heartbeat a lullaby in the flickering firelight. Her arms wrapped around him instinctively, and she allowed herself to sink fully into the exhaustion and satisfaction of the early morning, skin to skin, breath mingling with his. In that quiet, intimate cocoon, she drifted off, a contented sigh escaping her lips, still lying atop him, the storm outside reduced to a distant echo in the world they had created within these four walls.

Chapter Nine

Christian felt the subtle weight of her as she slipped into sleep, the rise and fall of her chest soft against his own. They were still connected, and it awed him—truly awed him—that she trusted him enough to rest so completely on top of him, vulnerable and unguarded.

His hands drifted instinctively down her back, tracing the curve of her spine. The warmth of her skin beneath his fingertips was impossible to resist. Every touch was reverent, deliberate, yet tinged with a desire that had nothing to do with conquest. He wasn't lying when he'd told her he had never felt this with another woman. He had been with countless beautiful women, shared fleeting moments of passion—but none of it had ever been like this. This—this closeness, this trust, this seamless connection—was extraordinary.

Christian lowered his head, resting his cheek lightly against hers, letting the quiet intimacy wash over him. The firelight flickered across her face, illuminating the delicate line of her jaw, the gentle rise of her lashes. For a long, suspended moment, he simply held her, letting the world fall away outside the cabin. The storm raged on, but inside, there was only the steady rhythm of her breathing, the subtle warmth of her body, and the profound realization that some moments—some people—were unforgettable in ways no number of fleeting encounters could ever match.

His brow furrowed as his thoughts flicked, reluctantly, to Clarissa. The thought was sharp, intrusive—he was engaged, legally bound, yet here, with Eliza resting atop him, feeling more for her than he had for anyone in years, every sense alight with desire and connection. Reality pressed hard against him.

Guilt hit, but not for Clarissa—he knew she had no real feelings for him, only a hunger for control, recognition, and the prize he represented. It was Eliza who stirred the ache in his chest. He hadn't been honest with her. When he told her no one was waiting, it had been a lie—one he had let pass, allowing her to believe she was the only one, the sole focus in this stolen, fragile moment.

And now, watching her so unguarded, trusting him enough to sleep in his arms, the weight of that deception gnawed at him, sharp and insistent. Each rise and fall of her chest, the warmth of her body against his, reminded him how much she deserved truth—yet here he was, tangled in desire and lies alike, unable—or unwilling—to pull away.

The irony stung. He had spent years searching for this kind of connection—the magnetic bond Henry and Mary shared, one so intense that every moment apart felt unbearable. And now his heart was laid bare, utterly exposed, pressed against the one person he wanted most, who had no way of knowing the whole truth.

How could he marry Clarissa when this—this fierce, consuming, undeniable connection—was possible with someone else? He remembered Henry talking about Mary: how he couldn't stand being away from her, how it was like a force beyond reason. Christian had never believed it could happen to him. Yet lying here with Eliza, he felt it—the same overwhelming, uncontainable force—but magnified, more intense than anything he had ever known.

A new ache coiled in his chest: desire, longing, and guilt entwined in a tight knot. He tightened his arms around her slightly, reluctant to let go, unwilling to break the fragile closeness, yet wishing he could rewind time and start this night with the truth laid bare. Every heartbeat whispered it: this was more than desire.

Was this love? His mind asked, almost afraid of the answer. He had never imagined feeling like this, so completely undone by someone he'd only known for days. Love was supposed to grow over time, with shared memories and experiences—but the pull he felt toward Eliza was instantaneous, undeniable, and consuming. Was it too soon? Foolish? Or was it the rare kind of love that could not be restrained, that struck like lightning and demanded surrender?

There she lay, asleep in his arms, trusting him enough to be vulnerable, and he felt a deep, aching responsibility to protect her—yet also an overwhelming urge to claim her, to mark this connection in every way he could. He pressed his forehead gently against hers, inhaling the faint scent of pine and the warmth of her skin, and finally allowed himself to face the truth he had been avoiding. Whatever this was, it was nothing like he had ever felt—and he could not imagine letting it go.

But reality pressed hard, like the snow piling outside the cabin. He was marrying Clarissa for his inheritance. Five years. No cheating. No scandals. How could he do it? He hadn't even been with her in nearly two months—and he had no desire to. Could he live a life of duty and emptiness while this—this fire, this connection with Eliza—blazed inside him? Could he ask a woman to wait, to sacrifice her own desires, while he was bound to another? He knew the answer before he even spoke it to himself: he couldn't. He wouldn't. And he also knew, with a certainty that thrilled and terrified him, that he would never resist her if given the chance again, married or not.

Exhausted, body and mind heavy from the storm outside and the one within, he let himself slowly slip into sleep. With Eliza lying across him, warm, soft, and utterly trusting, he held her a little tighter, letting the quiet of the cabin, the crackling fire, and the sound of her breathing lull him into a rest he knew would be brief—but for now, it was enough.

After spending the previous day entwined—sleeping in each other's arms, then making love again—Eliza woke wrapped in warmth, the lingering haze of sleep clinging to her. The last thing she remembered was being wrapped in Christian's arms, and for a heartbeat, disorientation flickered across her mind. Then she realised—he must have adjusted the blankets. He was behind her, strong arms curled around her, the fur draped over both of them. Despite the icy chill seeping through the cabin walls, she felt only heat—deep, encompassing warmth that made her chest flutter.

She stretched slowly, pressing against him almost instinctively. The subtle friction sent a shiver of awareness through her. She felt him stir, a low, deliberate movement that made her pulse spike. Sleepily, barely more than a breath, she whispered, "Christian…"

Instantly, his arms tightened, anchoring her against his chest. "I'm here," he murmured, low and rough, each word charged with need.

Encouraged, Eliza pressed back into him, her body curving perfectly against his. A guttural groan rumbled from his chest, vibrating through her back. "Eliza," he breathed, voice thick with hunger, his body responding to hers with raw, immediate desire.

Her hips shifted instinctively, the soft brush of movement against him making a startled moan escape her lips. "Mmm…"

Christian's hands slid up her sides, pausing to cup her breasts, thumbs brushing over the sensitive peaks, drawing tiny, involuntary shivers. Every motion was deliberate, reverent, yet charged with an urgency that made her pulse pound. She arched back, breath hitching, pressing closer as if trying to fuse herself entirely to him.

His lips found the curve of her shoulder, trailing heated kisses down her neck, hands never leaving her. Each press of his chest, each subtle grind of his hips drew shivers from her, her fingers tangling in his hair as if anchoring herself to him.

"Eliza…" he murmured against her skin, low and ragged, each word a plea as much as a declaration. "God… you feel incredible."

She tilted her head back, a soft gasp escaping as his fingers brushed the sensitive skin beneath her breasts, sparks of heat coursing through her. Her hips moved instinctively, pressing harder into him, testing, needing, driving him closer to the edge.

Christian groaned, his control unravelling, every nerve alight with need. He pressed closer, cupping her sides, feeling every shiver, every pulse beneath his hands. "I want you... again," he admitted in a rough whisper, words almost lost in the storm of sensation consuming them both.

Eliza's breath hitched at the raw honesty in his voice, at the way his hands and body moulded perfectly to hers. "Yes... please," she murmured, trembling, words laced with longing and surrender.

He didn't hesitate. Sliding carefully behind her, he entered her warmth with slow, deliberate ease, making her gasp, a soft, urgent sound escaping her lips. "Ohhh... Christian," she breathed, pressing back instinctively.

His lips claimed the curve of her neck with hungry, searing kisses. Each exhale, each brush of breath against her skin made her pulse spike. Then, just as suddenly, he withdrew slightly, only to surge forward again, their rhythm locking in an intoxicating, desperate harmony, every movement a conversation of desire and need neither could—or wanted to—resist.

Christian's hands roamed her body with deliberate hunger, sliding from her sides up to her breasts, cupping and kneading as he groaned low in his throat. Every shiver she gave, every gasp under his touch drove him further, until it felt as though he might lose himself completely in her.

Eliza arched back, silently urging him closer, deeper. Her breaths came in ragged, intoxicating gasps, each one pulling a groan from him that vibrated through her very bones.

"You feel... so perfect," he whispered against her neck, voice thick with need, reverence, and the raw hunger he had barely restrained. "Eliza..."

"Yes... Christian," she murmured, words spilling in a trembling rush, body pressing desperately against his.

He moved with her, matching every tilt, every press, rhythm intensifying, building, until the world outside—the storm, the cold, the cabin—vanished entirely. There was only the heat between them, the fire in their veins, the desperate, unspoken claim of bodies that had waited far too long for this closeness.

Christian's movements became more urgent, more possessive, each thrust measured yet impossible to control, as if their bodies alone dictated the rhythm. Every shudder, every gasp, every arch of her body sent jolts through him, igniting a fire he could no longer temper.

She arched into him, pressing flush against his body, every curve aligning perfectly, and he groaned—a raw, primal sound that rattled through her. "Eliza... God, you're mine," he whispered, husky, reverent, hands roaming, worshipping her skin, tracing the delicate slopes and soft hollows he had longed to know.

"I… I can't… Christian," she gasped, voice trembling, breath hitching with every movement. "I… want you… need you."

He pressed his lips to the shell of her ear, down to her neck, leaving hot, lingering traces that made her shiver. Her back arched instinctively, pushing against him, and he met her motion for motion, their bodies in perfect synchrony—want and need so intense it felt elemental. Every gasp, every whispered name, every frantic clutch of his hands spiralled them closer to a shared peak.

Christian tightened his hold, friction and heat consuming them both. "Eliza… I'm close…" His voice was rough, unsteady with want.

His fingers slipped between her thighs, pressing with deliberate intensity, and she cried out, low and urgent. "God… yes, Christian!"

Every gasp, every soft moan, ignited the flames that had smouldered since she had first fallen into his arms. His thrusts became frantic, driven by need, each movement deepening the connection between them, his body attuned to every shiver, every curve.

He teased her relentlessly—hands, lips, the unyielding rhythm of his body— driving her to the edge again and again until she arched and tumbled over the peak, shuddering in release, her cries mingling with his low, guttural growls. The world narrowed to firelight, the storm outside, and the two of them— surrendering completely to desire, to trust, to the uncontainable need that had drawn them together.

Christian groaned low in his throat, following her over the edge, body shuddering, every muscle taut and trembling. He collapsed beside her, letting the warmth of their entwined bodies sink in, chests rising and falling together in a quiet, shared rhythm that grounded them in the aftermath.

Eliza clung to him, arms wrapped around his torso, steady pressure anchoring her in a way she hadn't expected. Her breath came in ragged bursts, mingling with the faint scent of fire and pine lingering in the cabin. In that suspended moment, nothing existed beyond their closeness, the warmth, the simple miracle of being near each other.

"I…" she whispered, voice small, almost fragile. "That was… I've never felt like that before… not like this."

Christian's arms tightened around her, hands sliding over her sides as his lips rested gently against the curve of her neck. "Nor have I," he murmured, low and reverent, thick with feeling. "Eliza… you're extraordinary. I—" He swallowed hard, the weight of his confession almost choking him. "I've never wanted anyone like I want you."

Her body pressed closer, still warm and flushed from their shared heat. "Christian... this... I don't know what to say," she admitted softly, fingers tracing the line of his arm as though needing the contact to anchor her. "I've only known you for... days, but it feels like... like I've known you forever."

He pressed a kiss to her shoulder, then the side of her neck, savouring the trust and vulnerability she had placed in him, letting it settle deep in his chest. "I feel it too. Every second with you feels... inevitable," he whispered, husky. "I can't ignore it. And I don't want to."

Christian shifted slightly, tightening his embrace without smothering her, letting her body mould to his. Her back curved into him, her warmth seeping into him, and he let himself savour it—the softness, the steady pulse of her heartbeat against his, the fragile peace of their closeness.

"We'll figure this out," he murmured, a promise not just to her but to himself, low, reverent. "No matter what happens outside... in here, it's just us."

She exhaled a quiet, tremulous laugh, the sound trembling with relief and something softer, unspoken. "Okay," she whispered, fingers tightening slightly around his arm. For now, that was enough.

Christian stepped into the tiny bathroom first, the small space barely containing him as he washed, water warm against his skin. Steam curled into the corners, fogging the mirror, and he caught a glimpse of himself—dishevelled, flushed, fully aware of the lingering warmth from Eliza.

When he emerged, Eliza was stepping past him toward the bathroom. Without thinking, he reached out, hands sliding around her waist, pulling her gently but firmly against him. She froze, a soft gasp escaping, then melted into him as his mouth found hers in a long, slow, lingering kiss. There was no hesitation, only the quiet urgency of two people who had surrendered once and could feel the pull all over again.

She wrapped her arms around his neck, fingers tangling in his hair, pressing closer as if memorising every line, every heat of him. Christian's hands roamed her back and hips, holding her just enough to make her feel entirely his.

When they finally parted, foreheads pressed together, breaths mingling, the quiet crackle of the fire the only sound besides the distant howl of the storm outside.

Eliza tilted her head, green eyes shimmering in the firelight. "Good morning," she whispered, a shy smile tugging at her lips.

Christian grinned, brushing a loose strand of hair from her face. "Morning," he murmured. "Sleep well?"

Her lips curved into a soft, private laugh. "With you? Impossible not to."

He pulled her closer, one arm snaking around her shoulders. "I think I could get used to mornings like this," he said, low, teasing yet tender. "Though I might have to insist on being the first to wake you every time."

Eliza laughed again, light, and musical, pressing a quick, mischievous kiss to his jaw. "We'll see about that."

The storm had eased outside, but inside the cabin, the world had shrunk to just the two of them—warm, safe, and utterly magnetic. Every glance, every touch carried a promise neither dared voice… at least for now.

Chapter Ten

While Eliza was in the bathroom, Christian moved quietly around the small cabin, the pot of beans clinking lightly in his hands as he set it over the fire to heat. The rhythmic crackle of the flames mirrored the turmoil inside him. Every movement, every sound reminded him of her—her laughter, the curve of her lips, the way she had trusted him so completely.

He needed to tell her the truth. The words weighed heavier than the storm outside: he was engaged. But thoughts of Clarissa now filled him with a bitter detachment. How could he possibly marry her, knowing what he had felt last night, knowing what he felt every time he looked at Eliza? No inheritance, no promises, no fortune was worth sacrificing this—this sudden, fierce connection that had ignited between them.

He stirred the beans absentmindedly, the spoon clinking softly against the enamel. His gaze drifted to the small window, where the storm had finally eased, leaving a thick blanket of snow piled nearly halfway up the cabin walls. Outside, the world was silent and frozen—but inside, his thoughts churned like the tempest that had just passed. He had never imagined this could happen—not to him, not like this. Yet every fibre of his being screamed that it was real, undeniable, and more powerful than anything he had ever known.

Running a hand through his hair, he exhaled sharply, the weight of honesty pressing down on him. He had to tell her. She deserved nothing less. She deserved the truth, even if it risked everything between them. The thought of losing her, even for a fleeting moment, sent a pang through him. The fragile trust she had placed in his arms could stand on nothing but complete truth.

The beans hissed over the fire, filling the cabin with a warm, homey scent that mingled with the faint pine lingering in the air. Water ran in the bathroom, and he heard her movements—small, careful, entirely herself—and his pulse quickened. Soon, she would emerge, and he would have to speak. No hesitations. No half-truths.

He set the beans aside and leaned against the counter, firelight brushing his shoulders. I can't marry Clarissa. Not even for the inheritance. Not when this— this connection, this… feeling—is possible. I've never felt anything like it. I can't ignore it. I won't.

His hands clenched briefly, then relaxed, the tension coiling and uncoiling in his chest. When she stepped back into the cabin, he would tell her. The whole truth. Every word, every confession. And whatever came after, he would face it—because she had the right to know, because he couldn't live with anything less.

Eliza emerged from the bathroom, freshly cleaned, and dressed, the storm outside now a soft whisper against the cabin walls. Christian was at the counter, carefully ladling the warm beans into two bowls. The aroma mingled with the lingering scent of pine and fire, filling the cabin with comforting warmth.

She moved quietly behind him, slipping her arms around his waist and pressing herself to his back. "You looking after me… I like it," she said, a playful laugh threading through her words.

Christian stiffened for a heartbeat at the contact, then relaxed into her warmth. He turned slightly in her arms, brushing her hair with his lips. "I like it too," he murmured.

For a moment, they stayed like that, bodies pressed together, the unspoken tension stretching the seconds into something heavier, charged. Every instinct screamed to tell her now—to lay everything bare: the engagement, the truth, the dangerous pull that had him captivated.

As he placed the bowls on the tiny table, he made a quiet, resolute decision. As soon as they finished eating, he would tell her everything. He would tell her he was engaged—but only for a little longer. That the life he had planned, the inheritance he was meant to secure, was meaningless compared to what this— what they—could be. That he was willing to risk everything for a chance at love, at a connection he had never thought possible.

The inheritance was worth billions, yet he already had enough. What mattered now was Eliza—the way she trusted him, the way she made him feel alive in ways money or power never could. For the first time in years, he knew with absolute certainty that some things were worth far more than wealth.

They had just finished their simple meal. The cabin was bathed in the soft glow of the firelight, the storm outside now a distant memory. Inside, warmth and intimacy lingered like a tangible presence, wrapping around Christian and Eliza as they sat close, savouring the rare quiet. Their connection had deepened overnight, and Christian's chest ached with the truth he had to share. He needed to tell her everything—to lay bare the engagement he had hidden and the feelings that had grown far too strong to ignore.

As Eliza stirred the fire, he approached, heart hammering. His hand lifted, brushing gently against her cheek, and he spoke, his voice rough with emotion.

"Eliza," he began, gaze locking with hers, "there's something I need to tell you. Something important."

She looked up at him with that trusting smile that made his chest tighten. "Okay," she said softly. "You know you can tell me anything." Her words, her unwavering trust, sent a rush of heat through him. He had never felt a connection this strong with anyone—not like this.

Before he could speak again, a sudden roar shattered the fragile calm. The sharp, insistent beat of helicopter blades cut through the cabin, vibrating against the walls. Eliza's eyes widened in surprise, and Christian's heart sank. He had hoped for a private moment, a chance to be completely honest with her—but now that hope seemed to vanish into the cold air.

"They must be here to rescue us," Eliza murmured, hurrying to the window. Her breath fogged the glass as she peered outside. The snow had piled high, nearly halfway up the cabin walls, yet a helicopter hovered above, slicing through the whiteness. A man leapt from the landing skids, struggling through the deep snow toward the cabin door.

Christian's mind raced, his pulse hammering with frustration and disbelief.

"Mr. Harrington!" a voice called, cutting through the wind and snow.

"Yes!" Christian shouted back, voice tense.

He threw open the cabin door, and a gust of icy snow whipped inside, stinging their cheeks. The man stumbled in, snow clinging to his coat, eyes wide with relief.

"Thank God! We've been looking for you! Your fiancée is out of her mind with worry!"

Eliza froze, her hand gripping the back of a chair, confusion etched across her face. The words took a heartbeat to land—but when she looked at Christian, his expression, tight and unreadable, confirmed the dreadful truth.

"Fiancée," she whispered, disbelief and shock threading her voice.

Christian's jaw tightened, guilt and frustration warring in his chest. The moment he had waited for—when he could finally tell her everything—was gone. With it, the fragile possibility of what might have been, stolen away by a woman he was sure he could never love…and a secret he had kept far too long.

"Eliza…"

She couldn't bring herself to look at him. The word—*fiancée*—hit her like a physical blow, pain radiating through her chest, stealing her breath. Her eyes burned, threatening to spill tears she refused to let fall. Her throat tightened, every word stuck, and for a moment, she felt hollow, as though the ground beneath her had disappeared.

Christian moved toward her, hand reaching out instinctively, but she recoiled, stepping back as if distance could shield her from the truth. His dark eyes, usually so controlled, were raw with frustration and longing, but she couldn't face him—not yet.

The man who had come to rescue them cleared his throat. "We need to get you two in the chopper. We're not sure how long the sky will remain clear." His tone was urgent but careful, aware of the tension crackling between them.

Eliza drew in a shaky breath, forcing herself to move. She was running on little more than adrenaline and confusion, but she mechanically put on her coat, zipped it tight, and pulled on her boots, her hands trembling just slightly. She ignored the heat of Christian's gaze on her back as he did the same, pulling his coat around him with a controlled exhale, bracing himself for the ride ahead.

They moved slowly through the snow toward the helicopter, each step heavy with the weight of what had just passed in the cabin—and the unspoken future that now felt impossibly out of reach. With every crunch beneath their boots, Eliza's chest tightened, as though leaving the cabin also meant leaving a piece of herself behind.

The man accompanying them stepped up to her side, guiding her with professional calm. He adjusted her harness, checked the straps, and made sure everything was secure with practiced efficiency, all while Eliza's mind whirled with confusion, longing, and disbelief.

Christian followed immediately after, his movements precise but taut, every muscle alert. The cold air bit at his face, but it was nothing compared to the ache in his chest. He climbed into the helicopter behind her, settling into the seat with a controlled exhale, aware of the small space between them, the lingering warmth of her presence, and the silent, unspoken tension that refused to dissipate.

Even as the rotors whirred to life, whipping snow around them, every glance, every brush of fabric against fabric, reminded him of what had been left unfinished—the confessions he had yet to make, the truths he had yet to speak, and the connection neither of them could ignore.

The flight back to the chalet was a blur of motion and silence, the roar of the blades drowning out everything else. Christian's mind raced, circling every word he hadn't spoken, every confession he had hoped to make before the rescue. He stole glances at her, her profile outlined against the swirling snow outside, and the ache in his chest deepened. She was tense, rigid, but she hadn't moved away completely—a small mercy that teased him with the possibility of reconciliation.

Finally, the helicopter touched down at the chalet. Snow crunched underfoot as they disembarked, the cold air biting at their faces, grounding them in reality. The staff and Clarissa were already there, waiting. Eliza's heart hammered painfully in her chest, and Christian's hand brushed against hers as he guided her through the snow—subtle contact, charged with everything left unsaid.

They reached the warmth of the chalet, golden light spilling from the windows, promising comfort, and safety. But for Christian, it felt like stepping onto a stage. Clarissa rushed forward, throwing her arms around his neck with exaggerated relief. "Thank God! I was worried sick! I thought I'd lost you!" she exclaimed, voice high and dramatic, perfectly timed for effect.

Christian's jaw tightened. He knew her well enough to see through it. Every ounce of that worry was performative, designed to reinforce the image of the perfect fiancée clinging to the future heir of the Harrington fortune. Beyond the façade, he felt nothing—no genuine concern, no warmth, no connection.

His gaze flicked to Eliza. She had stopped a step behind, watching, her green eyes wide, lips pressed together as though holding herself back. When their eyes met, even briefly, he saw the hurt, the betrayal, the quiet anguish etched across her face. Then she looked away, quickly, as if to protect herself—or maybe him—from the emotions she could not show.

A sharp pang struck him in the chest. He felt like an utter bastard. Here he was, standing in the warmth of the chalet, with Clarissa clinging to him like a trophy, while Eliza—the woman who had made him feel alive in ways no one else ever had—stood outside, aching in silence. He wanted to reach for her, pull her into his arms, shield her from the pain—but the helicopter ride and the presence of others made it impossible. And yet, the guilt gnawed at him, a reminder that every choice he had made had consequences, the hardest being that he had just torn something precious from her without explanation.

Clarissa clung to him as though she had rescued him from certain death. "You had me so worried, Christian! I don't know what I'd have done if anything had happened to you."

Christian kept his expression neutral, polite, but his mind raced. He could feel Eliza's gaze on him from the corner of his eye—her shoulders tense, her hands gripping her coat, the faint tremor in her posture. He wanted to tell her everything, to explain, to pull her close, but Clarissa's arms made that impossible.

"Clarissa…" he said carefully, forcing calm into his voice. "Thank you for your concern. I appreciate it."

Her smile widened, perfectly rehearsed, but Christian caught the flicker of calculation in her eyes. Every move, every word, was designed to remind him—and everyone else—that she was the future Mrs. Harrington, that she belonged in his life.

Eliza stood frozen nearby, and the weight of her silent judgment struck him harder than anything Clarissa could have said. He saw the tears threatening in her eyes, the heartbreak she tried to hide. It pressed against his chest like a physical force.

He wanted to take her hand, pull her away, let her know the truth before she saw anything else—but the others' presence and Clarissa's tight hold made him hesitate. He swallowed hard, heart hammering, knowing that if he didn't act soon, the moment—maybe even the chance—would slip away.

As the staff moved around them, offering drinks and checking on the group, Christian's mind raced. He had to get Eliza alone, to speak, to tell her the truth: Clarissa wasn't the woman he wanted, wasn't the one he could love. Only Eliza had awakened something in him so deep, so raw, that denying it was impossible.

He caught her eye again, and this time let his gaze linger—silent, loaded with meaning. A promise. A warning. He would find a way. He would tell her everything—but first, he had to survive the polished facade that Clarissa insisted upon, the lies and expectations built around him since birth. He would not let this chance slip, not again.

Eliza shook her head when a staff member offered her a glass of juice. Her throat felt raw, tight with pain and heartbreak. "No, thank you," she said politely, offering a small, fragile smile before excusing herself and retreating toward the lift.

Christian's voice cut after her, low and urgent. "Eliza…"

She didn't turn. Didn't slow. Her legs carried her forward, each step a mix of resolve and despair. She pressed the button for her floor, deliberately putting distance between herself and him, between herself and Clarissa, and most of all, between herself and the man she had come to realise she loved.

The weight of it hit her like a physical blow. It was insane—completely irrational—how quickly she had fallen for him. Days. Mere days. And yet her heart claimed otherwise. She loved him. Truly. Irrevocably.

A bitter clarity washed over her. She had never truly loved Brad. His absence, his betrayal, the way he had abandoned her—it had all been a disguised mercy. By running away with Clair, he had left her heart unclaimed, opening the door for this—the possibility of love that was real, that made her pulse ache, that made her want and fear and hope all at once.

As the lift doors slid shut, Eliza pressed herself against the polished metal wall, fingers curling tightly around the rail for support. Her chest heaved with a shaky breath, and she closed her eyes, letting the bitter truth settle like a storm raging quietly inside her. Every nerve ached, a mixture of longing and despair. It hurt. It frightened her. But it was real.

For the first time in her life, she felt utterly certain of something—she could never stop loving Christian. Every moment with him, every touch, every glance, had carved itself into her heart. But the cruel reality pressed in like ice: he belonged to someone else. Not to her. Never to her.

The thought twisted in her chest, sharp and relentless. Her pulse thundered in her ears, tears threatening to spill, but she fought them back. She could not—would not—allow herself to hope. Not when her heart had already chosen a man who, in the world as it stood, could never be hers.

The lift continued its slow ascent, and she pressed her forehead to the cool metal, the tiny space feeling impossibly confining, mirroring the cage of her emotions. She had never known longing like this—so urgent, so consuming, and so entirely impossible. Yet despite it all, she whispered softly to herself, almost lost in the hum of the lift: "I love him… and it will never be enough."

Christian watched the lift doors slide closed, his chest tightening with frustration and despair. He wanted—needed—to reach her, pull her into his arms, tell her the truth, but he was trapped in the middle of the chalet, surrounded by staff, cameras, and Clarissa's ever-watchful presence. Every step toward her felt impossible.

His gaze flicked to Clarissa, still clinging to him with practiced worry, eyes calculating, touch coldly possessive. It was all for show, and he despised it—but he couldn't risk a scene, not yet. Not when Eliza was out of reach, and the fragile moment they'd shared was slipping further away with each passing second.

Christian ran a hand through his hair, jaw tight, anger and longing warring inside him. He had never wanted anyone like this—not in all his years, not even with all the women he'd known. Eliza had claimed something inside him he didn't even realise was missing, and now she was gone, leaving only the ache of absence.

He pressed a hand to his chest over the rapid beat of his heart and whispered under his breath, a confession only he could hear: "I can't lose her… not to anyone, not to this life, not to Clarissa."

The storm outside had passed, the snow piled high, but the storm within him raged on—raging for her, for the truth, for the chance he hadn't yet dared to take. He would find her. Soon. He would tell her everything. And when that time came, nothing—neither obligation nor circumstance—would hold him back.

For now, all he could do was wait, burning with a desire and a certainty he had never felt before, hoping that Eliza would hold on just long enough for him to reach her.

Chapter Eleven

Eliza stood beneath the pounding spray of the shower, her body wracked with sobs so fierce they stole her breath. She pressed her forehead to the cool tiles, water streaming over her face and mingling with her tears, but nothing could wash away the raw ache tearing through her chest. She had never known pain like this—soul-shattering, bone-deep, the kind that made it hard to stand, to breathe, to exist.

Christian. His name alone broke her. The thought of him with Clarissa—his fiancée—was unbearable, a knife twisting with every beat of her heart. She couldn't stay here. Not another hour. Not two more days. Running into them again would destroy her completely.

When at last she dragged herself from the shower, she caught sight of her reflection. Her eyes were swollen and red, cheeks blotched, lips trembling. She barely recognised the woman staring back. Pulling on her clothes with mechanical movements, she reached for her phone, fingers shaking. She searched desperately for a way out, and when she found an earlier flight, relief and sorrow collided, leaving her trembling all over again.

A train to the airport. A seat to London. A chance to disappear. She clung to the plan like a lifeline.

She packed quickly, folding her clothes with a precision born of determination, not care. Every item she placed in her bag felt like severing another tie—another reminder of the man she had let into her heart too quickly, too completely. She zipped the suitcase closed and forced herself to her feet.

At reception, the woman behind the counter blinked in surprise. "Checking out two days early, Mrs. Clarke?"

Eliza's heart lurched at the name—Brad's name, the one she should have worn as a wife, but never had. It stung, a reminder of betrayal, of dreams slipping through her fingers. She swallowed hard, forcing composure into her voice. "Yes. Family emergency."

The receptionist nodded sympathetically, processing the bill quickly. "Of course. Thank you for staying with us, Mrs. Clarke. Safe travels."

Eliza managed a thin smile she didn't feel. "Thank you."

Minutes later, she slid into the waiting vehicle, suitcase tucked at her side. As it pulled away from the chalet, she stared resolutely ahead, refusing to glance back. She couldn't risk seeing him—Christian—in the arms of another woman.

London awaited. A new life awaited. She clung to that fragile hope, even as her heart remained behind, broken, with the man she had loved far too quickly—and far too deeply.

An hour later, Christian finally shook himself free of Clarissa's endless prattle. She had clung to his arm since the rescue, performing worry like an actress on stage, and every nerve in him screamed to escape. At last, he did. He strode to the reception desk, heart hammering with urgency.

The young man behind the counter straightened nervously. "Good evening, Mr. Harrington. Can I help you?"

"Yes," Christian said, voice low, tight with impatience. "I need the room number for Eliza Preston."

The man tapped at his keyboard, eyes scanning the screen. After a moment, his brow furrowed. "I'm sorry, sir, but there's no guest under that name."

Christian leaned forward, irritation flashing in his eyes. "That's impossible. She's staying here. Check again."

More typing. More scrolling. Then the same helpless shake of the head. "No record, sir. I'm afraid not."

Christian's temper flared, barely contained. "Get me your manager."

The manager arrived within minutes, smoothing his jacket as though preparing for battle. "Mr. Harrington. What seems to be the problem?"

"I'll tell you what the problem is," Christian snapped. "The woman rescued with me today—Eliza Preston. I want her room number. Now."

The manager stepped behind the desk, checked the screen himself, then looked up, calm but apologetic. "I understand, sir, but I can't give you what doesn't exist. There is no one by that name checked in with us."

Christian stared at him, disbelief knotting in his chest. "You saw her this morning. She was here. You know she was."

"Yes," the manager admitted quietly. "I did see her. But as far as our records show, she was never registered. The only missing person reported to us was you, by your fiancée."

Christian's blood ran cold. His fiancée. Clarissa. Always Clarissa. And Eliza—vanished.

He stepped back, pulse hammering, a sick weight settling in his chest. Somehow, while he'd been trapped in Clarissa's clutches, forced to endure her theatrics, Eliza had slipped right through his fingers.

"She has to be here," he insisted, voice rough with disbelief. "She has to be in the hotel somewhere."

The manager straightened, uncomfortable under Christian's sharp stare. "Sir, I understand your concern. But there's no record of a Miss Preston in our system. We weren't even aware of her presence until she stepped off the helicopter with you. As far as our staff is concerned, she wasn't a guest."

Christian's jaw tightened, frustration and panic colliding. "Are you telling me," he demanded, voice low and dangerous, "that no one noticed when she disappeared?"

"That's correct, sir," the manager confirmed gently. "Your fiancée reported you missing. That was the first and only report we received. Until you returned, we had no knowledge of the young lady."

Clarissa's name. Clarissa's lies. Clarissa's shadow. And Eliza—alone, unseen, erased as though she had never existed. Eliza was worth a thousand Clarissa's— and she was slipping through his grasp.

A sudden thought struck him. He leaned forward, voice tight with urgency. "Has anyone checked out recently?"

The manager frowned, fingers flying over the keyboard before nodding. "Yes, sir. Only one guest. A Mrs. Clarke."

Christian's heart lurched. Mrs. Clarke? That didn't make sense. Eliza wasn't married. She couldn't be. His mind reeled, the name taunting him, refusing to align with what he knew.

"No…" he muttered under his breath, shaking his head. "That can't be her." But a sharp ache gnawed at his gut, whispering that it was. That she'd left under a name he didn't recognise—a name she hadn't trusted him enough to explain.

Damn it, Eliza… where are you? His chest tightened, anguish twisting like a blade, cutting deeper with every breath. I need to find her. And fast.

A few days later, Christian stepped out of his grandfather's lawyers' offices, the echo of polished marble and practiced voices still clinging to him. Moments ago, he had told them—calmly, unequivocally—that he had no intention of marrying Clarissa. The engagement was over. The words had tasted strange on his tongue, heavy with finality, yet beneath the weight was something startlingly light—liberation.

Reclining in the plush leather of his limousine, the city lights streaking past in a blur, Christian's thoughts returned obsessively to the past three days. He had spent endless hours in the chalet foyer, hoping—praying—that Eliza would appear. But she hadn't. Not once. Clarissa had whined incessantly about appearances, the optics of his prolonged absence, and he had told her flatly that he didn't give a damn.

Then, yesterday, back in London, he had told Clarissa outright: he couldn't marry her. Her response was crocodile tears, an overdramatic display of heartbreak he saw through instantly. Clarissa had never cared for him beyond the advantages of the Harrington name. When he told her she could keep the engagement ring—over a million pounds in value—her face had brightened immediately, opportunistic delight lighting her features. He hadn't cared. No fortune, no matter how vast, could make him marry her.

The lawyers had tried their usual tactics—reasoning, appeals to duty, reminders of legacy—but Christian's mind was made up. He couldn't accept a cold, loveless marriage now. Not when he had glimpsed what could be possible with someone who stirred his soul like Eliza did. Even though he couldn't find her, even though she was somewhere out there, unreachable, the memory of her— the weight of her trust, the warmth of her presence, the raw connection they had shared—had changed him.

He clenched his hands, frustration, and determination warring in his chest. Money, obligation, appearances—they all felt hollow compared to what mattered now. He would find her. He would tell her the truth. No half-measures, no secrets left unsaid.

The limousine slowed to a stop in front of Henry and Mary's townhouse. They had invited him for dinner, expecting Clarissa to be at his side—but if he never saw her again, it would be far too soon.

He stepped out, the crisp evening air doing nothing to cool the fire of resolve burning through him. Henry's butler opened the door with a polite bow.

"Welcome, Mr. Harrington. Mr. and Mrs. Windsor are in the drawing room," the man announced.

"Thank you," Christian said, giving a brief smile before stepping inside.

"Christian!" Henry came forward immediately, clasping his hand firmly. His gaze swept behind him, frowning. "Where's Clarissa?"

"Not coming. She probably won't be seen with me again," Christian replied, voice steady, though a flicker of relief passed through him.

Mary emerged from the room, eyes lighting up as she kissed him lightly on the cheek. "Why? What happened?" she asked, concern and curiosity mingling in her tone.

Christian exhaled, tension in his shoulders easing just slightly as he stepped fully into the warmth of the drawing room. The truth weighed on him, urgent and undeniable—but for the first time in days, he felt a measure of control. He would find her. He had to.

"I called it off," he said, voice calm but resolute.

Henry's shoulders relaxed, a hint of relief in his expression. "Thank God."

Christian arched an amused brow. "Tell me what you really think."

"You know I never liked her," Henry replied, a wry smile tugging at his lips.

Mary, however, looked concerned, her eyes narrowing slightly. "What happened?"

"My eyes were opened," Christian said, tone steady but charged.

Henry leaned closer, curiosity glinting in his eyes. "By who?"

Christian let out a dry laugh, shaking his head. "What makes you think someone else is involved?"

"Christian, I've known you since we were kids," Henry said, gaze sharp.

Christian held his hands up in mock surrender. "Okay, okay... I met someone."

Mary's eyes widened, a mixture of surprise and concern. "Someone...?"

Christian's lips curved into a small, tight smile. "Yes. And believe me, I've never felt anything like it."

Henry exchanged a knowing look with Mary, sensing there was far more to the story but choosing to stay silent. Christian's jaw tightened; determination flashed in his eyes. He wouldn't rest until he found her.

Mary sensed the tension between them. "I'll just go check on things while you two talk," she said gently, offering a small, understanding smile.

Christian leaned forward, pressing a brief, heartfelt kiss to her cheek. "Thank you, Mary."

She gave him a knowing nod and quietly left the room. The soft click of the door marked a subtle shift in the atmosphere.

Once she was gone, Henry's eyes sharpened, a half-smile tugging at his lips. "Well, spill. I can feel there's a story brewing here."

Christian ran a hand through his hair, exhaling slowly. "It's… complicated," he began, voice low but urgent. Then he let the truth tumble out. "I ran into her three times… and the third time, we got caught in the storm. We were trapped together, and…" He paused, swallowing hard as a flush crept over his face. "…the attraction between us—it's unlike anything I've ever felt. It's… overwhelming."

Henry leaned forward, elbows on his knees, eyes fixed intently on Christian. "Overwhelming how? You don't mean…"

Christian's gaze darkened, a raw, almost feral edge in his voice. "I mean—making love to her… it was a revelation. She's unlike anyone I've ever known. Every touch, every look, every moment—it felt alive. Real. I can't put it into words properly, Henry, but I've never felt this way with anyone. Not even close."

Henry let the words settle, nodding slowly, the gravity in Christian's tone impossible to ignore. "Sounds like you've met someone who's completely turned your world upside down. That's exactly how I felt when I met Mary."

Christian's jaw tightened, eyes distant as the memories replayed—the storm, the cabin, the heat, the closeness, the surrender. "She has… and I can't… I can't go back to pretending. Not with Clarissa, not with anyone else. I think… I love her."

"Well, where is she? You should have brought her," Henry pressed.

Christian shook his head slowly. "That's the complicated bit."

"Oh?"

"I can't find her," Christian admitted, the words tasting bitter.

"What? Why?"

He took a deep breath, voice rough. "When we were rescued, she found out I was engaged before I could tell her. The hurt in her eyes… Henry, it nearly killed me."

Henry leaned back, absorbing the weight of his friend's confession. He could see the torment etched into Christian's features—the longing, the remorse, the desperation. This wasn't just a fleeting infatuation; it had claimed him completely.

"That's… a lot," Henry said finally, voice quiet but steady. "But if she's the one, Christian… you'll find her. You have to."

Christian's eyes flicked up, a fire igniting behind the storm of guilt and loss. "I will. I can't let her slip away. Not now. Not ever."

Henry nodded, recognizing the unwavering certainty in his friend's voice. This was a turning point—one that would shape the rest of his life and the woman who, in just a few days, had become impossible to forget.

Christian leaned back slightly, eyes fixed on Henry. "You know, when you told me my inheritance wasn't worth being trapped in a loveless marriage, I thought you were mad. I didn't get it… not then. But now I do. I couldn't go through with it—not now, not when I've felt what it's like to be with someone who makes everything else meaningless."

Henry's gaze was steady, conviction shining in his eyes. "I told you, Christian. I wouldn't give Mary up for all the money in the world."

Christian exhaled slowly, a hint of a smile tugging at his lips, though his eyes still burned with longing. "That's exactly how I feel about Eliza. Everything else—status, money, appearances—it doesn't matter. Not one bit. All I know is I can't stop thinking about her. Can't stop needing her."

Henry's nod was firm, almost solemn. "Then you do what you have to do. You find her. Nothing else matters until you do."

Christian's jaw tightened, a fierce blend of determination and desperation hardening his features. His voice was low, steady, carrying the weight of his resolve. "I will find her. No matter what it takes. I won't let this—us—slip away."

Henry raised an eyebrow, half-amused, half-impressed. "I figured as much. You've never been one to let anything—or anyone—get away."

"I've already hired the best private investigator available," Christian continued, his tone sharp with conviction. "I don't care how much it costs, how long it takes, or how far I have to go. I will find her. She—Eliza—is worth everything. And I won't stop until I do."

Henry nodded slowly, the weight of Christian's words settling on him. "Then if you need anything—resources, connections, whatever it takes—just say the word. Consider it done. And I have to admit… I can't wait to meet this Eliza who's turned your world upside down."

Christian let out a long, measured exhale, a flicker of relief softening the tension in his shoulders. Yet even as he did, the fire in his eyes burned undiminished— a steady, determined blaze. He had made his choice, and there was no turning back. Every instinct, every thought, every heartbeat now aligned with one unshakable truth: he would find her, no matter what.

Chapter Twelve

Eliza stepped through the door of her small London flat, the familiar click of the lock doing little to settle the storm in her chest. Her feet ached, her body was weary, and the quiet of the apartment felt heavier than usual. It had been ten days since she had left St. Moritz, ten days since the storm, ten days since Christian had vanished from her life as completely as he had entered it.

She dropped her coat over a chair, sliding off her boots, but even the comfort of home did little to ease the emptiness gnawing at her. The apartment felt impossibly silent, the walls too close, the air too still. A part of her ached as though a vital piece of her had been left behind in that snow-bound cabin, wrapped in warmth, firelight, and the memory of him.

She sank onto the edge of the sofa, burying her face in her hands, letting herself inhale and exhale through the hollow ache that seemed to grip her chest. Each breath carried the weight of memories she couldn't shake—the sweep of Christian's hand across hers, the intensity that had burned in his eyes, the way he had made her feel seen, wanted, alive. The ache of missing him was sharp and insistent, a fire that tightened her chest and made her heart hammer, leaving her dizzy with longing. Something essential, something irreplaceable, had been ripped away, and the thought of never seeing him again felt almost unbearable.

But the bitter truth pressed in with equal force. Christian was promised to someone else. She had wanted to believe that what they had shared meant something to him, that the stolen night, the whispered words, the intimacy— they had all counted. Yet now, doubt slithered into her thoughts, cruel and relentless. Perhaps she had been nothing more than a fleeting escape, a convenient indulgence, an itch he had needed to scratch. That sting cut sharper than the memory of Brad abandoning her at the altar. At least Brad had been honest in his cowardice. Christian… he had been everything she wanted, everything she thought she could have, and yet now he was gone, leaving only questions and the raw ache of loss.

She exhaled shakily, pressing her palms to her face as if she could smother the tumult inside her. The room was quiet, yet the echo of his presence lingered, haunting her every thought, a ghost she couldn't shake. In that stillness, the full weight of her loss pressed down on her, and with it, a sharp, sobering clarity: the danger of allowing herself to feel again. Especially after two men—one who had abandoned her at the altar, the other who had ignited something she had never expected—had betrayed her trust in the span of a single week. Her heart ached not only for what had been taken but for the peril of opening it once more.

Her mind wandered reluctantly to practicalities, but even they seemed tinged with the shadow of him. She had just finished her final interview for her new job, the one she would start in the new year in a childcare facility. The last hurdle was the pre-employment blood screening scheduled for the twentieth of December—next week—and it felt surreal to have such mundane concerns amid the storm of emotions he had left behind.

Tomorrow, she would start a small part-time role as Santa's little helper in a luxury department store. Perhaps the busy days, the laughter of children, and the sparkle of holiday decorations would distract her from thinking about Christian so relentlessly. Perhaps—but she wasn't convinced. Deep down, she knew no festive lights or jolly giggles could fill the void he had left in her heart.

She lowered her hands from her face, letting the glow of the living room lamps wash over her. She felt the quiet hum of the city outside her window, the ordinary world continuing without pause, indifferent to the tempest inside her. And yet, in that quiet, the longing for him persisted, a constant, invisible thread pulling at her very core.

Christian stood in his high-rise office, the sprawling London skyline stretched behind him, though he barely noticed it. The weight of what he'd just learned about Eliza pressed down on him—a tangled mix of guilt, frustration, and raw panic twisting in his chest. Not only had her fiancé abandoned her at the altar, but he himself had been dishonest—betrayed her trust even as he fell deeper into something he couldn't ignore.

His phone buzzed on the polished desk. Without looking, he pressed the intercom button.

"Yes?"

"Mr. Windsor is here to see you," came the calm voice from the other end.

"Send him in."

Moments later, Henry strode into the office, taking a seat opposite Christian. His gaze was sharp, direct. "Any news on Eliza?"

Christian ran a hand down his face, exhaling a long, exasperated sigh. "The PI just left."

"And?" Henry prompted, leaning forward.

"She… she was supposed to be on her honeymoon," Christian said, voice tight, laden with anger and guilt.

Henry's eyes widened, disbelief etched across his face. "What? She's married?"

Christian slammed his fists onto the desk, jaw tight, teeth gritted. "No," he growled, voice low and ragged. "The bastard left her at the altar. And then I… I lied to her."

"Shit," Henry muttered, leaning back, running a hand over his face. "The poor girl. To be left like that… and then to have someone else lie to her. I'd be surprised if she trusted anyone again."

Christian's knuckles whitened as he clenched his hands harder. "I know. I feel like an utter bastard." He slammed his hand down again, the echo reverberating through the office. "Why didn't I tell her when I had the chance? Why didn't I just—just be honest? She deserved the truth, Henry. Not my half-measures, not my cowardice. She trusted me!"

Henry's expression softened, voice firm but calm. "Listen, Christian. You can't change the past. But you can do something about it now. You have to find her. You have to tell her everything. No more lies, no more half-truths. She needs to know who you really are—and what you feel."

Christian ran a hand down his face, exhaling sharply. "I can't stop thinking about her. Every moment without her is… unbearable. I've never felt anything like this for anyone. I can't lose her, Henry. Not now. Not ever."

Henry leaned forward, locking eyes with him. "Then stop thinking. Start acting. Find her, Christian. No excuses. No delays. And when you do… make sure she knows the truth from you. Every word, every feeling, every truth she deserves."

Christian nodded, determination hardening in his gaze. "I will. I'll find her. And this time… I won't let her slip away. Not for anyone, not for anything."

The city stretched out beneath the high-rise, streets buzzing with oblivious lives. The clatter of traffic and distant sirens were meaningless to him. For Christian, there was only one thought, pulsing through every vein, every nerve—Eliza. *Where are you?*

Henry stood, the weight of the conversation pressing lightly on his shoulders. "Come on. I'll take you to lunch. You look like you could use it."

Christian grabbed his jacket, sliding it on with tense, restless energy. "Okay… but as long as it comes with a strong drink," he muttered, voice low, as though the alcohol might steady the storm inside him.

Henry raised an eyebrow, half-amused, half-concerned. "Strong enough to handle the truth, or just strong enough to survive me?"

Christian allowed himself the barest hint of a smirk. "Both," he replied, following Henry out, each step echoing with the single thought he couldn't shake—*I will find her. No matter what.*

Eliza adjusted the jingling red-and-gold elf hat perched on her head and forced a smile at the little boy clutching his mother's hand. The luxury department store was a dazzling wonderland of Christmas cheer—twinkling garlands draped along marble bannisters, crystal chandeliers casting a festive glow over polished floors, and the mingling scents of cinnamon, mulled wine, and expensive perfume filling the air.

It was her first shift as Santa's little helper, and though the costume was more playful than dignified—green velvet dress, striped tights, bells on her shoes—there was something soothing about the distraction.

"Come along, sweetheart," she said, crouching to the boy's level, her voice warm though her heart still felt bruised. "Santa's waiting for you."

The child's eyes widened at the sight of Santa in his grand velvet chair, and Eliza felt a small flicker of pride at being part of the magic. She guided the boy toward the snowy set, then stepped back as the photographer clicked away.

Between children, she straightened decorations and offered candy canes to passing shoppers, letting the steady rhythm of the job carry her along. It was easier than thinking about Christian—about his hands, his kiss, his betrayal. Still, every time she caught her reflection in the polished shop windows, she barely recognised the woman staring back: someone trying desperately to smile while hiding the fracture lines beneath.

"Miss?" a little girl tugged at her skirt, big eyes fixed on the tray of sweets.

Eliza crouched again, handing her a striped candy cane. "There you go, darling. Merry Christmas."

The girl beamed, skipping back to her father, and for the first time all day, Eliza felt her smile reach her eyes. Maybe, just maybe, this job would help her rebuild. She needed to believe in something again—even if it was only the magic of Christmas in a glittering department store.

But as she straightened, smoothing her skirt, her gaze swept the floor beyond the grotto. For the briefest second, her heart lurched—because across the polished marble, she thought she saw him. Christian. Tall, commanding, magnetic even at a distance, utterly out of place among the swirl of Christmas shoppers.

Her breath caught, the tray of candy canes trembling in her hands. It couldn't be. Not here. Not now.

A child tugged at her striped tights, holding up a crooked drawing of Santa and his reindeer. "Look! I made this for him!"

Eliza bent down, and despite the hollow ache lodged in her chest, a laugh burst from her—soft at first, then light and bright—as the little boy proudly explained his picture. The sound startled her, as though she'd forgotten how laughter felt on her lips.

Christian and Henry strolled through the bustling department store, the polished marble floors gleaming beneath crystal chandeliers, the air thick with the mingled scents of pine garlands and expensive perfume. Shoppers moved around them in a blur of red bags and winter coats, but Christian barely noticed. This was one of many Harrington Group stores—empires of glass, steel, and commerce. Soon, none of it would matter.

He had made peace with that. The inheritance, the empire, the gilded legacy— it all meant nothing compared to what he had lost. All he wanted was Eliza.

Then it happened.

A sound cut through the carols and chatter—a laugh. Not just any laugh. Her laugh. Light, warm, edged with the sweetness he had replayed in his mind a hundred times since St. Moritz.

Christian froze mid-step, chest tightening, heart hammering. He turned to Henry, voice hoarse. "Did you hear that?"

Henry stopped, brow furrowed. "Hear what?"

The laugh came again—clearer this time, rising above the clamour.

Christian's pulse surged. He knew it. He knew it. "That's Eliza," he said, certainty burning in his voice. "I would recognise it anywhere."

Henry's eyes widened, following Christian's gaze as he scanned the crowd like a man starved.

Christian's eyes darted across the polished floors, the sweep of gilt banisters and towering Christmas trees blurring around him. His breath lodged in his throat, every muscle taut, straining to catch it again.

Henry laid a hand on his arm. "Christian, slow down—you could be mistaken. It's Christmas, half the city is in here. A laugh is just a laugh."

Christian shook his head, conviction blazing in his eyes. "No. Not hers. You don't forget something like that."

He pivoted, scanning through the swirl of shoppers, the line snaking toward Santa's grotto, the shimmer of tinsel, the chaos of children's laughter. The world pressed against him—too loud, too bright—until, soft and fleeting, like a bell just beyond reach, her laugh rang out again.

Christian's chest clenched as though the universe had shifted on its axis.

"She's here," he whispered, more to himself than to Henry, voice hoarse with hope and disbelief. "I can feel it."

Henry watched his friend's face transform with raw urgency. "Then find her," he said quietly.

Christian drew a sharp breath, chest tight, eyes scanning, waiting—knowing in his bones she was close.

His pulse thundered as he pushed forward through the crowd, every step carrying him closer. And then—he saw her.

Eliza.

She stood by the velvet rope of Santa's grotto, tray of candy canes balanced carefully in her hands, green velvet dress catching the glow of twinkling lights. She laughed at something a child had said, head tipped back slightly, the sound pure, unguarded. For a heartbeat, he froze, unable to breathe, watching as though she might vanish if he moved.

Everything else fell away—the carols, the chatter of shoppers, even Henry beside him. There was only her.

His chest ached with the force of it, with the certainty that he was staring at the woman he could never let go of again.

"Eliza…" he whispered, the name breaking from him like a prayer.

Henry followed his gaze, a slow, knowing smile spreading across his face. "Well, I'll be damned."

Christian didn't respond. He simply stood, rooted to the spot, drinking her in— Eliza, adjusting a little boy's Santa hat, laughing softly, utterly unaware of the storm she had just stirred in him. He couldn't move—not yet. The fear of losing her again, of her slipping away before he could reach her, kept him frozen. She was here. Real. Alive. And, finally, within reach.

His chest tightened with each heartbeat, a relentless reminder of how much he had missed her, how much he needed her now. And this time—this time—he would not let her slip away.

Henry's hand landed firmly on his shoulder, shaking him slightly. "Don't just stand there, Christian. Go to her."

Christian drew a slow, deliberate breath, swallowing the lump in his throat. He stepped forward, then another, measured and deliberate, anchoring himself to the polished brass railing beside him. His gaze never wavered from hers, drinking in every movement, every laugh, every flicker of life that made her utterly, painfully irresistible.

This was it. He could hesitate no longer.

Eliza knelt to adjust the little boy's Santa hat, laughing as he wriggled in protest. "There we go, perfect!" she said, voice warm. She handed him a candy cane and ruffled his hair gently, losing herself for a moment in the simple joy of the task.

Then she looked up—and froze.

Across the marble floor, two men stood, watching her. One of them tall, impossibly familiar, radiating the same commanding presence she couldn't mistake for anyone else. Christian.

Her heart lurched. She forced a small, professional smile at the child. "There you go, all done," she murmured, but her eyes couldn't leave him. He was watching her with that same intensity she remembered—the same raw, undeniable pull.

The other man—dressed sharply, standing slightly behind Christian—looked amused, eyes flicking between her and Christian.

Her stomach twisted with a mix of excitement and panic. She had only just started this job, and now here he was, appearing like a ghost from her past she never expected to see.

Her hands gripped the candy cane tray a little tighter, knees trembling, but she forced herself to speak to the child again. "Do you want to sit for a picture with Santa now?" she asked, voice steadier than she felt.

Christian didn't move. He just stared at her, frozen by relief and longing, until the man beside him lightly touched his shoulder and murmured something. Slowly, they began walking toward her, each step measured, hearts beating in quiet anticipation.

When they drew near, Christian's voice dropped to a low, almost reverent whisper. "Eliza… you're here."

She lifted her gaze, catching his eyes, and tried to steady her voice. "Hello, Christian." She forced calm into her tone, masking the ache of how much she had missed him, the sting of how deeply he had hurt her.

The man at Christian's side extended a hand, smiling warmly. "Hello, Eliza. I'm Henry Windsor. It's really good to meet you. Christian has told me all about you."

Her eyes shifted to the stranger, and after a brief pause, she shook his hand, careful but polite. "Nice to meet you, Henry. Eliza Preston."

Even in that small exchange, Christian felt it—the way she hesitated, the subtle flicker of guarded warmth in her eyes. A fragile bridge, tentative, yet enough to make him believe there might be a way back to her.

Eliza's gaze flicked back to Christian, mouth opening as if to speak, but before she could, her supervisor hurried over, concern etched across her face.

"Mr. Harrington is everything okay?" she asked, polite but questioning.

Christian straightened, giving a quick nod and calm smile. "Yes, yes, everything is fine," he said, voice steady, though his eyes never left hers.

Eliza blinked, confusion knitting her brows. Henry noticed immediately. "Christian… she doesn't know who you are?" he asked quietly, a hint of amusement in his tone.

Eliza turned to Henry, then back to Christian, shaking her head slowly. "I… no," she admitted, uncertainty and a flicker of hurt crossing her features.

Pain shot through Christian's chest, sharp and relentless, yet beneath it, a deeper ache—the knowledge that he had withheld the truth, and how desperately he longed to tell her everything.

She tilted her head, curiosity and suspicion lacing her voice. "Then… who are you?"

Before Christian could answer, her supervisor, Helen, stepped closer, smiling gently. "Eliza, dear… he owns this department store."

The words hung heavy in the air. Eliza's eyes widened, pieces clicking into place. Shock, hurt, disbelief—and the sudden, undeniable pull toward the man she had been missing for so long.

"I… I need to get back to work. Nice to meet you, Mr. Harrington," she said, voice tight, turning back to the children, clinging to something familiar.

"Eliza…" Christian began, but she ignored him, returning to the little ones with a measured calm that belied the storm inside her.

Chapter Thirteen

Henry placed a firm hand on Christian's shoulder, both a warning and a shove in one. "Come on, Christian," he said, tone sharp but measured. "You can't just stand there like a lovesick fool."

Christian exhaled, his gaze lingering on Eliza for one last heartbeat, committing her to memory, before letting Henry guide him away. The ache of her absence—even when she was just feet away—gnawed at him. He had glimpsed what could be, and keeping the truth from her had been a mistake he would not make again.

Back in his office, Christian sank into the leather chair behind his desk, running a hand through his hair. "I really stuffed up, didn't I?" he muttered, voice heavy with frustration and self-reproach.

"Yeah, you did," Henry replied, leaning against the edge of the desk. He studied his friend, noting the rare vulnerability in Christian's posture. "You didn't even tell her who you really were?"

Christian shook his head, a rueful smile tugging at the corner of his lips. "No. I liked that she didn't look at me like a bank balance. She... she saw me." His voice softened, almost to himself. "Really saw me."

Henry smirked knowingly. "Something tells me she wouldn't have cared anyway."

Christian's jaw clenched, determination flickering in his eyes. "No. She wouldn't. And I'm not going to waste another second. I need to fix this, Henry. I need her to know the truth—all of it. About me, about what I feel, about everything."

Henry nodded slowly, a hint of a grin returning to his face. "Then let's figure out how to get her back without scaring her off. You've already shown her glimpses of who you are. Now it's time to show her the whole man."

Christian leaned back, the weight of the plan settling over him. Finally, the chase had a purpose, and the prize—Eliza—was worth every risk.

The last echoes of children's laughter faded from the department store as Eliza hung up her Santa apron and slipped out of the small staff room. She tugged her coat tighter around her, the crisp December air biting at her cheeks as she stepped onto the street. Her thoughts were a jumble—Christmas, work, and the memory of Christian—but she pushed them aside. She had a life to start, boundaries to keep. She couldn't let herself be swept away again.

A shadow fell across her path, tall and unmistakable. She stopped, her heart skipping.

"Eliza."

She turned slowly, brushing a strand of hair from her face. "Christian." Her voice was calm, careful—controlled. "Please, I'm not interested in… whatever this is."

His eyes softened, hands almost pleading as he stepped closer. "Please. Just hear me out. Can we… have dinner tonight? One meal. No expectations, I promise."

Eliza's brows drew together, uncertainty flickering in her gaze. "I… I don't know. I don't think—"

"Just one dinner," he interrupted, voice low, insistent. "I need to explain everything. I lied, I hurt you, and I can't… I can't fix it without telling you the truth." His chest rose and fell with urgency. "Please, Eliza. Let me."

She studied him, the familiar pull in her chest threatening to betray her words. Part of her wanted to turn and walk away, to protect herself from the raw emotions he stirred. But the other part—the part that had missed him more than she thought possible—softened.

After a long, tense moment, she nodded, lips barely a whisper. "Okay. One dinner. But that's all."

Christian's face softened, a flicker of relief breaking through the intensity in his eyes, warming her despite her resolve. "Thank you," he breathed. "I need your address."

He held out his phone, hopeful. After a moment of hesitation, she took it. Fingers poised, she typed in her contact details, then handed it back, expression carefully neutral.

"Thank you," he murmured, slipping the phone into his pocket. "I'll pick you up at seven. I promise—you won't regret it."

"We'll see," she replied, tone clipped, though the slightest frown tugged at her lips. Without another word, she turned and walked away, the soft click of her heels fading into the evening air.

Christian stood frozen for a heartbeat, watching her retreating figure. His chest tightened with a mixture of relief and frustration. Every instinct screamed to run after her, to pull her into his arms and never let go. But he forced himself to breathe, to let her go for now. Even from a distance, he felt the pull of her presence, the memory of her laugh, the warmth of her touch, making the hours until seven feel like an eternity.

She won't regret it, he whispered to himself, gripping the phone tightly. Because this—her—this is everything. Tonight, I get to show her how much she matters.

He finally turned and walked back into the building, each step measured, anticipation coiling in his chest like a living thing. The promise of dinner—just one dinner—made the world feel suddenly lighter, brighter, and infinitely more hopeful.

Eliza stood before the mirror in her small London flat, fingers brushing the neckline of the dress she had chosen. It wasn't extravagant—just a simple, elegant navy sheath that hugged her figure without shouting for attention—but tonight it had to be perfect. She smoothed the fabric, twisted a strand of hair around her finger, then shook her head. Calm, she reminded herself. Just dinner. One dinner.

Her reflection stared back at her—eyes wide, lips slightly parted. The flutter in her chest was all too familiar, the same breathless stir she'd felt the first time Christian had looked at her. With a sharp exhale, she reached for her clutch, checked her phone. Seven o'clock. Exactly seven.

The quiet was broken by the soft, deliberate thud of footsteps in the hall. Each one echoed like a drumbeat against her ribs. Eliza froze, pulse quickening, then jumped at the knock that followed. For a long moment, she stood motionless, hands trembling, before forcing herself to open the door.

Christian stood framed in the glow of the corridor lights. His tailored coat fit perfectly across his broad shoulders, but it wasn't the cut of the fabric that stole her breath—it was his face. Hope, raw intensity, and something achingly tender flickered in his eyes. Something she hadn't dared dream she'd ever see again.

"I… you look… beautiful." His voice caught, almost faltered, and for an instant he looked undone. His gaze swept over her slowly, reverently, lingering until her knees felt weak.

Heat rushed to her cheeks. "Thank you," she whispered, forcing composure, fighting back the swell of emotion threatening to undo her.

Christian stepped closer, his voice low, as though the hallway itself might betray his heart. "I'm so glad you agreed. I know I don't deserve this… but I need tonight. I need to explain everything."

She studied him, torn between the armour of her resolve and the aching pull he always evoked. At last, she gave a short, careful nod. "I said I'd go. But I'm not sure this is a good idea."

His answer was swift, fierce, but quiet. "It is."

He extended his hand. For a moment she hesitated—but then her fingers slid into his. Warmth flowed into her, steady and certain, unravelling just enough of her doubt. "Thank you," he murmured, eyes locked on hers as though she were the only thing in the world. "I promise—you won't regret it."

They descended the narrow stairwell together, stepping into the crisp night air. Waiting at the curb was a sleek black limousine, gleaming beneath the streetlamps. The driver moved swiftly to open the door.

Eliza froze on the pavement, her hand still linked with his. Her stomach knotted. She didn't belong in this world of polished cars and easy wealth. It had never been hers.

Her voice came low, strained. "Christian, I don't…" She faltered, shaking her head, eyes flicking from him to the car. "I don't belong here."

Christian turned fully to her, their hands still entwined, the night curling cold around them. For a moment he simply looked at her—past the fear, past the guarded uncertainty, to the woman who had undone him.

"Eliza," he said softly, with a weight that made her chest tighten, "you don't belong in this"—he nodded at the car— "and neither do I. Not really. All of that—money, privilege, appearances—it's just noise. Empty noise." He stepped closer, gaze unflinching. "But with you… I belong. I've never felt that before. Not once in my life."

Her breath caught. She couldn't meet his eyes. The sincerity in his tone pierced straight through the walls she had built.

He brushed a stray curl from her cheek, touch so tender it nearly undid her. "Don't look at the car. Don't look at the life you think I live. Look at me. Tonight isn't about luxury—it's about us. Just us."

Her throat tightened, heart pounding hard enough to hurt. She wanted to believe him.

His voice dropped lower, raw, unguarded. "I don't care if it's the finest restaurant in London or fish and chips on a park bench. I just want to sit across from you. To talk. To explain. To make you see that what happened between us wasn't some passing moment. It was everything."

The city hummed beyond the quiet street, the driver waiting silently, patient. Eliza finally lifted her gaze, and what she saw in his eyes—hope, determination, and rare, aching vulnerability—made her knees weak.

Slowly, she nodded. "Okay," she whispered, voice unsteady. "But... for tonight only."

Relief broke across his face, a smile like sunlight through clouds. He held out his hand once more. "Tonight," he agreed softly, "is all I need. For now."

The limousine slid smoothly into the flow of London traffic, the low hum of the engine filling the silence between them. Eliza sat stiffly against the leather seat, her hands folded tightly in her lap, eyes fixed on the blur of city lights through the tinted window.

Beside her, Christian studied her profile—the elegant slope of her nose, the firm set of her jaw, the restless way her fingers worried at the hem of her dress. She looked calm, composed, untouchable. But he knew better. He had created the storm churning beneath that surface, and the weight of it pressed like stone against his chest.

"I've missed you," he said at last, the words breaking from him like a confession, low and rough in the quiet.

Her head turned just slightly, her gaze flicking to his before retreating back to the glass. "You don't get to say that."

The rejection stung, sharper than he'd expected, but he didn't flinch. "I know. But it's still the truth."

Her breath fogged faintly against the cool window, her reflection a pale echo of herself. "You were engaged, Christian. To someone else. Whatever happened between us—it shouldn't have happened."

He leaned forward, elbows braced on his knees, his eyes never leaving her. "I ended it. I ended everything with her the moment I realised what you meant to me. There was never a future with Clarissa. Not the kind I saw in a single moment with you."

Her chest tightened, her heart lurching against her will, but she forced her head to shake, refusing to let hope take root. "Words are easy. Promises are easy. I've heard them before—believed them before—only to be left behind. To realise I meant nothing."

Christian's jaw clenched, the sting of her pain carving into him. He shifted closer, his voice dropping, raw with sincerity. "You mean everything. I can't erase what I did—the secrets I kept, the truth I hid when I should have been honest. But I won't let you think you were a mistake. You never were. You never could be."

The limousine eased to a stop at a red light. Outside, the city glowed—Christmas lights draped across shopfronts, golden and bright—but inside, the air was heavy, threaded with everything unspoken.

Eliza turned then, meeting his gaze fully for the first time. Her eyes shone, vulnerable, wounded in a way that made his chest tighten until he could hardly breathe. For a heartbeat neither moved. Then, almost without thought, Christian reached for her hand.

She hesitated—just long enough to make his heart falter—but she didn't pull away.

Her touch seared him, warmth flooding through his veins, grounding him in the single truth that mattered: she was here. And he would spend everything he had, everything he was, to prove himself worthy of her.

The light changed. The car glided forward, carrying them deeper into the city—and closer to the reckoning they could no longer outrun.

Moments later, the limousine slowed before one of London's most exclusive restaurants, its glass façade glittering with festive amber light. A valet hurried to the curb. Christian stepped out first, the night air crisp against his skin, then turned back, hand extended.

Eliza paused on the threshold of decision. Then, with a breath she didn't realise she was holding, she placed her hand in his. His palm closed firmly around hers, the contact sparking a shiver through her—a dangerous reminder of what it felt like to belong to him. Even if she knew she shouldn't.

Inside, the restaurant glowed with understated opulence. Crystal chandeliers spilled golden light across tables draped in white linen, candles flickering like tiny flames of promise. Soft music threaded through the air as waiters glided past in crisp uniforms. Heads turned, one by one, as Christian Harrington entered—tall, commanding, wearing power like a second skin.

Eliza felt the weight of every glance. Heat crept up her neck as she shrank slightly into herself, suddenly conscious of the simple navy dress she'd chosen. She didn't belong here—not in this rarefied world where people spoke the language of fortunes and legacies over champagne, where Christian fit as if born to it.

Sensing her unease, he leaned close, his voice low and intimate. "Ignore them. Tonight, it's just you and me."

The maître d' appeared at once, bowing. "Mr. Harrington. Your table is ready."

They were ushered to a private corner, where the hum of the dining room softened into background music. Eliza settled into her chair, but Christian's gaze never wavered, steady, intent, unyielding.

"You don't believe me," he said gently.

Her laugh was quiet, edged with bitterness. "I don't. Because men like you don't fall for women like me."

His jaw flexed, but his tone was even, steady. "That's where you're wrong. From the moment I met you, nothing else mattered. Not the engagement. Not the life I thought I wanted. You changed everything, Eliza. And I'm not going back."

Her heart twisted at the raw conviction in his voice. Terrifying, because a part of her already believed him.

The waiter arrived with menus, breaking the spell. Eliza's eyes widened at the impossibly high prices, but Christian dismissed the man with a quiet word, ordering wine without even looking.

When they were alone again, she lifted her chin. "I don't need this. The champagne, the five-star meals, the limousines. I just need to know you're telling me the truth."

Christian's expression softened, the fire in his gaze giving way to something vulnerable. "Then let me prove it. Not with money. Not with promises. Just with us. One day at a time. Starting tonight."

Her throat tightened. For once, she didn't answer immediately. She only stared across the flickering candlelight, wondering if this was the moment her heart dared to hope again.

Her voice came out low, aching. "Why did you sleep with me when you were engaged? You told me there was no one waiting for you. That was a lie."

Christian flinched, the words cutting deep. His hand closed around his wineglass but didn't lift it. "I know. And I hate myself for it. But please… let me explain. From the beginning."

Eliza hesitated, chest rising too quickly, then gave a short, reluctant nod. One chance. She'd listen.

The wine arrived, the waiter retreating. Eliza lifted her glass, hands trembling slightly—then nearly choked when Christian's first words landed like a blow.

"I didn't even like the woman I was engaged to."

She coughed into her napkin, eyes wide. "Excuse me? You didn't like her?"

He leaned forward, elbows braced on the table, gaze locked on hers. "Not even a little. There was no love. No affection. Nothing but expectation and convenience. Clarissa was… convenient. That's all. And I should have told you. I should have been honest from the start."

Her hand shook as she lowered the napkin. "Then why lie?"

"Because I wanted to see you. Because I didn't know how to be honest without losing you before I'd even had a chance. You're not like anyone I've ever met, Eliza. You're alive. You make me alive. And I couldn't bear to lose that." His voice cracked with the weight of it.

Her heart pounded painfully, disbelief and longing twisting together. "So, all this time… you were living a lie?"

Christian shook his head fiercely. "No. I was blind. Until you. Until these past days. I never thought I'd feel this way—for anyone. And I didn't want you hurt because of my mistakes. But I can't hide it anymore. I can't hide how I feel about you."

Eliza's throat ached, her fingers curling against the linen tablecloth. She wanted to stand, to flee before he tore her apart again. But the intensity in his eyes pinned her where she sat, her pulse racing, escape impossible.

Finally, she drew a ragged breath. "Do you know why I was in St. Moritz alone?"

His brow furrowed, unease shadowing his features. "Yes."

Her head tilted, wary. "You do?"

He nodded once, voice low. "I hired someone to find you. I needed to. And this morning… I learned the truth."

Her lips parted, surprise softening her expression. Not anger. Not betrayal. Something else. Something fragile. He had cared enough to look for her.

"Well then," she whispered, her voice trembling, "you know I was supposed to be there on my honeymoon."

Christian's jaw clenched, but he nodded.

Eliza exhaled sharply, pressing the napkin to her palm as if to anchor herself. "My fiancé left me at the altar," she said flatly, each word slicing the air. "I didn't even want to marry him—not really. But I convinced myself it was safe. Expected. And then suddenly, it was gone before it began. I was standing there in a dress that meant nothing, staring at a life I didn't want, and he just… walked away."

Her voice broke, but she pressed on. "And then there was you. Twice. The storm. Fate mocking me. And then you lied." Her eyes shone, a tear threatening to fall. "You told me there was no one waiting for you. But there was."

Christian's chest ached, guilt twisting like iron. "Eliza, I—"

She shook her head, cutting him off, tears brimming. "I'd already been lied to by one man. But I trusted you. For a moment, I thought what we had meant something. And it did. It still does. But you weren't honest with me. Not when it mattered most."

The weight of her pain pressed down on him, relentless. Slowly, he reached across the table, his hand hovering inches from hers, trembling with restraint.

"I know," he whispered. "And I can't undo what I did. But from this moment forward, I swear—I will be nothing but honest. I never want to hurt you again. What I feel for you… it's real. More real than anything I've ever known."

Chapter Fourteen

Eliza's eyes searched his, wide and luminous, and for a heartbeat the world seemed to still. Candlelight flickered between them, shadows, and gold dancing across the table, while the low murmur of the restaurant faded into silence. In that suspended moment, it was only them—bound by a truth too raw, too undeniable, to turn away from.

Her chest rose and fell with a slow, measured breath. "You can't lie to me ever again, Christian," she whispered, her voice trembling with both fear and hope. "No more secrets. No more lies."

His gaze glimmered, a mix of steel and something softer—something only she seemed able to draw from him. He inclined his head, his voice low, steady. "I promise," he vowed, the words landing like an oath carved into stone.

Their meals arrived, the rich scent of roasted vegetables and warm bread filling the air. Christian began to speak, calm but deliberate, while Eliza listened, every word pulling her deeper.

"I asked Clarissa to marry me just after my grandfather passed, barely two months ago," he admitted, his fingers brushing against hers as he spoke.

Eliza's expression softened, unexpected sympathy slipping through. "I'm sorry," she murmured, reaching across the table to lay her hand over his.

His hand shifted, fully enclosing hers, grounding her in the warmth of his touch. "Thank you," he said quietly, a fleeting smile tugging at his lips. That fragile thread between them tugged tighter.

He leaned back, his gaze never wavering. "After my grandfather died, I felt… unmoored. Clarissa was there, pushing, expecting. It felt like the path was already drawn, and I—fool that I was—convinced myself it was what I should do. But even then, I knew. I never felt with her what I feel every moment I look at you, Eliza. Not once."

Her fingers remained in his, her eyes softening though wariness lingered.

"I lied in St. Moritz," he went on, his voice low, taut with regret. "I let you believe I was free, that no one was waiting for me. And the moment I saw the hurt in your eyes, I regretted it."

Her breath caught, her instinct urging her to pull back—but something in his raw honesty held her still. "Then why didn't you tell me?" she asked, her voice unsteady.

Christian exhaled, his shoulders heavy with truth. "Because I was a coward. Afraid that if I admitted the truth, you'd walk away before I even had a chance to hold you." His throat worked as he swallowed. "But that night, in the storm… Eliza, everything shifted. I realised I'd never wanted anyone the way I wanted you. Not ever."

Her chest tightened, her pulse fluttering like a bird desperate to break free. "Christian… you didn't even know me then, and yet—"

"I know," he cut in, his voice fierce with urgency. "But the moment I saw you, in the foyer—it was like lightning. A current tearing through me. I can't explain it. I've never felt anything like it in my life."

Her lips parted, the wall around her cracking. "I felt it too," she admitted, the words so soft they almost vanished between them.

Relief washed over his features, his body easing as though her confession had given him breath. "Then you understand," he said quickly, leaning closer. "Being near you, hearing your laugh, watching the way you light up a room— it was like waking after years of sleep. I didn't know how empty I was until you. And now… I can't go back."

Tears welled in her eyes, blurring the glow of the candles. "I want to believe you," she whispered, her voice trembling with the weight of both fear and longing.

His thumb brushed across her hand, gentle, reverent. "Then let me prove it," he murmured, every word threaded with sincerity. "I can't erase the lies, but I can give you nothing but truth from this moment on. I don't want to hurt you again, Eliza. I don't ever want to lose you."

For a moment, the world stilled again—the clink of silverware, the laughter, the music all dissolving into nothing. It was just them, bound in the fragile promise of something real.

Her gaze softened, her tears spilling freely, though her smile trembled with uncertainty. "Okay," she breathed. "But we take it slow, Christian. You can't rush me. Not after everything."

His chest rose on a shaky exhale, a smile breaking through the intensity in his gaze—tender, reverent. "That's all I can ask for," he murmured, his voice thick with emotion.

They sat across from one another, candlelight casting soft shadows across their faces, the quiet hum of the restaurant a distant blur. Christian reached for his glass of wine but paused halfway, his eyes locked on hers.

"So…" Eliza began cautiously, her fingers tracing the rim of her glass. "How did… Clarissa take it? The broken engagement?" Her voice was careful, but curiosity threaded through every syllable.

Christian let out a slow breath, a mixture of disbelief and dry amusement tugging at his features. "Crocodile tears, mostly," he said, his tone edged with restrained sarcasm. "She cried, wailed, carried on like she'd lost the love of her life. Until I told her she could keep the engagement ring."

Eliza lifted her glass, taking a measured sip, torn between laughter and disbelief.

He shrugged, a wry smile curving his mouth. "Worth just over a million pounds. That seemed to perk her right up."

Her eyes widened, the wine catching in her throat. She coughed, nearly choking. "A… a million pounds?" she sputtered, her voice breaking with incredulity.

Amusement flickered in Christian's gaze at her reaction. "Yes," he said softly, shaking his head. "All smoke and mirrors, Eliza. Every tear, every word—it was all theatre. And in that moment, I knew with absolute clarity what I didn't want. Not her. Not that life. Not ever."

Eliza dabbed at her eyes, still recovering, a reluctant laugh bubbling free. "Unbelievable. Crocodile tears for a million-pound ring. That's… absurd."

Christian leaned forward, the humour fading from his features, replaced by warmth and quiet conviction. "Absurd, yes—but the truth is, none of that matters to me. What matters… is you."

Her heart skipped, the quickening of her pulse betraying her, and for the first time in days, a spark of fragile hope flickered beneath the ache she carried.

"So… tell me about Brad," Christian prompted gently, his thumb brushing across the back of her hand.

Eliza drew in a shaky breath, then exhaled, a bittersweet laugh breaking from her lips. "We were together six months before he proposed. I thought it was love at first… but when the day came and he actually stood me up at the altar, I realised it wasn't love at all. Just… duty, expectation, panic. All the wrong reasons. And when he left, yes, it hurt—but in hindsight, maybe it was the best thing that could have happened."

Christian tightened his hold on her hand, his eyes intent, softened by something almost fierce. "Then I'm glad you're not married."

Eliza arched a brow, a teasing smile tugging at her lips despite herself. "Glad? Not suspicious about my taste in men? Not worried what kind of choice I might make next?"

He chuckled, a low, rich sound that warmed the space between them. "Honestly? After meeting you, I don't see how anyone else could ever measure up."

She laughed, lighter now, the sound musical, unguarded. "Flattery will get you everywhere, Mr. Harrington."

His gaze lingered on her, softened, hungry yet reverent, drinking in every flicker of her smile. "Then I'll take that as encouragement to keep trying," he said, his voice low, threaded with promise.

In that moment, with candlelight between them and the echo of her laughter still hanging in the air, the weight of the past seemed just a little lighter. Something new, fragile but exhilarating, was beginning to take root.

The rest of the meal unfolded in a rhythm that felt private, intimate—soft laughter slipping between them like shared secrets, glances that lingered too long, carrying silent promises neither dared voice. The world beyond their table faded: no clinking cutlery, no murmured conversations, no London beyond the glass walls—only them, suspended in possibility.

Christian's chest tightened as he watched her, memorising the light in her eyes, the curve of her lips when she allowed herself to forget the pain, even for a breath. He longed to tell her everything—about the inheritance, the deadline that loomed over the New Year like a storm cloud—but he forced it back.

It didn't matter. Not compared to this. He had already chosen. Wealth, legacy, empire—none of it meant a thing without her. And he would never let her believe for a moment that his love was entangled in contracts or obligations. She was his only truth.

As the candlelight flickered softly between them, Christian lifted his glass, his eyes still fixed on hers. Whatever tomorrow brought, he knew one thing with absolute certainty—he would never return to the half-life he'd lived before her. Not now. Not when he had finally found the only woman who made him whole.

The limousine eased away, leaving Christian and Eliza in the cool hush of the night. Their footsteps echoed softly along the corridor until they reached her flat.

Eliza's breath caught.

A man sat slumped on the floor against her door, suit rumpled, head bowed. At the sound of their approach, he stirred, lifting his gaze.

Her heart lurched in disbelief. "Brad?"

Christian stiffened beside her, his body taut with unspoken fury.

Brad staggered to his feet, eyes red-rimmed, voice hoarse. "Eliza… can we talk?"

Christian's fists curled at his sides, every muscle coiled, but he stayed silent. Not unless she needed him. Yet the fear gnawed at him—what if her silence meant Brad still had a hold on her?

Eliza lifted her chin, voice cold and steady. "Why, Brad? You made your choice the moment you ran off with Claire."

Shame flickered across his face. "I made a mistake. The biggest of my life. I should never have left you. I want you back."

She gave a hollow laugh, disbelief cutting through the ache. "You can't be serious." Her gaze sharpened. "Where's Claire?"

"Back in Australia," he said, shoulders slumping. "She didn't want to move here when I started my new job."

Eliza drew a sharp breath, betrayal flaring—but it didn't break her. It steeled her spine.

"Oh, I see. That's why you're here." Her eyes narrowed, voice edged with scorn. "She rejects you, and suddenly I'm the consolation prize?"

Brad shook his head quickly, desperation rising. "No—it's not like that, Eliza. I swear it isn't."

"I think it is." Her tone was calm, resolute, leaving no room for debate. "No, Brad. You don't get to do this. You don't get to vanish when it mattered most, then show up at my door when it suits you. You humiliated me. You left me to face everything alone. And I put myself back together without you."

"Eliza, please—" His voice cracked, raw with regret.

She held up a hand, stopping him cold. "No, Brad. I wish you well, truly. But it won't be with me. Not now. Not ever." Her eyes flicked briefly to Christian, then back to Brad. "I think you should leave."

Silence pressed against the walls. Brad's mouth opened as if to argue, but the finality in her gaze left him nothing. Shoulders sagging, he gave a defeated nod and walked down the corridor, each step echoing farther away until he disappeared.

Christian exhaled, finally releasing the tension he hadn't realised he'd been holding. His chest swelled with pride, relief, and a fierce, protective heat.

"Eliza…" His voice was low, reverent, as though speaking too loudly might shatter the fragile air. "Are you all right?"

She met his gaze. For a heartbeat, he feared she might crumble—but she drew a steady breath and nodded. "Yes. I'm fine."

Her fingers trembled slightly as she rummaged in her bag for her keys. Then, with a faint, tentative smile, she looked up at him. "Would you like some coffee?"

Relief softened his features, a small smile curving his lips. "I'd love some."

Inside, the quiet of her flat wrapped around them like a soothing balm after the tension of the hallway. Eliza moved to the kitchen, the soft clink of cups and the hiss of the kettle filling the silence, while Christian remained where he was, watching her. There was something captivating in the ordinary rhythm of her movements—the way her hair fell when she bent, the quiet determination in her hands—and he felt an ache, a mixture of longing and admiration.

When she returned with two steaming mugs, they settled side by side on the sofa, the warmth of the coffee mingling with the residual tension lingering in the air.

Eliza let out a small, rueful laugh, curling her fingers around the cup. "Well… that was unexpected."

Christian's lips curved into a faint, fond smile, his gaze never leaving hers. "Unexpected… but telling," he murmured. "You handled him with more strength than I think he'll ever understand."

Her chest tightened—not with hurt, but with a steadier, fiercer sense of hope.

"So… do you like your job? Santa's little helper?"

Eliza laughed, a light, melodic sound that made something stir deep within him. "It's okay… only for a little while. I start my new job in the New Year."

"Oh? And what is that?" he asked, leaning slightly forward, careful not to press too hard.

She smiled, pride softening her lips. "I'm an early learning teacher, I got a position at a childcare facility in Richmond."

Christian's eyes softened. "So… you like kids, then?"

"Yes," she said, nodding. Her smile faded slightly as a shadow crossed her face. "When Brad got the transfer to London, that's when he asked me to marry him. That's why I'm here. We were supposed to move in together—luckily, the lease was in my name. I applied to a few places, but this one sounded the best. I went for the final interview the other day. I just need to do the pre-employment blood screening next week, and then I start on January 5th."

Christian reached instinctively for her hand, brushing his thumb lightly across her knuckles. "I didn't even know you were in London. I was prepared to go to Australia to find you."

"Really?" she asked, surprise softening the edges of her hurt.

"Yes," he said simply, with quiet honesty.

She gave a small laugh, shaking her head. "And here I am, dressed as Santa's little helper, trying to convince toddlers that candy canes are magical… while you're out in the world, high-rise and all."

Christian chuckled, low, and warm. "I'd trade all my high-rises to see you laugh like that every day."

They shared a glance, a silent moment stretching between them. Then Christian asked, "How long have you worked with children?"

"Since I left school. I'm fully qualified now, which helps when trying to get a new job," she said.

"It's a big step, moving countries," he murmured.

"I can't say I wasn't worried," she admitted, "especially after the wedding debacle… doing it all on my own."

"You've planned all this… and you're making it work. I admire that, Eliza," he said, voice warm and steady.

She glanced at him, a flicker of something unspoken passing between them, allowing herself a small, tentative smile. "It's just… life. You do what you have to."

Christian's gaze lingered on her, fierce and gentle all at once. "I don't ever want to let you go again."

He finished his coffee, setting the cup down with a soft clink. "I better let you get your beauty sleep."

She smiled, shy and tender, and he felt the pull in his chest tighten. He wanted to stay, to linger in this moment, but he reminded himself of his promise—to take it slow, to follow her lead.

He stood, and she rose with him. "Thank you for dinner," she murmured, warmth in her voice making him ache.

"You're welcome," he said softly, relief and longing mingling in his tone. "I'm just glad you said yes."

At the doorway, he hesitated, brushing a stray lock of hair from her face. His thumb traced her cheekbone gently. "Eliza… can I kiss you goodnight?"

She nodded, lips parting slightly, breath hitching.

He leaned in, first pressing a gentle, lingering kiss to her knuckles—a playful, tender gesture—then rested his forehead against hers for a heartbeat, savouring her nearness.

When their lips met, it began sweet and soft, almost teasing, a delicate brush of warmth. Then, as she leaned into him with a shy but bold spark in her eyes, the kiss deepened, playful and passionate at once. She laughed lightly against his lips, and it ignited something inside him—a thrill, a joy, a promise of all the nights yet to come.

Her arms circled him, holding him close, fingers threading into his hair. His hands cupped her face, and for a moment they moved together in a rhythm both tender and teasing, a dance of desire and delight. It was a kiss that said far more than words could—hope, longing, and the certainty that they had found something worth holding onto.

Finally, they parted just enough to rest their foreheads together, breaths mingling, smiles tugging at their lips.

"Goodnight, Eliza," he whispered, husky but warm.

"Goodnight, Christian," she replied, lips curving into a shy yet radiant smile.

He lingered a moment longer, simply holding her, letting the quiet intimacy settle around them before finally stepping back, hearts still racing, eyes locked, and a world of unspoken words hanging between them.

Eliza adjusted the small Santa hat perched atop her head and smoothed the velvet of her festive costume. The luxury department store glittered with holiday decor—crystal chandeliers catching the light, polished marble floors reflecting the twinkle of elegant Christmas displays, and the scent of fresh pine and fine chocolate lingering in the air.

She smiled politely at the next child in line, handing out candy canes and small gifts, but her thoughts weren't on the children or the sparkling surroundings. They were on Christian. She found herself replaying their dinner—the warmth in his gaze, the feel of his hand against hers, the soft intensity in his voice when he had promised her no more lies. Her chest tightened at the memory, and she let out a quiet sigh, brushing a loose strand of hair behind her ear.

She looked up—and there he was. Christian—just on the other side of the red velvet rope, watching her. Her heart lurched. His tailored jacket draped perfectly over broad shoulders, his presence as commanding and magnetic as she remembered.

"Eliza," Christian called softly, his eyes locking onto hers.

She froze mid-step, her apron clutched tightly in her hands. "Christian! What… what are you doing here?"

He stepped closer, gaze warm, intense, impossible to ignore. "I was hoping you were free tonight."

Eliza blinked, searching his face. "Tonight? Why?"

"I'd like you to come to dinner at my home," he said, voice low, almost pleading. "I want you to meet my friends—Henry and Mary. You met Henry yesterday, remember?"

"Oh… yes," she murmured, recalling the charming, steady man who had accompanied him before.

Christian's expression softened, a flicker of vulnerability crossing his features. "Just dinner, Eliza. No pressure. I'd really like to spend more time with you."

She hesitated, eyes sweeping over the store—the glittering chandeliers, polished marble, bustling holiday shoppers—and then back to him. Her heart wavered between caution and longing. Finally, she gave a small nod. "Okay… dinner. I'd like that."

A warm, relieved smile spread across his face, lighting up the intensity in his eyes. "Great," he said.

"Can I have your address?" she asked, voice gentle, almost hesitant.

He smiled, slow and easy, making her heart skip. "Or… how about I pick you up from your apartment?"

"Okay," she whispered, feeling heat creep up her cheeks, aware of the curious glances from shoppers and staff nearby.

"I'll be there at seven," he said, tone steady, confident, yet warm. "Thank you, Eliza."

As he turned and strode toward the elevators, her pulse quickened, thoughts spinning with anticipation. Dinner at his home—the idea sent a thrilling shiver through her. Maybe tonight, just maybe, everything would start to make sense between them.

Chapter Fifteen

Eliza stood in front of her small bedroom mirror, tugging at the hem of her dress for the third time. The soft ivory fabric felt light and elegant—simple, yet perfect for the dinner where she would meet his friends. Her fingers trembled slightly as she brushed her hair, gathering it into a loose knot, strands falling softly around her face. Her pulse thrummed in her ears, each beat echoing the anticipation—the flutter of nerves and excitement she could no longer ignore.

She took a deep breath, smoothing the fabric one last time. "Okay, Eliza… just dinner. You can do this," she murmured to herself, forcing a smile into the mirror. She hoped fervently that his friends would like her.

A soft knock at the door made her jump. Her heart leapt into her throat, knees going weak. She set down the hairbrush and moved to open the door.

There he stood, framed by the warm hallway light, wearing a tailored coat that hugged his broad shoulders. His gaze was magnetic, filled with hope, intensity, and that rare tenderness that made her chest ache.

"You… you look… beautiful," Christian said, his voice faltering slightly as his eyes swept over her. The words were simple, yet heavy with a weight that made her breath catch.

"Thank you," she replied softly, a small, nervous smile curving her lips.

He stepped closer, lowering his voice. "I'm so glad you said yes. I'm really looking forward to you getting to know Henry and Mary—they're incredibly important to me."

She hesitated, heart torn between caution and longing. Finally, she gave a small, decisive nod. "I'm looking forward to it too," she admitted, voice trembling slightly.

"They'll love you," he said firmly, reaching out his hand. The warmth of his palm met hers, grounding her, making it impossible to pull away. Her cheeks flushed, and she let him guide her down the steps to the waiting limousine. The crisp night air brushed her skin as she slid into the car, her pulse racing in tandem with her anticipation.

Christian slid in beside her, their hands brushing in a fleeting, electric touch that left her breathless. As the car glided through the illuminated London streets, the city lights reflected in her eyes, carrying a fragile thrill of hope she hadn't felt in weeks.

They soon arrived at a luxury apartment block. The doorman opened the door with a professional smile. Christian stepped out first. "Good evening, Joe."

"Good evening, Mr. Harrington," the doorman replied.

Christian held out a hand to Eliza. "This is Eliza Preston. I hope we'll be seeing a lot more of her."

"Miss Preston, nice to meet you," Joe said, bowing his head slightly.

Eliza blushed, voice soft. "Hello."

"Call me Joe," he said kindly.

"Thank you, Joe," she replied, smiling.

Christian watched her, quiet pride in his gaze, as they walked through the grand lobby toward the elevator. Tonight felt like a beginning—one she wasn't sure she was ready for yet couldn't imagine resisting. Every step toward the lift tightened the flutter in her chest, a delicious mix of nerves and anticipation she couldn't quite name.

The elevator doors slid open, revealing a private cabin gleaming with polished brass accents and plush carpeting. The subtle hum of its mechanics seemed almost musical, and Eliza couldn't help but glance around, wide-eyed. This was a world far removed from her own—luxury so tangible it left her slightly breathless. She caught her reflection in the mirrored walls, straightening her posture as if she could will herself to belong here.

The elevator chimed softly as it ascended, rising steadily. When it reached its floor, the doors opened with a gentle hiss, revealing a vast, elegantly lit penthouse that seemed to stretch endlessly. Crystal chandeliers cast shimmering patterns across the marble floors, and the scent of fresh flowers mingled with the faint, comforting aroma of polished wood.

Eliza's hand flew to her mouth as she gasped. "You… you live here?" Her voice trembled between awe and disbelief, the space around them almost overwhelming.

Christian's lips curved in a small, amused smile, his hand brushing lightly against hers to guide her out of the lift. "Yes," he said simply, though the understated tone did nothing to lessen the grandeur surrounding them.

"Christian…" Her voice faltered, tinged with nervousness. "I don't…"

"Eliza, it's just an apartment. Nothing more," he said gently, his thumb brushing reassuringly over her knuckles. "I want you to feel comfortable."

Her eyes roamed the space again, taking in the sweeping living area, polished wooden floors, the soft glow of ambient lighting, and floor-to-ceiling windows framing the twinkling London skyline. The quiet elegance of the penthouse hummed with understated luxury, but it was Christian—tall, confident, beside her—that made her pulse race.

Then movement caught her eye. A man and a woman appeared from the terrace, hand in hand. The man—the same one from the other day—smiled warmly as his gaze landed on her. The woman, with a gentle, luminous presence, had the unmistakable curve of pregnancy, subtle yet undeniable.

Henry's eyes lit up as he approached, his steps purposeful but friendly. He took both of Eliza's hands, bending slightly to kiss her cheeks in a warm, familiar greeting. "It's so good to see you again, Eliza."

Her brows lifted in surprise, her voice soft but genuine. "Hello, Henry. It's good to see you too." His easy warmth made her feel unexpectedly at home, as if they were old friends reunited rather than mere acquaintances.

Henry turned slightly, gesturing toward the blonde woman at his side. "And this is Mary, my wife."

Mary's eyes sparkled as she stepped forward, embracing Eliza in a heartfelt hug. "It's so wonderful to meet you, Eliza. Christian has told us so much about you."

Eliza felt a flicker of warmth, a sense of belonging that surprised her. She returned the hug, voice soft but sincere. "It's lovely to meet you too, Mary."

Christian watched the interaction, a quiet pride in his eyes, as Eliza laughed lightly, the tension in her shoulders easing. She let herself be drawn into the easy camaraderie of Henry and Mary, her natural warmth and humour shining through. For the first time since arriving at his apartment, she allowed herself to imagine that this evening might not be as daunting as she had feared.

Mary took her hand gently, guiding her toward the terrace. "You two get us some drinks while I get to know Eliza," she said with a teasing smile.

Eliza glanced at Christian as Mary led her away, a mixture of nervousness and curiosity fluttering in her chest.

Henry leaned close to Christian, his voice low but tinged with amusement. "So… she's a beauty, Christian. That Santa's helper get-up doesn't even begin to do her justice."

Christian's lips curved into a small, knowing smile, his eyes following Eliza as she laughed lightly on the terrace. "I know," he said quietly—simple words, yet heavy with the truth of how he felt.

"She is giving you a chance?" Henry asked, nudging him gently.

"Yes," Christian admitted, a faint sigh of relief escaping him. "Thank God."

"Well, don't stuff it up," Henry warned, though the teasing lilt in his voice betrayed him. "She seems… really nice."

Christian nodded, turning toward the wet bar but his gaze flicked back to the terrace, lingering on Eliza as she took in the view, a tentative smile softening her features. "She is," he murmured.

Henry leaned closer, lowering his voice. "She's not used to this world, you know. She's smart, she'll adapt. But give her time. Just… reassure her."

Christian's chest tightened as he watched her laugh at something Mary said. "I will. I don't want to lose her again."

Henry's expression softened, understanding clear in his eyes. "She's warming up," he whispered. "It's all about patience. Mary needed time too. You just need to be there, steady, let her know she's safe with you."

Out on the terrace, the glittering city lights stretched endlessly before them. Mary squeezed Eliza's hand warmly. "I see you're not entirely comfortable with all this luxury?"

Eliza's cheeks flushed. "N… no. It's a bit overwhelming."

Mary's laugh was soft, easy, and understanding. "I felt exactly the same way when I first met Henry."

Eliza arched a sceptical eyebrow. "Really?"

"Yes, really," Mary replied, her tone warm and unpretentious. "I was a waitress when I met him. It took me a while to feel at ease in this kind of world."

Eliza let out a small, tentative smile, the tension in her shoulders easing slightly. "Oh… I see," she murmured. For the first time, she felt as though she might belong here, at least for tonight.

Mary nodded knowingly, releasing her hand but keeping her warm gaze on Eliza. "Just be yourself—that's more than enough. You'll fit right in soon enough."

Eliza laughed lightly, a spark of ease settling in her heart.

"So, Christian tells us you're Australian?" Mary asked, leaning back comfortably against the railing.

"That's right. A small town in Queensland," Eliza replied.

Mary's eyes twinkled. "Tell me—there aren't kangaroos hopping down the streets every morning, are there?"

Eliza chuckled, relaxing further. "No, you do see them occasionally in the suburbs, but usually at night or very early in the morning. They're more mischievous than dangerous."

The sound of Christian and Henry approaching drew her attention. Henry handed Mary a fruit juice, and Christian offered Eliza a glass of chilled white wine.

"Thank you," she said, smiling at him. Their fingers brushed briefly as she took the glass, and the spark of connection was unmistakable.

Henry leaned in, curiosity in his voice. "So… tell us a bit about yourself, Eliza."

Eliza shrugged lightly, her smile modest. "Not much to tell. I was born in Queensland, Australia. My parents aren't around anymore, and I don't have siblings. I'm an early learning teacher, and at the moment, I'm working in Christian's department store as Santa's little helper." She laughed softly, shaking her head at herself.

Henry leaned in, playful. "Is it true what they say about kangaroos?"

Eliza laughed again, a musical, easy sound.

Henry looked puzzled. "What?"

"I just asked her that," Mary said, laughing.

Christian's eyes followed her laughter, the warmth and light in her face making his chest ache in the best possible way. For the first time tonight, he allowed himself to believe this—tonight could be the beginning of something real and lasting.

Christian led Eliza to the dining area, where a beautifully set table awaited, flickering candles casting soft golden light that danced across crystal glasses. The scent of roasted herbs and fresh bread mingled with faint notes of holiday pine drifting in from the terrace, creating an atmosphere both festive and intimate.

Mary took Eliza's hand gently. "I hope you're hungry, dear. Christian has tried to make tonight very special."

Eliza smiled, her nerves easing under Mary's warm presence. "It smells amazing."

Christian gestured toward her seat. "Please, make yourself comfortable." He gave her hand a reassuring squeeze before taking his own seat beside her. Henry and Mary settled across from them, their easy smiles helping her relax.

As the meal began, conversation flowed naturally, punctuated by laughter and small anecdotes. Mary asked about Eliza's move from Australia, the children she taught, and her hobbies, while Henry teased Christian whenever he glanced at Eliza with obvious admiration.

Christian watched her intently, captivated by the way her eyes lit up when she spoke, the subtle gestures revealing her humour and thoughtfulness. He leaned slightly closer when speaking to her, keeping his voice low, savouring the intimacy of their shared side conversations.

"So… tell me more about the children you work with," Mary asked gently. "What age group do you teach?"

Eliza relaxed, slipping easily into conversation. "Two- to four-year-olds. They're mischievous, curious, endlessly energetic—but it's rewarding. They remind me to find joy in small things."

Christian smiled softly. "Sounds like a lot of fun… and you'd need a lot of patience."

She laughed lightly. "You'd be surprised. They keep me on my toes, but it's exactly the kind of challenge I love."

Henry leaned back, a teasing glint in his eye. "Christian seems… quite taken with you," he said lightly.

Christian's jaw tightened slightly, but his smile never faltered. "I am," he admitted simply. "And I'm making sure she knows it."

Eliza felt her cheeks warm, pulse quickening at the quiet intensity in his voice. She had missed this—the feeling of being truly seen, of being valued—yet she reminded herself to stay cautious, to guard her heart from past betrayals.

Mary caught the look between them and smiled knowingly. "You two have a connection," she said softly, without judgment. "It's rare, and it's beautiful. Just… take your time."

Eliza's gaze flickered to Christian, who offered a tender, reassuring smile. She felt something shift—a fragile sense of possibility.

The courses came and went, each bite punctuated by laughter, playful remarks, and lingering glances. Christian told stories of his travels, and by the time dessert arrived—a delicate chocolate torte with fresh raspberries—Eliza found herself leaning slightly toward him, her hand brushing his occasionally, savouring the warmth of his presence. Christian mirrored her subtly, careful not to overwhelm, yet every movement spoke volumes.

Finally, as the candles burned low and the last hints of dessert were enjoyed, Christian's hand found hers on the table, his thumb tracing gentle circles over her knuckles.

Henry cleared his throat, glancing at his watch with a teasing air. "Well, we should probably call it a night. It's getting late."

Mary laughed softly, her hand resting on her belly. "Yes, I tire more easily these days."

Eliza smiled warmly. "I can imagine. Are you looking forward to it?"

"Can't wait," Mary said, eyes sparkling. "We're debating whether to find out the baby's sex at our next ultrasound."

Henry grinned. "I want to know, but Mary is leaning toward keeping it a surprise."

Eliza chuckled, shaking her head. "I don't think I could wait—I'd want to know immediately."

Henry shot Mary a playful look. "See?" he said, grinning.

They all laughed together, the easy camaraderie making the goodbye bittersweet. Henry and Christian shook hands firmly. "Thanks for coming," Christian said sincerely, his eyes briefly meeting Eliza's.

Mary hugged and kissed Eliza warmly. "It was so lovely to meet you, Eliza. I hope we get to see you again soon."

"Thank you," Eliza said, her smile genuine. "I'd like that very much."

Henry gave a light kiss to her cheek. "Goodnight, Eliza," he said, and together he and Mary stepped into the lift. The doors closed, leaving Christian and Eliza alone.

Christian's voice dropped low, intimate. "Eliza… thank you for coming tonight. I don't take this for granted. Not for a second."

Eliza's heart fluttered, her pulse quickening. "I'm glad I came," she admitted softly, a shy but genuine smile tugging at her lips. "I… I really enjoyed myself. They're so lovely."

Christian's gaze softened, a fierce tenderness shining through. "I think they loved you too," he whispered, his thumb brushing lightly across her hand.

He extended his hand, a playful glint in his eyes. "Come out to the terrace for a while?"

Eliza hesitated for a moment, then placed her hand in his, letting him guide her away from the lift toward the wide terrace. The city stretched below them, lights glittering like stars scattered across the night. The wind was crisp, carrying the faint scent of winter, but beside him, she felt a warmth that outshone it all.

Christian drew her close, gently resting his forehead against hers. "Eliza," he murmured, voice soft, almost reverent, "I'm so glad you're here."

Her heart raced. She looked up at him, words unnecessary, and whispered, "Me too."

He leaned in, and their lips met in a soft, lingering kiss—tender but edged with quiet passion, filled with promise and the ache of the moments they'd been apart. Each heartbeat seemed to synchronise, a rhythm all their own.

When they finally parted, just enough to breathe, Christian rested his forehead against hers again, his hands cradling her gently. "I'll take you home now," he said softly.

Eliza nodded, a small, contented smile curving her lips. "Thank you," she whispered, feeling the fragile thrill of hope and the undeniable pull of what might be beginning between them.

The limousine glided smoothly through the quiet streets, the soft hum of the engine filling the space between them. City lights streaked past the windows in blurred ribbons, yet inside the car, time seemed to slow.

Eliza's hand rested lightly in Christian's lap, his fingers curling around hers with a warmth that made her pulse flutter. She stole glances at him, noting the relaxed confidence in the way he sat, the faint curve of his lips as he watched her, and the steady intensity in his eyes that made her chest tighten.

"You were wonderful tonight," Christian said after a pause, his voice low and warm, carrying a softness that made her breath hitch. "You... fit in perfectly with Henry and Mary. I think they already adore you."

Eliza's lips curved into a shy smile, though a flicker of hesitation lingered in her eyes. "I... I like them too," she admitted softly. "But I'll be honest—I was nervous."

"You had nothing to be nervous about," he murmured, his thumb brushing lightly across hers, a grounding, tender motion. "You're... amazing, Eliza."

Her chest tightened further, a blush creeping across her cheeks. "Christian…" she whispered, caught somewhere between the urge to lean in and the instinct to hold back.

He turned slightly toward her, gaze unwavering, full of sincerity. "I know it's a lot… all of this. I don't want to overwhelm you. But I can't pretend I don't feel it—not now, not ever."

Eliza exhaled slowly, trying to steady her racing heart. "I… I like being with you," she admitted, her voice soft. "But I'm still cautious."

Christian's smile softened, reassuring and gentle, tugging at the corners of his lips. "I'll take it slow," he promised. "I'll follow your lead. Always."

"Okay… thank you," she whispered, fingers tightening around his.

When they arrived at her apartment, he walked her to the door, each step deliberate, as if prolonging the moment. He leaned in, brushing his lips to hers in a soft, lingering kiss—sweet yet charged with all the unsaid desire between them.

Pulling back just enough to meet her gaze, he asked quietly, "Can I see you tomorrow night?"

Eliza's lips curved into a small, tentative smile. "I'd like that. But… something casual. All this luxury—being around you—it's a little overwhelming."

Christian chuckled softly, pressing a gentle kiss to the tip of her nose. "Anything for you," he whispered, his voice low and intimate.

For a moment, they lingered in the doorway. The city noises felt distant; the night stretched around them. Silence settled—not uncomfortable but charged—the space between them alive with possibility, anticipation, and the fragile, thrilling spark of something special.

Eliza found herself looking forward to every evening after work, knowing she would be spending time with Christian. The first night had been ice skating— laughter and the occasional stumble over the ice bringing them closer with every shared moment. She had clung to his steady hand, savouring the warmth of his palm against hers and the thrill of the cold wind biting her cheeks.

The second night was quieter, more intimate. They went to the movies, sitting side by side in the darkened theatre. She felt his presence behind her, the occasional brush of his arm, the subtle tilt of his head toward hers when a funny scene played out on the screen. It was comforting and exciting all at once.

On the third night, Christian had taken her to a small, charming café tucked away from the bustling streets. Soft lights cast a warm glow, and the scent of fresh bread and coffee mingled in the air, creating an atmosphere that mirrored the ease she felt when she was with him. They talked about everything and nothing, laughter spilling freely between them, and Eliza realised how rare it was to feel so completely at ease with someone.

Each evening, Christian walked her back to her small apartment, never pressing for more than a gentle goodnight kiss. It was perfect and maddening all at once. She wanted more—wanted to linger in his arms, to feel closer—but wasn't sure how to bridge the gap between desire and caution.

That third evening, as they shared dessert and sipped their coffee, Christian's gaze softened, growing serious. He reached across the small table, brushing a stray strand of hair from her face.

"Eliza," he said, his voice low but steady, "would you consider coming away with me this weekend? Henry and Mary will be there too. You'll have your own room if you want—no pressure. I just… I want to spend more time with you."

Eliza's breath caught, her heart thudding in her chest. She didn't pause to think about refusing. The idea of a weekend with him—close, unhurried, without the ticking clock of an evening—filled her with an ache she didn't want to ignore.

"Yes," she said softly, her eyes meeting his. "I'd like that."

Christian's face lit up, a mixture of relief and joy warming his features. He reached across, taking her hand gently, holding it as if he never wanted to let go. "Good," he murmured. "You have no idea how happy that makes me."

As they left the café and stepped into the crisp night air, her hand still in his, Eliza felt a flutter of anticipation. This weekend—time with Christian, laughter, quiet moments away from everything else—felt like the beginning of something she had been quietly yearning for. And, for the first time, she allowed herself to hope.

Chapter Sixteen

The drive out of London was quiet, comfortable in its own rhythm. Christian's hand rested lightly on the wheel, steady and confident, while Eliza sat beside him, her fingers occasionally brushing his as she stole glances at him. The city lights faded behind them, replaced by open countryside, winding roads, and the soft golden glow of the late afternoon sun.

"You're quiet," Christian said softly, his eyes still on the road. "What's on your mind?"

Eliza let out a small sigh, a smile tugging at her lips. "How happy I am. I'm looking forward to seeing Mary and Henry again… and spending time with you, of course."

He glanced at her, that familiar small, knowing smile tugging at his lips. "They're looking forward to seeing you too. And you know I love spending time with you."

Her pulse quickened, a warmth spreading through her chest, and she let out a small, melodic laugh. "I'm glad. I'll say thank you now just in case I forget later."

He chuckled, reaching over to take her hand, lifting it gently to his lips. His kiss was soft, reverent, sending a shiver up her arm. "You're welcome," he murmured.

When they arrived at the country home, Eliza's breath caught. The house was warm and inviting—cozy yet elegant, the scent of fresh flowers mingling with the faint crackle of a fireplace. Mary came bustling down the stairs, her smile radiant, hand resting lightly on her rounded belly.

"Eliza! It's so lovely to see you again," she said, enveloping her in a gentle, lingering hug.

Eliza's cheeks warmed, but she smiled, allowing herself to relax into the embrace. "It's wonderful to see you too, Mary."

Henry appeared shortly after, his grin steady and friendly, eyes sparkling with good humour. He kissed her cheek warmly, then added with a teasing lilt, "Welcome! I'm glad to see you haven't gotten sick of Christian yet."

"Never," Eliza said softly, glancing at Christian with affection.

Christian's hand found hers, fingers entwining in a quiet, grounding gesture. "I'm grateful," he said, his voice low and warm, the sincerity in his gaze making her heart flutter.

The evening unfolded effortlessly. They played board games, sipped hot chocolate by the fire, and lingered in quiet conversations in cozy corners of the living room. Christian's attention never wavered from her. His fingers brushed hers whenever they met across the table, his hand lingering on her shoulder as he passed by—a subtle, constant reassurance.

At one point, Mary leaned over, her eyes sparkling with mischief. "You two look so good together."

Eliza felt her cheeks flush, a delicious heat rising through her, caught somewhere between embarrassment and delight. Christian's thumb brushed against her knuckles, his gaze locking with hers. "I think so too," he murmured, voice low, filled with warmth and quiet certainty. The intimacy of the moment made her pulse race, and she realised just how much she wanted him close.

Later that night, after Henry and Mary had retired to their room, Christian walked beside Eliza toward her allocated bedroom. The hallway stretched ahead, quiet, and dimly lit, each step echoing softly in the stillness of the house. Eliza's heart thudded in her chest, a fierce, unspoken longing rising within her. She stopped, turning to face him, her eyes searching his—vulnerability and desire mingling in her gaze.

Christian's hands lifted to her waist, drawing her gently into his arms. He leaned down, brushing his lips against hers in a soft, tentative kiss—testing the waters. But before he could pull away, as he had so many times since finding her again, Eliza's arms wrapped around his neck, anchoring him. She deepened the kiss, letting every emotion, every withheld longing spill into it.

For a moment, Christian hesitated, taken aback by the intensity of her surrender, then responded, his arms tightening, pulling her closer. The kiss deepened, urgent and tender all at once. When he finally pulled back slightly, forehead resting against hers, she felt the warmth of his breath on her skin. His lips trailed down her jawline, pressing soft, lingering kisses along her neck. Eliza's head tilted back instinctively, a shiver of anticipation running through her.

"Stay with me tonight," she whispered, barely audible but weighted with intent.

Christian froze, chest rising and falling as he absorbed her words. He lifted his head slowly, looking into her eyes, dark with reverence and awe. "Are you sure?" His voice was low, reverent, treasuring every syllable.

"Christian," she said softly but firmly, her hands cupping his face, drawing him closer, "I want to be with you. Really be with you."

A slow smile tugged at the corners of his lips, mingled with a depth of longing she had never seen. "I want to be with you too," he murmured, pressing another searing kiss to her lips—a promise of every moment, every night to come.

Eliza opened her door, hand slipping into his, pulling him gently into her room. The door clicked softly behind them, key turning to seal them in a bubble of stillness where nothing else existed.

Christian paused, eyes dark with awe and desire, drinking in the sight of her— the soft curve of her jaw, the shine in her eyes, the way her hair framed her face. He cupped her cheek, brushing a strand behind her ear, thumb tracing lightly over her skin.

Eliza's pulse quickened, breath catching as though the air itself had thickened. She pressed her palms to his chest, feeling the solid muscle beneath his shirt, the steady beat of his heart against her hands. Warmth seeped into her, igniting something deep and uncontrollable. Slowly, deliberately, she pressed him back until his shoulders met the cool wood of the locked door.

A quiet groan escaped Christian's throat as his hands slid to her waist, fingers flexing against the curve of her hips. But Eliza wasn't interested in caution— her need had taken over, urgent, and fierce. She leaned closer, her body fitting against his as if they had been made for this closeness, this reunion.

Her hands travelled upward, trailing from his chest to his shoulders, clasping around his neck. Her touch was both possessive and pleading, saying she could no longer keep the distance between them.

"Eliza…" His voice was low, roughened with desire and reverence. He whispered her name as both a prayer and a warning.

And then his lips were on hers—urgent, searching, unstoppable. The kiss stole her breath, a fierce collision of longing and memory, as though all the weeks of restraint had broken open at once. She responded without hesitation, lips moving with his in equal urgency, answering the hunger that had burned between them since they had found each other again.

She responded with a low moan, her body trembling as she tightened around him, urging him deeper. Time seemed to suspend; the world outside the room vanished, leaving only the two of them, intertwined in a frantic, desperate, but tender dance. Every movement spoke of weeks of longing, of passion restrained and finally unleashed, each touch a promise, each gasp an admission.

Christian lowered his head, kissing her collarbone, her shoulder, her neck— everywhere she could feel his mouth, marking her as his, while his hands held her firmly, worshipping her curves, memorising every inch. She arched against him, soft cries escaping her lips, and he matched her, moving with her, anticipating every subtle shift, every tremor of need.

"Christian… God… yes…" Her words dissolved into a breathless moan, and before she could finish, his mouth was on hers, urgent and claiming, devouring her lips with a hunger that matched her own.

His movements became frantic, deep, and relentless, every thrust driving them closer to the edge. The sound of their ragged breaths filled the room, mingling with their moans and the soft scrape of skin against skin. Each motion carried weeks of longing, weeks of restraint, and the need to be closer than ever before.

"Eliza…" he groaned, his voice raw, almost desperate, vibrating against her lips. His hands gripped her hips, holding her taut as he pushed harder, faster, chasing the same desperate release.

Her fingers threaded through his hair, tugging him closer as a shiver tore through her body. "Yes… oh God… yes…"

And then it hit—her climax, wild and consuming, a torrent of pleasure that left her trembling and breathless. She screamed into his mouth, their teeth and tongues clashing in frantic rhythm, her body arching impossibly against his.

Christian groaned, his own release following moments later, his movements a final, powerful drive that sent them both over the edge. They collapsed together, pressed close, her chest rising and falling against his, the storm of their passion leaving them trembling, spent, and utterly entwined.

He held her against him, forehead resting against hers, murmuring her name over and over as the tremors of their shared ecstasy slowly faded, leaving only the warmth of their bodies and the quiet, sacred intimacy of the moment.

He held her pressed against the door, his body a solid, protective weight, forehead resting against hers. His breaths mingled with hers, low and steady, as he murmured her name over and over. The tremors of their shared ecstasy slowly ebbed, leaving behind only the warmth of their bodies, the rhythm of their heartbeats, and the quiet, sacred intimacy of the moment.

Eliza's voice was barely a whisper, soft and awed. "That was…"

"Incredible," Christian finished for her, his lips brushing hers in a gentle, lingering kiss.

"Yes," she breathed, her hands resting lightly against his chest, as if trying to memorise the feeling of him.

He nuzzled her temple, a soft smile tugging at the corners of his lips. "I can't believe we didn't even make it to the bed," he murmured, his voice low and husky. "I just… I couldn't wait another second for you."

Her eyes fluttered closed, and she melted into him, the aftershocks of their passion giving way to something steadier—trust, warmth, and the quiet understanding that this was only the beginning. She pressed a soft kiss to his cheek, her lips lingering against his skin.

"I felt the same," she whispered, her voice barely audible, yet filled with sincerity. Her hands rested against his chest, tracing the lines of his muscles, memorising the solid reassurance of him.

Christian's arms tightened around her, holding her as though she were his entire world. "You're mine," he murmured into her hair—a vow wrapped in devotion, a promise of forever.

She tilted her head, a shy smile tugging at her lips. "And you're mine," she whispered, allowing herself to savour the simple, perfect certainty of that moment.

The silence between them wasn't empty—it thrummed with the lingering heat of passion, the fragile weight of new trust, and the unspoken promise of all that was yet to come. Every heartbeat, every shallow breath carried with it a quiet, urgent longing.

Christian traced lazy patterns along her back, his gaze tender but unwavering. He felt it then—an ache that went beyond desire, something deeper, something that whispered of permanence. The words hovered on his tongue, unguarded and raw: *I love you.* He wanted to tell her; to let her know she had become the centre of his life, the axis around which every thought and plan now revolved. But instead, he let the silence speak, let the weight of his touch, the steady warmth of his embrace, and the certainty in his eyes tell her what he could not yet voice.

Gathering her gently into his arms, he carried her to the bed, never breaking their closeness, lowering her with reverence as though she were something fragile and irreplaceable. He brushed a soft kiss to the tip of her nose, lingering there for a moment before slipping away to the bathroom.

When he returned, there was a mischievous glint in his eyes. Scooping up the scattered clothes, he held up her torn lace panties with exaggerated solemnity. "I suppose I should apologise for this," he said, his tone mock-serious.

Eliza burst out laughing, the sound warm and melodic. "You're not sorry."

Christian's chuckle rumbled low in his chest as he eased back onto the bed beside her, stretching out and pulling her into the curve of his body. "No," he admitted with a teasing smile, "I'm not." His arm draped around her waist, possessive yet gentle, as though holding her was the most natural thing in the world.

Their laughter softened, giving way to a quiet warmth that filled the room like candlelight. Every brush of his fingers, every breath shared between them, deepened the intimacy, weaving something more lasting than the heat of passion.

And he wasn't sorry. Not for a second. Because this—*her*—was unforgettable. The memory of her taste, the echo of her laughter, the ache of wanting her even now—it was all burned into him, tightening his chest with both longing and fierce contentment.

He leaned in, nuzzling her temple, his breath warm against her skin. A sigh escaped him, low and reverent. "You have no idea how much I've wanted this… wanted you."

Eliza tilted her head, brushing her lips against his shoulder. "I think I do," she whispered, her voice unsteady but sure. "Because I feel exactly the same."

Christian's chest tightened, and he pressed a lingering kiss to her temple, holding her closer. "Then we don't have to pretend anymore," he murmured, his fingers tracing slow, tender circles against her back. "We can just… be us."

"I would like that," Eliza breathed, her fingertips drawing idle patterns across his chest. Her gaze met his, steady and earnest. "But promise me something."

"Anything," he said softly, already meaning it.

"No over-the-top extravagance," she whispered, a faint but resolute smile curving her lips. "I'm not interested in all that. I just want you. Nothing else matters."

For a long moment he simply looked at her, the truth of her words sinking into him. Every other woman he had known had wanted the trappings—the glitter, the glamour, the gifts. But Eliza wanted none of it. She just wanted him.

Slowly, a tender smile curved his lips, his eyes warm with reverence. "You're remarkable," he said, his voice low and steady. "And I promise… I'll never forget how honoured I am that you want me—for me."

Chapter Seventeen

The next morning, Christian made his way down to the dining room, soft sunlight spilling across the polished floors. He had just left Eliza to take a shower and get ready, and their morning together still lingered in his mind. It had been tender, slow, and intimate—different from the fiery passion of the night before, yet every bit as consuming. A small, satisfied smile tugged at his lips as he remembered the way she had looked at him, the warmth of her body pressed against his.

Henry was already there, leaning casually against the counter with a mug of coffee in hand. "Morning," he greeted easily.

"Morning," Christian replied, his eyes bright.

Henry raised an eyebrow, a knowing smirk playing at the corner of his mouth. "You look happy."

Christian laughed softly, sinking into a chair. "I am… God, Henry, I'm in love. And it feels… incredible. Completely unbelievable."

Henry chuckled, shaking his head. "Well, about time, mate. I can see it in your face."

Christian leaned back, letting the quiet contentment wash over him. "She's… extraordinary. I can't believe she's mine."

"Have you told her?" Henry asked, curiosity softening his tone.

Christian shook his head. "Not yet. She wanted to take things slow, and I don't want to overwhelm her."

Henry nodded approvingly. "Probably the right move."

Christian ran a hand through his hair, a trace of tension crossing his features. "I want to ask her to marry me, but… I'm worried. If she finds out about the inheritance, she might feel pressured."

Henry's eyebrows shot up. "She doesn't know… or the deadline?"

"No," Christian said firmly. "And it's not about her. I made the decision to let it go before I even found her again. I don't want it to affect us."

"So… you're giving it up completely? No second thoughts?"

"I gave it up," Christian said, voice steady. "It was never about the money— it's the legacy. Built by my grandfather, my father… it's part of who I am. But none of that matters if I can't have her in my life."

Henry leaned back, letting the words hang in the morning air. "Sounds like you've made the right choice then. And honestly if she is as remarkable as I think she is… she'll understand. She's not after money, Christian. She's after you."

Christian exhaled slowly, a small, shy smile tugging at his lips. "I know. She made me promise no extravagance, but somehow… that just makes me want to give her everything I can."

Henry's expression softened. "Mary was exactly the same. It's rare, for men in our position, isn't it? To be loved for who you are, not for what we can give them?"

Christian nodded, eyes distant, filled with awe. "It's extraordinary… I honestly can't imagine my life without her. Every laugh, every glance—it's like nothing else matters."

Henry clapped him lightly on the shoulder, a teasing smile tugging at his lips. "Then don't waste another second. Cherish her. Every single day. Trust me… she will be worth it."

Christian's smile deepened, warmth radiating from him as he leaned back in rare, unguarded serenity. "I will," he murmured. "Trust me, Henry. I will."

Just then, Mary and Eliza entered the room, morning sunlight catching the edges of their hair. Both greeted them cheerfully.

Henry moved to Mary, brushing a gentle kiss across her cheek. "Good morning," he said warmly.

Christian's attention was already on Eliza. He stepped forward, eyes meeting hers with a mixture of tenderness and longing, and pressed a soft, lingering kiss to her lips. For that moment, the world seemed to shrink around them, the quiet intimacy of the morning wrapping them in a bubble that belonged to just the two of them.

Eliza smiled against his mouth, her hands brushing lightly along his arms as they pulled apart, a shared warmth lingering in the space between them.

Christian pulled out a chair for her, fingers brushing hers as she settled in. The small gesture made her heart flutter, and she caught his eye with a shy, teasing smile.

Mary set down a plate of freshly baked croissants, the buttery aroma filling the room. "I hope you're hungry, Eliza," she said warmly. "Breakfast is my favourite part of the morning."

"I am," Eliza replied, her gaze flicking repeatedly to Christian, who met her eyes with a soft, intense warmth and a small smile.

Henry poured coffee for everyone, the rich aroma mingling with the gentle hum of conversation. They chatted easily about the weekend ahead, teasing Christian about his sometimes "over-ambitious" driving, while Mary laughed, debating whether to find out the baby's gender or keep it a surprise.

"We could take a drive through the countryside," Henry suggested, "maybe a walk through the estate grounds, then try that little riverside café for lunch."

Christian added, "Or ice-skating Sunday morning. Eliza and I had a great time earlier this week."

Eliza smiled. "That all sounds lovely." Then a practical thought nudged her. "As long as I'm back in London by nine Monday morning—I have my pre-employment blood screening."

Mary touched her arm lightly. "When do you start your new job?"

Eliza's eyes brightened. "Fifth of January. I'm really looking forward to it. It feels like a fresh start."

Christian's hand brushed hers under the table, a quiet, reassuring gesture. "They will be lucky to have you," he murmured, eyes warm, making her chest flutter.

"I hope so," she whispered, a small, shy smile tugging at her lips.

Mary leaned forward, curiosity sparkling. "So, what are your plans for Christmas, Eliza?"

Eliza glanced at Christian, uncertainty in her tone. "I'm not sure. I usually spend it with friends in Queensland. I... haven't really thought about it this year."

Christian gently squeezed her hand, voice low and earnest. "I hope we'll spend it together."

A flutter of excitement warmed her, and she nodded, smile widening. "I'd like that."

Henry grinned teasingly. "Well, you have to come to Christmas lunch at ours. It won't be the same without you."

Eliza laughed softly, glancing at Christian, who gave her an encouraging, knowing look. "Looks like I'll have a very full holiday," she said, nerves mixing with happiness.

Christian's eyes met hers again, a quiet promise lingering there. "You'll never be bored," he murmured.

Eliza walked into the clinic at five minutes to nine, her heels clicking softly against the polished floor. The weekend still lingered in her mind—the laughter, the warmth, the easy camaraderie with Henry and Mary, and, most of all, the quiet, intoxicating closeness she had shared with Christian. Every moment with him felt effortless, yet charged with something deeper, something neither of them had rushed but both had savoured.

She knew, without a shadow of a doubt, that she loved him. She had felt it from the stormy night in St. Moritz, that raw, undeniable connection—but he hadn't said the words yet, and so she kept her feelings carefully guarded. Still, thinking of him now, her chest warmed with a mixture of hope and certainty— she believed that, given time, he could grow to love her just as fiercely as she loved him.

Taking a deep breath, she smoothed her blouse and stepped forward, trying to focus on the present. Today was just a routine pre-employment blood screening—but in her mind, it felt like a quiet, pivotal moment, a hinge on which the next chapter of her life might swing.

Her name was called, pulling her from her anxious thoughts. She followed the nurse into the small, clinical room, the faint scent of antiseptic lingering in the air. The nurse gestured to the chair, and Eliza sat, rolling up her sleeve. Her heart thrummed in her chest, nervous anticipation prickling at her as the nurse prepared the blood draw.

"Just a quick prick, and we'll be done," the nurse said with a comforting smile.

Eliza nodded, focusing on the faint hum of the fluorescent lights. The needle pricked her arm—sharp, but brief—and she squeezed her eyes shut. When it was over, she felt a mix of relief and lingering nerves. She thanked the nurse and left the clinic, clutching her small bag, already shifting her thoughts to the day ahead.

By mid-morning, she was back at the department store, slipping into her Santa's helper apron and greeting the children with practiced cheer. The bustling holiday chaos—the jingling bells, the laughter, the excited chatter—was a welcome distraction. She smiled as little hands tugged at her dress and small voices squealed with delight, momentarily setting aside the personal whirlwind that had begun that morning.

Just as Eliza was about to take her brief lunch break, Christian appeared at her section of the store, leaning casually against the counter. The sight of him made her heart lurch, leaving her momentarily breathless.

"Eliza," he murmured, his eyes lighting up the instant they met hers. Without hesitation, he bent down and pressed a soft, lingering kiss to her lips.

"Christian!" she exclaimed, a warm blush creeping up her cheeks. "You shouldn't do that... here."

"Why not?" he asked, a teasing curve tugging at his lips, his gaze locked on hers.

"Because..." she faltered, unsure how to explain the fluttering, unsteady feeling he always provoked in her.

"I don't care who sees, Eliza," he said firmly, his hand brushing against hers. "I'm not hiding how I feel about you."

"Are you sure?" Her voice was tentative, a mix of awe and apprehension.

He leaned in again, kissing her a little longer this time, his lips soft but insistent. When he finally pulled back, his forehead rested against hers. "One hundred percent," he whispered.

She let out a small, shy laugh, fingers brushing the back of his hand. "As long as you're comfortable with it," she said, her eyes sparkling with both affection and amusement.

Christian's smile deepened, a quiet, satisfied curve tugging at his lips. "With you? Always."

Eliza returned the smile, warmth spreading through her chest.

"I have a late meeting tonight," he continued, his tone soft, carrying just a hint of regret. "So, I won't be able to see you. But don't forget tomorrow night—Henry's surprise birthday dinner." Mary had mentioned it over the weekend, and now it felt exciting to be part of it.

Eliza pressed her lips into a small, wistful smile, a flicker of disappointment crossing her features. "Okay... I'll look forward to it," she said, keeping her voice light.

"I'll pick you up at six," he added, a reassuring sparkle in his eyes.

He leaned down once more, pressing a soft, lingering kiss to her lips, and she felt the warmth of his presence linger even as he stepped back.

"See you tomorrow, Eliza," he whispered, giving her hand a gentle squeeze before turning and walking away, leaving her with a fluttering heart and the sweet ache of anticipation.

That night, Eliza sat in her small flat, the soft glow of her phone screen illuminating her face. She scrolled absentmindedly through the news feed, missing Christian with a familiar ache in her chest.

Then her breath caught. There it was—her and Christian, captured in a photo as they kissed, the moment frozen for the world to see. Her pulse quickened as she read the headline in bold letters:

BILLIONAIRE HARRINGTON HEIR SPOTTED KISSING SANTA'S LITTLE HELPER!

Christian Harrington, the dashing heir to the Harrington fortune, was seen sharing an intimate kiss with a young woman dressed as Santa's little helper at London's Harrington Department Store yesterday, sparking whispers across the city.

The lucky lady has been identified as Eliza Preston, a temporary festive helper at the store, whose cheerful presence has caught more than just shoppers' attention. Eyewitnesses say the couple appeared completely absorbed in one another, seemingly oblivious to the busy holiday crowd around them.

This public display comes just weeks after Harrington's recent broken engagement, and while neither party has commented, insiders are already speculating that the spark between Harrington and Preston may have played a role in his sudden split.

A source close to Harrington revealed, "Christian hasn't looked this happy in years. There's something about her that has clearly captured his heart."

Fans and media alike are left wondering if this is the beginning of a new romance or simply a festive fling destined to make headlines.

Eliza's fingers trembled over the screen, her heart hammering in her chest. Heat flared across her cheeks—embarrassment, disbelief, and a flicker of worry all tangled together.

She hadn't expected this. The headline, the photo… being with Christian in private had been one thing, sharing moments just between them, but seeing it splashed across the city felt like a jolt straight to her chest.

What would he think? He'd said he didn't want to hide how he felt, but this… this was a whole other level. The thought twisted her stomach, a swirl of excitement and dread threatening to overwhelm her.

Her thumbs hovered nervously over the phone. Finally, she typed a short message, every word trembling with anticipation:

Christian… when you have a moment, can you please call me?

She hit send and bit her lower lip, staring at the screen as the seconds crawled by. Her mind raced—*what if he was angry? Or worried? Or… what if he found it funny?*

Less than two minutes later, her phone buzzed. Eliza's heart leapt the instant she saw his name glowing across the screen. She answered it at once, though she had to steady her voice.

"Hello?" she breathed, her tone trembling just slightly.

"Hello, sweetheart." Christian's deep, warm voice wrapped around her like a balm. "Are you okay?"

She exhaled shakily, relief and nerves tangling inside her. "Um… I'm fine. Have you… seen the article?"

"No," he replied, curiosity threading his words. "What article?"

"There's a picture of us… kissing," she admitted quickly, hesitant, her stomach flipping as heat rushed to her cheeks.

Christian chuckled, low, and amused, and the sound loosened some of the tightness in her chest. "And that worries you?"

"I… I'm just not used to it," she confessed, chewing on her lip. "And I don't know how you feel about it."

"Eliza," he said firmly, but with a warmth that steadied her, "I don't care. I don't care if the whole world knows how I feel about you."

Her breath caught, relief flooding her, though a flicker of doubt lingered. "Are you… sure?"

"One hundred percent," he murmured, his voice low and certain. "Nothing about this changes how I feel. Not for a second." Then, softer, touched with concern, he added, "But, unfortunately, attention like this comes with me. Are you okay with that?"

Her answer came without hesitation. "I don't care, Christian. I want to be with you."

For a heartbeat, silence stretched between them—intimate, weighted with meaning. When he spoke again, his voice was tender, reverent, threaded with promise.

"Good," he whispered. "Because I intend to spend every day making sure you never, ever have a reason to doubt me."

Eliza let out a soft, contented sigh. "Alright."

"Unfortunately, I have to go for now," he said, a reluctant edge in his tone betraying how much he didn't want to hang up. "But I'll see you tomorrow, okay?"

"Okay… goodnight, Christian," she murmured, a small smile tugging at her lips even though he couldn't see it.

"Sleep well, sweetheart," he said, his voice warm and lingering just long enough to make her heart flutter.

She ended the call and held her phone close for a moment, a soft smile spreading across her face as she imagined him thinking of her too.

The next day, Eliza had just stepped into her flat, her feet aching from the day, muscles tugging with faint weariness, yet a flutter of anticipation stirred in her chest. She missed Christian terribly—last night had felt far too long, and she had longed for him through every quiet, lonely hour.

Just as she was about to step into the shower, her phone buzzed. She picked it up, hope tightening her chest. Unknown number. Her heart skipped. Maybe… just maybe, it was Christian.

"Hello?" she said cautiously, her voice tentative.

"Hi, Miss Preston? This is Dr. Singh from the clinic regarding your pre-employment blood tests," came the calm, professional voice on the other end.

Eliza's stomach fluttered nervously. "Yes… is there a problem?"

"No, not a problem," Dr. Singh replied gently. "But your blood test shows the presence of hCG."

Eliza blinked, confusion knitting her brows. "hCG… what does that mean?"

"It indicates that you're pregnant," he explained carefully. "It's very early, though—too early to measure exact gestational milestones. Based on your levels, you're approximately three weeks along. We recommend a follow-up in about a week to confirm and monitor your progress properly."

Eliza froze, the words pressing down on her chest like a weight she couldn't lift. She sank onto the edge of the bath, her fingers trembling as they rested in her lap. "Pregnant?" she whispered, barely audible, her mind reeling in disbelief.

"Yes," Dr. Singh confirmed softly. "We wanted to inform you as soon as possible so you can follow up with your GP or obstetrician. Everything looks normal so far, but it's important to be monitored."

Eliza managed a shaky, "Okay… thank you," before ending the call. She rested her forehead in her hands, pressing her palms to her face as a storm of thoughts collided inside her.

Her mind went instantly to Christian—the storm, the night in St. Moritz, the way he had held her, kissed her, made her feel seen, wanted, cherished. And now, the impossible, breathtaking truth—a new life was growing inside her.

She had missed only three pills, caught between the chaos of the blizzard and her hurried escape from St. Moritz.

Fear, wonder, and a fragile thread of joy tangled in her chest, setting her pulse racing. Her thoughts flickered between exhilaration and dread, uncertainty, and awe. Everything had changed in a single heartbeat, yet beneath the confusion, a small, luminous hope began to take root.

What would he think? Her lips pressed together, teeth biting lightly at her lower lip. She had heard too many stories of women being judged, of intentions questioned—especially when a wealthy man was involved. *Would Christian suspect she had planned this?* The thought sent a shiver of nervous dread through her.

Eliza sank further, letting her hand rest instinctively on her stomach. Her fingers curved gently over the soft swell of her belly, and a whisper rose in her mind, almost reverently: *Christian's baby.*

Her breath caught in her throat, a shiver of anticipation and awe running through her. For a moment, the world outside her flat vanished. All that existed was the warmth of that possibility, the delicate life she carried, and the love she had come to feel—so fierce, so certain—that it made her chest ache with longing and hope.

She closed her eyes, letting the weight of it all settle, and for the first time allowed herself to imagine a future with him—and with this child—woven together, fragile, terrifying, and utterly exhilarating.

Chapter Eighteen

Eliza stepped into the shower, letting the warm water cascade over her, the steam curling around her like a fragile shield. She pressed her forehead against the cool tiles for a moment, gripping the edges of the shower wall as tears slid down her cheeks. Thoughts of Christian overwhelmed her—how fiercely he had held her, kissed her, made love to her—and now this impossible news.

What if he thought she was trying to trap him? She shook her head violently, the thought twisting painfully in her chest. She loved him—she was certain of that—but the fear of misunderstanding, of losing him before she could even tell him, made her sob quietly.

After a long, trembling shower, she wrapped herself in a towel and moved to her bedroom, drying her hair and pulling on the dress she had chosen for Henry's birthday dinner. Simple, elegant, nothing extravagant—but tonight, she barely noticed the fabric against her skin. Her mind was consumed with worry. She considered calling Christian to cancel, telling herself she needed time to think, time to process everything before facing him.

Then a steadier thought pushed through the storm of panic, fragile but insistent. No. She couldn't let fear dictate her choices. She loved him—deeply, irrevocably—and she trusted him, even if a small, irrational part of her still trembled. She would wait. She would wait to tell him, and in the meantime, she would focus on the evening ahead, on enjoying their time together, on keeping things normal. She tried to steady her racing thoughts, repeating it like a mantra.

But the words felt hollow against the tide of anxiety coursing through her. Her stomach fluttered nervously, and her hand tightened around the hairbrush she was holding. Convincing herself wasn't enough. Every beat of her heart reminded her of the secret she carried, the life she now nurtured, and the love she didn't want to risk.

By six o'clock, Eliza stood at the door of her flat, smoothing her hair one last time, her fingers trembling ever so slightly. Her heart thudded in her chest, a tangled mix of anticipation and the unspoken worry she hadn't yet allowed herself to confront.

A sharp knock made her jump. Her pulse quickened as she opened the door—and there he was. Christian. Impeccably dressed, radiating confidence and warmth, his smile lighting up the doorway the instant he saw her.

"Eliza," he murmured, voice low and full of affection. Without hesitation, he bent down and captured her lips in a soft, lingering kiss. Tender but charged, it sent a shiver through her, made her stomach flutter, her chest ache with a delicious longing. She pressed closer, letting the familiar comfort of his presence chase away—if only for a moment—the gnawing worry she carried.

When they finally pulled apart, his forehead rested against hers, eyes searching hers with quiet, steady devotion. "You look incredible," he whispered, every word reverent, as though each were a promise.

Eliza managed a small, shy smile, tucking a strand of hair behind her ear. "You look… perfect," she admitted softly, trying to mask the churn of anxiety inside her. She hoped her smile would be enough.

He noticed. His gaze lingered on her a heartbeat longer than usual—a flicker of something unspoken in his eyes—but he said nothing. He assumed her quietness was still about the article, the sudden surge of public attention. It would take time for her to grow comfortable beneath the world's gaze. Reaching for her hand, he gave it a gentle squeeze, his voice soft but steady. "Shall we?"

Eliza nodded, forcing a smile, pushing down the swirl of emotions inside her. Tonight, she would be with him. She would laugh, enjoy the warmth of friendship and love. And she would wait—wait to tell him until the moment felt right.

As they walked toward the limousine, side by side, she leaned slightly against him, drawing comfort from the familiar strength of his presence. The unexpected news could wait. Tonight was about Henry.

The surprise had been a resounding success—Henry had absolutely no idea. The apartment buzzed with laughter and chatter; at least ten couples had gathered, the party in full swing, glasses clinking, music playing softly in the background. Christian moved through the crowd with effortless charm, attentive to friends and guests alike, his smile dazzling and warm. But Eliza, though thrilled to be there, felt subdued, quiet—a shadow of worry lurking behind her eyes.

Mary, ever perceptive, noticed immediately. She pulled Eliza aside as soon as she could, her voice gentle yet concerned. "Are you okay, Eliza?"

Eliza's smile faltered, just slightly. "Yes… I'm fine," she said, though the tremor in her voice betrayed her.

Mary's gaze softened, understanding in her eyes. "I hope you think of me as a friend, someone you can trust," she said quietly, brushing a light hand over Eliza's arm.

Eliza's chest tightened. She desperately wanted to confide in someone, to release the secret gnawing at her all afternoon, but she couldn't tell Christian—not yet. She hesitated, then whispered, barely audible over the hum of music, "If I tell you… it's only between us."

Mary's warm eyes softened further. "Of course, Eliza. Anything you say in confidence stays with me."

Eliza swallowed hard, her voice trembling. "I… I just found out I'm pregnant."

Mary's eyes widened, and a radiant smile spread across her face. "Oh, that's wonderful!"

Eliza shook her head, panic still tight in her chest. "No… it's not."

Mary frowned slightly, concern flickering. "It's not Christian's? It's someone else's?"

"No… no, it's his," Eliza whispered, hands clenching at her sides. "But I don't know how to tell him. I'm scared of how he'll react."

Mary reached out, taking her hands gently. "Eliza, he cares about you. He'll be thrilled. Trust me."

Eliza bit her lip, scepticism clouding her features, tears welling in her eyes. "I don't know… he might…"

Before she could finish, Christian appeared, his presence sudden yet grounding. His eyes immediately caught the tremor in her shoulders, the glistening tears threatening to fall. "Eliza… is everything okay?" His voice threaded with concern as he stepped closer.

Eliza blinked, caught between fear and relief. Mary gave a gentle squeeze, her smile steady and reassuring. "You should talk to Christian," she said softly, then gave him a knowing look before stepping away, leaving them alone.

Christian's gaze softened, warm and unwavering, as his hand instinctively reached for hers. "Eliza… talk to me. I can see you're upset. Is it about the article?" he murmured, his voice low and tender, each word careful, patient.

Eliza's heart hammered in her chest. She shook her head, the truth so close, yet still just out of reach. She drew in a shaky breath, steadying herself with the weight of his care and Mary's gentle encouragement.

Finally, her voice barely above a whisper, she said, "I… I need to tell you something… in private."

Christian's eyes softened even further, a mixture of patience and concern in his gaze. "Of course," he replied gently. "We can go to Henry's study."

He guided her gently down the hall to Henry's study, the noise of the party fading with each step. Once inside, he closed the door behind them and turned to her, eyes soft but urgent. He reached for her hands, holding them firmly yet tenderly. "Talk to me, Eliza," he said, low, steady, full of concern.

She swallowed hard, meeting his gaze. "You know how I had to get a blood test for my new job?"

"Yes," he replied, brow furrowing slightly.

"They… they found something."

Christian's hand tightened around hers, worry flickering in his eyes. "You're not ill, are you?"

"No, no," she said quickly, her voice unsteady. "I'm fine. I'm healthy… but—" She drew in a shaky breath, her heart thundering in her chest. "I'm pregnant. It's… it's yours."

The words hung between them, delicate and weighty all at once—like fragile glass suspended in air, shimmering with both fear and wonder.

For a moment, Christian didn't move. Then his eyes widened, the shock giving way to something softer—astonishment, reverence, a dawning tenderness that stole his breath. He reached up, cupping her face in both hands, his thumbs brushing her cheeks as if she were something precious.

"Eliza…" he breathed, voice rough with emotion. "Are you—really?"

She nodded, tears welling despite herself, the weight of the secret finally shared. "Yes. It's yours, Christian. It's our baby."

For a moment, silence held them, heavy with the enormity of it, before Christian pulled her into a tight embrace, lips brushing the top of her head. "Our baby," he murmured over and over, as if speaking it aloud made it more real. "Eliza… I… I love you. I love you so much."

His words tumbled out, raw and urgent, pressing against her like a tangible force. Christian's hands cradled her face, thumbs tracing the curve of her cheeks as if memorising every detail. "You've changed my life, Eliza," he continued, voice thick with emotion. "I've never felt like this about anyone. You… you are everything."

Tears spilled freely down her face. She pressed herself against him, pulse racing with a chaotic mix of relief, fear, and wonder. Yet beneath the rush of emotion, a quiet, insistent doubt lingered. She clung to him, but a small voice whispered: *Is he saying this because of the baby?*

Not long ago, a man had promised her love and forever, only to break it. The memory stung sharply, reminding her that even passionate words could sometimes be empty.

She lifted her head just enough to meet his gaze, desperate to see the truth there, to read sincerity in his eyes. Christian's expression was open, unguarded, alive with joy and longing, every line of his face illuminated by the intensity of his feelings.

And yet… the shadow of doubt lingered. She pressed closer, letting herself feel the strength of his embrace, the security of his arms, the palpable happiness radiating from him. She wanted to surrender completely, to trust him with everything—but a fragile part of her remained cautious, wary of letting hope outrun certainty.

Even in that closeness, her heart beat in two rhythms: one racing with love, the other pulsing with caution. She held both in the quiet tension of being utterly, dangerously alive in his arms.

Then, unexpectedly, his voice broke the silence. "Marry me."

Her eyes widened, shock freezing her. "Christian… no," she whispered, voice barely audible. Her mind spun—*was he only asking because of the baby?*

"Why not?" he pressed gently, searching her face. "I love you. You love me, don't you?"

"Yes, but…" Her voice faltered, tears threatening again. "I—I don't want you to feel obligated to marry me because of the baby."

Christian's expression softened, hands tightening around hers. "Eliza," he said, low, earnest, unwavering, "I loved you long before we knew about this little life. I'm not asking because of the baby. I'm asking because I want you—for the rest of my life. Not for what's coming… for what we already have."

Her heart clenched, torn between doubt and the undeniable truth in his gaze. She wanted to believe him, desperately. And yet the weight of fear and past hurts held her back, whispering caution even as her body ached to say yes.

Christian leaned closer, forehead resting against hers, warm and steady. "I'm here, Eliza. Always. You don't have to answer now. Just… feel this moment. Feel us. And when you're ready, you'll know."

Her breath hitched, eyes closed, letting the warmth of his words and the weight of his touch settle over her. Every fibre ached to believe him, to surrender to the joy he radiated—but a small, stubborn part held back, whispering caution into the corners of her heart.

When they rejoined the party, Christian's smile came easily—warm, radiant, threaded with quiet triumph—while Eliza's was careful, composed, concealing the flicker of uncertainty that still shadowed her eyes. Laughter and conversation swirled around them, the room alive with music and light, yet inside her, a quiet storm of hope, fear, and disbelief still raged.

Christian felt it—saw the tension in her shoulders, the way her hand lingered in his but didn't quite rest. He was elated, dizzy with the knowledge that they were creating a life together, but he understood she needed time. So, he didn't press, didn't demand. He would simply stand beside her—steady, patient, certain that one day soon she would see what he already knew.

They belonged together. Always had. Always would.

The next day was Eliza's day off, and though the flat was quiet, her mind was anything but. She couldn't stop thinking about Christian—the way he had stayed the night, the tenderness of his arms around her, the way his love had poured into her until dawn. She loved him—she knew she always would. *But could she truly trust that his love was real, lasting, unshaken by circumstance?*

She was folding laundry when a sudden knock at the door made her jump. Wiping her hands on her jeans, she opened it to find Mary standing there, her expression gentle and warm.

"I hope you don't mind," Mary said softly. "I wanted to see how you're doing after last night."

Relief warmed Eliza's chest. "I don't mind at all—it's very kind of you. Please, come in."

Mary stepped inside, and after offering a smile, Eliza asked, "Would you like some coffee?"

"I'd love some," Mary replied.

Soon they were settled on the sofa, mismatched mugs in hand, the rich aroma of freshly brewed coffee curling through the room.

Mary's gaze was steady, warm, and perceptive. "I noticed how happy Christian looked after you told him the news."

Eliza's lips curved faintly. "He was. He even asked me to marry him."

Mary's eyes widened, delight shining through. "Oh, Eliza—that's wonderful!"

But Eliza's smile faltered. She shook her head. "No, it's not... not really. I don't know if he asked because he truly loves me, or because of the baby." Her voice cracked. "Brad said he loved me too—and then he left me at the altar."

Mary's expression softened, her tone firm yet gentle. "Christian is not Brad."

"I know," Eliza whispered, fingers tightening around her mug. "But the memory of that betrayal… it left a scar. One I'm not sure will ever fade."

Mary set her half-full mug gently on the coffee table, eyes never leaving Eliza's. Her face grew serious, almost troubled. "There's something you should know."

Eliza frowned, confusion flickering across her features. "About what?"

Mary hesitated, then exhaled slowly, as though weighing loyalty against what she felt Eliza needed to hear. "Henry would kill me if he knew I was telling you this. But I think you deserve to know: Christian loves you—more than you realise."

Eliza's brow knit, uncertainty sparking in her gaze. "Why do you say it like that? As if you're so certain. How could you possibly know?"

Mary leaned forward slightly, her tone careful, deliberate. "When you met Christian… you knew he was engaged to Clarissa."

"Yes," Eliza murmured, stomach tightening.

"He was engaged to her for one reason," Mary said sadly. "A reason that was unfair to him, but he felt trapped—like she was his only option."

Eliza's breath caught. "I don't understand…"

Mary's eyes locked on hers, serious yet gentle. "Christian's grandfather passed away recently."

Eliza nodded, absorbing the news, a mix of comprehension and apprehension stirring in her chest.

Mary continued, her tone thoughtful. "The reading of his will was… a shock to Christian. He's now the sole heir to the Harrington fortune. But his grandfather… he wasn't exactly a fan of Christian's choices, his lifestyle."

Eliza tilted her head, curiosity piqued. "What do you mean?"

"His grandfather wanted Christian to settle down, marry, and have children. But Christian… he never met anyone he truly loved, and he refused to compromise. He said he would never marry without love, no matter the pressure."

Eliza's lips curved slightly. "Just as it should be."

Mary nodded, a faint smile touching her eyes. "Exactly. But his grandfather, stubborn and rigid as he was, put a clause in the will: if Christian didn't marry before the new year, he would be disinherited."

Eliza's eyes widened. "That's… ridiculous. And cruel."

Mary's expression softened, her gaze warm with understanding. "It was both cruel and unreasonable. His grandfather had expectations and despised it when Christian stood up to him. But Christian… he's always stayed true to his heart. The only thing that could sway him would be his legacy. The Harrington fortune is worth billions, but he doesn't care about the money. What he does care about is the legacy his grandfather and father built. That's why he got engaged to Clarissa—to fulfill the stipulations in the will."

Eliza's eyes widened further, comprehension dawning. "That explains why Christian told me he never loved Clarissa."

Mary nodded gently. "I don't think he ever liked her, not really. She was ambitious, from a good family, and she… she thought she was the right choice. That's all."

Eliza shook her head, incredulous. "That's an awful lot of pressure for anyone."

"Yes," Mary agreed softly, "but Christian was willing to go along with it… until he met you."

Eliza frowned, confusion knitting her brows. "I… don't understand."

Mary smiled faintly, leaning closer, as if sharing a secret. "When he met you, he fell in love—truly, deeply. And he realised he couldn't marry Clarissa. Not honestly, not with his heart where it belongs. So, as soon as he returned from St. Moritz, he ended it."

Eliza's breath caught. "But… that's ridiculous. Doesn't that mean he would lose his inheritance?"

Mary's eyes gleamed with admiration. "Yes. It does. But he was willing to lose it… for you."

Eliza's hand went to her chest, pulse quickening. "For me…" she whispered, barely believing it.

Mary reached out, giving her hand a reassuring squeeze. "Yes, Eliza. For you. That's how much he loves you."

Eliza sat back slightly, letting the words wash over her like a warm tide. Her mind raced yet somehow felt steadier. After a long pause, she whispered, almost to herself, "Why… why didn't he tell me?"

Mary's gaze softened, understanding her turmoil. "He made the decision on his own before he even found you again. He told Henry that he couldn't—he simply couldn't—marry for anything less than love once he knew what it truly felt like. And he didn't tell you because he didn't want you to feel responsible for him losing his inheritance. That was his choice, his alone. It was never about you having to make a decision—he wanted it to be his, from his heart."

Eliza swallowed hard, letting Mary's reassurance wash over her, a mix of awe and relief settling in her chest. The weight she'd been carrying eased slightly, though a flicker of vulnerability remained. "He... he loves me that much?" she whispered, her voice barely audible.

Mary's eyes softened. "Yes. I've only known Christian for just over two years, and I've never seen him this happy, this... content. You've brought him something no one else ever could."

Eliza sank back, stunned, her mind reeling with the depth of Mary's words. After a pause, her own voice tumbled out before she could stop it. "I have to marry him," she said quickly, urgency and panic threading her tone. "So he doesn't lose his inheritance."

Mary's expression turned gentle but firm. "Eliza... you can't. It's too late. There are only nine days until the deadline, and in England, you can't even get a marriage licence that quickly. It takes at least twenty-eight days."

Eliza's brow furrowed. "But... surely if the lawyers knew we were getting married, that would count?"

Mary shook her head, squeezing her hand reassuringly. "No. The will is ironclad—Christian had it checked thoroughly. But that's not why I'm telling you this. I wanted you to understand just how much he truly loves you. That's what matters."

Tears of joy welled in Eliza's eyes. She looked at Mary, voice trembling with the fullness of her heart. "I love him... with all my heart. I never thought I could love someone as much as I love Christian."

Mary smiled, warm and certain. "I know you do, Eliza. And I promise... you two will be very, very happy together."

For a moment, the women sat in quiet understanding, the air between them warm with shared affection and hope. Then Eliza's gaze shifted, a sudden spark of determination lighting her features. Her breath caught as an idea began to form.

"Wait..." she said, her voice quickening with excitement. "There's a way."

Mary tilted her head, intrigued. "What do you mean?"

Eliza took a deep breath, reaching for Mary's hands. "I know how he can secure his inheritance... and still follow his heart. But... I'll need your help—and Henry's. Will you help me?"

Mary's expression softened, admiration and affection shining in her eyes. "Of course, Eliza. Whatever it takes, we'll help you."

Eliza squeezed her hands, relief, and gratitude flooding through her. "Thank you. I couldn't do this alone. I just… I want him to have everything, without losing what matters most."

Mary gave her a reassuring smile. "Then we'll make sure it happens. We'll figure this out together."

Eliza exhaled slowly, a mixture of hope and resolve settling over her. For the first time in days, she felt a path forward—one that could preserve Christian's legacy and protect the love that had grown between them.

Chapter Nineteen

Henry walked into Christian's office, his usual confident stride carrying a faint air of amusement, though the corners of his mouth betrayed a secret he seemed eager to share.

"What do I owe the pleasure of this visit?" Christian asked, glancing up from his laptop, curiosity flickering in his steady gaze.

Henry dropped into the chair opposite his desk, sprawling comfortably as if the office were his own. "I came to check on the soon-to-be daddy," he teased, a mischievous smile tugging at his lips.

Christian's grin spread wide, unguarded, his eyes bright with a rare light. "I still can't believe how lucky I am," he admitted, voice low but fervent.

"I'm genuinely happy for you, Christian," Henry said, the humour in his tone giving way to sincerity.

"Thanks, Henry," Christian replied warmly, the weight of gratitude carried in those two simple words.

Then Henry leaned forward, lowering his voice in a way that made Christian's brows rise. "Actually... I came to ask a favour."

"Anything, Henry. You know that." Christian's tone was easy, confident, but touched with the affection of brotherhood.

"Mary needs to be in Las Vegas tomorrow."

Christian blinked, straightening slightly. "Tomorrow? It's Christmas Eve. Why Las Vegas?"

"There's a family emergency," Henry explained, his expression sobering. "Her mother's sister is ill."

Concern softened Christian's features. "I didn't realise she had family there."

Henry gave a faint shrug. "She doesn't talk about it much. But... I was hoping we could use your jet."

"Of course," Christian said instantly, no hesitation in his voice. "Anything for her."

Relief softened Henry's face. "Mary actually thought you and Eliza should come too. She said we probably wouldn't be back in time for Christmas dinner, so why not all celebrate together in Las Vegas?"

Christian leaned back, letting the suggestion sink in. For a moment, silence stretched, then a slow smile curved his lips. "I'll ask Eliza tonight. When do you want to leave?"

"Around ten tomorrow morning. That would get us there by noon, local time."

Christian nodded, already piecing together the details in his mind. "Done. I'll talk to Eliza tonight, and we'll make it happen."

Henry clapped him lightly on the shoulder, affection shining through. "Thanks, Christian. You're a lifesaver."

Christian's smile deepened, tender yet assured. "You don't need to thank me. You know I'd do anything for you—and Mary."

That evening, Christian arrived at Eliza's flat right on time, his smile lighting the doorway the instant she opened it. He looked as he always did—impeccably dressed, composed, exuding quiet authority—but tonight there was something different in his eyes. A spark of anticipation, threaded with warmth and an intimacy that softened his usual precision.

"Eliza," he murmured, stepping inside before she could speak. He drew her into his arms, his kiss unhurried, tender, lingering just long enough to send a shiver through her and anchor her in the comfort of him. "How are you feeling, sweetheart?"

Eliza tilted her face up to him, a faint, tired smile curving her lips. "A little tired," she admitted.

His hand found its way to her stomach, his touch feather-light, reverent. "I hope you're not overdoing it," he said softly. "You've got precious cargo now."

A quiet laugh escaped her, gentle and full of affection. She covered his hand with hers. "I know. That's why I was hoping we could just stay in tonight."

"Anything you want," he murmured, his thumb brushing small circles across her skin, his voice low and full of promise.

"You really need to stop spoiling me," she teased, her tone lighter now, though her eyes shone with affection.

"I can't help it," he said, kissing the tip of her nose with playful devotion. His voice shifted, deepening slightly, carrying a weight that made her pulse flutter. "Actually… there's something I wanted to ask you."

Her heart skipped, curiosity and nerves intertwining. "Oh? What is it?" she asked softly, almost wary.

"Henry came to see me earlier," Christian began, warmth threading through his voice, "and apparently Mary needs to be in Las Vegas tomorrow. She suggested… we all go. Spend Christmas Eve together. You, me, Henry, Mary. What do you think?"

Eliza's breath caught, her pulse quickening as a smile blossomed across her lips despite the heaviness she carried inside. "Las Vegas?" she echoed, wonder edging her tone. "That sounds… incredible. I've never been there."

Christian's grin widened at her reaction. He gathered her into another embrace, holding her close as if to share his own excitement. "I knew you'd love the idea. Just the four of us—a holiday adventure we'll never forget."

Eliza laughed softly, letting herself imagine it, though beneath the flicker of excitement a knot of tension remained. Secrets, she knew, had a way of surfacing—and she couldn't hide hers forever. "I… I think I'm excited," she admitted, her voice tinged with both wonder and the faintest shadow of unease.

He pressed a kiss to her temple, his forehead resting against hers as if to seal the moment. "Good," he whispered. "Now… come on, you need rest. I'll take care of dinner. You just relax."

"Thank you, Christian," she said softly, cupping his cheek, her thumb grazing the warmth of his skin. "I love you so much."

"And I love you," he replied, his lips finding hers once more—slow, reverent, filled with a certainty that wrapped around her heart and almost, almost chased away the secret that still lingered at the edges of her happiness.

The next morning was bright and clear, the December chill clinging to the air as Henry, Mary, Christian, and Eliza made their way across the private tarmac. The sleek, silver Harrington jet gleamed in the morning sunlight, a dazzling emblem of power and privilege that seemed almost unreal to Eliza. She tightened her scarf around her neck, the crisp wind nipping at her cheeks, and tried not to stare too openly at the impossibly elegant aircraft waiting to carry them.

Christian slipped his arm around her waist as they approached, leaning close to murmur in her ear. "Ready for your first flight on a private jet, sweetheart?"

Eliza's lips curved into a soft smile, her voice carrying a mixture of awe and delight. "Ready… but I still can't believe this is real."

Henry chuckled from a few steps ahead, tossing her a knowing look. "Trust me, Eliza, the first time is always surreal. You'll get used to it."

Mary swatted him lightly on the arm. "Don't tease her. It's special."

As they reached the stairs, Christian offered his hand, steadying Eliza as she ascended. Her fingers lingered along the polished railing, heart fluttering with a mix of nerves and excitement. Once inside, she paused, taking in the cabin with wide eyes.

The interior exceeded every expectation—sleek leather seats arranged like a lavish living room, broad windows flooding the space with light, soft carpeting underfoot that made every step feel indulgent. Polished walnut accents gleamed warmly, and a subtle, expensive scent—cedarwood mingled with leather—permeated the air.

Eliza slowly turned in place, voice hushed. "Christian… it's beautiful."

His smile softened as he watched her, pride and tenderness mingling in his gaze. "I wanted you to see this world… my world. And share it with me."

He guided her toward the plush cream-coloured seats, sweeping a hand across the cabin as if presenting it solely for her. "Over there is the lounge area—plenty of space to stretch out if you want to nap during the flight. That's the dining table—we'll have lunch catered once we're in the air. And back there," his lips curved into a playful smile, "is the private suite. Perfect for when you need a little privacy."

Eliza's cheeks warmed at his teasing tone, and she gave him a gentle shove. "Christian Harrington, are you trying to scandalise me at thirty thousand feet?"

Henry, overhearing, laughed outright. "I think that's exactly what he's doing."

Mary rolled her eyes with fond amusement, settling into one of the armchairs. "Men."

Eliza laughed, though beneath it her chest swelled with something deeper. This wasn't just luxury—it was intimacy, an invitation into Christian's private world, one few people ever glimpsed. She slid into a seat by the window, drinking in every exquisite detail.

Christian lowered himself beside her, taking her hand and pressing a soft kiss to her knuckles. His voice dropped to something only she could hear. "I love seeing your eyes light up like this. You make me want to show you everything."

Her throat tightened with emotion. "I don't care about the jet, Christian," she whispered, squeezing his hand. "I care about you. Just being with you."

His smile deepened, the kind that reached his eyes and softened every sharp edge of his features. "And that," he murmured, brushing his lips over hers in a quick, tender kiss, "is exactly why I want to give you the world."

Moments later, the engines roared to life, a low hum reverberating through the cabin as the jet prepared for take-off. Henry poured champagne for himself and

Christian, while Christian signalled the attendant to bring sparkling water for Mary and Eliza. Eliza accepted her glass gratefully, her other hand never leaving Christian's.

As the jet began to taxi, her heart raced—not from fear, but from the dizzying sense that her life was shifting yet again. Weeks ago, she never could have imagined herself here—on a private jet, with Christian by her side, flying across the world with friends who had become family.

When the wheels finally left the ground and the jet soared into the wide, endless sky, Christian leaned close, his lips brushing her ear. "Welcome to your first Harrington flight, my love. Just the beginning of our adventures."

As the earth fell away beneath them, Eliza felt the words apply to more than the journey to Las Vegas. They were building a life together—a life full of risk, love, and possibilities she barely dared to imagine.

Once the seatbelt sign clicked off and the cabin relaxed, the attendant glided down the aisle with trays of coffee and pastries. Laughter and chatter quickly filled the space, as natural as if they were in Henry and Mary's living room rather than thirty thousand feet in the air.

Henry leaned back, swirling champagne lazily in its crystal glass. "Well, Eliza, first impressions? Still dazzled by Harrington luxury?"

Eliza laughed, shaking her head as she bit into a flaky croissant. "Dazzled, yes. But I'm trying very hard not to look like I've never sat in a seat this comfortable before."

Mary chuckled warmly. "Don't let him tease you. The first time Henry brought me on this jet, I spent half the flight opening and closing the drawers because I couldn't get over how smooth they were."

Henry groaned. "Must you tell that story every time?"

"Yes," Mary said sweetly, sipping her coffee.

Christian leaned toward Eliza with a grin. "Don't worry, sweetheart. You're much more composed than Mary was."

Mary gasped in mock outrage. "Excuse me?"

Henry pointed across the table. "I'll admit it. She squealed when the table folded out from the wall."

"I did not squeal!" Mary protested, cheeks pink as the others laughed.

Christian raised a brow. "You did."

Mary's eyes narrowed playfully. "Careful, Christian. I know stories about you too."

Henry chuckled. "So do I."

Christian placed a dramatic hand over his heart. "And yet, here I am, trapped with the three of you at thirty thousand feet. My reputation is doomed."

Eliza giggled, shaking her head. "Oh, I think your reputation can survive a little playful banter."

Christian turned to her, his smile softening into something more private. "I suppose you're right. Besides, you're the only one whose opinion matters to me."

Heat rose to her cheeks at the intensity in his gaze, and she quickly sipped her water to steady herself. Mary caught the moment, smiling knowingly, before turning back to Henry.

Christian leaned closer, voice low and intimate. "Come with me."

Her eyes widened, pulse skipping. "Where?"

He tilted his head subtly toward the rear of the jet. "Just for a few minutes. I want you to see something."

She hesitated only long enough to glance at Henry and Mary, who were engrossed in their own conversation. Then she allowed Christian to take her hand, heart thudding as he guided her down the aisle toward the private suite.

The moment the door clicked shut, the sounds of laughter and engines dulled to a hush. The suite was surprisingly spacious, with a wide bed dressed in crisp linens, soft lighting, and a window framing the endless blue sky beyond.

Eliza turned slowly, breath catching. "Christian… this is incredible."

He wasn't looking at the suite—he was looking at her, expression tender, reverent, and charged with heat.

"It's just a room," he murmured, stepping closer, cupping her face. "You're what makes it extraordinary."

Her pulse fluttered wildly as his lips met hers, unhurried but electric, filled with all the love and intensity he carried. She melted against him, fingers curling into his shirt, the rest of the world slipping away.

His kiss deepened, hands sliding from her face to her waist, drawing her closer. The world outside—the endless blue sky, the low hum of the jet—faded into insignificance.

Time became irrelevant. Every touch, every sigh, every whispered word threaded tenderness and passion so tightly together they were inseparable. When they finally stilled, tangled together in the hush of the suite, Eliza rested her head against his chest, listening to the steady beat of his heart.

"I think I could stay here forever," she whispered.

Christian's arms tightened around her. "Then forever it is," he murmured, words vibrating against her like a private vow.

Eventually, they pulled away, straightening clothes and exchanging soft, private smiles before returning to the others. Henry grinned knowingly. "Took you long enough," he teased.

Christian rolled his eyes, smirking. "We were, uh… inspecting the jet," his tone innocent, though the glint in his eye betrayed him.

Eliza laughed, linking her arm with his. "Yes, it's very… spacious," she added, recalling their private moments with mischief.

Mary chuckled, shaking her head. "Hopelessly in love, that's for sure."

Christian looped his arm around Eliza, drawing her closer as the attendant arrived with trays of food for lunch. The aroma of pastries, fresh fruit, smoked salmon, and coffee filled the cabin, and the laughter and chatter resumed, mingling with the quiet intimacy that lingered between Christian and Eliza, a thread of love running quietly but unmistakably through the group.

"Lunch is served!" the attendant announced with a bright smile, setting the trays down with careful precision. Plates of golden croissants, delicate sandwiches, and colourful fruit bowls were arranged neatly, accompanied by sparkling water and freshly squeezed juice.

Eliza's eyes lit up, a mix of awe and delight. "This looks incredible," she said, taking a seat beside Christian, who returned a playful, indulgent smile.

"Only the best for my passengers," Christian said, reaching for a croissant and offering it to her with a flourish, his eyes twinkling.

Henry and Mary exchanged amused glances across the table. "Well," Mary said, shaking her head with a soft laugh, "I suppose we can let them be spoiled for the next few hours."

As they began eating, the conversation flowed naturally—stories from the past week, light teasing, and plans for the coming holiday festivities. Yet throughout it all, Christian and Eliza shared secret smiles, fleeting touches of fingers across the table, and glances full of quiet understanding. Even amidst the cheerful chatter and clinking of cutlery, the warmth and intimacy between them lingered like a subtle, unspoken thread.

Chapter Twenty

After finishing their lunch, Christian and Henry moved to the lounge area, sinking into the plush seats with steaming cups of coffee in hand. Christian's expression was contemplative, his fingers tapping lightly against the armrest as his gaze drifted toward the cabin windows.

"So…" Henry began, leaning back in his seat, casual yet alert, "you really mean it, don't you?" His tone was easy, but his eyes searched Christian's carefully, seeking the weight behind his words.

Christian gave a small, wry smile, amusement flickering in his gaze. "About what?"

Henry smirked knowingly. "About Eliza. You're completely smitten. Utterly, hopelessly in love."

Christian's features softened, a warmth threading his low, steady voice. "I've never felt like this about anyone, Henry. She's… everything I didn't even know I was missing. And now…" He shook his head slightly, a tender smile tugging at the corner of his lips. "Now, all I want is to make her happy. Every single day. All of it."

Henry nodded, a wide grin spreading across his face. "Good. That's what I like to hear. You deserve her, and she deserves you."

Christian exhaled slowly, the tension in his shoulders easing. "Thanks, Henry. I just… I want to be certain I'm doing everything right. I can't afford to mess this up."

Henry chuckled softly. "You won't. And no regrets about your grandfather's will?"

"None," Christian said firmly, his gaze steady.

Henry leaned forward, curiosity lighting his eyes. "And… long term? Can you see a future with Eliza?"

Christian's smile softened, eyes drifting to a distant place as though he were picturing their life ahead. "Yes. The moment she told me she was pregnant, I asked her to marry me. She thought I was asking just because of the baby, but I'm not. She's the one, Henry. I know it in my heart. I just… I don't want to push. I want her to choose me, fully, freely. She's everything to me, and I want every moment with her to be because she wants it too."

Henry's grin widened, pride and relief evident in his expression. "Then you're exactly where you're meant to be. Trust her—and trust yourselves. That's all that matters."

Christian leaned back, letting the words settle, a quiet, contented light in his eyes. "I will. I have to."

Meanwhile, Mary and Eliza had moved to the far corner of the cabin, heads bent together over a small table. Eliza's fingers twisted nervously in her lap, her mind racing with the plan she and Mary had carefully perfected over the past few days.

"Okay," Mary said gently, placing a reassuring hand over Eliza's. Her voice was soft, yet full of confidence. "Here's how it goes. Henry will have the driver take us to the chapel—we scoped out a beautiful little one in downtown Las Vegas. We'll make ourselves scarce so you can propose to Christian in private. And when he says yes…"

Eliza's chest tightened, a wave of doubt threatening to crash over her. "He might not say yes," she murmured, voice trembling slightly.

Mary tilted her head, eyes steady and warm with certainty. "Of course he will."

Eliza shook her head, uncertainty flickering across her face. "But… what if he wants to wait? Maybe for a prenup or something?"

Mary raised an eyebrow, her tone gentle yet probing. "Would that bother you? A prenup, I mean?"

Eliza exhaled, fingers clenching briefly. "No… I don't care about any of that. I'll sign anything he wants me to. But I can't pretend it wouldn't cross his mind. I'm not naive—I know someone in his position would consider it."

Mary's expression softened, a faint, reassuring smile tugging at her lips. "Honestly, I don't think he'll even give it a second thought. And if he does, he won't let it stop him. So… when he says yes, we go straight into the chapel. We'll be there to witness it."

Eliza's voice dropped to a whisper, filled with tender conviction. "I'm only doing this for him. I love him. I know I'll love him forever, and I want to marry him. But I don't want him to give up his legacy… not for me. I can't let that happen."

Mary squeezed her hand reassuringly, eyes warm and understanding. "Then this is perfect, Eliza. He loves you—he'll say yes. And you'll both get everything: your love, your life together, and his legacy intact. It'll be perfect."

Eliza let out a shaky breath, a mixture of hope, fear, anticipation, and determination flooding her. She nodded slowly, letting the plan crystallise in her mind. This was it. Her whole life could change forever in a matter of hours.

Taking a deep breath, Eliza allowed Mary's confidence to anchor her. "Alright… I can do this. I can do this for us—for him."

Mary's hand squeezed hers again. "Exactly. And Eliza… no matter what, I'll be right here. And so will Henry. We've got your back."

Eliza smiled, relief and determination settling over her. For the first time in hours, the fluttering in her chest felt like excitement instead of fear. The plan was set—and soon, everything could change. She only hoped that Christian would feel the same way and that she wasn't about to make a complete fool of herself.

With several hours still left in the flight, Christian noticed Eliza's eyelids drooping slightly and the faint flush of fatigue on her cheeks. He reached over, brushing a strand of hair from her face, his gaze soft with concern.

"I think you should have a lie down," he murmured, his voice low and gentle. "You were up early, and I don't want you overdoing it."

Eliza looked up at him, a tired smile tugging at her lips. "I'm fine, really… just a little sleepy."

Christian shook his head, the corner of his mouth quirking into a playful, yet tender smile. "No arguments. You're coming with me to the suite. You'll rest, and I'll keep you company."

Before she could protest, he took her hand, guiding her down the aisle toward the private suite at the rear of the jet. The door clicked softly behind them, cutting out the cabin's chatter. The room was quiet and cozy, with soft linens and plush seating bathed in gentle, ambient light.

Eliza sank onto the bed, stretching out comfortably, and Christian settled beside her, leaning back against the headboard. He took her hand in his, pressing a light kiss to her fingers.

"You look exhausted," he said softly, brushing a lock of hair from her forehead. "Let me take care of you for a bit. Close your eyes, breathe, and rest. I'll be right here."

Eliza exhaled, the tension in her body melting slightly under his attentive gaze. "I could get used to this," she murmured, snuggling closer to him.

Christian chuckled softly, wrapping an arm around her shoulders. "Good. Because I plan to spoil you, every chance I get."

She laughed quietly, warmth spreading through her chest, and let herself sink into the comfort of his presence. The hum of the engines beneath them and the soft light of the suite created a cocoon of calm and intimacy.

As she closed her eyes, Christian leaned down, pressing a tender kiss to her temple. "Rest, my love. We've got hours to enjoy this flight… and plenty of adventures ahead."

Eliza rested her head against his shoulder, feeling the steady beat of his heart beneath her cheek. "With you… I feel like I can face anything," she whispered.

Christian's arm tightened around her protectively, his lips brushing her hair. "And I'll be right here, every step of the way," he murmured. "Always."

Eliza's breathing evened out as sleep claimed her, her body curling slightly against his side. Christian stayed still, careful not to disturb her, his eyes tracing the peaceful lines of her face. Her hair fell in soft waves across the pillow, her lips slightly parted, and for a moment, the world outside the suite ceased to exist.

He let out a slow breath, pressing a gentle kiss to the top of her head, his mind wandering. This… this is right, he thought, feeling a swell of certainty deep in his chest. He had agonised over decisions before, over the legacy of the Harrington fortune, over family expectations—but now, looking at her, he knew he had chosen correctly. His grandfather's will, the pressures, the engagements, the compromises—none of it had mattered the way this did.

Christian's hand drifted to rest lightly on her waist, the warmth of her body grounding him. Yet, a shiver ran down his spine at the memory of how close he had come to marrying Clarissa. The thought made his stomach twist in discomfort—the thought of a life built on duty rather than love, on obligation rather than truth. He could almost see the ceremony, feel the hollow congratulations, hear the polite smiles masking disappointment. The mere possibility of it now made his skin crawl.

He shuddered slightly, shaking the memory away, and pressed his forehead gently against hers in the quiet darkness of the suite. "Never," he whispered to himself, voice rough with relief and lingering disbelief. "Never again. I can't believe I almost… I almost…" He trailed off, unable to finish the sentence, the relief of having escaped that life mingling with the profound gratitude of having found Eliza.

His eyes softened as he watched her sleep, her chest rising and falling in rhythm with the calm hum of the jet. This is everything, he thought. Her. Us. Love. Life. This is real, and I will never let it go.

For long moments, he simply stayed there, holding her close, memorising the curve of her shoulders, the gentle rise of her cheeks, the quiet vulnerability that made her so achingly beautiful. The world outside could wait; here, in the quiet intimacy of the suite, he allowed himself to savour the certainty, the safety, and the overwhelming happiness of having chosen right—not because of a will, not because of an obligation, but because of love.

And in that quiet, cocooned space, Christian made a silent vow: he would spend the rest of his life protecting her, cherishing her, and never, ever taking a single heartbeat of their life together for granted.

Christian nudged Eliza gently, his voice low and warm. "Sweetheart…"

"Mmm," she murmured, still caught between sleep and wakefulness, her head resting lightly against his shoulder.

"We're landing soon," he added softly, brushing a strand of hair from her face.

Eliza's eyes fluttered open, the soft cabin light and the gentle hum of the jet filling her senses. She blinked a few times, taking in the sight of Christian beside her—his hair slightly tousled, his expression relaxed yet alert, the faint crease of concern softening into tenderness as he looked at her.

"Already?" she whispered, stretching lightly and letting a small yawn escape. "I didn't even notice the time…"

Christian smiled, leaning closer to press a brief, reassuring kiss to her temple. "Did you have a good sleep?"

"I did, thank you," she replied, returning the gesture with a soft kiss to his cheek, her fingers brushing lightly over his jaw.

Christian gave her hand a gentle squeeze, his thumb tracing soothing circles over her knuckles. "Good. We'd better get settled in our seats for landing."

He helped her to her feet, brushing a strand of hair from her face again. "You look delightfully tousled," he said with a playful glint in his eye, unaware of the surprise Eliza was quietly orchestrating.

Eliza's lips curved into a smile, her pulse quickening as a thrilling mix of anticipation and nervous energy spread through her. She let him steady her, their hands still intertwined, feeling the comforting weight of him at her side. "I'm ready," she murmured softly.

Together, they made their way toward the front of the cabin, joining Mary and Henry, who were already seated. Mary offered Eliza a knowing smile, the kind that hinted she was fully aware of what was about to unfold.

Christian gave Eliza's hand one last reassuring squeeze, oblivious to the plan she was about to put into action. "I can't wait to show you around," he murmured, his tone full of warmth, anticipation, and just a hint of curiosity.

The landing was smooth, the wheels kissing the tarmac before the jet taxied to a halt. Customs was quick and efficient, leaving them with more than enough time to move on to the next part of their journey.

Outside, a sleek black limousine waited, gleaming in the midday sun. Henry spoke quietly with the driver, giving instructions in measured tones, while Eliza leaned slightly toward Christian, keeping him distracted with playful conversation. She wanted him engaged, unaware of the surprise waiting for him.

Sliding into the back seat, Eliza settled beside Christian, the soft leather enveloping her as she reached for his hand. Mary and Henry took the seats across from them, creating a comfortable, intimate arrangement for the ride.

The limousine glided smoothly onto the open road, the warm afternoon sun streaming through the windows and casting a gentle glow over the cabin. Eliza kept up her chatter, laughing at Christian's jokes and teasing remarks, her other hand brushing his lightly, a small reminder of the closeness they shared.

Christian leaned back, relaxed but curious, glancing out the window at the passing cityscape of Las Vegas. The sprawling streets, mid-afternoon traffic, and clear sky made it feel like a different world from the quiet hum of the jet.

"So, Henry… what hotel did you book us into?" Christian asked casually, though a subtle spark of curiosity—and perhaps suspicion—flickered in his eyes.

Henry chuckled, leaning back slightly. "The Waldorf Astoria. You'll love it. I've stayed there before."

Christian nodded, the corner of his mouth lifting into a small, knowing smile, though his gaze flicked briefly toward Eliza. She returned his look with a soft, secretive smile of her own, her pulse quickening. Her fingers tightened around his hand under the plush seat, a silent signal of her anticipation and the secret she carried.

The limousine glided smoothly through the wide streets of Las Vegas, sunlight bouncing off the polished buildings, the city sprawling endlessly around them. Each turn, each quiet stretch of road, seemed to hum with promise. Christian relaxed into the leather seat, unaware that every twist and bend was guiding them toward a moment that could change everything—for them both.

Eliza stole a glance at him, her heart fluttering at the thought of what was about to happen, a mix of excitement, nerves, and hope mingling in her chest. She squeezed his hand again, a gentle reassurance… and a quiet invitation for what was to come.

The limousine slowed to a gentle stop in front of a small, charming building tucked away on a quiet street. Christian blinked, confusion knitting his brow as he peered out the window. "Where… where are we?"

Henry cleared his throat, his expression casual but with a knowing glint in his eyes. "Mary and I will step out for just a minute."

Christian's gaze flicked between Henry and Mary, suspicion rising. "Why? What's going on?" His voice was calm, but the edge of uncertainty made it clear he was on alert.

Mary smiled warmly at him, her eyes sparkling with gentle amusement, and Henry gave a small nod. "Trust us. Just stay put for a moment."

Before Christian could protest, they both stepped out of the limousine, leaving the doors closed and the engine humming softly.

Christian turned to Eliza, who was sitting beside him, her fingers brushing lightly against his. She met his gaze with a quiet, mischievous smile, her pulse racing with anticipation.

"Eliza…" he began, his voice low, a mixture of curiosity and caution threading through each word. "What's happening?"

She didn't answer immediately, letting the moment stretch, letting him feel the weight of the mystery and the thrill of the unknown. Her hand tightened around his, just enough to give him a hint of what was coming, her eyes shining with both love and a fierce, unshakable determination.

Christian's brow furrowed slightly as he studied her, sensing that something significant—something unforgettable—was about to unfold.

Eliza took a steadying breath and lifted both of his hands into hers, holding them as if anchoring herself as much as him. "Christian… when we first met, it felt like you and I had known each other forever."

"I felt the same," he murmured, his voice low and earnest, his eyes locked on hers.

She swallowed, her heart pounding, and continued, "I love you with all my heart… but I know about your inheritance, and I could never be with you if I caused you to lose so much."

Christian's eyes widened, worry flashing across his face. "Eliza…" he began, reaching for her, his tone edged with concern, fearing she was pulling away.

She lifted a hand and placed her finger gently against his lips, silencing him. "No… listen. Christian Harrington," she said, her voice steady and full of conviction, "will you marry me—today, right now?"

For a heartbeat, the world seemed to stop. Christian stared at her, shock giving way to awe, then a smile broke across his face—bright, irrepressible, full of joy and relief. "Eliza…" he whispered, his voice thick with emotion, "are you… serious?"

She nodded, her eyes glistening with tears of hope and love. "I'm very serious. I love you. I want to spend every moment with you, without regrets, without holding back."

Christian's grin widened, and he pulled her into a fierce, exhilarating embrace, laughter and relief mingling with the pounding of his heart. "Then yes," he said, his voice steady, trembling only with happiness. "A thousand times yes!"

Christian kissed her with a hunger and tenderness all at once, each movement reverent yet fierce. Between kisses, his voice was a low, desperate whisper, repeating the words she loved to hear. "I love you… I love you…"

Eliza melted against him, her hands threading into his hair, her heart swelling with a joy she had never imagined. Every brush of his lips, every press of his body against hers, spoke volumes of the depth of his devotion.

When she finally pulled back, breathless, her eyes shining with love, Christian rested his forehead against hers, still holding her close. "We better let Henry and Mary know," she murmured, a soft smile curving her lips.

"They were in on this?" Christian asked, confusion flickering through his expression.

Eliza laughed, the sound light, full of happiness and wonder, her fingers tracing circles over his chest. "Yes," she said simply, her voice brimming with love. "They helped me plan it all."

Christian's eyes widened, then softened, and a smile tugged at his lips. "I should've known," he said, shaking his head, still holding her close. "I'm… I'm just so lucky—so unbelievably lucky."

Eliza pressed her forehead to his, laughter and tears mingling. "No, Christian… we're lucky. All of us. But most of all, us."

He brushed his thumb over her cheek, eyes searching hers. "Forever us," he whispered.

"Forever us," she echoed, her heart soaring, knowing in that moment that nothing—neither time, nor money, nor circumstance—could ever change the love they had found.

Chapter Twenty-One

Christian stepped out of the limousine first, reaching back to help Eliza with effortless grace. She took his hand, letting him guide her to the curb, her pulse still racing from the thrill of the proposal. Waiting there, Mary and Henry's faces lit up with anticipation.

Eliza beamed, her fingers still entwined with Christian's. "He said yes," she announced, her voice trembling with joy and relief.

Mary let out a delighted cheer, rushing forward to envelope both Christian and Eliza in a warm, heartfelt hug. "Oh, you two! I'm so happy for you!" she exclaimed, her eyes sparkling.

Henry grinned broadly, leaning down to plant a quick kiss on Eliza's cheek before turning to Christian. "Congrats, mate," he said, shaking his hand firmly and giving him a friendly pat on the back. "You did good."

Christian laughed, the sound full of warmth, and pulled Eliza closer to his side. "Thanks, Henry," he said, his eyes crinkling with genuine happiness. "Couldn't have done it without you two schemers," he added, looking toward Mary, who only laughed in response.

Eliza's heart swelled as she looked at him, and then at her friends who had helped make this perfect moment happen. The small chapel in Las Vegas might have been unexpected, but with Christian by her side, and the love and support surrounding them, everything felt exactly right.

Mary and Henry stepped aside, giving the newly engaged couple a clear path as they approached the small, charming chapel. Sunlight streamed through the stained-glass windows, scattering fragments of ruby, sapphire, and amber across the polished wooden floor. The chapel was quaint, intimate, and impossibly perfect—exactly the kind of place that made Eliza's heart flutter, a delicious mix of nerves and anticipation tightening in her chest. Every detail—the scent of polished wood, the soft echo of distant footsteps, the gentle warmth of the afternoon sun—seemed designed to hold this moment in suspended perfection.

Christian's hand never left hers, their fingers interlaced like a promise carved in gold. He bent slightly, brushing a stray lock of hair from her face, his gaze soft but intense, tender yet charged with something deeper. "Ready?" he whispered, his voice low, carrying both reassurance and a quiet thrill that made her pulse quicken.

Eliza nodded, cheeks flushed, eyes sparkling with a mixture of awe and certainty. "I've never been more ready for anything in my life," she whispered, her voice trembling with a fragile, exhilarating excitement.

They reached the front of the chapel, where the officiant waited with a warm, encouraging smile. Mary and Henry lingered quietly at the back, giving them the illusion of privacy while their own joy and anticipation radiated just beneath the surface, like sunlight through clouds.

The ceremony was brief, but every word carried weight, every pause brimming with the quiet magic of their love. Eliza and Christian's eyes never wavered from each other's, their gaze anchoring them as they spoke their vows. Each word flowed naturally, tinged with reverence, intimacy, and exhilaration—a promise sealed not just in sound, but in the unspoken rhythm of their hearts.

The officiant cleared his throat gently, his eyes twinkling at the obvious devotion between them. "Then by the power vested in me, I pronounce you husband and wife. You may kiss the bride."

Christian laughed softly, a sound that trembled with pure joy, and drew Eliza close. "Finally," he murmured, before capturing her lips in a kiss that stole her breath, made her knees weak, and set her heart soaring. Time seemed to stretch and bend, the world narrowing to just the two of them, tangled in the intensity of this perfect, electric moment.

Outside, Mary clapped softly, tears glinting in her eyes, while Henry let out a low whistle and shook his head in admiration. "They're perfect together," he said, voice full of awe and delight, a grin spreading across his face.

Hand in hand, newly married, Christian and Eliza stepped out of the chapel into the bright afternoon. The sun seemed to shine just for them, illuminating the world as if celebrating their union. Their hearts pounded in unison, every beat a declaration of love, every glance a reaffirmation of the promises made. The limousine waited, sleek and gleaming, ready to whisk them away, but in that suspended moment, nothing else mattered.

Just the two of them. Their love realised. Their future stretching before them like an open road bathed in light. Every heartbeat, every shared smile, every tender squeeze of the hand whispered a single, undeniable truth—they had found their forever in each other. And for Christian and Eliza, that forever began right here, right now, in the warmth of the sun, the quiet joy of family beside them, and the limitless possibilities that lay ahead.

The newlyweds slid into the plush leather seats of the waiting limousine, Christian still holding Eliza's hand, their fingers entwined as naturally as breathing. Sunlight spilled across the city streets outside, golden, and bright, though the afternoon bustle hadn't fully taken hold. For a heartbeat, it felt as if the world had paused just for them.

Mary and Henry settled across from them, grinning like proud accomplices. "So," Mary said, her eyes alight with mischief, "how does it feel to be officially married?"

Eliza laughed softly, giving Christian's hand a squeeze. "Surreal… amazing… and a little terrifying," she admitted, her cheeks still glowing from the ceremony and that dizzying kiss that seemed to echo in her chest.

Christian leaned in, his eyes twinkling. "Terrifying?" he teased. "I was going to say life-changing. But terrifying works too."

Eliza nudged him playfully, her laughter bubbling out.

Henry chuckled, shaking his head. "You two look like you belong together. Always have."

Mary reached for Henry's hand, her smile softening. "See? I told you he'd say yes. And look at him—he hasn't stopped grinning since you asked."

Christian turned towards Eliza, draping an arm along the seat, his other hand still laced with Eliza's. His voice dropped, low and intimate. "I can't help it. I've been waiting my whole life to find her. And now…" His gaze locked with Eliza's, fierce and tender all at once. "…she's mine."

Eliza's heart swelled, her throat tightening with emotion. "I'm yours, Christian. Always," she whispered, pressing her palm to his chest, feeling the steady thrum of his heartbeat beneath her touch.

The limousine glided smoothly through the streets, the quiet hum of the engine wrapping around them like a cocoon. Christian bent closer, brushing a kiss against her temple, then her cheek. "I can't wait to spend every day proving that I'm yours," he murmured.

Eliza tilted her head, catching his lips in a lingering kiss, sweet but edged with promise. "I think I'll hold you to that," she said, her eyes sparkling with love and playful challenge.

Mary and Henry exchanged a look across the aisle, their smiles impossible to hide. "We'd better get to the hotel so you two can have some time alone," Henry teased, his tone full of good-natured amusement.

Christian chuckled, dropping his head in agreement. "For once, I agree with Henry," he said in a low, teasing voice, giving Eliza a wink that made her blush.

The limousine rolled on, carrying them forward, but for Christian and Eliza, the city outside faded into a blur. Nothing else mattered—not the world, not the obligations that waited, not even the future. In that moment, in that stolen bubble of bliss, there was only them—Christian and Eliza. Married. In love. And utterly, completely together.

The limousine slowed to a graceful stop in front of the hotel, its sleek glass façade gleaming beneath the afternoon sun. Bellhops hurried forward, but to Eliza, the world around them blurred. Her pulse fluttered as Christian stepped out first, tall and composed, then turned and offered his hand.

She placed hers in his, and the moment their fingers touched, she felt that same electric certainty that had carried her through the chapel. Christian helped her down as though she were the most precious thing in the world.

"You're my wife now," he murmured, the words tasting foreign but thrilling on his lips. His thumb brushed across her knuckles, his gaze locked on hers. "I plan on reminding you of that every chance I get."

Heat bloomed in Eliza's cheeks, her heart flipping at the intensity in his voice. "I don't think I'll need reminding," she whispered, leaning closer as if the rest of the world had vanished.

Mary and Henry followed behind, grinning like conspirators. Henry clapped Christian on the shoulder. "We'll leave you two lovebirds to settle in. Enjoy the honeymoon phase."

Mary hugged Eliza once more, her eyes shimmering. "You deserve every moment of this happiness." Then, with knowing smiles, the pair disappeared inside, giving them space.

Christian led Eliza through the grand hotel doors, the cool air rushing around them, scented faintly with lilies and polished wood. The lobby glittered with chandeliers and marble floors, but Christian's attention never wavered from her. His hand remained firm at her back, guiding her gently but possessively toward the private elevator waiting for them.

Inside, as the doors slid shut, he turned to her, crowding the space just enough that her breath caught. His eyes, dark with emotion, traced every line of her face. "Mrs. Harrington," he whispered, savouring the title, "this is the beginning of forever."

Eliza's lips parted, her chest tight with wonder and desire. She rose onto her toes, brushing her mouth against his in a kiss that deepened almost instantly—slow, hungry, and filled with everything they hadn't yet had a chance to say.

By the time the elevator chimed at their floor, Eliza's pulse was racing, her cheeks flushed with anticipation. Christian pulled back just enough to brush his lips against hers, murmuring softly, "Our room awaits." The words carried a weight she felt in her bones—the threshold of their first night as husband and wife.

The suite door clicked open, the hush of luxury spilling out to greet them. Soft golden light illuminated the spacious room, where a bottle of champagne waited chilling in a silver bucket beside two crystal flutes. Floor-to-ceiling windows revealed the stretch of Las Vegas below, though the city lights were just beginning to stir.

Before Eliza could take it all in, Christian swept her up into his arms. She let out a startled laugh, her arms instinctively wrapping around his neck.

"Christian!" she gasped, her voice filled with delight.

His smile curved slow and possessive as he carried her across the threshold. "It's tradition, Mrs. Harrington," he murmured, savouring the name as though it were the finest wine. "And I wouldn't dream of starting our marriage without it."

Eliza pressed her cheek against his shoulder, her heart pounding with joy. "You make me feel like the heroine in one of those fairy tales."

"You are," he said simply, his voice husky as he carried her deeper into the suite. "My fairy tale. My forever."

Christian set Eliza carefully on the bed, but his hands lingered, sliding slowly down her arms as if he couldn't quite let her go. His eyes drank her in—every line of her face, every flicker of her expression—as though he were memorising her all over again.

Eliza's breath caught, her heart racing under the weight of his gaze. She reached for him, tugging lightly at his tie, her fingers trembling but sure. "Come here, husband," she whispered, the word sending a thrill through both of them.

Christian's answering smile was molten. He leaned down, capturing her lips in a kiss that started soft, reverent, but deepened quickly, heat sparking between them like kindling catching flame. His hand slid into her hair, cradling her head, while the other pressed against the small of her back, pulling her closer.

Eliza sighed into the kiss, her body arching instinctively toward his. Her hands explored the broad span of his shoulders, the steady strength she'd come to rely on. "I love you," she murmured against his mouth, every word trembling with sincerity.

He pulled back just enough to look into her eyes, his forehead resting against hers. "I love you more," he said, his voice raw, husky, as if the truth of it burned inside him. "And I'll spend every day proving it."

Their lips met again, slower this time, lingering, savouring. His jacket slipped away, her hands helping, their laughter mingling between kisses. The world beyond their suite—the city, the lights, the future—fell away. There was only this: the two of them, tangled in love and passion, discovering what it meant to belong wholly, completely, to one another.

The champagne on ice went untouched. The city lights glittered unseen below. And in the quiet cocoon of their wedding night, Christian and Eliza wrote the first lines of their forever, each touch, each whispered promise binding them closer, sealing their love in a way no ceremony ever could.

The next day dawned bright and clear—Christmas Day. Their suite still carried the lingering glow of the night before, but by late morning they were getting ready to meet Mary and Henry for Christmas lunch.

As Eliza fastened her earrings in the mirror, Christian came up behind her, sliding his arms around her waist and pulling her gently against his chest. His chin brushed her shoulder, his eyes warm yet troubled.

"With all the excitement yesterday," he murmured, "I just realised… I never got you a Christmas present." There was a hint of guilt in his voice, as though the thought weighed heavily on him.

Eliza turned in his arms, tilting her head to look up at him. Her hand came up to cup his cheek, her thumb stroking lightly over his jaw. "I don't need a present, Christian," she said softly, her smile tender. "I already got mine."

He arched a brow, curiosity flickering in his eyes. "Oh? And what was that?"

Her lips curved with mischief as she leaned closer, her voice dropping to a playful whisper. "I got a billionaire for Christmas."

Christian blinked, then laughed, the tension melting from his shoulders. He caught her mouth in a quick, joyful kiss before resting his forehead against hers. "Well, Mrs. Harrington, I can't compete with that. But for the record, I think I got the better deal."

Eliza's laughter rang out, light and happy, filling the room with the kind of joy that didn't need ribbons or wrapping paper.

Hand in hand, they stepped out together, ready to share Christmas with Mary and Henry—but carrying the secret glow of knowing they had already given each other the greatest gift of all.

Epilogue

Five years later…

Christian stood quietly in the doorway of the nursery, his gaze softening at the sight before him. The early morning light filtered through the curtains in a gentle cascade, washing the room in a golden glow that seemed almost otherworldly. Eliza sat in the rocking chair, their six-month-old son nestled against her as she nursed him, her voice humming a soft, soothing tune that made the air feel sacred—like a moment set apart from time itself.

For a long while, Christian simply watched. He watched the curve of her tender smile as she gazed down at their child, the tumble of her hair spilling loose around her shoulders, and the serenity that radiated from her with such quiet strength. His chest ached in the best way, stretched to its limit with a love so full it nearly hurt.

His thoughts slipped backward—unbidden, vivid—to the day she had proposed to him in Las Vegas. Even now, five years later, he could hardly believe his fortune. That this brilliant, beautiful woman had chosen him still felt like a miracle he had no right to claim. Yet here she was: his wife, his anchor, the centre of a life overflowing with laughter, warmth, and devotion. Their clever, mischievous daughter, Kimberly, already four, was happily away at a sleepover with Henry and Mary's little girl. And now they had Jonathan—tiny, perfect, the final piece of their family puzzle.

Gratitude surged through him so fiercely that it tightened his throat. He didn't know what he had done to deserve this happiness, but he vowed silently, as he did every morning, never to take it for granted.

Just yesterday the lawyers had confirmed what once seemed impossible: Harrington & Co was officially his, free and clear. The stipulations of his grandfather's will—*marry before New Year's Eve, remain married for five years, no infidelity, share a household*—had all been fulfilled. The company was now his legacy. He shuddered at the thought of what might have been: five years chained to Clarissa in a hollow marriage, his life stripped of meaning. Instead, fate had led him here—to love, laughter, and a home that pulsed with joy.

He remembered their quick Christmas Eve wedding, unpolished yet perfect in its simplicity. Later, he had tried to give Eliza the grand ceremony he thought she deserved. She had only smiled, her eyes glistening as she told him, *'I already have the man of my dreams. Why would I want another wedding? The first one was perfect.'*

The same had happened with the engagement ring. He had tried to present her with something dazzling enough for a Harrington bride, but she had wagged her finger and laughed, telling him, *'Don't you dare, Christian. I don't need a huge rock to remind me of what I've got.'* She had placed a hand over her still-flat belly, whispering, *'If—and only if—you see something that you think I'd truly love, something with meaning, then give it to me. But if not, I'm perfectly content with this.'* She had lifted her hand, showing the plain platinum band that matched his, the rings she and Mary had bought the day before the wedding.

A month later, he had found it: a modest emerald solitaire, simple yet luminous, the exact shade of her eyes. *'I saw it and thought of you,'* he had told her as he slipped it on her finger. She had gasped, kissed him breathless, her gratitude shining brighter than any jewel. She never asked for anything. But that only deepened his desire to give her everything.

"Morning, sweetheart," Eliza's soft voice pulled him back to the present. She shifted Jonathan gently, burping him against her shoulder before lifting her gaze. Her eyes caught the light, luminous and loving. "Merry Christmas."

Christian's heart caught. He crossed the room in a few strides and knelt beside the rocking chair, cupping her cheek as he kissed her gently, reverently, tasting the warmth of her smile.

"Merry Christmas, my love," he murmured against her lips. His hand brushed over Jonathan's tiny back before returning to hers. "Did you sleep well, sweetheart?"

"I did—and so did Jonathan." Eliza's fingers smoothed over their son's downy hair before she lifted her gaze back to Christian, her expression tender. "Did you?"

His smile deepened, his voice low and intimate. "I always do—with you in my arms."

They lingered there, suspended in that quiet bubble of peace, before Eliza's expression shifted, excitement sparking in her eyes. Yesterday, they had marked their fifth anniversary quietly with Henry, Mary, and their daughter Jessica—a perfect reminder of how far they had come. Christian thought of how Eliza had once insisted on working right up until a month before Kimberly's birth, despite his protests that they already had more than enough. *'I didn't marry you to live a life of privilege without purpose,'* she had told him. And though now she was content to stay home and raise their children, she poured her energy into loving him, spoiling him in every way she could.

That same spark of determination shone in her now as she carefully handed Jonathan into Christian's arms. "I have something for you," she said, her smile bright and mischievous.

Adjusting the baby into the crook of his arm, Christian let her guide him into the living room, his free hand twined with hers. The penthouse glittered with Christmas warmth, the towering tree twinkling with ornaments that cast a kaleidoscope of light across the polished floors. Eliza bent, reached beneath the branches, and pulled out a neatly wrapped package.

"Here," she whispered, placing it in his hand before taking Jonathan back so he could open it.

Christian kissed her softly, reverently, then turned to the gift. He unwrapped it carefully because every present from Eliza, no matter how small, carried her heart. Inside lay a framed photograph: Eliza, Kimberly, and Jonathan captured in a candid moment of laughter and light. His entire world, caught in one image.

His throat tightened as his fingers traced the glass.

"I thought you could put it on your desk at work," Eliza said shyly, her pride glimmering through her voice. "So, you'll never forget how much we love you."

Christian looked up, eyes shining, and kissed her again, his voice husky with emotion. "As if I ever could forget."

He lingered over the photograph, then back to Eliza, then down at Jonathan sleeping peacefully in her arms. The glow of the tree haloed her face, and his chest swelled so full he thought it might burst.

"You always know exactly what I need," he whispered, pressing a kiss to her temple. "But you didn't think you'd be the only one with a gift, did you?"

Surprise flickered across her face. "Christian… you already gave me everything I could possibly want. I don't need—"

"I know," he said softly, cupping her cheek. "That's the thing, Eliza. You never ask. But that only makes me want to give you more."

He rose, crossed to the tall cabinet by the windows, and returned with a slim velvet box. Kneeling before her, he opened it slowly.

Eliza gasped, her breath catching.

Inside lay a delicate necklace, a single emerald pendant circled by a halo of tiny diamonds. The green glowed with the exact shade of her eyes—the same shade he had fallen in love with years ago.

"I saw it and thought of you," he murmured, echoing the words from long ago. "Not because it's valuable, but because it reminded me of your strength, your beauty… and the way you've given me a life I never dreamed I'd deserve."

Her eyes shimmered with tears. "Christian, it's beautiful… but you and the children are all I'll ever need."

He smiled, fastening the clasp at her neck. "And you're mine, Eliza. But let me spoil you, just a little."

The emerald settled above her heart, catching the glow of the tree lights. He gazed at her, memorising how the gem drew out her eyes, how she seemed to shine brighter than the room itself. Then he kissed her—softly, reverently—sealing the gift not just with love, but with a promise that went deeper than words.

"Merry Christmas, sweetheart," he murmured.

Eliza's smile glowed as she whispered back, "Merry Christmas, my love. But you didn't have to get me anything. I tell you every year…" Her eyes twinkled with mischief. "…I already got a billionaire for Christmas."

Christian laughed softly, shaking his head as though he'd never tire of hearing it. He framed her face in his hands, his own eyes brimming with devotion.

"And I got something far rarer—my forever."

The End

Echoes of Deception

Alison Reid

A complete standalone romance

Previously published individually

Chapter One

Ashley Sintaro, sixteen years old, tall, and graceful with long chestnut-brown hair, striking blue eyes, and a flawless complexion, walked into the main office of her father's company, Sintaro Furniture. Though already blossoming into a stunning young woman, Ashley wasn't vain; she was known for her caring, gentle spirit and her unwavering loyalty to her father, Samuel Sintaro, the company's owner.

The large open-plan office was alive with activity, sunlight streaming through the floor-to-ceiling windows and reflecting off sleek desks scattered across the room. Each desk was a hub of bustling energy, filled with the clatter of keyboards and the hum of conversations. Ashley's gaze, however, honed in on a single desk—the one belonging to Beau Tramain.

Beau, at twenty years old, stood out in any crowd. Over six feet tall, with an athletic build, deep green eyes, and an easy confidence, he exuded a quiet charm that had caught Ashley's attention since the day he started working at Sintaro Furniture six months ago. Her quiet admiration had grown into a subtle crush, though she kept it to herself.

Summoning her usual cheerful confidence, Ashley strolled up to his desk, a radiant smile lighting up her face. "Hi, Beau! How are you?"

Beau glanced up from his paperwork and laptop, his gaze softening the moment he saw her. "Hi, Ashley. How was school?" Though he tried to keep things professional, he couldn't deny the magnetic pull he felt toward her natural charm and warmth. Still, he reminded himself of their age difference—she was just sixteen.

"It was good, thanks," Ashley replied, effortlessly hopping up to sit on the edge of his desk. She leaned in slightly, her playful confidence catching Beau off guard. "Although I've got a mountain of homework waiting for me. Not exactly thrilled."

Beau chuckled, his admiration evident in his expression. "You'll manage. You always do. Hard work seems to be in your DNA."

Ashley shrugged, brushing off the compliment with a casual laugh. "Yeah, I guess so. Lucky me, right?" She glanced toward the window, where dark storm clouds were beginning to gather. "I was hoping Dad could drive me home before this storm hits. I really don't want to show up looking like a drowned rat."

Beau grinned, the corners of his mouth twitching with amusement. "I don't think you could ever look like that, no matter what."

Ashley blushed; her cheeks tinged with a rosy hue. "Thanks, but trust me, it's possible." She tilted her head as a thought struck her, her eyes lighting up. "Oh! Did I tell you? I got the lead in the school play!"

"Really?" Beau's brows lifted in genuine delight. "That's amazing! What play are you doing?"

"Romeo and Juliet," Ashley said, practically vibrating with excitement. "And guess who's Juliet?"

Beau's smile widened. "Of course you are, Angel Face. That's perfect for you." He'd started calling her that recently—a nickname that suited her so well it had a way of making her blush every time. "So, who's your Romeo?"

Ashley's excitement dimmed slightly, her expression faltering. "A guy named Bruno," she said, her tone less enthusiastic. "Not exactly thrilled about it."

Beau tilted his head, intrigued. "Why not?"

Ashley rolled her eyes dramatically. "He's just… ugh. He's kind of a sleaze. He keeps asking me out, and honestly, I'm not interested. My friends think I'm crazy because apparently, he's the cutest guy in school. But I don't see it. Plus, the way he looks at me—it's like he's sizing me up. It's creepy."

Beau's expression darkened, a protective instinct kicking in. "He hasn't done anything inappropriate, has he?"

"Not really," Ashley admitted, though her voice carried an edge of discomfort. She hesitated before adding, "But during rehearsals, he gets way too into the kissing scenes. It's so gross." She shuddered visibly. "Like, dude, it's acting. Chill!"

Beau's jaw tightened, his green eyes darkening with concern. "Has your teacher said anything to him?"

"She has, but it's like he doesn't know how to take no for an answer," Ashley sighed. "It's exhausting."

Before Beau could respond, the sound of approaching footsteps interrupted their conversation. Both of them turned as Samuel Sintaro, Ashley's father, stepped into the office, his commanding presence immediately drawing attention. Dressed in a tailored suit that complemented his salt-and-pepper hair, Samuel exuded authority and warmth.

Catching sight of his daughter, Samuel's stern expression softened, his love for her evident in his warm smile. "Hi, sweetheart," he greeted, leaning down to kiss her cheek. Ashley wrapped her arms around him in a tight hug, the familiar scent of his cologne reminding her of home.

"Hi, Dad. Busy day?" she asked, tilting her head up to meet his gaze, her smile bright and genuine.

Samuel chuckled, brushing a strand of her chestnut hair behind her ear. "Never too busy for you, sweetheart."

Their bond had deepened over the last two years, ever since the devastating loss of her mother in a tragic drowning accident during a family vacation. Samuel had poured all his love and energy into being both a father and a source of comfort for Ashley, and she, in turn, had become his rock—a reminder of the love they'd shared as a family.

Ashley glanced out the window at the darkening sky. "I was hoping you could drive me home. Looks like the storm's already starting."

Samuel was about to reply when Beau's voice cut in from behind his desk. "I can take her, Samuel. I need to stop by one of our suppliers, and it's on the way."

Samuel turned to Beau with a grateful smile. "That would be perfect. Thanks, Beau." He looked back at Ashley, his eyes softening. "Is that okay with you, sweetheart?"

Ashley nodded, smiling at Beau. "Yep, no problem. Thanks, Beau. I really appreciate it."

Beau stood, grabbing his keys and coming around his desk. "Alright then, let's get going."

Before leaving, Ashley gave her father another hug. "See you at home, Dad. Don't be too late—I'm cooking your favourite tonight."

Samuel's eyes lit up with delight. "That's my girl! I'll be home on time, I promise."

Beau led the way to his car, the rain already falling in steady sheets. Ever the gentleman, he opened the passenger door for Ashley, shielding her with his jacket. She slid inside, giving him an appreciative smile.

"Thanks," she said softly.

Beau closed her door and hurried to the driver's side, starting the engine and pulling out onto the slick street. The rhythmic sound of the rain against the windshield filled the car as they drove in comfortable silence.

After a moment, Beau glanced at her, his tone more serious. "Do me a favour, Angel Face."

Ashley turned to him, curiosity in her eyes. "Sure, what is it?"

"Promise me you'll tell your dad if Bruno keeps bothering you," he said, his green eyes briefly leaving the road to meet hers.

Touched by his protectiveness, Ashley smiled. "I will. But don't worry—I can handle Bruno."

Beau didn't look entirely convinced but chose to let it drop for now. He shifted his focus back to the road, watching the rain come down harder. "Lucky you're getting a ride—it's pouring out there."

Ashley laughed, glancing out the window at the torrential downpour. "See? I told you I'd have been a drowned rat."

Beau chuckled, a smile tugging at his lips. As he pulled up in front of her house, he slowed to a stop and turned to her. "Here we are—safe and sound."

Ashley hesitated for a moment, then leaned over and kissed him on the cheek. "Thanks, Beau. For everything."

Beau froze, momentarily caught off guard, but before he could react, Ashley was already out of the car, dashing toward her front door.

He watched as she fumbled for her key and disappeared inside, closing the door behind her. For a moment, Beau remained in his car, his thoughts lingering on the unexpected kiss and the warmth it left behind. Finally, he shook his head, started the engine again, and drove off, the image of her bright smile etched into his mind.

Inside, Ashley set her bag on the hook by the door and rummaged through it for her books. As she walked past the entryway mirror, she paused, catching sight of her reflection. Her long, chestnut-brown hair was slightly damp from the rain, framing her bright blue eyes and flushed cheeks.

She studied herself for a moment, tilting her head. She'd always thought of herself as pretty but not stunning—not like the girls Beau might notice. A wistful sigh escaped her lips as she thought of him.

Why couldn't I be older?

The thought of his warm green eyes and the way he called her Angel Face sent a shiver down her spine. She wondered what it would feel like to kiss him, to have his arms wrapped around her. But she was only sixteen—practically a kid in his eyes.

Still, a flicker of hope sparked in her chest. Maybe in a few years, he'll see me differently.

She grimaced at the thought, torn between longing and the reality of their age gap. With a deep breath, she pushed the feelings aside and focused on her books.

For now, she had homework to do and a dinner to cook—but Beau Tramain would remain a pleasant daydream for the time being.

Four weeks flew by in a whirlwind of schoolwork, late-night study sessions, and intensive rehearsals for Romeo and Juliet. The night of the big performance arrived, bringing with it an electric mix of excitement and nerves. Ashley stood backstage, adjusting her costume, trying to steady her breathing. She knew her lines perfectly and had worked hard to embody Juliet's passion and innocence. Yet, one nagging worry clouded her thoughts—Bruno.

Throughout rehearsals, his behaviour had been a persistent thorn in her side. He had a tendency to push boundaries, especially during their on-stage kisses, which had prompted several stern warnings from their drama teacher. But those warnings had done little to curb his overenthusiasm, and Ashley dreaded the thought of him ruining her big night.

Still, she refused to let Bruno dampen her spirits. Peeking out from behind the curtain, her heart swelled at the sight of her father, Samuel, sitting in the front row next to Beau. Her dad had gone out of his way to secure the best seats and seeing him there filled her with warmth and pride. But her gaze lingered on Beau, whose presence stirred a different emotion—one that left her stomach fluttering.

The thought of Beau watching her kiss Bruno made her palms sweat. She didn't want him to misunderstand and think she had feelings for Bruno. Deep down, she knew Beau was the only one who mattered to her. She just hoped he would see her as more than a kid someday.

A tap on her shoulder snapped her out of her thoughts. Kelly, dressed as Lady Montague, grinned at her. "Are you ready, Ash? This is your moment!"

Ashley smiled, though her nerves prickled. "Yep, I'm ready. Are you prepared to keep your 'son' in check?"

Kelly laughed, her eyes twinkling with mischief. "Romeo has a mind of his own, and you're the only thing on it. Good luck with that."

Ashley rolled her eyes, her laugh tinged with exasperation. "That's exactly the problem."

Kelly nudged her playfully. "I still don't get why you're not into him. He's the cutest guy in school!"

Ashley raised an eyebrow, her voice firm. "Not my type."

Kelly smirked knowingly. "Let me guess—Beau is?"

Ashley blushed but didn't deny it. "I know he's too old for me, but I can dream."

As the curtain rose, Ashley threw herself into the role of Juliet, captivating the audience with her grace and authenticity. The play unfolded beautifully, but when the pivotal kissing scenes with Bruno arrived, her dread materialised. He leaned in too closely, holding her longer than necessary, his enthusiasm bordering on possessiveness.

By the time the final act arrived—where Romeo kisses Juliet's lifeless body goodbye—Ashley's patience wore thin. Bruno's intensity made her skin crawl, but she endured, focusing on delivering her best performance.

When the final curtain fell, the audience erupted into applause, a standing ovation filling the theatre. As the cast lined up to take their bows, Bruno wrapped an arm around Ashley, pulling her closer than she liked. Her discomfort was palpable, and her eyes instinctively found Beau in the front row.

His expression was stormy, his green eyes blazing as he glared at Bruno. The intensity in his gaze made her heart race, and she suddenly felt a surge of comfort knowing he was there.

Backstage, the energy was electric as the cast celebrated their success. Although Ashley's smile faded as she spotted Bruno approaching her near the costume rack. She clenched her fists, her pulse quickening with irritation.

"Great job tonight, babe," he said, smirking as he stepped closer.

Ashley's eyes narrowed. "I'm not your 'babe,' Bruno. Back off."

His smirk didn't falter. Instead, he wrapped his arms around her waist, his grip firm. "You'll come around eventually," he said, his voice low and cocky. "We're perfect together."

Before she could push him away, Beau appeared like a storm. In one swift motion, he grabbed Bruno by the collar and yanked him back.

"She said no," Beau growled, his voice dangerously calm.

Bruno's face twisted in anger. "Who do you think you are? This is none of your business!"

"It's my business when someone I care about is being harassed," Beau replied, stepping protectively in front of Ashley.

Bruno scoffed. "Ashley's my girlfriend. Stay out of it."

Ashley's voice rang out, steady and defiant. "I'm not your girlfriend, Bruno. Leave me alone."

Beau's jaw tightened, his voice firm. "Get lost, Bruno. If I hear you've bothered her again, you'll regret it."

Realising he was outmatched, Bruno sneered. "Whatever. She's not worth the trouble anyway." With a final glare, he stormed off.

As the tension eased, Beau turned to Ashley, his green eyes soft with concern. "Are you okay?"

Ashley nodded, though her hands trembled slightly. "Thanks to you."

Without thinking, Beau pulled her into a hug, his arms wrapping around her protectively. She melted into his embrace, her heart pounding as she felt the steady beat of his.

When she looked up, their eyes met, and before she could process what was happening, Beau leaned in, brushing his lips softly against hers. The kiss was brief but electrifying, leaving her breathless.

When he pulled back, Beau looked both apologetic and conflicted. "I'm sorry, Angel Face," he murmured. "Your dad and I are waiting for you in the car park."

Ashley watched him walk away, her mind spinning.

Ten minutes later, she stepped into the car park, her cheeks still flushed from the unexpected kiss. Her father greeted her with a warm hug.

"You were incredible, sweetheart. Best Juliet I've ever seen," Samuel said proudly.

Beau nodded, his expression unreadable. "You were amazing, Ash."

Ashley smiled shyly. "Thank you."

Samuel's brow furrowed. "But that Romeo… he seemed a bit too into his role. Is he your boyfriend?"

"No way!" Ashley exclaimed, horrified. "He's more like an octopus."

Samuel's concern deepened. "Do I need to have a word with him?"

"It's handled, Dad. Don't worry," Ashley assured him, carefully avoiding mentioning Beau's involvement.

As they drove home, Ashley glanced out the window, a quiet smile tugging at her lips. Her thoughts lingered on Beau's kiss, the memory sparking a hope she couldn't quite ignore.

Chapter Two

For the next two years, Beau and Ashley's relationship remained steady and uncomplicated, though devoid of any overtly intimate moments. Their bond deepened through countless shared dinners, weekend barbecues, and Ashley's frequent visits to the office. Now eighteen, Ashley had grown into a confident, intelligent young woman, though her feelings for Beau had only intensified over time.

With senior prom just weeks away, a question had been weighing on her mind, leaving her both excited and anxious. Several boys had already asked her to be their date, including Bruno—who hadn't given up his pursuit—but none of them mattered. Her heart was set on someone else. Someone who had been a constant presence in her life, someone she trusted and admired.

Beau.

However, asking him felt like stepping into uncharted territory. What if he said no? What if he thought the idea was ridiculous? Ashley's heart raced, her palms growing clammy at the thought of Beau's possible reactions. She replayed countless scenarios in her mind, each one more anxious than the last.

Since her eighteenth birthday, Beau seemed busier than ever, taking on more responsibilities in her father's absence while he travelled for work. She hadn't seen much of him lately and couldn't help but wonder if he was avoiding her. Had something changed between them? The thought left her unsettled.

She also knew the age limit for prom attendance was twenty-two, meaning Beau would be eligible. If she wanted him to be her date, the ball was in her court. She had to ask. Summoning every ounce of courage, Ashley resolved to do just that.

The next afternoon, she found herself standing outside the office of Sintaro Furniture, her heart pounding as she rehearsed what to say. Taking a deep breath, she pushed open the door and stepped inside.

Beau was at his desk, focused on paperwork, his fingers flying over the keyboard. The sight of him, with his light brown hair slightly tousled and his shirt sleeves rolled up, sent a flutter through her chest.

"Hi, Beau," she greeted, her voice tinged with nervousness.

Beau looked up, his smile lighting up his face as it always did when he saw her. "Oh, hey, Ash! What brings you here?" But as he noticed the tension in her posture, his expression softened with concern. "Is everything okay?"

"Oh, yes, nothing's wrong," Ashley assured him quickly, her hands fidgeting at her sides. "I just... wanted to ask you something."

Beau stood, coming around to lean casually against the front of his desk. His athletic frame and easy confidence only made her more acutely aware of her nerves. Crossing his arms, he gave her an encouraging smile. "What is it? Ask away."

Ashley hesitated, her heart thudding in her chest. She glanced down at her hands, trying to steady herself. "So… prom is coming up soon," she began, her voice wavering slightly.

Beau raised an eyebrow, his smile turning curious. "Ah, the big senior prom. Are you excited?"

"I guess," Ashley replied, managing a small laugh. "But, um… I haven't decided who I'm going with yet."

Beau tilted his head, his green eyes studying her. "Really? I'd have thought the boys would be lining up for a chance to take you."

"They are," she admitted, blushing. "But none of them feel right. There's only one person I want to go with."

Beau's smile faltered slightly, replaced by a look of intrigue—and perhaps a hint of apprehension. "Oh? Who's the lucky guy?"

Ashley took a deep breath, her eyes locking with his. "It's you, Beau. I want you to be my date."

For a moment, Beau froze, his green eyes widening in surprise. He straightened from where he leaned against the desk, his expression unreadable.

Ashley's stomach churned with anxiety, her heart pounding so loudly she was sure he could hear it. *This was a mistake,* she thought. *He's going to say no.* She braced herself for rejection, biting her lip to steady her nerves.

"I would love to," Beau finally said, a smile breaking across his face. His green eyes sparkled with an enthusiasm that made Ashley's heart skip a beat.

"Really? You will?" she asked, her voice a mix of relief and disbelief.

"Of course I will," Beau replied, his tone sincere. "I'd be honoured to take you, Angel Face."

A warm blush spread across Ashley's cheeks as she returned his smile. "Thank you, Beau," she said softly, her voice barely above a whisper.

Pushing away from the desk, Beau walked over to her, his tall, athletic frame towering just slightly over her. He gently took her hands in his, their warmth sending a thrill through her. Pulling her closer, his voice dropped to a soft murmur. "I've been waiting for you to turn eighteen," he said, his green eyes locking with hers.

Before Ashley could process his words, Beau leaned down and pressed a soft, tender kiss to her lips. The world seemed to still in that moment, the air around them charged with an intensity that took Ashley's breath away.

A shiver ran through her as Beau's arms circled her waist, pulling her closer. She instinctively wrapped her arms around his neck, her fingers tangling lightly in his hair. The kiss deepened, slow and deliberate, as Beau's lips coaxed hers apart. When their tongues met in a sweet, gentle dance, a soft, involuntary moan escaped her, vibrating against his mouth. The sensation sent a rush of warmth and excitement through her, her heart racing uncontrollably.

After what felt like an eternity yet no time at all, Beau pulled back slightly, his forehead resting against hers. His eyes, filled with a mix of tenderness and desire, searched hers. "I've been waiting two years for that moment," he said, his voice low and sincere. "And it was even better than I imagined."

Ashley felt her cheeks burn as she looked down, shyly avoiding his gaze. "It was… nice," she whispered, her voice trembling slightly.

Beau chuckled softly and tilted her chin up with his hand, gently forcing her to meet his eyes. "Nice?" he teased, a playful smile tugging at the corners of his lips. "Angel Face, it was perfect."

Ashley couldn't help but smile, though her cheeks still burned. "Thank you," she murmured, unsure what else to say.

"You're beautiful, you know that?" Beau said suddenly, his voice filled with earnestness.

Ashley blinked, taken aback by his compliment. "Do you really think so?" she asked, her voice hesitant.

"Absolutely," he replied, his gaze unwavering. "And I can't wait to show you off at your prom."

Her blush deepened, and she glanced away, feeling a mix of pride and bashfulness. "I should probably let Dad know," she said, her voice light but uncertain.

Beau's grin turned mischievous. "No need for that. I asked him a couple of weeks ago if I could take you out, and he gave me the green light."

Her eyes widened in surprise. "You did?"

Beau nodded, his smile softening. "I wanted to make sure he was okay with it first. He told me, and I quote, 'As long as you promise to treat my girl right.'" He leaned in, brushing a featherlight kiss against her lips before pulling back. "Looks like you beat me to it, though."

Ashley laughed, the sound light and musical. "I guess I did," she said, her confidence growing. "But I'm glad I did."

"Me too," Beau replied, his voice warm and affectionate.

Ashley glanced at the clock on the wall, realising she still had a lot to prepare for the prom. "I should go," she said with a smile. "I have a lot of shopping to do."

Before she turned to leave, she stood on her tiptoes and pressed a soft kiss to Beau's lips, her heart fluttering as she felt him smile against her.

"See you soon," she said, her voice filled with excitement as she walked out of the office, leaving Beau standing there, watching her with a look of pure contentment on his face.

As the door closed behind her, Beau let out a soft chuckle and shook his head. "Angel Face," he murmured to himself, "you're going to be the death of me."

Ashley met Kelly at the mall, her excitement bubbling over as they prepared for their mission to find the perfect prom dress. She could barely contain herself as she spotted Kelly approaching their usual meeting spot. Her eyes sparkled with anticipation, and before Kelly even had a chance to say hello, Ashley blurted out, "Guess who's taking me to prom?"

Kelly stopped in her tracks, her eyes widening at the question. She studied Ashley's radiant expression and grinned knowingly. "It has to be Beau," she said, her voice laced with certainty.

Ashley's shoulders sagged slightly at how quickly Kelly had guessed, but she couldn't help the wide smile that followed. "Yes! Isn't it amazing?"

Kelly squealed in delight and pulled Ashley into a tight hug. "It's more than amazing! You must be on cloud nine."

"I am," Ashley admitted, her cheeks flushing with happiness.

"Well," Kelly said, grabbing her friend's hand with an excited gleam in her eyes, "then we have to find you a dress that's absolutely jaw-dropping. Let's go!"

They dove into the nearest boutique, giggling as they rifled through racks of shimmering gowns. It wasn't long before they turned their hunt into a full-on adventure, moving from store to store, trying on dress after dress, each more dazzling than the last.

After hours of searching, they finally found the ones. Ashley chose a breathtaking A-line gown in a rich royal blue, its off-the-shoulder neckline perfectly accentuating her graceful collarbone. The delicate embroidery along the bodice added just the right amount of elegance. Kelly, on the other hand, selected a soft pink gown with a plunging V-neckline and subtle sparkles that shimmered as she moved. Both dresses hugged their figures in all the right places, making them feel like royalty.

To complete their looks, they found matching two-inch heels in coordinating colours—blue for Ashley and pink for Kelly. The shoes struck the ideal balance between style and comfort, ensuring they'd be able to dance the night away. Before leaving the mall, the girls booked hair and makeup appointments to be done at Ashley's house on prom day. Kelly's date planned to pick her up from there, making it the perfect hub for their pre-prom preparations and a fun photoshoot.

A couple of nights later, the sound of the front door closing echoed through the house as Samuel called out, "Ashley, I'm home!"

Ashley's face lit up, and she dashed down the stairs, her excitement bubbling over. She threw her arms around her father in a warm, tight hug. "I missed you, Dad," she said, her smile stretching wide.

Samuel chuckled, hugging her back before settling at the kitchen table. Ashley busied herself making him a cup of coffee, the comforting aroma filling the room as Samuel shared stories from his business trip. His voice was animated as he described the successful deals he'd secured and the interesting people he'd met.

As he sipped his coffee, Ashley took a deep breath, steadying herself. "Dad," she began, her voice hesitant but determined, "I wanted to tell you something. I asked Beau to be my date for prom. I hope that's okay."

Samuel set his cup down, his expression softening. "I know, sweetheart," he said, smiling warmly. "Beau called me right after you left the office to let me know. And actually, a couple of weeks ago, he asked for my blessing to take you out on a date. I told him yes, as long as he respected you and took care of you."

Ashley blinked in surprise. "He did?"

"He did," Samuel confirmed, his eyes twinkling. "Beau's a good man, Ashley. I trust him. And I can see how much you two care about each other."

Relief washed over Ashley, and she smiled brightly. Samuel reached out, placing a reassuring hand on hers. "I'm okay with it," he continued. "Just promise me you won't rush into anything. He is older than you, and I want to make sure you're both thinking this through."

"I promise, Dad," Ashley said, her voice filled with sincerity. She leaned over and kissed his cheek. "Thank you for trusting us. I really like Beau, and I know he'll treat me right."

Samuel smiled, squeezing her hand gently. "That's all I need to hear. Now," he added with a teasing glint in his eye, "tell me about this dress you picked out. I want to hear every detail."

Ashley laughed, her heart light and full of joy as she launched into an enthusiastic description of her royal blue gown and the plans she and Kelly had made. For the first time, she felt like everything was falling perfectly into place.

The day of the prom finally arrived, and Ashley and Kelly were brimming with excitement. Beau had told Ashley he would pick her up in a limousine and had graciously invited Kelly and her date, Daniel, to join them. The idea of a glamorous ride set the tone for what they hoped would be an unforgettable evening.

The afternoon was a whirlwind of activity as Ashley and Kelly got their hair and makeup done at Ashley's house. The stylists worked their magic, giving Ashley an elegant French twist with soft tendrils framing her face, while Kelly's hair was styled in loose waves pinned back with delicate clips.

When it was time to put on their dresses, both girls gasped at their reflections.

Kelly stared at Ashley, her mouth slightly open. "Wow, Ash, you look... absolutely stunning! Like a princess."

Ashley's cheeks flushed as she beamed. "Thank you, Kelly! You look amazing too—Daniel is going to be speechless."

Kelly laughed, her cheeks tinged pink. "Let's hope he doesn't faint."

As the two admired each other, the doorbell rang. Kelly peeked out the window. "That's Daniel. I should head downstairs."

Just then, Samuel appeared in the doorway. He smiled warmly at Kelly. "You look lovely, Kelly. Daniel's waiting for you downstairs. I just need a moment with my daughter."

Kelly nodded, flashing Ashley a supportive smile before leaving the room.

Samuel stepped closer to Ashley, his eyes glistening with pride. He took her hands in his, his voice soft. "Ashley, you look breathtaking, sweetheart. You remind me so much of your mother."

Tears welled up in Ashley's eyes. "Thank you, Dad."

Samuel gently handed her a tissue. "No tears now; we can't ruin that beautiful makeup. I have something for you." Reaching into his pocket, he pulled out a small jewellery box and opened it to reveal a pair of sapphire drop earrings set in white gold.

"These were your mother's," he said, his voice thick with emotion.

Ashley's hand flew to her mouth. "Oh, Dad, they're beautiful!" She kissed his cheek before carefully putting them on. Spinning to face him, she asked, "How do they look?"

Samuel's smile broadened. "Perfect. You're perfect. I'm so proud of you, Ashley."

"Thanks, Dad," she whispered, her heart swelling.

The doorbell rang again, and Samuel offered his arm. "That must be Beau. Are you ready?"

Ashley nodded, her excitement building as they descended the stairs together.

Beau stood in the foyer, adjusting his tuxedo when he heard footsteps. He glanced up, and the sight of Ashley descending the stairs made him freeze. She looked radiant, her royal blue gown shimmering under the lights.

As she reached him, Beau smiled, his voice low and filled with awe. "Angel face, you look absolutely stunning. You take my breath away."

Ashley's cheeks warmed. "Thank you, Beau. You look incredibly handsome."

Beau chuckled, his green eyes twinkling. "I clean up okay, don't I?"

"I'd say better than okay," she teased.

"I have something for you," he said, producing a small velvet box. Inside was a sapphire pendant on a delicate white gold chain.

Ashley's breath hitched. "Oh, Beau, it's beautiful! You didn't have to—"

"I wanted to," he interrupted, his smile soft. "May I?"

Ashley turned, holding her breath as Beau fastened the necklace. Leaning down, he pressed a light kiss to the nape of her neck, sending a shiver down her spine.

"Thank you," she murmured, her voice barely above a whisper.

Samuel cleared his throat, reminding them of his presence. "Beau," he said, his tone serious, "take care of my girl."

Beau met his gaze with sincerity. "You have my word, Samuel."

The limousine ride to the prom was filled with laughter and excitement. Kelly and Daniel were equally enthralled by the experience, but Ashley barely noticed anyone else. Her hand rested in Beau's; their fingers intertwined as they exchanged quiet smiles.

When they arrived at the venue, Beau stepped out first, offering his hand to help Ashley. As she emerged, he leaned down and kissed her softly. "You look absolutely breathtaking, angel face."

Blushing, Ashley whispered, "Thank you."

Inside, the night was everything Ashley had dreamed of. Beau was attentive, twirling her around the dance floor, stealing kisses on her cheek and forehead, and whispering sweet compliments that made her heart flutter.

The announcement for prom king and queen came mid-evening. Kelly rushed over to Ashley, her eyes sparkling. "Ash, you're going to be prom queen—I just know it!"

Ashley groaned. "Please, no. I don't want to be queen, and I definitely don't want to dance with Bruno."

Kelly waved off her concerns. "It's just one dance. Besides, you deserve this."

When the names were announced, Ashley's heart sank. Bruno Vincent was prom king, and her name followed shortly after as prom queen.

Beau kissed her cheek. "Go on, angel face. The sooner you get it over with, the sooner you're back in my arms."

On stage, Ashley accepted her crown with a smile that didn't quite reach her eyes. As Bruno led her to the dance floor, he pulled her close—too close.

"Keep your hand where it belongs, Bruno," Ashley said sharply.

"Relax, Ash. You look amazing tonight," he replied with a smirk.

The dance ended, but not before Bruno leaned in and kissed her without warning. Furious, Ashley pushed him away and stormed off.

Beau was by her side instantly. "Fresh air?" he asked gently.

"Please," Ashley replied.

Outside, under the stars, Beau wrapped his arms around her. "You're safe with me," he murmured, pressing a kiss to her temple.

Ashley looked up at him, her anger melting away. "I know."

Their lips met in a kiss that was sweet and passionate, the perfect end to a night neither of them would forget.

Chapter Three

That summer was the best of Ashley's life. She and Beau were inseparable, their days filled with laughter, tender kisses, and quiet moments that felt like forever. Whether they were exploring quaint little towns, sharing ice cream on the boardwalk, or cuddling on the couch during movie nights, every moment with Beau felt magical. Their bond grew deeper with each passing day.

Beau's respect for her and her values made her fall for him even more. He exercised remarkable restraint, carefully maintaining boundaries, and never pushing for more than what she was comfortable with. It wasn't just about his respect for Ashley—it was also about the respect he held for her father, Samuel, whose trust he didn't want to betray. It touched Ashley's heart, making her feel safe and cherished. Beau made her believe in the kind of love she had only read about in books.

But as the golden days of summer began to wane, a shadow loomed over their happiness. The time was approaching for Ashley to leave for college, and while she held onto the hope that their love would withstand the distance, Beau had other plans.

One evening, as the sun dipped low on the horizon, painting the sky in hues of pink and orange, Beau took Ashley to her favourite spot—a secluded clearing by the lake where they had shared so many special moments. Ashley sensed something was different; his usual warmth was tinged with a quiet sadness.

Sitting side by side on the soft grass, Beau took her hands in his, his green eyes serious yet filled with tenderness.

"Ashley," he began, his voice steady but low, "there's something I need to say, and I need you to hear me out."

Her heart clenched. "What is it?" she asked, her voice barely above a whisper.

Beau sighed, running a hand through his hair before meeting her gaze. "You're about to start an incredible new chapter in your life. College is a time to explore, to grow, and to experience things you never have before. And I... I don't want to hold you back."

Ashley stared at him, confusion clouding her expression. "Hold me back? Beau, you're not holding me back. I want to share this chapter with you."

He shook his head, his grip on her hands tightening slightly. "Angel Face, it's not that simple. Long-distance relationships are hard. I don't want you to feel tied down while you're there. I want you to meet new people, date, and see the world with fresh eyes. You deserve that freedom."

Her chest tightened, tears welling up in her eyes. "Are you saying you want to break up?"

"I'm saying I don't want you to miss out on anything because of me," he replied, his voice cracking. "You need to go to college unattached. It's the best thing for you."

Ashley's tears began to fall, her voice trembling. "But I don't want to date other people. I don't want anyone else, Beau. I want you."

He cupped her face gently, his thumbs brushing away her tears. "I care about you more than you know. But this isn't about what we want right now—it's about what's best for you in the long run. Four years is a long time, Ash. You'll change, and so will I. It wouldn't be fair to either of us."

"Fair?" she echoed, her voice breaking. "Do you think this is fair to me? To us?"

Beau's own eyes glistened, but he held firm. "If it's meant to be, we'll find our way back to each other. But for now… you need to go."

Ashley's heart shattered as she realised, she couldn't change his mind. She looked at him, searching for any sign of doubt in his resolve, but all she saw was love—a love so deep that he was willing to let her go for her own sake.

"I thought you cared about me," she whispered, her voice trembling.

"I do," Beau said, his voice breaking. "More than anything. That's why I have to do this."

The days leading up to her departure were agonising. Beau was there to help her pack, offering support even as they both avoided the inevitable. On her final night at home, he held her tightly in his arms, neither of them wanting to let go.

When the time came to say goodbye, Beau stood in the driveway, watching as Ashley's car disappeared down the road. She glanced back once, her tear-streaked face meeting his. He raised a hand in farewell, his heart aching as she turned away.

Ashley arrived at college feeling as though a part of her heart had been left behind. The vibrant campus and new experiences couldn't fill the void Beau's absence left in her life. Every day, she replayed their final conversation in her mind, clinging to the hope that maybe, just maybe, they would find their way back to each other.

For now, though, all she had were memories of a summer love that had left an indelible mark on her heart.

College life was a difficult adjustment for Ashley, and the first few months were far from easy. The demands of her classes, combined with the weight of being away from home and the heartbreak of losing Beau, often felt overwhelming. At first, the loneliness was unbearable. She cried herself to sleep more nights than she cared to admit, the ache of missing him a constant companion.

Determined to move forward, Ashley eventually began dating other guys. None of these relationships were serious or lasting—they were more of a distraction than anything else. She went on a few dates, laughed at bad jokes, and tried to convince herself that she was fine. But every time she glanced at her phone, half-expecting a text from Beau, her heart reminded her otherwise.

Fortunately, her roommate and close friend, Kelly, became her anchor during those trying times. Kelly had a knack for bringing lightness into the room when Ashley needed it most. Late-night chats, spontaneous ice cream runs, and Kelly's unwavering support helped Ashley find her footing. Their shared dorm room became a sanctuary, a place where Ashley could let her guard down.

By the time the holidays arrived, Ashley was eager to return home, hoping to find a sense of peace. Instead, she found that Beau was actively avoiding her. The distance he maintained was more painful than she had expected. Whenever their paths did cross—usually in her father's office—he greeted her with polite indifference. He was always "busy," shuffling through paperwork or engrossed in a call, making it clear he had no intention of reconnecting.

Despite his cold demeanour, Ashley couldn't stop thinking about him. Beau's absence only solidified how deeply her feelings for him ran. The hurt lingered, and every passing interaction—or lack thereof—left her wondering if she'd ever truly get over him.

In her final year of college, Ashley returned home for the holidays, hoping for a reprieve from her hectic schedule. One afternoon, she and Kelly decided to go shopping, eager to make the most of their break. They wandered through the aisles of a local boutique, laughing and chatting, when Ashley suddenly froze.

There, just a few feet away, stood Beau. He was with a petite brunette, her sleek brown hair falling just past her shoulders. She clung to Beau's arm with a possessive ease, her warm brown eyes darting around the store. Her smile was bright, effortless—completely unaware of the storm brewing inside Ashley.

Ashley's heart plummeted. Her laughter faded, replaced by a lump in her throat she couldn't swallow. Before she could react, Kelly spotted them.

"Hello, Beau. How are you?" Kelly called out; her voice cheery but laced with a protective undertone.

Beau looked up, his expression unreadable. He nodded politely. "Hi, Kelly. Ashley," he said, his tone distant as his eyes flickered briefly to hers. "How's college going?"

Ashley forced a small smile, though her voice came out softer than she intended. "Good, thanks."

Kelly took over the conversation, filling the awkward silence with idle chatter about school and holiday plans. Ashley barely listened; her gaze fixed on the floor as she fought to keep her emotions in check.

As Beau talked, his arm remained draped casually over the brunette's shoulders. Ashley felt a sharp pang in her chest every time Sarah glanced up at him, her expression adoring.

After a few moments, Sarah tugged on Beau's arm, her tone sharp and impatient. "Come on, Beau. Let's go," she said, her voice cutting through the tension.

Beau hesitated for a fraction of a second before giving a curt nod. "Take care," he said, his words directed at no one in particular as they walked away.

Kelly waited until they were out of earshot before turning to Ashley with an incredulous look. "Wow, she's a bit of a bitch, isn't she?"

Ashley managed a weak nod, her emotions too raw to respond. She changed the subject quickly, desperate to bury the pain that was bubbling to the surface.

That night, Ashley cried herself to sleep, her heart shattering all over again. The image of Beau with Sarah haunted her, a painful reminder that the life she had once imagined with him had slipped through her fingers.

For the rest of the holidays, Ashley avoided any mention of Beau. She busied herself with family and friends, pouring her energy into anything that would keep her from thinking about him. But no matter how hard she tried, the memory of that encounter lingered, a quiet ache that refused to fade.

At last, college came to an end. Ashley had successfully completed her four-year degree in Business and returned home, eager to begin the next chapter of her life. Though she had achieved a major milestone, there was still a lingering emptiness in her heart, a quiet ache that reminded her of the love she had lost. The world seemed to be moving forward, but she felt like she was stuck in place, trying to find her footing amidst the overwhelming sense of what could have been.

She did her best to avoid the office, telling herself it was time to focus on her future. But there were moments when she couldn't avoid it—when family events brought her face-to-face with Beau. Whenever that happened, he would try to strike up a conversation, his smile warm yet distant, as if he were trying to bridge the gap that had grown between them. Ashley, however, was resolute in her decision to protect herself. She wasn't ready to face the emotions he stirred inside her, emotions she had carefully hidden away. Her response was always the same: she didn't have time to talk.

A month after her return, as the holidays neared, Samuel invited Beau over for dinner. Ashley instantly disagreed with the idea. Her gut told her it was a bad idea, but she didn't argue. Instead, she resigned herself to it, focusing on her responsibilities in the kitchen. She spent the evening cooking, cleaning, and staying busy, all in an attempt to avoid any emotional confrontation.

As dinner wound down, Samuel excused himself to retire early. Beau remained behind, his presence filling the empty space in the house in a way that made Ashley uncomfortable. When he approached her later that evening, she could feel the weight of his gaze on her.

"Ashley, can we talk?" Beau's voice was quiet but pleading.

She kept herself busy with the dishes, trying to appear calm, though her hands trembled slightly. "Do we have to?"

"Ashley, please..." he continued, his voice softer now, almost like he was begging. "Angel face."

Ashley stiffened at the familiar nickname, the one that had always made her feel safe and loved. But not anymore. "No," she said firmly, her voice cracking with a pain she could not hide. "Don't call me that."

Beau, sensing the emotional distance, stepped closer, his hands gently settling on her shoulders. He turned her to face him, his expression full of regret. When he saw the tears in her eyes, his own softened. He pulled her into his arms, holding her tightly as if to make up for all the time lost. "Oh, angel face, I'm so sorry," he murmured, his voice filled with emotion.

Ashley stiffened in his embrace, the old feeling of comfort warred with the anger and hurt that had built up inside her. She pulled back slightly, her voice sharp despite the tenderness in his arms. "Why? What are you sorry for?" she asked, her words cutting through the air. "You have nothing to be sorry for. You told me you'd move on, and so have I."

Beau's grip tightened, his eyes darkening. "What do you mean? You've moved on?"

Ashley's heart raced, but she kept her expression cold. She forced herself to lie, to make him feel the sting of her words. "Bruno and I are seeing each other now. It's getting serious."

Beau recoiled, his face a mixture of disbelief and frustration. "Bruno? Are you out of your mind?" His voice cracked with the intensity of his emotions.

Ashley's temper flared, the years of pent-up frustration and pain spilling over. "What's that supposed to mean?" she snapped, her voice sharp with anger. Her fists clenched at her sides, ready for a fight.

Beau shook his head, desperation creeping into his tone. "He's not the right guy for you."

Ashley crossed her arms, her posture defensive, but a rush of warmth swept through her despite the anger. "Oh, and who is, Beau? You?" She lifted an eyebrow, daring him to respond.

Beau stared at her, his eyes searching hers as if trying to figure out what was really going on beneath the surface. After a tense silence, he made a decision. Without warning, he pulled her into his arms, his grip firm and insistent. "Yes, me," he murmured, his voice raw with emotion.

Before Ashley could process his words, his lips crashed down onto hers in a kiss that was both desperate and longing. It was forceful, a kiss that demanded attention, one that made her forget everything around them. The world seemed to disappear in the heat of his touch, and for a moment, she could almost convince herself that nothing had changed.

Ashley stiffened at first, her mind racing as memories of their past flooded back. But the moment soon melted away, her body betraying her as she let out a soft moan. She instinctively wrapped her arms around his neck, pulling him closer, unable to stop herself. The kiss deepened, intense and filled with a desperate need they had both kept hidden for so long.

Beau softened his kiss, his lips moving in a slow, sensual rhythm, his tongue tracing hers in an intimate dance. It was as if he was savouring the moment, a mixture of desire and apology blending with every movement. He pulled away just slightly, his breath ragged, and murmured against her lips, "I've waited so long for you, angel face."

The words sent a shiver down Ashley's spine, and before she could fully process them, he took her lips again, this time more urgently, his arms wrapping around her waist, pulling her tightly against him as he deepened the kiss. Every nerve in Ashley's body came alive, her senses ablaze with the heat of him. She tangled her fingers in his hair, holding his head firmly, as if afraid he might pull away—though she knew, deep down, that he had no intention of doing so.

The kiss deepened, becoming more desperate, as Beau's hands slid down her waist, then to her hips, pulling her even closer. The pressure of his body against hers made his desire unmistakably clear, and it ignited a fire within Ashley she hadn't felt in so long.

"Beau, please…" she whispered, her voice thick with longing. She wasn't even sure what she was pleading for, but the ache in her chest demanded release.

"I know, angel face," he murmured softly, his lips leaving hers just long enough to meet her gaze. His eyes were dark with passion, and his voice was a mixture of longing and desperation. Then, with renewed intensity, he captured her mouth again, pouring every ounce of pent-up passion into the kiss.

Chapter Four

The room seemed to fade away as they lost themselves in each other. Just as their bodies pressed closer, the shrill ring of Beau's phone pierced the silence, cutting through the moment like a harsh reality check. Reluctantly, Beau raised his head, his hands still holding Ashley close, unwilling to fully let go. He glanced down at her flushed cheeks, her lips swollen from their kiss, before finally answering the call.

"Hello?" he said, his voice hoarse, still tangled in the aftermath of their kiss.

Ashley's heart sank at the sound of the name that followed. "Sarah, you need to stop. It's over," Beau said, his voice edged with exasperation.

The mention of Sarah hit Ashley like a cold slap, and suddenly the warmth between her and Beau felt distant. She pulled away from him, the anger and hurt welling up inside her, and she swiftly turned her back, busying herself with stacking the dishes in the dishwasher. Beau's hands lingered on her hips for a moment, but he let her go, his eyes still watching her intently, his expression full of frustration and regret.

"It's been two months, Sarah," Beau continued, his tone firm, as if trying to convince himself as much as her. "You have to let it go." He ended the call and exhaled deeply, his face tense.

Ashley didn't turn around. She closed the dishwasher with finality, her movements deliberate as she avoided his gaze. The tension in the air was thick, and she could feel the storm brewing within her. Beau took a step forward, but she cut him off before he could speak.

"No, Beau," she said firmly, her voice steady despite the rush of emotions crashing within her. She glanced over her shoulder, meeting his gaze for the first time since the kiss. "We've both moved on."

Beau's eyes widened, his disbelief evident. "You can't seriously be involved with Bruno," he said, the words heavy with judgment.

Ashley felt her temper flare at his tone. "Oh, really?" she shot back. "Were you not serious about Sarah?"

Beau ran a hand through his hair, frustration etched on his face. "No, I wasn't. And she knew that. I was very clear from the start."

Ashley's heart twisted at the ease with which he dismissed his past with Sarah, as if it meant nothing. She shook her head, her eyes full of hurt. "You treated me like a stranger for four years, Beau. Do you have any idea how that felt?"

"I had to, Ashley," he said quietly, his voice softening as he stepped closer. "You have to understand that."

Ashley looked at him, her brow furrowed in confusion. "Why should I understand? I never wanted any of this... any of the heartbreak."

Beau's expression darkened, but he stepped closer, his gaze locking with hers. "Angel face, we belong together—you know that as much as I do."

The weight of his words hung in the air between them, but Ashley took a shaky breath, stepping back slightly. "I thought I did," she murmured, her voice faltering. "But you're the one who told me to let you go. So I did."

Beau reached for her hand, his voice raw with emotion. "I know," he said softly. "But I can't be without you anymore. I was wrong. We belong together."

Ashley looked down at their entwined fingers, her heart heavy with doubt. "What about the next time, Beau? When things get complicated?"

"There won't be a next time," he said softly, pulling her gently into his arms. She didn't resist, resting her hands on his chest as he gazed deeply into her eyes. "I want to be with you, Ashley. For good."

Her heart ached at his words, but she had to speak her truth. "You hurt me, Beau. Badly."

"I know," he replied quietly, his eyes full of regret. "And I'm so sorry. I was hurting too."

She looked at him, disbelief and sorrow filling her chest. "You didn't seem to be."

Beau closed his eyes briefly, as if the weight of his past mistakes pressed down on him. "I just hid it better than you," he murmured, his voice thick with regret.

Ashley rested her head against his chest, the warmth of his embrace soothing some of the turmoil within her. "You can't hurt me like that again."

"I won't," he promised, his voice firm, as he tightened his arms around her. "But you've got to get rid of Bruno for me."

Ashley shivered slightly, a chill running through her at the mention of the name. "I'd never really go out with him."

Beau lifted her chin gently, his eyes filled with a playful spark, though the vulnerability was still there. "So, you lied."

A smile tugged at her lips despite herself. "Yes… I wanted you to feel a fraction of what I felt."

"Well, it worked," he said, kissing her deeply once more. When he pulled back, his lips brushed against hers as he murmured, "Don't do it again."

Ashley smiled softly, a hint of regret flickering in her eyes. "I won't."

Over the next month, Beau and Ashley's bond grew deeper, strengthened by a shared understanding and commitment. Their relationship flourished in ways neither of them had anticipated. They spent countless hours talking, laughing, and making memories, yet the level of intimacy they both craved remained just beyond their reach. It wasn't a lack of love; it was something else, something more profound that they both felt but couldn't quite articulate.

One evening, as they sat on the couch together, the warmth of the fire casting soft shadows across the room, Ashley finally asked what had been weighing on her heart.

"Beau," she said gently, her voice filled with curiosity and tenderness, "why are you holding back? I don't understand."

Beau's expression softened, and he reached for her hand, his thumb tracing delicate circles across her skin. "Angel face," he began, his voice low and steady, "I want your first time to be special. I don't want to rush something that's meant to be beautiful, something that marks the beginning of the rest of our lives."

Ashley's gaze met his, earnest and unwavering. "But it already is special, Beau," she said, squeezing his hand. "It will be special because it will be with you. Nothing could make it more perfect than that."

To her astonishment, Beau's face shifted, and he suddenly dropped to one knee in front of her, his eyes gleaming with love, his heart exposed in a way Ashley had never seen before. For a moment, time seemed to stop. She looked down at him, her breath catching in her throat as he reached into his pocket and pulled out a small, velvet box.

"Ashley," Beau began, his voice thick with emotion, "I love you more than anything in this world. Will you make me the happiest man alive and be my wife?"

Ashley's heart leapt in her chest, the reality of the moment crashing over her like a wave. Tears welled up in her eyes, and her smile bloomed like the sun after a storm. "Yes, Beau! A thousand times, yes!" she cried, her voice filled with joy and disbelief.

Beau's hands trembled with happiness as he stood, slipping the sparkling diamond solitaire ring onto her finger. He pulled her into his arms, and in that moment, they kissed—deeply, passionately, the kiss that sealed their future. It was a kiss full of promises, of dreams long held, and now finally within their grasp. Nothing else mattered in that moment but the two of them, together, their hearts intertwined.

News of their engagement spread quickly, and the excitement was palpable. Friends and family rallied around them, celebrating the love that had finally found its way back. However, not everyone shared in their joy. Sarah and Bruno, each for their own reasons, made their disapproval loud and clear. Sarah's bitterness was as evident as ever, while Bruno, though he masked it with a forced smile, made no attempt to hide his distaste for the engagement. Their negativity, however, had no effect on Beau and Ashley. They had waited too long for this, and nothing could spoil their happiness.

As the days passed, Beau and Ashley began to plan their wedding with a sense of urgency, eager to start their life together. They decided on an intimate ceremony, one that reflected their bond, set just eight weeks away. The timeline felt perfect, as if the universe had aligned to guide them toward this moment.

One week before the wedding, Ashley and Beau celebrated with their respective bachelor and bachelorette parties.

Kelly had gone all out organising Ashley's bachelorette party. As her best friend and bridesmaid, she had carefully planned every detail to ensure it would be a night to remember. They arrived at a lively, upbeat club, where the music was loud and the atmosphere electric. It wasn't long before Ashley found herself surrounded by her closest friends, laughing, dancing, and enjoying the night. The drinks flowed, the music pulsed through her veins, and for the first time in a long while, she felt carefree, surrounded by love and celebration.

As Ashley looked around at the familiar faces of her friends—Kelly, Jenna, Megan, and the others—she couldn't help but reflect on everything that had led her to this moment. The years of uncertainty, the heartbreak, the misunderstandings, and the waiting. It had all brought her here, to this place, this time, with Beau. He had become her home, the one person who had always stood by her, and now she was about to marry him. The thought filled her with overwhelming happiness. Despite everything, despite all the pain, she had found the one who was worth the wait.

As the night wore on, the crowd around them thickened, and the energy seemed to swell in every direction. Ashley's heart swelled too, full of hope for the future. Beau was the person she'd been searching for all along, and the love they had built was strong. Slow and steady, it had grown into something unshakable, something that could withstand anything life threw at them. She was ready for this next chapter.

But just as she was beginning to lose herself in the music and the joy of the night, a familiar voice cut through the buzz of the club.

"Hi, Ashley," Bruno's voice sounded behind her, sharp and unexpected.

Ashley stiffened, her smile faltering as she turned to face him. His smirk was as irritating as it was familiar. "What are you doing here, Bruno?" she asked, her voice edged with annoyance.

"I just came to congratulate you," he said, his tone feigning sincerity, but there was an underlying tension in his eyes.

"Thanks, Bruno," Ashley said, her response curt as she tried to keep things polite, even though her patience was thinning.

There was a long, uncomfortable pause, and then Bruno's next words were quiet, almost too soft to hear above the music. "Can I talk to you for a second?"

Ashley glanced at her friends, who were busy laughing and chatting among themselves, oblivious to what was happening. She didn't want to cause a scene, but the unease in her gut told her this wasn't going to be a pleasant conversation. She stood up slowly, a sense of foreboding settling over her. "Fine, but make it quick," she muttered, bracing herself for whatever he was about to say.

Bruno led her away from the table, his hand lightly resting on her arm as he guided her to a quieter spot in the club. Before Ashley could fully process what was happening, he pulled her into his arms, and without any warning, pressed his lips roughly against hers.

Ashley froze in shock. Her hands shot to his shoulders, pushing with every ounce of strength. It took some doing but eventually she managed to break free, her heart pounding in her chest as she slapped him hard across the face, the sting of it matching the fury in her veins.

"Seriously, Bruno, stop it!" she exclaimed, her voice shaking with a mix of anger and disbelief.

Without waiting for a response, she spun on her heel and marched back toward her table, her legs unsteady with adrenaline, but her determination unwavering. She needed to get away from him, from that moment, from the person he used to be.

Kelly, who had been watching the scene unfold from a distance, immediately stood up as Ashley approached, her face etched with concern. "Are you okay, Ash?" she asked, her voice soft and gentle.

Ashley winced, her lips sore from the force of the kiss, and the emotional toll of the entire encounter. But she didn't want to show how shaken she really was. She forced a smile, though it didn't quite reach her eyes. "I'm fine. Just… don't worry about it," she said, her voice steady but distant as she sat back down.

The rest of the night was a blur. Ashley tried to shake off the encounter, but the lingering sense of disgust gnawed at her. Bruno had no right. She looked at Kelly, who gave her a sympathetic but knowing look, and tried to push the unsettling feeling to the back of her mind.

For Beau, his bachelor party turned out to be a night of quiet reflection. Amid the laughter, drinks, and camaraderie with his friends, his mind continually drifted back to Ashley. He was about to marry the woman of his dreams—the one he had fought so hard for, the one he knew would be by his side for the rest of his life. It felt surreal, yet deeply fulfilling, to think that despite all the struggles and heartache they'd endured, he had found his forever.

His best man had arranged a hotel room for the evening, a space where the guys could watch sports, drink, and relax before the big day. The atmosphere was lively, and everyone was in high spirits, including Bruno, who had shown up with a polite but strained smile to offer his congratulations. Beau appreciated the gesture, though the tension between them hadn't gone unnoticed.

As the night wore on, the conversations blurred, and the laughter became nothing more than distant background noise. The guys slowly filtered out, each heading to their own rooms or off to find other things to do. Beau's last clear memory was of having one final drink with Bruno, a quiet moment amidst the chaos.

The next morning, Beau woke up with a pounding headache and a heavy sense of disorientation. He lay in an unfamiliar bed, the room shrouded in dim light and stillness. The clock on the nightstand indicated it was already late, but the world outside felt distant and out of reach. He was alone, dressed only in his trousers, while his shirt lay discarded on the sofa across the room. The bed was a chaotic mess, and his mind struggled to make sense of the previous night. It all felt like a distant haze—fragmented flashes of laughter, blurred faces, and the faint echo of conversations. His best man, the guys—everyone had disappeared, leaving him to face the aftermath in solitude. The silence in the room pressed down on him as he rubbed his temples, trying to remember what had happened, but the pieces just wouldn't fall into place.

Groaning, Beau rubbed his temples, the sharp throb of his hangover settling in. He closed his eyes for a moment, trying to clear his head, but it was hard to focus on anything except the overwhelming weight of the day ahead.

Chapter Five

Ashley spent the rest of the weekend recovering from the party, doing her best to reclaim some normalcy amid the aftereffects of a night filled with emotions, laughter, and lingering tension. While she had kept up a brave face during the event, the exhaustion caught up with her quickly. Every muscle in her body felt drained, and she couldn't bear the thought of Beau seeing her like this. She had to maintain the image of the glowing, excited bride-to-be, even though she barely had the energy to keep her eyes open.

They stayed in touch over the phone, each of them nursing the aftermath of their wild nights. Neither had fully recovered yet, but their connection was enough to ease the tension of the day. When the phone rang that afternoon, Ashley hesitated for a moment before picking up. Her voice was hoarse from the hours of talking and laughing the night before.

"Hey, Beau," she said, forcing a cheery tone despite the weariness that clung to her. "How's your head?" she asked, trying to sound light-hearted, though it was clear she wasn't feeling much better.

Beau chuckled softly, his voice reflecting the exhaustion he was still battling. "Let's just say I'm glad the wedding's not tomorrow," he sighed, the humour in his voice barely masking the fatigue. "A week's recovery sounds pretty good right now. I didn't think it was possible to feel this bad and still be standing."

Ashley leaned back against the couch with a soft groan, her feet sore from the endless dancing. "I get that," she said with a weak smile, her voice barely above a whisper. "My feet are killing me from all the dancing. I think I wore myself out trying to keep up with Kelly."

Beau's voice lightened, the teasing tone creeping back in despite his exhaustion. "Sounds like a night to remember," he said with a smile she could almost hear through the phone. "But I'm glad you're taking it easy today. I miss you. I love you."

Ashley's heart fluttered at his words, a wave of warmth spreading through her despite her tiredness. "I love you too," she replied softly, a genuine smile tugging at her lips. "I miss you and can't wait to marry you."

There was a brief, comfortable silence before Beau spoke again, his voice rich with emotion. "I can't wait to marry you," he said, the longing in his words palpable.

"I think I better go," she murmured, almost apologetic. "I need a shower and a nap to sleep it off."

Beau's voice softened, full of concern. "Get some rest, angel face," he said, his words tender and reassuring. "Sleep well."

Ashley allowed herself a small, tired smile, comforted by the gentleness in his voice. "I will try," she whispered, feeling her exhaustion seep into her words. "Love you."

"Love you too, angel face. Talk soon," Beau replied, the warmth of his words lingering long after the call ended.

Early Monday morning, Ashley opened an envelope that arrived at her home, expecting nothing more than a simple piece of mail. But as she pulled out the contents, her heart shattered into a million pieces. Inside were photographs of Beau in bed with Sarah, her straddling him in a raw, intimate moment.

For a moment, Ashley clung to the hope that these photos were from the past, perhaps before they had rekindled their relationship. But as she studied the image closer, her stomach twisted. On Beau's wrist was the watch she had given him just a few weeks ago for his twenty-sixth birthday. There was no denying it—the betrayal was recent.

Simultaneously, Beau received a text from Sarah, sending him a photo of Ashley and Bruno locked in a kiss, one that appeared as passionate as the one in the photos. Confused and hurt, Beau's mind raced. The more he looked at the image, the deeper his sense of betrayal grew.

That afternoon, as the office emptied for the day, Ashley arrived with the envelope in hand, determined to confront Beau about his night with Sarah. She barely stepped inside before Beau's voice rose in anger.

"Care to explain?" Beau demanded, shoving his phone into her hands.

Ashley's heart sank as she looked at the photo, instantly recognising the moment from her bachelorette party. Her breath caught in her throat, and she swallowed hard, trying to keep her composure. "It's not what it looks like," she said quickly, but her voice faltered, knowing how weak her defence sounded.

"It looks pretty clear to me," Beau shot back, his anger and betrayal evident in every word.

Ashley opened her mouth to explain, but before she could, he cut her off. "How could you, Ash?" His voice cracked, the hurt sharp in his tone.

The shock quickly turned into fury. Ashley could hardly believe he would accuse her of betrayal without letting her explain—especially when she was holding an envelope that contained proof of his own infidelity.

"Did you sleep with him?" Beau's voice was cold, his words cutting through her like ice.

Ashley recoiled, her own anger flaring. "Are you joking?" she snapped, disbelief and hurt flashing in her eyes.

"Do I look like I'm joking?" Beau's eyes bore into hers, his expression as hard as stone.

Her breath hitched as she took a deep breath. "Would it even matter if I had?" she shot back, her voice trembling with both fury and sorrow. "You've already made up your mind about me."

"Of course it would!" Beau exploded, his pain and jealousy dripping from each word.

The words stung, but Ashley, crushed and exhausted, refused to defend herself. She couldn't find the strength to argue, knowing deep down that Beau had no right to question her loyalty when his own actions had already shattered any trust between them.

Her silence spoke louder than words, and Beau took it as an admission. His expression hardened. "We're done, Ashley. I can't forgive this."

"Just like that?" Her voice cracked in disbelief, still struggling to process his coldness.

Beau's gaze was cold, dismissive. "What did you expect, Ashley?"

Ashley's voice shook with a raw bitterness as tears welled in her eyes. "I expected the man I love to trust me," she bit out, her pain evident in her words. "I expected him to be faithful."

The weight of his betrayal settled on her chest like a crushing weight. Her hands shook as she yanked the engagement ring off her finger, holding it out to him. "Here," she said, her voice thick with emotion.

Beau's eyes flickered to the ring, but he didn't reach for it right away. His voice was cold, his bitterness raw. "What would I want it for?" he snapped, then with a malicious grin, he added, "Maybe you should keep it, Ashley. After all, you've earned it."

Without another word, Ashley walked out, the unopened envelope still in her hand, the engagement ring heavy in her trembling grasp. She made a decision then—not to defend herself, not to beg for his trust. She realised, in that moment, that the man she had loved didn't trust her, when it was he who couldn't be trusted.

The news of Ashley and Beau's breakup spread quickly, leaving everyone stunned. Friends and family were left reeling, unable to comprehend what had just happened. But amidst the chaos, two people seemed almost to revel in it.

Kelly was at Ashley's door within hours, her face etched with concern. "What happened, Ash?" she asked, her voice soft but filled with worry.

Ashley's eyes filled with tears as she explained the painful truth—the photograph of her and Bruno and Beau's accusations of cheating. Her words trembled, the hurt still raw.

"But I know the real story," Kelly said, her voice rising in frustration. "I'll go tell him what really happened. He needs to hear the truth."

Ashley shook her head, her voice steady but firm. "No."

Confusion flickered in Kelly's eyes. "Why not? You love him."

"I do," Ashley whispered, her voice breaking as she spoke the words. "I did… not anymore."

Kelly's expression shifted from confusion to disbelief. "I don't believe you," she said, frustration evident in her tone. "Something else is going on. What is it, Ash? Tell me."

Ashley handed her the envelope, her hands trembling as she did. Kelly opened it, her face falling as she saw the contents. "That bastard!" she muttered under her breath, her fists clenching with fury. "Wait until I see him."

"No!" Ashley's voice cracked as she rushed to stand in front of Kelly. "You can't say anything. Promise me."

"Why not? He needs to know the truth."

"Because it's humiliating," Ashley sobbed, the weight of everything crashing down on her at once.

"Oh, Ash," Kelly whispered, pulling her into a tight hug. "You don't deserve this."

Ashley wiped her eyes, pulling back slightly to look at Kelly. "Promise me you won't tell anyone. Please, Kell. Promise."

Kelly looked at her friend, her own anger simmering beneath the surface. "Okay," she said softly, her eyes filled with fury but her voice calm. "I promise."

A week passed after the breakup, but Beau's disappearance left Ashley in a whirlwind of confusion and hurt. He vanished without a word, without an explanation or apology. Just like that, he was gone. She was left to pick up the pieces of her broken heart, but life had a way of moving forward, even when the ache felt impossible to bear.

It would be five long years before Ashley saw Beau again—and by then, everything between them had irrevocably changed.

Ashley Sintaro, dressed in black, stood at the gravesite, her posture rigid, yet her heart heavy with sorrow. The cold wind whipped through her hair, but she barely noticed. Her gaze was fixed on the freshly turned earth before her—her father's grave beside her mother's, the final resting place of the two people she had loved most in this world. The tears on her face were the only outward sign of the turmoil inside. Samuel Sintaro, her father, had been her rock, the one person who always knew how to make everything seem okay. But now he was gone, leaving an emptiness that felt suffocating.

Her thoughts raced back to just a week ago, when she had cradled her father's lifeless body in her arms after he'd collapsed from a heart attack, his last breath stolen from him too quickly. The shock of it still hadn't fully worn off. How could someone so strong, so full of life, be gone in an instant? Ashley had barely had time to process the grief before her entire world seemed to crumble. The house they'd shared for so many years now felt like a hollow shell, each room echoing with memories of the family that once filled it.

A soft touch on her shoulder broke through her spiralling thoughts. Kelly, her best friend, was standing beside her, her presence a small comfort in the overwhelming silence.

"It's time to go, Ash," Kelly's voice was gentle, but firm, filled with love and concern.

Ashley's eyes were still locked on the headstone as fresh tears welled up, her voice barely a whisper. "I have no one left, Kell. Why did this happen? What did I do to deserve this?"

Her words trembled, each one laced with a sorrow so deep, it felt like it might swallow her whole. It was as though she had been abandoned by life itself—no family, no guideposts to show her the way forward. All she had was a mountain of grief, and it was too much to bear alone.

Kelly squeezed Ashley's shoulder, her touch warm and reassuring. "I'm here for you, Ash. Always," she said, her voice rich with the kind of unconditional support that Ashley knew she could rely on, no matter what.

Ashley turned to face Kelly, the tears falling freely now, and for a moment, she let herself lean into her best friend's embrace. Her sobs came in heavy waves as she buried her face in Kelly's shoulder. "I love you, Kell," she whispered through the tears, her voice breaking, every word heavy with the weight of loss.

"I love you too," Kelly murmured, holding Ashley close, letting her cry. She didn't try to fix anything, knowing there was nothing that could be fixed right now—just comfort, just presence. "You don't have to go through this alone."

"I don't know what to do now," Ashley admitted quietly after a few moments, her voice raw with grief.

Kelly stroked Ashley's back, offering what little solace she could. "You'll find your way, Ash. It's going to take time, but you need to give yourself that time."

Ashley nodded shakily, her breath still unsteady. She knew Kelly was right. There was no way to rush through the pain, no shortcuts. But that didn't make it any easier. She wiped her eyes, managing a small, watery smile, though it barely reached her eyes. "I know," she whispered, but there was a hint of determination in her voice now, as if she was starting to understand that life, despite its cruelty, would go on.

With a deep breath, Ashley turned away from the gravesite, her feet feeling heavier than ever as she walked toward the car, where Kelly's husband, Daniel, was waiting with the back door open. He offered her a silent, sympathetic smile, but he knew there was nothing to say. She slid into the back seat, the cool leather of the seat greeting her like an uncomfortable reminder of everything that had changed. Kelly and Daniel took their places in the front, and as the car slowly pulled away from the cemetery, Ashley stared out the window, her thoughts a jumbled mess, her heart aching with every mile they travelled toward her family home.

At the house, the wake was already underway. The quiet hum of voices filled the rooms, punctuated by polite laughter, though it felt hollow, forced. The visitors who arrived, offering their condolences and kind words, seemed like strangers to Ashley. She smiled weakly and nodded, murmuring her thanks, but it all felt distant. The weight of her grief made it hard to focus on anything else. She went through the motions, playing the part of a dutiful daughter, but inside she felt numb, as if everything had turned to fog. Every gesture, every word felt mechanical. The ache of losing both her parents, of being left alone in the world, was too great to allow for any real connection to the people around her.

Ashley sank into the living room couch, too exhausted to care about the crowd. Her heart felt hollow, and for the first time, she realised that no matter how many people were there, the only thing she truly needed—her parents—was gone. The grief, raw and unrelenting, was the only thing left to fill the space.

Beau Tramain lingered in the shadows of the trees at the edge of the graveyard, his eyes fixed on the woman who had once shattered his heart. The sight of her stirred a storm of emotions he thought he'd long buried. Even in the midst of her grief, Ashley was as captivating as ever, though the pain etched into her features was impossible to miss. She was the same woman he had loved—no, obsessed over—yet she felt like a distant memory now, one that he couldn't quite escape, no matter how hard he tried.

Her long, chestnut-brown hair, gathered in a simple ponytail at the nape of her neck, framed her delicate face. Her flawless, porcelain skin bore no signs of age or wear, untouched by time or sorrow, as if she remained the same person he had known. Yet, the absence of her usual warmth and radiance was palpable. Dark sunglasses shielded her striking blue eyes from both the harsh sunlight and any prying gaze, making it harder for him to read her. Despite her attempts to mask her emotions, the faint tremble of her hands as they rested by her sides betrayed her grief.

Her slender, tall figure seemed more fragile now than it ever had before. He noticed how her shoulders slumped slightly, as if the weight of the world had settled on them in a way he hadn't seen before. Despite the vulnerability in her posture, there was still a quiet grace about her. She stood beside Kelly, her best friend, who seemed to offer the only stability left in her life. She was resolute yet delicate, a woman shattered by loss, yet carrying herself with an elegance that was impossible to ignore.

Beau's chest tightened as he observed her. He knew how deeply she had loved her father. Samuel Sintaro had been more than just a father to her; he had been her protector, her guide, her constant. The man had held a place in Beau's heart too, one forged through years of admiration and gratitude. Samuel had been the one to offer Beau a chance when no one else would, to teach him what it meant to be a man of integrity. He owed Samuel not just for the lessons, but for the life he had been given—one that had shaped him into who he was today. No matter the history between him and Ashley, Beau knew he couldn't forget the debt he owed to the man who had inspired him in so many ways.

Ashley was now left with nothing but the aching memory of her father's love. Beau could see it in her posture, the way she stood motionless beside her friend, her eyes fixed on the ground. She hadn't married, and now, she was entirely alone. The thought hit him with an unexpected force. She's truly alone now.

The bitterness that had once consumed him now felt small, insignificant in the face of the crushing loss she was enduring. Beau had always felt abandoned by Ashley, betrayed in the worst possible way. But standing there, witnessing her mourning, a part of him realised that they had both been abandoned, in different ways, by the people they loved most.

As he watched her slip into the back of the car with Kelly, memories began to surge in his chest. The way she had smiled at him when they first met, the feeling of her hand in his, the way she had lit up his life and made him feel like he was worth something. That part of him—the part that had been impossible to leave behind—reached out for her in the quiet moments between them. In the years since their separation, Beau had convinced himself that he'd moved on, that the ache of her loss had dulled. But watching her now, he knew the truth: no one had come close to replacing her. No one had made him feel the way she had.

He would soon have to face her again, after five long years. She would be standing in front of him, no longer the woman he had once known. So much had changed, but the way she haunted him, the way she stayed in his mind long after she was gone, hadn't.

Once the car disappeared down the winding path, Beau stepped out from the shadows of the trees and made his way toward the gravesite. His footsteps were slow, deliberate, as he walked through the quiet, empty cemetery. The world around him seemed to hold its breath as he stood before the headstone, staring at the names etched into the cold stone.

Samuel and Helena Sintaro. Gone.

The silence around him felt suffocating, heavy with all the words that could never be said. The grief that Ashley felt mirrored his own, though their losses were different, their pain unique. He, too, had lost people who meant the world to him, people who had shaped his life. But nothing compared to the loneliness that came with losing someone who had been your anchor, your reason for moving forward. He understood, perhaps for the first time, what Ashley had felt all these years. She had been left with no one to turn to, just as he had.

Beau stood there, the weight of everything sinking in. He thought of the future that could have been, the future they had once talked about together, and he realised it would never be. For both of them, the dreams they had once shared had been buried with the people they loved. The road ahead was unclear, uncertain. But in that moment, he knew one thing: just like Ashley, he was adrift, trapped in the echoes of a past that refused to let go.

They were both alone, but in their solitude, there was an understanding between them—one forged by shared loss, by time, and by the silence that spoke more than words ever could. Beau didn't know what the future held, but for the first time, he understood that they were bound together, not by the love they once shared, but by the emptiness that would forever linger between them.

Chapter Six

Two months had passed since her father's funeral, and Ashley found herself sitting in the plush, dimly lit office of Henry Sinclair, the family solicitor. The room, lined with imposing bookshelves, seemed to close in around her, the shadows from the afternoon sun casting long, melancholic patterns on the walls. The faint smell of leather-bound books mixed with the faint scent of polished wood.

Henry, his glasses perched low on his nose, glanced up from the papers before him with a quiet sigh. "I've found a buyer for your father's business," he announced, breaking the silence.

Ashley managed a weak smile, the words feeling distant, as though they belonged to someone else. "That's good news," she said, though she couldn't fully feel the weight of the sentiment.

"However," Henry continued, his tone a little heavier, "there's one condition to the sale."

Ashley's brow furrowed, her attention sharpening. "A condition? What is it?"

She'd already made the difficult decision to sell Sintaro Furniture—a place so filled with memories it threatened to suffocate her. The business was her father's legacy, but it no longer felt like a part of her future. At twenty-seven, with no parents left and no husband, she was searching for something new, something that didn't tie her to the past. She had to move forward, no matter how daunting it felt.

"The buyer requires that you stay on for a month to help with the transition," Henry explained, shifting uneasily in his chair. "The sale won't be finalised until that period is complete, and the condition will be included in the contract."

Ashley paused, the news settling into her mind. It was unexpected, but not unreasonable. "Do you think the deal is worth accepting?" she asked, her voice quiet, trying to gauge his opinion.

Henry's gaze softened as he nodded, his expression full of reassurance. "Yes, absolutely. It's a very generous offer. With this, you'll have the financial security you need for the rest of your life. Your father's success left a remarkable legacy."

Ashley absorbed his words, her mind working through the implications. It wasn't just about money—it was about moving on. "A month isn't too long," she finally said, a small resolve firming in her chest. "It'll give me some time to figure out what's next."

Henry smiled, a look of approval crossing his face. "Excellent. I'll inform the buyer and get the contracts ready for your review."

Ashley rose from her seat and extended her hand, feeling a brief but sincere sense of gratitude. "Thank you, Henry. Just let me know when everything's prepared."

After exchanging pleasantries, she stepped out of his office, the cool air of the afternoon brushing against her face. For the first time in months, she felt a tiny flicker of hope—a signal that perhaps the next chapter of her life was beginning.

She walked to her car, the weight of the past two months still heavy on her shoulders but now accompanied by a small sense of direction. As she drove toward Sintaro Furniture, she couldn't help but feel a surge of nostalgia. The sight of the building loomed ahead, bringing with it a flood of memories— memories of her father, of the life she had once known. She hadn't spent much time at the office since his passing. She trusted her team to handle the day-to-day operations, but today, she was here to tie up the loose ends.

Taking a steadying breath, she pushed open the door to the office, the familiar chime of the bell above the entrance sounding a little too loud. Inside, the office was quiet, save for the rustling of papers. She found Daniel at his desk, deeply absorbed in a stack of paperwork.

"Good afternoon, Daniel. Everything alright?" Ashley asked, her voice light despite the heaviness she still felt.

He looked up, a warm smile instantly spreading across his face. "Oh, hey, Ash. The delivery of the Italian furniture got delayed because of customs. It'll arrive around midday tomorrow."

"That's fine," she replied with a small sigh. "I actually came by to tell you something—Henry found a buyer for the business."

Daniel's expression shifted briefly, but he nodded without missing a beat. "Okay."

Ashley paused, watching him for a moment. She wanted to reassure him, to make sure he didn't feel like he was losing something too. "I'm sure you'll still have a place here. You're great at what you do," she said, trying to sound more confident than she felt.

Daniel smiled warmly; the kind of smile that made her believe he truly meant it. "I'm not worried, Ash. I'll be fine, no matter what happens."

Her heart lifted a little at his words. Daniel, with his unshakable optimism, was one of the few constants in her life. He had been a rock when everything around her had crumbled, and his easy-going nature always had a way of making her feel grounded, even when the world felt like it was falling apart.

"How's Kelly?" Ashley asked, a gentle smile forming on her lips as she thought of her best friend.

Daniel chuckled softly. "Mornings are still rough. She's been dealing with a lot of morning sickness, but she's better by the afternoons."

Ashley's smile widened at the news. Kelly's pregnancy with their second child was an exciting development. Brian, their firstborn, was already three years old and full of life. "Tell her that if she needs anything, she shouldn't hesitate to call," Ashley said warmly.

"I will," Daniel replied, his eyes lighting up with affection. "And Brian's been keeping her busy, too. That little guy's a bundle of energy."

Ashley laughed, the sound filling the room. "I bet he is." For a moment, she felt a lightness in her chest, as though the weight of her own concerns had been lifted, even if only briefly.

"Alright, if everything's under control here, I'll be on my way," she said, standing up and smoothing down her skirt.

"You're still coming to Brian's birthday party tomorrow, right?" Daniel asked, his eyes full of hope.

"I wouldn't miss my godson's birthday party for the world," Ashley replied, her smile genuine. "I'll be there early to help you and Kelly with everything."

Daniel grinned. "Thanks, Ash. We'll see you then. Have a good night."

After exchanging goodbyes, Ashley left the office, the weight of the day slowly beginning to lift. She felt the tiniest sense of peace, a small but significant step forward. Tonight, she would focus on something other than loss. She would focus on what was still good in her life.

Walking into her empty house always left Ashley with a deep, unshakable sadness. The silence was overwhelming, like a thick fog that crept into every corner, amplifying the void that had settled inside her. It was the kind of silence that didn't offer comfort but instead magnified the absence of everything she had lost.

She made herself a simple dinner—something easy, something that didn't require much thought. The quiet hum of the kitchen was a welcome distraction, but it didn't last long. After eating, she made her way to the living room, her feet dragging as if the weight of the world pressed down on her shoulders.

She sank into the couch, trying to find comfort in the soft cushions, but the restlessness in her mind wouldn't let her settle. The ache in her chest, the one that seemed to follow her everywhere, throbbed steadily, a reminder of the emptiness she couldn't escape. With a soft sigh, she reached for the remote, the motion almost mechanical. She needed something to take her mind off the ache, to fill the silence with something other than her own thoughts. She flicked through channels aimlessly, desperate for any distraction, anything that might offer a reprieve from the sadness she could never outrun.

But nothing seemed to work. The television glowed in front of her, but her mind was elsewhere, lost in a fog that wouldn't clear. She was too tired to fight it tonight. Another restless night of sleep was inevitable.

Chapter Seven

The next morning, Ashley woke early and prepared a light breakfast, her movements automatic, though her mind was far from focused. After finishing, she slipped into a breezy sundress, one of the few things that still made her feel somewhat normal. She grabbed the wrapped present for Brian and headed out the door, determined to make the most of the day and immerse herself in the festivities for her best friend's son's third birthday.

Arriving at Kelly and Daniel's house, Ashley knocked lightly on the door. Almost immediately, Kelly's cheerful voice rang out from inside. "Come in, Ash!"

Ashley stepped into the warmth of the kitchen, where Kelly greeted her with a kiss on the cheek. Flour dusted her hands, evidence of her busy morning preparing. "Hi, Kell! How's the morning sickness?"

Kelly chuckled lightly. "It's not too bad now. I only throw up once in the morning now, so I'm surviving."

Ashley smiled sympathetically, but the tiredness in Kelly's voice tugged at her heart. "Glad to hear it's easing up a bit. What can I help with?"

"Could you chop up the salad? It's all in the fridge," Kelly said, gesturing to the open refrigerator.

"Absolutely, no problem," Ashley replied, moving toward the fridge to gather the ingredients. "Where's my little man?"

"Oh, he's outside, watching Daniel inflate balloons," Kelly said, her tone light.

Ashley chuckled. "I bet he's loving that!"

Kelly laughed, too. "Who, Daniel or Brian?"

"Either one works for me!" Ashley smiled as she finished preparing the salads and placed them in bowls, setting them in the fridge. "I think I'll go check on my little man."

"No worries, I'm almost done here. I'll be out soon," Kelly said, busying herself with the final touches for the party.

Ashley made her way to the backyard, and just as she stepped outside, Brian came running toward her, his face lighting up with pure joy. "Ash! Ash! It's my birthday!"

Bending down, Ashley scooped him up and swung him around, laughing as she felt his small arms wrap around her neck. "I know! You're growing up way too fast!"

Brian planted a big, sloppy kiss on her cheek, his grin stretching from ear to ear. "I know! I'm three now!" he exclaimed, his excitement infectious.

Ashley smiled, her heart swelling with affection. She greeted Daniel with a wave and a smile, then took Brian inside to give him his present. As he eagerly tore off the wrapping paper, his eyes lit up at the sight of the big Tonka truck.

"You can play with it in your sandpit!" Ashley said, her voice full of joy as she handed it to him.

"Thank you, Ash!" Brian shouted, planting another sloppy kiss on her cheek before racing off to show Daniel.

Ashley watched him go; her heart filled with warmth as she thought about how far he had come in just three short years. After a while, she rejoined Kelly and Daniel to help set up the tables, arranging the food and chairs as guests began to trickle in.

The house quickly filled with the sounds of chatter and laughter, the kind of noise that reminded Ashley that, despite everything, life kept moving forward. She stood back for a moment, taking it all in, before the sudden sound of a familiar voice broke her thoughts.

"Hello, Ashley."

Ashley turned, her stomach tightening at the sight of Bruno, his usual confident smirk plastered on his face as he sauntered toward her.

"Hi, Bruno. How are you?" she asked, forcing a smile as he leaned in to kiss her cheek.

"I'm good. How have you been?" he asked, his voice low, as though he had every right to be so intimate with her.

"Good, thanks," Ashley replied, internally cringing as his lips brushed her skin. She wished she could wipe the spot where he kissed her, but she kept her composure.

"When are you going to go out with me, Ash?" Bruno pressed, his tone almost pleading.

"Not this again, Bruno. Please, just accept that it's never going to happen," she said firmly, her patience running thin.

Bruno dramatically placed a hand on his chest, feigning hurt. "You wound me! I'm a good-looking guy, and you're a good-looking girl. I think it's time to accept that we're meant for each other."

Ashley rolled her eyes. "I don't think so. I'm not looking to become just another notch on your belt."

Bruno grinned, a hint of arrogance in his gaze. "You know you wouldn't be. You're different. I'm just going out with the others while I wait for you." He paused, his smile becoming smug. "You can't still be holding that kiss from your hen night against me. It's been five years."

Ashley's anger flared, and for a moment, she considered slapping him. Instead, she clenched her teeth, speaking through them, "Of course not, Bruno. You just caused the breakup of my engagement. But that's exactly what you wanted, wasn't it?"

Bruno's expression faltered for a moment, but he quickly recovered. "It wasn't like that, Ash. I was just congratulating you. It's not my fault Sarah sent a photo to Beau." He sighed, exhaling dramatically. "I wouldn't have ended things with you just because a male friend congratulated you. If he broke up with you over that, he clearly never trusted you or loved you in the first place."

Ashley took a deep breath, silently acknowledging that Bruno had a point, but she would never admit it to him. "I've loved you since high school, and I still do. When are you going to put me out of my misery?" he pressed, his gaze unwavering.

Ashley met his eyes, her resolve firm as steel. "Bruno, I said no then, and I say no now. We were never meant to be together. We just wouldn't suit."

"Why, Ash?" he asked, his expression softening, as if he truly didn't understand.

"You know why," she replied sharply, her voice firm. She quickly added, "I don't want to talk about this anymore. How is your mother?"

Bruno shrugged casually. "She's fine. I think she's trying for her third husband now."

Ashley smiled, trying to keep the conversation light. "What happened to the second husband?"

"Oh, she got rid of him about six months ago. They're filing for divorce soon," Bruno replied with a shrug.

"She moves on quickly," Ashley remarked, her voice laced with confusion.

"She doesn't like being alone," Bruno informed her, his tone matter of fact.

After chatting for a little while longer, Ashley finally excused herself, her patience with him wearing thin.

Later, after the last of the guests had left, Ashley cradled a sleepy Brian in her arms, feeling the comforting warmth of his small body against hers.

"Hey, Kell," she called softly, "Do you want me to put him in his room? He looks beat."

"Yes, please, Ash," Kelly replied gratefully.

Ashley carried Brian upstairs and gently laid him in his bed, draping a soft throw blanket over him. She pressed a tender kiss to his forehead before quietly heading downstairs to help with the cleanup.

Once everything was in order, Ashley prepared to leave. Kelly and Daniel thanked her, both grateful for her help.

"No problem," Ashley said with a smile. "It was a wonderful day."

After saying her goodbyes, she headed home, where she took a shower and prepared for bed. Settling under the covers, she reached for the romance novel on her nightstand, her fingers lingering on the spine. She opened it and began to read, but her mind drifted.

As she read, Ashley realised how unfulfilled she felt. She was a beautiful, successful woman, with everything she could possibly need—except the one thing she craved the most: love. She couldn't shake the ache in her chest, a constant reminder of what had once been with Beau Tramain. The memories crept in, bittersweet, and no matter how hard she tried, no one seemed to measure up.

The desire for a loving partner, someone to share her life with, and the hope of one day having children of her own—a dream that seemed so distant— remained deeply buried in her heart. But it flickered still, fragile and faint, just like the memory of a love she had never quite let go of.

A few weeks later, all the paperwork for the sale of Sintaro Furniture had been finalised, and today was the day the new owner was set to arrive and take over. Ashley had transitioned from her old desk in the main office to a new one in the outer office, where she would assist with the handover process for the next month. Once everything was complete, she planned to leave Boston behind and set out to explore the world, a fresh start in search of rediscovery.

As Ashley organised her desk, Daniel appeared, offering a warm smile. "Ready for the new owners?" he asked.

"As ready as I'll ever be," Ashley replied, her voice trembling slightly. She hadn't yet met the new owner and was left to wonder whether he would be kind to both the staff and the business.

A familiar voice suddenly broke through her thoughts. "Good morning, Ashley."

Ashley's heart skipped a beat, her entire body going still. That voice, the one she had never quite forgotten, sent a shiver down her spine. Slowly, she lifted her gaze and saw him standing in the doorway—Beau Tramain.

At just over six feet tall, Beau looked as effortlessly handsome as she remembered, with tousled light brown hair that gave him a carefree, untamed look, like someone had just run their fingers through it. His striking green eyes locked onto hers with a mischievous sparkle, and his high cheekbones framed lips that always seemed to be smiling or about to kiss. He was undeniably gorgeous—and he knew it.

Ashley's breath hitched as she took in his appearance. He was dressed in a dark blue business suit that was impeccably tailored, highlighting his athletic build. She was used to seeing him in casual jeans and a T-shirt, but today, dressed so sharply, he took her breath away. He looked absolutely glorious.

"Beau… hello," Ashley managed, her voice a little shaky as her heart raced.

It had been five long years since she'd last seen him. Never in a million years had she expected their paths to cross again.

Beau entered the main office with his usual confident stride, his presence commanding attention. Turning back toward Ashley, he gave her a casual, almost playful smile. "Give me five minutes to get settled, and then you can introduce me to everyone," he called over his shoulder before shutting the door behind him.

Standing in the outer office, Ashley's mind was reeling. Her pulse pounded in her ears as a flood of old emotions rushed in—emotions she thought she had long since buried. Beau's return had shaken her more than she could have imagined, and she felt a mixture of shock, confusion, and something else she wasn't ready to name.

Daniel looked at Ashley with wide eyes, his surprise evident. "Did you know it was Beau who bought the business?"

Ashley shook her head, still processing the sudden appearance of her past. "No, I had no idea," she replied softly. The sale had been conducted under a corporate name, so she hadn't known who the buyer was.

"Wow, he looks amazing," Daniel continued. "I heard he made a ton of money in his IT business."

Ashley furrowed her brow in confusion. "How do you know that?"

Daniel shifted awkwardly. "Kelly kept an eye on his progress," he admitted, then quickly added, "but she didn't want to say anything to you because she knew how hurt you were."

Ashley's lips curled into a small, somewhat forced smile. "That's okay," she said, though part of her felt betrayed by Kelly's silence.

"He's a millionaire now, you know," Daniel added, clearly eager to share more.

Ashley's mind was elsewhere, distracted by the rush of memories. She absentmindedly responded, "Is he? That's nice," her voice distant, not really interested in his financial success. She was far more consumed by the shock of seeing Beau again, the sight of him reminding her of all the history they shared.

Her thoughts were racing—how was she going to cope with the next month? The mere idea of working alongside Beau, especially with the emotions still churning inside her, filled her with a sense of dread. She had no idea how she would maintain her professionalism when every glance from him seemed to stir up feelings she thought she had left behind. And what if those feelings resurfaced? She wasn't sure she could handle it.

Chapter Eight

Meanwhile, in the main office, Beau had set his briefcase down on the desk and pulled out his laptop, settling into the role of the new owner. When he was in the outer office, his gaze had fell upon Ashley. He couldn't help but notice how stunning she looked. Time had been kind to her—she was more beautiful than ever, though she seemed to be trying to hide it.

His eyes lingered on her, and he found himself wondering how she would react to his return. Part of him longed to pull her into his arms and kiss her senseless, but he quickly reminded himself that would not be wise, not yet. It had been five years since their painful breakup. The last thing he wanted to do was complicate matters again, but the pull between them, the undeniable connection, was still there. He just wasn't sure how he was going to navigate it.

Ten minutes passed, and Beau still hadn't emerged from his office. With a deep breath, Ashley decided to check in. She glanced at Daniel, managing a nervous smile. "Wish me luck," she said quietly, knowing she'd need every ounce of composure.

She knocked on the door and waited for the soft "Come in" before opening it and stepping inside. Beau didn't look up. "Close the door and sit," he instructed, his tone brisk.

Ashley complied, the coolness in his voice sending a chill through her.

Finally, he glanced up, and his expression softened just a fraction. "First, I want to offer my condolences for your father's passing. I was shocked and deeply saddened to hear about it."

Ashley lowered her head as tears welled in her eyes. "Thank you," she murmured, her voice tight with emotion.

"I attended the funeral," Beau continued, his voice gentler now, "but under the circumstances, I didn't make my presence known."

Her head snapped up, her eyes wide with surprise. "You were there?"

He nodded. "I was. I respected Samuel deeply. He was good to me, and I'll always be grateful for that. His death was a real loss."

Ashley sat in silence, overwhelmed by the unexpected revelation. After a moment, she managed to say softly, "He liked you too."

Beau rose from his desk, his gaze lingering on her briefly. "Alright, let's get started. You can introduce me to everyone now."

Ashley followed him back to the outer office, her emotions swirling as she led him to meet the team. Many of the employees were still with the company from the time Beau had worked there, and they greeted him with warm smiles and handshakes. Yet, as they glanced at Ashley, their expressions shifted, reflecting their concern. They remembered how devastated she had been after Beau left and now seeing them together again felt surreal.

The introductions stretched on through the morning. By lunchtime, Ashley was exhausted from forcing polite smiles and suppressing the emotions threatening to surface.

As they returned to the office, Beau announced, "I'll take you to lunch so we can go over the transition plans."

Ashley hesitated, already feeling drained. "That's not necessary. I can wait here, and we can discuss everything later."

But Beau was firm. "No, I have to leave after lunch and won't be back until tomorrow. Lunch it is."

Resigned, Ashley nodded, following him to his sleek black BMW. Her headache, which had started as a dull ache earlier, was now pulsing behind her eyes.

At the Italian restaurant, they were seated in a quiet corner. Beau got straight to business. "I want to ensure we maintain a professional atmosphere this month and leave our past where it belongs."

Ashley nodded quickly. "Of course."

"Good." He picked up his menu, his tone turning cold. "For now, all employees will remain in their positions. No one needs to worry about their jobs."

Ashley sighed in relief at this news, grateful that at least the staff wouldn't face uncertainty. She picked up her menu, though her appetite was non-existent.

The waiter arrived, and Beau ordered ravioli, while Ashley opted for a Caesar salad.

"You used to have a much healthier appetite," Beau remarked, his sharp gaze studying her. "You've lost a lot of weight."

Ashley stiffened, irritation flaring. "Things change," she replied curtly, wishing he hadn't commented on her appearance.

As they ate, Beau outlined his expectations for the month. Ashley listened, though her throbbing headache made it difficult to focus. When he mentioned hiring a business manager, Jason, to take over the day-to-day operations, she nodded weakly, unable to muster much of a response.

By the time they left the restaurant, Ashley was feeling increasingly unwell. The bright sunlight outside struck her like a hammer, making her dizzy. Her vision blurred, and she staggered.

"Please, not now," she thought desperately, but it was too late. Everything went black.

Beau reacted instantly, catching her as she collapsed. "Bloody hell!" he muttered, scooping her up effortlessly.

Jason, who had just arrived, rushed over. "Is she alright?"

"She'll be fine," Beau said, his jaw tight. "I'll take her home. You head to the factory and meet with Daniel."

With Ashley cradled in his arms, Beau carried her to his car and gently placed her in the passenger seat. As he drove to her house, he glanced at her pale face, concern tightening his chest. He retrieved the key from her bag and carried her inside, memories of the home flooding back—late nights with Samuel and Ashley, laughter, and warmth he hadn't felt in years.

Laying her carefully on the couch, Beau went to the kitchen and returned with painkillers and water. "Here," he said softly, handing them to her.

Ashley sat up slowly, feeling humiliated. "Thank you," she whispered. "I'm sorry. It came on so suddenly."

"You haven't outgrown the migraines," Beau said, his voice tinged with concern. He remembered how stress always triggered them. "Have they been worse since your dad passed?"

She nodded. "Yes. It's been a lot to deal with."

Beau's expression softened. "I'm not surprised. Losing someone like Samuel…" He paused, then added gently, "Take it easy, Ashley. You've been through enough."

Her gaze lifted to meet his, confusion and vulnerability written on her face. "Why are you here, Beau? Why did you come back?"

He hesitated, a flicker of something unspoken passing through his eyes. "That's a conversation for another time," he said quietly, his voice low and filled with meaning.

Ashley searched his face, looking for answers, but his expression remained unreadable. Yet, in his gaze, there was a quiet intensity that left her both uneasy and curious.

Suddenly, there was a sharp knock at the front door, and it swung open. "Ashley?" Kelly called out; her voice tinged with concern.

Beau turned toward the sound. "In here," he responded.

Kelly entered the living room, freezing in her tracks as her eyes landed on Beau. Her expression immediately hardened. "So, it is you," she said, her tone dripping with accusation.

Beau straightened, caught off guard by her hostility. "Yes… it's me. Hello, Kelly," he said, trying to keep his voice calm.

"Don't 'hello' me. Get out," Kelly snapped, her glare unwavering.

Beau blinked, surprised by the icy reception. He had always thought Kelly liked him—or, at the very least, tolerated him. What he didn't know was that Kelly was the only person Ashley had confided in about the photos she'd received five years ago, the ones that had shattered her heart. Kelly had wanted to confront Beau back then, but Ashley had made her promise not to.

"Kelly?" Beau said, his confusion evident.

Kelly stepped closer, her protective stance clear. "You heard me. Leave. You've done enough damage to Ashley for a lifetime."

"Kelly…" Ashley murmured weakly, attempting to intervene, but the pain from her migraine made it difficult to form coherent words.

Kelly softened momentarily as she glanced at her friend, but her anger reignited as she turned back to Beau. "I couldn't believe it when Daniel told me you were back. And now here you are, acting like nothing happened. You don't get to waltz in and hurt her all over again. Leave."

Beau's jaw tightened as his gaze flickered between the two women. "What lies have you been telling people about me, Ashley?" he asked, his voice low and cold.

"She doesn't lie," Kelly shot back, stepping between them. "Now get out before I call the police."

Beau looked at her, bewildered by the venom in her voice. With one last glance at Ashley, who had her eyes squeezed shut in discomfort, he turned and left without another word.

As the door closed behind him, Kelly exhaled sharply and moved to help Ashley. "Come on, let's get you to bed," she said gently, guiding her friend upstairs. Once Ashley was tucked under the covers, Kelly smoothed her hair and promised to return the next day.

The following morning, Ashley awoke feeling slightly better, though the lingering ache in her head reminded her of yesterday's events. She padded downstairs and was nibbling on a piece of toast when another knock sounded at the door.

With a sigh, she set her plate down and opened the door to find Kelly holding her son, Brian. "Hi, Ash," Kelly greeted with a warm smile. "Mummy said you weren't feeling well," Brian chimed in, his little arms reaching out for a hug.

Ashley's face lit up as she scooped him into her arms. "I'm okay, sweetheart. Just a little headache."

Brian kissed her cheek sloppily and hugged her neck. "You need to get better!" he declared.

Ashley laughed softly. "I will. You're the best medicine."

Kelly stepped inside, her sharp gaze sweeping the room. "How are you really feeling?"

"I'm fine," Ashley insisted, though her weak smile gave her away.

Kelly's brow furrowed as she peeked into the fridge. "Ash, you've got nothing in here. When was the last time you ate a proper meal?"

Ashley sighed. "I'll go shopping later."

"No, you won't. I'll run out and grab some groceries," Kelly said firmly, setting Brian down on the couch.

Ashley protested, but Kelly waved her off. "Brian can keep you company. I'll be back soon."

After Kelly left, Ashley and Brian settled into the living room. The boy snuggled close, regaling her with stories about daycare and his dad's silly antics. They were laughing when another knock sounded at the door.

"Come in!" Ashley called out, expecting Kelly. But when the door opened, Beau stepped inside.

Ashley froze. "Oh, I thought it was Kelly."

Brian's small arms tightened around her as he eyed Beau suspiciously. "Who's that?" he whispered.

Ashley gave him a reassuring squeeze. "This is Beau. He's a friend."

Brian frowned. "Like a bow tie?" he asked quietly, still wary.

Beau chuckled and crouched to meet Brian's level. "Sort of. Nice to meet you, little man" he said warmly, extending his hand.

Brian buried his face in Ashley's shoulder, mumbling, "That's what Ash calls me."

Ashley smiled and rubbed his back. "He's a bit shy with new people."

Beau straightened, his gaze softening as he looked at them. "I didn't realise you had a child," he said, his tone carefully neutral.

Ashley's cheeks flushed. "Oh, no, he's Kelly and Daniel's son. But I wish he were mine," she added, tickling Brian and making him giggle.

Beau exhaled, relief flickering across his face. "Well, he's a lucky kid to have you around." He glanced at Brian. "I just wanted to check on you, Ashley. See how you were feeling."

Brian, emboldened by Ashley's presence, finally piped up. "She's better! I'm taking care of her."

Ashley kissed the top of his head. "And you're doing an amazing job, sweetheart."

Beau smiled. "I can see that. Thanks for looking after her."

Brian beamed, hugging her tight. "I love Ash."

Ashley hugged Brian close. "And I love you forever," she whispered, then looked up at Beau. "Thanks for checking in. I'm feeling much better. I'll be back at the office tomorrow."

Beau nodded, standing. "No need to rush—just focus on getting better." He smiled at Brian. "It was really nice to meet you, Brian."

Brian, feeling braver, held out his hand. "Nice to meet you too."

Beau took his tiny hand and shook it gently, smiling warmly. "You too, buddy." With one last look at Ashley, he turned and quietly left.

Chapter Nine

Ashley arrived at the office early the next day, the silence offering a welcome reprieve before the bustle of the day began. Seated at her desk, she hesitated for a moment before pulling out the delicate chain hidden beneath her blouse, a locket dangling off it.

She opened the locket, revealing Beau's picture on one side and a photo of the two of them together on the other. Her thumb grazed over his face as a wave of emotions surged—loss, anger, and the faint echo of love she tried so hard to suppress.

"Morning," a cheerful voice broke through her reverie.

Ashley startled, snapping the locket shut and tucking the chain back under her blouse. She looked up to see a man with an easy smile and bright eyes standing in the doorway.

"Morning," she replied, mustering a polite smile as her heart settled.

The man extended his hand. "You must be Ashley. I'm Jason Jackson—it's great to finally meet you. Feeling better today?"

"Yes, thank you," she said, shaking his hand. His warmth and boyish charm were immediately disarming. He seemed to be around her age, and his relaxed demeanour put her at ease.

"Well," Jason said, his grin widening, "since we'll be working together, let's start with something important—how do you take your coffee?"

Ashley couldn't help but smile. "White with two sugars."

"Coming right up," he said with a wink before heading toward the break room.

Daniel strolled into the office just as Jason stepped out, a mischievous glint in his eye. He leaned casually against her desk, arms crossed. "Looks like you've got yourself an admirer," he teased.

Ashley raised an eyebrow, suppressing a smile. "I've only just met him," she protested lightly.

"True," Daniel conceded, "but he was pretty curious about the 'beautiful young woman' who fainted on Monday." He grinned, waggling his eyebrows. "I'd say he liked what he saw."

Ashley rolled her eyes, a small laugh escaping despite herself. "You're impossible."

"Guilty," Daniel said with a wink before heading off toward the kitchen.

Left alone, Ashley leaned back in her chair, the faintest smile still tugging at her lips. For the first time in what felt like ages, the weight on her shoulders felt just a little lighter.

Jason returned a moment later, holding two steaming cups of coffee. He handed one to Ashley before pulling up a chair and sitting across from her desk. "So, Ashley, tell me a bit about yourself," he said, his tone casual yet genuinely curious.

She took a sip of the coffee, savouring the warmth. "Not much to tell, really. My father owned the business, and after he passed, I thought it was time to let it go."

Jason's expression softened, his light-heartedness giving way to empathy. "I'm really sorry about your father. You must've been close."

"We were," Ashley said quietly, the ache in her chest momentarily surfacing.

They spent the next few minutes exchanging stories, and Ashley found herself relaxing in Jason's company. She learned he was a year older than her, single, and had a talent for making her laugh with his effortless wit.

They were laughing at one of Jason's anecdotes when the office door opened, and Beau walked in. His confident stride faltered briefly as his gaze landed on Ashley, her head tilted back in laughter at something Jason had said. His jaw tightened imperceptibly, and his sharp green eyes flicked to Jason before settling on her.

Jason straightened in his chair, his easy-going demeanour shifting to one of professionalism. "Morning, Mr. Tramain," he greeted, his tone crisp.

Beau inclined his head curtly, his sharp gaze flicking between Jason and Ashley before finally settling on her. "Morning, Jason." His voice softened slightly. "Morning, Ashley."

Ashley felt the weight of his attention and cleared her throat, her cheeks warming. "Good morning," she replied, her voice quieter than she intended.

Beau's expression remained unreadable. "Ashley, can I see you in my office for a moment, please?" His tone was calm, almost gentle, but there was an undercurrent of something else—something unspoken.

Ashley's posture tensed, the subtle shift in her demeanour immediately catching the attention of both Jason and Daniel, who had just returned. "Yes, of course," she said, her voice calm and steady, though the flicker of anxiety in her eyes didn't go unnoticed.

Rising from her chair, she followed Beau into his office, quietly closing the door behind her.

The door clicked shut behind her, leaving Jason and Daniel alone. Jason's brow furrowed as he turned to Daniel, his curiosity evident. "What's going on there?" he asked, sensing the charged atmosphere that had lingered even after they left.

Daniel sat back in his chair, his expression thoughtful. "They've got history," he said, his tone low.

Jason tilted his head, intrigued. "What kind of history?"

Daniel hesitated, choosing his words carefully. "They were engaged once. He ended it a week before the wedding."

Jason blinked, the revelation catching him off guard. "Seriously?" He glanced toward Beau's closed office door, his voice softening. "And now he owns her father's business?"

Daniel shrugged. "No one knows why he came back or what he's after. But Ashley… she's been through hell because of him."

Jason processed this, his expression pensive. "She seems like a genuinely lovely person. I can't imagine why anyone would let her go."

Daniel smiled faintly, noting the sincerity in Jason's tone. "She is. She's my wife's best friend, and I can tell you this much—Ashley deserves someone who sees her for who she is and treats her right."

Jason's gaze lingered on the office door for a moment longer, a flicker of determination in his eyes. "Whoever ends up with her," he said quietly, "is going to be incredibly lucky."

Daniel studied him for a beat before nodding. "You're right about that."

Ashley sank into the chair opposite Beau's desk, the tension in the room pressing down on her as she waited for him to speak. He remained standing, his hands gripping the edge of his desk, his posture stiff, and his intense gaze fixed on her.

"Are you feeling better?" he asked softly, the gentleness in his tone doing little to ease the knot in her chest.

"Yes, thank you," she replied, her voice composed, though her eyes remained focused on a spot somewhere past his shoulder.

Beau studied her for a moment before continuing, his tone sharpening. "Why did Kelly go off on me the other day?"

Ashley's fingers curled into her lap, feigning indifference as she looked away. "I don't know."

"You do know, Ashley," he pressed, stepping closer. Gently, he tipped her chin up with his fingers, forcing her to meet his eyes.

She flinched at the contact, a flicker of discomfort crossing her face. "Maybe you should ask her," she murmured, her tone evasive.

His gaze didn't waver. "I am asking you," he said quietly, his voice steady but insistent.

With a heavy sigh, Ashley relented. "She's angry because, when we broke up, she was the one who had to deal with the aftermath. She saw how much it destroyed me."

Beau's expression softened, a flicker of guilt crossing his face. He stepped back, lowering himself into his chair as the weight of her words sank in.

"I was shattered too, Ashley," he said finally, his voice low but firm.

Her eyes narrowed, her tone cold. "If you say so."

His jaw tightened. "You don't believe me."

She shrugged, her indifference cutting. "What difference does it make now?"

Beau leaned forward; his frustration evident as he tried a different approach. "Why haven't you married?"

Ashley's eyes flashed with irritation, his question hitting a nerve. "That's none of your business."

Ignoring her protest, he pressed on. "I'd bet it's for the same reason I haven't."

She crossed her arms, her voice sharp. "Oh? Enlighten me."

"Because," he said, his tone steady and deliberate, "you and I have unfinished business."

Ashley froze, his words throwing her off balance. She stared at him, disbelief etched across her face. "I thought you made it perfectly clear how you felt about me when you ended our engagement and walked away."

Beau's expression hardened, his tone turning icy. "That was because you cheated on me."

"No, I didn't." Her voice was steady, her gaze unwavering. "You assumed I did."

His brow furrowed as confusion flickered across his face. "What? Why didn't you tell me this back then?"

She shook her head, her voice laced with exhaustion. "Because you'd already decided I was guilty. There was no point in fighting you."

Beau shot to his feet, his frustration boiling over. "So, our relationship wasn't worth fighting for?"

Ashley met his gaze, her voice soft but resolute. "Not after I found out what you did."

His confusion deepened. "What are you talking about? I didn't do anything, Ashley."

She let out a slow breath, her shoulders sagging under the weight of her emotions. "You don't get it, Beau. And I don't have the energy to explain it to you now." Rising from her chair, she fixed him with a calm but firm look. "This isn't the time or place for this conversation."

Without waiting for a response, she turned and walked toward the door. Opening it with purpose, she left the office without a backward glance.

Beau remained frozen in place, his mind racing as he tried to piece together what had just happened. Frustration and disbelief swirled within him, the feeling of missing something vital gnawing at him.

Back at her desk, Ashley lowered herself into her chair, her movements controlled despite the storm still brewing inside her. She took a deep breath, trying to push the encounter aside.

Daniel approached; his brow creased with concern. "Ash, are you okay?"

She offered a faint, almost mechanical smile. "I will be."

Turning to Jason, who wore a faint look of concern, she straightened her posture, masking her unease with a determined expression. "So," she said, her voice steady, "where do we begin?"

Jason, picking up on her need to shift gears, offered a reassuring nod. "Let's get started," he replied, his tone a balanced mix of warmth and professionalism.

As they dove into work, Ashley felt the tension slowly begin to lift, though the echoes of her conversation with Beau still lingered in the back of her mind. When Beau left the office shortly after, her relief was palpable, but the unresolved questions continued to cloud her thoughts.

By the time Ashley got home just after five, she was ready to leave the chaos of the day behind. She kicked off her heels by the door, dropped her bag on the counter, and headed straight for a shower. The hot water washed away the tension clinging to her, and by the time she changed into her favourite comfortable shorts and a singlet, she felt somewhat lighter.

As she padded into the kitchen, the thought of cooking dinner brought a sense of normalcy she desperately needed. She pulled out a cutting board and some vegetables, ready to throw together a quick stir-fry. But just as she was about to start chopping, a knock at the door interrupted her thoughts.

Her heart sank when she opened it to find Beau standing there. Dressed casually in jeans and a plain T-shirt, he looked disarmingly at ease, though his expression was anything but.

"What are you here for, Beau?" she asked, crossing her arms as frustration crept into her voice.

"We need to talk," he replied, his tone serious. Without waiting for an invitation, he stepped forward, brushing past her.

Ashley's jaw clenched, but she stepped aside, closing the door behind him. "Oh, by all means, come in," she said, her voice laced with sarcasm.

Beau moved into the living room and settled into an armchair. His posture was tense, his hands clasped tightly together as if to steady himself. Ashley sat on the couch across from him, arms crossed, her expression guarded.

The silence stretched before Beau finally spoke, his voice steady but carrying a note of frustration. "Why didn't you defend yourself when I asked if you slept with Bruno?"

Ashley let out a slow breath, her gaze dropping to the floor. "Beau, this is pointless," she said softly. "There's no reason to dig all this up now."

"I disagree," he said firmly, leaning forward. "If you're telling me the truth, then I made the biggest mistake of my life."

Her eyes flicked up to meet his, her expression unreadable. "It doesn't matter, Beau. If you hadn't ended it, I would have."

He froze, clearly startled. "What are you talking about?"

Before she could respond, a voice came from the hallway, startling them both. "Because you're a cheat and a liar," Kelly said, stepping into view. Her arms were crossed, and her gaze was sharp and unwavering.

Beau turned; confusion etched across his face. "What the hell, Kelly?" he demanded. "Ashley was with Bruno that night. She's the one who betrayed me."

Kelly's face turned red with fury. "She did not!" she yelled, her voice echoing through the room.

Beau's eyes narrowed as he turned back to Ashley. "Tell her," he said coldly. "Tell her the truth. Tell me the truth."

Ashley shrank under the weight of his gaze, tears welling in her eyes. Before she could speak, Kelly stepped in.

"I already know the truth," Kelly said icily. "I saw Bruno corner her that night. She wasn't at fault for any of it. And you—" she pointed a trembling finger at Beau, her voice rising, "you were off with Sarah! Don't you dare turn this on her!"

Beau's face went pale. "Sarah?" he repeated, stunned. "What are you talking about?"

Kelly took a steadying breath, her fury barely contained. "I saw the photos, Beau. You and Sarah, in that hotel room. Don't act like you don't know."

Ashley let out a choked sob, her shoulders shaking. Kelly rushed to her side, sitting down and wrapping a protective arm around her.

Beau stood frozen, his face a mix of confusion and disbelief. "What photos?" he asked, his voice quieter now.

Ashley looked up through her tears, her expression a mixture of heartbreak and exhaustion. "In my top drawer," she whispered, her voice trembling. "Next to the bed."

Kelly's eyes widened. "You kept them?"

Ashley nodded weakly. "I had to," she said, her voice barely audible. "To remind myself not to go after him."

Beau stared at her, his mind racing. He had no idea what was in those photos, but the weight of her pain hit him like a tidal wave. He opened his mouth to speak but found himself at a loss.

As Kelly hurried upstairs to retrieve the photos, Ashley turned her gaze to Beau, her eyes filled with pain and lingering anger. Her voice was quiet, but the weight of her words pressed down on him. "I came to confront you that day," she said, her tone trembling. "But before I could say a word, you accused me of cheating. When you asked if I'd slept with Bruno… I didn't answer because I wanted you to hurt as much as you hurt me."

Beau flinched, her words hitting him harder than he anticipated. He opened his mouth to respond, but the sound of Kelly's hurried footsteps descending the stairs stopped him.

Kelly reappeared, holding a worn envelope, her expression tight with anger. She thrust it into Beau's hands, her voice sharp. "Here. Now tell me it wasn't you who cheated."

Beau took the envelope, his movements slow and tentative, as though he were handling something fragile. The first item that slipped out was his engagement ring—the one he had given Ashley.

His breath caught. He looked up at her, his voice barely audible. "You kept it."

Ashley nodded, tears streaking her cheeks. "It meant something to me, Beau," she said, her voice breaking.

Beau stared at the ring for a moment before carefully reaching into the envelope again. His hands trembled as he pulled out the photos. The images were sharp and vivid—showing Sarah and him in an intimate moment. His expression shifted from shock to confusion, then to something more complex—a mix of regret and disbelief.

Overwhelmed, Beau sank into the nearest armchair, the photos heavy in his hands. His voice was hollow when he finally spoke. "This… this isn't me. I never did this."

Kelly crossed her arms, her tone cutting. "How can you still deny it? Look at your wrist in those pictures—you're wearing the watch Ashley gave you for your birthday. Weeks before you ended things."

Beau's eyes darted back to the photos, honing in on the watch. His face tightened, his mind racing. "Ashley," he said, his voice strained and raw, "this… it didn't happen. I don't know how these photos exist, but I swear—this isn't real."

Ashley stared at him, her tears slowing but her expression unreadable. "How do you explain it, then, Beau? How do you explain the dates, the watch, the woman straddling you?"

"I don't know!" he blurted, his frustration evident. He ran a hand through his hair, his thoughts spiralling. "I don't know how these photos came to be, but I know this—none of this is real. I swear to you, Ashley, I would never… I didn't do this."

Kelly stepped forward, her patience wearing thin. "You expect her to believe that? After everything you've put her through. Get out, Beau. You've done enough damage."

Beau turned to Ashley, his eyes pleading. "Ashley, please. I need you to believe me. I'll prove it. I'll find out who did this, who planted these lies, but I need you to give me a chance."

Ashley wiped her cheeks, her voice quiet but firm. "I don't know if I can believe you, Beau. Not after all this time."

Kelly moved between them, her protective instincts flaring. "She doesn't owe you anything. Just leave her alone."

Beau hesitated, looking like he wanted to say more, but the finality in Kelly's tone silenced him. Slowly, he stood, his movements heavy with defeat. Without another word, he turned and walked out, the envelope still clutched in his hand.

As the door closed softly behind him, Beau felt the cold air hit his face like a slap. He stood on the porch for a moment, his mind racing. The photos—the damn photos—had shattered everything. But they weren't real. They couldn't be.

Walking down the driveway in a daze, he resolved to uncover the truth. Someone had gone to extraordinary lengths to destroy his relationship with Ashley, and he would find out who. He didn't know where to start, but he knew one thing for sure: this wasn't over.

Inside, Ashley sat back on the couch, her head in her hands. Kelly knelt beside her, wrapping an arm around her shoulders.

"You okay?" Kelly asked softly.

Ashley shook her head, her voice cracking. "I don't know what to believe anymore."

Kelly's jaw tightened as she glanced toward the door. "We'll figure it out," she said firmly. "But you don't need him to get closure. You have me, okay?"

Ashley nodded weakly, leaning into her friend's support. But even as Kelly's comforting words filled the silence, Ashley couldn't shake the doubt lingering in her heart. What if Beau was telling the truth? And if he was... who was behind the photos?

Chapter Ten

Ashley and Jason were engrossed in their work at her desk when Beau strode into the office. "Morning, everyone," he greeted, his tone warm but underpinned by a sharp edge that made the atmosphere crackle with tension.

Ashley's cheeks flushed as memories of their last confrontation rushed back. She quickly straightened in her seat, willing herself to remain composed. "Good morning," she replied, her voice steady but devoid of warmth.

Daniel and Jason exchanged polite greetings, though their glances toward Beau were wary. The room was thick with unspoken words.

Beau's gaze lingered on Ashley, softening slightly. "Ashley," he said after a beat, "could I see you in my office? Please?" His voice was gentle, almost apologetic.

Ashley hesitated, her stomach twisting, but she nodded. "Of course." Rising from her chair, she followed him, acutely aware of Jason and Daniel's curious stares trailing her.

Once inside Beau's office, she closed the door and perched on the chair opposite his desk. She folded her hands tightly in her lap, her posture guarded. Beau remained standing, leaning against his desk, his expression unreadable.

"Are you okay?" he asked, his voice soft.

"Yes, thank you," she replied curtly, avoiding his gaze.

Beau exhaled slowly, his jaw tightening. "Ashley, I…" He paused, searching for the right words. "I can't express how sorry I am that you saw those photos." His voice broke slightly, betraying the depth of his emotions.

"Beau, please," she interrupted, shaking her head. "I don't want to do this right now."

He stepped closer, his tone pleading. "Just let me finish."

Ashley's shoulders tensed, but she gave a slight nod, signalling him to continue.

"I don't know how this happened," he began, his voice thick with frustration, "but I swear to you, those photos are fake. Someone wanted to tear us apart, and they succeeded. I'll find out who did this, Ashley. I promise you."

Her lips parted in disbelief, but she quickly pressed them into a thin line. "Beau…" she started, her voice trembling. "How can you expect me to believe that? After everything?"

"Because it's the truth," he said, his voice firm. "I loved you, Ashley. I still do. And I would never do something like that to you."

Her heart clenched at his words, but the wall she had built around herself remained steadfast. "Okay," she said flatly, rising from her seat. "Can I go now?"

Beau's shoulders sagged as if the weight of her dismissal physically bore down on him. "Yes," he said softly.

She turned toward the door, her hand on the handle, when his voice stopped her.

"It worked, Ashley."

Her brows furrowed, and she turned slightly, confused. "What worked?"

"When you didn't deny sleeping with Bruno," he said, his tone tinged with regret. "It hurt me more than you know."

She stared at him for a long moment, her emotions churning. But instead of replying, she opened the door and left, leaving Beau standing in the wake of his words, alone and uncertain.

Beau sank into his chair, running a hand through his hair as his thoughts spiralled. After leaving Ashley's house that night, he had been consumed by a restless need for answers. The photos haunted him, their clarity and precision erasing any room for doubt in Ashley's mind. But Beau knew the events they depicted hadn't happened.

He replayed the night of his bucks' party over and over in his mind, searching for clues. He remembered waking up in a hotel room, disoriented, with no memory of the hours after his final drink with Bruno. His shirt had been carelessly draped over a couch, but his trousers had remained on. At the time, he dismissed it as the result of a typical drunken night.

Now, though, that blank space in his memory felt ominous. Someone had orchestrated this—someone had ensured that Ashley would find those photos and believe the worst of him.

The fury that simmered beneath his regret finally bubbled to the surface. He slammed a fist onto his desk, his mind racing. He had wasted five years, and for what? Misunderstandings, betrayal, and heartbreak.

The memory of seeing Brian, the little boy Ashley adored, flashed in his mind. Beau had initially assumed Brian was her son, and the thought had been like a dagger to his heart. But now, knowing the truth, it hurt even more. That little boy had brought Ashley so much joy, and Beau had robbed himself of the chance to share in that joy with her.

He leaned back in his chair, his chest tight. Ashley would be an incredible mother, he thought. The image of her with Brian only solidified that belief. He had always imagined her as the mother of his children.

But now, as he sat in his office, the weight of lost years pressing down on him, Beau knew he couldn't undo the past. He could only fight for the truth—and for Ashley. Whoever had destroyed their relationship wouldn't get away with it.

He just had to figure out where to start.

Later that day, Beau sat in a dimly lit office, the air thick with tension as he met with a seasoned private investigator, Dennis Cooper. Beau had brought the photos along, and he could feel the weight of them as he handed them over. The investigator studied each one carefully, his brow furrowing with focus. After a long silence, Dennis finally spoke, his voice low and deliberate.

"Something's not right here, Beau. These photos don't add up," Dennis said, pointing to one of the images. "Your face isn't directed toward the camera, but in every shot, your eyes are closed. If these were real, at least one photo would likely show your eyes open, maybe a blink or something. But there's nothing."

Beau leaned forward, his anxiety rising with each word the investigator spoke. "What does that mean?"

Dennis continued, flipping to the next image. "Look here. Your hand is resting on the woman's breast but notice her hand—it's placed over yours. It almost looks like she's holding your hand there. The position of your elbow is too bent, as if someone propped it up artificially. If you were actually touching her, your arm would be more extended. Your other arm is just by your side, not engaged in the moment at all. In a real situation like this, both hands would be involved, right? But it's as if this was staged."

Beau swallowed hard, the chill of realisation creeping through him. Dennis wasn't done.

"And then there's the sheet," he said, pointing to the way it draped over the woman's leg. "The way it's tucked up your side—it's not natural. You're probably not even naked underneath. "The way everything's arranged suggests that someone went to great lengths to make this look like an intimate moment, but it's all for show, not reality. This scene is staged. And let's be real—no one would willingly let someone photograph them in such a compromising position."

Beau sat back in his chair, his heart sinking. He stared at the photos, trying to process what Dennis was saying. The world he thought he understood was crumbling around him. These photos, these undeniable pieces of evidence that had destroyed everything he'd worked for with Ashley, were elaborate fabrications. But who would do this to him, who did this to Ashley?

Dennis's next question cut through the fog of confusion. "Did you or your fiancée have any enemies? Anyone who might have been opposed to your engagement?"

Beau's mind raced, his thoughts snapping to two people who had made their dislike known. "Yes. Two people," he said with conviction. "My ex-girlfriend, Sarah Helman, and someone who had a history with Ashley, Bruno Vincent. They were both vocal about their discontent. In fact, it was Sarah who sent me the photos of Ashley with Bruno, kissing. That was the catalyst for everything."

Dennis nodded thoughtfully, taking in the details. "It's becoming clearer now. Sarah has the motive, but Bruno, too? It seems pretty clear what happened here. You've been set up, Beau. Someone's gone to great lengths to sabotage you."

Beau's hands clenched into fists. The anger that had simmered beneath the surface for so long now surged up. He had to act, and fast. "I need irrefutable proof," he said, his voice sharp with urgency. "A confession or undeniable evidence. Ashley won't accept anything less, and honestly, I don't blame her. She deserves the truth. I need to clear my name before it's too late."

Dennis leaned forward, his gaze steady. "I can help you with that. But this is going to take time. The people who did this won't admit it easily, and they'll try to cover their tracks. We'll need to dig deeper, find the connection between them, and prove it was all a setup."

Beau nodded, determination hardening his resolve. "Do whatever it takes. I can't let Ashley think I did this to her. I need to fix this."

As Dennis outlined the next steps, Beau felt a mix of hope and dread. The path ahead would be treacherous, but for Ashley, he was willing to face anything. There was no going back now—he had to find the truth, no matter how dark it turned out to be.

Ashley spent the day going over purchasing procedures for their overseas suppliers with Jason. He was easy to work with—his humour and quick wit providing the perfect distraction from the stress of the day. Every time they found themselves alone, Daniel would tease her about Jason's apparent interest, and she'd laugh it off, pretending it didn't affect her.

To Ashley's relief, Beau left the office before lunch and didn't return for the rest of the day. By five o'clock, Daniel had also wrapped up for the day, leaving

Ashley and Jason to finish their work. As they sorted through paperwork and shut down their computers, Jason suddenly caught her off guard.

"Ashley, would you consider going out to dinner with me sometime?"

She smiled, a warm feeling blossoming in her chest at the idea. "I'd love to," she replied, surprised at how much she genuinely liked the thought. She liked Jason more than she'd been willing to admit.

Jason grinned widely. "Great! How about Friday night?"

"That sounds perfect," she said, scribbling her address on a piece of paper before handing it to him.

He glanced at it, nodding. "Thanks. How about I pick you up at six?"

"Sounds good," she agreed, a little spark of excitement igniting inside her. As they wrapped up, she felt lighter than she had in weeks.

Later that evening, after a quiet shower, Ashley slipped into a simple sundress before heading to the kitchen to start dinner. She was just about to serve herself when she realised, she had made extra. Cooking for herself and her father had always been second nature, so she figured she'd save the leftovers for another night.

She set the table for one, but with the thought of dinner with Jason on Friday, she couldn't help but smile to herself. For the first time in a while, the idea of something new—and possibly exciting—felt like a welcome change.

Just as Ashley was about to sit down to eat, there was a knock at the door. Surprised, she opened it to find Beau standing there, casually dressed in black tailored trousers and a white polo shirt, his appearance effortlessly handsome and relaxed.

"Hello," Ashley greeted, masking the shock in her voice with calm composure.

Beau offered a tentative smile, his eyes lingering on hers. "I hope you don't mind. I just wanted to talk to you about something."

Ashley, feeling lighter than she had in weeks—thanks in no small part to Jason's company—stepped aside to let him in. "Okay," she said, her tone warm despite the unease she felt at seeing him again. "I just finished cooking. Would you like some dinner?"

Beau's expression softened, clearly touched by the invitation. "I'd love some. I've really missed your cooking," he said, his voice laced with sincerity.

They moved to the kitchen, and Ashley plated a portion for him, placing it across from her at the table. "Would you like some wine?" she asked, glancing at him as she poured.

"I'd love some," he replied, his smile returning.

Ashley opened a bottle of red wine, pouring them both a glass. As she placed one in front of him, Beau took a sip, his gaze thoughtful as he looked around the room, as if taking in the space that had once been shared between them.

They began to eat, and for a brief moment, the conversation flowed easily. Beau's voice broke through the comfortable silence. "You seem happy today," he observed, his tone curious.

Ashley smiled softly; her mood lifted by the small joy of the moment. "I feel... lighter," she said quietly, her words more vulnerable than she intended.

Beau seemed to notice the shift in her mood, his own expression turning serious. "That's good," he said, but there was an undercurrent of tension in his voice now. "There's something I need to tell you. I've hired a private investigator."

Ashley paused, her fork frozen mid-air, her heart rate picking up as she set it down. She met his eyes, confusion and curiosity welling up.

"The photos are fake, Ashley," Beau continued, his voice steady, though a touch of desperation slipped through. "I'm going to prove it to you. I have to."

Ashley felt her pulse quicken as she processed his words. She stared at him, trying to make sense of it all. "If... and I mean if that's the case," she began, her voice uncertain. "We broke up..."

He finished the sentence for her, his frustration evident. "For no reason. Yes."

Ashley took a slow sip of her wine, trying to digest the weight of his admission, but still, she couldn't quite bring herself to believe him. "Why would someone do that? If you're telling me the truth," she added, the doubt lingering in her voice despite the hope his words sparked.

Beau's gaze was intense, his jaw clenched as he looked at her. "I have some ideas, but I can't prove anything yet."

A sudden thought struck Ashley, and her eyes widened as pieces began to fall into place. "Bruno...? Sarah...?"

Chapter Eleven

Beau didn't say anything at first. He only nodded, his silence heavy with confirmation.

Ashley shot to her feet, the chair scraping loudly across the floor. "That can't be right," she exclaimed, a mixture of disgust and anger surging through her. "Why would anyone do that?" Her voice broke as tears welled in her eyes. The enormity of the betrayal hit her all at once.

Beau stood, stepping toward her, his expression mirroring her own frustration and helplessness. "I don't know," he murmured, his voice thick with emotion. "I can't fathom why anyone would do that. But they did." He stopped in front of her, reaching out as if to offer reassurance, but he didn't know how to fix this.

Ashley looked him in the eye, the storm of emotions swirling within her, and asked with a rawness that broke through her defences, "You're telling me the truth, aren't you?"

Beau held her gaze, his voice unwavering and sincere. "Yes, Ashley. I swear, I would never have done anything like that to you. Ever."

Tears began to spill from Ashley's eyes, the weight of everything—the photos, the lies, the hurt—overwhelming her.

Beau stepped forward, wrapping his arms around her, pulling her into a gentle embrace. She rested her head on his chest, letting the tears fall in silence. He didn't speak. He just held her, offering the kind of comfort only his presence could give.

As the tears slowed, Ashley pulled back, wiping her eyes. Beau didn't resist, allowing her space to gather herself. "This is unbelievable," she whispered, her voice shaky. "I can't process this."

Beau nodded, his gaze softening with understanding. "I know. It's a lot to process, but I promise, I'll get to the bottom of it."

His eyes then fell to the delicate chain around her neck. Gently, he lifted it, pulling the locket from beneath her dress. His fingers brushed against it, and he paused, taking in the sight.

Ashley held her breath, her cheeks flushing.

"You kept the locket," Beau murmured, his voice laced with disbelief. "You still wear it."

She nodded, her face turning a deeper shade of red. "Yes. I only take it off to shower."

A flicker of hope shone in his eyes. He opened the locket, finding the old photos they had taken together still inside. His gaze moved from the pictures back to her, a quiet wonder crossing his features.

"I couldn't let them go," she whispered, her voice soft and vulnerable.

Beau carefully closed the locket, his fingers lingering on it for a moment before he released it. They sat back down, both lost in their thoughts. The conversation resumed only in the soft clink of their silverware, the meal an unspoken acknowledgment of the fragile hope that still lingered between them—a hope that maybe, just maybe, they could find their way back from all this.

They finished their meal in companionable silence, the conversation fading as they both sipped their wine, savouring the warmth of the evening. After a while, Ashley stood to clear the plates, her movements slow as she tried to process everything that had just been revealed. She poured them both more wine, the liquid calming her nerves, before leading Beau into the living room.

They sank into the couch, the quiet stretching between them, both lost in their thoughts. Ashley felt a strange tension in the air, as though they were teetering on the edge of something fragile. It was she who finally spoke, her voice trembling slightly with uncertainty.

"You understand that I'm finding this incredibly hard to accept," she said, her eyes cast downward as she fiddled with her wine glass, unable to meet his gaze.

Beau nodded, his expression soft and understanding. "Yes, I know it's hard. Trust is something that's not easily given, especially after everything that's happened. But I will prove it to you, Ashley. I will make sure you know the truth. And then... then we can leave it behind us." His tone became quieter, almost hopeful. "And maybe, we can move forward."

Ashley's heart fluttered at his words, a mixture of relief and uncertainty battling within her. She raised an eyebrow, her curiosity piqued despite herself. "What do you mean by that?"

Beau set his wine glass down on the coffee table and shifted closer to her, his movements slow and deliberate. He kneeled in front of her, taking her hand gently in his. His eyes searched hers, an earnestness in his gaze that was impossible to ignore.

"I want us to move forward... together," he said, his voice barely above a whisper, his hand still warm against hers.

Ashley's breath caught in her throat, her pulse quickening. She pulled her hand back slightly, her chest tightening. "I don't know if I can do that, Beau."

The hurt in his eyes was undeniable, but there was understanding there too. He sat back on his knees, not pressuring her, just waiting for her to find her way through the whirlwind of emotions that seemed to have taken over both of them. "I know," he said softly. "But once I prove it—once you know that I never lied to you about this—I hope we can talk more about it. And then we'll see where we go."

Ashley's hands trembled as she held her wine glass. Beau gently took it from her hand, setting it on the side table before reaching up to touch her face. His fingers were gentle as he cupped her cheeks, giving her a moment to pull away if she needed. She didn't. She felt drawn to him, despite the fear gnawing at her heart.

His lips met hers softly, a tender kiss that sent a shiver down her spine. When he pulled back, his eyes searched hers, filled with a raw sincerity. "I've never stopped loving you, angel face."

His words cut through the stillness, and tears welled up in Ashley's eyes as the weight of his confession hit her. She blinked rapidly, trying to push them away, but it was impossible. The pain, the longing, the history they shared—all of it rushed back to her in a flood.

Without thinking, Ashley leaned forward, meeting his lips with an urgency that surprised her. It felt like madness, like she was walking a tightrope without a safety net, but she couldn't stop herself. His kiss remained gentle, but she didn't want gentle. She wanted to feel something—anything that could make sense of the chaos inside her. Wrapping her arms around his neck, she pulled him closer, her breath coming faster.

Beau's hands slid around her waist, pulling her in as their kiss deepened. "Angel face," he whispered against her lips, his voice low and husky. His tongue traced the edge of her lips, and she parted them, eager to let him in.

The kiss turned hungry, fierce, as their bodies pressed together, the warmth of each other's closeness igniting something deep inside. Ashley's fingers tangled in his hair, pulling him closer as she lost herself in the kiss. Her heart hammered in her chest, her mind momentarily blank as she drowned in the sensation of him, their breaths mingling, growing faster with the building urgency between them.

But then, something inside her snapped her back to reality. Her chest tightened with panic, and she pulled away from him, her hands pushing against his chest.

"No," she gasped, her voice trembling with desperation. "I can't... I can't do this again."

Beau looked at her, confusion clouding his expression. He hesitated before slowly pulling back, his heart aching as he searched her face. "What's wrong? Did I...?"

Ashley stood quickly, stepping away from him. She wiped her eyes, her breath shaky as she tried to steady herself. "I can't get hurt like that again, Beau. I can't..." Her voice broke, the vulnerability she was trying to hold at bay slipping through. "I can't go through that again. I was broken. And I'm still not healed."

Beau's expression softened with pain, and he rose to his feet, his hands outstretched as though wanting to comfort her but unsure how to. "Ashley, I swear to you, I will never hurt you again," he said, his voice steady, full of conviction. "I never wanted to hurt you in the first place."

Ashley shook her head, taking a few steps back, her heart heavy. "You said that before, Beau. You promised me that. And look what happened." Her words were bitter, but the anger that once fuelled them was now replaced by something far deeper—fear, confusion, and heartbreak.

She turned toward the window, staring out at the darkness, but her thoughts were far from the night outside. Her mind raced with memories of the past, the hurt, the betrayal, and the unanswered questions that continued to gnaw at her.

Beau stood still behind her, regret weighing heavily in the air between them. "I know I hurt you, Ashley," he said softly, his voice a mix of regret and sorrow. "But it wasn't what I wanted. None of this was what either of us wanted."

Ashley turned to face him again, her eyes searching his. "You don't understand," she whispered, her voice fragile. "I was broken. I still don't think I'm healed."

Beau's gaze softened, his own heart aching as he stepped closer, his voice thick with emotion. "I feel the same way, Ashley. I've never stopped thinking about you. I've never stopped loving you."

She shook her head, tears threatening to fall once more. "This... this is too much, Beau," she whispered. "I can't handle this. Not now."

Beau could feel the walls she was putting up, and he stepped closer, his voice soft with urgency. "We belong together, angel face. We always have. I've loved you for eleven years, I'll never stop.

Ashley's eyes filled with emotion; her chest tight with the weight of everything between them. "Please, just stop," she whispered, her voice breaking. "I need time. I can't do this now."

Realising how close she was to her breaking point; Beau softened his approach. "When I have proof… when you see the truth, will you at least talk about us?" His voice carried a quiet plea, the last thread of hope he clung to.

Ashley studied him for a moment, then nodded, her voice steady but full of the burden she carried. "Yes," she replied softly. "But I need to be honest with you. I've just agreed to start seeing someone."

The flicker of hurt in Beau's eyes was brief but undeniable. Before he could say anything, Ashley added, her tone gentle but firm, "I'm not saying this to hurt you. I just want to be upfront with you. I owe you that much."

Beau nodded; his face tight with emotion as he absorbed her words. "Alright," he said quietly, swallowing his pain. "I'll go."

Ashley walked him to the door, the silence between them thick with the weight of everything left unsaid. Just before he left, he leaned in, pressing a soft, lingering kiss to her cheek. For a moment, they stayed like that, as if trying to hold on to something that was slipping through their fingers. Then, with one final glance, Beau stepped out the door, leaving Ashley standing alone in the quiet, her heart a storm of conflicting emotions she wasn't sure how to navigate.

Ashley woke up early, her sleep restless and fractured. She had barely closed her eyes before her mind started racing, replaying every word of her conversation with Beau. If he was telling the truth—that someone, maybe Bruno or Sarah, had faked those photographs—then that would mean years of unnecessary pain. But what if the photographs were real? What if he'd lied? Why would Beau lie about something so important? The uncertainty gnawed at her, pulling her in every direction.

Frustrated with herself, she sat up in bed, gripping her sheets tightly. "Just stop overthinking it already!" she muttered under her breath. Her heart thudded in her chest, but she couldn't find a way to quiet her mind.

She dragged herself out of bed and into the bathroom, the cold water of the shower helping to clear her head, though the questions still lingered, stubbornly refusing to let go. After dressing, she grabbed a quick breakfast and drove to work, the early morning fog still hanging in the air as she navigated the empty streets. The silence in her car gave her space to think—too much space. By the time she pulled into the office parking lot, her thoughts had only gotten more tangled.

She arrived before anyone else, the building still quiet as she stepped inside. She grabbed a coffee from the break room, trying to find some semblance of comfort in the simple routine. Settling at her desk, she opened her emails but couldn't focus. Her mind kept circling back to Beau. The idea that he could have been telling the truth about those photographs, about the manipulation behind them, was a concept she wasn't sure she could accept. What if she had let her bitterness cloud her judgment for years?

"Ashley, you're here bright and early!" Jason's cheerful voice broke through her thoughts as he walked in, wearing his usual morning grin.

She managed a faint smile in response, looking up from her desk. "Morning," she replied, her tone weary. "Early, yes. Bright? Not so much."

Jason gave her a concerned look, his eyes softening as he noticed the exhaustion in her expression. "Rough night?"

"You could say that," Ashley sighed, rubbing her temples as if trying to ease away the weight of it all.

Jason's gaze softened further, but he quickly tried to lighten the mood. "Are we still on for tonight?" he asked, though there was an undercurrent of something else in his tone—perhaps curiosity, or concern.

Just as she was about to answer, the door to the office opened, and Beau walked in. He froze for a moment, his eyes landing on Ashley, and something flickered across his face—hurt, confusion, maybe even a little resignation. But just as quickly, it was masked by a practiced neutrality.

"Morning," he said, his voice tight but even.

Ashley felt her cheeks flush, her heart skipping in her chest. "Morning," she replied softly, almost as if the simple greeting was more of a plea than anything else.

Jason didn't miss the exchange, raising an eyebrow as he studied them both. "Morning," he added, his gaze shifting between Ashley and Beau with quiet curiosity.

Beau gave a tight, strained smile before retreating into his office, closing the door behind him with a soft click.

Jason turned to Ashley, a knowing look in his eyes. "Is everything okay between you two?" he asked, his tone gentle but probing.

Ashley forced a smile, trying to maintain some semblance of normalcy. "Yeah, all good," she said, though the words felt hollow, a lie even to herself.

Jason seemed to sense the tension but didn't press further. "Alright, but if you ever need to talk, you know where to find me. I'm a pretty good listener."

She gave him a small, grateful smile. "Thanks—I might take you up on that."

As the hours passed, the office grew busier, and Ashley tried her best to keep herself focused on work. The day flew by in a blur of paperwork, phone calls, meetings, and the occasional burst of laughter from the team. Still, she couldn't shake the unease swirling inside her. Every time she caught sight of Beau, her thoughts went back to their conversation, to the things he had said, to the things she still wasn't sure she could believe.

Before she knew it, the clock struck four, and Jason glanced over at her from his desk.

"Six o'clock still good?" he asked, his voice light, though there was a hint of anticipation in his eyes.

"Absolutely," Ashley replied with a smile, though it didn't quite reach her eyes. "I'd better get going—I'll see you then."

As Jason left for the day, Ashley took a deep breath, trying to steady herself. She wasn't sure what she was hoping for tonight—an escape, maybe, or the clarity she hadn't been able to find in the chaos of the past few days. But whatever it was, she needed something to break the tension that seemed to have taken root inside her.

She gathered her things and headed for the door, determined to put the doubts in her mind on hold, at least for a few hours. What she needed right now wasn't answers—it was space.

Chapter Twelve

Ashley arrived home shortly after; her mind still tangled in thoughts from the evening. She needed to unwind, to clear the mental fog that had settled over her all day. Deciding to indulge herself, she ran a warm bath, allowing the steam and soothing water to ease away the tension in her muscles. The quiet of her home, combined with the soft scent of lavender from the bath salts, helped calm her mind—though the doubts still lingered in the back of her thoughts.

Afterward, she emerged from the bathroom feeling refreshed and more grounded. She began the process of styling her long hair, pulling it up into a sleek French twist. A touch of makeup to enhance her features followed—subtle but enough to feel put-together. She slipped into a cream silk pantsuit, the fabric draping effortlessly over her frame. Black heels completed the look, with a sleek black purse as the finishing touch. As she caught her reflection in the mirror, she couldn't help but pause, surprised at how good she looked. She hadn't expected to feel so confident, but the polished image staring back at her was a welcome reminder of her strength, even in uncertain times.

At exactly six o'clock, there was a knock at her door. She took one last look in the mirror, steadying herself before opening it. Jason stood there, his eyes lighting up as they met hers.

"Wow, you look amazing," he said, his voice tinged with genuine admiration.

Ashley felt her cheeks warm, a smile tugging at her lips. "Thank you."

"Ready to go?" Jason asked, his tone light and eager.

"Yes," she answered, locking the door behind her before stepping out into the evening air. Jason opened the passenger door for her, and she slid into the seat, fastening her seatbelt. He did the same on the driver's side before starting the car and pulling out of the driveway.

"So, where are we headed?" Ashley asked, her curiosity piqued.

"Hope you're in the mood for seafood," Jason replied with a grin.

"I love seafood," she said, her smile widening at the thought. She could already imagine the fresh taste of the ocean, and it felt like the perfect way to unwind.

Fifteen minutes later, they entered an elegant seafood restaurant, its ambiance soft and intimate. The low hum of conversation mixed with the clink of glasses and silverware, creating a warm, inviting atmosphere. They were led to a secluded, candlelit table set for two in the corner, far from the bustle of the main dining room.

"This is beautiful," Ashley commented, glancing around, taking in the refined décor. "I've never been here before."

Jason smiled, clearly pleased with her reaction. "I'm glad I could bring you somewhere new."

The waiter arrived promptly, handing them menus before asking, "What would you like to drink?"

"I'll have a glass of Chardonnay," Ashley answered.

"I'll have the same, thanks," Jason added.

After the waiter returned with their drinks, they placed their orders. Ashley took a small sip of her wine, letting the crisp, refreshing taste linger before turning back to Jason.

"So, tell me about yourself, Jason," she asked, leaning in slightly with a curious smile.

Jason returned her smile, clearly enjoying the conversation. "Alright. I'm an only child—my parents live in New York, and they're both doctors."

"I'm surprised you didn't follow in their footsteps," Ashley remarked, her brow furrowing slightly.

He chuckled. "No way—I can't stand the sight of blood."

"Really?" Ashley laughed, clearly amused.

"Yes, really," Jason grinned. "I wanted to help people, but I figured I could do that without the whole 'blood and guts' thing."

Ashley couldn't help but laugh, enjoying the easy back-and-forth. "So, how did you end up working for Beau?"

"I started working for him about four years ago, right after his IT company took off," Jason explained. "I've been helping with some of his other ventures since then."

"And how did you end up with this assignment?" Ashley asked, intrigued.

Jason shrugged, a playful look in his eyes. "Beau asked me to take it on. He said it was important."

Ashley tilted her head, studying him for a moment. "You seem like a really sharp guy. Honestly, I feel like your talents are wasted running a furniture company."

"I was surprised too," Jason admitted with a laugh. "But Beau said it was important, so I agreed. Plus, we're usually based in New York, so Boston's a bit of a change for me."

"Do you like it here?" she asked as their appetisers arrived.

"It's different," Jason said, taking a bite of his dish. "A lot quieter than what I'm used to, but I don't mind it."

Ashley chuckled. "Give it time—you'll probably get bored here."

Jason raised an eyebrow. "Maybe, but I don't mind the slower pace for now."

As they ate, the conversation shifted. Jason asked, "So, now that your father's company has been sold, what's next for you?"

Ashley sighed, pushing a bite of her food around her plate. "Honestly? I have no idea. I don't have any family left, but my best friend is like family to me. I was thinking about travelling for a while, but Kelly's pregnant, and she might need me around."

"That's Daniel's wife, right?" Jason confirmed, his expression softening.

"Yeah," Ashley nodded, her smile warm as she spoke about Kelly. "We've known each other since high school. She's been there for me through both my parents' deaths and…" Ashley's voice faltered as the weight of the words hit her. "And my breakup with Beau."

Jason leaned forward slightly, his gaze gentle. "Daniel mentioned you two have some history. Sounds like it was rough."

"You could say that," Ashley replied, her tone darkening. "Unfortunately, it's all been dredged up again." She paused, glancing down at her plate. "I really don't understand why Beau bought the company."

"I don't know either," Jason said, taking a sip of his wine. "He did mention it was important to him, but he didn't elaborate."

Ashley let out a quiet sigh. "Enough about Beau," she said softly, eager to shift the focus away from the painful past.

Jason nodded in understanding. "Alright."

The waiter arrived with their main courses, and they both fell into a comfortable silence, savouring the flavours of their meal. As they ate, Ashley hesitated before asking, "Are you close to your parents?"

Jason's expression softened. "Not really. Doctors work long hours, and I had nannies growing up." He grimaced slightly. "It sounds like you were very close to yours."

Ashley smiled gently. "Yes, I was. My mother drowned when we were on a family vacation when I was fourteen."

Jason's face changed, empathy flooding his expression. "Oh, that's terrible. That must have been very hard."

Ashley's smile was tinged with sadness. "Yes," she whispered, her voice tight. "It devastated my father. We were all very close, but dad and I became even closer after my mom died."

He regarded her carefully, his voice soft. "What happened to your father?"

Ashley's gaze dropped briefly, the pain of the memory flashing across her face. She took a slow breath before answering, her voice thick with emotion. "He came home from work one day. I greeted him at the door, and he kissed me on the cheek. Then, all of a sudden, he collapsed in my arms. He died of a massive heart attack." A tear escaped, slipping down her cheek. "It was very quick."

Jason reached across the table, gently taking her hand. "I'm so sorry."

Ashley dabbed her eyes with her napkin, her voice barely above a whisper. "Sorry."

Jason shook his head. "Don't be. I envy what you and your father had. You were lucky."

Ashley met his gaze, her eyes distant for a moment before her smile softened. "I know," she said quietly. "I was."

He squeezed her hand before releasing it, sitting back in his chair. "Have you lived here your whole life?" he asked.

Ashley smiled faintly. "Yes, I've never left the U.S. That's one of the reasons I've been thinking about travelling."

Jason's interest piqued. "Where would you like to go?"

Her smile widened. "The Greek islands would be my first stop. Have you been?"

"I have, actually," Jason said with a nostalgic look. "It's absolutely beautiful there."

The evening continued with easy conversation, filled with laughter, and shared stories of places they had both visited. After dessert, Jason drove Ashley home, and they lingered for a moment outside her door.

"Would you like to come in for coffee?" Ashley asked, her voice warm.

"That would be lovely," Jason replied, his eyes lighting up.

Inside, Ashley kicked off her shoes and made coffee, then they settled into the cozy living room. Jason glanced around, taking in the space. "This is a big house for just one person," he remarked. "Are you planning to keep it?"

Ashley sighed softly as she took a sip of her coffee. "I've thought about selling it, but… I'm not ready to let go of it yet."

"A lot of memories here, I take it?" he asked gently.

Ashley smiled, her eyes distant. "Yes, a lot of memories."

Jason asked carefully, "How long were you with Beau?"

Ashley was momentarily caught off guard by the question. Her eyes flickered downward as she gathered her thoughts, hesitant to dive into the past. "I met him when I was sixteen," she began, her voice softening with the memory. "We started dating when I was eighteen, but after high school, I went off to college for four years. We broke up during that time." She exhaled, the weight of those years lingering. "When I came back, we reconnected and picked things up where we left off. Then, a few months later, he asked me to marry him." She paused, the memory of that moment bittersweet. "We were only engaged for two months before…"

Jason's voice was gentle but steady as he finished the sentence for her, "He cheated on you."

Ashley blinked, a wave of shock crossing her face. She hadn't expected him to be so direct. "Wow, Daniel really has told you a lot," she said, forcing a small smile, though there was an ache behind it.

Jason nodded, his expression sincere. "He knew I was interested in you," he said plainly. "And from what he told me, I can't understand why anyone would hurt you."

Ashley's eyes widened, a little surprised by his openness. "Oh," she said, taken aback.

Jason leaned forward, his tone earnest as he added, "You're a beautiful woman, Ashley. You're not just kind and smart, but you're also independent and strong. I don't know why anyone in their right mind would cheat on someone like you." He paused, a thoughtful expression crossing his face. "Honestly, I can't figure out why you're still single."

Ashley blinked, her heart stirring with a mix of emotions. "Wow, you really don't mince words, do you?"

"I prefer to be honest," Jason replied, shrugging slightly. "It's not something I'm good at avoiding."

Ashley let out a soft laugh, an appreciative gleam in her eyes. "I really admire that. It's such a rare quality these days."

They shared a brief moment of understanding before Jason placed his empty coffee cup on the table and stood up. His movements were deliberate, purposeful as he crossed the room, coming to a stop just in front of Ashley. He reached out, taking her hands gently into his as she set her own cup aside. With a quiet strength, he pulled her to her feet.

His voice was low, a subtle intensity in his words. "Now, I need to ask you something."

Ashley's heart seemed to skip a beat as she whispered, her breath catching slightly, "Yes?"

Jason's eyes softened, a faint smile tugging at the corners of his lips. He took a deep breath before asking, "Can I kiss you?"

Ashley's response came without hesitation, simple but full of meaning. "Yes."

Jason's grip on her hands tightened slightly as he leaned in, his body inching closer to hers. His lips brushed against hers, soft and tentative at first, before a growing warmth spread between them. Ashley leaned into the kiss, her fingers curling against his chest as she felt the steady beat of his heart. As the kiss deepened, Jason's arms slid around her waist, pulling her closer, the connection between them intensifying. For a moment, it felt like time stood still.

Ashley's palms rested against his chest, her breath mingling with his. She could feel the quiet rhythm of his heartbeat under her touch, grounding her in the moment. When they finally pulled apart, Jason's forehead gently rested against hers, his eyes darkened with desire and something deeper. "Wow," he murmured, his voice thick with emotion. "I should go, before I can't leave."

Ashley smiled softly, though her heart felt a little more conflicted than before. She reluctantly pulled back from him, her voice steady but warm as she said, "Thank you for a lovely evening."

Jason nodded, stepping toward the front door, a lingering smile still on his face. "I had a great time too," he said as he paused, looking over his shoulder. "I hope we can do it again sometime."

Ashley opened the door, her hand resting on the handle as she stood in the threshold, her voice soft but sincere. "I'd like that."

Jason turned back, his eyes locking with hers as he stepped closer, leaning in to press one last, soft kiss to her lips before pulling away. "Goodnight," he said with a warmth that seemed to linger between them.

"Goodnight," she whispered as she watched him step out into the night, the door clicking closed behind him.

As the echo of his footsteps faded, Ashley's smile faded too. She gathered the empty coffee cups and made her way to the kitchen, her mind spinning with a thousand thoughts. She absently washed the cups, her fingers tracing the edges of the ceramic as if searching for clarity. Jason's kiss had been gentle, tender—nice even—but it hadn't made her heart race the way Beau's kisses used to. Should she pursue something with Jason? The thought was tempting, but it felt uncertain, like she was moving too quickly. Her emotions were still tangled up in the past, in Beau.

She set the clean cups aside, a sigh slipping from her lips as she shook her head. Everything felt so complicated lately, and she didn't know if she was ready to unravel those tangled threads. Would she ever be ready? She leaned against the counter, her mind a whirl of questions she didn't have answers to.

Chapter Thirteen

Ashley's mind was a whirlwind of emotions. The photographs, could she rekindle her relationship with Beau? As much as she tried to convince herself that she was done, the pull she felt toward him remained undeniable. That same magnetism that had drawn her to him all those years ago was still there, as strong as ever. But what did that mean for her now? Was she willing to risk it all, to dive back into the whirlwind of passion and pain? Or was it time to walk away for good?

The thought gnawed at her as she climbed the stairs toward her bedroom, the weight of uncertainty heavy on her shoulders. She couldn't shake the feeling that she was on the precipice of a decision, but she didn't know what the right choice was.

Then, a knock at the door stopped her in her tracks.

It was nearly eleven o'clock—who could be visiting at this hour? Her heart began to race, the sense of unease growing with each passing second. She turned slowly, her mind already racing with possibilities. With a mixture of dread and anticipation, she descended the stairs, her steps slow and deliberate. As she reached the door, she paused, glancing through the window beside it.

Her breath caught.

Beau stood there, looking up at the window, his expression unreadable but intense. Her heart skipped a beat as she hesitated. Her hand hovered over the door handle, torn between wanting to see him and knowing that letting him in could make everything more complicated.

But in the end, she couldn't resist. With a deep sigh, she opened the door.

The moment their eyes met, everything else seemed to fade away. Beau stepped forward, his gaze locking onto hers with a mixture of longing and desperation. A soft exhale escaped his lips as he took in her appearance. "You look beautiful," he said, his voice low, almost reverent.

Ashley felt a rush of warmth spread through her chest, though she quickly masked it with caution. "Beau, you shouldn't be here," she murmured, her voice barely above a whisper.

His eyes softened, but there was an urgency in his movements as he stepped inside. Before she could protest, he closed the door behind him, locking it swiftly. His hands were on her before she could say another word, pulling her into his arms and pressing her firmly against him. The intensity of his touch sent a shock through her system, but it wasn't just physical—it was emotional too, the weight of everything they'd shared before coming crashing back into the present.

"You look stunning, angel face," he whispered, his lips dangerously close to hers.

Ashley's heart pounded in her chest, her breath catching. "You shouldn't be here, Beau," she repeated, though there was less conviction in her words now. The magnetic pull between them was too strong.

Beau's hand gently cupped her cheek, his thumb brushing over her skin before moving to her hair. His fingers worked the delicate knot that had held her hair in place, and it tumbled around her shoulders in soft waves. His touch was deliberate, slow, as if savouring every moment of their closeness. "You still want me, don't you, angel face?" he murmured, his voice low and velvet soft. "Because I want you. I've never stopped wanting you."

Ashley's breath hitched. She tried to protest, but her voice faltered. "Beau…"

He leaned in closer, his lips brushing against hers in a teasing, tantalising motion. "Tell me to leave," he challenged, his breath mingling with hers. "Say the words, and I'll go."

But Ashley couldn't do it. Her body was betraying her, urging him closer. Her eyes locked with his, a silent plea. She didn't want him to leave. All she wanted was for him to kiss her.

"Kiss me, angel face," Beau whispered, his words thick with desire.

Without hesitation, Ashley closed the distance between them. Her lips met his in a soft, eager kiss, the connection instant and electric. Beau's breath hitched at the sensation, and he groaned softly, the sound filled with need. His kiss deepened, becoming urgent, a silent expression of everything unspoken between them. Ashley's heart raced in her chest, her hands trembling slightly as they slid up his neck, pulling him closer.

As the kiss deepened, Ashley's arms wrapped around his neck, fingers threading through his hair. Their breaths became quicker, more desperate, the kiss a raw, passionate dance of hunger and familiarity. Every movement felt like a culmination of everything they had been—of everything they had yet to resolve.

When Beau's tongue gently sought entry, Ashley parted her lips, allowing him to deepen the kiss. A soft moan escaped her throat as the intensity between them grew. Her fingers tangled further in his hair, her body pressing against his as if she could melt into him.

The kiss felt timeless—like it had been waiting to happen for so long. In that moment, the world outside no longer existed. It was just the two of them, locked in this heated connection, the past and future lost in the heat of their embrace.

Beau finally pulled back, his lips trailing a path of soft kisses down her neck. "You have no idea how much I want you, angel face, we have waited so long," he murmured against her skin, his voice rough with desire. His lips burned a trail of fire down her throat before returning to her mouth, where their kiss deepened again, slower this time, each movement deliberate and filled with an aching need.

Ashley's mind swirled in a haze of desire and uncertainty. She couldn't tell if it was love, lust, or something else entirely that kept pulling her back into his orbit. But at that moment, she didn't care.

Beau lifted Ashley effortlessly into his arms, never breaking the kiss, as though the world around them had dissolved. He moved toward the stairs, his lips still capturing hers in a fervent embrace. As they reached her bedroom, he set her gently on her feet, pulling away just enough to look into her eyes.

His fingers slid into her long hair at the nape of her neck, drawing her head closer, as he lowered his mouth to her lips again, this time more tenderly, cupping her face with his other hand. Their lips met in a soft, almost reverent kiss, yet it was charged with a building intensity. Desire flooded through them both, and without thinking, Ashley's arms wrapped around his neck, pulling him closer again, her kiss becoming deeper, more urgent, much more passionate.

The heat between them exploded, a wild, fiery surge that left Ashley breathless and exhilarated. His lips were demanding, possessive in their fervour, and with every movement, she felt a tremor of longing that swept through her entire body. She could feel the hard press of his body against hers, and the world around them faded into nothingness as they lost themselves in the heat of the moment.

Beau gently broke the kiss, his lips trailing a path down to her ear. His breath was warm against her skin as he whispered softly, "Tell me you want me, angel face."

Ashley's breath hitched, a moan escaping her lips as she replied, "I want you… please, Beau."

His body trembled with the intensity of her words. "I want you too, sweetheart. God, I want you so much." His lips moved along her neck, his kisses hot and insistent. As he spoke, his hands slid down her body, cupping her bottom and pulling her tightly against him. She could feel the undeniable evidence of his desire pressing against her, the heat and urgency unmistakable.

Beau settled onto the edge of the bed, guiding Ashley into his lap, his lips finding hers again with renewed passion. As they kissed, his hands moved to the buttons of her blouse, slowly undoing each one until the fabric slipped open, revealing the lace beneath. His hands found her breast, kneading gently, his thumb grazing over her taut nipple through the lace.

"Beau, please," she whispered, a plea wrapped in a soft moan.

He slid his hands around her back, unclasping her bra and letting it fall away. His lips traced a heated path down her throat, lingering in the hollow between her collarbone before dipping lower. His mouth found her breast, his tongue circling her sensitive peak before pulling it gently between his lips, licking and sucking with an exquisite tenderness.

"Oh, Beau, please," she breathed, her fingers tightening in his hair, her head falling back.

Against her skin, he murmured urgently, "You're so beautiful... you taste incredible."

Beau's mouth moved to her other breast, his tongue swirling over her sensitive peak before drawing it into the moist warmth of his mouth. As his lips worshiped her, his hand slid down her stomach, deftly unfastening her pants. He slipped his hand inside, finding her soft, heated centre.

"You're so wet, angel face," he murmured against her breast, his voice thick with desire.

"Yes, Beau... yes," she gasped, her body responding to his touch.

His fingers glided through her slickness until he found the firm bud of her pleasure. He circled it gently, sending waves of sensation radiating through her.

"Beau..." she whispered, her voice trembling with need and anticipation as she cradled his head against her.

"Yes, angel, just like that," he murmured, his lips trailing from her breast to the curve of her elegant neck. His fingers moved with perfect precision, their touch setting every nerve alight. The tension within her spiralled higher, coiling tightly until she was perched on the brink.

Then, like a flood breaking through, a wave of intense pleasure crashed over her, leaving her breathless and quivering in his arms.

She cried out his name, voice trembling with pleasure. "Beau... yes."

"Angel face, you're so responsive—you're driving me crazy," he whispered before claiming her mouth in a deep, passionate kiss that stole her breath away.

With a sense of urgency, she tugged at his shirt, eager to feel his skin beneath her fingertips. He pulled his T-shirt over his head, and her hands spread across his chest, exploring every inch. "Oh, yes," she whispered, revelling in the warmth of him.

Beau gently lifted her to her feet, sliding her pants down her long legs. Then, he eased her blouse off her shoulders, and she stood before him, bare and beautiful. His gaze was full of awe as he whispered, "You're so beautiful, angel face."

He pulled back the covers and lifted her, laying her gently onto the bed. Quickly, he shed his jeans and underwear before joining her, stretching out beside her. His hand continued its gentle worship of her breast, his thumb brushing over her taut nipple, as his mouth possessed hers in a kiss that grew deeper, more intense with each shared breath.

Slowly, he began a reverent journey down her body, his lips leaving a heated trail. Pausing at her breasts, teasing one with tender, lingering kisses, his tongue circling and flicking over her sensitive skin before moving to the other. Her breath quickened, anticipation building with each movement. His mouth traced lower, gliding over her flat stomach, until he reached the sensitive skin at the apex of her thighs.

Gently, he parted her legs, his warm breath teasing her before his mouth found her core, his tongue exploring her folds with a rhythm that left her trembling.

"Beau... please," she gasped, clutching at his hair as he deepened his ministrations.

He moved with exquisite precision, licking and sucking, sending waves of pleasure through her. She arched beneath him, her breathing quickening as he pushed her closer to the edge. "You taste like the sweetest honey," he murmured against her skin, his voice thick with desire, before his lips returned to their intoxicating rhythm.

With one final stroke, she shattered, a powerful release surging through her as she cried out his name. He didn't stop, savouring every moment until her shudders faded and she lay breathless and sated beneath him.

He trailed soft, lingering kisses along her body as he slowly moved up, settling between her thighs. He took her mouth in a deep, searing kiss, his voice a low murmur against her lips. "Tell me you want me, angel face."

Her breath was shaky. "I want you, Beau. Please... now."

A soft, desperate groan escaped him as he positioned himself at her entrance, then with one firm thrust, he entered her.

Ashley gasped, a sharp pain catching her by surprise. "Oh!" she cried, her voice filled with both shock and discomfort.

Beau froze instantly, his gaze searching her face. "Ashley! You're a virgin?" he asked gently, concern etching his features.

Tears sprang to her eyes, and Beau noticed immediately. His expression softened as he gently wiped them away with tender kisses. "Don't cry, angel face," he whispered. "It's okay, sweetheart."

He pressed gentle kisses along her face, his soothing touch helping her relax. When he felt her ease beneath him, he slowly began to move, pulling out just a little before easing back in. Her eyes flew open, a soft gasp escaping her lips, surprised at the sensation. "Oh…"

Beau withdrew slightly, then eased back in, repeating the movement with a gentle rhythm that deepened each time. "Wrap your legs around me, angel," he murmured urgently.

She did, tightening her hold around him. "That's it," he whispered, his movements becoming more assured as he guided her through the rhythm. "Beau… please… yes," she breathed, her voice filled with longing.

He quickened his pace, each motion drawing them closer, until her body instinctively matched his rhythm, moving with him in perfect harmony.

Her fingers dug into his back. "Yes… please, Beau," she gasped.

He picked up his pace, driving them both higher with each movement until she shattered in a powerful climax, her body trembling beneath him. Feeling her release, he let himself go, his own pleasure cresting as he stiffened and released a deep, low groan, surrendering to the exquisite moment.

As their breathing gradually steadied, Beau rolled onto his back, pulling Ashley with him so she lay draped over his chest. He kissed her deeply, a slow, lingering kiss that conveyed everything words couldn't.

"That was amazing, angel face," he murmured against her lips.

"Mmm," she replied, too blissfully exhausted to say more, a satisfied smile spreading across her face.

Ashley drifted into a deep, blissful sleep. Beau pulled the sheet over them, pressing a gentle kiss to the top of her head.

The realisation that she had been a virgin made his mind reel—at twenty-seven. But more than anything, he felt an overwhelming sense of privilege and protectiveness. She had trusted him, and he knew in his heart that he didn't want to let her go, ever. She was his, always had been, and he would cherish her.

Chapter Fourteen

Ashley stirred, lying on her side with a heavy arm draped around her waist and the warmth of a body pressed close against her back. Memories of the night before flooded over her, bringing a blush to her cheeks.

Beau, sensing her wakefulness, murmured, "Good morning, angel face." His hand slid slowly up her stomach, settling over her breast.

A shiver of desire sparked at his touch. "Morning, Beau," she replied softly.

Beau's fingers kneaded her breast, pinching its peak gently between two fingers.

"Oh…" she gasped, instinctively trying to pull away and get out of bed.

But Beau slid his other arm beneath her, catching her other breast with a soft, possessive grip. "Where do you think you're going?" he murmured, his voice low and teasing.

Ashley's mind fogged with pleasure, and her resistance melted away as she sank back into the mattress, a soft moan escaping her lips.

Beau's hand drifted from her breast, tracing a slow path down to the apex of her thighs. He pulled her firmly against him, his hard, thick arousal pressing into her firm flesh of her bottom. His fingers slid between her slick folds, expertly finding her most sensitive places, making her breath hitch and her body melt into his touch.

"You're already ready for me, aren't you?" he murmured, his breath warm against her ear as he trailed soft kisses down her neck.

"Yes," she whispered breathlessly, surrendering fully to the sensations he was stirring within her.

He intensified the pressure between her thighs, his other hand still kneading her breast and teasing her hardened nipple. She writhed under his touch, unable to contain the rising wave of sensation.

"Let go, sweetheart," he whispered, his voice coaxing.

"Yes…yes…" she gasped, and finally, a powerful climax tore through her, leaving her breathless and trembling in his arms.

At his urging, she turned in his arms, and he captured her mouth in a searing kiss, full of raw want and passion. Her hands roamed over his chest and down his back, exploring his warmth and strength. Then, to his surprise, she pushed him back onto the bed, straddling him without breaking the kiss.

Slowly, she traced a path from his lips to his ear, then down his neck, her mouth warm and teasing against his skin. She nipped, licked, and sucked her way to his broad chest, savouring every inch. A deep, rumbling groan escaped him, sending a thrill through her as she smiled in satisfaction.

She moved to his nipple, gently sucking and flicking her tongue over it, drawing a low, husky, "Oh yes, angel face," from his lips.

Smiling against his skin, she slowly shifted to the other side, savouring every moan and groan that rumbled up from deep within him as she teased and tasted him.

She kissed her way slowly down his taut stomach, her hands exploring the lines of his hips and the strength of his chest. As she slid her bare breasts down his torso, he trembled beneath her touch, every movement igniting a deeper response in him.

Her hair spilled over his stomach as she wrapped her delicate hand around his thick, solid length, flicking her tongue teasingly over the tip.

"Ashley," he groaned, his voice a low rumble. "You don't have to…"

"Mmm, but I want to," she murmured, meeting his gaze with a hint of mischief. Then, without hesitation, she took him into her mouth, her lips and tongue sending a shudder through him as she began to move.

"Oh angel, yes," he gasped, his voice thick with need.

She responded eagerly, her mouth sliding up and down his velvety skin as she sucked and licked, savouring every reaction. His moans filled the air, spurring her on, each sound urging her to take him deeper, driving them both to the edge.

His hand threaded through her hair, holding her for a moment before pulling her up. "Enough," he murmured, his voice strained.

Ashley looked at him, a hint of disappointment in her eyes. "Why?"

"I need to be inside you… now," he breathed, his desire clear.

Without hesitation, she straddled his hips, positioning him at her entrance. Slowly, she slid down, both of them groaning in ecstasy as they became one, the sensation taking over their senses.

"You feel incredible," he groaned, his voice thick with desire.

She began to move, slowly rising and falling, her body meeting his with each rhythmic thrust. "Oh yes," she breathed, the pleasure building between them.

As she moved, she bent down, capturing his lips in a kiss brimming with passion. His hands gripped her hips, guiding her, his touch a constant reminder of his control. The kiss deepened, their bodies moving in perfect harmony.

Then, sitting up, she quickened her pace, her own hands finding his, her breaths ragged. His hands moved to her breasts, kneading and worshiping her as she pushed herself harder, faster. She could feel the tension coiling tighter inside her, the edge of release close.

With a final cry, throwing her head back, she shattered, her body quaking in ecstasy. As she let go, he took full control, his grip on her hips tightening as he thrust into her a few more times before his own climax overtook him, his release coming in powerful waves.

"Ashley," he gasped, his breath catching as his arms enveloped her. He slid his hands up and down her back, the motion soothing and gentle, grounding her.

"I didn't know it could feel like this," she whispered, her voice filled with awe.

He pressed a soft kiss to her temple, his tone tender. "Only with you, angel face."

And he was right—he had never experienced the same depth of satisfaction and pleasure with another woman. What he felt with her was unlike anything he'd known before.

"Ashley," he said softly, his voice tinged with uncertainty. "I love you."

She stiffened in his arms, and he felt the hesitation in her. She didn't look at him, nor did she move from where she lay on his chest.

"Ashley…" He sighed, his words earnest. "Don't say anything. I know you need time, but I had to tell you—I love you. I've never stopped loving you."

"I'm not ready, Beau," she whispered against his chest, her voice trembling. "I'm scared."

He tightened his arms around her, his grip reassuring. "I know, Ashley. And I'll be patient. I promise."

"Thank you," she murmured, her voice barely audible as she slowly got up from his embrace and walked toward the bathroom, tears welling in her eyes.

Ashley turned on the shower, stepping under the warm spray. The water cascaded over her, soothing not just the physical ache that lingered in her muscles, but also the emotional weight that had been pressing down on her chest for days. She closed her eyes for a moment, letting the sensation of the water against her skin calm her racing thoughts, wishing she could wash away the confusion and uncertainty that had been plaguing her heart.

After rinsing her body clean, she reached for the shampoo bottle and carefully lathered it into her hair. The rhythm of her actions felt meditative, a small reprieve from the chaos of her mind. As she rinsed her hair and turned off the water, she stepped out of the shower and wrapped a towel around her damp hair, using another to dry her skin. The plush softness of the robe hanging on the back of the door felt like a comfort as she slipped it on, tying the belt snugly around her waist. The familiar sensation of the fabric against her skin grounded her, offering a small measure of peace.

When she stepped back into the bedroom, Beau was sitting on the edge of the bed, his gaze lifting to meet hers. He extended a hand toward her, his eyes full of something she couldn't quite read. For a moment, she hesitated, unsure of what to do with the unspoken tension that hung between them. But then, something inside her softened, and she walked toward him, placing her hand in his.

Without a word, Beau wrapped his arms around her waist, pulling her into him and resting his head gently on her breast. Instinctively, Ashley's fingers began to thread through his hair, her touch slow and soothing, offering him a comfort she couldn't fully explain. There was something in the way he fit so easily against her, as though they had always belonged in this quiet, tender moment.

The silence stretched between them until Ashley finally broke it. "You go shower," she said softly. "I'll make us some breakfast."

Beau looked up at her, his gaze intense, yet softened by something deeper. Without a word, he stood, pulling her into a kiss—gentle, but with a possessiveness that made her heart race. She melted into him, savouring the closeness, before he pulled away, his eyes lingering on hers as if he wanted to say something more, but didn't. Then, without another glance, he turned and made his way into the ensuite to take his shower.

A few minutes later, after finishing his shower and getting dressed, Beau made his way downstairs. The smell of breakfast wafted through the air, and he found Ashley standing at the stove, busy finishing the meal. Her back was to him, and he couldn't help but admire the way she moved, her quiet confidence radiating in the simplest of tasks. Without a word, he approached her from behind, sliding his arms around her waist and pulling her gently against him. He nuzzled her hair aside, placing a soft kiss on the side of her neck.

"That smells wonderful," he murmured, his voice low and warm, carrying a sense of admiration. "And so do you."

Ashley turned in his arms, smiling up at him. She wrapped her arms around his neck, her cheeks flushing a soft pink. "Thank you," she whispered, her voice barely above a breath.

Beau chuckled softly, his fingers brushing gently against her skin. "I love how you blush. I'm glad you never grew out of it."

Her smile deepened, her heartwarming at the familiarity of his words. She kissed him gently on the lips. "Sit, I'll serve," she said with a lightness in her voice.

Reluctantly, he released her, watching as she moved to prepare their breakfast. He took a seat at the table, eyes never leaving her as she placed two plates in front of them, one for him and one for herself. She poured them each a cup of coffee, the rich aroma filling the room.

"You still drink it black?" she asked with a teasing smile.

"Yes, thank you," he replied, feeling a warmth spread through him at the way she remembered even the smallest details about him. It was the kind of attention he had always appreciated, the little things that made him feel seen in ways he hadn't known he needed.

"This looks amazing," he said, eagerly eyeing the food. "I'm starving."

She laughed, shaking her head in amusement. "You're always starving," she teased, setting down her own plate and taking a seat across from him.

"And you used to eat like a bird, if I remember correctly," he said, grinning as he dug into his breakfast.

They both laughed, the sound of it filling the room, easy and comfortable. It felt like old times, when things had been simpler, when they hadn't yet tangled themselves up in the complexities of life.

"With you around, no food ever went to waste," she added with a playful wink, cutting into her own meal.

They ate in comfortable silence, savouring the food, the coffee, and the shared space between them. The conversation was effortless, just a quiet rhythm of familiar exchanges that seemed to fit like a well-worn song. When Beau finished his plate, he glanced over at Ashley's, noticing that she hadn't touched the last bit of her food.

"Are you going to eat that?" he asked with a teasing smile.

Laughing, Ashley slid the plate toward him without a word. He smiled in response, picking up the last bite and finishing it, while she shook her head in amusement.

"Always the same," she said, her voice full of affection.

He grinned, setting down his fork. "Some things never change," he said softly, meeting her gaze across the table, his eyes full of something deeper than mere nostalgia. It was warmth. It was home. And for a moment, the world outside didn't matter.

After they cleaned up, the weight of the morning began to settle in, and for the first time, Ashley felt a creeping unease. She turned to Beau, the question in her eyes before the words slipped out. "What now?" she asked, her voice quiet, laced with uncertainty.

Beau, sensing her shift in mood, took her hand gently in his. Without a word, he led her to the living room, guiding her to the couch. They sat facing one another, the space between them still charged with the intimacy of their morning. His hand rested in hers, warm and steady, as his eyes met hers with a softness that belied the serious tone of his next words.

"I have to ask, angel face," he began, his voice uncharacteristically soft yet steady. "Why were you still a virgin?"

Ashley froze, her cheeks flushing a bright crimson. Her gaze dropped to her lap, her fingers nervously twisting together as embarrassment flooded through her. "Beau…" she murmured, her voice barely audible, full of discomfort.

"Please," he urged, his voice coaxing, a gentle insistence that she couldn't ignore. "Tell me."

The weight of his request hung in the air between them, and after what felt like an eternity, Ashley sighed softly. "You were the only one I've ever had those feelings for," she said, her words faltering. "And I've never been interested in… random sex." Her voice dropped even lower, barely above a whisper, the weight of her confession making her chest tighten.

Beau smiled softly, the warmth in his expression only deepening as he pulled her into his arms. His embrace was a silent promise, full of understanding. "I'm glad," he murmured, his voice full of tenderness.

Ashley pulled back just enough to look at him, confusion clouding her features. "You are?"

"Of course I am," Beau replied, as though the answer was as obvious as breathing. "I feel privileged that you'd trust me with your body—and only me." His words, simple and genuine, melted away the last traces of her anxiety.

Ashley shifted in his embrace; her face still flushed with embarrassment. "Can we not talk about this anymore?" she asked, her voice small, almost apologetic. The conversation had taken a vulnerable turn, and she wasn't sure how much more of herself she could give just yet. She quickly changed the subject, her voice lightening in an attempt to steer the conversation away. "What are you doing today?"

Beau, ever perceptive to her moods, didn't push further. Instead, he smiled, his eyes softening as he responded, "Hopefully spending it with you."

A slight frown creased her forehead as she replied, "I have to babysit Brian tonight. It's Kelly and Daniel's date night."

"Can I stay and help?" Beau offered; his voice laced with sincerity. "He's a nice kid. I wouldn't mind."

Ashley hesitated, her gaze flickering toward the door as if contemplating the possibility. "I suppose," she said, though uncertainty tinged her voice. "I'm not sure how Kelly will feel about it."

Beau's smile dimmed slightly, understanding her hesitation. "Understandable," he replied, trailing off for a moment before his eyes brightened. "Let's go for a drive and see where it leads us. I promise I'll get you home in time for babysitting."

Ashley's curiosity piqued, but she still felt wary. "Okay," she said, her tone cautious yet intrigued.

She changed into a pair of long shorts and a blouse, grabbing a jacket just in case the weather turned cooler. Beau waited patiently for her, his presence calm and steady. When she was ready, they left together the world outside seeming a little less uncertain with each step they took.

Their drive took them toward Lake Winnipesaukee, a place from their past. Beau's hand rested gently on the steering wheel, his thoughts seemingly elsewhere, while Ashley watched the scenery pass by. It wasn't long before they pulled into a parking lot near the Sewall Woods Trail Loop.

"We used to come here every summer, remember?" Ashley asked, a nostalgic smile tugging at her lips as memories of their past filled her mind.

Beau nodded, a soft smile forming on his face. "Yes, I remember. You used to try to race me."

Ashley's laughter was light and carefree as she remembered. "Oh, remember that time I hid in the bushes?" she teased, eyes gleaming with mischief. "You went crazy looking for me."

"You scared the crap out of me," Beau replied, feigning a look of mock worry. "I thought I'd lost you for good."

Ashley smiled to herself, the memory vivid and comforting. "You know, that was the day I knew you loved me."

Beau stopped walking, the words hitting him in a way he hadn't expected. He gently lifted her chin, so she was looking up at him, his expression soft but serious. "Really? You didn't know before that?"

She shook her head, her eyes softening with the weight of the moment. "I knew you liked me, but when I saw the look on your face that day, I just knew. I already loved you, but I wasn't sure if you felt the same way…"

His hand cupped her cheek tenderly, and his voice became steady, almost reverent. "Angel face, I've loved you since you were sixteen."

Ashley's eyes widened in surprise, her breath catching at his admission. "Really?"

Beau nodded, a faraway look in his eyes as he recalled the memory. "Yes. I remember the exact day it happened." He paused, a smile tugging at his lips as he continued. "It was when you played Juliet in the school play. I remember ripping Bruno away from you… I wanted to kill him that day."

Ashley laughed, the sound full of warmth and affection. "That's the day I knew I loved you," she confessed, her voice full of awe.

Beau's heart swelled at the truth in her words, and without another thought, he leaned in and kissed her softly, the kiss tender but full of meaning. "I knew you were too young, so I tried to avoid being alone with you as much as I could," he said, as they resumed walking. "I didn't want to put you in a position where you could get hurt."

Ashley gave him a sidelong glance, her voice teasing. "I noticed that."

He chuckled lowly, the sound warm and familiar. "I was so caught off guard when you asked me to take you to prom. But I had already talked to your father, so I was relieved when you asked me."

Her curiosity piqued, Ashley couldn't help but ask, "I never did ask—how did Dad take it? You asking me out, I mean."

Beau's expression shifted into one of amusement as he recalled the conversation. "Oh, that was an uncomfortable conversation," he laughed. "I was terrified. I was a grown man, but still, your father was intimidating."

"Why?" she asked, intrigued.

"He was shocked at first, and then I think it all clicked for him," Beau explained, his voice softening. "He said to me that you cared about me a lot. I didn't know that. I knew you liked talking to me, but I didn't know you cared, as he put it."

Ashley smiled, a soft laugh escaping her lips. "Really? I thought I was being too obvious."

Beau shook his head, a smile tugging at his lips. "No, you weren't. But that night at your prom, that's when I started to realise it. I was worried the whole time we dated, knowing you were going off to college soon."

Ashley kicked at the dirt, the memory still fresh in her mind. "Yes, you broke my heart when you ended things."

"I had to, angel face," Beau said earnestly, his tone steady. "You had to experience college to the fullest, to live your life without feeling held back."

Ashley sighed, a wistful smile tugging at her lips. "Ha, ask Kelly. I just pined for you the whole time. And when I did go out with a guy, they actually repulsed me. I thought there was something wrong with me."

Beau's eyes softened with affection as he cupped her face, his voice gentle but full of love. "Don't ever think that. There's nothing wrong with you. You're perfect."

The silence between them was comfortable as they continued walking, the woods around them peaceful and quiet. "Then I came home, and you were with Sarah. I thought I was going to die of a broken heart," Ashley confessed, her voice barely above a whisper.

Beau stopped, his gaze softening with regret. "Sorry, sweetheart. But I can tell you now that was a huge mistake. She was seriously not right for me—she became a little obsessed. I broke it off with her the day we ran into you at the mall. I thought you had moved on, but when I saw how hurt you looked, that's when I thought there was hope for me."

Ashley glanced up at him, a small smile tugging at her lips. "I hadn't moved on... not at all."

Beau smiled, relief flooding through him. They continued their walk, the air between them light and easy, each step a reminder of how far they'd come.

Chapter Fifteen

By the time they finished their walk, it was nearly lunchtime, and both were hungry. They stopped at a small café on the way back and sat down to a simple but pleasant meal. As they ate, Beau's phone buzzed with an incoming call.

"Hello," Beau answered, his voice steady and serious as he listened for a moment. Then, a slow smile spread across his face. "That's fantastic." He glanced down at his watch, eyes lighting up. "Can you meet me at the hotel bar in an hour?" He paused, his smile widening as he listened again. "Perfect, we'll be there." He hung up, still beaming.

Ashley raised an eyebrow, intrigued. "Good news?"

Beau's smile grew, his eyes gleaming with excitement. "I hope so," he replied, his voice laced with anticipation. "All will be explained when we get there."

Beau and Ashley arrived at the hotel and made their way through the dimly lit lobby toward the bar, where a man was waiting. He was middle-aged, slightly balding, and dressed in a plain brown suit that did little to mask the quiet authority he seemed to carry. Despite his unassuming appearance, there was a subtle strength in his posture—an air of someone who knew how to handle delicate matters.

Beau turned to Ashley with a calm, reassuring look. "Ashley Sintaro, this is Dennis Cooper. Dennis, this is Ashley."

Dennis extended his hand with a firm grip, his eyes warm but careful. "Hello, Miss Sintaro."

Ashley hesitated for just a moment; the confusion she'd been feeling on the drive here hung over her like a heavy fog. She shook his hand, offering a polite smile but unable to fully mask her unease. "Hello," she said, her voice quiet but respectful.

Dennis smiled back, his expression steady. "It's good to meet you." Without further preamble, he led them to a secluded table in the bar, where they sat down. The lighting here was softer, more intimate, but Ashley still felt out of place. Dennis slid a folded piece of paper across the table to Beau.

"I think you should read this," Dennis said, his voice businesslike, but there was a hint of something else in his eyes—something that made Ashley's curiosity spike even further.

Beau took the paper without hesitation, his expression serious as he began to read. His eyes flicked over the text quickly, scanning the words with practiced focus. After a moment, he looked up at Dennis, his brow furrowed. "It wasn't hard to find her?"

Dennis gave a slight nod. "No, it wasn't difficult at all. She's married now, with two kids. When I spoke to her, she was... open. Felt a lot of guilt about what she'd done. Took no time at all for her to tell me everything."

Beau's expression softened, a flicker of satisfaction crossing his features. He handed the paper to Ashley, his eyes briefly meeting hers. "You need to read this," he said, his voice quieter now, filled with a kind of resolve.

Ashley took the paper hesitantly, her fingers trembling slightly as she unfolded it. She could feel the weight of the moment pressing on her chest, the anticipation thick in the air. She began to read, her mind racing to process each sentence, each revelation.

Dear Beau,

I hope this letter finds you in a place of understanding. These words are difficult to write, but I feel it is necessary to tell you the truth. My intention is not to excuse my actions but to take full responsibility and provide clarity about what happened on the night of your bucks' night.

Bruno contacted me with a plan to break your engagement with Ashley. At first, I hesitated, but my emotions at the time clouded my judgment, and I foolishly agreed to go along with his scheme.

We first went to where Ashley was celebrating her hen's night with her friends. Bruno approached her under the pretence of congratulating her. Although reluctant, she agreed to step away from the group. While alone, Bruno grabbed her against her will and kissed her. I took a photo of this kiss, but what you didn't see was Ashley's outrage—she slapped him across the face, hard. It wasn't her fault, Beau. None of it was.

Afterward, we went to where you were celebrating your bucks' night. Bruno gained access to your hotel room under the pretence of congratulating you and drugged your drink. Once you were unconscious, he helped you to the bed. That's when I arrived, and together, we staged the scene to make it appear as though we were engaged in sexual activity. Bruno took the photographs.

Throughout the night, Bruno repeatedly spoke of his obsession with Ashley. He claimed that these photos would "prove" she was meant to be with him and would show her the "truth." His obsession drove the entire scheme.

The following Monday, after the photos were developed, Bruno asked me to deliver them to Ashley's house. Regretfully, I complied. He then had me send the photograph of him and Ashley to your phone.

Beau, my actions were driven by personal pain, but that does not excuse what I did. When you ended our relationship to reunite with Ashley, I felt hurt and angry. In that vulnerable state, I allowed myself to be manipulated by Bruno, and I made decisions that I will regret for the rest of my life.

I share this not to justify my actions but to take ownership of them. I understand the harm I've caused, and I can only hope that this confession offers some clarity and a step toward healing.

I am truly sorry, Beau—for the pain, the betrayal, and the position I put you in. I accept full responsibility for my actions. Now that I am a wife and mother, I understand what I took from you and Ashley, and I regret it deeply. I truly hope you and Ashley have found the happiness you deserve.

Sincerely,

Sarah Gleason (née Helman)

Tears streamed down Ashley's face as she struggled to comprehend the lengths someone would go to hurt another person. Her heart ached under the weight of betrayal, each revelation feeling like a fresh wound. She clutched the letter tightly, as if its existence could somehow make sense of the chaos swirling around her.

Beau reached out; his touch gentle as he handed her a napkin. "Here," he said softly, his voice steady yet filled with concern. She took it, dabbing at her tears while he held her hand, grounding her with his presence.

Dennis, observing her distress, cleared his throat and spoke in a subdued tone. "Miss Sintaro, I'm deeply sorry you've had to endure this."

Ashley forced a small, shaky smile, her voice barely above a whisper. "Thank you." She turned her gaze to Beau, her eyes glistening with sorrow and confusion.

Beau returned her look, his lips curling into a faint, reassuring smile, though she could see the turmoil in his own eyes. After a moment, he turned back to Dennis. "Have you approached Bruno yet?"

Dennis nodded, his jaw tightening as he reached for his notebook. "I did. Tried to confront him, but as soon as I introduced myself and explained why I was there, he wasn't having it. His exact words were"—Dennis flipped to the page, his tone sharpening as he read aloud— "'That bastard Tramain shouldn't have come back and come between me and Ashley.'"

He closed the notebook with a snap, his frustration evident. "Then he told me to get off his property before he called the police." Dennis exhaled deeply; his brow furrowed. "He made it crystal clear he wasn't going to cooperate. But now that we've got Sarah's letter in hand, I'll be confronting him again. This time, he won't be able to dismiss me so easily."

Ashley stood abruptly, her chair scraping against the floor. "Excuse me," she muttered, her voice trembling. She needed air, space—anything to keep from crumbling completely in front of them.

She made her way to the restroom, each step heavy with the weight of her emotions. Once inside, she entered a stall, locked the door, and squatted against the wall. The world felt like it was collapsing around her. Silent sobs wracked her body as her head was in her hands, the overwhelming grief and anger finally spilling out. How had it come to this? How could someone be so cruel, so manipulative?

She wasn't sure how long she stayed there, but eventually, her tears slowed, and she forced herself to stand. Splashing cold water on her face, she stared at her reflection in the mirror. Her eyes were red and swollen, but there was a flicker of determination beneath the surface. She wouldn't let this break her.

By the time she returned to the table, Beau was alone, his expression shifting to one of deep concern the moment he saw her. He stood, waiting for her to approach, then pulled her into his arms without hesitation.

Ashley sagged against him, her walls crumbling as she allowed herself to lean on him. He held her tightly, his embrace steady and protective, offering her a moment of solace amid the chaos.

After a few moments, Beau spoke, his voice low and comforting. "I just need to grab a quick shower and change. Then I'll take you home, okay?"

Ashley nodded silently, her emotions too raw for words.

He took her hand, leading her toward the elevator. She followed in a quiet daze, her thoughts swirling as they ascended to his room. Once inside, she made her way to the armchair and sat down, curling into herself as Beau disappeared into the bathroom.

The sound of running water filled the room, leaving her alone with her thoughts. She replayed the day's events over and over, the truth of Bruno's obsession and Sarah's betrayal sinking in deeper with each passing moment.

When Beau finally emerged, dressed in black trousers and a light blue polo shirt, he walked over to her and knelt down. Taking her hands in his, he pulled her gently to her feet, wrapping his arms around her waist.

Ashley looked up at him, her eyes filled with regret. "I'm sorry," she whispered, her voice barely audible.

Beau frowned, confusion flickering across his face. "What for?"

She hesitated, her lips trembling. "For the photos… for everything." Her voice cracked. "I should've seen it. I should've known."

His expression softened; his eyes filled with understanding. "Ashley, don't," he said gently. "None of this was your fault. It wasn't mine either. We were both victims in this."

"But we let it happen," she said desperately, her tears threatening to fall again. "We played right into their hands."

Beau cupped her face, his thumb brushing away a stray tear. "Maybe we did," he admitted, his voice steady. "But that's over now. We can't change what happened, but we can move forward. Together."

Before she could respond, he lowered his head, capturing her lips in a kiss that was deep and full of unspoken promises. Ashley's arms instinctively wrapped around his neck, pulling him closer as the world faded away.

When they finally broke apart, Beau rested his forehead against hers, a soft chuckle escaping his lips. "We better stop before I lose control," he teased, a wicked grin tugging at the corners of his mouth. "I might forget to get you home on time."

Ashley let out a small laugh, the sound surprising her. For the first time in hours, the weight on her chest felt a little lighter.

Beau grinned and took her hand, leading her toward the door. "Come on, before I change my mind."

As they exited the room, he grabbed the letter, tucking it safely into his pocket. The drive to Ashley's home was quiet, the tension between them replaced by a fragile sense of peace. But as they pulled up to her house, the unspoken question lingered between them: where do they go from here?

Chapter Sixteen

When they arrived at Ashley's house, she went upstairs to shower and change, while Beau waited downstairs in the living room. Fifteen minutes later, she reappeared wearing a fitted, knee-length dark blue dress that highlighted her elegance. Despite her calm demeanour, there was a flicker of nervousness in her eyes.

Beau smiled when he saw her. "You look stunning," he said warmly.

Ashley blushed faintly and sat beside him on the couch. They turned on a movie to pass the time, their conversation light as they waited for Kelly, Daniel, and little Brian to arrive.

Just before six, the doorbell rang. Ashley answered it, greeted by Brian's bright smile as he stretched his arms toward her. "Ash! Ash!" he exclaimed, his joy infectious.

Ashley scooped him up, laughing. "Hello, little man! How are you?"

"I'm good!" he said enthusiastically. Then, noticing Beau, his eyes lit up. "Bowtie is here, Ash!"

Ashley chuckled. "Yes, he is."

Beau stepped forward, offering Brian a high-five. "Hey, buddy."

Brian grinned and slapped Beau's hand. Meanwhile, Kelly's expression was guarded as she crossed her arms and addressed Ashley. "Daniel said that was Beau's car in the driveway. Why is he here?" Her tone was sharp, suspicion laced in her words.

Daniel, standing behind her, shot Ashley an apologetic look but said nothing.

Before Ashley could answer, Beau stepped forward and handed Kelly a folded piece of paper. "This might help explain," he said evenly.

Kelly frowned, taking the paper reluctantly. "What's this?"

Ashley urged her gently, "Just read it, Kell."

Kelly unfolded the paper and began reading. Her sceptical expression shifted to one of shock, her eyes widening as she processed the contents. Daniel leaned over her shoulder, scanning the words. His face hardened with anger as he finished. "That's insane," he said, his voice tight with outrage.

Kelly gasped and turned to Ashley. "Oh my God, Ashley… I didn't know." Her gaze moved to Beau, and her demeanour softened. "Beau, I'm so sorry. I—"

Beau held up a hand to stop her. "It's okay, Kelly. You were just looking out for your friend. I can't hold that against you."

Relief washed over Kelly, and she stepped forward, wrapping Beau in an impulsive hug. He returned it warmly, his smile reassuring.

Ashley watched the exchange with a quiet smile, her heart feeling lighter.

Daniel placed a comforting hand on Ashley's shoulder. "You okay, Ash?" he asked gently.

"It's a lot to process," she admitted, her voice soft. "But… yeah, I think I'll be okay."

Kelly's expression turned furious. "This is unbelievable! What kind of person does something like that?"

Brian, sensing the tension, looked up at Ashley with wide eyes. "Why is Mommy mad?" he asked.

Ashley crouched down, pulling him into a hug. "She's not mad at you, sweetheart. Someone did something mean to me, and it upset her."

Brian's small arms tightened around her neck. "Are you okay, Ash?"

Ashley kissed his cheek, her smile warm. "I am now that you're here." She looked at Kelly and Daniel. "You two go enjoy your date night. This little guy will be just fine with us."

Brian giggled as Ashley tickled his sides. "Yeah, I'll be fine!"

After Kelly and Daniel left, Ashley and Beau settled into babysitting mode. Brian grabbed a book and climbed onto Ashley's lap, his face eager. "Read to me, Ash?"

"Of course, little man," she said with a laugh, opening The Very Hungry Caterpillar.

Beau watched from the armchair as Ashley animatedly read the story, helping Brian turn the pages. The sight filled him with a quiet warmth, her ease with the child stirring emotions he hadn't allowed himself to fully feel before.

When the story ended, Ashley asked, "What do you want for dinner, Brian?"

"Chicken nuggets, please!"

Ashley laughed. "Alright. Why don't you play catch with Beau while I cook?"

Brian eagerly grabbed his ball and tugged at Beau's hand. "Come on, Bowtie!"

Beau followed him to the hallway, glancing back at Ashley with a grin. "Wish me luck."

In the kitchen, Ashley prepared chicken nuggets for Brian and a spaghetti dinner for herself and Beau. When everything was ready, she called out, "Dinner's ready!"

The three of them ate together, Brian chatting non-stop between bites. Afterward, Ashley took him upstairs for a quick bath and got him into his pyjamas. When they came back downstairs, Brian crawled onto the couch and snuggled up against Ashley.

"Ash lets me fall asleep here," he murmured sleepily.

Beau chuckled, ruffling the boy's hair. "You're one lucky kid."

Brian grinned at Ashley. "My mom says I'm lucky 'cause Ash is the best person ever."

Ashley's heart melted, and she smiled softly as Brian's eyes fluttered closed. She draped a blanket over him, her movements gentle.

Beau leaned closer and whispered, "He's right, you know."

Ashley looked at him, her expression tender. "Thank you," she said quietly.

They moved to the kitchen for coffee, leaving Brian to sleep peacefully. As Ashley poured their cups, Beau broke the silence. "He really adores you."

She smiled. "I adore him too."

After a pause, he asked, "Do you want kids someday?"

Ashley blinked at the question but nodded. "Yeah. I thought I'd have a family by now."

"Me too," Beau admitted softly.

Their conversation shifted to lighter topics until Kelly and Daniel returned around eleven. Daniel carried a sleeping Brian to the car while Kelly hugged Ashley and Beau. "Thank you both so much," she said warmly.

When they were alone again, Ashley turned to Beau, her voice gentle. "Come on," she said, slipping her hand into his. "Let's go to bed."

"Good morning," Beau said, his voice warm as his gaze lingered on Ashley's serene face. Her eyes fluttered open, hazy with sleep, and she looked up at him.

"Morning," she murmured softly, a faint smile curling her lips. "How long have you been watching me?"

"Long enough to know you're absolutely beautiful," he replied, his voice low and full of affection.

Before Ashley could respond, Beau leaned down, capturing her lips in a deep, passionate kiss. She sighed against him, her hand instinctively moving to rest against his chest as his warmth enveloped her.

When he finally pulled back, Ashley's cheeks were flushed, and she let out a breathless laugh. "Really, Beau? We'll never get out of this bed if you keep that up."

He grinned, mischief sparking in his eyes. "And what's so wrong with that?"

Ashley raised an eyebrow, though her blush deepened. "We didn't get much sleep last night," she pointed out, though the playful smile on her lips betrayed her scolding tone.

Beau leaned closer, his grin wicked. "Are you complaining?"

She feigned indignation, putting a hand over her heart. "Of course not," she teased, laughing softly.

Beau pulled her closer, his arms wrapping around her waist as she settled against him. They lay there for a while, basking in the quiet intimacy of the morning, savouring the rare stillness between them.

Eventually, hunger drove them from the comfort of the bed. They made their way downstairs, where Ashley began preparing breakfast. As she cracked eggs into a pan, Beau leaned casually against the counter, watching her with a fond smile.

"I need to go to New York for a few days," he said after a moment, his tone casual.

Ashley glanced over her shoulder at him and smiled. "Okay," she replied simply, focusing on flipping the eggs.

There was a pause, and Beau's voice softened with an edge of hope. "Would you come with me?"

Ashley froze, the spatula hovering mid-air. She turned to face him, surprise flickering across her features. "Oh, I don't know…" she began, her voice trailing off.

Noticing the uncertainty in her eyes, Beau stepped forward, his expression gentle. "It's alright," he reassured her. "Maybe next time. I need to leave tomorrow morning, but I'll be back by Wednesday."

Ashley nodded slowly, her lips curving into a small, tentative smile. "Okay," she said softly, returning to her cooking.

When it was time for him to leave, Beau kissed her gently on the lips, his lips lingering for a moment before he pulled back. His eyes searched hers, filled with unspoken affection. "I'll see you Wednesday," he murmured.

Ashley's smile widened as she walked him to the door. "Take care," she called after him, waving as his car disappeared down the driveway.

Around six that evening, a knock at the door interrupted Ashley's quiet routine. Expecting Beau—she opened the door with a welcoming smile. But her expression quickly faltered when she saw who stood on her doorstep.

"Bruno?" she asked, her voice sharp with surprise and unease. "What are you doing here? You're not welcome."

Without waiting for an invitation, Bruno shoved past her, slamming the door shut behind him. Ashley stumbled back, her pulse quickening as dread settled in her chest.

"Get out, Bruno," she demanded, her voice firm but tinged with fear.

He sneered, his dark eyes locking on her. "Oh, I'm not going anywhere," he said coldly. "I'm sick of playing games, Ashley. Or should I call you 'Angel Face'? That's what he calls you, isn't it?"

Her stomach turned at the mocking tone. "I don't know what you're talking about, but you need to leave," she said, her voice trembling slightly now.

Bruno took a step closer, his presence suffocating. "I've been patient long enough," he hissed, his voice dripping with venom. "You and him—it ends tonight."

Ashley backed away, her heart racing as panic clawed at her throat. "Bruno, stop. Don't do something you'll regret," she pleaded, her voice shaking as she realised the dangerous intent in his eyes.

But Bruno's expression darkened further, his hands clenching into fists. "Regret?" he growled, his voice a low, menacing rumble. "The only regret I have is letting this go on for so long."

He advanced on her, leaving Ashley no choice but to retreat further into the house. Her mind raced as she tried to think of a way out, her instincts screaming at her to act quickly.

"Bruno, please—"

"Shut up!" he barked, his voice booming, the sudden outburst making her flinch.

Ashley's eyes darted to her phone on the counter just a few feet away, but Bruno caught the movement and smirked, blocking her path.

"No calls, Angel Face. No Beau to swoop in and save you this time."

Terror gripped her as she realised, she was trapped.

Chapter Seventeen

Tuesday morning arrived, and by 10am, Ashley still hadn't shown up to work. Daniel, already uneasy about her unexplained absence on Monday, had tried to dismiss his concerns, assuming she might have gone to New York with Beau. However, when Kelly called on Tuesday morning at 10:30am, her anxious tone sent his worry surging.

"Daniel, is Ashley at work today?" Kelly asked, her tone tight with worry.

"No, she still hasn't come in," Daniel said, his voice tinged with concern. "Yesterday, I told you I figured she was with Beau, but now… I'm not so sure anymore."

"I've been trying to call her since last night, but she's still not answering," Kelly said, the worry in her voice intensifying. "I'm really starting to get scared, Daniel. You know she wouldn't go anywhere without telling me. Can you call Beau and find out if she's with him?"

"Okay, I'll let you know what I hear," Daniel promised, already feeling a knot of unease forming in his stomach.

Kelly, unable to sit still, decided to act. "I'm going to her house. I'll let you know what I find," she told Daniel before hanging up and grabbing her purse and rushing out the door, Brian perched on her hip.

"What's wrong, Mommy?" Brian asked, his big eyes filled with concern as Kelly buckled him into his car seat.

"I'm not sure, sweetheart. I just need to check on Ash," Kelly replied, her voice tight.

As Daniel hung up, Jason had overheard. "You're really worried about Ashley, aren't you?"

Daniel frowned deeply. "Ashley's been completely off the grid. Kelly's been trying to call her since last night after I mentioned she wasn't at work yesterday. Ashley wouldn't just disappear without telling Kelly—it's not like her at all."

Daniel dialled Beau's number. The phone rang twice before Beau answered.

"Hello?" Beau's voice was calm, almost distracted.

"Beau, it's Daniel," Daniel said, skipping pleasantries.

"Daniel? What's up? Is everything okay there?" Beau asked, his tone still casual but with a hint of curiosity.

Daniel hesitated, then blurted out, "Is Ashley with you?"

Beau's tone immediately shifted, sharp and alert. "No, why? What's going on?"

"She hasn't been to work yesterday or today, and Kelly says she's not answering her phone," Daniel explained.

Beau's silence on the other end of the line was deafening before he finally said, "I've been in meetings since I got here and I tried calling Ashley last night, but it was late, so I wasn't concerned when she didn't answer, I'll try to call her now. Let me know if you hear anything."

"Will do," Daniel replied, hanging up.

Kelly arrived at Ashley's house and noticed her car still parked in the driveway. Relief was fleeting as she approached the door, her gut screaming that something wasn't right.

Fumbling with the spare key Ashley had given her months ago, Kelly tried to keep calm. Brian, sensing her unease, clutched her hand. "Why are we going to Ash's, Mommy?"

"I just need to check on her, honey," Kelly said, her voice shaking slightly.

Unlocking the door, Kelly stepped inside. The house was eerily silent, the air heavy with an unsettling stillness.

"Ashley?" she called out, her voice echoing through the quiet space. No response.

Kelly's eyes scanned the living room as she moved further inside. Lights were on in the kitchen and living room. On the hall table, a letter sat propped against a lamp. Her heart pounded as she picked it up, her hands trembling. The note was brief:

I am going away with a friend to clear my head.

Ashley.

Kelly stared at the letter, her heart sinking. This felt wrong. Ashley wouldn't just leave without telling her—especially not like this. As her gaze drifted, Kelly noticed a broken gold chain on the floor beneath the hall table. Her breath caught. It was Ashley's locket—the one she never took off unless she was sleeping or showering. A chill ran through Kelly as she crouched to pick it up, the unsettling weight of her discovery pressing down on her. Something was very wrong.

"That's Ash's necklace, Mommy?" Brian asked, his small hand tugging at Kelly's sleeve as he looked at the chain in her hand.

Kelly forced a reassuring smile for her son's sake, folding the note and slipping it into her pocket. "I know, sweetheart. She must have dropped it. Don't worry."

But worry was all Kelly could feel. She quickly pulled out her phone and called Daniel, keeping her voice low. "I found a note," she said, her tone tense. "It says she went away with a friend to clear her head, but it doesn't sit right. I found her locket on the floor in the hallway."

Daniel was silent for a moment before responding, his voice grim. "Her locket? She never takes that off unless she has to. If it's there, she didn't leave on her own."

"She wouldn't just vanish without telling us," Kelly insisted, her voice shaking. "Not me, not you, and definitely not Beau. She hasn't answered her phone. This isn't like her. Something's wrong, Daniel. I can feel it."

"I'll call Beau again," Daniel said, his determination clear. "We'll figure this out. Don't panic, Kelly. We'll get to the bottom of this."

Hanging up the phone, Kelly's hand shook slightly as she glanced down at Brian, her resolve hardening. "Let's go home, baby," she murmured, trying to keep her voice steady for him, though her mind was already spinning with worry. Something was terribly wrong—she could feel it deep in her gut.

They were just about to step out of the door when Ashley's home phone rang, and Kelly's heart skipped a beat. She rushed back to grab the receiver, hoping beyond hope that it was Ashley on the other end. "Ashley?" she answered, her voice desperate.

"It's Beau," came the reply, his tone tense. "Kelly, what's going on? Daniel just told me you found Ashley's locket."

The sound of Beau's voice almost shattered Kelly's composure. "Oh, Beau, when's the last time you saw Ashley?" she cried, her voice breaking with panic.

"I left her place on Sunday afternoon," Beau responded, confusion creeping into his words.

"She's gone, Beau," Kelly said urgently, fighting to hold back the tears. "No one has seen her since then."

Beau's voice sharpened with alarm. "Gone? What do you mean? What happened?"

Kelly quickly relayed everything—about the note she found, the locket left behind, Ashley's car still sitting in the driveway, and the sinking feeling that Ashley would never leave without at least letting someone know. "I know something's wrong," Kelly said, her voice trembling but firm. "This isn't like her."

Beau was silent for a moment, taking in her words, the weight of the situation sinking in. "I'm coming back," he said decisively.

The urgency in his voice fuelled a new wave of dread. Beau felt unease crawling up his spine. His mind raced with all the worst-case scenarios as he quickly booked the earliest flight back to Boston. The night was the soonest he could fly, but he would be back by late tonight, no matter what.

The moment his plane touched down, Beau drove straight to Kelly and Daniel's house, his knuckles white as they gripped the steering wheel. When he arrived, Kelly opened the door, her face a mixture of relief and anxiety.

"Oh, Beau, thank goodness," she said, stepping aside to let him in.

Inside the house, the weight of the silence hit him first. In the living room, Brian sat cross-legged on the floor, his small fingers absently pushing a Matchbox car back and forth. His little face was pinched with worry, and when he looked up and saw Beau, his eyes welled up with tears.

"Beau," Brian whimpered, his voice cracking. "Ash is gone."

Beau's heart clenched at the sight of the boy's distress. He knelt beside him, wrapping his arms around the small frame and pulling him close. "I know, buddy," Beau said softly, his voice rough with emotion. "But we're going to find her. I promise."

Brian sniffled, his tiny body trembling in Beau's arms. "Where is she? Why isn't she here?"

Beau didn't have an answer, but he held the boy tighter, trying to offer him comfort, even though his own heart was racing with worry. "We'll figure it out, I swear. We're not giving up on her."

As the night stretched on, Beau knew that this wasn't just a missing person situation—it felt like something far darker, and the fear gnawing at him was only growing stronger. But he couldn't let that show. Not in front of Brian. Not in front of Kelly.

They were going to find Ashley, no matter what it took.

"Bruno, please—you have to let me go! This is madness!" Ashley's voice was strained, her chest tight with fear as she tugged at the ropes binding her to the bed. Her wrists were raw, and the effort only seemed to make the ropes tighter, the knots more stubborn.

Bruno stood over her, his face hardening into an icy mask. "I don't think so, Ashley," he said, his voice low and chilling. "It's time you accepted that we belong together. I've waited long enough… and then he had to show up and ruin everything again." His eyes darkened, venom dripping from his words at the mention of Beau's name.

Ashley's chest tightened, panic clawing at her throat. "Why are you doing this?" she pleaded, her voice cracking as she desperately tried to understand the twisted reasoning behind his actions.

Bruno's expression softened for a brief moment, though it only seemed to make him more unstable. He reached out, brushing a hand over her cheek. Ashley flinched instinctively, but he ignored it, as if he hadn't noticed. "You must know, Ashley," he said, his voice eerily calm, "I've loved you since high school. I've always known you were meant for me. And you've always known it too."

Ashley recoiled, shaking her head in disbelief. "You're hurting me, Bruno," she whispered, her voice faltering with pain and despair. "This isn't love."

Bruno's eyes flashed with anger, and he gripped her chin, forcing her to meet his gaze. His touch was rough, unyielding, and his lips twisted into a snarl. "Don't say that," he hissed through clenched teeth, his breath hot against her skin.

Before she could protest, he leaned down, capturing her lips in a brutal kiss. She tried to pull away, but his hold was ironclad. Her lips burned from the force of it, and when she tasted the metallic tang of blood, her heart raced with panic. His desperation only made him hold on tighter, and every struggle she made seemed to push him further into his madness.

Tears blurred her vision as she gasped for breath, her voice barely a whisper. "How long do you plan to keep me here?"

Bruno pulled away slightly, his gaze shifting to one of sickening tenderness. He traced a finger down her cheek, the touch almost too soft for the violence in his eyes. "As long as it takes for you to understand that we're meant to be together," he murmured, his hand trailing down her neck, then lower over her collarbone. He moved his hand slowly over her body, his touch both possessive and invasive, until it rested at the hem of her dress. "You're so beautiful, Ashley. You must know that don't you?"

Ashley fought to keep her face expressionless, but her body tensed, dread pooling deep inside her. Her pulse pounded in her ears, and she could feel the weight of his gaze on her skin.

"Bruno, stop. Please, stop," Ashley forced herself to say, her voice trembling but firm. She couldn't let him see her break. "Is this really how you want things to be?"

His lips curled into a twisted smile. "Of course, I'd prefer it if you wanted to hold me too. And you will, Ashley. I'm certain of it."

Her heart hammered in her chest as she searched for any opportunity to keep him talking, to distract him long enough to think of a way out. "Where are we, Bruno? Who owns this place?"

"This was my father's place," he replied smugly, standing taller as he looked around the dimly lit cabin. "It's mine now, and soon, it'll be ours when we're married." He leaned down, pressing a lingering kiss to her cheek despite her obvious discomfort. She couldn't stop herself from shuddering, but he didn't seem to care. "It's the perfect place for us to start our life together," he added with a twisted gleam in his eye.

Ashley's mind raced. No, I can't let this happen. She needed to stall, to keep him distracted long enough to find a way out. "You know Kelly won't believe that note I left—the one you forced me to write," she said, trying to plant a seed of doubt in his mind. "She won't just let it go."

Bruno's hand froze on the doorknob as he turned back to look at her, his eyes narrowing with a sneer. "I need to leave you here for now," he said coldly, his voice void of emotion. "If people start noticing I'm missing, they might put the pieces together. Don't worry—I'll be back soon."

With that, he stepped outside, the door slamming shut behind him, leaving Ashley alone in the heavy silence. The sound of the bolt sliding into place echoed in her ears as it locked her in.

Ashley's heart raced as the reality of her situation sank in. She was trapped.

She surveyed the room, her eyes adjusting to the dim light. The cabin was sparse—barely furnished—and the air smelled faintly of mildew. Her hands were tightly bound to the bed, her legs tied just enough to give her limited movement. The ropes bit into her skin with every attempt to free herself, and the locked door was an insurmountable barrier. There were no windows to escape through, only small, shuttered panes that offered no hope.

A small bottle of water sat on the floor next to the bed, but there was nothing else—no food, nothing to help her survive this nightmare. In the corner, a metal bucket made her stomach turn as she realised its grim purpose.

A chill ran down her spine as she steeled herself. I can't give in to fear. I have to find a way out.

Every minute felt like an eternity as she began to plan her next move. If she could free herself from the ropes, she might be able to get to the door. But the thought of Bruno returning kept her on edge. She had to think fast—time was running out.

Chapter Eighteen

Ashley had been missing for four agonising days now, and Beau was slowly losing himself in the torment of uncertainty. The thought of anything happening to her, the terror that she could be hurt—or worse, dead—chilled him to his core. His sleep was fitful, filled with nightmares, and his mind was consumed by a constant barrage of worst-case scenarios. Every time his phone buzzed, his heart skipped a beat, only to plummet with disappointment when it wasn't news about her. Kelly and Daniel had insisted he stay with them, offering what little comfort they could, but their home felt empty, like a hollow shell, without Ashley safe by his side.

The police had done little to help, dismissing Kelly and Beau's fears as overblown, largely because of the note Ashley had left. Despite their insistence that Ashley would never leave without telling anyone, the authorities had remained unmoved. "She just needed some space," they'd said. The idea that she'd simply taken off seemed plausible to them, but to Beau and Kelly, it was a betrayal of everything Ashley stood for. It was completely out of character for her to leave without so much as a word to anyone, especially her closest friends. Beau knew they couldn't rely on the police to find her—if he was going to get answers, he'd have to take matters into his own hands.

He and Kelly had spent countless hours calling hospitals, motels, hotels— anywhere that might have a trace of Ashley. Every lead came up empty. Desperation clawed at Beau's chest, making it hard to breathe. He couldn't sit idly by any longer. He had to find her. In a final attempt, he decided to confront Bruno, the man who seemed to have a tangled past with Ashley. Despite the tension between them—the fake photos, the lies, and the manipulation—Beau needed to know if Bruno knew anything. Finding Ashley was his only priority. Everything else could wait.

When Beau had arrived at Bruno's house, he found the man lounging carelessly in his chair, a drink in hand, as if he had no care in the world. Beau wasted no time with pleasantries. "Where is she, Bruno?" he demanded, his voice low but sharp with the intensity of his worry.

Bruno had barely lifted an eyebrow, his lips curling into a mocking sneer. "Why would I know where she is? She's your girlfriend, not mine," he said, his voice dripping with disdain.

Beau's fists clenched, but he held back, focusing all his energy on staying calm. He couldn't lose control—not when Ashley's life was on the line. "If you see her, can you at least let me know?" Beau asked, his voice strained, fighting to keep the anger at bay.

Bruno leaned back in his chair, almost taunting him with his casualness. "Why would I? You took her from me. Maybe she's finally realised she's sick of you," he sneered, eyes flickering with something that might have been jealousy or malice.

Beau's body went rigid, every muscle tense, but he didn't let his anger show. Kelly placed a calming hand on his arm, her touch grounding him in the midst of his fury.

"Bruno, please," Kelly said, her voice steady but pleading. "We just need to know if you've heard or seen anything. Anything at all."

Bruno turned to her, his expression softening, though only slightly. "Sorry, Kelly," he said with a careless shrug. "I don't know where she is."

Kelly's desperation reached a new height. "Please," she said, pleading, "if you know anything, just tell us. We just want to find her."

Bruno's gaze flickered momentarily, but he remained aloof. "Alright, alright," he replied with a dismissive shrug. "I'll let you know if I hear anything, but I doubt she'll be reaching out to me."

As Beau and Kelly left Bruno's house, Beau could barely hold his emotions in check. The bile of frustration bubbled up inside him, but he forced the words out in a clipped tone. "He knows something, Kelly. I can feel it. There's no way he doesn't."

Kelly nodded; her face drawn with concern. "I think so too. But what can we do about it? We've tried everything."

Beau's eyes hardened, determination settling in his gut. "We get my PI on this. It's time to stop waiting for the authorities to do something. We need answers now."

Once they were safely back in Beau's rental car, he immediately pulled out his phone and dialled. "Mr. Cooper, I need your help. Ashley Sintaro is missing," he said, his voice clipped with urgency. "Can you meet me as soon as possible?"

He paused, listening to the response on the other end, then added, "I'll text you the address. We need you here as quickly as possible."

After hanging up, Beau turned to Kelly, his voice laced with the frustration he was trying to control. "He'll be here in an hour. Let's just hope we get some answers."

Kelly's face was a mixture of hope and exhaustion. "I just don't understand. We've got no leads, no clues. It's like she disappeared into thin air," she said, her voice small and filled with fear.

Beau's jaw tightened as he explained the situation to Mr. Cooper, highlighting their absolute certainty that Ashley hadn't left of her own volition. She wouldn't just vanish like this, not without any trace, not without saying goodbye to someone who meant so much to her.

Mr. Cooper, a no-nonsense investigator known for his quick action, nodded thoughtfully. "We'll start with this Bruno character. He's the obvious lead, and I'll have my team dig into it right away," he said. His calm demeanour contrasted with the urgent tension in the room, but his words were reassuring, nonetheless. He noticed Kelly's weary expression, the raw emotion that was barely contained in her eyes. "Don't worry, Miss. I'll do everything in my power to find her. I won't stop until we get some answers."

Tears welled in Kelly's eyes as she nodded. "Thank you, Mr. Cooper. I just... I just hope she's okay. It's been four days now and no word. I don't know how much longer I can stand this," she said, her voice cracking with emotion.

Mr. Cooper gave her a sympathetic look before rising from the table. He extended his hand to Beau, his voice firm but filled with reassurance. "I'll be in touch as soon as I have any information. We're going to find her."

Beau grasped his hand firmly, his resolve harder than ever. "I appreciate it. I won't stop looking either. She's out there, and I'll get her back."

Two days passed in an agonising haze before they finally heard from Mr. Cooper.

On Sunday morning, the doorbell rang, and Kelly, still haggard from sleepless nights, hurried to answer. Standing on the porch was Mr. Cooper, sharp in a crisp suit, looking every bit the professional.

"Morning, Miss. I'm looking for Mr. Tramain," he said, his voice businesslike but softened by the circumstances.

"Yes, he's here. Please, come in," Kelly replied, stepping aside to allow him in. She led him through the quiet house to the living room where Beau and Daniel were deep in conversation. They both looked up as the door opened, and the hope in Beau's eyes was impossible to hide.

"Mr. Cooper," Beau said, standing quickly, his voice laced with urgency. "Please, tell me you've found something."

Cooper's face was as serious as ever as he handed Beau a folded piece of paper. Kelly and Daniel watched anxiously, their faces a mix of hope and fear. The air in the room was thick with tension.

"Bruno Vincent has been under surveillance," Cooper began, his tone measured. "He hasn't been going anywhere unusual—just home, work, and a few businesses around town. If he knows where she is, he's not checking on her. So, if he's the one who has her, that's a real concern."

Beau's heart sank as he read the paper, but Cooper wasn't done yet. "However, we've uncovered something important. We discovered a property owned by Bruno's father, which was left to Bruno in his will. It's in a remote part of the country. I think it's worth investigating."

Beau's heart pounded in his chest. This could be the break they were looking for. Cooper looked directly at him. "I'm heading out there now. Would you like to accompany me?"

"Yes," Beau said without hesitation, standing taller, his jaw set with determination.

"I'm coming too," Daniel added, already on his feet, ready to go. His expression was fierce, just as it had been when he first heard about Ashley's disappearance.

Kelly's face twisted with anguish. "If he's hurt her…" she trailed off, her voice breaking. "I swear, I'll kill him." She collapsed into an armchair, tears streaming down her cheeks, her hands shaking as she tried to hold herself together.

Daniel immediately knelt beside her, his hand gently resting on hers. "We'll find her, sweetheart," he said softly, his voice steady and reassuring.

Kelly managed a watery smile, grateful for his strength, but her heart was breaking.

Mr. Cooper cleared his throat, signalling that it was time to go. "We should leave now. It's about a two-hour drive, and we need to get there before it gets dark."

Just then, little Brian wandered into the room, his wide eyes taking in the worried expressions of his parents and Beau. Beau crouched down and scooped him up, holding him close, his voice calm but filled with determination. "We're going to look for Ash, Brian," he said gently. "I need you to be strong for your mom while we're gone."

Brian wrapped his small arms around Beau's neck, holding on tightly. "Bring her back, okay?" he whispered, his voice small but filled with a child's desperate hope.

Beau's throat tightened, and he nodded firmly. "I'll do my best, buddy. I promise."

With a final hug, Beau set Brian down and joined Mr. Cooper and Daniel. As the three men left, Kelly and Brian watched them go, clinging to the fragile hope that they would return with good news.

Meanwhile, in the grim isolation of the cabin, Ashley was beyond exhaustion. Her body ached, her skin cracked, and her spirit was near breaking. She had been tied to the bed for six long days and seven nights, the rough ropes scraping her skin raw. She had tried to free herself countless times, but the ropes were unforgiving, and each failed attempt left her more defeated than the last. Her limbs had gone numb, her head swam with dizziness, and Bruno hadn't returned once to check on her.

Her limited water had run out two days ago, leaving her parched, her throat dry as sandpaper. She had been forced to use a bucket you relieve herself, a repulsive experience that had made her stomach churn. The smell of it lingered in the air, filling her lungs with its stench, and she could feel the bile rise in her throat each time she took a breath. Even the simplest actions, like shifting in her dress, had become unbearable. She couldn't even adjust her underwear properly—what if Bruno found her like that? The thought made her skin crawl.

The nights were cold, bitterly so, and she shivered uncontrollably, unable to sleep, her body trembling as she lay there, exhausted and broken. Hope was slipping away, and a haunting thought gnawed at her: was Bruno planning to leave her here to die? Was she truly alone?

Ashley's thoughts were interrupted when she heard the unmistakable sound of footsteps on the veranda outside the cabin. The slide bolt clicked, and the door creaked open, a beam of light spilling into the darkness. She clung to a fragile hope—could it be someone coming to rescue her?

But that hope shattered like glass when Bruno stepped into the cabin, a grimace on his face as he looked around. "Ugh, it smells in here," he sneered, his voice filled with disgust. Ashley's blood boiled, a wave of humiliation and anger flooding her chest.

She forced her dry throat to speak, her voice cracking from dehydration. "What did you expect, you animal? Leaving me here for days with no food or enough water?" She tried to stand, but dizziness struck her, and she staggered, her vision blurring.

Bruno's face twisted in frustration. "Don't talk to me like that," he snapped. "It's your boyfriend's fault I couldn't get here sooner. They were watching me. But they finally left." He smirked, as though his presence were some kind of favour. "So here I am."

Anger flared inside Ashley like a wildfire. "I hope you get caught, you bastard," she spat, though her voice trembled with weakness. "You make me sick."

Bruno's face darkened, and before she could react, he stormed over and struck her hard across the face. The blow sent her crashing to the floor, the pain radiating through her skull as she gasped for breath.

He paused, looking down at her, a flicker of something almost like guilt in his eyes. But it quickly disappeared, replaced by cold indifference. He dropped beside her and tried to pull her into his arms. "Sorry, sweetheart," he muttered, his voice softer, almost apologetic.

Ashley recoiled, pushing him away with whatever strength she had left. "Get off me, you animal," she hissed, her voice weak but laced with disgust. "I hate you. You deserve to be in jail. You make me sick."

Bruno's face twisted in fury. "You bitch," he growled, and with a swift motion, he kicked her hard in the ribs.

Ashley screamed in agony as her body crumpled beneath the force of the kick.

"Stop it!" Bruno yelled, his voice cracking with frustration. "Stop making me hurt you!"

Ashley glared up at him, her pain only adding to the fire burning inside her. "I don't care what you do to me," she spat, her voice shaking with defiance. "You disgust me. Kill me, I'd prefer that over being with someone like you."

Bruno's rage erupted in a violent fury. His fists flew, landing punch after punch, each blow more forceful than the last. "You're mine! You always will be!" he screamed.

Ashley's body was battered, bruised, and bloodied, but her thoughts remained focused on Beau. She thought of his love, his warmth, his promise. The regret that she hadn't told him how she truly felt—the words she hadn't said when he had confessed his love to her—haunted her.

She felt the punches land, each one sinking her deeper into the abyss, but in the fleeting moments of clarity, she held on to the thought of him. And as her vision blurred, she lost her fight to stay awake, her body giving in to the relentless pain. One last thought of Beau—his face, his smile—and then darkness claimed her.

Chapter Nineteen

Beau and Daniel followed Dennis Cooper in the rental car, the tension in the air palpable as they made their way toward the cabin. Beau's grip tightened on the wheel as his mind raced with thoughts of Ashley—hoping, praying that they were going to find her alive and safe. The road ahead seemed endless, the minutes stretching out like hours, and every passing second added to his growing unease.

About ten minutes into the drive, Beau's phone buzzed. He glanced at the screen, seeing Dennis Cooper's name flash across it. He quickly answered.

"Beau, it's Dennis," the voice on the other end was sharp, urgent. "We've got a lead. My team just informed me that Mr. Vincent's car is headed in the same direction as us. We put a tracking device on it, and it's about ten minutes ahead of us. If Ashley's there, we'll find her."

Hope flared in Beau's chest, though it was tempered by anxiety. "Then let's get there, fast."

"We're on it," Dennis confirmed before hanging up.

Beau's foot pressed harder on the accelerator as the car surged forward. Daniel remained quiet; his hands tight around the seat as the weight of the situation hung heavy between them.

An hour and a half later, they arrived at the destination, a secluded, run-down cabin surrounded by dense forest. They parked next to Bruno's car, which sat idly in front. Dennis's eyes scanned the area, and his colleague stepped out of the car with a brief nod, both men immediately drawing their weapons.

Beau's heart pounded as the adrenaline kicked in. He couldn't wait any longer. He had to get to Ashley. "Let's go," he said, his voice low and intense. "Stay close. We move fast," Dennis ordered, his eyes flicking to Beau and Daniel. "Be careful. We don't know what we're walking into."

The narrow walking track ahead was barely visible beneath the overgrown plants, and the silence of the forest was oppressive. Every footstep felt like it echoed. As they neared the cabin, Beau's breath caught in his throat—the scream that pierced the stillness was unmistakable. It was Ashley.

"Ashley!" Beau's heart leapt into his throat. Without thinking, he broke into a sprint, his legs carrying him faster than he thought possible. Behind him, he could hear Dennis and his colleague following quickly, but nothing mattered except reaching her.

He burst through the door, and the sight that greeted him almost stopped his heart. Bruno was on top of Ashley, his fist raised, striking her with cruel violence. He didn't even notice Beau's arrival until it was too late.

In a flash, Beau lunged at Bruno, grabbing him by the shoulders and yanking him away. Bruno was sent sprawling to the floor, his head snapping back with the force of Beau's punch. Beau didn't hesitate—he stood over Bruno, fists clenched, chest heaving with rage, but his eyes immediately darted to Ashley, who lay motionless on the floor.

His knees hit the ground beside her, his hands shaking as he pressed his fingers to her neck. His breath caught in his throat when he felt the faintest pulse—she was alive. Barely.

"Ashley," he whispered, his voice breaking. He fumbled with a pocketknife Dennis handed him, slicing through the ropes that bound her wrists and ankles. His stomach churned as he saw the raw, angry marks on her skin. The sight only fuelled his anger further, his body trembling with the need to make Bruno pay for every second she'd spent in this hell.

Her body was limp in his arms, and he couldn't wait another second. "We need to get her to the hospital," he said, his voice hoarse, his grip tightening on her fragile form. He turned to Dennis, who was now securing Bruno with handcuffs. "Can you handle him?" Beau asked urgently.

"I've got it," Dennis replied, his tone cold and professional as he approached the subdued Bruno.

Without waiting another moment, Beau scooped Ashley into his arms, cradling her close to his chest. Every second counted. "You need to drive," he ordered Daniel, who nodded, already heading toward the vehicle.

The drive to the hospital was a blur. Beau held Ashley close in the back seat, his eyes never leaving her. The sight of her bruised face and bloodied lips made his stomach twist with fury. He felt helpless, but the one thing he could do was make sure she survived.

"Is she okay?" Daniel asked, glancing back in the rearview mirror, his voice tight with concern.

Beau's voice was thick with emotion as he replied, "She's breathing, but she's unconscious. We need to get her help fast."

They arrived at the hospital in record time, Daniel pulling directly into the emergency department. Beau leapt out of the car, his hands shaking as he lifted Ashley from the backseat and gently placed her onto a stretcher. A nurse was already there, gesturing for them to hurry inside.

A doctor rushed to meet them, her face grim. "What happened?"

"She was kidnapped and was being held captive," Beau said, his voice strained with barely controlled panic. "She hasn't regained consciousness since we found her."

The doctor nodded and signalled for the stretcher to be moved. "We'll take it from here. You'll need to wait here." With that, they whisked Ashley away, and Beau was left standing in the sterile waiting area, his heart hammering in his chest.

Daniel joined him, his face tense with worry. "I need to call Kelly?"

Beau rubbed his face, his mind still racing. "Yeah. Let her know we found her. But... we don't have any answers yet. It could be hours."

Daniel nodded, pulling out his phone to make the call. A few minutes later, he returned with a solemn expression. "She wants to come, but I told her to wait until we know more."

Beau nodded, grateful for the understanding. But the waiting was torture. He paced the room, his mind spinning with thoughts of Ashley—hoping she would pull through, hoping she would be okay.

And above all, Beau silently promised himself that he would never let anyone hurt her again.

"Ashley, can you hear me?" a female voice called out, unfamiliar yet urgent.

Faint murmurs surrounded her, a symphony of frantic voices, blending into one chaotic blur. Her body screamed in pain—her face, her ribs, every inch of her felt like it was on fire. Where was she? Panic clawed at the edges of her consciousness, but it wasn't until the images of Bruno's angry shouts and the sickening blow hit her like a wave that everything came flooding back.

Bruno.

The horror of his touch. The fear that had almost crushed her.

"Ashley, I need you to open your eyes," the voice coaxed, calm but firm.

She tried. Her eyelids felt like they weighed a thousand pounds, heavy and unyielding. She fought to open them, to focus, but they refused to obey.

"Ashley, can you squeeze my hand?" the voice persisted, and then—comforting and warm—a hand slipped into hers.

She willed her fingers to move. It took every ounce of her strength, but slowly, barely, they twitched. A small, tentative squeeze.

"Good, Ashley. That's good. Now, can you open your eyes for me?" the voice encouraged, steady and gentle.

She tried again. Her eyelids fluttered open briefly before slamming shut again, too heavy to keep open.

"That's it," the voice praised. "You're doing great, Ashley. Just keep going."

The voice grew more authoritative as it addressed someone nearby. "She needs an IV, stat. Cut these clothes off. Start cleaning the lacerations on her wrists first."

The words blended into the haze, and before Ashley could grasp onto them, darkness enveloped her once again.

When she woke next, everything was blurry. Her vision was like a fog, and her head throbbed in time with her pulse. Slowly, the world began to come into focus. A woman hovered over her, her face calm and reassuring, a stark contrast to the chaos Ashley had just escaped.

"Hello, Ashley. Welcome back," the woman said gently.

Ashley tried to speak, her throat raw and dry, but the words wouldn't come. Her lips moved faintly. "Where..." She croaked, barely able to get the question out.

"You're in the hospital," the woman explained. "I'm Dr. Fraser. You've been through a lot. We had to put in an IV because you were severely dehydrated, and we're treating the lacerations on your wrists and body." She smiled warmly, a kind light in her eyes. "You're safe now. Once we finish here, there are a few people eager to see you."

Ashley's mind tried to focus, the name that had been echoing in her head barely escaping her lips. "Beau..."

Dr. Fraser's smile softened further. "Mr. Tremain was the one who found you and brought you here. He's been waiting for news about you. He's very worried, Ashley."

Meanwhile, Beau was in a storm of his own. The minutes felt like hours, each one stretching on endlessly, pulling him further into his anxiety. He paced restlessly, barely able to sit still. His hands clenched and unclenched; his body wound tight with tension. Daniel sat across from him, his eyes filled with concern, knowing just how much was riding on this moment.

The door to the waiting area opened, and a doctor appeared, her expression serious but not entirely grim. Beau's heart lurched in his chest. This was the moment that could change everything.

The doctor walked toward them, glancing between Beau and Daniel. "Mr. Tremain?" she asked, her voice steady but with a hint of softness.

Beau sprang to his feet, his voice tight with desperation. "Is she okay? How is she? What's happening?" His words tumbled out in a rush, his body trembling with worry.

The doctor paused for a moment, her gaze softening as she observed the strain in his expression. "She's stable," she said, her voice calm and reassuring. "Very weak and severely dehydrated, but she's awake and conscious. She has bruising and lacerations on her face and body, which we've cleaned and dressed as best we can. Fortunately, she wasn't sexually assaulted. She's very fortunate you found her when you did."

A wave of relief crashed over Beau, and he sank back into the chair behind him, his legs giving way beneath him. He gripped his knees to steady himself, trying to catch his breath. Daniel's hand rested on his shoulder, grounding him in that moment.

"She's going to be okay?" Daniel asked softly, his voice filled with the same fear that gripped Beau's chest.

The doctor offered a small, reassuring smile. "Yes, she should make a full recovery. We've started her on IV fluids to treat the dehydration, and we'll keep her under observation overnight. She's going to be sore for a while, and it will take time for her to heal fully. She is asking for you. A nurse will let you know as soon as you can see her."

Beau closed his eyes, releasing a shaky breath. He didn't know if he could ever let go of the tension that had kept him on edge since they found her. But for now, the most important thing was clear: Ashley was alive. She was going to be okay.

And that was a promise he would keep to her—he would make sure nothing and no one would ever hurt her again.

Chapter Twenty

Finally, Beau was allowed to see Ashley. The moment he stepped into her hospital room, a tidal wave of emotion crashed over him, nearly knocking him off balance. His chest tightened, his breath hitched, and the burning in his eyes threatened to overwhelm him. He had prepared himself for this moment, but nothing could have steeled him against the sight of her.

Ashley lay motionless in the hospital bed, her pale skin a stark contrast to the bruises and cuts marring her face and arms. An IV line was taped to her arm, and bandages were wrapped snugly around her wrists, covering the cruel marks left behind. Each injury screamed of the pain she had endured, a silent testament to her strength. Yet, despite it all, she was alive, and that alone was enough to bring Beau to his knees.

He approached her bedside slowly, his footsteps hesitant as though crossing some invisible threshold. The soft beeping of the monitors filled the room, a steady rhythm that felt almost like a lifeline. His throat tightened as he reached her, and for a moment, he simply stood there, taking her in.

Then, as if sensing him, Ashley's eyelids fluttered. Slowly, her eyes opened, their usual brightness dimmed but not extinguished. Her gaze wandered the room before landing on him. Recognition flickered across her face—brief, but undeniable.

"Ashley," Beau whispered, his voice trembling as he sank into the chair beside her. His hand hovered over hers, hesitant to touch her fragile form. "I'm here, angel face. I'm right here."

Her lips parted, a soft sound escaping them. "Beau…" she breathed, her voice a faint whisper, laced with exhaustion. Her eyes searched his face, as though grounding herself in the only thing that felt real.

He reached out, carefully taking her hand in his, his touch feather-light. "You're safe now," he murmured, his voice thick with emotion. "You're going to be okay. I promise."

Tears welled in his eyes as he leaned closer, unable to look away from her. The fear lingering in her gaze tore at his heart, but beneath it, he saw something else—something fragile yet resilient. Love.

"I thought I'd lost you," he confessed, his voice breaking. "I can't lose you, Ashley. I won't."

Her fingers twitched in his grasp, squeezing weakly. Despite the exhaustion etched into her face, a small, tremulous smile appeared. "I love you," she whispered, her voice barely audible but filled with quiet determination.

Beau couldn't hold back anymore. He leaned in, pressing his forehead gently to hers. "I love you, Ashley. I've always loved you," he said, his words a vow, a promise.

For a moment, the world outside the room faded away, leaving only the two of them in their fragile, shared space. The pain and fear that had dominated the past days melted into the background, replaced by a glimmer of hope. No matter what lay ahead, Beau knew one thing with certainty: he would never let her face it alone.

Ashley felt utterly drained, her body ached, and her wrists and ankles stung with every small movement. Yet, the moment Beau entered her hospital room, his familiar presence washed over her like a balm. Everything felt right again, even in the wake of the terror she'd endured. His warm, steady hand in hers was her anchor, grounding her in the safety of the present.

In that fragile moment, Ashley believed everything would be okay.

Her head throbbed, her body heavy with exhaustion. Earlier, when the doctors and nurses had treated her, their kind words and gentle touches had been a lifeline. But one question had shaken her to her core: Had she been sexually assaulted? The implications of the question had hit her like a truck, making her realise just how much worse things could have been. A shiver coursed through her at the memory, but she clung to the fact that she had been spared that particular nightmare.

Beau's hand tightened around hers as though sensing her thoughts. His voice was calm, soothing, when he spoke. "Bruno?" she rasped, her throat dry and voice barely audible.

Beau's jaw tightened, his anger flickering in his eyes before he quickly masked it. "The police have him," he assured her, his tone steady. "He'll never hurt you again, Ashley. I promise."

Tears welled up and slipped down her cheeks. "Thank you," she whispered, her gratitude as deep as her exhaustion.

Though her words warmed Beau's heart, guilt lingered like a shadow. He didn't feel like the hero she believed him to be—he only felt like the man who had failed to protect her in the first place.

Just then, the door opened, and Daniel entered with Kelly, who held little Brian in her arms. The boy's wide eyes lit up when he spotted Ashley, though his joy quickly turned to uncertainty when he saw her bruised and bandaged face.

Ashley tried to smile for him, but her energy was fading fast. Her eyelids fluttered shut, the weight of sleep pulling her under. Beau knelt beside Brian, his voice soft and reassuring. "Ash is just really tired, buddy. But she's getting better."

Brian's lip quivered, and Kelly leaned in, whispering gentle words into his ear. Gathering his courage, Brian reached out with his small hand, carefully touching Ashley's cheek. His voice was shaky but full of love. "I love you, Ash. The police got the bad man, okay?"

Even in her near-sleep state, Ashley murmured faintly, "Thank you, little man." The words were barely audible, but they brought a small smile to Brian's face.

Recognising how much rest Ashley needed, Kelly and Daniel quietly ushered Brian out of the room, promising to visit again soon.

When the others left, Beau remained. He eased into the chair by her bedside, his hand never leaving hers. Even when the nurses hinted, he should go, he refused to budge. His determination prompted the doctor to step in, eventually granting him permission to stay.

Throughout the night, Beau sat vigil, his eyes fixed on Ashley's sleeping form. He watched the steady rise and fall of her chest, the faint movements of her fingers as if she were dreaming, and the bruises that marred her beautiful face. Every mark fuelled his resolve—he would never let anyone hurt her again.

When morning came, Ashley stirred. Her eyes fluttered open, greeted by the soft light of dawn streaming through the window. The first thing she saw was Beau, slumped slightly in the chair, his hand still holding hers.

"Beau?" she whispered, her voice raspy but steady.

His head snapped up, relief flooding his face. "Morning, angel face," he said softly, his lips curving into a smile. "How are you feeling?"

She gave a faint smile in return. "Better. Sore, but better."

Her gaze travelled over him, taking in the dark circles under his eyes and the stubble on his face. "You don't look so good," she teased weakly. "You need sleep."

"Not without you," Beau said firmly, his voice filled with tenderness.

Before Ashley could argue, the door opened, and the doctor entered with a warm smile. "Good morning, Ashley. How are you feeling today?"

"Better," Ashley replied, sitting up slightly with Beau's help.

The doctor nodded. "That's good to hear. You're well enough to go home today. I'll have the nurse remove your IV and finalise your discharge papers. You'll need to rest as much as possible, stay hydrated, and eat light meals. Recovery will take time, listen to your body, don't push yourself."

Beau's jaw tightened with determination. "Don't worry, Doctor. I'll make sure she's taken care of."

The doctor smiled knowingly. "I don't doubt it." She left the room, leaving the two of them alone.

Ashley turned to Beau, her voice soft but full of gratitude. "Thank you for staying. For saving me."

Beau leaned in, pressing a gentle kiss to her forehead.

Soon, Ashley was settled in Beau's car, the soothing hum of the engine filling the air. His careful, deliberate movements reminded her of how much he cared—each action conveying his determination to shield her from any further harm. He treated her like fragile glass, but rather than resenting it, she felt safe.

When they arrived home, she was surprised to find Daniel, Kelly, Jason, and Brian waiting on the porch. Their smiles were warm and welcoming, a stark contrast to the lingering darkness in her mind. Beau quickly got out, moving to her side of the car to help her out. His hands were steady and sure as they guided her to her feet, his touch a grounding presence.

Ashley looked at Jason as the others began to filter inside. "Can I talk to you for a moment?" she asked, her voice soft but clear.

Jason nodded, following her to a quiet corner of the yard. His expression was kind, though his gaze flickered toward Beau before meeting hers. "Looks like your past finally caught up with you," he said gently, a hint of teasing in his tone.

Ashley blushed, lowering her gaze. "I'm sorry, Jason. I didn't mean for things to get so… complicated."

Jason shook his head, his smile unwavering. "Don't be. I'm just relieved you're okay. And honestly, Ash… I'm glad you're happy. It wasn't the right time for us. It never would've been." He hesitated, then added with a wry chuckle, "Although I'll admit I didn't expect him to be the one to steal your heart."

Touched, Ashley leaned in and kissed him on the cheek. Out of the corner of her eye, she caught Beau watching them, his jaw tight with restrained emotion.

Jason noticed too, and he chuckled, nodding toward Beau. "I should probably go before he gets the wrong idea and decides to punch me."

They shared a quiet laugh, a rare moment of lightness after all the darkness. Jason gave her shoulder a reassuring squeeze, his voice gentle. "Take care of yourself, Ash, it was really nice to get to know you." With a final, lingering look, he got into his car and drove away.

As Jason disappeared down the street, Ashley turned to find Beau waiting patiently by the door. She could see the flicker of relief in his eyes when Jason left. Together, they walked inside, where Brian immediately ran to her, his small arms wrapping tightly around her legs.

Ashley crouched to his level, pulling him into a proper hug. "I missed you, little man," she said, her voice thick with emotion.

Brian beamed up at her, his eyes bright and innocent. "I missed you too, Ash! Beau said he's gonna protect you so no more bad men can hurt you."

Ashley's gaze shifted to Beau, her eyes soft and filled with warmth. "I'm lucky, aren't I?"

Brian nodded enthusiastically. "Yes! Super lucky!"

Not long after, Daniel, Kelly, and Brian said their goodbyes, each giving Ashley a gentle hug and Beau a knowing pat on the shoulder. "Take care of her," Daniel murmured as he left.

Once they were alone, Ashley turned to Beau. "You should go too," she said gently. "You've got work—"

"Not anymore," Beau interrupted, his tone firm but calm. "Jason's heading back to New York to oversee things there, and I've handed over control of your father's company to Daniel."

Ashley blinked, stunned. "What? Beau, you didn't—"

"I did," he said simply, lifting her hand to his lips and kissing it. "We've already lost so much time, Angel Face. I'm not losing any more. We belong together, and I'm staying."

Tears welled in Ashley's eyes as she leaned into him, resting her head against his chest. His arms wrapped around her securely, holding her like she might vanish if he let go.

Her voice trembled as she admitted, "I need a shower... I need to wash him off my skin." A violent shiver ran through her as the disgust crept into her voice.

Beau didn't hesitate. "Alright," he said, his voice steady as he helped her to her feet. "Let's get you upstairs."

In the bathroom, Beau adjusted the shower to the perfect temperature, his every movement calm and deliberate. Carefully, he removed the bandages from her wrists and ankles before helping her out of the clothes Kelly had brought from the hospital. He undressed too, his focus entirely on her needs. There was no hesitation, no embarrassment—just care.

Under the warm spray of the water, he washed her gently, his hands soothing and deliberate as they worked away the grime and the memories. Each touch was slow, deliberate, and healing. When he reached her hair, his fingers massaged her scalp in rhythmic circles, easing the tension that had been building for days. Ashley sighed softly, her body relaxing under his tender ministrations.

Once she was clean, Beau wrapped her in a towel, carefully patting her dry before drying himself.

"I could get used to this," Ashley teased, her voice lighter now but still full of gratitude.

Beau smiled, brushing a damp strand of hair from her face. "Good," he replied softly. "Because I plan to take care of you for the rest of your life."

Her heart fluttered at his words, and she leaned in to kiss him gently on the lips. "Thank you," she whispered.

After helping her into a comfortable nightgown, he bandaged her wrists with practiced care. "Your ankles?" he asked, his tone serious.

"They're fine," she assured him. "Just my wrists."

As he worked, a flicker of anger crossed his face. "I still can't let go of what he did to you," Beau admitted, his voice tight.

Ashley reached for his hand, her touch grounding. "You have to, Beau. Don't let him take up space in your heart or your mind. He's not worth it. I'm safe now."

His shoulders relaxed slightly, though the tension didn't fully leave him. "I love you," he said simply, his voice raw with emotion.

"I love you too," Ashley replied.

Beau helped her into bed, promising to bring her soup. When he returned, she ate slowly, exhaustion dragging at her every movement. Afterward, she drifted into a restless sleep.

But when she cried out in the middle of the night, trapped in the claws of a nightmare, Beau was there. He gathered her into his arms, whispering soothing words until her trembling subsided.

"You're safe," he murmured, pressing a kiss to her hair. "I've got you."

In his embrace, Ashley found peace again, her fears gradually fading away as she drifted back into a deep, dreamless sleep.

Chapter Twenty-One

Over the next week, Beau became Ashley's rock, his unwavering presence guiding her through the slow but steady process of recovery. He made sure she ate nutritious meals, gently encouraged her to take small walks to regain her strength, and most importantly, he listened. Each conversation they shared became a stepping stone, helping her navigate through the tangled emotions and fears that had gripped her.

Daniel, Kelly, and little Brian visited every afternoon, their warm, familiar presence a comfort to Ashley. Brian would climb onto her lap with his favourite storybook and listen to her read to him with the endearing enthusiasm only a child could muster. Kelly often brought homemade soups or light casseroles, and Daniel would offer quiet but heartfelt encouragement. Their visits brought a sense of normalcy, a reminder of the love and support surrounding her.

As the days passed, Ashley grew stronger. The bruises and cuts that once marked her body began to fade, her physical wounds slowly healing. The emotional scars, however, took more time. Nightmares still haunted her, but they grew less frequent as Beau held her in his arms every night, his steady heartbeat and soothing whispers grounding her in safety.

One quiet evening, as they sat on the couch with a soft blanket draped over them, Ashley looked up at him. Her eyes, though still carrying a shadow of pain, were soft and full of emotion. "I love you, Beau," she said, her voice trembling with sincerity. "I didn't think I'd ever get to say that to you again."

Her gaze faltered, and she took a shaky breath, her fingers nervously twisting the edge of the blanket. "I thought he was going to kill me," she admitted, her voice breaking. Tears welled in her eyes as she whispered, "I actually asked him to kill me. I told him I'd rather be dead than be with him."

Beau's heart clenched at her words, the weight of her pain pressing heavily on his chest. He reached out, gently cupping her face with both hands. His thumbs brushed away her tears as he spoke, his voice steady but thick with emotion. "Ashley, you're here. You're alive. And you're so much stronger than you realise. What he did doesn't define you. You survived, and that takes more courage than I can put into words."

Ashley let out a small, shaky sob, leaning into his touch. "I don't feel strong," she murmured, her voice barely audible.

"You don't have to feel it," Beau said gently. "You just have to keep going, one step at a time. And I'll be with you every step of the way."

She smiled faintly through her tears, the warmth of his words wrapping around her like a protective shield. "Thank you, Beau," she whispered.

He pressed a soft kiss to her forehead, holding her close as the room fell into a peaceful silence. In that moment, Ashley felt something she hadn't in a long time—hope.

By the fifth night, Ashley felt stronger—not just physically, but emotionally too. Her bruises were fading, her cuts were healing, and with Beau's constant care, her nightmares were becoming less frequent. But there was one thing that hadn't changed: Beau hadn't made love to her since she'd come home from the hospital.

They would hug, kiss, and share tender moments, but whenever things began to deepen, he would gently pull away with the same careful words:

"I don't want to hurt you," or "You're still recovering."

At first, she'd understood, even appreciated his restraint. But now, it was driving her crazy. She didn't want to be treated like she was fragile anymore. She needed more than his care; she needed all of him.

That night, as Beau stepped into the shower, Ashley sat on the edge of the bed, her mind racing. Enough was enough, she decided. If he wouldn't take the first step, then she would.

She slipped out of her robe, her heart pounding, and quietly padded toward the bathroom. Steam billowed out as she opened the door, the sound of running water masking her approach. Beau stood with his back to her, washing his hair, his broad shoulders glistening under the warm spray.

Without hesitation, Ashley stepped into the shower, her movements deliberate. The heat of the water cascaded over her as she slipped her arms around his waist, pressing herself gently against his back.

Beau stiffened for a moment, surprised, but before he could say a word, Ashley leaned in and began pressing soft kisses along his shoulder blade, her lips trailing upward toward his neck.

"Ashley…" he murmured, his voice a mix of surprise and something deeper.

"Shh," she whispered against his skin, her hands sliding up his chest. "I need you, Beau. All of you."

He turned slowly, water streaming down his face, his eyes locking with hers. "You're still—"

"Don't," she interrupted, placing a finger against his lips. "I'm not fragile, Beau. I want you. I need you."

Her words hit him hard, and for a moment, he just stared at her, the water falling between them. Then, with a groan that came from deep in his chest, he reached for her, pulling her close as his lips found hers.

The kiss was slow and deep, full of all the pent-up desire and emotion they'd both been holding back. His hands roamed her body with a reverence that made her heart ache, his touch both careful and insistent.

"I was trying to protect you," he murmured against her lips.

"I don't need protecting from you," she whispered back, her hands tangling in his wet hair.

Beau's restraint shattered, and he kissed her with a passion that left her breathless. The shower's warmth surrounded them as their bodies pressed together, every touch and caress speaking the words they couldn't say aloud.

When they finally stepped out of the shower, wrapped in towels and the heat of each other's presence, Beau lifted her into his arms and carried her to the bed. He laid her down gently, as though she were the most precious thing in the world, and leaned over her, his gaze searching hers.

"I love you, Ashley," Beau said as he lay beside her, his voice thick with emotion. "You have no idea how much I've wanted you this past week. It's taken everything in me to hold back."

Her eyes softened, and she reached out, cupping his cheek with a tenderness that made his chest ache. "I'm right here," she whispered, her voice steady but filled with longing.

For a moment, Beau simply looked at her, his hand brushing a strand of damp hair from her face. Then, as if a dam had broken inside him, he pulled her into his arms and kissed her. It wasn't a tentative kiss—it was deep, intense, and filled with all the passion and need he'd been suppressing.

Ashley responded immediately, her hands tangling in his hair as she pressed herself closer to him. The kiss grew fiercer, and the space between them disappeared as if the entire week of holding back had built to this singular, undeniable moment.

"I didn't want to hurt you," Beau murmured against her lips, his hands sliding down to her waist, pulling her flush against him.

"You're not," she whispered back, her voice trembling with both desire and certainty. "You could never hurt me, Beau. Please… don't hold back."

The intensity in her voice left no room for doubt, and Beau's hesitation melted away. He kissed her again, this time slower, more deliberate. His hands moved over her with a mix of reverence and hunger, as if rediscovering every inch of her.

Ashley gasped softly at his touch, her body arching beneath his. She had waited for this moment, and now, every caress, every kiss, felt like a renewal of their connection—a reclaiming of what had almost been lost.

Beau took his time, his movements tender yet filled with an unrelenting passion. He worshiped her with his hands and lips, ensuring that every moment was about her, about reminding her of how much she meant to him.

"You're everything to me," he whispered as he leaned over her, his gaze locking with hers. "Everything."

Ashley's heart swelled at his words, and she pulled him closer, her voice trembling with emotion. "I love you, Beau. I've always loved you."

Their love made the moment all the more powerful—an intimate union of trust, passion, and healing. They moved together with a rhythm that felt natural, as if they had always been meant for this.

When they finally lay entwined, their breaths mingling and their bodies warm from the afterglow, Ashley rested her head on Beau's chest. She traced lazy circles on his skin with her fingers, feeling his steady heartbeat beneath her touch.

Beau kissed the top of her head, his arms tightening around her. "I've wanted to show you how much I love you every day this week," he admitted softly. "But I didn't want to rush you."

She tilted her head to look at him, her smile soft but teasing. "Well, maybe next time don't wait so long. I might not always have the patience to wait for you to figure it out."

Beau laughed, the sound deep and warm, and he kissed her forehead. "Noted," he said, his voice filled with a mix of love and amusement.

As they lay there in the quiet of the night, their breaths evening out, Ashley felt a sense of peace she hadn't felt in weeks. She was home—not just in the physical sense, but in Beau's arms, where she knew she truly belonged.

Sunday morning, exactly one week after she had been rescued, Ashley woke to the soft warmth of the sun streaming through the windows. Her body felt stronger, the aches of recovery still there but less pronounced. As she made her way downstairs, Beau was right behind her, his hand a steady presence on her back.

She paused at the bottom of the staircase, her breath catching in her throat as she looked into the living room. The entire space was transformed. Every available surface was covered in vibrant flowers—lilies, roses, orchids, and daisies in every colour imaginable, their fragrances filling the air. It was like stepping into a dream, a sea of beauty and life after everything she'd endured.

Her eyes widened as she turned to Beau, her voice barely a whisper. "What's all this?"

Beau smiled, a warmth in his eyes that made her heart flutter. Without a word, he dropped to one knee before her, his hands moving to retrieve something from his pocket. Ashley's gaze dropped to his hand as he revealed a stunning sapphire and diamond ring, set in platinum, catching the light in the most dazzling way.

"Angel face," he began, his voice thick with emotion, "I love you. I think I've loved you since the day I met you. Will you make me the happiest man alive and marry me—as soon as possible?"

Ashley's hand flew to her mouth, tears springing to her eyes before she could stop them. The overwhelming wave of emotion—the relief, the love, the joy—came rushing over her. She sank to her knees in front of him, her arms instinctively wrapping around his neck as she pressed her lips to his in a kiss filled with all the words she couldn't say.

"Yes," she whispered between kisses, her voice thick with happiness and gratitude. "Yes, please."

Beau grinned, his heart soaring at her response. He carefully took her hand, sliding the ring onto her finger with such tenderness it made her chest tighten. Then, he lifted her hand to his lips, pressing a soft kiss to the sapphire stone, his eyes never leaving hers.

"I love you," he murmured, his voice full of reverence and passion.

Ashley smiled through her tears, her heart full. "I love you too."

Without breaking the moment, Beau pulled her into his arms, kissing her deeply, as if to show her just how much she meant to him. The kiss was long and tender, filled with every ounce of love, relief, and passion he'd felt for her over the years and especially these last few days.

As they finally pulled away, both breathless, Ashley gazed at the ring on her finger, then back at Beau. "You've been planning this?" she asked, a playful smile tugging at her lips despite the tears still glistening in her eyes.

Beau chuckled, his fingers gently brushing away a tear that had slipped down her cheek. "I knew I couldn't wait forever. I just needed the right moment. And now… there's nothing holding us back."

Ashley laughed softly, the sound full of joy. "I can't believe this is real," she whispered, her heart racing with the possibilities of the future they would build together.

Beau stood, pulling her up with him and into another tight embrace. "It's real, Angel Face. And we're going to make the most of every single moment."

They stayed there for a long moment, wrapped up in each other, before Beau finally pulled back, his expression soft but serious. "So… what do you say? Will you marry me soon, Ashley?"

She nodded, her heart bursting with happiness. "Yes. Yes, I will."

Beau's smile grew impossibly wider, and he kissed her again, this time softly, reverently, as if sealing a promise that no matter what, they would always have each other. Their love had been tested by the darkest of circumstances, but now, there was nothing but light ahead of them.

Epilogue

Ashley and Beau were married two weeks after the proposal, in a small, intimate ceremony surrounded by their closest friends. It was a quiet affair, with only those who had supported them through the hardest of times by their sides. There was no grandiose event, no extravagant décor. Just the two of them, promising forever in front of the people who truly mattered.

Ashley looked radiant as she stood at the altar. Her beauty was undeniable, but it was more than just her appearance. There was a light in her eyes, a joy that had blossomed over the past month as she healed, physically and emotionally. She was glowing, a mixture of love, relief, and hope. Beau couldn't take his eyes off her. In that moment, he knew he had made the right decision, that he was exactly where he was meant to be.

Her dress was simple but elegant, a soft ivory silk that clung to her curves in all the right ways. Her hair, styled simply in loose waves, framed her face perfectly. Beau's heart swelled as he watched her approach, his breath catching in his chest. This was the woman he would spend the rest of his life with, and nothing could ever take that away from him.

The ceremony itself was short, sweet, and filled with emotion. Beau had written his vows from the heart, speaking softly but with conviction as he pledged his life to Ashley. Her vows were just as heartfelt, a promise to always stand by him, to love him through every moment of their lives. As they exchanged rings, the weight of the promise they were making to each other settled in—this was the beginning of a new chapter for them both.

After the ceremony, they shared a quiet moment together, just the two of them, before heading to the reception. It was an intimate gathering at a small venue, with a few close friends and some of their colleagues. The atmosphere was warm, filled with laughter, love, and the shared joy of everyone there. Daniel, Kelly, Brian, and Jason were all there, smiling widely, each offering their congratulations to the newlyweds.

Beau and Ashley had agreed from the very beginning that they didn't want bachelor or bachelorette parties. After everything they had been through the last time, they both agreed that they didn't want to take the risk. They had no need for wild parties, no desire for anything extravagant. Their love was enough.

Later that evening, after the last of their guests had left and the lights had dimmed, Ashley and Beau stood together in the quiet of the empty hall, just the two of them. Beau pulled her close, his arms around her waist as he kissed her forehead softly.

"Did you ever think we'd make it here?" Beau asked, his voice low and full of wonder.

Ashley smiled up at him, her hand resting gently on his chest. "No, I didn't. And now here we are, married."

Beau kissed her softly, his lips lingering on hers. "Here we are," he repeated, his voice filled with awe. "And I'm never letting you go."

Ashley laughed softly; her heart lighter than it had ever been. "Good," she whispered. "Because I'm never letting you go either."

Twelve months later, Beau helped Ashley out of the car and gently placed their three-day-old daughter into her arms. His heart swelled with pride as he kissed Ashley on the lips, then leaned down to press a soft kiss on his daughter's head. "Welcome home, my two favourite girls," he said warmly, his voice filled with love.

Inside, their friends Daniel, Kelly, Brian and their nine-month-old daughter, Sally, were waiting. The living room was alive with warmth and laughter, the perfect setting for their new family to celebrate together. As Ashley carefully settled into an armchair, Kelly bent down to kiss her cheek, her smile wide and sincere. "Welcome home, Ash. She's absolutely beautiful! Have you decided on a name yet?"

Ashley glanced at Beau; his pride so evident as he beamed at their daughter. "Beau suggested we name her Helena, after my mother," she replied, her voice soft and filled with emotion.

"That's perfect," Kelly said warmly, her eyes sparkling. "A beautiful name for a beautiful little girl."

Just then, Brian approached with a thoughtful expression, eager to take a look at the baby. "Hi, Ash," he said, his face suddenly clouded with a touch of sadness. "Hi there, Helena."

Ashley immediately noticed the change in his demeanour and gently asked, "What's wrong, sweetheart?"

Brian hesitated, looking up at her with wide, worried eyes. "Do you still love me now that you have your own baby?"

Ashley's heart melted at the vulnerability in his voice. She looked over at Beau, who stepped in to hold their daughter, allowing Ashley the chance to pull Brian onto her lap. "Oh, sweetheart," she murmured, her hand tenderly stroking his hair. "You will always be my little man. No matter how many babies I have, I'll always love you and Sally."

She gave him a playful tickle, causing him to giggle. "Will you still love me when you're all grown up?"

Brian nodded, his small face lighting up with a smile, before turning to Beau with a mischievous grin. "I was going to marry you, but I guess I can't now."

Laughter filled the room as Beau ruffled Brian's hair, his grin broad and affectionate. "Don't worry, buddy. Someday, you'll find a wonderful girl, just like I was lucky enough to find Ashley."

"Really?" Brian's eyes brightened with hope, and Ashley could see the joy in his expression.

"Really," Beau promised with a wink, pulling Brian into a one arm playful hug.

The laughter slowly faded, and soon they found themselves alone, standing in the quiet of Helena's nursery, gazing down at their daughter as she slept peacefully in her crib. The soft rise and fall of her tiny chest filled the room with an almost surreal calm.

Ashley leaned back into Beau, feeling the comfort of his arms securely wrapped around her waist. His presence was a constant source of warmth and safety. He lowered his head, his breath warm against her ear. "Are you happy?" he whispered, his voice filled with tenderness.

"Mmm," she murmured, leaning further into him, the weight of the moment sinking in. "I've never been happier." She turned in his arms, meeting his gaze, her eyes full of love. "Are you?"

He smiled; his expression so full of contentment that it made her heart flutter. Beau pressed a soft kiss to her lips, the kind that spoke of years of shared memories, of love built in quiet moments like this one. "You made me the happiest man alive when you said 'I do' on our wedding day. And every day since, you've only made me happier."

Ashley smiled, her heart swelling with love for the man who had stood by her through everything. "We've come so far, haven't we?" she whispered.

Beau nodded, his thumb tracing gentle circles on her waist. "From that very first moment I saw you, I knew you were the one. And now, we have this— our family."

Looking over at their daughter, then back at Beau, Ashley's heart was full. "I wouldn't trade our life for anything."

"Me neither," Beau said softly, his voice a quiet promise. They stood together in the stillness, wrapped in each other's love, knowing that no matter what the future held, they would face it together—with their hearts full of love for each other and for the little family they had created.

The End

Shattered Dreams

Alison Reid

A complete standalone romance
Previously published individually

Chapter One

Flynn Oakland leaned back in his leather chair in the study at Oakland Park, the late afternoon sun spilling molten light across the polished wood floors. The tall windows framed the gardens outside, the lake shimmering faintly in the distance, but the beauty of the estate could not pierce the weight pressing down on him. The silence of the room was almost suffocating, broken only by the faint creak of the leather beneath him and the occasional whisper of wind through the trees.

His hand drifted through his thick black hair, restless, as his blue eyes roamed the room he had known since boyhood: shelves lined with rare first editions, the glint of polished mahogany, and the stern, approving gazes of Oakland ancestors staring down from their portraits like an unyielding tribunal. Every detail spoke of legacy, power, and expectation—but tonight, every detail felt hollow.

At thirty-three, divorced, with everything money could buy, he should have felt free. Instead, emptiness coiled tight in his chest, an ache no success could quiet. He had chased achievement until he was breathless, but the triumphs only echoed back at him, meaningless.

His gaze fell on the envelope lying on his desk, crisp and heavy, his name penned in the neat script of Henry Rockwell—lawyer, family confidant, and father of the only woman Flynn had ever truly loved. His throat tightened even before he reached for it.

The paper crackled under his fingers as he tore it open. The documents inside confirmed what he already knew but hadn't wanted to face: his marriage was officially over.

Two years. Two years wasted in a union that had been nothing but performance. Yasmin had adored his money, his name, the glittering social world attached to both—but never him. The whispers of other men had reached his ears often enough to sting, though they cut less deeply than the truth he'd always known. He had never loved her, and she had never wanted him for more than the doors his name could open.

The memory of his wedding surfaced unbidden: obscene extravagance, flowers priced like mansions, gowns chosen not for beauty but for status. Gwen Oakland had presided over it all with approval sharp as steel. Yasmin had smiled through the spectacle, playing her role to perfection, and Flynn had played his— dutiful son, broken man, willing sacrifice.

He pressed the decree flat on the desk, his jaw clenching. He never would have married Yasmin had his heart not already been in ruins. But his mother had urged it, insisting Yasmin was *'perfectly suitable'*, and he—bleeding, raw, and desperate to numb the hollow ache of loss—had listened.

Loss had a name.

Pippa.

The sound of it inside his mind was enough to make him flinch. He closed his eyes, and there she was—emerald eyes, a laugh like sunlight breaking through clouds, the warmth of her hand curling into his as though it belonged there forever. He had loved her in a way he had never thought himself capable of, fierce and certain, as though the future had already been written for them both.

And then she had destroyed it.

The night he planned to propose, when he had rehearsed every vow of forever, she had vanished. Not with tears or hesitation, but with a letter. A single page that bled him dry.

Flynn reached into the bottom drawer, pulling out the worn, folded paper. Its edges were frayed, the ink faint from the passage of time, but the words inside remained sharp as glass. He unfolded it with reverence and dread, as if it were both relic and weapon, and began to read for what must have been the thousandth time.

Flynn,

I've tried to fight this, tried to ignore the truth I can no longer deny. But I can't stay, and I can't let you continue to believe in something that isn't real.

His vision blurred as memory overlaid reality: the summer house lit with lanterns, Pippa's laughter echoing as she leaned into him, whispering she could never leave him.

I don't love you the way you think I do. I care for you, I always will, but not in the way a woman should care for the man she is meant to spend her life with.

Liar. His chest tightened until he could barely breathe. He remembered the glow in her eyes, the way she looked at him as though he were the only man alive. He remembered the promise in her kiss, the tenderness that now read as betrayal. *Had it all been a performance?*

You deserve someone who can give you everything you need, everything your heart wants—and I am not that person.

He pressed his fist against his mouth, swallowing the raw ache. His mother had told him once that love was weakness. Perhaps she had been right.

Please understand that this is for the best. I cannot be the person you hope I am. I cannot be the person you love. Holding on will only bring us both pain.

Pain was all that had ever remained.

I am leaving, and you must try to move on. Believe me when I say it's not easy for me, but it's necessary. You deserve happiness—true happiness—and I am not the one to give it to you.

—Pippa

The last stroke of her name felt like a blade every time. He folded the letter with aching care, sliding it back into the drawer as though he could cage the past. But the memories always escaped.

The emerald engagement ring, untouched in its velvet box, gleamed faintly from the desk's corner. He picked it up, thumb brushing the stone, a mirror of her eyes. A symbol of the future he had been denied.

That was the night he had stopped believing in love. And tonight, he vowed again: never again would he allow anyone close enough to destroy him. Never again would he hand over his heart like a weapon to be used against him. He would guard it, lock it away, build walls higher than even Pippa's memory could scale.

The knock on his study door was soft, polite on the surface. But the presence behind it was anything but. Flynn didn't need to ask who it was.

"Come in, Mother."

The door opened, and Gwen Oakland swept into the room. Her silk blouse gleamed under the fading light, pearls at her throat immaculate, her tailored suit as crisp as her posture. She moved with the controlled elegance of a queen entering her throne room, every step measured, every glance sharp.

"You look exhausted," she observed coolly. "Divorces are untidy. But that is why I'm here. We need to discuss how to move forward."

Flynn leaned back, arms folded across his chest. "*We?*"

"Of course." Her brow arched with faint disapproval. "Appearances matter. The Oaklands cannot afford whispers. It is time to consider a stronger match— a woman who will—"

"No."

The single word cut through the room like a blade. For the briefest moment, Gwen faltered. Her lips parted before composure returned, every line of her face tightening. "Excuse me?"

Flynn stood, his tall frame radiating the authority she had long claimed as her own. He moved to the window, the skyline glittering behind him, before turning back, eyes like ice.

"I said no. I'm done letting you arrange my life as if I were a pawn. Yasmin was your choice, your manipulation. And it was a mistake I'll never repeat."

Her hand tightened on the desk. "Flynn, you're being dramatic. Yasmin may not have been ideal—"

"She was a disaster." His voice cracked sharp across the room. "And you knew it. But you pushed because she was *suitable*. Because she suited you. I paid for that mistake with two years of my life. I will not pay again."

For the first time in years, Gwen truly studied him—not as a son to command but as a man standing in opposition. Her eyes narrowed, calculating, cool. "You sound certain."

"I am." His tone was final, every syllable deliberate. "My life is mine. My choices are mine. And I don't want your advice on women, on marriage, on anything. Your influence ended with Yasmin."

A long silence stretched between them. Then Gwen straightened, smoothing an invisible crease from her blouse, her composure immaculate. Only her eyes betrayed her, burning with quiet fury.

"You're making a mistake," she said at last, her voice cool as winter. "Oaklands cannot afford to disregard tradition. Reputation is everything. You will learn that again, in time."

She turned, heels clicking in sharp staccato against the polished floor as she swept from the study. Flynn remained rooted where he stood, jaw tight, listening to the echo of her retreat until it dissolved into silence.

He exhaled slowly, dragging a hand through his hair, the tension in his shoulders refusing to ease. For years he had bent to his mother's will, too hollowed by loss, too broken to resist when she had pressed her advantage. But he was not that man anymore. Tonight, had proved it. The confrontation hadn't freed him entirely—those chains ran deep, forged by grief, duty, and years of manipulation—but something had shifted.

In the ragged wake of their clash, he felt it: a fissure in the walls that had long held him captive. Beneath the layers of bitterness and resignation, something stirred—a dangerous, fragile spark that felt perilously close to hope.

The sunlight slanted through the floor-to-ceiling windows, casting golden stripes across the polished wood. For Flynn, it should have felt comforting— but it only reminded him of what he had lost.

Half a continent away, another life moved in parallel. The sunlight slanted across the San Francisco studio, golden and deliberate, catching every crystal, every seam, every shimmer of fabric. Pippa moved among the racks with practiced precision, adjusting the fit of a sparkling evening gown on their client, renowned actress Miranda Hale. Each touch was confident, exact—every detail mattered.

"Hold still, Miranda," Pippa murmured, eyes sharp as she scanned the dress for the slightest flaw. "The shoulder seam needs to sit perfectly, or it will read crooked on camera."

Chloe hovered nearby, sleek tablet in hand, eyes flicking between schedule and gown. For three years, she had been Pippa's right hand, her silent partner in running the studio with precision and grace. Together, they had built a world of order from chaos—a sanctuary of fabric, form, and focus.

Miranda twirled in front of the mirror, laughter light and appreciative. "Perfection, as always, Pippa," she said, warmth in her tone. "You make me look like I belong on the red carpet."

Pippa allowed herself a faint smile but didn't pause her work. Perfection wasn't a gift—it was a demand she placed on herself. Her mind, however, was already elsewhere, the edges of memory tugging at her attention like wind at the hem of a gown.

The sharp vibration of Pippa's phone rattled across the counter, slicing through the hum of the studio like a bell. She glanced at the screen, her stomach twisting when she saw the area code: New York. Her pulse quickened, a familiar tension coiling in her chest.

Chloe, sensing the shift before Pippa spoke, leaned closer. "Pippa?" she asked carefully, her eyes scanning for the unease she knew too well.

Pippa lifted the phone, steadying her voice even as her hands trembled slightly. "Hello?"

"Hello—this is New York Presbyterian Hospital. Is this Pippa Rockwell?"

Her throat closed, words sticking. "Yes… speaking."

"We're calling about your father, Henry Rockwell. He's had a heart attack. He's awake and responsive, but he should not be alone. We recommend you come as soon as possible."

The words struck like a physical blow, stealing her breath. Her grip tightened around the phone, knuckles whitening. "Is he stable?" she asked, voice tight and trembling beneath the veneer of calm.

"He is," the nurse replied, "but he needs family here. Can you come?"

"Yes," Pippa said firmly, swallowing the rising panic. "I'll be there."

Chloe was instantly at her side, steadying her with gentle hands. "Oh, Pippa… we'll get you there. You just focus on him. You don't have to face this alone."

Pippa drew in a shaky breath, the weight of years, distance, and memory pressing down. San Francisco had become her fortress, her sanctuary—a world she had built with meticulous care, control, and independence. New York, by contrast, was a battlefield she had long avoided. Streets, lights, buildings—they were all haunted by memories of Flynn, of loss, of a love that had broken her in ways no one here had ever seen.

Chloe's hand lingered in hers, a tether to the present. "I'll pack your bag. You just focus on your father."

Pippa nodded, her resolve forming between fear and duty. "Alright. We need to leave as soon as possible."

Half an hour later, the bright San Francisco light streaming through the studio windows felt impossibly heavy, almost tangible, as if the city itself were reluctant to let her go. Every street, every familiar building pressed against her memory, tugging at threads she had long tried to sever. But her father needed her. And New York was waiting—whether she was ready or not.

The plane's engines hummed beneath her seat, a steady vibration that seemed to echo the fluttering unrest in her chest. Pippa sank into the soft leather of first class seat, her fingers interlaced in her lap, knuckles pale from tension. Outside, the California coastline slipped away, cliffs and beaches blurring together, giving way to endless white clouds that stretched like frozen oceans below. The sunlight spilled over the cabin in strips, catching glints of gold in her hair and reflecting off the polished tray table, almost too bright, almost too real.

Beside her, Chloe buckled in, offering a reassuring smile, though her eyes betrayed worry. "You'll be okay, right?" she asked, her voice low, careful. "With your dad... and..." She hesitated, her gaze flicking sideways, the unfinished thought heavy between them. "You'll probably see him."

Pippa's lips thinned, a tight line across her face. She drew in a shallow breath, chest tightening as if the air itself were resisting her. "I don't know," she admitted, voice barely above a whisper. "I've stayed away for three years. I thought avoiding New York would make it easier, but..." She trailed off, words dissolving into the hum of the engines.

Chloe's hand reached over, threading her fingers through Pippa's in a grounding squeeze. "You've been strong, Pippa," she said, voice soft, steady. "You've built a life here. You've kept yourself busy, held it all together. But this—" Her hand pressed lightly against the back of Pippa's hand. "This you can't control. You just have to take it one step at a time."

Pippa nodded faintly, though her gaze remained fixed on the clouds outside, distant and untouchable. New York wasn't just streets and buildings—it was the place where Flynn still lived, where every heartbreak, every unanswered question lingered like smoke in the corners of her mind.

"You're going to see him," Chloe said, firm yet gentle. "Maybe even talk to him. Are you ready?"

Her jaw clenched, fingers flexing in search of an anchor. "I don't think anyone can be ready to see someone like Flynn again," she admitted, voice taut with old memory. "Three years, and he still feels like he's everywhere. But I have to be strong—for my father. That's what matters."

"Then that's what we'll do," Chloe said, nodding, her hand still holding hers. "One step at a time. And I'll be right there with you. You're not alone."

Pippa closed her eyes, leaning into the steady hum of the engines, the subtle sway of the plane, and Chloe's quiet strength. She drew in a long, measured breath, exhaling slowly, as if the act alone might tether her to reality. "Okay," she whispered. "I'll get through this. I have to."

Outside, the clouds blurred into rivers of white and silver. Inside, Pippa's mind slipped backward, tracing a path through memory.

The Oakland summer house. The garden after a storm, leaves glistening with droplets that caught sunlight like shards of glass. The air was heavy with rain and the faint perfume of wet earth. Flynn had stood on the veranda, tall, sure of himself, yet softened in the way he looked at her, a tenderness reserved for no one else.

"You know," he had said, teasing, his voice threaded with intent, "one day... maybe we could tell them. Maybe we could be together. Forever."

Her heart had leapt, the word ringing like a vow. She had imagined breakfasts in bed, laughter echoing through sunlit hallways, long walks under fading skies—a life she had believed would belong to them alone. His smile had lit her whole world.

And then there had been Gwen. Pippa could still hear the steel-threaded sweetness of his mother's voice, smooth and lethal all at once. "If Flynn were to marry someone deemed... unsuitable, someone not of the family's station or discretion... he could be stripped of control, denied his inheritance entirely."

Money, titles, social standing—Pippa had never cared for them. But Gwen's quiet, almost conspiratorial warning had landed like a blow. "You could be the reason he loses everything."

Her world had fractured in that instant. Fear—raw, choking, relentless—had silenced her heart. The words burned themselves into her mind. And in that quiet estate room, she had made the impossible choice: she had written the letter instead. Lied with her own hand. Chosen to protect him by destroying them both.

She could still imagine his face reading it—those piercing blue eyes clouded with shock, confusion, hurt. She had begged him, in her own way, not to come after her. And she had left before he could.

Three years later, the ache remained, sharp and insistent, yet beneath it stirred something new—a flicker of steel, a spark of determination she hadn't felt in years.

"Hey..." Chloe's hand on her arm drew her back to the present, grounding her in the cabin, in the hum of the engines, in the steady rhythm of reality.

Pippa opened her eyes, offering a fragile, wan smile. "I will be okay. Just... remembering," she said, swallowing hard. "Three years of remembering. And now... I have to face it all again."

Her gaze lifted to the clouds outside, distant and untouchable, but deep within, a spark ignited. She would go. She would face New York. Her father. Flynn. Every memory, every fear. All of it.

She had no choice.

Chapter Two

The plane shuddered gently as it began its descent, the city skyline slowly rising to meet them through the oval window. Pippa pressed her palm against the glass, her heart hammering as if it might leap from her chest. Manhattan stretched below her, familiar yet foreign after three long years—its streets, towering skyscrapers, and sweeping bridges all etched with memories she had tried desperately to bury.

Chloe leaned close, voice barely a whisper. "Almost there. You'll be okay."

Pippa nodded, forcing a slow, steadying breath. Her chest felt tight, her fingers trembling faintly against the armrest, betraying the calm she tried to project. Flying back to New York hadn't been a decision made lightly. Every mile closer to the city was a mile closer to Flynn—the man who still haunted her heart, the one she had left behind to protect both him and herself from Gwen's calculated manipulations.

The plane's wheels hit the tarmac with a muted thud, and the vibration shivered through her seat. The engines roared in reverse thrust, slowing the aircraft, and Pippa's stomach twisted with a mix of nerves, dread, and anticipation. Around her, other passengers murmured and fidgeted, the cabin alive with quiet energy, but she felt none of it. The ordinary bustle washed past her unnoticed, swallowed by the pressure in her chest—the relentless weight of a past she had sworn to leave behind pressing down as she returned to the city she had spent years avoiding.

Chloe's hand found hers again, warm and grounding. "No matter what happens, I'm right here," she murmured.

Pippa closed her eyes briefly, letting the reassurance seep into her like sunlight, though her mind inevitably drifted to the hospital, to her father's room, and unavoidably—to Flynn. *Would he even recognise her? Would he remember the way she had left, the letter that had shattered him entirely? And most frighteningly—would she have the strength to stand in the same room with him without the walls she had painstakingly built crumbling?*

The plane taxied toward the gate, the skyline sharpening into crisp detail. Stone and glass facades gleamed under the late afternoon sun, the hum of the city vibrating even through the tyres on the tarmac. Pippa's pulse quickened. Stepping off the plane meant stepping straight into a past that had never fully released her, a city that held both her father and the man she had never stopped loving.

Chloe squeezed her hand one last time. "Ready?"

Pippa inhaled deeply, unclenching her fingers. "As ready as I'll ever be," she whispered, her voice barely audible above the cabin noise.

The cabin door opened with a hiss, and the first rush of crisp New York air hit her face, carrying the familiar tang of city life beneath the antiseptic smell that clung to the plane. Step by step, she moved toward the exit, toward her father, toward the city—and toward the man whose presence still tugged at her heart with the power of old gravity.

The sliding glass doors of New York-Presbyterian Hospital parted with a soft whoosh, and Pippa stepped into the cool, antiseptic air of the hospital lobby. The scent of sanitiser and polished floors made her stomach twist—a harsh contrast to the faintly sweet, bracing perfume of the city she had left behind years ago.

Chloe stayed close, guiding her through the maze of sterile hallways. "Follow me," she said quietly. "Room 407. That's where he is."

Pippa barely registered the bustling staff, the hurried patients wheeling past, the murmur of voices and the squeak of carts. All she could see was her father's pale face, the sharp lines of a hospital bed, the fragile rhythm of a life interrupted.

They reached the elevator, and as the doors began to close, Chloe's hand found hers, warm and steady. "You okay?" she asked softly.

Pippa nodded, forcing a deliberate, controlled breath. *Stay strong,* she repeated in her mind like a mantra. But with each step closer to her father's room, the knot in her chest tightened, a slow, insistent ache that refused to ease, weaving itself through every fibre of her body.

Chloe was the only other person who knew the truth behind why she had left Flynn—the lie she had carried for years—and she felt it pressing down on her now, mingling with fear and anticipation of what awaited in New York.

The elevator doors opened, and the hallway stretched out before them, stark and clinical under the harsh fluorescent glow. Polished linoleum reflected the hurried movement of nurses, the occasional call of a room number, the rolling of carts and distant hum of hospital machinery.

And then she saw it: Room 407. Her father's room. The place that held the man she adored—and the possibility of something else she had long tried to avoid. Three years she had kept herself away from New York, terrified of running into Flynn, of facing the memories he carried, of confronting the lingering ache of seeing him—maybe with someone else.

Pippa knocked gently before opening the door, her fingers trembling ever so slightly.

Henry Rockwell looked up from his hospital bed, exhaustion and pain etched into his features, but a spark of relief lit his eyes as he saw her. "Pippa," he whispered, hoarse, raspy. "You came."

She crossed the small distance to his bedside, squeezing his hand gently. "Of course I did, Dad. I'm here."

For a brief moment, she let herself focus solely on him—the man who had always been her anchor, whose presence made the world steadier. Yet even as she settled beside him, a shadow lingered at the edge of her thoughts: *Flynn.*

Down the hall, Flynn stepped out of the hospital café, the warm scent of coffee clinging to his coat. He had been halfway through a cup, trying to shake the lingering fatigue of a long morning, when movement caught his eye.

She was there.

Pippa.

At first, he thought it a trick of the fluorescent lights or his tired mind. But no—there was no mistaking her. Taller than he remembered, lean and graceful, dark hair tumbling down her back, catching light with every subtle movement. She moved with effortless elegance, the quiet poise that had always drawn him in, that had once made him ache with longing.

He froze, coffee trembling in his hand. His chest tightened, a raw, physical ache coursing through him. She hadn't noticed him yet, and that alone—the thought of her unaware, the storm she could unleash simply by existing—made his pulse spike.

Three years. Three long years had passed, and yet she still had the power to stop him cold in his tracks. Her beauty, her presence, the weight of unspoken memories—it was almost unbearable. Reality, sharper and crueller than the fantasies he had rehearsed, pressed against him.

He gripped the coffee like a lifeline, forcing himself to breathe. *Control,* he told himself. But he knew—deep down—that the illusion had already shattered the moment he saw her.

Pippa.

The name whispered through him, a ghost of the past that still claimed him, even if she did not. Every instinct screamed to move, speak, reach. But he stopped himself. *No.* Not after everything. Not after the letter that had shattered him.

All he felt now was heartbreak, betrayal—the hollow, festering ache of knowing she had never loved him as he had loved her. That much was clear. She had proven it with a single letter, cold and final, leaving him gutted and discarded.

He would not let her see that she still held power over him. Not now. Not ever. He had learned how to shield himself, to harden every soft edge she had once touched. He would remain guarded, untouchable, distant.

And yet... his feet betrayed him. They carried him down the hall, every step fuelled by a rage he couldn't smother, until he stood before Room 407. The sterile white door loomed ahead, unremarkable but heavy, weighted with ghosts. His hand tightened on the handle, heart pounding like a war drum beneath his ribs, and then—he opened it.

"Hello, Pippa."

She stiffened instantly, as if she had felt the charge of his presence before she even turned. Slowly, deliberately, she faced him.

"Hello, Flynn."

Their eyes collided, and for a moment the years dissolved—the longing, the fury, the regret, all tangled into one brutal knot. It was there, raw and undeniable, straining the air between them.

Flynn didn't move. He didn't speak. He just looked at her.

Damn her. She was more beautiful than memory allowed. Her eyes, greener than he remembered, cut into him like blades. Her hair, dark and thick, cascaded down her back in a way that made his fingers ache with the memory of what it felt like—threaded through his hands, spread across his pillow.

The memory struck like a blow—the last summer before she had vanished. Weeks before her betrayal arrived in ink and paper. She had been so young then, innocent in ways that made him both protective and powerless. He remembered the breathless urgency of that night, her whispered confession, *I love you*, the way her body had trembled but trusted him completely. She had been his. Entirely his.

And then she had gutted him.

The letter. The words that had turned everything they were into ash.

Flynn forced a breath through his clenched teeth, dragging himself back to the present. He reminded himself why he was here—her father, not her. *Never her.* The memory of her love was a lie, one she had wielded like a weapon before walking away without so much as a glance back.

Still… the ache lingered. It burned. His body remembered even if his pride refused to. And beneath his fury, beneath the walls he had built to cage the ruin she had left behind, a dangerous truth pulsed—he still wanted her.

Flynn's jaw clenched, the muscles taut beneath his skin, and his fingers tightened around the coffee cup until it threatened to crush beneath his grip. *No.* He would not give her the satisfaction—not this time. Not when every beat of his heart, every ounce of longing for her, had cost him nothing but pain.

He held himself rigid, his gaze locked on hers, rage, desire, and grief twisting into one merciless knot inside him. And with brutal determination, he told himself—*again*—that she was dead to him. That the girl he had once loved was gone. That whatever tether still bound them was nothing more than memory.

She would never break him again.

Pippa broke the silence, her voice careful, tentative, almost hesitant, as if each word were a fragile thread she feared might snap.

"I… I heard you got married. Congratulations." Her words were careful, measured, but the memory behind them pressed heavy. She remembered when her father had told her—only six months after she left—that he was getting married. Back then, she had told herself he must not have loved her as much as she had believed, that he could move on so quickly. And in those six months, Pippa hadn't even attempted to date; she couldn't. Her heart had been too shattered, too raw, still tethered to the memory of him.

Flynn's jaw clenched hard, the muscle ticking as he turned to look at her fully. Those blue eyes—once the safe place she'd known better than her own reflection—were now cold, unyielding, carved into steel. "Divorced now," he said briskly. The words were clipped, flat, deliberately stripped of warmth. Delivered like a fact, not a confession.

The answer hit her like a blast of icy wind. She blinked, caught off guard, breath catching as the weight of it pressed into her chest. "Oh… sorry," she murmured softly, the apology fragile, instinctive, because she had no idea what else to say.

Flynn didn't move. Didn't blink. He just stared at her, eyes sharp, assessing, merciless. Then his gaze dropped briefly to the polished floor before snapping back, harder, colder, as though daring her to keep looking at him—daring her to remember what she'd thrown away.

The air between them grew heavy, a charged current that hummed and coiled until her lungs felt tight. Pippa forced herself to breathe, to stand straighter, to summon the practiced composure she'd worn like armour for years. She started again, trying to smooth the edges of her voice.

"I didn't mean to—"

"Don't." His voice cracked across the room, low and sharp, slicing her words in half. He gave his head a single, cutting shake, deliberate and final. "Not here. Not now. I don't need your congratulations or condolences. I never did."

The rebuke lashed across her skin, hot and humiliating. She swallowed hard, her stomach twisting into a hard, unyielding knot. She had expected tension. She had braced herself for bitterness. But nothing had prepared her for this— this calm, razor-edged fury that made every syllable feel like a verdict passed.

Still, she nodded slowly, masking the sting, forcing her tone into the same neutral steadiness she used with difficult clients. "I understand."

But she didn't. She couldn't.

The silence that followed was deafening, the walls seeming to close in on them, heavy with memory and loss. The years of love, the years of silence, the lies, the heartbreak—it all pressed down, crowding the narrow space between them. And though neither moved, neither spoke, every unspoken word lingered there like smoke, suffocating, impossible to escape.

Flynn didn't immediately notice the other woman in the room. His gaze was locked on Pippa, unrelenting, merciless. Every detail struck him at once—the cautious lift of her chin, the guarded calm in her green eyes, the elegance that clung to her like a second skin. She was more beautiful than he remembered, and it infuriated him. Because beauty had been the snare, the illusion. The trap he'd walked into with his whole heart wide open.

Then movement cut across his line of sight. The other woman stepped forward, smooth and confident, her smile polite but edged with something protective. She extended her hand.

"Hello, I'm Chloe. Pippa's assistant."

Flynn blinked, the interruption pulling him just enough out of his private storm. He looked at the hand she offered, then at her face—calm, steady, unflinching. With deliberate precision, he clasped her hand in a firm, quick shake. "Flynn Oakland." His tone was clipped, cool, carrying the authority of a man who wasn't here to make friends.

Chloe's grip didn't falter. She met his gaze without a flicker of hesitation, and that subtle defiance stirred a faint flicker of interest before his attention dragged back to where it belonged—on Pippa. Always Pippa.

He studied her posture, noting the tension in her shoulders, the way her fingers tightened slightly at her sides. She thought she was hiding it. She wasn't. He knew her tells as well as his own. And seeing them now—those quiet cracks in her composure—ignited a surge of bitter satisfaction. *Good.* Let her squirm. Let her feel something of what she had left him with.

"You look… well," he said at last, his voice low, roughened by the anger he refused to unleash. The words were not a compliment but an observation, laced with an edge that made them sound almost accusatory.

"Thank you. So do you." Her reply was careful, steady, but he caught the flicker in her eyes—the one that always gave her away.

The silence that followed pressed heavy between them. The muted hum of hospital life faded into nothing. All that existed was the sharp crackle of tension, the weight of three wasted years, and the bitter truth lodged in his chest—that he still wanted her, and he hated himself for it.

Pippa's breath caught before she spoke again. "I… I didn't expect to see you here." Her voice was quiet, uncertain, a confession wrapped in caution.

Flynn's mouth curved—not in a smile, but in something closer to a sneer. "Neither did I." His tone was flat, hard, but the flare of emotion in his eyes betrayed him, if only for a moment. Rage. Longing. Hurt so deep it had hardened into armour.

They stared at each other, two statues carved from history, bound by memories that refused to die. Flynn's jaw tightened, his hands flexing once at his sides, aching to close the distance and shake the truth out of her. But he stayed still, his voice locked behind his teeth.

Chloe shifted subtly to Pippa's side, silent but watchful, her presence a quiet reminder that Pippa was not alone this time.

Pippa inhaled shakily, as if trying to steady her heart. "I—" She faltered, words slipping away under the weight of everything between them.

Flynn's gaze hardened again, his expression turning to stone. Whatever softness had threatened to surface vanished as quickly as it came. He would not be weak. He would not let her see.

The silence that followed was brutal, heavy with everything unsaid—betrayal, heartbreak, desire. And in that unyielding tension, one thing was certain. This was not closure. This was the spark of a fire neither of them was ready for.

The silence broke when Henry finally spoke, his voice steady but edged with fatigue, cutting through the thick tension that had wrapped itself around the room.

"I was with Flynn when I collapsed."

Pippa's head snapped toward her father, her breath catching in her throat. Fear carved itself across her face, erasing every trace of composure she had fought to hold onto since the flight. "What… what have the doctors said?" Her voice trembled, low and urgent, betraying the storm of panic she had kept buried.

Henry shifted slightly against the pillows, the faint wince in his expression betraying the dull ache that pulsed through his chest. "They think it might be a blockage in one of my arteries," he said carefully, weighing each word. "It isn't catastrophic—yet. But if it's ignored…" He paused, letting the unfinished thought hang heavy in the air. "They're running tests, monitoring me closely. But they've warned I may need a procedure. A cardiac catheterisation, to clear the artery. Routine, they call it. Still…" His breath thinned. "It's a procedure. And I'd rather have you here, Pippa."

Her stomach knotted hard. The fragile dam she had built inside herself finally cracked, sending a rush of helpless fear through her. She reached for his hand, threading her fingers through his, clutching it with quiet desperation. His skin was warm, steady, grounding, yet the thought of losing him hollowed her out.

"Dad… we'll get through this," she whispered fiercely, forcing her voice steady when her insides quaked. "We'll make sure the doctors do everything. You'll be alright."

Flynn, who had stayed silent at the foot of the bed, stepped forward then. His movements were controlled, precise, but Pippa didn't miss the taut line of his shoulders, the restraint in every step. His voice, when it came, was calm—almost professional—but beneath it was that protective undertone she remembered all too well.

"They'll take care of you, Henry," he said evenly, blue eyes fixed on the older man, though the tension coiled in him was impossible to miss. His gaze flicked briefly, sharply, toward Pippa. A silent acknowledgment. A reminder. But his focus snapped back to her father before it could linger.

Henry gave a faint smile, gratitude softening the harsh lines in his face. "I knew you'd come, Pippa. That's what matters most. I wasn't scared because Flynn was with me. But it's easier now—with you here too."

Her throat tightened. Pippa nodded, blinking hard, squeezing her father's hand again as though sheer force of will could keep him tethered to her. Still, she felt Flynn's eyes on her, heavy, unwavering, and against her better judgement, there was comfort in knowing he was there. Even if that comfort was laced with pain.

Chapter Three

Flynn leaned back slightly, resting his arms on the chair, but his gaze never left her. The years between them pressed into the silence—thick, unyielding—but for the moment it held like a fragile truce, one neither dared to break. His jaw shifted, and when he finally spoke, his voice had softened by a fraction.

"Where are you staying while you're in New York?"

Her breath stilled. The question, casual on the surface, landed with weight. She twisted her fingers in her lap, uneasy. "I… I don't know yet," she admitted quietly.

Henry's voice cut in, calm but resolute, the tone of a man accustomed to being obeyed. "You'll stay in the cottage on the estate. It's quiet, private. And close enough that I can see you whenever I need to."

The words hit Flynn like a blow he hadn't expected. His body stilled, though his jaw clenched hard, betraying the bristle of emotion he didn't show. Pippa—back on Oakland land. The cottage. Under his roof. Memories surged—laughter in the gardens, summer evenings by the lake, the night she left him without a word. He drew a slow, deliberate breath, forcing the storm inside him into stillness.

When he spoke, his voice was calm, measured, but edged with steel. "Your father's right. It's the best option. You'll have privacy. And we'll be close enough if anything happens."

Henry's lips curved faintly, a quiet reassurance in his smile as he patted Pippa's hand. "See? Even Flynn agrees. Trust me, darling. This is what's best for everyone."

Pippa's gaze drifted toward the window, out to the skyline she had once left behind. The mention of Oakland Park—its sweeping grounds, echoing halls, the ghosts waiting for her in every corner—tightened her chest until she could barely draw breath. She had buried those memories, sealed them away. But stepping back into that house meant unearthing all of it. Flynn. The truth. The past she had spent years running from.

She shut her eyes for a moment, drawing in a slow, measured breath. For her father's sake—for his peace of mind—she could endure it.

"Alright," she said at last, her voice quiet but steady, masking the tremor inside. "I'll stay there."

The words hung in the air like a promise she already regretted, one that tethered her back to the very place she had sworn never to return.

Flynn and Pippa sat in the back seat of the limousine, the supple leather cool beneath them, its faint scent of polish a sterile contrast to the storm of memory and regret pressing in on all sides. The car was quiet—too quiet—its insulated hush only amplifying the tension that thrummed in the narrow space between them.

Chloe occupied the seat across, composed but alert, her gaze flicking between them with quiet precision. She didn't intrude—her presence alone was enough, steadying the fragile balance between past and present.

The city blurred beyond the tinted windows, streetlights streaking like fractured constellations. Pippa's eyes remained on the passing scenery, but her focus was inward. Her hands twisted in her lap, knuckles whitening, echoing the anxious storm in her chest. Each heartbeat felt louder than the hum of the engine, each block drawing her closer to a place she had once sworn never to return.

Flynn's gaze stayed fixed ahead, sharp and unyielding, but the tension in his shoulders and the tight grip on the seat betrayed the calm exterior. The silence between them wasn't empty—it was a living weight, thick with memories, unspoken words, and the ache of betrayal neither had yet confronted.

Pippa shifted slightly, the brush of fabric loud in the hush. Their eyes met for a fleeting second, colliding with heat, memory, and longing before she tore them away. She swallowed hard, forcing a steady exhale, pretending calm she didn't feel.

The gates of Oakland Park rose ahead, wrought iron glinting in the fading light, flanked by stone pillars bearing the crests of generations. Pippa pressed her palm to the glass, a shiver tracing her spine as anticipation and dread twisted in her chest. Each familiar curve of the driveway, every sculpted hedge, tugged at buried memories—sunlight on Flynn's hair, the reverent intensity in his blue eyes, laughter echoing across lawns, fingers brushing, stolen kisses by the lake.

The limousine slowed as it neared the small cottage, its tyres crunching on the gravel. Pippa's pulse quickened, a mix of longing and apprehension tightening in her chest. The cottage appeared almost unchanged—neatly trimmed hedges, freshly painted shutters—but imbued with life, with echoes of mornings spent with her father. And then there were memories of Flynn—the secret smiles, whispered promises, the innocence of love once thought unbreakable.

The driver opened the car door, and the crisp evening air brushed against her. The familiar scent of polished wood and faint floral polish greeted her, safe yet brimming with memories. Flynn stepped out beside the car, the late afternoon sun glinting off his tailored suit. He moved with the precision that had always unsettled and reassured her simultaneously.

"If you need anything, just let me know," he said, calm and measured, but threaded with the quiet authority that had drawn her in years ago.

"We will, thank you," Pippa replied, voice light but careful, fingers twitching slightly at her sides. Chloe offered a small, reassuring smile, silently standing guard over her friend.

Flynn's gaze softened slightly, a hint of warmth tugging at his lips. "Come to dinner tonight," he said, controlled, effortless.

"Oh, we don't want to impose," Pippa replied quickly, composure maintained though her chest tightened.

"Don't be silly," he countered, eyes unwavering. "Mother would be glad to see you."

Pippa stiffened. *Gwen—the woman whose whispered manipulations had shattered her future—would not be glad see her?* The thought twisted in her stomach. Chloe's steady presence was a quiet anchor, but the storm of anxiety, anger, and curiosity remained, coiling inside her.

Drawing a slow, deliberate breath, she pressed a hand to her chest. "Okay," she said finally, low and steady, a reminder that she was no longer the fragile girl she had been.

Flynn inclined his head in faint approval, eyes lingering just a beat longer, controlled yet carrying a flicker of something she couldn't place—concern, curiosity, a shadow of memory buried beneath his calm exterior. "Good," he said evenly. "Drinks at seven."

A small, fragile smile tugged at Pippa's lips. "Okay," she whispered. Chloe's fingers brushed lightly against hers, grounding and reassuring. She drew another deep breath, the scents of grass, flowers, and sun grounding her in the present, though the ache of the past refused to soften.

For a moment, she allowed herself to stand quietly, absorbing the beauty of the cottage and the estate beyond. The world seemed suspended, caught between a past she had tried to bury and the uncertain present she now had to navigate.

"Alright," she whispered to herself, more a promise than a statement. Hand pressed once more to her chest, she steeled herself for the storm ahead— memories, old feelings, and inevitable encounters with Flynn. One step at a time, she reminded herself.

Chloe's steady gaze met hers, a silent reassurance. Pippa gave the smallest nod. She wasn't alone. Not entirely.

With a final glance at the familiar cottage, she pushed open the door, stepping inside to the faint scent of polished wood and home, bracing herself for everything—and everyone—that awaited beyond.

Pippa set her suitcase down near the door and ran a hand along the smooth edge of the hall table, feeling the grain of the polished wood beneath her fingers, letting the reality of being back sink in with each quiet touch. Every surface, every familiar curve of the cottage, whispered fragments of the past she had tried to leave behind.

Chloe perched on the sofa, leaning back slightly, her posture relaxed but alert, eyes sweeping the room before settling on Pippa with a small, amused smile that carried both affection and mischief.

"It hasn't changed," Pippa murmured softly, exhaling through her nose as tension, nostalgia, and a trace of exasperation tangled in her chest. The cottage was exactly as she remembered—timeless, safe, yet infused with memories she wasn't sure she was ready to confront.

Chloe tilted her head, a faint smirk curving her lips. "I see why you fell for him," she said, her tone low, teasing, yet touched with something gentler beneath the playfulness. "Flynn... he's far more handsome than you ever let on."

Pippa's chest tightened, a heat rising to her neck, her pulse stuttering. The familiar ache—part longing, part apprehension—stirred unbidden. "Chloe..." she whispered, shaking her head lightly, half-scolding, half-in awe. "Don't start."

Chloe laughed quietly, sinking further into the cushions, eyes still fixed on Pippa with an intensity that was part curiosity, part protective watchfulness. "I'm serious. He's magnetic. I can see why you..." Her voice trailed off, leaving the thought suspended in the warm, sunlit room, charged with unspoken understanding.

Pippa's fingers curled into the edge of the sofa, her nails pressing lightly into the fabric as the memories surged forward. Being back inside this cottage—the one that had held so many firsts, so many stolen afternoons with Flynn—was overwhelming, too immediate, too real. Chloe's words, innocent as they were, only made the truth sharper: Flynn had never stopped being Flynn. And, somewhere deep inside, he had never stopped being hers either—despite the years, despite the betrayals, despite the letter she had written to protect him.

The cottage seemed to hold the weight of the past and the tension of the present in every sunlit corner. Dust motes floated lazily through shafts of late afternoon light, settling on polished wood and familiar furniture, as if time itself had paused, waiting for Pippa to step fully back into its embrace. She sank lightly into an armchair, letting herself feel it—the warmth, the nostalgia, the silent, persistent pull of what had once been and what might still be. Every creak of the floor beneath her, every subtle scent of polished wood and faint floral polish, carried memories she had tried so hard to forget; laughter echoing through hallways, whispered promises beside the lake, the gentle brush of his hand against hers.

Chloe, still perched on the sofa across from her, legs crossed, posture relaxed yet alert, studied her carefully. "Are you going to be okay… seeing his mother again?" she asked, her voice soft, probing just enough to pierce the surface without forcing a response.

Pippa exhaled slowly, eyes fixed on the floor as if it might hold the answer, tracing an invisible pattern with the tip of her finger along the armchair's fabric. "The last time I saw her," she began, voice tight with memory, each word carefully measured, "she told me I wasn't good enough for her son. That I would never be… worthy. I don't think she's going to be happy seeing me any more than I am happy seeing her."

The words hung in the room, heavy with the sting of past rejection. Pippa's hands twisted nervously, tugging at the hem of her sleeve, a subtle tremor betraying the carefully constructed calm. Chloe's gaze softened, unwavering, offering silent support, a tether to the present when the ghosts of the past threatened to pull Pippa under.

Pippa closed her eyes for a moment, drawing in a shuddering breath, letting the faint scent of polished wood and blooming garden outside settle around her. For all the fear and tension knotting her chest, she knew one thing with clarity: she would face Gwen tonight, and she would not crumble—not entirely. Not here, not now.

Chloe leaned forward slightly, a thoughtful crease forming between her brows. "Have you thought about telling Flynn the truth? About why you left?"

Pippa's lips pressed into a thin line, a bitter shadow flickering across her expression. Her gaze drifted to the window, where the late afternoon light filtered softly through the curtains, casting long shadows across the polished wood floors. "What would be the point?" she murmured, her voice low, almost swallowed by the quiet of the cottage.

Chloe's eyes softened, and she leaned back, studying her friend with gentle persistence. "He's divorced now… and I know you still care about him."

Pippa's fingers curled lightly in her lap, tracing the edge of the armchair's cushion. "I do," she admitted softly, almost to herself, the words tasting bitter on her tongue. "But he's moved on. He got married six months after I left. I don't think he has any feelings for me anymore. Not the way he used to."

The silence that followed was thick, heavy with memory. Chloe reached across, her hand brushing Pippa's in a quiet, grounding gesture. "It doesn't mean you stop mattering," she said gently. "Feelings are complicated. And Flynn... he's not exactly predictable, is he?"

Pippa managed a faint, wistful smile, the tension in her shoulders easing just slightly. "No," she whispered, voice barely audible, "he's not."

The cottage seemed to settle around them, warm sunlight spilling across the floors and furniture, illuminating the familiar space in a comforting glow. Pippa hugged her knees to her chest, letting the quiet lull wash over her. The soft tick of the mantel clock and the faint rustle of leaves outside marked a deliberate, measured passage of time—far removed from the tension that had followed her across the country.

Chloe's voice cut through the quiet, soft but steady. "Do we need to dress for dinner?"

Pippa exhaled a small laugh, fragile but genuine. "Oh yes," she said, glancing toward the window. "Gwen won't let you eat if you're not appropriately dressed. She's... a stickler for appearances."

Chloe arched an eyebrow, a playful glint in her eyes. "She sounds like a real witch."

Pippa's smile turned wry, bittersweet. "She is," she admitted softly, letting a shadow of memory cross her face. "I tried to get on with her once, but... I wasn't high enough on the social ladder. She made that very clear."

Chloe shook her head, chuckling softly, sympathy and amusement mingled in her expression. "Wow. Sounds like fun."

"Fun isn't the word I'd use," Pippa replied, voice low, wistful, almost a whisper. "But it's why I left... why things ended the way they did." She traced a finger along the arm of the chair, feeling the smooth wood beneath her touch. "I suppose tonight will bring all that back."

Chloe leaned forward again, elbows resting on her knees, eyes sharp yet warm. "Then we survive. One step at a time. I've got your back, Pippa. And who knows? Maybe Gwen isn't quite as terrifying as you remember."

Pippa let out a soft, self-deprecating laugh, fingers twisting the cushion. "I doubt that very much," she murmured, though a small smile tugged at her lips. "But... having you here makes it easier to face."

Chloe's eyes softened, pride and gentle teasing glimmering in them. "Well, you're not the same girl you were three years ago," she said warmly. "You've built a name for yourself—one of the most successful stylists in the country. That's no small feat, Pippa."

Pippa's smile widened slightly, the corners of her mouth lifting despite the lingering tension. "I suppose that's true," she admitted, a hint of pride threading her voice. "Still… standing in front of Gwen tonight? That's a whole different kind of challenge."

Chloe leaned back, arms crossed but gaze unwavering. "Then you'll meet it the way you meet everything else—head-on, with style, grace, and a little fire. And I'll be right there, making sure you don't get swallowed by her theatrics."

Pippa chuckled, a flicker of warmth spreading through her chest. "I don't know what I'd do without you," she murmured, the familiar trust and reliance in her voice unmistakable.

"You'd survive," Chloe replied confidently, a playful spark in her tone. "But lucky for you, you won't have to find out."

The sun dipped lower, casting the room in a softer glow, and for a brief moment, the weight of the past, the tension of the present, and the uncertainty of the evening ahead seemed a little lighter—held in check by friendship, loyalty, and the quiet strength of Pippa herself.

Chapter Four

Pippa stood before the full-length mirror in the sunlit bedroom of the cottage, the soft evening light filtering through sheer curtains and casting warm golds across the room. She had chosen a sleek, deep emerald dress that hugged her figure without being overtly revealing, the fabric flowing just below her knees. The neckline was modest yet elegant, and the subtle shimmer of the material caught the light with every movement. Her hair was loosely pinned back, wisps softening her face, and her makeup understated, enhancing the green of her eyes and the gentle curve of her lips.

She adjusted the delicate silver bracelet around her wrist and took a slow, grounding breath, fingers trailing along the polished wood of the dresser. Her gaze drifted to the window, falling on the summerhouse nestled quietly at the garden's edge, partially hidden by tall hedges. Her chest tightened with a sharp, unbidden memory—the first time Flynn had kissed her there, beneath the warm summer sun. She could see it as if it were happening again: the gentle pull, the brush of his hand against hers, the warmth of his lips, the heady, nervous intimacy of that fleeting, perfect moment.

A shiver ran down her spine, heart thumping, as the summerhouse seemed to hold the ghosts of laughter, whispered names, and first love. She pressed her palm lightly against the glass, grounding herself, drawing in a slow breath. Tonight, she told herself, she had to step forward—not just into the evening, but into the world where Flynn, and all the memories he carried, awaited.

Descending the narrow staircase, the soft carpet muffled her footsteps. Chloe was already waiting at the bottom, seated with quiet composure on the sofa. The warm glow from the chandelier above painted soft shadows across her poised frame, her eyes scanning the room before settling on Pippa with a faint, teasing smile that carried both affection and mischief.

"Ready?" Chloe asked, her tone light yet edged with curiosity, a protective undertone threading each word.

"Ready as I'll ever be," Pippa replied, smoothing the skirt of her dress, trying to calm the flutter of nerves twisting in her stomach. Chloe's steady presence beside her was an anchor, though it did little to quiet the storm of anticipation and old unease.

"You look amazing, Pippa," Chloe said, approving, her eyes flicking over her friend with subtle delight.

Pippa returned the smile, feeling a flicker of warmth. "So do you. Gwen can't complain, can she?" Her voice was light, teasing, but beneath it lingered the old tension—the memory of the woman whose approval had once felt like judgment itself.

Chloe chuckled softly, a comforting sound in the quiet room. "Not unless she wants to start a war," she murmured, half-joking, half-serious.

Pippa nodded, a faint grin tugging at her lips. With a final deep breath, they moved together toward the door, stepping out into the evening, where the sprawling estate awaited—and with it, the family she was about to face.

The sitting room of the main house was hushed, the late afternoon sun casting long shadows across the polished wooden floors. Flynn stood near the tall window, hands clasped firmly behind his back, eyes tracing the sweeping gardens beyond, though his focus was elsewhere. The clock on the mantel chimed six forty-five, its measured tone filling the space like a quiet herald.

"She'll be here any minute now," he murmured under his breath, voice low, almost swallowed by the cavernous room. "Pippa… and her friend." His jaw tightened, shoulders squaring as though bracing for impact.

From the wing chair, Gwen lifted a delicate hand, rings glinting faintly in the fading light. Her posture was impeccable, the epitome of poise, yet her eyes carried that familiar, cold sharpness Flynn had always found unnerving.

"I don't understand why you insisted on having dinner with Pippa and her friend," she said smoothly, deliberate, her words carrying the faintest edge of steel. "We are not friends, Flynn. You know that."

Flynn turned slowly to face her, jaw tight, posture precise, unyielding. "Mother," he said evenly, voice calm but firm, "I expect you to be civil. I truly don't understand why you carry so much animosity toward Pippa after all these years."

Gwen's lips curved slightly, cruelly measured, almost predatory. "She broke your heart, sweetheart," she said softly, deliberate, each word weighted with accusation.

Flynn's fingers flexed at his sides, but he did not flare, did not move. His gaze remained steady, controlled, though the storm within him simmered just beneath the surface. "She left, yes. But you didn't like her then," he said quietly, deliberately, "and you were… happy she left."

Gwen shifted in the chair, the soft rustle of silk filling the brief silence. "Like it or not, she upset you when she left," she replied, narrowing her eyes. "And now you invite her back into our home for dinner? After everything?"

Flynn exhaled slowly, letting each word land with precision. "She is here as a guest, Mother. Nothing more. I am asking you, as my mother, to behave with basic courtesy. That is all. She has enough to worry about with Henry being ill."

Gwen's gaze lingered on him, a flicker of something unreadable crossing her face—disapproval, surprise, perhaps the faintest trace of reluctant respect. "We shall see," she said finally, voice cool, controlled, though subtle curiosity threaded through it.

Flynn turned back toward the window, fingers brushing along the polished frame. The driveway stretched out before him, gravel catching the last light of day. Pippa would arrive soon, Chloe too. And with them would come the storm: old memories, unresolved tension, and emotions Flynn had long buried, now stirring quietly with each passing second.

He ran a hand through his hair, steeling himself. "Let's get this over with," he muttered under his breath, almost to himself, as the house seemed to hold its breath, suspended in anticipatory silence.

Outside, the path from the cottage to the main house stretched before Pippa, familiar yet fraught with anticipation. The gravel crunched softly beneath her heels, each step sounding sharper than it should in the still evening air, echoing faintly across the manicured gardens. The warm glow from the grand windows flickered through the trees, casting elongated shadows that seemed to reach for her, pulling her forward into a past she wasn't sure she was ready to confront.

Beside her, Chloe moved with confident ease, the subtle brush of her arm against Pippa's at intervals a quiet, grounding reassurance. "You've got this," she murmured, voice calm, yet edged with the quiet steel of certainty—a reminder that Pippa was not alone.

Pippa drew in a slow, measured breath, letting the scent of freshly cut grass and the heady perfume of blooming roses mingle with the faint, lingering fragrance of the evening air. Her chest tightened as memories rose unbidden: the warmth of summer afternoons, laughter spilling from the summerhouse, stolen glances and whispered names. She kept her eyes fixed on the path ahead, refusing to let them stray toward the secluded summerhouse at the garden's edge, where those memories lurked like ghosts waiting to ensnare her heart. Tonight, she reminded herself, was about Gwen. Flynn. The walls of the estate and the shadows they carried.

The massive oak doors of the main house loomed ahead, imposing yet elegant, carved with ornate patterns that spoke of generations of Oaklands who had walked these halls. As the doors opened, Mr. Harcourt stepped forward, tall, dignified, every inch the composed but warm presence she remembered from her childhood. At first, his expression bore the same practiced neutrality, but when his eyes met hers, a subtle warmth flickered across his face, softening the stern lines and lending a rare ease to his bearing.

"Miss Pippa," he said, voice low, rich with gentle authority, carrying a hint of genuine pleasure. "It has been far too long."

Her chest tightened, a tremor of unexpected comfort threading through the nervous flutter of anticipation. "Hello, Mr. Harcourt," she said softly, her voice steadier than the emotions churning beneath it. "It's… good to see you again."

The butler's lined face broke into a rare, genuine smile—one that seemed to reach his eyes and soften years from them. When she stepped forward, he opened his arms without hesitation. The embrace was brief but heartfelt, a gentle reminder of a time when she had felt welcome within these walls.

"And it's very good to see you, Miss Pippa," he said as they drew apart, his tone warm but perfectly measured, as if mindful not to overstep the unspoken boundaries that still hung in the air. His gaze lingered for a heartbeat longer than politeness required—kind, steady, quietly protective. "Welcome back to Oakland Park."

The words were simple, yet they carried a weight that settled deep in her chest. For a moment, the restless ache inside her eased, replaced by something fragile but real—a sense of belonging she hadn't allowed herself to feel in years. Mr. Harcourt had always liked her, always treated her with quiet respect even when others had chosen distance or disdain. That constancy now felt like an anchor in the storm of memories and emotions threatening to pull her under.

Beside her, Chloe's eyes softened, a faint smile curving her lips as she glanced between them. She seemed to understand—without needing words—the quiet relief that passed through Pippa at that small, dignified welcome

She turned slightly toward Chloe, her voice warm despite the tightness in her chest. "This is my friend, Chloe," she said, a hint of pride softening her tone as she made the introduction.

"Welcome to Oakland Park, Miss Chloe," Mr. Harcourt said warmly, his tone formal but kind.

"Thank you, Mr. Harcourt." Chloe smiled at him, her poise effortless, her eyes bright with quiet curiosity.

Mr. Harcourt stepped aside with a subtle flourish, his pride evident though never ostentatious. His voice carried the calm dignity of a man who had served this house—and those within it—for a lifetime. The simple gesture, the soft gravity of his words, felt like an acknowledgment of something more: that Pippa belonged here, that her return was not a disruption, but a restoration.

As they crossed the threshold into the grand foyer, Pippa's pulse quickened. Each polished floorboard beneath her heels seemed to echo through the vast space, each step a steady drumbeat marking her return. The air smelled faintly of lemon polish and old wood, touched by the warmth of lamplight spilling across marble and brass. Somewhere in the distance, the grandfather clock ticked, slow and deliberate, measuring the seconds between what had been and what was about to unfold.

Her gaze swept the familiar expanse—the sweeping staircase, the high archways, the quiet opulence that had once both dazzled and confined her. The weight of memory pressed close, but so too did a fragile steadiness, a sense that she was no longer the uncertain girl who had once fled these halls.

She drew a slow breath, Chloe's quiet presence a steadying force beside her. Whatever awaited beyond these doors—past confrontations, buried truths, lingering heartache—she would face it. Head-on.

The past was here, yes. But so was she. And for the first time in years, resolve— slender, luminous, and unyielding—flickered to life within her, lighting the path forward.

Flynn stood in the sitting room beside the mantel, posture impeccable, every line of his body taut with controlled tension. Gwen sat regally on the sofa, pale silk catching the fading light, hands folded precisely in her lap, expression as unyielding as polished marble. Her gaze swept over Pippa like a measured appraisal, every movement calculated, every glance precise.

For a heartbeat, Flynn's eyes found Pippa's, and the years dissolved. Summerhouse kisses, laughter by the lake, whispered promises that had once seemed eternal—all flared to life in an instant. She was breathtaking in emerald, the dress hugging her figure without boldness, the subtle shimmer catching the light as if to announce her presence. Her green eyes, bright and sharp, held shadows of the quiet strength that had undone him from the very start.

"Good evening," Pippa said, voice steady, though her fingers brushed the side of her dress as if drawing courage from the fabric itself.

"Good evening," Gwen replied smoothly, rising with the effortless grace of one who had spent a lifetime perfecting composure. Her eyes swept over Pippa with polite scrutiny, evaluating rather than welcoming. "It's been… some time."

Flynn's jaw tightened, muscles flexing beneath his calm exterior. He felt the weight of Gwen's assessment, the sharp edges of her disapproval, and a flare of protective anger rose, quick and silent. He would not—*could not*—allow her to make Pippa feel small under his watch.

Before tension could thicken further, Chloe stepped forward with measured warmth. "Chloe," she said, extending her hand with a calm confidence that seemed to push back the atmosphere of judgment. "Pippa's assistant."

Gwen's smile was faint, brittle, a mask stretched tight over subtle curiosity. "Assistant?"

"Yes. I work with Pippa," Chloe said, voice assured, steadying, unshaken.

"And what do you do now, Pippa?" Gwen asked, voice polite, but laced with the soft edge of scrutiny.

"She's one of the most respected stylists in the country," Chloe interjected, smooth, protective.

A flicker of surprise crossed Gwen's face, quickly masked by civility. "Oh? Well, you have certainly… moved up in the world."

Pippa stiffened slightly, the echo of old judgments pressing against her spine. Flynn's eyes narrowed just enough, jaw tightening, a silent signal that he would not allow his mother's veiled insults to pass unchecked. "She didn't just move up," he said quietly, voice firm, deliberate. "She built a career most only dream of." His gaze softened on Pippa for the briefest heartbeat before snapping back to Gwen, daring her to challenge him.

Gwen's lips curved into a flawless, measured smile. "Of course. Quite impressive," she murmured, civility heavy with judgment.

They moved into the dining room, light pooling across the polished mahogany table. Flynn claimed the head, rigid, the tight line of his jaw a silent testament to the storm he contained. Gwen took her place to his right, hands folded, gaze sharp and assessing. Pippa and Chloe sat to his left, every subtle glance and shift noted, every flicker of emotion observed and unspoken.

"Sherry?" Gwen's voice cut through the quiet, smooth, deliberate—a razor wrapped in velvet. She poured a glass, letting her gaze linger on Pippa, weighing her carefully.

"Please," Pippa said, voice steady, fingers twisting lightly in her lap. Chloe's presence was a subtle anchor, reassurance in the tension-laden space.

Gwen's eyes swept her once more, cool and calculating. "It's remarkable how time changes people. Some… more than others."

Pippa lifted her chin slightly, steady. "Time does change us. Sometimes in ways we never expect."

Flynn sipped from his glass, shoulders stiff, the tension in his posture betraying the storm beneath. Gwen's words, polite and barbed, pressed against the fragile truce he'd painstakingly constructed. He felt the ache of memory rise—Pippa's laugh, the light of the lake on her skin, the warmth of her hand in his—yet he restrained himself, measured and coiled, unwilling to give her mother the satisfaction of seeing his emotions break.

"And your personal life, Pippa?" Gwen continued, smooth, probing. "One hopes someone so focused on her career has not entirely neglected matters of the heart."

"Life teaches lessons in its own time," Pippa replied, calm, subtle defiance threading her words. "I've learned to take them as they come."

Flynn's gaze flicked to hers, just long enough to convey the unspoken acknowledgment of shared history before he returned to his glass. Chloe offered a quiet interjection, protective but light. "She has plenty of options. Men are drawn to Pippa."

Gwen's smile did not falter, though a flicker of recognition crossed her face, fleeting and almost imperceptible. "Well, I hope your choices have served you well. One must be careful in… matters of the heart."

The words hung, civility masking the current of tension crackling beneath. Flynn's hand hovered near his glass, fingers curling, releasing—a silent rhythm of control. Every muscle in his body was taut, restrained, yet protective of Pippa, guarding her silently against his mother's veiled barbs.

Memory surged sharp and sudden—Pippa's smile that had once made the world impossibly bright. He wanted to reach across the table, to tell her he had never stopped wanting her, never stopped remembering. But the shadow of her leaving, the emptiness she had left behind, kept him still.

Pippa felt the subtle shift in him, the tension beneath his civility, warmth creeping along her spine, yet she remained composed. The space between them hummed with unspoken longing, regret, and desire, all carefully measured against civility.

Gwen's words continued, smooth, layered with steel: "Tell me, Pippa, how does one maintain such… poise and composure in a world so full of distractions?"

"I've learned to focus," Pippa said evenly, chin raised, a quiet defiance threading her tone. "And to make the most of every opportunity."

Flynn's jaw clenched subtly. His gaze flicked from Gwen to Pippa, softening for just a heartbeat, a silent promise that he was holding back far more than words could contain. The truce he maintained was deliberate, but the storm beneath—anger, longing, protectiveness—radiated quietly through every controlled movement.

The tension hummed in the room like a wire drawn too tight. Every glance, every word, was charged with the weight of what had been, and what still lingered unspoken between them. Pippa's heart raced, breath shallow, yet she remained composed. Tonight, the dance of civility had only just begun—and beneath it, emotions long buried waited, patient and relentless.

When dinner finally drew to a close, Pippa exhaled slowly, a long, shuddering release that carried away only part of the tension coiled tight in her chest. The soft clatter of silverware and the rustle of chairs gave way to the quiet of the estate evening. Moonlight spilled across the grounds, painting the lawns in pale silver, casting long shadows through the hedges and trees. The scent of night air, cut grass, and faint roses mingled with the residual warmth from the dining room, grounding her after the storm of civility and veiled barbs she had endured.

"Well," Chloe said after a few steps, voice low but firm, steel threading beneath the warmth, "she's a cow."

Pippa laughed softly, a mix of incredulity and release, the sound trembling slightly in the night air. "I told you," she murmured, shaking her head, a small, wry smile tugging at her lips.

Chloe's eyes sparkled with quiet mischief. "Worse than I imagined. I felt like slapping her—right across the face."

Pippa chuckled again, the tension loosening fractionally in her shoulders. "It's hard to believe someone can be so… meticulously cruel," she admitted, the words spilling in a whisper as if confessing a secret. Her pulse still throbbed with the memory of Gwen's smooth, barbed remarks, the deliberate weighing of her worth—or lack thereof—against Flynn's approval.

The moonlight traced silver patterns along the winding path, glinting off the gravel and manicured hedges. Each footstep sounded impossibly loud in the hush of the night, echoing softly across the gardens. For the first time since arriving at Oakland Park, Pippa allowed herself a small, private smile, fragile as spun glass. She had survived dinner—endured the measured barbs, the subtle provocations, the careful scrutiny—and had remained unbroken, upright and composed in a room that had once threatened to swallow her whole.

Yet even as she walked, Flynn's presence lingered in her mind. Not in the form of words or gestures from dinner—he had remained deliberately controlled—but in every memory, every half-glance, every carefully measured reaction. He had watched her, protected her, restrained the storm that curled beneath his polished exterior, and in doing so reminded her of the pull that had never fully faded. The ache of unfinished business hummed quietly beneath the surface, persistent, demanding acknowledgment she was not yet ready to give.

At the cottage door, Chloe paused, a conspiratorial smile tugging at her lips. "Good night, Pippa. Try to get some rest." Her footsteps faded upstairs, leaving a comforting hush in her wake.

Pippa lingered in the dim hallway, the house quiet but her mind anything but. Sleep felt impossible; her thoughts were too sharp, too alive. She pulled a light shawl over her shoulders, the fabric brushing softly against her arms, and stepped quietly outside, the door closing with a faint click behind her.

Chapter Five

The cool night air brushed against her skin, prickling along her arms and neck, stirring goosebumps that raced like tiny sparks of memory. She walked slowly, deliberately, letting her eyes adjust to the silvered gardens. Each familiar curve of the path, each sculpted hedge, seemed to whisper in the language of the past, thrumming with echoes of laughter, arguments, and stolen promises. And there, framed by the dark silhouettes of trees, she saw it—the summerhouse.

It waited like a quiet sentinel, serene yet brimming with ghosts: stolen glances, whispered names, the warmth of hands pressed too close, and the heat of first kisses lingering in the air like perfume. Her breath caught, sharp and unbidden, and her chest tightened with a mixture of anticipation, dread, and the lingering pull of what had been—and what might still ache to be.

Pippa paused on the threshold, pressing a trembling hand lightly against the cool wood of the doorframe. The night seemed to hold its breath with her, the scent of roses, wet earth, and distant jasmine curling around her senses, mingling with the faint, ghostly glow of sunlight she could almost touch in memory. Every nerve hummed, taut with awareness, caught between the fragile peace of the cottage and the gnawing ache of Flynn's phantom presence.

She slid inside, letting the door click softly behind her, the sound impossibly loud in the hush of the summerhouse. The room felt suspended in time— shadows pooling over the worn wooden floorboards, the scent of polished wood mingling with faintly sweet echoes of the garden outside. She sank onto the edge of the bench, folding her knees close, letting the night press in around her. For the first time since dinner, she surrendered to the full weight of memory, raw and unshielded: longing that coiled in her chest, regret that burned in her veins, desire that trembled beneath her skin, and the bittersweet ache of everything she had lost—and left behind.

And somewhere, deep and insistent, she felt Flynn's shadow stirring, a silent, unyielding tether that threaded through her thoughts. The night, the moonlight, the quiet estate—they all conspired to awaken it, to pull her back to a past that refused to let go.

Pippa hadn't been sitting long when the soft crunch of footsteps on gravel reached her ears. Her pulse leapt, sharp and insistent, every nerve suddenly alive, prickling with both dread and anticipation. She hadn't expected anyone—but part of her, buried deep beneath reason, had known he might come.

Flynn appeared in the doorway, the moonlight catching the hard angles of his tailored suit, glinting off the sharp line of his jaw. His expression was unreadable, but his blue eyes—piercing, exacting, and impossibly familiar—swept over her.

An ache stirred in her chest, the same magnetic pull she had spent years trying to dull, now reignited like a live wire beneath her ribs.

"Pippa, what are you doing here?" His voice was low, measured, controlled, each word laced with reprimand—and something else, softer, almost hidden beneath the layers of anger he had so carefully constructed over the years.

She rose, smoothing her dress with trembling fingers, unsure whether she was greeting him or bracing herself for the storm she knew was coming. "Flynn," she whispered, the single word carrying a weight she hadn't intended to place upon it.

He stepped fully inside, closing the door with a soft click, and for a heartbeat the summerhouse held only them—moonlight pooling across the worn wooden floors, shadows curling around their stillness. His jaw was tight, posture taut with restraint, yet his eyes softened ever so slightly, tugging at the years she had spent trying to forget him, unraveling the careful barriers she had built.

"I wasn't expecting you," she said, her voice careful, precise, though beneath it quivered the nervous anticipation that had been coiling in her chest since she arrived.

He took a measured step closer, hands brushing the seams of his trousers in a subtle rhythm of restraint, the tension between them almost physical. "I didn't expect to find you here either," he said, voice low, carrying a hint of irritation that barely masked something more vulnerable. "And yet… I'm not surprised."

The space between them seemed charged, alive with unspoken memories and the quiet ache of everything they had left unsaid. Every heartbeat, every breath felt impossibly loud in the hush of the night, and Pippa realised, with a mix of longing and despair, that the years had done nothing to sever the bond that still tethered them together.

Pippa swallowed hard, the air catching in her throat as her chest tightened painfully. That familiar tension—the one that had always coiled between them like a live current—rose again, sharp and electric. "I should—" she began, her voice faltering as she moved toward the door, her pulse drumming loud enough she could almost hear it.

Flynn's gaze softened—just barely, a flicker that revealed more than he meant to—before hardening again, cold, deliberate, as though the softness itself had angered him. "Why are you here?" he asked, his tone low but edged with steel. The question carried layers—warning, accusation, and something darker, protective. "Are you going to tell me the real reason you left? You walked away once. I won't let that happen again… not without understanding why."

Her throat tightened around the words she'd promised herself she'd never say aloud. She had rehearsed this moment a hundred times in silence, but now, standing in the same air he breathed, every carefully built defence trembled. "Flynn…" she murmured, fingers brushing the worn edge of the bench for balance. "I left because I had to. Because it was the only way to protect… everything."

He exhaled slowly, his breath heavy with restrained fury. His hands flexed at his sides, the movement taut with control. "Protect what?" he asked, his voice quiet but dangerous. "Yourself? Me? Or someone else?" The words were precise, clipped, yet the undercurrent of betrayal ran through them like a blade.

Pippa's chest constricted. The memory of that night—the final words, the look in his eyes—pressed on her like a physical weight. "I thought it was the only way," she whispered, the confession trembling out of her. "To keep everyone safe. To stop everything from falling apart. I never stopped caring, Flynn. Not for a single day."

He stepped closer, and the air between them thickened, pulsing with everything they hadn't said. His nearness stirred something fierce and painful—desire tangled with regret. His gaze locked onto hers, unrelenting. "Do you have any idea what I felt when you left?" His voice was low, rough, vibrating with emotion he was barely containing. "The emptiness. The anger. The silence of this place without you…" He stopped, jaw tightening, swallowing hard before forcing control back into his voice. "And now you're here—standing in our summerhouse—as if nothing has changed. As if you belong here."

Pippa's breath hitched, her heart pounding so fiercely she thought he might hear it. "I didn't mean to upset you," she managed, though her voice trembled with everything she didn't dare say. "I came back because—because I needed to. My father…"

He studied her for a long moment, his expression a storm of anger and longing, every muscle drawn taut with restraint. Then, slowly, almost reluctantly, the rigid line of his shoulders eased. His next words came out rough, quieter, tinged with a dangerous kind of intimacy. "Fine," he said, his gaze still locked on hers. "If that's the story you want to tell… then we'll play it your way."

Her pulse thundered, each beat a drum of anticipation and fear. The tension between them was sharp, irresistible, coiling around them like electricity in the quiet room. And yet, in that charged silence, she understood something undeniable: beneath the anger, beneath the bitterness, beneath the brittle restraint, he was hurting. Because of her.

For a long, suspended moment, they simply stood there—two people tethered by years of love, regret, and desire. The summerhouse seemed to shrink around them, the walls holding echoes of laughter, whispers, and stolen kisses from years past. Moonlight spilled across the floor, tracing pale silver streaks over the sharp angles of Flynn's jaw and the curve of Pippa's shoulders, turning every movement into a silent, aching conversation. Every heartbeat felt amplified; every breath a fragile thread straining against the weight of three long years.

Flynn's hands clenched at his sides, polished wood pressing under his fingertips like the only thing grounding him. His piercing blue eyes bore into hers, sharp, unyielding, yet heavy with a quiet torment. "I never believed your letter, Pippa," he said at last, low and rough, the edges of his voice carrying the bitter weight of sleepless nights and unanswered questions. "I read it over and over… and every time, I can't make sense of it. You loved me one day and the next… you didn't. So, which was it? Did you ever love me at all?"

Her chest constricted as if he had reached inside and gripped her heart. She pressed her hands lightly against her stomach, grounding herself against the tidal wave of emotion. "Flynn… I—" Her voice faltered, the words lost in the gravity of his gaze.

"Don't," he snapped, though the force behind it was measured, controlled. "Don't start with excuses. I don't want to hear that you left to protect me—or anyone else. Don't tell me you had to go. I won't believe it. Not for a second."

Her lips parted, a whisper trembling through the tension. "I did love you," she said, fragile yet unwavering. "I left because I thought… I thought it was the only way to save you from the chaos I was bringing into your life. I thought walking away would protect everything you cared about."

He laughed, bitter and hollow, the sound reverberating through the quiet room like a slap. "Protect me?" he repeated, each word cutting into her. "You left me. You left me to wonder if I ever mattered at all. And now you stand here, telling me you loved me, and you expect me to… what? Forget everything?"

Tears pricked at the corners of Pippa's eyes, but she blinked them back, forcing herself to meet his gaze. "I can't undo the past," she whispered, voice raw but steady. "But I did care. I always have."

Flynn's jaw tightened, his body taut, yet his voice softened ever so slightly, betraying the ache he had carried silently all these years. "Then why?" he asked, quieter now, each syllable heavy with betrayal. "Why would you write that letter, claim you didn't love me? You knew I loved you. You knew it would break me."

Her fingers twisted lightly at the seam of her dress, grounding herself. "I had to," she admitted, soft and urgent. She could never tell him the truth about his mother—not ever. "I was afraid… afraid that staying would destroy you, destroy us. I thought leaving was the only way to protect you."

He stepped closer, the air between them thick with heat and unspoken desire. His gaze softened briefly, a fleeting shadow of the man she had loved, yet the bitterness never fully lifted. "You destroyed me to protect me," he scoffed, voice taut with anger and longing. "By leaving, by saying what you said… you left a hole I've been carrying every day since."

"I know," she whispered, stepping closer, letting the memory of what they had been guide her. "And I'm sorry, Flynn. I know it doesn't fix anything. I can't change the past."

He exhaled slowly, jaw clenching and unclenching, fists tightening then relaxing, a storm raging behind his eyes. "You think showing up now… looking more beautiful than you ever have, walking into my life again… makes it all okay?" His voice trembled just enough for her to hear the vulnerability beneath the anger. "You think I can just forgive—and forget—three years of pain?"

Pippa closed the distance carefully, deliberate, leaving just enough space for him to breathe but not enough to escape. "No," she admitted, voice firm despite the flutter of her pulse. "I don't expect forgiveness. I don't expect us to pick up where we left off. But I need you to know, Flynn—I did care. I did love you. I left because I thought it was the only way to protect you—not because I didn't care."

"You let me make love to you, Pippa. You were innocent," he said, low, raw, trembling with the ache of memory. "You told me you'd love me forever. But your love didn't even last a day."

He stared at her, every muscle taut, every instinct screaming—anger, longing, regret, desire—entwined into one unyielding knot. Silence fell thick around them, broken only by their steadying breaths and the faint creak of the floor beneath their feet, as though the house itself were holding its breath for the reckoning yet to come.

Then, without warning, he closed the distance like a predator, hands gripping her shoulders with a rough, urgent insistence. He pulled her into him with a force that left her breathless, her heart hammering against her ribs as if trying to escape. The world around them vanished, leaving only the scorching heat of him and the impossible ache of everything they had denied.

His lips collided with hers—hard, searing, and demanding—driving into her mouth with a ferocity that stole her breath. It was a kiss that screamed of years of restraint, of nights spent aching for a touch that had been forbidden, of words they had never dared to speak. Pippa's body went rigid for a fraction of a second, stunned, then surrendered, melting into him, matching his hunger with her own.

Her fingers dug into his chest, nails scratching, as a shiver of fire raced through her veins. His hands tightened at her waist, pressing her impossibly close, tilting her back just slightly, pulling her deeper into the storm of need. The kiss shifted—less anger, more desperation, more raw, trembling desire, a need so intense it bordered on pain.

She kissed him back with growing boldness, letting herself sink into the ache she had carried for years. Her hands threaded into his hair, tangling, tugging, urging him closer, while her body pressed fully against his, every curve and line of him etched into memory. She gasped against his lips, the sound mingling with his own ragged breath, each inhale a promise, each exhale a surrender.

Her arms wrapped fully around his neck, pulling him impossibly close. His hands roamed her back and waist, holding her tight as if letting go would undo both of them. The kiss deepened, messy, urgent, and consuming—tearing down every wall they had built, scorching the air between them, a perfect, stormy collision of longing, regret, and unrelenting desire.

But then—suddenly—he pulled back. The world lurched beneath her feet, and Pippa stumbled, chest heaving, eyes wide, desperately searching his. The fire that had ignited between them flickered out like a candle snuffed too soon, leaving only the hollow ache of absence in its wake.

Flynn's chest rose and fell rapidly, his breaths shallow, jagged. His eyes—stormy, haunted, turbulent—flicked away from hers. His jaw was tight, fingers flexing at his sides, as though he was trying to restrain a storm raging inside him. Desire clashed with bitterness, love with rage, longing with fury—every emotion colliding in one impossible instant, leaving him raw and exposed.

Pippa pressed a trembling hand to her chest, trying to steady her pounding heart, her lips still tingling from the kiss that had scorched them both. She stared at him, breathless, suspended between yearning and the sharp sting of his abrupt withdrawal. For a long moment, they remained like that—two halves of a fractured whole, hovering on the edge of what had been and what might be lost forever.

Flynn's chest heaved again, as if the kiss had torn open a wound he had long hidden. He stepped back sharply, the intensity in his gaze hardening into steel. His hands clenched at his sides, every muscle coiled with tension, jaw locked.

"I'm not falling for you again," he said, low, razor-sharp, each word trembling with anger he couldn't fully hide—even from himself. "I did that once. It won't happen again."

Pippa blinked, lips parted, heart hammering. Before she could respond, he continued, every syllable measured but laced with bitter fire:

"Do not come back here," he warned, eyes flashing with pain and fury intertwined. "You can stay at the cottage—for Henry's sake—but stay out of the summerhouse. This place... it's mine. I won't let it be used to reopen old wounds. Not again."

His words landed like blows, sharp and final. Pippa's stomach twisted, desire and longing clashing with the sting of his anger. She wanted to protest, to tell him she hadn't come back to hurt him—but the raw edge in his voice silenced her, tightening her chest with every beat.

Flynn's gaze flicked to hers for a brief, torturous instant—a flash of everything he felt, everything he'd wanted to say, restrained by years of hurt and bitterness. Then, with a slow, deliberate exhale, he shifted slightly, rigid as a drawn bow, the tension coiled through every line of his body. He had set his boundary, drawn his line, and now forced himself to hold it—even as desire and regret tore at him from within.

Pippa's lips trembled; a fragile whisper of emotion caught in her throat. Every fibre of her being screamed to stay, to reach for him, to tell him she hadn't come to wound him—but the raw anger and pain in his eyes, the hard edge of his voice, held her frozen in place.

With a heavy, reluctant heart, she stepped back, deliberate, measured, each movement a battle against the longing that clawed at her. The summerhouse, once their sanctuary, now pulsed with memory, every shadow and slant of moonlight whispering of a past she could no longer touch.

Finally, she reached the door, fingers brushing lightly against the polished frame as if drawing strength from it. She walked slowly, each step a quiet surrender, the soft echo of her footsteps lingering in the heavy air. She paused, took a steadying breath, and closed the door behind her, the click sharp, hollow—a sound that seemed to reverberate far deeper than it should.

Flynn stood frozen, chest tight, a storm of desire, frustration, and longing twisting inside him. The ache of her absence burned sharper than ever, a reminder that some wounds could not be soothed, some fires refused to be extinguished, and that the moment they had just shared had only made the hunger between them more unbearable.

Her lips lingered on him in memory—the taste of her, delicate, intoxicating, impossible to forget. He could still feel them pressed to his, warm and insistent, a lingering echo of everything he had lost. The memory of the last time he had kissed her—the trembling, the promise, the shy confession—flared in his mind, raw and unrelenting.

The late afternoon sun shimmered across the lake at Oakland Park, scattering molten gold across the water and dappled leaves. Pippa's laughter floated lightly as she stepped over the soft grass, the hem of her sundress brushing her knees. Flynn walked beside her, taller, strong, yet gentle, letting his hand graze hers now and then—a teasing, deliberate touch that sent warmth pooling in her stomach.

"You always walk like the world might tip if you step too hard," he murmured, lips tugged in a faint smile.

Pippa rolled her eyes, unable to hide her grin. "And you, Mr. Oakland, always think you know everything," she replied, nudging him lightly.

He caught her elbow, holding her gaze, dark eyes soft yet intense. "I don't think I know. I know," he said, voice low, threaded with months of restrained longing.

They followed the curve of the lake, sunlight glinting like scattered jewels on the water. A breeze carried the scent of wildflowers and earth, wrapping around them, cocooning them in their own private world. Conversation dwindled to murmured smiles and lingering looks, hearts already speaking in ways words could not.

When they reached the cottage, the space quiet and intimate with her father away, Pippa stopped at the door. Her fingers tightened around his, her eyes luminous with nerves and desire. "I'm ready," she whispered.

Flynn's hand cupped her cheek, thumb brushing lightly across her skin, his gaze searching hers. "Are you sure?" His tone was reverent, careful, as if this moment could shatter if not handled gently.

Her breath caught. "Yes… I want you. I want this… I want you to be my first and only," she breathed, the words trembling with need.

He leaned in slowly, lips meeting hers in a gentle, tentative kiss. Pippa's body responded immediately, pressing closer, melting into his warmth. The kiss deepened, urgent yet controlled, a dance of trust and desire, teasing and claiming all at once. Her hands threaded through his hair, tangling in the soft strands, nails grazing his scalp, while his hands traced the curve of her waist, drawing her into him, memorising the shape of her body.

Wordlessly, they stepped inside, moving upstairs. Sunlight slanted through the curtains, painting their skin with warmth. Flynn's lips sought hers again, slow, explorative, tasting, memorising, while his hands traced the line of her neck, shoulders, and back. Pippa's breath hitched as every touch made her pulse race, her heart hammering with longing she had held back for months.

Gently, he lowered her onto the bed, lips never leaving hers, hands cupping, stroking, anchoring her to him. She pressed into him, surrendering to the heat of his body, the strength of his arms, the intimacy of each careful movement. Their bodies shifted together naturally, instinctively, the closeness electric, every brush of skin a promise.

Pippa gasped softly when he kissed the curve of her shoulder, the nape of her neck, and when their bodies joined fully, the intensity of their connection sent a thrill through her she had never known. Flynn moved slowly, reverently, giving her time to adjust, to feel safe, to feel cherished. Every touch, every kiss, every gasp of breath was wrapped in the warmth of trust and love.

When they finally lay entwined, breathless, hearts pounding together, Pippa rested her head against his chest, feeling his heartbeat beneath her ear. A serene smile spread across her lips, soft and luminous. "I love you," she whispered, steady, certain.

"I love you too," Flynn replied, pressing a gentle kiss to her temple, a tether and a promise. "Always."

"I will always love you," she said, voice low, carrying every ounce of hope and devotion she felt. In the quiet room, with the lake sparkling beyond the windows and the sunlight glowing around them, they finally let themselves believe that their love—tender, passionate, and unshakable—could be everything they had ever dreamed.

But that was yesterday—or so it seemed now, in the cruel light of memory.

Her love had only lasted a day. The very next day, she was gone. She had left him, leaving behind that devastating letter that shattered his heart, words he had read again and again, each line a knife twisting deeper into the wound. The echo of her voice, the warmth of her touch, the promises they had made—all of it was gone, replaced by the cold, bitter ache of betrayal.

Flynn's jaw tightened as the memory pressed against him, unrelenting. He could still feel her lips on his, hear the tremor in her voice, see the hope in her eyes—and yet, he knew the truth now: she had left, and he had been left to bear the weight of what could have been.

Chapter Six

By the time Pippa reached the cottage, her hands were trembling. She slipped inside, turning the key in the lock with a sharp, final twist—as if a simple bolt of iron could bar the storm still raging inside her. Silence enveloped her, heavy and suffocating after the searing closeness of Flynn's nearness.

Upstairs, the moonlight spilled through her window, silvering the room in ghostly calm. She raised her fingers to her mouth, tracing the tender curve of her lips. They were still swollen from his kiss—a kiss that had undone her, unravelled every defence, whispered of a life she still longed for but could never claim.

Her breath came unsteady, chest rising and falling as she caught her reflection in the glass. The woman staring back was flushed, shaken, alive in a way she hadn't been in years. And that, she realised bitterly, was the most dangerous truth of all.

She wanted to tell him. To confess that she had never stopped loving him, that all she wanted was a lifetime in his arms. But she couldn't—not when the price was everything he had worked for, everything that was his birthright. Not when her love could be the reason he lost it all.

Her mind dragged her back—back to the day her dreams had shattered.

Pippa sat stiffly in the drawing room, her hands folded tightly in her lap. Gwen reclined in the high-backed chair opposite her, the afternoon sun glinting off the crystal in her hand. Her expression was smooth, polite—but cold, deliberate, calculating.

"Pippa," Gwen began, voice soft but firm, "I've heard… rumours that you and Flynn are becoming… close."

Pippa swallowed, feeling the heat rise to her cheeks. "We… we care for each other," she admitted cautiously.

Gwen's eyes narrowed slightly, a flicker of steel beneath her calm. "Care, yes. But love can be so dangerous, can't it? Especially in our world, where appearances, family, and legacy matter more than mere affection."

Pippa stiffened. "I don't understand."

"You will, child." Gwen leaned forward, the motion subtle but commanding. "You know Flynn's father is gone. May he rest in peace. But you may not realise how meticulously his estate was arranged. Everything—the trust, the

company shares, the family holdings—was designed to protect the Oakland legacy. And there are… stipulations.”

Pippa's stomach twisted. “Stipulations?”

“Yes.” Gwen's lips curved in a tight smile. “The trustees—men of law and experience—are bound to uphold the terms. If Flynn were to marry someone deemed… unsuitable, someone not of the family's station or discretion… he could be stripped of control, denied his inheritance entirely.”

Pippa's heart lurched. “But… that's impossible. Flynn… he'd never—”

“Wouldn't he?” Gwen interrupted gently, though there was an edge to her tone. “Do you think the law bends for love? Do you think the trustees, the board, the family's associates would overlook a marriage that might embarrass the estate, tarnish the name?”

Pippa bit her lip, silent.

Gwen's voice softened, almost intimate, and she leaned closer, lowering it to a whisper. “Pippa, I don't say this to frighten you unnecessarily, but—if you and Flynn go through with this… you could be the reason he loses everything his father left him. Everything he's been promised, everything he's worked for, could vanish in a heartbeat.”

Pippa's hands tightened in her lap. The weight of it pressed down on her chest. She wanted to argue, to defy Gwen, but the words died in her throat. She had never wanted to hurt Flynn, never imagined putting his future at risk—but now… now it felt almost inevitable.

Gwen sat back, letting the silence stretch, letting Pippa feel the full measure of her warning. “I'm sure you understand why I have to be honest with you,” she said, voice silky. “Some loves… are too dangerous to pursue.”

Pippa nodded mutely, a storm of longing, fear, and frustration roiling inside her. She left the room quietly, every step weighted with the impossible choice that now lay before her: follow her heart—or protect the only life she wanted Flynn to have.

Pippa sat alone in her room, the late afternoon sun slanting through the curtains, casting warm stripes across the floorboards. The echo of Gwen's words still lingered in her mind, sharp and precise, slicing through every memory she had of Flynn: the laughter, the stolen glances, the way his hand had felt in hers along the lake.

Her chest ached with the weight of the impossible. *I can't tell him. I can't.* The thought repeated itself like a mantra, each repetition hollow and final. How could she explain that her love, fierce and real as it was, might cost him everything his father had left him? That every dream he had for his future—

every ounce of inheritance, every ounce of freedom—could vanish because of her?

Tears pricked at the corners of her eyes, but she blinked them away. She had to be strong. I have to protect him. Even if it kills me to do it.

Her fingers trembled as she gathered paper and pen. She had to leave, but she couldn't face him. Not now, not ever with Gwen's shadow still pressing down. The letter would have to speak for her, the truth she could not say aloud, the love she could not afford to reveal.

She wrote slowly, each word a careful, deliberate fracture of her heart:

Flynn,

I've tried to fight this, tried to ignore the truth I can no longer deny. But I can't stay, and I can't let you continue to believe in something that isn't real.

I don't love you the way you think I do. I care for you, I always will, but not in the way a woman should care for the man she is meant to spend her life with.

You deserve someone who can give you everything you need, everything your heart wants—and I am not that person.

Please understand that this is for the best. I cannot be the person you hope I am. I cannot be the person you love. Holding on will only bring us both pain.

I am leaving, and you must try to move on. Believe me when I say it's not easy for me, but it's necessary. You deserve happiness—true happiness—and I am not the one to give it to you.

—Pippa

She folded the letter with trembling hands, pressing it flat as though the crease could somehow hold her resolve together. Her lips pressed briefly to the paper, a silent kiss, a goodbye she could not voice.

Her chest ached as she packed a suitcase. Every item she placed inside felt like another layer of herself she was leaving behind, every movement a reminder of the life she could not share with him.

Standing at the door, she took a deep breath, her fingers lingering on the knob. I can't face him. I can't let him see me like this. He would never understand… not fully.

With one final, shuddering breath, she stepped into the corridor, leaving the room—and her heart—behind. The letter she had left would have to speak for her: her confession, her farewell, and her silence, bound together in ink she could never take back.

Outside, the evening air wrapped cool against her flushed cheeks, the estate hushed in its quiet grandeur, as though holding its breath. When the Uber pulled up, headlights cutting across the gravel, Pippa forced herself forward. The crunch beneath the tyres as the car rolled away was soft, almost merciful, yet each turn of the wheels dragged her further from Flynn, from the only future she had ever wanted.

She pressed her forehead lightly to the glass, the great house shrinking behind her, swallowed by shadow and distance. Her chest ached with the unbearable truth: sometimes love—no matter how fierce, no matter how forever—was not enough.

Blinking hard, Pippa wrenched herself back to the present, pressing the memories deep into the corners of her mind where they could do no more damage—for now. Upstairs, in the quiet sanctuary of her bedroom, she sank heavily onto the edge of the bed, the weight of the day pressing against her chest. The room felt still, almost expectant, as if holding its breath along with her.

There could be no more wavering. No more allowing herself to linger on what had been lost or what might have been. Her father needed her—his health and strength depended on her steadiness, on her resolve. She had to be the anchor, the calm in the storm, the steady presence that would guide him back to safety. And when that was done, she would leave New York behind, retreating from the echoes of a life that had both thrilled and wounded her. The sooner, the better.

But her thoughts betrayed her, drifting inevitably to Flynn. She had heard the raw edge of pain in his voice, seen the tight line of his jaw, the storm simmering behind his blue eyes tonight. She knew she had wounded him deeply, and the knowledge twisted in her chest. He didn't deserve that—not from her, not ever. And yet, despite everything, the ache of longing and love that had never truly faded still throbbed within her. She loved him with all her heart, had loved him then, and still loved him now, though the consequences of that love were bitterly clear.

Pippa rested her face in her hands for a long moment, inhaling slowly, letting the quiet of the room ground her. The evening had left her raw, exposed, and painfully aware of the past she could not undo. She drew in another deep breath, forcing herself upright, shoulders squared, heart steadying. For her father, for herself, she would remain strong. For Flynn... she would carry the memory of that love in silence, hoping that, someday, time might ease the ache they both still bore.

The early morning light filtered through the blinds, striping the quiet hospital room in soft bands of gold and grey. Pippa sat at the edge of her father's bed, fingers entwined with his, grounding herself in the familiar warmth of his hand. Chloe perched in the chair beside her, coffee long forgotten in her lap, eyes alert and watchful. They had taken an Uber straight from the cottage—the less she saw Flynn while she was here, the better, for both him and her.

The steady beep of the heart monitor filled the space, a constant, low hum that underscored the fragility of the moment. Every breath, every shift in Henry's chest seemed magnified in the quiet room.

Henry's eyes fluttered open, confusion mingling with the remnants of sleep and pain. "Pippa… Chloe… morning," he croaked, his voice rough but steady. He gave her hand a faint squeeze, his grip weaker than she expected, yet full of affection.

"Morning, Dad," Pippa whispered, brushing a strand of hair from his forehead. Her voice trembled ever so slightly, betraying the worry she tried to hide. "How are you feeling?"

"I—" He started, then coughed softly, wincing as his hand pressed against his chest. "Better, I think… a bit dizzy."

Chloe leaned forward instinctively, concern etching her features. "That's normal, Henry. Just rest. We're right here." Her hand hovered near his, a silent offer of support.

The door opened with a soft click, and a man in a crisp white coat entered, clipboard in hand. His expression was calm and professional, yet there was a quiet warmth in his eyes that seemed to soften the sterile edges of the hospital room.

"Good morning, Mr. Rockwell. Miss Rockwell," he greeted, then turned toward Chloe with a gentle nod. "And you must be…?"

"Chloe," she replied, brushing a loose strand of hair from her face as she offered a polite smile.

"Chloe," he echoed, returning her smile with one of quiet reassurance before focusing back on Henry. "I'm Dr. Patel. I've reviewed your tests from last night." He paused briefly, the kind of pause that preceded something heavy.

"You have a significant blockage in one of your coronary arteries. It's serious enough that we'll need to address it promptly to prevent further complications."

Pippa's chest tightened, the words landing with the dull, inevitable weight of something she had feared but not wanted to name. She tightened her hold on her father's hand, grounding herself against the rush of worry that threatened to spill over.

"It's going to be all right, Dad," she said softly, though her voice trembled ever so slightly.

Chloe reached across the bed and laid a gentle hand on Pippa's shoulder, the simple gesture speaking volumes—solidarity, reassurance, love. Pippa drew strength from it, forcing a steady breath, her heart warring between fear and the determination to stay strong—for him.

Henry blinked slowly, trying to process the news, his hand still clutching hers. "So… surgery?" His voice was low, uncertain, carrying the weight of vulnerability he rarely allowed.

Pippa's chest tightened, the words echoing in her mind like a drumbeat. She squeezed his hand firmly, willing her own fear into the background. "What… what does he need to do?" Her voice trembled slightly, betraying the knot of worry twisting in her stomach.

Dr. Patel's gaze swept between the two women, calm but firm. "The best course of action is a coronary angioplasty," he explained, his tone measured. "We'll insert a small balloon catheter to open the blocked artery, often followed by a stent to keep it clear. For someone in otherwise stable condition, it's routine. But timing is crucial. Any delay increases the risk of a heart attack."

Henry shifted slightly in bed, wincing as the memory of last night's pain flared briefly across his features. "Will… I be okay?" His voice was quieter now, a fragile whisper, carrying the fear he rarely admitted.

Dr. Patel's expression softened fractionally, reassuring yet precise. "You have every reason to expect a successful recovery," he said. "The procedure is minimally invasive, and complications are uncommon when performed promptly. The key is scheduling it as soon as possible and adhering to post-procedure care."

Pippa swallowed hard, nodding, feeling the air in the room constrict around her. "When… when can we do it?"

"As soon as the team is prepped," the doctor replied, his tone steady and reassuring. "We'll move quickly this morning if you're ready. We'll explain everything beforehand, answer any questions, and make sure Henry is as comfortable as possible."

Chloe reached over, her hand settling on Pippa's shoulder like a lifeline. "He's going to be fine," she murmured, soft but firm, though the worry lingering in her eyes betrayed her own fear.

Pippa drew a deep, grounding breath, the weight of responsibility pressing onto her shoulders like a physical weight. She looked at her father, meeting the trust and hope in his eyes, and felt a quiet determination ignite within her. "We'll do it," she said, voice steady despite the tremor in her stomach. "Let's get it done."

Henry gave a faint, weary smile, squeezing her hand in return. "You always take care of me, don't you, Pippa?" His words were a whisper, but heavy with love and gratitude.

"I always will, Dad," she whispered back, leaning forward to brush a gentle kiss across his temple. The warmth of her touch carried a quiet strength, defying the anxiety knotting in her chest.

Dr. Patel nodded, satisfied. "Alright. Let's get started." He motioned toward the door. "The nursing staff will help prep Mr. Rockwell, and we'll take it step by step. You're in good hands."

Pippa sat back for a moment, glancing at Chloe. Outside, the city moved on, indifferent, the hum of traffic distant behind the hospital walls. But here, in this quiet, sterile room, every second mattered. Every heartbeat. Every decision.

Her father's life depended on her presence, on her steadiness. And she would do everything she could—everything—to make sure he got it back.

The morning sun crept further through the blinds, spilling light across the room. For the first time, Pippa let herself anchor in that quiet certainty: nothing else mattered, not the past, not Flynn, not the lingering ache in her heart. Only her father. Only now.

Pippa sat in the small waiting area just outside her father's room, hands folded tightly in her lap, shoulders slightly hunched as if bracing herself against the weight pressing down from every direction. The hum of fluorescent lights overhead mingled with the distant beeps of monitors, the occasional rolling cart, and the soft murmur of nurses—an industrial lullaby that seemed to echo the rhythm of her own anxious heartbeat. Chloe had gone to fetch coffee, leaving her alone with the thoughts that had been clawing at her since yesterday, insistent and unrelenting.

Her fists clenched in her lap, the warmth of her palms pressing into her knees as she tried to will away the ache in her chest. Flynn. His kiss. The way his eyes had locked onto hers, filled with betrayal and longing, as though she had ripped his heart from his chest and crushed it in her hands. Her lips tingled still, the memory a raw, smouldering burn she could neither ignore nor escape.

And yet... she could not face him. Could not risk the ruin of everything he had worked so hard to build—the family, the estate, the legacy, and the fragile balance of his life that she had already disrupted once. The thought of scandal, of disruption, of undoing him in any way made her chest tighten further.

Her mind turned to the letter she had written three years ago, the words etched with desperate self-preservation. *I don't love you the way you think I do.* Each syllable had been a dagger to his heart, a lie wrapped in the guise of truth, written to protect him even as it destroyed her. She had convinced herself it was the only way to save him from her own presence, from the chaos she feared she would bring.

Pippa pressed her forehead into her hands, drawing slow, measured breaths. "It has to be this way," she whispered, a threadbare mantra to steady her racing thoughts. "I can't... I can't risk his future. Not for me. Not for us." The sterile walls seemed to absorb her words, reflecting her desperation back at her, a reminder of the impossible choice she had made.

The scrape of shoes on tile and the soft click of the door announced Chloe's return. She set the coffee beside Pippa and rested a warm hand on her shoulder, grounding her. "He's in good hands," she said softly, voice steady, a tether against the storm of worry inside Pippa. "You're here. That's what matters."

Pippa nodded, swallowing hard, but her gaze drifted back to the closed door of her father's room. Every muffled sound—the scrape of a nurse's shoe, the whisper of a voice—made her chest constrict. She longed to run, to vanish like she had before, but the stakes were infinitely higher this time. Her father's life hung in the balance, and she could not abandon him—not now.

She drew a slow, grounding breath, recalling the letter curled in her mind like a nightmare she would never fully escape. Soon, she would have to leave New York. Soon, she would have to step back into a life that made sense, a life apart from Flynn, a life that demanded the sacrifice of the love she still carried quietly, painfully, in her heart.

But the memory of his blue eyes—their haunted depth, the yearning, the pieces of her heart she had never truly given him—refused to let her go. Even in the sterile hospital corridor, even with the weight of duty pressing down, she could feel his presence lingering, an invisible tether she could not sever.

Pippa sipped the lukewarm coffee Chloe had brought, letting the bitterness anchor her in the present. Her hands rested over her lap, fingers fidgeting lightly against the paper cup. She whispered to herself, barely audible, "I love you, Flynn... and I always will. But sometimes love... isn't enough."

The words settled over her like a stone—heavy, true, unyielding.

The soft click of the door interrupted her reverie. A nurse stepped out, her expression calm and professional, offering a small nod. "Everything's ready. You can see him for a moment before we take him in."

Pippa rose, shoulders squaring, chin lifting, the muscles in her jaw tightening with resolve. She followed the nurse back, each step a quiet testament to the battle raging inside her: love and duty, desire and restraint, the heart she could not fully give, and the life she could not yet abandon.

With each step, the weight of her past and the responsibility of the present converged, reminding her that some choices were made not for happiness, but for the ones she loved most. And for Henry, she would stand steadfast, even if it meant the world outside, and the man who still haunted her heart, remained just out of reach.

Chapter Seven

The steady beeping of monitors filled the pre-op room, a mechanical counterpoint to the uneven rhythm of Pippa's breaths. Her father lay calm beneath the stiff hospital sheets, though a faint crease marred his brow, betraying the worry he tried to hide. Nurses moved briskly around him, checking vitals, adjusting lines, their clipped words blurring into background noise.

Pippa smoothed a stray lock of hair from his forehead, her touch trembling. "Dad… I'll be right here when you wake up, I promise," she whispered, her lips brushing his temple. She lingered there, as though memorising the warmth of his skin, the contours of the face she loved most.

Henry's fingers twitched, curling faintly around hers. "I'll be fine, Pipp," he murmured, voice weak but steady, a ghost of a smile tugging at his lips. "Go wait with Chloe… I don't want you worrying."

Reluctantly, she let go. The nurses wheeled him away, their voices fading down the corridor. When the door shut behind them, silence rushed in, loud and suffocating.

Pippa followed Chloe into the waiting area, her steps heavy, her heart pounding. They sank into stiff plastic chairs, side by side, while the minutes dragged on mercilessly. Each tick of the clock was a hammer on her nerves. Her fingers twisted together, white-knuckled, while her mind chased every possible *what if*.

The hiss of the automatic doors made her flinch.

She looked up.

Flynn.

Tall, composed, devastatingly familiar. His dark suit fit with effortless precision, his shoulders squared with the confidence of a man used to commanding a room. But his eyes—blue, storm-filled, sharp as glass—swept the waiting area and locked onto her instantly.

"Pippa."

Just her name. Low, almost a breath. But it cut through her chest as though he'd spoken a lifetime of accusations and regrets in that single word.

Chloe rose, offering him a polite nod. "I'll… give you two a moment," she murmured before slipping quietly down the hall, her footsteps fading until only silence remained. Pippa felt it immediately—the shift in the air, the sudden gravity of being alone with him.

Flynn moved toward her, each step measured, deliberate. His jaw was rigid, his eyes unreadable, but the authority in his stance was undeniable. Pippa's pulse stuttered. She clasped her knees, willing herself not to shrink beneath the intensity of his gaze.

He stopped in front of her, close enough that she could feel the pull of his presence—the same magnetic force that had once undone her completely.

"How's your father?" he asked, his voice low, controlled. It wasn't gentle, but it wasn't cold either—something raw and unspoken lingered beneath the surface. "Is he—will he be all right?"

She swallowed hard, forcing steadiness into her tone. "They just took him in. The doctors said it's routine. He's… in good hands."

Flynn's jaw tightened, the muscle ticking as his gaze flicked briefly to her hands before returning to her face. For an instant, his fingers twitched, as if he meant to reach for her—but he caught himself, curling them into a fist at his side.

"Good," he said finally, the word clipped, roughened by something he couldn't quite disguise.

Pippa managed a fragile smile. "Thank you for coming."

His eyes darkened. For a fleeting heartbeat, she saw a shadow of the man she had once loved—the boy who had kissed her under the old oak tree, who had looked at her as though she was the only thing in his world. But the warmth vanished as quickly as it appeared, replaced by something colder, harder.

"I'm not here for you, Pippa," he said flatly. His voice carried steel, but beneath it, she heard the faintest tremor—pain, tightly contained. "Don't mistake this for anything. I came for Henry. He deserves that. But you—" his gaze cut over her, slow and deliberate, lingering where it hurt most— "you've already taken enough from me."

The words struck like a physical blow. Pippa's breath faltered, her chest constricting. She had prepared herself for his anger, for the sharp edges of his resentment—but hearing it still tore something open inside her.

Flynn sank into the chair beside her, the motion deliberate, heavy. He was close enough that she could feel the heat of him, the faint brush of his sleeve against her arm, but he angled his body away, a wall of rigid self-control. His hands flexed once, the veins in his forearms standing out before he forced them still.

The silence between them was thick—filled with the sterile hum of machines, the distant shuffle of nurses' shoes, and the ghosts of everything they had once been.

And still, she felt it. That pull. The invisible thread that had always connected them—frayed, battered, but not broken. His nearness made her ache; it awakened memories she had buried, desires she had tried to forget.

But his anger was armour, his bitterness a fortress she could not breach. He sat beside her, close enough to touch, yet impossibly far away—two people bound by love and history, divided by pain neither knew how to undo.

Chloe returned quietly, setting a coffee beside Pippa before settling herself on the other side. Her presence was a gentle anchor, grounding Pippa in the room's sterile reality. The soft clink of the cup against the table barely registered over the tension humming like a wire between Pippa and Flynn.

So, Pippa sat there, side by side with them, staring at the clock on the far wall, forcing herself to focus on its mechanical ticking rather than the way Flynn's hands flexed restlessly, or the way his eyes flicked toward her only to dart away again. Every glance, every breath, was a silent war—love and anger, longing and regret, all suspended in the sterile glow of the waiting room.

Hours passed in slow, dragging increments. The sterile hum of the waiting room, punctuated by distant beeps from monitors beyond the walls, became the only rhythm Pippa could cling to. She had barely touched her coffee, fingers curled tightly around the paper cup, knuckles white, as if the warmth might ground her otherwise racing thoughts. Chloe sat close, her presence calm and steady, occasionally offering a quiet word or a gentle squeeze of Pippa's hand, but even her reassurance could not fully ease the ache that clutched Pippa's chest.

Flynn's presence was silent yet commanding. He leaned back in the chair beside her, body angled just enough to respect distance, but his stormy blue eyes flicked toward her frequently, brief and loaded glances that spoke of restrained emotions: anger, longing, regret, and desire tangled together, coiled beneath his composed exterior. He hadn't spoken of their history since arriving, but the tension radiating from him was undeniable, a current Pippa could neither ignore nor escape.

Chloe's hand brushed hers again, a soft anchor. "It's going to be fine," she said gently, though Pippa could hear the worry threading her calm tone. "They'll take good care of him. He's strong."

Pippa gave a small, grateful smile, yet it felt fragile. Her eyes wandered to the closed doors thinking of the operating theatre, imagining her father inside, unaware of time slipping past. Every tick of the clock was a drumbeat of anxiety, each second stretching longer than the last, a reminder that Henry's life—and the fragile balance of her own emotions—hung in the hands of others.

Flynn shifted slightly, his gaze lifting to hers. There it was again—the storm in his eyes, raw and unfiltered, the lingering fire that had once consumed them both. No words passed, but Pippa understood, he was here for Henry, yes, but the weight of the past pressed down on both of them. Anger and hurt mingled with a longing that neither could fully voice.

The minutes dragged. Pippa's thoughts swirled, memories clawing at her—laughing by the lake, whispered promises, the brush of his hands, the ache of leaving him behind. She pressed her palm to her forehead, willing herself to breathe, to be present, but every heartbeat reminded her of what she had lost and what she might never regain.

Then the doors opened. The doctor appeared, crisp in his white coat, clipboard in hand, expression calm but precise. Pippa's stomach dropped, a fluttering catch of breath betraying her nerves. Flynn was instantly on alert, rising from his chair with an ease born of habit and urgency, his posture rigid yet charged with barely contained emotion. The sharp edge of fear lingered in his gaze.

The doctor stepped forward, clearing his throat. "Miss Rockwell? Mr. Oakland?" His eyes flicked between them, steady, careful. "The surgery went exactly as expected. Your father responded well to the procedure. There were no complications."

Relief crashed through Pippa like a wave. She sagged into her chair, gripping the armrests as her heart raced, a tremor of exhaustion and gratitude running through her. Flynn exhaled sharply, tension in his shoulders loosening fractionally, though the storm in his eyes remained, focused entirely on her.

"He's in recovery now," the doctor continued, voice steady, precise. "He'll need careful monitoring and rest, but he's stable. You can see him shortly."

Pippa nodded, swallowing hard, the tight knot in her chest loosening just slightly. She dared a glance at Flynn, noting the subtle shift in him—his posture still taut, his jaw clenched, yet the shadow of relief flickered through the storm of emotions she saw reflected in his eyes. For a heartbeat, it was as if the weight of everything unsaid, every wrong, every longing, had lifted just enough to allow them to breathe.

And yet, even in that moment, the tension lingered—palpable, electric, a silent promise that the past was far from settled, and the storm between them was only temporarily restrained.

A nurse appeared in the doorway, her smile professional but kind. "Mr. Rockwell is awake. You can see him now, but only a few at a time, please."

Chloe immediately rose and slipped her hand into Pippa's, giving it a reassuring squeeze. "Come on," she murmured gently. "Let's go see him."

Pippa's heart thudded unevenly as she followed her friend down the corridor. She opened the door to Henry's room with a soft click, and the sterile tang of antiseptic enveloped her. The rhythmic beeping of monitors and the faint hiss of oxygen grounded her in the present, though her chest tightened at the sight before her.

Henry lay propped against a mound of pillows, his skin pale, his frame thinner than she remembered, but the steady rise and fall of his chest brought instant relief. A thin hospital sheet covered him, tubes and wires running like lifelines from his body to the machines beside the bed. His eyes fluttered open as she approached, and a tired but genuine smile curved his lips.

"Pippa…" His voice was hoarse, a whisper of its usual strength, but still warm enough to make her heart ache. "You're here."

"Always, Dad," she whispered, leaning down to press a gentle kiss to his forehead. Her fingers lingered against his arm, feeling the faint but steady pulse beneath fragile skin. "The doctor said everything went well."

Henry's lips curved into a small, grateful smile. His trembling hand lifted to brush a strand of hair from her face, fatherly instinct shining even through his weakness. "I knew it would be," he murmured, though fatigue tugged at his words.

Behind her, Flynn remained near the door, tall and contained, his presence unmistakable. She didn't have to turn to know he was there—she felt him. The tension in his shoulders, the restless flex of his hands, the intensity of his gaze. He didn't move at first, but his nearness filled the space like a storm pressing against the walls.

Chloe, sensing the undercurrent, stepped aside, giving Pippa the space she needed.

Finally, Flynn moved forward, each step deliberate, until he stood at Henry's bedside. His voice was careful, measured, when he spoke. "Henry." A faint nod, almost formal. "It's good to see you awake. Glad you're doing well."

Henry's eyes flicked toward him, studying him for a heartbeat before softening. He gave a small, knowing smile that tugged at the corner of his mouth, the kind of smile that suggested he saw more than either of them wanted him to. "Thank you, Flynn," he rasped. His gaze slid back to Pippa, and his expression grew quietly earnest. "Look after her for me."

Heat rushed to Pippa's cheeks. She gripped her father's hand more tightly, her voice firm but tender. "I can look after myself, Dad."

Flynn's jaw tightened, the words catching somewhere between pride and bitterness. He stepped back slightly, his tone quiet, almost to himself. "I'll be right outside. If you need anything, Henry… just let me know."

Henry nodded faintly. "Thank you."

Chloe touched Pippa's shoulder lightly, then slipped out of the room with Flynn, leaving her alone with their father. The silence that followed felt both a relief and a weight.

Pippa sank into the chair beside his bed, her fingers wrapping gently around his. The weight of the day pressed down on her shoulders—the worry, the exhaustion, the bittersweet pull of Flynn's presence. But here, now, only her father mattered.

Henry's eyelids grew heavy, drifting closed as the medication pulled him back toward rest. His grip slackened in hers, but she didn't let go.

She leaned back, exhaling slowly, brushing a loose strand of hair behind her ear. For a moment, the world outside—the anger, the longing, the fear—fell away.

It was just her and her father. And that was enough.

Chloe and Flynn walked side by side down the long hospital corridor, their footsteps muted against the polished floor. The hum of fluorescent lights filled the silence between them, mingling with the faint aroma of coffee drifting from the café kiosk at the end of the hall. Despite the sterile chill, the air between them was warm with unspoken friction.

"So," Chloe said at last, her tone deceptively casual, though her eyes flicked toward him with quiet sharpness. "You've been holding up surprisingly well… for someone who makes it clear he'd rather Pippa hadn't come back."

Flynn's jaw ticked, a muscle working as he kept his gaze fixed ahead. "Subtle," he muttered dryly.

Chloe gave a small shrug, unfazed. "It's obvious you're holding a grudge."

His lips pressed into a thin line. "I've got good reason to."

She slowed her pace just enough to glance fully at him, her voice calm but edged. "I know you think you have."

The words made him cut her a sharp look, suspicion and irritation simmering in his stormy blue eyes. Chloe didn't flinch. She knew more than he realised— about his mother, about the letter, about the sacrifice Pippa had made. But Pippa's plea for silence echoed in her mind: *'Don't tell him. Please, Chloe. I don't want him hurt.'*

Flynn exhaled through his nose; his hands shoved deep in his pockets. "I suppose I should expect you to be on Pippa's side," he said flatly.

"Of course I'm on her side," Chloe replied evenly. "She's my best friend. But being on her side doesn't mean I'm against you, Flynn." She let her words linger, deliberate, before adding, "It just means I see things you're refusing to."

He looked away, eyes hardening as though building walls against the weight of her meaning. Chloe didn't push further—yet—but her silence was layered, heavy with truths she wasn't allowed to speak.

Together they reached the end of the corridor, the low hum of the coffee machine filling the pause. Flynn ordered without looking at her, but Chloe studied him, seeing not just the anger but the hurt beneath it. A hurt Pippa had never stopped carrying herself.

And Chloe wondered—just how much longer either of them could survive the storm they kept locked between them.

Meanwhile, back in Henry's room, the door opened with a soft click, and Dr. Patel stepped inside. His usual professional composure carried a touch of warmth this time, a small smile tugging at the corners of his mouth.

"Miss Rockwell," he greeted, his tone gentle but sure, as he crossed to her side. "I just wanted to reassure you once more—your father's surgery went exceptionally well. Everything proceeded exactly as we hoped."

Relief broke over Pippa like a sudden tide, her chest heaving as if she had been holding her breath for hours. "Thank you," she whispered, her voice thick, gratitude softening every syllable. "Truly, Dr. Patel. You've given him back to me… I don't even know how to thank you."

Her trembling hands reached instinctively for his, clasping them briefly. The doctor's smile deepened, a flicker of something warmer than professionalism sparking in his eyes.

He hesitated a fraction, then cleared his throat. "If… you'd ever consider stepping away from hospital walls for an evening," he said carefully, "I would be honoured to buy you a drink sometime."

Pippa blinked, startled by the unexpectedness of the invitation. Her lips parted, then curved into a small, shy smile despite the heaviness of the morning. "I… I'd like that," she said softly, almost surprised at herself.

Dr. Patel slipped his phone from his pocket, offering it with a hopeful smile. "Then perhaps your number?"

Pippa's breath caught, her pulse skittering. She glanced down at the device in his hand, her cheeks warming with a mixture of nerves and—if she was honest—something dangerously close to excitement. She took the phone from him and with quick fingers, she typed in her number, saving it under the playful nickname *Pipp*. For a fleeting moment, her lips curved, an indulgent smile tugging upward at the corners. She hadn't smiled like that in far too long.

When she handed it back, Dr. Patel's expression brightened, a flicker of satisfaction passing behind his otherwise professional composure. Just as his fingers brushed hers, the door opened with a soft, deliberate push.

Dr. Patel straightened, instinctively tucking the phone into his pocket—a small, innocuous gesture, but one that suddenly felt weighted, significant.

Flynn stepped inside, Chloe close behind. Instantly, the air changed—dense, electric—like the moment before a thunderstorm breaks. The faint hum of the machines filled the silence as Flynn's storm-blue gaze swept the room, landing first on Pippa. It lingered—just a heartbeat too long—before sliding to Dr. Patel. His eyes followed the motion of the doctor's hand, catching the phone disappearing into the pocket of his coat. The muscle in his jaw tightened, a slow, deliberate flex that spoke of barely restrained control.

"Everything alright in here?" His voice was calm, smooth as polished steel, but the razor edge beneath it was impossible to miss.

Chloe hesitated in the doorway, her hand brushing the frame as her eyes darted between the three of them. Her brows lifted just slightly, the kind of subtle, knowing gesture that said she had walked straight into something she wasn't meant to see—but instantly understood.

Pippa's stomach twisted. The sharp tension in the air felt almost tangible, pressing against her ribs until it was difficult to breathe. She forced her fingers to unclench from where they had curled tightly by her side, nails leaving faint crescents in her palms. Her gaze dropped to her father—sleeping peacefully, blissfully unaware of the quiet storm building around his hospital bed.

"Yes," she said quickly, her voice steady but just a shade too bright, too controlled. "Everything's fine."

The silence that followed was brittle, a taut thread stretched between them all— each aware that one wrong word might snap it. She could feel Flynn's stare on her like heat, scorching and unyielding. It carried accusation, confusion, and something far more dangerous—a possessive edge he couldn't quite hide. Her heart hammered harder, each beat a painful reminder of the unresolved past between them.

Dr. Patel cleared his throat softly, breaking the silence with professional grace. "Well... I'll leave you to your family," he said, bowing his head slightly. His tone was careful, polite, but the faint awkwardness in the way he stepped back betrayed that even he had felt the shift.

He slipped toward the door, offering Pippa one last faint smile before disappearing into the hall.

And still, Flynn didn't look away.

The door clicked shut, and the quiet that followed was suffocating. The steady beep of Henry's monitor filled the silence, each pulse amplifying the tension that hung thick in the air.

Flynn's gaze pinned her where she stood. "So," he said at last, his tone clipped and razor-edged, "you're giving your number to doctors now?"

Pippa's head jerked up, heat flooding her cheeks. "That was nothing," she said quickly, her voice pitched a shade too high. "He was just being kind."

A low, humourless laugh slipped from him, sharp as glass. "Kind," he echoed. He shifted his stance, broad shoulders squaring, hands shoved deep into his pockets as though they were the only thing keeping him tethered. "Strange how kindness looks an awful lot like asking you out."

Her pulse thundered, anger sparking against the guilt that already gnawed at her chest. "You don't get to stand there and judge me," she whispered fiercely, her voice low but cutting, mindful of her father's fragile rest a few feet away.

For a beat, his mask faltered. The storm in his eyes cracked open—hurt, jealousy, something rawer lurking just beneath the surface. He leaned forward slightly, voice roughened. "I'm not judging you, Pippa. I'm just… standing here watching you move on."

The words sliced through her. Her breath caught, her lips parted, but no reply came. She couldn't meet his gaze—not when the truth blazed between them like wildfire, scorching everything in its path.

From the corner, Chloe cleared her throat, her arms folded, expression sharp. "Maybe this isn't the time," she said softly but with enough steel to make them both remember where they were.

But Flynn didn't look away. His eyes stayed locked on Pippa's, unyielding, burning with everything he wouldn't say—and everything she couldn't.

Chapter Eight

They stayed with Henry for a little while longer, lingering in the quiet warmth of the hospital room, savouring the steady rise and fall of his chest, the soft rhythm of the monitors, the reassurance that he was safe. Pippa held his hand, feeling the faint pulse beneath her fingers, while Flynn lingered near the door, a silent anchor—alert, watchful, restrained, but undeniably tense. Every so often, his eyes flicked to her, stormy and unreadable, betraying the weight of emotions neither of them dared speak aloud.

Finally, Flynn broke the silence, his voice low and deliberate. "Come home in my limousine—it'll be more comfortable than an Uber."

Pippa hesitated, glancing at Chloe, who offered a subtle shrug and a small, encouraging smile. "Thank you, Flynn," Pippa said, her voice steady despite the flutter of nerves in her chest. "That's very kind of you."

He inclined his head, expression unreadable, and led them out of the hospital. The ride back to the estate was thick with unspoken words. Flynn and Pippa sat together in the back seat, the leather seat cool beneath them, while Chloe occupied the seat across, offering only the occasional reassuring smile. Flynn's stormy blue eyes kept flicking toward her, lingering for a heartbeat too long before glancing away, and every time, Pippa's pulse stuttered. She kept her gaze fixed on the passing city lights, fingers clasped tightly in her lap, silently willing herself to remain composed.

The limousine's quiet was only punctuated by the soft hum of the engine and the occasional shift of Flynn's weight. Tension coiled between them, heavy, magnetic, impossible to ignore. Chloe, sensing the storm in the air, remained calm, letting them navigate the silence in their own way.

When they finally reached the estate, Flynn had the driver pull up at the cottage. He stayed seated, tall and still, as the chauffeur opened the door for them. Pippa's fingers brushed against the cool metal handle as she climbed out, offering him a faint, polite nod. "Thank you," she murmured, her voice quiet but sincere.

"You're welcome," Flynn replied, jaw tight, eyes unreadable. He shot a measured glance at Chloe and added, "Take care."

Chloe offered a small, knowing smile. "Thank you."

The limousine drove off, leaving the two women on the quiet gravel driveway. Inside the cottage, Chloe leaned casually against the counter, a teasing glint in her eyes. "So…" she began, crossing her arms, "did gorgeous Dr. Patel ask you out?"

Pippa's cheeks warmed, and she bit her lip, caught off guard despite having anticipated the question. She shook her head slightly, a small, wry smile tugging at her lips. "Not yet," she murmured softly, the words barely above a whisper. "He asked if I'd like to get a drink with him sometime."

Chloe's grin widened, mischievous and knowing. "Not yet? Hmm… that man is bold, I'll give him that. You going to let him try?"

Pippa leaned back against the counter, exhaling slowly, her fingers tracing the edge of the surface as if grounding herself. Thoughts of the morning, of her father's surgery, and the tense ride with Flynn still tangled in her mind. "I… don't see why not," she admitted quietly. "There's… no reason for me to say no. And it's not like it's going to go anywhere serious. We'll be going back to San Francisco once Dad feels better."

Chloe gave her a gentle, reassuring pat on the shoulder. "Fair enough. Just… a bit of fun, you know? God knows you deserve a bit of fun. You don't go out on dates enough, Pipp."

Pippa allowed herself a small laugh, the sound light but tinged with the residue of nerves and tension. "I suppose I haven't," she admitted, her voice softer, reflective. "It's… been a while since I thought about anything other than work or… family. This…" She gestured vaguely to the room, to the morning's chaos, to everything she'd been juggling. "…might actually be nice."

Chloe's eyes softened, a rare flicker of seriousness breaking through her teasing smile. "You deserve it, Pipp. Just promise me one thing—don't let anyone… especially Flynn—make you feel guilty for taking a moment for yourself."

Pippa met her friend's gaze, a small, grateful smile tugging at her lips. "I promise," she whispered, though the promise felt heavier than words, carrying a quiet determination to let herself breathe, even if only for a little while.

Yet, even as she allowed that thought to settle, a small, unbidden tug of longing stirred in her chest. Flynn's stormy eyes, the tight line of his jaw, the weight of everything left unsaid—they lingered at the edges of her mind, a ghost she couldn't quite shake. She shook her head slightly, pressing her fingers against her temples as if to dispel the memory, forcing herself to focus instead on the tiny spark of possibility Dr. Patel's invitation offered—a brief, harmless escape from the weight of everything else, a momentary reprieve from the storm of her own heart.

Later, as Chloe and Pippa settled at the small kitchen table for a light evening meal, the quiet hum of the estate surrounding them, Pippa's phone buzzed insistently. She picked it up, eyes scanning the screen. A message from Dr. Robert Patel blinked back:

Drinks tomorrow afternoon, around 5pm...?

A small smile curved her lips despite herself. She tapped out a reply, fingers hovering for a heartbeat as she considered the moment.

Love to. I'll be at the hospital in the afternoon.

Almost immediately, another message appeared:

Perfect. I'll meet you at the front of the hospital.

Pippa lowered her phone, letting out a soft breath. The simple exchange—a harmless plan, just a drink—felt almost thrilling in its normalcy. Chloe, noticing the faint upward tug at her friend's lips, gave her a small, knowing smile.

"You're smiling," Chloe teased, her voice light but warm.

Pippa's cheeks warmed. "It's nothing," she murmured, though the flutter in her chest betrayed her. "Just... a drink."

Chloe's eyes sparkled with mischief and approval. "A drink, huh? Well, Pip... I think you deserve it. Just a little bit of normalcy—and maybe a little fun, too."

Pippa nodded, letting herself savour the tiny moment of anticipation. For the first time in days, the weight pressing on her heart felt a little lighter. Yet even as she ate, the memory of Flynn's presence—the way he had watched her, restrained yet impossibly magnetic—crept at the edges of her mind, reminding her that some things couldn't be ignored so easily.

She took a sip of water, her fingers tightening slightly around the glass, and whispered to herself, "Just a drink... nothing more."

And yet, somewhere deep inside, she knew the heart rarely obeyed such rules.

Flynn sat in his study, the soft glow of a single desk lamp casting long shadows across the room. The estate grounds were lit up beyond the tall windows. His fingers drummed lightly against the polished wood of the desk, though his mind was far from focused on the papers and files stacked neatly before him.

He could still see it, sharp and clear—the fleeting moment in Henry's hospital room when Dr. Patel had slipped his phone into his pocket after Pippa had handed it back. He was only guessing that she had entered her number, at the doctor's polite request, but he didn't need confirmation. The faint curve of her lips as she had done it—the small, almost imperceptible smile—burned into his memory. And really, why wouldn't he ask her out? She was beautiful. Unforgettable. Impossible.

Flynn's jaw tightened, irritation and something darker, unnamed, twisting through his chest. He leaned back in his chair, eyes narrowing at the shadows crawling across the study walls. He hated himself for the tightening in his chest, for the sudden stab of jealousy that made his pulse spike, even as he reminded himself with grim logic—she wasn't his. Not anymore. Maybe she never had been.

But the thought of another man—any man—receiving even a fragment of her attention, even in the most innocent, casual way, felt like a knife pressed against his ribs. His hands clenched into fists on the armrests, nails digging into leather. *I'm not falling for this again. I did that once. Never again.*

He rose abruptly, pacing the study in long, precise strides, each step echoing the storm that churned within him. Anger, bitterness, longing—they tangled together, a vicious, roiling knot he could neither unravel nor ignore. He stopped at the window, gripping the sill, eyes tracing the lights across the estate grounds. *I can't... I won't...* he exhaled sharply, jaw tight, body taut as steel. *She's here for Henry. That's it. Nothing else.*

And yet... the image of her refused to be dismissed. Her delicate hands, her laughter just out of reach, the warmth in her eyes when she looked at anyone who mattered to her—they lingered, haunting him. He shook his head, pressing his palms to the window frame, muscles coiled, mind racing. The war between reason and desire raged quietly but relentlessly, leaving him restless, furious, and painfully aware of what he still wanted—and had lost.

He sank back into the chair, running a hand through his hair, letting the shadows of the study swallow him. Outside, the city went on, indifferent, oblivious. Inside, Flynn Oakland wrestled with a truth he could not yet speak, a truth that burned hotter with every thought of her: no matter how much he tried to deny it, Pippa still held a piece of him. A stubborn, unyielding piece that refused to let go.

Flynn's thoughts were still tangled in shadows of Pippa when his phone buzzed sharply against the polished mahogany of his desk. He glanced down, frowning as the name flashed across the screen: **Marion Hayes**—one of the board members for the *Children's Hope Foundation Gala*, a charity he directed.

He hesitated before answering, already anticipating the controlled charm she would bring to the conversation. "Marion," he said, his voice clipped, though polite.

"Flynn! There you are," Marion's tone was warm, insistent, the kind of cheer that suggested she had rehearsed it countless times. "I've been trying to pin you down for months. I simply *must* see you before the gala—only five days away. It's going to be quite the event this year, and I expect my director to make an appearance... and, well, keep me company."

Flynn's jaw tightened. He leaned back in his chair, running a hand through his hair. *'Keep me company',* she said, like it were a casual suggestion, a favour to her—and yet, in her mind, it was an obligation. "Marion," he said carefully, voice level but firm, "I appreciate the invitation, but I'll be attending the gala as part of my duties on the board. That will have to suffice."

"Oh, Flynn," she cooed, playful yet persistent, "you always say that. But you and I both know it's not quite the same as spending a little evening together beforehand. Just a quiet dinner—no work, no speeches, no charity business. Just us."

His stormy blue eyes darkened, tension threading through the polite mask he wore. "Marion, I'm afraid I can't. I have other commitments that evening... and personal matters I need to attend to."

A brief pause, then Marion's tone softened, but the persistence didn't waver. "Personal matters, hmm? I see... well, I'll let you off the hook this time but do keep me in mind. Five days, Flynn—try to keep your calendar open."

He exhaled slowly, gripping the edge of his desk until his knuckles whitened. "Noted," he said finally, the single word heavy with more meaning than Marion could ever guess. He ended the call and set the phone down, jaw tight, eyes narrowing into slits.

For a moment, the memory of Pippa flared like wildfire—her delicate hands brushing his own, the subtle curve of her lips, the laugh that had haunted his chest for years. The idea of her spending an evening with anyone else, especially Dr. Patel, felt like a physical ache.

Flynn rubbed his temples, leaning back against the leather of his chair, but the thought wouldn't leave him. Dr. Patel... taking Pippa out. On a date. The image gnawed at him, igniting something sharper, rawer—jealousy, possessiveness, protectiveness all tangled together.

No. He forced the word through clenched teeth. *I won't let this happen. Not again. Not him. Not anyone.* His hands curled into fists at his sides, the leather armrests cutting into his palms as his pulse quickened.

He paced the study, long, measured strides echoing against the polished floor, mind racing. Every scenario flickered through his thoughts—Pippa laughing across the table from someone else, leaning in closer than she ever leaned toward him, allowing another man to touch even a fragment of what he had once claimed as his own.

The thought made his chest tighten, his body coiled with tension, a storm barely restrained. *She's here for Henry. That's it. Nothing else.* He muttered the words aloud, but even as he did, he knew how unconvincing they sounded.

He stopped at the window, gripping the sill, the city lights of New York sprawling beneath him like a glittering battlefield. She belonged to no one— yet every fibre of him ached with the knowledge that he still wanted her, and that no one, not Dr. Patel, not Marion Hayes, would take that from him without a fight.

Leaning back against the window frame, muscles taut, jaw clenched, he closed his eyes for a moment. The war between reason and desire raged relentlessly, leaving him restless, angry, and painfully aware of the one truth he couldn't escape: Pippa still held a piece of him, as stubborn and unyielding as ever, and he knew he needed to let go.

Chloe joined Pippa in the kitchen, her presence warm and grounding in the soft morning light. "Morning, Pippa," she said, sliding a mug of coffee across the counter toward her. "Sleep well?"

"I did, thanks," Pippa replied, accepting the cup with a small smile, letting the rich aroma fill her senses.

Chloe leaned against the counter, sipping her own coffee. "Good. I've had a few calls this morning... seems like people are already aware you're in New York." She raised an eyebrow, the corners of her mouth twitching with amusement. "And apparently, they're very keen to see you. Gabriella Rossi and... let's see... Celeste Monroe. They want some time with you."

Pippa's lips curved in a wry smile, amused despite the lingering exhaustion. Gabriella Rossi, the A-list actress known for her red-carpet elegance, and Celeste Monroe, the chart-topping singer with a penchant for daring style choices—both reaching out to her while she was in town was flattering, but also slightly overwhelming.

"I suppose I could make some time in the afternoons," Pippa suggested, swirling her coffee in the cup. "I don't want to overcommit, but I can fit a few meetings in while I'm here in New York."

Chloe's grin widened, her eyes sparkling with efficiency and just a hint of mischief. "Leave it to me. I'll organise it all—schedules, locations, even the catering if needed. You just focus on showing up and looking fabulous."

Pippa chuckled softly, grateful for Chloe's unwavering support. "Thanks, Chloe. Honestly, I don't know what I'd do without you."

Chloe waved her hand dismissively. "You'd survive," she said, smirking, "but let's be honest—you'd survive, but you'd be stressed to the point of losing your mind. So, consider me your sanity insurance."

Pippa laughed, the sound light and warm in the sunlit kitchen. "Sanity insurance… I like the sound of that."

Chloe's smile softened, and she clinked her mug gently against Pippa's. "Alright, we'll get some work done while we're here. New York won't know what hit it."

Pippa laughed, the sound light and bright, a brief reprieve from the weight of the morning. "I'll be heading to the hospital this afternoon," she said, taking a slow sip of her coffee. "And… I'm meeting Dr. Patel for drinks afterward."

Chloe arched an eyebrow, amused. "Oh? Already making plans, are we?" She shook her head with a teasing smile, then her expression softened. "Don't worry, I'll make sure your schedule works. We'll keep your mornings free for your father—he should be coming home in the next couple of days. Afternoons can be for work and meetings, while he rests and recovers."

Pippa nodded, a quiet sense of relief settling over her. "Thanks, Chloe. It's good to know I won't have to worry about juggling everything at once."

Chloe leaned back against the counter, folding her arms with a satisfied smirk. "That's what I'm here for—keeping your life on track while you focus on the important things. And maybe sneaking in a little fun along the way."

Pippa smiled, letting herself relax into the easy rhythm of their morning, feeling the weight of responsibility balanced by the reassuring presence of her friend.

Pippa leaned back slightly, considering. "Since we're going to need transport while we're here… could you organise a hire car for the duration of our visit? I may need to take Dad to doctor's appointments and run a few errands."

Chloe nodded, thoughtful. "Good idea. Ubers are fine for short trips, but having your own transport will make everything so much easier—and faster. I'll get it sorted, so you don't have to worry about it."

Pippa smiled, relieved. "Perfect. That'll make things a lot smoother."

Chloe grinned. "Exactly. Consider it done. You focus on your dad—and maybe a little on yourself, too."

Pippa glanced at the clock, then back at her coffee. "I'll be leaving in a couple of hours. Not sure what time I'll be back."

Chloe chuckled, a teasing glint in her eyes. "Hopefully late."

Pippa rolled her eyes, though a faint smile tugged at her lips. "I will not be too late. Don't let your imagination run wild."

Chloe raised an eyebrow, still grinning. "We'll see about that."

Pippa left Chloe in the kitchen and headed to the bathroom, washing her hair and taking her time with her routine. When she was done, she dressed carefully for her visit with her father and her drinks with Robert. She chose a soft, cream-coloured silk blouse that skimmed her figure, paired with tailored navy trousers that lent a quiet elegance. Her hair fell in gentle waves over her shoulders, and a subtle touch of makeup highlighted her eyes and lips, giving her a polished, effortless glow.

As she took a final glance in the mirror, a flicker of thought crossed her mind—Flynn. She could still see the tension in his eyes from the hospital, the way his jaw had tightened when she smiled at Robert. She pushed the memory aside, willing herself to focus on Henry first, on the mundane necessities of her life in New York, and on Robert later. But she knew, even as she pulled on her shoes, that Flynn's stormy gaze would not easily leave her mind.

Satisfied, she took a deep breath, steadying herself. Tonight, she reminded herself, was about balance—her father, her responsibilities, and maybe, just a little, herself.

Chapter Nine

Pippa stepped into the back of the waiting Uber, the city blurring past as she made her way to the hospital. Her thoughts drifted between her father, her responsibilities, and the evening ahead. She tried to push aside the memory of Flynn, focusing instead on Henry—on the steady rise and fall of his chest, the small, reassuring movements that reminded her he was safe.

When she arrived, she made her way quietly to her father's room. Henry's eyes lit up when he saw her. "Pippa," he said, voice warm despite the lingering fatigue. "You're here."

"Of course, Dad," she whispered, brushing a strand of hair from his forehead. They spoke softly, catching up on the day's events, laughter mingling with tender concern. Henry was in good spirits, joking lightly about the hospital food and teasing her about keeping Chloe in line.

A nurse appeared, clipboard in hand. "Mr. Rockwell is recovering well," she said. "If all continues as it has today, he should be able to go home tomorrow morning."

Relief washed over Pippa, her shoulders loosening slightly. "That's wonderful news," she said, squeezing her father's hand. "You'll be home soon, Dad."

By ten to five, Pippa knew it was time to leave. She hugged her father gently, lingering in the moment. "I'll see you tomorrow, okay?" she whispered.

"I'll be ready," he replied, smiling.

With a final squeeze of his hand, she left the room and made her way to the hospital's front entrance. The late afternoon air was cool against her skin, carrying the faint hum of city life. She scanned the entrance, and there he was— Dr. Robert Patel, standing casually near the revolving doors, a small smile on his face.

"Wow," he said as soon as he saw her, his eyes lighting up. "You look amazing."

Pippa felt a faint warmth rise to her cheeks. She smiled, brushing a loose strand of hair behind her ear. "Thank you," she said softly, letting the tension of the day ease just enough for a spark of anticipation.

Dr. Patel offered his arm with a polite, easy charm. "Shall we?"

Pippa hesitated only a moment before taking it. The brush of his hand against hers sent a faint thrill up her spine, though she immediately chastised herself. *Focus on today. Focus on a drink. Nothing more.*

They walked down the steps together, the city casting long shadows across the pavement. The streets of New York were alive with motion—taxis honking, late-afternoon pedestrians hurrying by—but in that small bubble of space between them, the world felt quiet, contained.

"You've had a long day," Robert said, glancing at her with genuine concern. "Hospital visits aren't exactly relaxing."

Pippa let out a small laugh, shaking her head. "You could say that again. But it's worth it. He's doing well, and he'll be home tomorrow. That's what matters."

Robert nodded, his fingers brushing lightly against hers as they walked. "Good. I'd hate for him to have a grumpy daughter dragging herself through the city tonight."

Her lips curved into a small smile. "Grumpy? Me?" she teased softly.

He chuckled, a low, warm sound. "Oh yes. The grumpiest. Though I think you wear it well."

Pippa felt her cheeks warm despite herself. She caught herself glancing toward the street, almost expecting to see Flynn appear somewhere, stormy eyes locked on her. She shook her head and focused back on Robert. *Don't think about him. Not now.*

They reached the elegant glass doors of the rooftop lounge where they were to have drinks, the soft glow from inside spilling onto the sidewalk. Robert held the door for her, a small, gallant gesture that made her smile.

"After you," he said smoothly, his blue eyes meeting hers with a mixture of confidence and warmth.

"Thank you," she murmured, stepping inside. The buzz of conversation, the soft clinking of glasses, and the warm amber lighting felt immediately comforting. She let out a slow breath she hadn't realised she was holding, feeling the day's tension ease just slightly.

And yet… the memory of Flynn's stormy eyes lingered at the edges of her mind, a quiet, insistent pull she couldn't ignore. For a moment, she wondered how different tonight might have been if he were here instead.

Robert's voice drew her attention back. "What would you like to drink?"

"Espresso martini, please," she replied, letting herself focus, if only for a few minutes, on something else—a kind smile, a gentle presence, and the promise of an evening that, at least for now, belonged entirely to her.

They found a cozy table near the edge of the softly lit lounge. Robert waved a waiter over, and their drinks arrived almost immediately, the dark, rich liquid glinting under the warm light.

"So… do I call you Doctor?" she asked with a teasing chuckle, swirling the martini lightly in her glass.

"Robert, please," he replied smoothly, the corners of his mouth tugging into a faint grin.

She raised her glass slightly. "Cheers," she said softly.

"Cheers," he echoed, the clink of their glasses punctuating the moment.

They took a sip, the first taste of coffee and vodka sparking a tiny warmth that seemed to ease the tension of the day. Pippa leaned back in her chair, letting the hum of the lounge and the soft murmur of other patrons wash over her. For just a moment, the weight of Henry's surgery, the pull of Flynn, and everything else seemed to fade.

Robert studied her over the rim of his glass, a curious, amused light in his eyes. "You seem… lighter than when I saw you at the hospital," he observed.

Pippa smiled, a small, almost shy curve of her lips. "I think seeing him stable… knowing he'll be home tomorrow, it's a relief." She paused, then added lightly, "And this drink isn't hurting, either."

Robert laughed softly, warm and low. "I'll take that as a compliment to my choice of venue," he said, leaning back in his chair just slightly, giving her space but keeping the attention focused entirely on her.

Pippa caught herself studying him in return—the easy confidence, the kind eyes, the subtle charm. For tonight, at least, she let herself relax, enjoying the safe, gentle spark of attention that had nothing to do with obligation or heartbreak.

"So… do you often ask your patients' visitors out for drinks?" she asked, arching an eyebrow, a teasing lilt in her voice.

He chuckled, a warm, low sound that made the edges of her chest lift slightly. "Would you believe… you're the first?"

She studied his face, searching for signs of deception, some hidden motive, but found none. The sincerity in his gaze, the faint warmth at the corners of his mouth, put her slightly at ease. "I'm honoured," she said softly, a small, genuine smile tugging at her lips.

"So," he said, leaning back just a fraction, resting an arm on the back of the chair, "do I call you Pippa… or Pipp?"

"Whichever you're comfortable with," she replied, letting her fingers trace the rim of her glass, enjoying the way the martini glimmered in the soft light.

He grinned, a teasing spark in his eyes. "I think I'll start with Pipp. Short, sweet... and memorable, like you."

Pippa laughed lightly, a flush creeping across her cheeks despite herself. "Careful, Dr. Patel. That kind of flattery is dangerous."

"Dangerous?" he repeated, mock horror on his face. "I thought it was charming."

"Charming," she corrected, "but also potentially manipulative." She leaned back slightly, giving him a playful, scrutinising look.

He raised his hands in mock surrender. "Guilty as charged. But only if it works," he said, eyes twinkling.

She tilted her head, lips curving, enjoying the effortless banter. "I suppose I'll have to keep an eye on you then. Wouldn't want to fall victim to your 'charm,'" she teased.

"Not at all," he replied smoothly, leaning slightly forward, voice low and conspiratorial. "I'm more interested in your company than anything else. Consider tonight just... a taste of good conversation and a better drink."

Pippa's fingers tightened slightly around her glass, her pulse quickening, but for once, she allowed herself to simply enjoy the moment. No guilt, no lingering ache from Flynn's stormy eyes—just laughter, warmth, and the thrill of something new teasing at the edges of her careful heart.

Pippa swirled her espresso martini, the bitter-sweet aroma grounding her as she allowed herself a rare moment of ease. Across the table, Robert leaned back slightly, a relaxed smile tugging at his lips, his eyes attentive, curious, like a canvas waiting for the first stroke of inspiration.

"You really have a way of making people feel... themselves," he said, voice smooth and warm.

Pippa tilted her head, a playful glint in her eye. "Well, I spend my life styling people who are terrified of looking foolish. Celebrities, socialites—they're all convinced one wrong outfit will ruin their lives." She laughed softly. "So, I've learned how to calm the panic while making them look amazing."

Robert chuckled. "And you do it well, I'll bet."

She shrugged, letting her fingers trace the rim of her glass. "It's my job to know exactly what someone needs before they do. A good stylist anticipates, predicts, and occasionally pretends they didn't notice a wardrobe disaster coming from a mile away."

His gaze lingered on her, appreciative and light, and Pippa felt a warm flush creep up her neck. She reminded herself to focus on tonight—Henry was resting, Flynn was off somewhere, and this was a harmless reprieve.

"So," Robert said, lifting his glass slightly, "Pipp… what's the most outrageous request a client has ever made?"

Pippa laughed, shaking her head. "Oh, that's easy. Someone wanted their outfit to channel a 1920s movie star—but with a modern twist. I spent a good ten minutes debating whether to laugh or cry before I decided to do it anyway."

"You did it?" Robert asked, clearly intrigued.

"Of course," she said, smiling. "I may be a stylist, but I'm not heartless. Mostly."

He grinned, leaning closer. "I like that. A little heart, a little mischief. Dangerous combination."

Pippa caught herself studying him in return—the easy confidence, the kind eyes, the subtle charm—and felt a flicker of delight. For tonight, she could relax, indulge in the rare pleasure of attention that had nothing to do with crisis or obligation.

"And you?" she asked, leaning forward, playful. "Any quirks your patients don't know about?"

Robert chuckled again, eyes glinting. "A few. But you'd have to stick around to find out."

Pippa laughed softly, the sound bright in the quiet café corner. Yet, even as she enjoyed the moment, she couldn't fully banish the memory of Flynn: the storm in his eyes, the tension in his jaw, the way he still owned a piece of her heart.

Somewhere between the safe warmth of Robert's attention and the pull of her past, she was caught in a quiet tug-of-war—between what she wanted and what she knew she couldn't have.

He grinned. "If I'm being completely transparent, I had a bit of an ulterior motive in asking you out tonight."

"Oh?" Pippa leaned forward, intrigued. "Do tell."

Robert's smile deepened, mischievous now, and he tapped the side of his glass. "Well… I have a gala on Saturday night. The Children's Hope Foundation Gala. And," he added, shrugging with a playful flourish, "I need a date. I was hoping… you might consider going with me."

Pippa blinked, caught off guard. Her fingers paused mid-twist on the straw. "Oh? And here I thought we were just having drinks to unwind after a long day," she said, amusement dancing in her voice.

"Unwinding is part of it," he said smoothly, leaning closer. "But I figured, why not kill two birds with one stone? Drinks tonight, and maybe some gala fun on Saturday?"

Pippa laughed, shaking her head, a mix of delight and disbelief warming her. "A gala, huh? That sounds… intriguing. And you want me as your date?"

"Yes," he said simply, his grin widening. "I promise to behave, at least for the cameras."

She tapped her glass lightly against his. "Well then… consider it tentatively accepted. But only if you can keep up with my dancing."

Robert raised an eyebrow, mock-serious. "Challenge accepted."

The corner of Pippa's mouth lifted into a genuine smile. For the first time that day, she felt a lightness she hadn't realised she was craving—an evening, even a weekend, that might just belong entirely to her.

They lingered over their drinks, letting the warm buzz of espresso and conversation settle around them. Pippa twirled her glass, watching the ice clink softly, while Robert leaned back, eyes bright with interest.

"Another?" he suggested, a hint of teasing in his voice.

Pippa shook her head, smiling. "I think one more is enough for me tonight. I'm feeling the effects already."

Robert laughed softly. "Fair enough. How about dinner then?"

Pippa hesitated, a yawn threatening at the corner of her lips. "I… I think I'll pass tonight. It's been a long day at the hospital, and I'm a little tired." She added with a small smile, "But I'd be happy to go with you to the gala on Saturday."

His eyes lit up, a genuine smile spreading across his face. "Saturday it is then. I promise it'll be fun."

When the conversation lulled, he offered smoothly, "May I take you home?"

Pippa shook her head, brushing back a strand of hair. "No, thank you. I'm happy to take an Uber."

He nodded, a small crease forming between his brows, but didn't press. Instead, he stayed beside her, talking softly until the familiar hum of the approaching Uber filled the street outside.

When the car pulled up, Pippa gathered her bag, slipping it over her shoulder. Robert followed her to the door, his presence quiet, protective, and steady.

Before she stepped inside the car, he leaned slightly and pressed a gentle kiss to her cheek. "I look forward to Saturday night," he murmured, his voice warm and low.

Pippa's heart fluttered at the touch, a smile tugging at her lips. "So do I," she whispered, settling into the car as the driver started the engine.

As the car pulled away, Robert watched for a moment, then turned back toward the city streets, already counting down the hours until Saturday.

Pippa arrived back at the cottage, the crunch of gravel under her shoes announcing her return. When she pushed open the door, the soft glow of the lamp in the lounge spilled across the floor. Chloe was curled up on the sofa, a throw over her legs, half-watching the television with a bowl of popcorn in her lap.

Chloe looked up, eyes narrowing in mock suspicion. "You're home early… far too early."

Pippa laughed, kicking off her heels by the door. "Late enough. Don't start."

Chloe muted the television, sitting up straighter. "Mhm. So?" she prompted, a wicked little smile tugging at her lips.

Pippa crossed the room and dropped onto the armchair opposite. She tucked her hair behind her ear, trying—and failing—to hide the flush still warming her cheeks. "He asked me to go to a gala on Saturday night."

Chloe's grin spread wide. "Oh really." She leaned forward, propping her chin on her hand. "That sounds… fancy. Black tie, champagne, the whole New York society scene?"

Pippa gave a small shrug, trying for nonchalance but betraying herself with the sparkle in her eyes. "It's the Children's Hope Foundation Gala. He said he needed a date."

"Oh, darling," Chloe teased, shaking her head. "He didn't just *need* a date— he wanted *you* on his arm."

Pippa rolled her eyes, though her smile gave her away. "It's just one evening."

"Uh-huh." Chloe smirked, tossing a piece of popcorn into her mouth. "One evening in a gorgeous gown, at a glamorous gala, with a very handsome doctor who clearly likes you. Yep, totally casual."

Pippa's laugh filled the room, soft but genuine, as she pulled a cushion into her lap. "You're incorrigible."

"And you're blushing," Chloe shot back, triumphant.

Pippa shook her head, pressing the cushion tighter against her. "It was nice to be seen as… a desirable woman," she admitted quietly, her voice carrying a vulnerability she rarely shared. Her gaze dropped to the cushion in her lap, fingers smoothing over the fabric. "It's been a long time."

Chloe's teasing smile softened, her expression warming with sisterly affection. "Well, you are. And it's about time someone reminded you of that."

Pippa's lips curved faintly, though the words settled heavier than she wanted to admit. She hugged the cushion to her chest, as if anchoring herself.

"Flynn is not going to like this when he finds out," Chloe said gently, her tone careful now.

Pippa exhaled, the breath shaky. "Chloe, it's time I let that go. I can't… I can't keep ruining his life. Dr. Patel—it's not going to turn into anything serious. We live in different cities. But maybe it's time I try to move on."

Chloe tilted her head, studying her. "Don't you think that should be Flynn's decision to make?"

Pippa's throat tightened, her gaze dropping to the cushion. "How can I ask him to go against the only family he has left? To risk losing everything that was his birthright?" Her voice wavered, pain flickering in her eyes. "I just can't do it."

Silence stretched for a moment before Chloe leaned forward, her eyes locking on Pippa's. "You didn't answer the real question."

Pippa looked up, startled. "What do you mean?"

"Do you still love him?" Chloe asked softly but firmly, the words landing like a stone between them.

Pippa froze, her lips parting as if to reply, but no words came. The truth burned in her chest, raw and undeniable, but voicing it felt impossible. She turned her face away, blinking hard, her silence the only answer Chloe needed.

Chloe sighed, her expression gentling again. "Then don't fool yourself, Pipp. Moving on isn't as simple as agreeing to have a drink with someone else."

Chapter Ten

The next morning, the rental car arrived—a sleek black SUV that Chloe immediately approved of. "Much better than juggling Ubers," she said with satisfaction as she signed for it.

Pippa, phone pressed to her ear, nodded distractedly. She had just hung up with the hospital, relief softening her features for the first time in days. "Dad's being discharged today," she announced, her voice light with excitement.

"Perfect," Chloe replied, keys jingling in her hand. "Let's go bring him home."

The drive to the hospital was brisk, both women quiet but buoyed by anticipation. When they arrived, Henry was ready and waiting, dressed in comfortable clothes with a discharge packet tucked under his arm. His smile was tired but radiant as he spotted them.

"Look at my girl," he said warmly, his voice a little raspy but full of life. "Breaking me out of here."

Pippa rolled her eyes fondly. "You've been spoiled enough, Henry. Time to get you back to real food and fresh air."

Slipping her arm through his, she steadied him as they walked. "We've got everything set up for you at the cottage, Dad. You'll be able to rest properly."

The ride back was gentle, Chloe driving while Pippa fussed over her father in the back seat. Henry chuckled at her constant checking, though his hand closed over hers in quiet gratitude.

Once home, they settled him onto the sofa in the cottage's cozy living room, propping him with pillows and draping a blanket over his legs. Pippa moved about with restless energy—pouring water, checking his medication bag, adjusting the pillows just so—her every movement threaded with relief and nervous care.

Not long after, a knock sounded at the door. All three of them looked up at once.

Pippa's heart gave a small, unsteady leap.

Chloe rose to answer it, her steps cautious. She opened the door to find Flynn standing there, tall and composed, his storm-blue eyes sweeping past her almost immediately to land on Pippa and Henry.

"Morning, Flynn," Chloe said neutrally.

"Morning." His voice was low, steady, his expression unreadable. "I called the hospital. They said Henry had been discharged and was on his way home."

Henry's smile spread, tired but genuine, as he straightened a little on the sofa. "Flynn," he greeted warmly. "Good of you to come."

Flynn gave a small nod, his gaze never straying far from Pippa.

She remained still, her hand resting lightly on her father's arm, her pulse quickening at the sight of him framed in the doorway. For a beat too long, the room seemed to shrink around the three of them.

At last, Pippa broke the silence, turning gently to her father. "We'll leave you two to talk, Dad. Chloe and I will just be in the kitchen making tea." Then, forcing herself to glance at Flynn, she added quietly, "Would you like some?"

His eyes held hers for the briefest second before he answered. "Yes, please."

In the kitchen, Pippa busied herself with the kettle, keeping her hands occupied as though the ritual of making tea might steady her racing heart. The sound of water filling the pot seemed louder than usual in the silence.

Chloe hopped up onto one of the stools, arms folded, eyes fixed on her friend. "You're rattled," she observed matter-of-factly.

Pippa shot her a look over her shoulder. "I am not."

"You are," Chloe countered, smirking. "You get that little crease between your brows when you're trying too hard to look calm. It's basically your tell."

Pippa huffed, setting the kettle on its base with more force than necessary. "It's just… complicated. He caught me off guard, that's all."

"Mm-hmm." Chloe leaned forward, chin resting in her hand. "Complicated, or unfinished?"

Pippa froze for half a second, her fingers brushing the tea tins on the counter. "Chloe," she warned softly.

Her friend's smile softened, though the glint in her eyes didn't fade. "You don't have to say anything. But the way he looked at you just now? I don't think Flynn's as done as he wants everyone to believe. And judging by that blush creeping up your neck…"

Pippa turned back to the kettle, ignoring the heat in her cheeks. "This isn't about him. It's about Dad. That's all that matters right now."

"Of course," Chloe said easily, though her tone carried a quiet challenge. "But don't think for one second that he doesn't notice every move you make. Because he does. And so do I."

The kettle clicked off, filling the air with a sharp pop. Pippa let out a slow breath, pouring the hot water into the teapot. Her hands were steady now, but her pulse wasn't.

"Tea," she said firmly, as though the simple word could close the subject.

Chloe only smirked. "Tea. And maybe a little truth."

In the living room, Henry shifted against the cushions, pulling the blanket higher on his lap. Though his face was pale from the surgery, his eyes carried the sharp glint of a man who missed very little.

Flynn stood near the mantel, his stance composed, hands loosely in his pockets. But Henry saw it—the tension etched into his shoulders, the way his jaw clenched and released as though restraining something heavier than words.

"You didn't have to come this morning," Henry said after a moment, his voice low but warm. "But I'm glad you did."

Flynn's gaze softened briefly as it landed on him. "Of course I came. You're family, Henry."

A faint smile curved Henry's lips, though it carried a weight Flynn couldn't quite decipher. "Family," Henry echoed, the word laced with meaning. He adjusted the blanket over his lap, his sharp eyes studying Flynn carefully. "You and Pippa... you've been circling each other like two wary cats since the day she set foot back in New York. I may be old, but I'm not blind."

Flynn stiffened, his jaw tightening. "Henry—"

The older man lifted a hand, stopping him gently. "I'm not saying this to meddle. But can't you two sort this out? I see how you look at her. And I see how she looks at you."

Flynn exhaled slowly, his gaze drifting toward the kitchen door as though he could feel her presence even through the walls. "Some things aren't that simple. Your daughter made her choice—and it wasn't me," he murmured, his voice steady but edged with something raw, betraying the conflict simmering beneath.

Henry studied him for a long moment, his brows drawing together. "I'll never understand what happened. One moment you two were inseparable, and the next... she was gone."

"Believe me, Henry, I was as confused as you," Flynn said, his voice low, almost bitter. "But we both have to move on." Was he trying to convince Henry—or himself? He wasn't sure anymore. What he did know was that he couldn't afford for Pippa to pull him back in. His heart had already taken a hard enough beating.

"Sometimes," Henry said quietly, "the things that are hardest… are the ones worth the complication."

The faint clatter of cups carried from the kitchen, a reminder that the women would return any moment. Flynn straightened, his features settling back into the familiar mask of composure.

But Henry's words lingered, heavy and unspoken, filling the silence between them.

The door to the kitchen swung open, carrying with it the comforting aroma of fresh tea. Chloe came in first with the tray, her movements brisk and practical, while Pippa followed close behind, balancing cups and saucers with careful precision.

Flynn's shoulders shifted almost imperceptibly, the mask sliding firmly into place, smoothing away the rawness Henry had drawn from him moments before. By the time Pippa looked up, his expression was calm, controlled—as though nothing had been said at all.

"We thought you might like this," Chloe announced, setting the tray down on the low table. Her eyes flicked between Flynn and Henry, sharp enough to sense the lingering charge in the room, though she said nothing.

"Perfect timing," Henry said warmly, his tone a shade too light, a subtle attempt to ease the heaviness. He reached for the cup Pippa offered him, his hand brushing hers. "Thank you, love."

"You're welcome, Dad," she murmured, her eyes straying briefly to Flynn. His gaze was already on her, steady, unreadable, and for a moment it felt as though the air between them thickened, pressing in around her ribs.

Chloe cleared her throat deliberately, breaking the moment. "Well, this looks cozy," she said, seating herself with a wry smile.

Pippa passed Flynn his cup, their fingers grazing in the exchange. A spark flared, quick and unwelcome, and she pulled back a heartbeat too fast. Flynn's jaw flexed, but he said nothing, lifting the tea to his lips with studied nonchalance.

Henry, watching the quiet exchange from his nest of pillows, hid a knowing smile behind the rim of his cup, the corners of his eyes crinkling with amusement.

Chloe leaned back slightly, taking the lead in the conversation. "So, Pippa's going to be busy while she's here. She's scheduled a few appointments in the afternoons," she said, voice bright but measured, giving Pippa a subtle glance.

Henry nodded approvingly, his expression softening. "I'm glad you haven't let me pull you away from your work entirely," he said, his tone gentle, a hint of pride in his voice.

Pippa smiled, brushing a strand of hair behind her ear. "We can leave you to rest in the afternoons while we get some work done. You need your energy back, Dad."

Flynn's stormy eyes flicked to her briefly before returning to the conversation. "You must be sought after if people know you're in New York," he remarked, his voice calm, but there was a subtle note of admiration woven in.

Chloe's lips curved in a proud, almost conspiratorial smile. "She is," she confirmed, her gaze landing on Pippa with unmistakable warmth. "Everyone wants a bit of Pipp's magic."

Pippa felt a faint heat rise to her cheeks but kept her composure, offering only a small, wry smile as she sipped her tea. The room settled into a comfortable rhythm, conversation flowing easily between Chloe, Henry, and Flynn, while the unspoken tension between her and Flynn lingered like a charged current just beneath the surface.

The rest of Flynn's visit, Pippa didn't say much. Henry and Flynn carried most of the conversation, with Chloe chiming in now and then to keep things light. When Flynn finally rose and took his leave, the silence he left behind felt heavier than the footsteps that carried him out.

Afterward, Pippa busied herself with what she knew best—caring for her father. She made sure Henry was comfortable, propping his pillows, adjusting the blanket, setting his medication within reach. Chloe prepared soup and warm crusty bread, and the three of them shared a quiet, simple lunch together before Henry drifted into a doze in his chair.

By late afternoon, it was time for work. Their destination: the penthouse apartment of Gabriella Rossi, an A-list actress with a reputation for commanding every red carpet she set foot on.

The building itself was as sleek as its inhabitants—glass and steel soaring into the sky, with a doorman who greeted them by name after Chloe had arranged everything in advance. The elevator ride was swift and silent, whisking them up to the top floors where Gabriella's penthouse spanned nearly the entire level.

When the elevator doors opened, they were met with a view that took even Pippa's breath away. Floor-to-ceiling windows wrapped the open living space, flooding it with the golden hues of the setting sun. Sculptural furniture in soft creams and metallics sat like artwork against the sprawling city backdrop. A faint scent of jasmine lingered in the air, delicate but luxurious.

Gabriella swept into the room a moment later, barefoot, her silk lounge set flowing elegantly around her tall frame. Her dark hair was caught in a careless bun that only enhanced her natural allure—effortless, luminous, as though she'd stepped out of a magazine without trying. She kissed Pippa on both cheeks with breezy European charm, her perfume lingering like an expensive whisper.

"Finally," she sighed dramatically, her Italian accent wrapping around every word like silk. "The premiere is next week, and I need something that screams cinema goddess, not last season's fashion casualty."

Chloe laughed softly as she unzipped the first garment bag, while Pippa's demeanour shifted seamlessly into professional focus. She set her sleek styling kit on the glass coffee table, arranging jewellery trays and opening her tablet, the curated cookbook already glowing with options.

"You won't be anyone's casualty," Pippa said smoothly, her voice steady, reassuring. "I've pulled three looks—an ethereal Elie Saab, a sophisticated Ralph & Russo, and something a little daring from Alexander McQueen. We'll see how each one moves and then fine-tune the details."

Gabriella's eyes sparkled, her smile wicked and delighted. "Perfect. I knew you would understand me. The critics must remember the film, but the world must remember me."

Pippa's lips curved in the faintest of smiles as she slid a gown from its bag, the silk unfurling like liquid moonlight between her hands. "Trust me, Gabriella," she said softly, knowingly. "They won't forget you."

As Chloe moved gracefully around the penthouse, arranging stilettos and velvet clutches in neat pairings, the air filled with the soft rustle of fabric, the gleam of sequins catching the light, the quiet thrill of anticipation.

And in that moment, surrounded by glamour and possibility, Pippa felt herself return to her element. Here she wasn't just Henry's daughter, or the woman tethered to memories of Flynn—she was Pippa Rockwell, stylist to the stars, shaping elegance out of chaos and giving women the armour to command a room.

Gabriella disappeared behind a folding screen with the Elie Saab gown draped over her arm. The soft whisper of silk followed her, and moments later she emerged, the fabric cascading over her like liquid starlight. The gown's delicate embroidery caught the penthouse lighting, shimmering as she moved.

Gabriella struck a dramatic pose, one bare foot peeking out from beneath the hem. "Well?" she demanded, her tone imperious but her eyes sparkling with mischief. "Do I look like a goddess—or a lampshade?"

Pippa circled her slowly, her gaze sharp and critical in the way only a stylists could be. She adjusted the strap on Gabriella's shoulder, smoothed the fabric at the waist, then stepped back, appraising. "The silhouette is breathtaking, and the colour is luminous on your skin. But the hemline needs lifting by two inches if you want to glide instead of trip. And I'd pair it with the diamond teardrops from De Beers, not the chandelier earrings you wore at Cannes. You need elegance, not distraction."

Chloe, crouched by the array of heels, held up a satin pair in a muted champagne. "These will elongate your frame without fighting the dress."

Gabriella's lips curved as she slipped into them, pivoting in front of the mirror. She studied her reflection, head tilting thoughtfully, then glanced at Pippa. "You're right. Again. Always. You have an eye like no one else."

Pippa smiled faintly but kept her professional poise. "It's not about me. It's about making sure the world sees you. And in this gown, they won't see anyone else."

The actress gave a little satisfied hum, twirling once, the skirt fanning in a glittering sweep. Chloe snapped a quick photo on her phone to capture the movement, her grin widening.

Gabriella turned back to Pippa, her expression softening beneath the glamour. "You know, cara, I trust you with everything. You don't just dress me—you make me believe I can conquer a red carpet."

Pippa's throat tightened briefly at the sincerity in her voice, but she smoothed it away with a serene smile. "That's the goal. The gown is only the frame. You are always the portrait."

Gabriella laughed, delighted, before sweeping back behind the screen to try on the next option. The penthouse buzzed with energy, fabric rustling, heels clicking, jewels glittering in neat rows—and Pippa felt that familiar rush of satisfaction. This was where she thrived: bringing vision to life, crafting confidence with silk, sequins, and steel-edged instinct.

When Gabriella reemerged the second time, it was in the Alexander McQueen gown. The dress was bold, sculptural, with sharp lines at the bodice that flowed into a dramatic train. Midnight black, threaded with subtle metallic accents, it was a piece that whispered danger and dominance rather than softness.

Gabriella's nose wrinkled the moment she caught sight of herself in the mirror. "Mamma mia," she muttered, throwing her arms wide. "I look like I am auditioning for a villain in a Bond movie. No?"

Chloe bit back a laugh from the sofa where she perched, one hand pressed to her lips. "Well, it does have… presence," she offered diplomatically.

Pippa, however, didn't flinch. She rose, moving closer, her hands smoothing down the dramatic lines of the gown, adjusting the fall of the train. Her eyes narrowed with focus. "Presence is the point," she said calmly. "This isn't soft glamour—it's power. And sometimes, Gabriella, power is what makes people remember you long after the photos fade."

Gabriella turned, studying herself from another angle, her lips pursed. "But is it me? I do not want to frighten the critics."

Pippa smiled faintly, resting one hand on the actress's shoulder. "You won't. You'll intrigue them. This isn't a gown for someone who wants to blend in— it's for a woman who owns every inch of the carpet she walks. And you, Gabriella, can pull it off better than anyone I know."

For a moment, the actress was quiet, her gaze flicking from her reflection to Pippa's steady expression. Then, slowly, her lips curved into a mischievous smile. "You are dangerous, cara. You make me believe I can be anything."

"Not anything," Pippa corrected softly, adjusting the line of the bodice one last time. "Everything."

Chloe finally let her laugh escape, shaking her head. "She's got you there, Gabriella."

The actress gave a delighted little spin, the gown's train slicing dramatically across the floor. "Maybe I will keep this one… for Venice. Yes, Venice will not know what hit it."

And as she swept back behind the screen once more, Pippa allowed herself the smallest, most private smile. This was what she did best—giving her clients more than just clothes. She gave them armour, artistry, and, most of all, belief.

As Gabriella twirled one last time, Pippa adjusted a stray fold of silk, smoothing the fabric over the actress's shoulder. Her eyes lingered on the way the gown moved, how the metallic threads caught the light.

Chloe, sitting cross-legged on the sofa with a cup of tea in hand, arched an eyebrow and smirked. "You know, Pipp, the way you talk about these gowns… I swear you describe them like they're men."

Pippa froze mid-adjustment, a faint blush rising to her cheeks. "Excuse me?" she asked lightly, though a corner of her mouth twitched.

Chloe leaned back, eyes sparkling. "You know exactly what I mean. *This one has power… this one has presence… this one makes them remember*. You're practically whispering love letters to a dress."

Pippa let out a small laugh, shaking her head. "I'm just… passionate about my work, Chloe. That's all."

Chloe raised a hand in mock surrender. "Sure, sure. Passionate. But maybe one day, you'll talk like that about someone you're allowed to love again."

Pippa's fingers stilled on the silk, and she looked down, a faint hush of longing in her chest. "Maybe," she whispered, voice soft, almost lost to the hum of the penthouse.

Chloe gave her a knowing smile, the teasing glint in her eyes softening. "Just don't hide it forever, Pipp. The right person… well, they deserve to hear you."

Pippa offered only a small, thoughtful smile in return, adjusting the gown one last time. For now, the world was fabric and light, texture and colour. But in the quiet corners of her heart, some things—unspoken, unfinished—remained.

By the time Gabriella was settled in her chosen gown, with Chloe double-checking shoes and accessories, Pippa and her assistant gathered the styling kit, carefully packing away the day's work. The penthouse had quieted, the buzz of excitement fading to a calm hum.

As they stepped into the elevator, Chloe stretched, letting out a contented sigh. "Another successful day. You make it look effortless, Pipp."

Pippa smiled faintly, adjusting the strap of her bag. "It's fun, really. But… it's got me thinking. I need to get myself a gown for the gala on Saturday."

Chloe's eyebrows lifted, a mischievous smile tugging at her lips. "Oh? Already planning your entrance, are we?"

Pippa laughed softly, shaking her head. "Nothing like that. I just… need something appropriate, elegant. Something that says I know how to wear a gown without tripping over it. I don't want to embarrass Robert."

Chloe chuckled softly. "I'll help you. We'll find something stunning."

Pippa grinned, letting the thought settle, feeling a rare flicker of excitement as she imagined herself in a beautiful gown, an evening that promised a little distraction from the weight of everything else.

"And," Chloe added as the elevator doors opened onto the street, "we'll make sure you're the one who turns heads. Just don't forget, Pipp—you deserve a little fun too."

Pippa let the words linger in her mind, a small, private promise as they stepped out into the crisp New York afternoon, the city bustling around them. The gala could wait… but for the first time in a long while, she allowed herself to look forward to something purely for herself.

Chapter Eleven

The next day, her father seemed a little stronger, his spirits lifted by being back home. Pippa focused on him, enjoying the calm routine of checking his medications, sharing quiet conversation, and helping him settle comfortably in the living room. Each smile from him felt like a small victory, grounding her in the present.

In the afternoon, with her father resting, Pippa and Chloe ventured out for a little indulgence: gown shopping for the gala. The boutiques of New York were alive with energy, fabrics and colours dazzling under the soft lighting. After trying on several options, Pippa's fingers lingered over a floor-length gown in a champagne hue—elegant, understated, yet undeniably striking.

Chloe's eyes sparkled as she took in the dress. "Pipp… this is perfect. You'll shine."

Pippa turned to the mirror, letting the soft fabric drape over her, imagining herself at the gala, the city lights glinting, a night that might just let her feel… normal again. A small, hopeful smile tugged at her lips. "Yes," she murmured softly. "This is the one."

The next morning passed in quiet, steady rhythm. Pippa devoted herself entirely to her father, ensuring he rested comfortably, refilling his water, fluffing his pillows, and sharing soft conversation. Henry's presence grounded her, each small smile and laugh a reminder of why she was here. The morning slipped by, gentle and unhurried, the city outside the cottage fading into a soft hum.

In the afternoon, Chloe and Pippa set out for their next appointment. They were meeting Celeste Monroe, the chart-topping singer known for her daring, often boundary-pushing style, at the private lounge of a sleek Manhattan hotel. The lobby gleamed with marble and glass, a quiet sophistication that contrasted with the vibrant, colourful energy Celeste carried.

When they arrived, Celeste was already there, reclining on a velvet chaise in a suite-like room off the lounge. Metallic accessories glinted in the soft lighting, her platinum hair falling in effortless waves over her shoulders. She wore a cropped leather jacket and sequinned leggings—audacious and unapologetic.

"Finally," she said with a wide grin, sliding from the chaise with a dancer's grace. "I was starting to think you'd forgotten me. Two weeks to the awards and I need to look like someone who owns the stage, not someone who wandered in off the street."

Pippa smiled, quickly setting her styling kit on a nearby console and pulling out swatches, shoes, and accessories. "Don't worry, Celeste. We'll make sure the cameras don't know what hit them. I've already curated a few looks that are bold but still uniquely you."

Chloe moved gracefully around the suite, placing shoes and jewellery trays, offering a supportive glance at Pippa. The buzz of the room shifted instantly, filled with the controlled chaos of creativity, colour, and fashion.

As Pippa approached Celeste with a sequinned gown in her hands, the singer's eyes lit up. "Yes! That's it! I can feel the spotlight already."

For a few hours, the penthouse-like suite became their world—Pippa guiding, adjusting, selecting, and shaping the looks that would define Celeste's presence at the awards, while Chloe assisted, keeping everything organised and flowing. For Pippa, it was a welcome reprieve from the weight of New York's social expectations and her own private heartache—a world where her talent spoke louder than anything else.

Pippa held the sequinned gown against Celeste's frame, stepping back to study the effect in the floor-length mirror. "See how the light hits the embroidery here? It's going to shimmer like wildfire on the red carpet," she explained, her hands adjusting a delicate strap.

Celeste spun slowly, her eyes sparkling with delight. "Oh, Pipp… you always know exactly what I need! Honestly, how do you do it? I'd probably show up in something that looked like a glitter explosion gone wrong."

Pippa laughed, brushing a loose strand of hair behind her ear. "It's all about balance, Celeste. You want to be bold, but not chaotic. The camera loves confidence, not chaos."

Chloe chimed in from the side, holding up a pair of metallic heels. "And these will give you the extra height without killing your feet, trust me."

Celeste kicked her shoes playfully. "I will survive for fashion—and only for you two." She plopped onto the chaise, patting a spot beside her. "Honestly, Pipp, being styled by you is like having a fashion fairy godmother. I feel like I could walk through fire in these gowns and still look amazing."

Pippa smiled, tucking a seam into place. "That's the idea. By the time you step on that stage, they won't just remember the performance—they'll remember the look."

Chloe rolled her eyes fondly. "And maybe, just maybe, Pippa can get a little reminder that she's talented enough to take her own spotlight seriously. Right, Pipp?"

Pippa gave a small grin, feeling a faint warmth creep into her cheeks. "Oh, I take my own work seriously," she said, though her voice held a soft amusement. "I just… like seeing it come alive on someone else sometimes."

Celeste leaned forward, eyes twinkling. "I don't know what I'd do without you, Pipp. You make fashion feel like magic."

For the next hour, the room became a whirlwind of fabric, sequins, and laughter. Pippa guided Celeste through each gown, offering small tweaks, swapping accessories, and smoothing hems. Chloe floated between them, fetching shoes, jewellery, and a fresh bottle of water, ensuring the process flowed effortlessly.

By the end, Celeste stood before the mirror in the final look, a perfectly balanced fusion of daring style and elegance. She turned to Pippa, eyes bright. "You've done it again. I feel unstoppable."

Pippa allowed herself a small, satisfied smile, brushing a curl of hair back from her face. "That's the goal. Remember, confidence is your best accessory."

Chloe clapped her hands lightly. "Alright, ladies, I think we've conquered another styling mission. Time to let Celeste strut her stuff… and maybe take a little break before Pipp goes back to keeping the city's elite looking perfect."

Pippa chuckled softly, the buzz of accomplishment filling her. For a few hours at least, the weight of New York, of heartbreak, and of responsibility felt lighter. She was simply Pippa Rockwell—the stylist who could make magic, one gown at a time.

Saturday morning was bright and warm, sunlight streaming through the cottage windows and spilling across the living room. Pippa stretched leisurely, savouring the rare moment of quiet before the whirlwind of the evening. Her phone buzzed on the side table.

A message from Robert lit up the screen:

Good morning, Pipp. Just wanted to confirm your address—I'll be picking you up at 6:30 this evening. Looking forward to tonight.

She smiled faintly, a flutter of anticipation in her chest. Typing back quickly, she replied:

Setting her phone aside, Pippa moved to the kitchen, where Chloe was already bustling about, arranging a simple breakfast. The warm, golden morning light highlighted the cottage's cozy corners, giving her a sense of calm she hadn't felt in days.

Chloe glanced up from pouring coffee and raised an eyebrow. "So… the big night is finally here. Nervous?"

Pippa shook her head, letting a small grin tug at her lips. "Excited. And maybe just a little curious." She paused, brushing a strand of hair behind her ear. "It's going to be fun, Chloe. A little escape… and a chance to be someone other than Pippa Rockwell, caretaker and stylist."

Chloe chuckled, pouring two mugs of coffee. "Just promise me you'll enjoy yourself. That's an order."

Pippa took the mug, warmth spreading through her hands. "I will," she said softly, letting the thought of the evening settle around her like a promise she was finally ready to keep.

Outside, the city hummed softly under the bright morning sky, and for the first time in weeks, Pippa felt a lightness she hadn't allowed herself in a long time. Tonight, the gala, the glitter, the music—it would all be a world apart, and she was ready to step into it.

Chloe sipped her coffee, glancing at Pippa with a knowing expression. "By the way… your dad mentioned something interesting this morning."

Pippa raised an eyebrow, curious. "Oh? What's that?"

"He said Flynn has been coming by every afternoon to check on him," Chloe said casually, though her eyes flickered with amusement.

Pippa set her mug down, a faint flush warming her cheeks. She looked away, focusing on the sunlight spilling across the counter. "Probably… to avoid me," she murmured softly, a small, rueful smile tugging at her lips.

Chloe tilted her head, raising an eyebrow. "Avoid you? Or maybe trying to see you without getting caught?"

Pippa shook her head gently, letting out a soft sigh. "No… it's probably for the best. I don't want to hurt him any more than I already have. I've done enough damage." Her voice was quiet, edged with regret and a heavy resignation that Chloe could hear.

Chloe's gaze softened, and she reached out to squeeze Pippa's hand gently. "Are you sure you're doing the right thing, Pipp? You still love him. He should get to decide what happens next."

Pippa's fingers tightened around hers, a faint tremor betraying the storm inside her. "Chloe… if he ever found out that his mother was the reason I left… it would crush him."

Chloe's eyes flashed with frustration. "That woman's a cow, Pipp. He doesn't deserve any of this."

"I know," Pippa murmured, her lips pressing into a thin line. "But she's the only family he has left. And I can't be the one responsible for him losing his birthright."

Chloe shook her head slightly, a mixture of exasperation and empathy in her expression. "He might not care about any of that. He might see past the wealth, the property… all of it—and realise that you're the one who matters."

Pippa's gaze dropped, her voice barely a whisper. "Maybe… maybe he would at first. But what if he resents me later? For all of it—losing the property, the money, the prestige… everything that was supposed to be his?"

Chloe leaned in, firm but gentle, her hand brushing against Pippa's. "Pipp… you can't live your life in fear of what might happen. You've loved him for years—that counts for something. Whatever he feels, resentment or not, it's his choice to make, not yours to bear alone."

Pippa swallowed hard, Chloe's words pressing on her heart like a weight she couldn't shake. She looked away, staring out the window at the bright New York morning, her voice a soft, almost inaudible murmur. "I just… I can't risk it."

Chloe didn't answer. She let the silence hang, steady and unjudging—a quiet solidarity that somehow said more than words ever could. Pippa closed her eyes for a moment, drawing a shaky breath, letting the warmth of Chloe's presence anchor her amid the storm of her thoughts.

Flynn was in his study at the estate, the morning sun streaming through the tall windows, casting long, sharp shadows across the polished floors. He was reviewing papers at his desk, the quiet punctuated only by the soft rustle of pages. The door opened with a gentle click, and his mother stepped in, elegant as ever, her presence filling the room.

"Are you taking a date to The Children's Hope Foundation Gala?" she asked, her tone deceptively light, her eyes calculating.

"No," Flynn replied sharply, his eyes still glued to the documents in front of him, voice clipped.

"You shouldn't go alone," his mother said smoothly, tilting her head with a faint, knowing smile. "You're the director of the charity. It would be proper to take someone—Marion Hayes, perhaps."

He finally lifted his gaze, jaw tightening, the frustration evident in the set of his shoulders. "No way. That woman is relentless. I won't subject myself to that."

"She would make a perfect wife," she said smoothly, unbothered by his rising irritation.

"Mother—enough. My love life is none of your concern. I told you after the divorce that your meddling is no longer required," Flynn said firmly, voice low but edged with frustration.

She arched a brow, the faintest smirk tugging at her lips. "I merely want what's best for you, Flynn."

He slammed a hand on the desk, shaking his head. "And I am perfectly capable of deciding that for myself. Now, if you'll excuse me, I have work to finish."

As his mother's footsteps faded, Flynn exhaled slowly, sinking back into his chair. And yet, for the briefest moment, his thoughts betrayed him: Pippa. Her stormy eyes, the curve of her lips, the way she moved through a room with effortless elegance—she was the only woman he would want at his side for the gala. No, the only woman he wanted with him, ever.

If only things had been different. His chest tightened at the thought, a bitter knot of longing and anger twisting inside him. She had left him, and he still didn't know if she had ever truly loved him. After that afternoon in the cottage, after the words she had whispered in her bed, he had planned to ask her to marry him. She had said she would love him forever... and then she was gone the next day. He still couldn't understand why.

The study fell silent once more, the sprawling estate bathed in the warm late-morning sun. Inside, Flynn wrestled with the storm of emotions he refused to name—a tangle of heartache, fury, and desire that would not be quieted.

He had been visiting Henry every afternoon, deliberately keeping himself occupied, deliberately avoiding Pippa. Because every time he saw her, the ache in his chest deepened—the longing to touch her, to hold her close, to reclaim what he had lost. But he knew the danger all too well. One wrong move, one moment of weakness, and it would be his ruin. She had already hurt him once, and he could not risk being ensnared again, pulled back into the orbit of a woman who held his heart as if it were her own possession.

Yet even with that resolve, the memory of her lingered in every shadow of the room, every shaft of sunlight across the polished wood, a reminder of what he had lost—and what he still wanted.

Pippa stepped into the quiet of the bedroom, the soft light from the window brushing over the champagne folds of her gown. She paused, letting the fabric settle around her feet, the full skirt pooling gracefully. The strapless lace bodice hugged her figure perfectly, delicate and intricate, sparkling faintly as it caught the light.

Her dark hair cascaded over her shoulders in loose waves, framing her face, and the diamond drop earrings shimmered subtly, catching every flicker of sunlight. She took a slow, deliberate breath and moved toward the full-length mirror.

The reflection that greeted her stole her words. She looked exquisite. Every detail—the elegance of the gown, the gentle curve of her neck, the soft glimmer of the earrings—made her feel like a woman transformed, confident, radiant, untouchable.

Pippa tilted her head slightly, studying her own expression. There was a spark in her eyes she hadn't seen in months, a quiet thrill of anticipation. Tonight, for once, the world would see her as more than a daughter, a stylist, or someone defined by the past. Tonight, she was simply… Pippa.

She let her hand drift to the bodice, smoothing the lace, and whispered softly to her reflection, "Not too late for a little magic, is it?"

"Pipp, Dr. Patel is here," Chloe's voice called from downstairs, warm and teasing.

Pippa's pulse skipped. She gathered her clutch, sliding her phone and credit card inside, and took a steadying breath. The soft rustle of fabric accompanied her as she smoothed the champagne folds of her gown and descended the staircase.

Robert stood near the doorway, his gaze sweeping over her as she approached. His stormy eyes lingered just a moment too long, taking in the strapless lace bodice, the full flowing skirt, the diamond earrings sparkling against her dark waves. He said nothing yet, but the intensity in his stare spoke volumes.

Henry, seated comfortably in the living room, caught sight of her and smiled, a mixture of pride and affection in his eyes. "You look beautiful, Pipp," he said gently.

Chloe, standing nearby, winked knowingly. "That's more like it," she murmured, a sly grin tugging at her lips.

Robert finally broke his silence, his voice low and deliberate. "You look... stunning," he said, the single word carrying both admiration and something warmer, a promise of attention for the evening ahead.

Pippa felt a faint warmth rise to her cheeks, the flutter of excitement mingling with nerves. For a moment, she allowed herself to just stand there, the centre of their admiration, and enjoy it.

Pippa bent slightly to give Chloe a quick hug. "Thanks for everything," she murmured, her smile soft and genuine.

Chloe squeezed her hand and winked. "Go dazzle him."

Pippa turned to her father, pressing a gentle kiss to his cheek. "Don't wait up," she teased lightly, her tone warm but playful. Henry chuckled, the corners of his eyes crinkling with amusement.

She walked back toward Robert, who had been watching quietly. He extended his arm with a gentlemanly flourish. "Shall we?" he asked, his voice steady, eyes flicking to hers with an approving gleam.

Pippa slid her hand into the crook of his arm, letting him guide her gracefully through the front hall. The evening air greeted them as they stepped outside, the limousine waiting, sleek and polished, ready to carry them into the night.

As the door closed behind them, the city unfolded before her, glittering and alive. The lights reflected off the sleek black hood of the car, painting the interior with a soft, golden glow. Pippa leaned back slightly, letting herself take it all in—the hum of the engine, the warmth of Robert's hand steady at hers, the thrill of a night that promised something extraordinary.

For a moment, the weight of responsibility, the lingering tension from New York, even the memory of Flynn—all of it faded. Tonight was hers. Tonight, she could simply be Pippa Rockwell, seen and celebrated, swept into the glamour of the city and the promise of the evening ahead.

Chapter Twelve

The entrance to the Children's Hope Foundation Gala glittered beneath a canopy of golden lights, the red carpet alive with the staccato pulse of camera flashes and the murmur of New York's elite. The night air shimmered with perfume, champagne, and ambition—a heady blend of wealth and willpower that promised both opportunity and ruthless judgment. Every step along the velvet rope felt like walking across a stage, where every glance could crown or condemn in the same breath.

Flynn stepped from his sleek black town car, the door held open by a gloved attendant. His polished shoes met the carpet with deliberate ease, each stride measured, confident, commanding. The crowd noticed—they always did. Broad shoulders filled the perfect cut of his midnight-blue tuxedo, the crisp white shirt framing the strong line of his throat, the black bow tie sharpening the elegance of his jaw. Dark hair, neatly combed but never stiff, caught the light as he moved, while his storm-blue eyes surveyed the throng with the quiet precision of a man who understood both his influence—and its cost.

If he felt the weight of the gazes that followed him, he didn't show it. Flynn carried himself with that effortless composure born of habit and control, a man who could silence a room without speaking. Yet beneath the tailored calm, something restless stirred—a tension he'd carried for days, coiled beneath his skin, hidden behind the polish and restraint demanded by evenings like this.

"Flynn!"

The voice cut through the hum of conversation like a practiced cue. Marion Hayes glided toward him, a ripple of emerald silk and confidence. Her gown shimmered beneath the lights, sequins catching every flicker of flashbulb, while her sleek blonde hair cascaded over one bare shoulder. She was elegance crafted for display—every smile rehearsed, every movement calculated—but it was the ambition in her eyes, cool and bright, that truly defined her.

"You finally made it," she said, sliding her arm through his without hesitation. Her perfume rose around him—jasmine, spice, a hint of something sharper— and she tilted her face toward his with a knowing smile.

Flynn's jaw flexed, though he didn't pull away. "Marion," he greeted, his tone clipped and impeccably polite—the single word a measured wall.

"You didn't bring a date," she teased, satisfaction glinting in her eyes. "Perfect. You can stay by my side tonight. We'll give the photographers something to talk about."

He exhaled slowly, the faintest ghost of amusement touching his lips though it never reached his eyes. Marion Hayes was everything his mother approved of—cultured, well-connected, ambitious to her core. But she was also everything he no longer wanted. Her charm was weaponised, her allure practiced. And she wasn't her. She wasn't the woman whose absence still haunted him in the quiet hours when composure failed.

As Marion guided him toward the gala entrance, Flynn's gaze swept the glittering crowd. Donors, CEOs, politicians, and celebrities moved through the ballroom like polished chess pieces, each conversation a strategy, each smile a calculated move. The low hum of laughter and glassware filled the air, but beneath it pulsed the same undercurrent of competition that always followed power.

They moved together easily, like a well-rehearsed duet. Hands were shaken, compliments exchanged, and every flash of a camera captured precisely what the world expected of Flynn Oakland—control, charisma, and an untouchable sheen of success.

Marion's laughter chimed beside him, practiced and deliberate. She leaned lightly into his arm, her touch a constant reminder of the performance she was determined to perfect. "You'll introduce me to your board members, won't you?" she murmured, her voice a silken plea. "I want them to remember me."

Flynn's expression remained composed, though his eyes moved with quiet precision, scanning the room for an escape he couldn't quite take. "Of course," he replied evenly, offering polite nods, the consummate host wrapped in a fortress of distance.

Marion's painted lips curved as she gestured toward a nearby table gleaming with crystal and silver. "And later, we'll make sure they hear about my new project. Your company. Our connection. It's such a natural fit."

Flynn raised a single eyebrow, the gesture smooth and controlled. "Naturally." His voice held just enough warmth to be courteous, but the coolness beneath it was unmistakable. To her, this was theatre. To him, endurance.

Marion leaned closer, her breath brushing his ear. "I like this version of you," she whispered. "So polished. So… untouchable."

He allowed the faintest smile, sharp enough to slice cleanly through the charm in her tone.

"Untouchable," he murmured, meeting her gaze, "has its advantages."

As they drifted from group to group, shaking hands and exchanging perfectly rehearsed pleasantries, Flynn's mind betrayed him. It wandered—unbidden, unrelenting—to someone else. Someone who lingered in the corners of his thoughts no matter how tightly he tried to shut her out. The ghost of a woman whose memory had never dulled, only deepened. And lately—this past week especially—her absence had pressed harder than ever, a dull ache beneath his polished composure.

Yet under the glittering chandeliers, beneath the scrutiny of New York's finest, he locked the thought away. Forced it down. Forced her down. Every glance, every smile, every word with Marion became an act of discipline—appearances to maintain, masks to wear, an endless choreography of wealth and influence.

Still, even as he smiled for the cameras, as champagne glasses clinked and laughter swelled around him, a faint tension lived in his frame. It was there—in the rigid set of his shoulders, in the way his jaw ticked just once before stilling again. His storm-blue eyes held the perfect calm expected of him, but beneath their polished surface, a shadow stirred.

He was present only in form, the embodiment of control and success. But his thoughts—his heart—belonged elsewhere.

To a memory.

To a moment.

To the woman who had once undone him completely.

The sleek limousine glided to a stop before the steps of the Children's Hope Foundation Gala, its polished black surface catching the shimmer of a thousand lights like liquid glass. The air outside pulsed with glamour and expectation—a symphony of camera flashes, murmured greetings, and the faint sparkle of champagne carried on the cool evening breeze.

Pippa drew a slow, steadying breath, letting the smooth champagne silk of her gown settle elegantly around her. When the door opened with practiced precision, she was met by Robert's outstretched hand—steady, sure, and reassuringly familiar. He looked effortlessly composed in his tailored tuxedo, the crisp bow tie accentuating the clean lines of his jaw. There was something quietly grounding in his presence, a calm she could lean into when nerves threatened to rise.

She slid her arm through his, her heels clicking softly against the marble as they stepped onto the red carpet. Instantly, the world erupted in flashes—white light bursting like lightning as photographers called out for smiles and angles. Pippa lifted her chin, posture graceful and poised, a serene smile curving her lips even as her heart thrummed beneath the silk of her gown.

"Just follow my lead," Robert murmured, his voice low and confident against her ear. The quiet authority in his tone steadied her pulse.

Together, they moved through the storm of cameras with practiced ease. Robert's hand rested lightly at the small of her back, guiding her forward with subtle assurance. His attention never wavered—protective, composed, watchful. The flashes caught them mid-step, her elegance mirrored by his quiet strength, two figures moving in unspoken sync.

At the grand doors, Robert glanced down at her, a restrained smile softening his features. "Ready for tonight?" he asked, the question carrying a note of private warmth.

Pippa laughed softly, brushing a loose curl behind her shoulder. "As ready as I'll ever be."

Inside, the gala glowed with opulence. Soft laughter rippled beneath the swell of classical music, crystal glasses chimed like distant bells, and a thousand muted conversations wove through the air in a symphony of wealth and charm. Chandeliers spilled golden light across the marble floors, scattering reflections that danced like firelight across sequinned gowns and polished shoes.

Robert paused near the stage, exchanging nods and handshakes with the event organisers. Every motion was effortless—authority wrapped in courtesy, confidence tempered by grace. He spoke easily, his laughter low and genuine, the kind that drew people in rather than demanded attention.

Pippa watched, an unexpected thrill coursing through her as she took in the way he carried himself—self-assured, elegant, magnetic. For tonight, beneath the chandeliers and the hum of admiration, he seemed entirely in his element. And for the first time in a long while, she allowed herself to simply watch him, to feel the quiet pull of connection in a room full of strangers.

As Robert introduced her to a few of his colleagues, Pippa's thoughts drifted despite her best efforts. Images she had tried to bury—Flynn's storm-blue eyes, the hard line of his jaw, the echo of their last encounter—rose unbidden, slipping through the fragile barriers she'd built around herself. She took a careful breath, forcing the memories down, willing herself to focus on the gala, on the conversation, on the man at her side who deserved her attention. But a stubborn pull lingered low in her chest—a quiet ache that whispered some ghosts never really stayed buried.

Just as she steadied her smile, a familiar voice broke through the hum of chatter.

"Pippa?"

She turned, her expression brightening as genuine warmth replaced her practiced composure. "Victoria!" she exclaimed, her smile widening.

Victoria Langford moved toward her; the sequins of her pale rose gown scattering light like shattered glass. Her eyes sparkled with delight. "I can't believe it's really you. What are you doing in New York?"

"My father…" Pippa began softly. "He had a heart attack."

Victoria's hand flew to her chest. "Oh, Pippa, I'm so sorry."

"He's recovering now, thank goodness," Pippa reassured her, a faint breath of relief softening her voice.

Victoria's shoulders eased, her smile returning. She reached forward for a quick, friendly hug. "I'm so glad he's alright."

Pulling back, Pippa gestured toward her companion. "This is Dr. Robert Patel—the doctor who saved him."

Robert extended his hand, all calm professionalism wrapped in quiet confidence. "It's a pleasure to meet you, Victoria."

"And this," Victoria said, turning with pride, "is my husband, Marcus."

Marcus Langford—tall, polished, and effortlessly self-assured—offered a courteous nod and a firm handshake. "A pleasure, Pippa. Victoria has spoken very highly of you."

"The pleasure's mine," Pippa replied warmly. "It's lovely to finally meet you."

Victoria's laugh was light, melodic, a familiar echo from another, simpler time. "I'm so glad we've run into each other. The last time you styled me—for that Cannes after-party—people were still talking about that gown months later. You made me feel like I was walking on air."

Pippa laughed softly, her shoulders easing. "You made it effortless, Victoria. That's the secret."

"Oh, stop—you're too modest," Victoria said, waving a jewelled hand with mock reproach. "Tell me you're staying a while. I know at least three women who would kill to have you dress them for the winter charity circuit."

Pippa's smile was gentle, touched with restraint. "I'm here for my father. Work… comes second right now."

"Of course," Victoria nodded quickly, her expression softening but her enthusiasm undimmed. "Still, it's such a treat to see you. The city always feels a little brighter when you're in it."

While the women chatted, Marcus and Robert had fallen into easy conversation nearby—philanthropy, board strategies, mutual connections. Their polished tones merged effortlessly into the elegant hum of the ballroom.

But across the glittering expanse, amid the swirl of tuxedos and champagne gowns, one man had gone utterly still.

Flynn stood half-turned from his own conversation, his glass suspended midair, his focus caught—held fast—by a vision in champagne silk.

Pippa.

She stood beneath the grand chandelier, the champagne satin of her gown shimmering like liquid sunlight. Her dark hair spilled in soft waves over one shoulder, catching the light as she turned. She was laughing—unguarded, melodic—and the sound floated above the music, delicate and devastating.

For one suspended heartbeat, the chandeliers, the orchestra, the low murmur of the city's elite—all of it fell away. There was only her.

She looked incandescent—alive in a way that made everything else fade into insignificance. Flynn couldn't move. The crowd around him blurred into colour and motion while his pulse roared in his ears. It was as though the years between them had folded in on themselves, leaving only that sharp, familiar ache of memory and want.

Pippa, unaware of the gaze fixed upon her, leaned toward Victoria, her lips curving in that quiet, knowing smile that had once undone him completely.

The night had barely begun, yet already the air seemed to shift—subtly, unmistakably—charged with the gravity of two lives slowly drawn back into each other's orbit. Some collisions, he thought distantly, were never truly accidents.

He had only just managed to free himself from Marion's relentless talk of wintering in St. Moritz when his gaze swept the ballroom again—and stopped cold.

And then he saw him.

Robert Patel.

The doctor leaned close, saying something meant only for her. Pippa's lips curved into another soft smile, her eyes bright with laughter—the kind of unguarded joy Flynn hadn't seen in years, the kind that once belonged only to him.

The sound of it reached him across the room, clean and merciless, slicing through the armour he had spent years perfecting. Heat surged at the back of his neck. His chest tightened, tension coiling deep and sharp inside him.

She was radiant—untouchable—and her world no longer revolved around him.

And God help him, it gutted him to see it.

His jaw flexed, the muscle in his cheek ticking as he forced his expression into something neutral, controlled. She had once promised him forever. And now here she was, laughing with another man—beautiful, poised, utterly self-contained—while he stood rooted to the floor, furious at himself for still wanting the woman who had broken him.

Marion's voice droned beside him, flirtatious and hollow, but her words dissolved into meaningless sound. Flynn heard nothing. His world had narrowed to one sharp, unwavering point across the room: Pippa Rockwell. The woman who had ruined him—and the only woman he had ever truly wanted.

His fingers tightened around his champagne glass until his knuckles whitened. He didn't drink. He couldn't. He was too busy trying to breathe through the slow burn of want and anger twisting inside him.

"Darling."

The word sliced cleanly through the noise, low and familiar. Gwen.

She appeared at his side with the poise of someone born to command a room, her emerald gown whispering against the marble floor, diamonds glittering at her throat like cold fire. "You're not listening to Marion," she murmured, her tone light, almost amused. Her hand brushed his sleeve in a gesture both maternal and possessive.

Then she followed his gaze.

"Well," she said softly, her lips curving, "I was wondering how long it would take before she found her way back into your world."

Flynn's jaw tightened further, his voice clipped. "I don't want to discuss this here, Mother."

"Of course you don't," Gwen replied, her tone velvety and sharp all at once. She lifted her glass with effortless grace, taking a slow sip before continuing. "But if you'll allow me one piece of advice—don't let her distract you. A woman like that..." Her smile cooled. "...brings only chaos."

The words landed like sparks against dry tinder—too practiced, too knowing—and Flynn felt the echo of old anger flare beneath his ribs. But across the room, Pippa laughed again at something Robert said, her smile soft, unguarded, devastating. No amount of Gwen's polished warnings could erase that sound.

She was still the only woman who could undo him.

His mother's voice cut through his thoughts again, smooth and calculated. "Darling," she said, her tone shifting, silk over steel. "You mustn't let her undo you again." Her hand came to rest on his arm once more, her grip feather-light but unyielding. "And fortunately, you don't have to."

Her eyes glinted, a knowing satisfaction gleaming in them. "You already have someone far more suitable."

Before he could respond, Gwen lifted her chin, her gesture as commanding as a maestro. "Marion, dear!"

Marion Hayes, momentarily distracted in another conversation, lit up and swept back toward them. Sequinned emeralds caught the light with every confident step, her hand brushing Flynn's sleeve as though he belonged to her by default.

"There you are," she purred, sliding seamlessly into his orbit.

"Perfect," Gwen said smoothly, her smile gracious but edged with satisfaction. "The two of you make such a striking pair. Everyone can see it."

Flynn forced a polite nod, jaw tight, knuckles whitening around the untouched champagne glass. Across the ballroom, Pippa stood radiant in her champagne gown, leaning toward Robert, entirely present with him as if the world beyond that circle did not exist.

And now, with Marion clinging to his arm and Gwen orchestrating the scene with subtle mastery, Flynn felt more imprisoned than ever—captured in his own gala, a spectator to a life that could have been his yet remained heartbreakingly out of reach. Every heartbeat echoed with the cruel reminder that some losses never truly fade.

His eyes never left her. Each laugh, each tilt of her head toward Robert, was a blade twisting in his chest. He had imagined this moment countless times over the years—seeing her across a crowded room, radiant and untouchable—but always with the hope it would be him. Not another man. Not Robert Patel, calm, assured, leaning toward her as though she were the only person in the world.

Marion's hand tightened on his arm, a sharp reminder of the persona he was expected to maintain. She whispered something playful, flirtatious, but he didn't respond. Every sense was tuned to Pippa: the way her gown shimmered in the chandelier light, the subtle curve of her neck, the laugh that haunted the corners of his memory. She was alive, vibrant, unclaimed—and yet claimed, at least for now, by another.

Gwen's presence beside him was a cold anchor. Her eyes, sharp and calculating, flicked toward Pippa, then back to him, silently testing his restraint. He clenched his jaw, resisting the urge to storm across the room and reclaim what had always been his. Politeness, appearances, legacy—everything demanded he remain still, a spectator, a man bound by duty and decorum.

The crowd swirled around him, a glittering mass of faces, glasses, and laughter, yet all he could see was Pippa. Every movement she made seemed deliberate, a secret choreography he recognised instinctively. His chest tightened—a mix of longing, regret, and raw, unacknowledged desire. Years of walls and control crumbled in the glow of chandeliers and the hum of New York's elite.

He swallowed, forcing himself to breathe, to notice Marion's perfumed presence, Gwen's cold reminders, the glinting crystal glasses before him. Yet every pulse, every heartbeat, every flicker of light seemed to whisper her name.

A shiver ran down his spine—not from cold, but from the intensity of wanting her and knowing he couldn't have her. Robert laughed softly at something she said, and Flynn's hand tightened around his glass as though he could crush it to match the tension coiling in his chest.

"Careful, darling," Gwen murmured, silk over steel. "Control yourself." Her gaze lingered on Pippa, then back to him, unyielding. "Remember why you're here. Remember who you have at your side."

Flynn nodded once—polite, rigid—but his storm-blue eyes betrayed none of the chaos within. Marion's smile was bright, victorious, oblivious to the battle raging across the room. Meanwhile, Pippa, radiant and unaware, moved through the gala with effortless grace, utterly untouchable—and utterly unforgettable.

Every second stretched, each one a reminder of the past and the impossible present. Flynn, standing tall and polished in his midnight-blue tuxedo, felt caught between two worlds: the life he was expected to inhabit, and the one his heart still longed for, burning quietly across the glittering ballroom.

Chapter Thirteen

The music swirled through the ballroom, soft strings weaving over the hum of conversation and laughter. Pippa leaned slightly toward Robert as they navigated the glittering crowd, her champagne gown catching the light with every step. His voice, low and easy, threaded warmth and attentiveness into each word, and she found herself laughing more freely than she had in weeks.

"You really shouldn't have remembered that," she said, shaking her head at a story Robert had teased from her earlier.

"I did," he replied, a faint smirk tugging at his lips. "And I'll never let you forget it." His dark eyes held hers for a moment, and she felt that familiar flutter of comfort—a tether grounding her amid the gala's glitter and noise.

"Alright, I think it's time we find our table," she said, tilting her head toward the elegantly displayed floor plan near the entrance.

"Lead the way," Robert said, offering his arm with quiet attentiveness that made her heart lift. "I've got you."

They threaded through the elegantly dressed guests. Robert's hand rested lightly at the small of her back whenever they navigated tighter spaces. At each turn, he whispered gentle directions: "Left here… a step aside there," his voice calm, composed, protective. She laughed softly, grateful for his steadiness amid the glittering chaos.

Finally, they reached their table. Pippa's stomach lurched. Her nameplate gleamed under the soft light, and beside it… she froze.

Flynn. Gwen. And Marion, impossibly close to Flynn, her sequinned gown catching the chandelier light as she leaned in, laughing at something he said.

"Oh." Pippa blinked, cheeks warming. "Well… this is… unexpected."

Robert followed her gaze, a flicker of recognition crossing his face. He reached for her hand briefly, giving it a reassuring squeeze. "Looks like we'll have an interesting evening," he murmured, tone light but protective.

Pippa forced a small smile, though her stomach twisted. Across the table, Flynn's storm-blue eyes flicked toward her, sharp and unreadable. Marion's laughter bubbled like liquid gold beside him, her hand brushing his arm as though the space between them belonged solely to her. And Gwen… Gwen's gaze settled on Pippa, calculating, the polite smile just thinly veiling an edge of malice.

"Well, isn't this… cozy?" Gwen purred, voice smooth, sharpened with subtle menace. "How fortunate that all of you are at the same table. Fate—or perhaps a lesson in civility."

Pippa's chest tightened. She opened her mouth, but Robert leaned in slightly, voice low, calm, measured.

"Gwen, it's lovely to see you," he said, dark eyes steady on hers. "I'm sure we'll have a pleasant evening together."

Gwen's smile faltered for the briefest moment, though she pressed no further. Marion, sensing the shift, laughed lightly, her gaze glued to Flynn. Pippa exhaled, grateful for Robert's quiet deflection.

"Shall we sit?" Robert asked, nodding toward the chairs, his hand brushing hers again.

Pippa followed, forcing her pulse to steady as she slid into the seat beside him. Across the table, Flynn's gaze lingered on her a heartbeat too long, while Marion leaned closer, all casual charm and possession. Gwen's presence was constant, sharp and deliberate—a silent reminder of the subtle games at play.

Robert leaned in slightly, whispering just for her. "Ignore them. Let's focus on us tonight."

She nodded, grateful for his calm presence, though she knew that sitting so close to Flynn, Marion, and Gwen would test every ounce of her composure. Each flutter in her chest, every lingering glance from Flynn, was a temptation she had no right to indulge.

The table glittered with crystal glasses, polished silverware, and the soft glow of candlelight reflecting off the marble centrepiece. Nearby guests' chatter mingled with the string quartet's soft notes, yet Pippa's attention remained divided—half on Robert's reassuring presence, half on the others across the table.

The first course arrived—a delicate arrangement of seasonal vegetables and smoked salmon—and small talk began in a practiced, careful rhythm.

"So, Pippa," Gwen said, her voice smooth, the words curling around the edges of civility, "New York must feel very different from San Francisco. I hope it's not too much of a shock."

Pippa smiled politely, feeling a subtle tension coil in her stomach. "It's… different, yes. But it's lovely to be here for my father." Her gaze flicked to Robert; he gave a reassuring nod.

Gwen's lips curved into that faint, knowing smile. "And yet, you find yourself at a gala rather than at your father's bedside. Interesting priorities, don't you think?"

Before Pippa could respond, Robert leaned slightly toward her, voice low, smooth, protective. "Gwen, I'm sure Pippa has her hands full already. Tonight, let's just enjoy the evening." His tone was calm but firm, the subtle authority making Gwen pause for a heartbeat before offering a polite, noncommittal smile.

Marion chimed in, her honeyed voice directed at Flynn but loud enough for Pippa to hear. "And tell me, Flynn, how's the season shaping up? You must have so many projects on the horizon. I'd love to hear all about them."

Flynn's jaw tightened fractionally, but his words stayed measured. "Quite busy, as always. But it's a pleasure to be here." His eyes flicked briefly to Pippa before returning to Marion, and she felt that familiar tug of memory twist in her chest. She let it ache quietly, unwilling to act, unwilling to give him the satisfaction of seeing her want him.

Pippa sipped her sparkling water, forcing herself to breathe slowly. She kept her attention on Robert, who leaned in toward her, a subtle, confidential smile playing on his lips. "Don't let them get under your skin," he murmured, his hand brushing hers again. "Focus on the moment. On us."

She allowed herself a small smile in return, grateful for his steadiness. Across the table, Gwen's gaze lingered like a quiet challenge, while Marion's flirtatious laughter and casual closeness to Flynn seemed designed to provoke. But Robert's presence acted as a shield against the storm of tension.

Dinner drew to a close with the soft clinking of cutlery against fine china and murmured farewells. Pippa and Robert lingered at their plates a moment longer, exchanging a few last words, their hands brushing occasionally across the table.

"Everything okay?" Robert asked quietly, concern flickering in his dark eyes, a reassuring corner of his lips lifting.

Pippa nodded, a small smile tugging at her lips. "Yes, thank you. The food was wonderful... and the company, well..." Her gaze drifted toward Flynn, Marion, and Gwen, and she forced a steadying breath. "...challenging, but enlightening."

Robert chuckled softly, a deep, warm sound. "I'll take that as a compliment." He finished his water, setting the glass down carefully.

They sat as the waitstaff moved efficiently, clearing plates and refilling glasses in a seamless ballet. The chandeliers above cast soft, golden light across the gleaming floor, highlighting the gala's elegance.

Pippa straightened her gown, smoothing the delicate folds of champagne silk over her shoulders. Robert's presence at her side was steady, grounding, and she drew a quiet breath, preparing herself for the next part of the evening.

The maître d' stepped forward, tapping the microphone. "Ladies and gentlemen, if I may have your attention… our keynote speaker this evening, Dr. Robert Patel."

A ripple of polite applause swept through the room. Robert rose, straightened his jacket, and moved toward the podium with unhurried confidence. Calm, assured, and effortlessly composed, he commanded attention without needing to claim it.

Pippa's gaze followed him. The soft hum of conversation faded beneath the quiet murmur of anticipation.

Robert adjusted the microphone. "Good evening, everyone. It's an honour to speak tonight on behalf of the Children's Hope Foundation…"

His voice carried easily—warm, measured, and sincere. Pippa found herself drawn in by his quiet authority, by the natural rhythm of his words. There was a steadiness about him, a grounding presence she found comforting. For tonight, she told herself, she could keep her thoughts of Flynn locked away, however painfully.

Across the table, Flynn sat rigid, one hand loosely around his champagne glass, the other tapping a restless rhythm against his thigh. The music, the chatter, the rustle of silk—it all blurred into background noise. His gaze, fixed and unyielding, found her across the room.

Pippa laughed softly at something Robert said—a warm, genuine sound that wrapped around Flynn like a memory he couldn't shake. Her dark hair caught the chandelier light, molten against the pale silk of her gown. Every tilt of her head, every subtle movement, drew him in deeper.

Flynn's jaw tightened. She looked radiant. Not merely beautiful—radiant. As if she belonged here, as if she always had. Yet it wasn't her poise that stole his breath—it was her ease. The way she laughed, fully present with Robert, her grace unstudied, effortless.

Marion's hand tightened on his arm, her voice honeyed and incessant, but he barely heard her. Across the table, Gwen's sharp eyes flicked toward Pippa every few seconds, lips curved in that familiar expression of genteel disdain. Flynn barely registered that either. Nothing existed beyond the woman in champagne silk.

The pull of her was magnetic—old and unbroken. The years apart hadn't dulled it; if anything, it burned hotter. The way she smiled, the light in her eyes—it was almost unbearable.

His chest constricted. She's with him. She laughed with him. And I— He forced his fingers to unclench around the glass, the crystal stem slick beneath his grasp. Not now. Not here. He wouldn't let the woman who had once shattered him see how easily she still could.

But his body betrayed him. His gaze lingered, tracing the delicate line of her neck, the subtle way her fingers brushed an invisible strand of hair from her shoulder. Beneath the restraint, the truth pulsed like a heartbeat—she still had power over him. Even now—especially now—she could undo him with a glance.

Robert's voice drew to a close, his speech met with generous applause. The sound swelled, then softened, as he returned to Pippa's side.

She looked up at him, eyes bright with admiration. "That was wonderful," she said softly, tucking a loose curl behind her ear.

Robert smiled, his gaze steady on hers. "Thank you," he murmured. "But I have a feeling the evening's highlight isn't over yet."

As the orchestra began its next piece—a waltz rich and graceful—the music unfurled across the ballroom like silk. Robert turned to her with a quiet smile.

"May I have this dance?" he asked, his voice low, meant for her alone.

Pippa's heart fluttered. She hesitated only a heartbeat before nodding, a soft laugh escaping her lips. "I'd be delighted."

He offered his arm. She slipped her hand into his, the steadiness of his touch grounding her as he led her toward the dance floor.

The world around them—the chatter, the chandeliers, the shimmer of crystal—blurred into insignificance. For this moment, it was just the two of them, moving together beneath the golden light.

And from across the room, Flynn watched—silent, still—as the woman he had never stopped loving was carried into another man's arms.

Robert's hand rested lightly at her waist, guiding her with effortless grace, while her hand found his shoulder. Each turn, each step, was fluid and precise—a quiet extension of the connection between them.

Pippa caught her reflection in a mirrored panel. Her champagne gown shimmered with every turn, soft waves of hair tumbling over her shoulders. Robert's gaze followed her movements, calm and magnetic, grounding her in a way both comforting and thrilling.

For the first time since arriving at the gala, she allowed herself ease—laughter, genuine enjoyment. The tension coiled around her chest loosened, replaced by the warmth of Robert's presence.

And then she felt it—the prickle of awareness that she wasn't completely free of her past.

Across the ballroom, Flynn stood like a statue, posture rigid, hands clenched loosely around his glass. His eyes never left her.

Pippa felt a sharp pang, a reminder of all she'd tried to bury. She pressed it down, focusing on Robert and the gentle rhythm of the dance.

He leaned in, murmuring against her ear, "Just follow my lead. Let the world fade for a while."

She smiled, letting herself be carried by the motion, though her chest ached with quiet longing. Somewhere across the room, Flynn was watching—and despite her best intentions, part of her wished he weren't.

Flynn's jaw tightened again. Every laugh, every tilt of her head, every subtle glance toward Robert hammered against the restraint he fought to maintain. Possession, longing, memory—they collided, sharp and unrelenting.

Marion leaned closer, her laughter light and practiced, but Flynn barely noticed. Gwen's knowing smirk flitted in the corner of his vision, but he ignored it. All he could see was Pippa.

She was radiant. Alive. Laughing. Dancing. And with every step, the distance between them stretched, twisting in ways he couldn't control.

He gripped his glass tighter, knuckles whitening, refusing to move—not yet. Not publicly. Not where Robert could see. But he made a silent promise: he would speak with her. Soon. He had to.

The orchestra swelled, the music wrapping around Pippa and Robert like a tide, carrying them effortlessly across the floor. She laughed softly at a teasing remark Robert whispered, the sound innocent yet intoxicating.

Flynn's eyes narrowed, his chest tightening with frustration and longing. Every fibre of him wanted to be there—to pull her close, to make the world vanish until only they existed. Yet he remained rooted, a silent sentinel at the edge of the dance floor, watching her with careful, aching intensity.

The dance flowed—elegant, measured, unhurried—and Pippa allowed herself to sink into the music, into the warmth of Robert's hand at her waist. But deep down, the ache remained—a stubborn reminder that Flynn's gaze still held her, even from across the room.

And for all the beauty of the ballroom—the chandeliers, the laughter, the glimmering perfection—nothing could erase the truth pulsing quietly within her: no matter how hard she tried to bury it, Flynn's presence still had the power to undo her.

Flynn couldn't bear it. Not for another second.

A spark ignited inside him—cold, sharp, unyielding. If she could laugh with another man, let herself be charmed and carried in someone else's arms, then so could he. He would.

Marion stayed at his side, her perfume cloying, her laughter warm and practiced, her hand clinging to his arm as though it were hers by right. Perfectly poised. Perfectly willing. Perfectly convenient.

"Marion," Flynn said evenly, tilting his head just enough to catch her attention.

She smiled, tilting her chin, eyes bright with expectation. "Flynn?"

He didn't hesitate. "Dance with me." His tone was smooth, controlled, threaded with subtle command.

Her brows lifted in brief surprise before she masked it with a dazzling smile. "I'd love to."

He offered his hand. She slipped hers into it, light and eager, and he led her onto the floor. His posture was easy, authoritative, every inch the man in control—but his mind was nowhere near the woman at his side.

His eyes searched. Found her.

Pippa.

She hadn't noticed him yet, still caught in Robert's orbit, still smiling, still shining. But Flynn saw everything—the curve of her lips, the softness in her expression, the slight lean toward the doctor as if she belonged there. A flare of jealousy stabbed through him, bright and raw, but beneath it pulsed something darker, heavier: clarity.

He couldn't have her. Not now. Not ever.

But he could remind himself he wasn't broken beyond repair. He could still choose, still move, still command a room—even if every step felt like walking a tightrope above a chasm he couldn't name.

The music swelled, sweeping Marion into his arms. She laughed at something he murmured, hand brushing his shoulder as if she owned the space. Flynn leaned in just enough for the crowd to see—for Pippa to notice. Because whether he admitted it or not, every calculated smile, every subtle touch, wasn't for Marion.

It was for her.

Flynn didn't stop. He laughed lightly at Marion's next remark, leaning close, his hand grazing hers in a gesture so intimate it might have been mistaken for real. The world might have believed it. But his focus—his heart—remained locked on the one woman who wasn't his.

Chapter Fourteen

Pippa let herself glide across the ballroom floor with Robert, the music flowing around them in a silken tide. Chandeliers scattered pools of golden light across the polished marble, casting everything in a soft, dreamlike haze. Her champagne gown shimmered with each step, laughter spilling from her lips at something Robert whispered—a sound that surprised even her. Light. Unburdened. It loosened a tension she hadn't realised she'd been carrying all night.

Then, through the blur of silk gowns and shifting tuxedos, her gaze caught on a figure across the room.

Flynn.

And he wasn't alone. Marion clung to his arm as they moved together, laughing—close, effortless, perfectly composed.

Across the floor, Pippa's chest tightened, a jolt of electricity sparking through her as she felt the unmistakable pull of his gaze. She looked up—met those storm-blue eyes for a single, searing heartbeat—and then looked away, forcing her attention back to Robert. But the ache in her chest burned sharper than before, impossible to ignore.

This was how it had to be.

In the three years since she'd walked away, she hadn't let anyone close. Dating had been casual, fleeting. Forgettable. Intimacy—once effortless—had become a closed chapter. No one had ever measured up. No one ever could. Not when Flynn lingered like a ghost in the quiet corners of her heart.

But him? He had moved on. Married someone else. Six months after she'd left.

The truth cut beneath her composure like ice under the skin. Clearly, she hadn't meant as much as she once believed. The ache in her chest hardened, forming the mask she wore now—elegant, untouchable, seamless as the gown draped across her body.

He would not see how deeply he'd broken her.

Robert's quiet warmth steadied her, drawing her back. "Everything alright?" he murmured, his breath brushing her ear, anchoring her in the moment.

"Yes," she said, smiling softly. Too softly. The expression didn't quite reach her eyes. "Everything's fine."

But her gaze betrayed her. Again and again, it drifted back to Flynn—laughing, charming, moving with Marion as though their shared past had never existed. Each glance was a blade, a reminder of what she had lost… and what she could never reclaim.

She drew in a deliberate breath, forcing her spine straight, her hands tightening lightly around Robert's. *Stay away. Don't give him a second thought. For his sake—and yours—maintain distance.*

The orchestra swelled, weaving through the low hum of voices and laughter. Pippa moved with Robert gracefully, poised, the picture of composure. Yet beneath the polish, a storm churned. Every flicker of her eyes toward Flynn betrayed her resolve, tracing him—always him—across the glittering floor.

Longing. Frustration. Disbelief.

So, this is how easily he moves on.

Every smile aimed at Marion, every touch, every laugh—it was unbearable. He could flirt so openly in front of her, while she spun in another man's arms, as if their history had been nothing at all.

She gripped Robert's hands a little firmer, steadying herself on his presence. *It's his choice. He's moved on. He doesn't belong to me anymore.*

She repeated the words like a shield, even as her heart refused to obey.

When the orchestra's final notes softened into silence, the ballroom stilled, and Pippa's steps slowed. Her chest rose and fell with careful breaths as she looked up at Robert, her smile calm, polished, but shadowed by the weariness pressing against her ribs.

"Robert," she said softly, almost hesitant, "I… I think I'd like to go. I'm feeling a bit tired."

His head turned instantly, expression attentive, concerned, free of judgment. "Of course," he said, his voice steady as he offered his arm. "Let's get you home."

Pippa nodded, smoothing the folds of her champagne gown as though the gesture could quiet the turmoil inside her. With Robert's calm presence beside her, she moved through the glittering crowd, offering polite smiles, never lingering. His steady arm anchored her as the music and laughter trailed behind.

From across the ballroom, a pair of storm-blue eyes tracked her every step. Flynn didn't move. Didn't speak. Marion leaned closer to him, her laughter spilling light and unguarded, but his gaze was fixed—unyielding, piercing—on Pippa. She felt it, sharp as a blade, pressing against her chest, but she forced her chin higher and her steps to remain measured.

Outside in the foyer, the cooler air wrapped around her, a welcome balm against the suffocating brightness of the gala. She allowed herself to lean slightly into Robert's quiet strength. "Thank you," she murmured, her voice low, gratitude unspoken yet sincere.

Robert's smile was warm, confident, reassuring. "Always," he said simply. "I'll see you home safely."

At the curb, he held the limousine door for her, hand steady as she slipped inside, the satin of her gown whispering against the leather seats. He closed the door gently, then settled beside her, his presence filling the quiet space with calm assurance.

"Comfortable?" he asked, reaching to brush a loose strand of dark hair from her face.

"Yes," she breathed, the sigh carrying more than fatigue. The weight of the ballroom—the stares, the music, the ache of seeing Flynn—began to lift as she sank back into the plush seat.

Robert studied her in the dim glow of the car, noting the tension in her hands resting against her lap, the distant cast of her gaze. "Did you enjoy yourself tonight?" His voice was warm, protective, gently coaxing her back to the present.

Her lips curved into a small, tired smile. "I did… thank you."

For the first time that evening, Pippa exhaled fully, her shoulders softening as the city lights streaked past. The glittering chaos of the gala felt a world away, replaced by Robert's steady presence and the quiet rhythm of the car. She closed her eyes, letting the silence wrap around her like a balm, telling herself she was safe—for now.

Meanwhile, inside the ballroom, Flynn disentangled himself from Marion's clinging hold. She tilted her chin, lips curved in a practiced pout, her hand gliding down his arm as though she could anchor him there.

"Flynn, don't be so cold. We barely danced," she teased, her sequinned gown sparking beneath the chandeliers like liquid fire.

"Maybe another time," he said smoothly, tone courteous but clipped. A brief, controlled smile flickered across his lips—measured, polite, but utterly devoid of warmth—before he straightened, already turning away.

Marion's sultry protest faded behind him, her voice swallowed by Gwen's calculated charm as his focus sharpened elsewhere. The laughter, the music, the glittering swirl of the gala—all blurred into insignificance. All he felt was the hollow ache she had left behind. Pippa. Her absence weighed on the room more than her presence ever had.

"Leaving so soon?" Gwen's voice reached him, deceptively light, but her sharp gaze missed nothing.

"Yes," Flynn replied evenly, though the slight clench of his jaw betrayed him. "I'll send the car back for you."

Her lips curved in the faintest, knowing smile, enough to make his spine stiffen. She didn't press, didn't need to—her silence spoke volumes.

But Flynn's attention was already fixed on the ballroom doors. The thought of Pippa, slipping away into the night, pulled at him with an urgency he could no longer ignore. Every instinct screamed: follow her. Stop her. Demand the answers that had haunted him for years.

He moved, steps purposeful, each one carrying the decision already made.

Flynn reached the doors just in time to see the sleek black limousine gliding to the curb. His chest tightened, a sudden, sharp ache twisting through him. There she was—the soft shimmer of her champagne gown catching the streetlights, hair cascading over her shoulders, framed by the car's open door.

For a moment, he froze, every muscle taut, every instinct screaming to call her back. Then, as if the universe were answering his unspoken command, his own limousine slid up behind hers, door swinging open with quiet, practiced precision.

Without hesitation, he climbed in, the leather seat cool beneath him, the engine's low purr steadying his racing heart. His storm-blue eyes fixed on the car ahead, jaw tight, hands gripping the edge of the seat as the city lights glinted off polished chrome.

He didn't speak. He didn't plan. He simply let the car ease forward, closing the distance between him and the woman who had haunted every corner of his mind for years. Tonight, there would be no hesitation, no polite restraint. He was going after what had never truly been his to lose—and yet he had always wanted.

The limousine slowed into the driveway, and Pippa slipped out gracefully, Robert following close behind. The night air was crisp, carrying the distant hum of the city, while the soft glow from the cottage windows welcomed them like a beacon.

"Here we are," Robert said, his eyes warm, steady, full of that quiet attentiveness she had come to rely on. He guided her gently toward the front door, then stepped aside with a slight bow of his head. "May I—?"

Before she could respond, he leaned down just enough to brush his lips lightly against hers. Pippa froze for a heartbeat, caught off guard, then softened ever so slightly into the kiss—allowing it, acknowledging it—but she made no move to deepen it. It was a gesture of reassurance, a quiet connection, not an invitation.

As they parted, both slightly breathless from the subtle intensity, neither noticed the sleek black limousine gliding past the driveway at that exact moment. Inside, Flynn's storm-blue eyes tracked the glow from the cottage, the faint shimmer of her champagne gown catching the reflection of the porch light. His jaw was tight, hands gripping the seat, a knot of jealousy and longing twisting sharply in his chest.

Pippa, unaware of the other presence, turned to Robert with a soft smile. "Thank you for tonight," she murmured. "It was… lovely."

Robert's gaze lingered on her, steady, protective, quietly intense. "Thank you for being my date tonight," he said, his voice soft but sincere. "I'd really like the chance to take you out again—properly."

Pippa's lips curved into a faint, wry smile. "I'm not sure how long I'll be in town," she replied, her tone light but edged with hesitation. "We'll see what happens."

Robert smiled, a quiet warmth in his eyes. "I'll call you and hope for the best," he said, bending slightly to brush a gentle kiss against her cheek. "Good night, Pippa."

"Good night, Robert," she replied softly, fingers brushing the fabric of her gown as she savoured the brief, steadying connection.

He straightened, offering one last warm glance before moving toward the waiting limousine. The door closed with a soft thud, and the engine purred to life. Pippa lingered on the doorstep, watching the sleek black vehicle glide away into the night, taillights disappearing down the quiet driveway. The air was cool against her skin, carrying a mixture of lingering warmth and the soft ache of something unspoken.

She exhaled slowly, pressing a hand to her chest, letting the moment settle— until a harsh, unmistakable voice cut through the quiet night.

"Did you have a nice night?" Flynn's voice was tight, each syllable sharp, his storm-blue eyes flashing with barely contained edge.

"Oh… Flynn! What are you doing here?" Pippa's pulse quickened, her breath catching in surprise.

"You and Robert looked… cosy," he said, jaw tight, jealousy lacing every word.

Pippa lifted an eyebrow, meeting his glare evenly. "So did you… and Marion," she replied coolly, deliberate—a quiet challenge threaded through her calm.

Flynn's eyes narrowed, his chest tightening at her deflection, but he didn't respond immediately. The silence between them crackled, heavy as the night air around them.

"Did you enjoy kissing him?" he asked, low, sharp, edged with possessive fire.

Pippa's chest constricted. "How did you—"

"You didn't exactly hide it," he cut in, stepping closer, his stormy gaze unreadable, unrelenting.

"It's none of your business. You have no right to spy on me," she shot back, trying to keep steady, though the tremor she couldn't hide betrayed her.

"I wasn't spying," he said, voice hardening, closing the distance between them, every step taut with unspoken need.

The night seemed to shrink around them. Every heartbeat, every sharp inhale magnified. Pippa felt herself caught, a spark of something fierce and dangerous igniting as Flynn's eyes held hers, unyielding.

"Why did you leave, Pippa? And don't tell me you didn't care," he demanded, voice low, rough, edged with barely contained anger.

"I had to," she whispered, voice tight, fragile.

"That's not a reason. You didn't like me dancing with Marion any more than I liked you dancing with Robert," he shot back, frustration cracking his tone beneath the weight of desire.

"You're imagining things," she said, though her pulse betrayed her.

"Am I?" His voice dropped, rasping, closer now, each word pressing against her skin.

Without warning, his hands slid to her waist, drawing her flush against him. Heat radiated from his body, pressing her into a tension she had long denied, every inch of her senses ignited. Years of longing, regret, and restrained desire coiled between them like a live wire, humming with dangerous electricity. Pippa's breath caught in her throat, shallow and trembling, as every rational thought dissolved in the pull of him.

Then his lips claimed hers—first gentle, testing, almost reverent, as if seeking permission. And then, as if some dam had burst, the kiss deepened with smouldering intensity. Tenderness and raw need fused in every movement; his mouth was warm, demanding, intoxicating. His tongue traced hers with a precision that stole her breath, leaving her senses alight with fire.

Her hands shot to his shoulders, gripping the firm weight of his jacket, anchoring herself even as every nerve screamed for more. She felt the press of him, the hard plane of his chest against hers, the way his arms encircled her with a possessive certainty that left her trembling. Desire, anger, and grief long buried ignited all at once, a fierce, searing ache that ran through her, coiling around her heart.

Her body melted against him, soft and pliant, yet electric with the force of feeling she had tried to suppress. Her heart hammered, pulse racing, a mix of want and fear, shock and yearning. Every brush of his lips, every inhale of his scent, every faint shiver running through her skin screamed of a passion she had not allowed herself to feel in years. The sharp tang of need mingled with the ache of memory, the taste of him igniting a longing she had thought safely buried, until now.

Finally, she pulled back, gasping, hands pressed to his chest. "Flynn… stop," she breathed, shaky but firm. She didn't want the kiss to end—not really—but it had to. This fire between them was dangerous, too much for the fragile boundaries she had built.

"Why? Tell me the truth, Pipp," he murmured, hoarse, urgent, pulling her toward him, eyes burning with the fire that had haunted her dreams for years.

"We can't go there, Flynn." She stepped back, voice trembling under the weight of restraint.

"Pippa—" He reached for her again, but she dodged, a mix of fear and frustration in her movements.

"Please, Flynn. Stop. This… this can't happen."

"Why?" he snapped, raw anger threading each word.

Her chest tightened, every pulse screaming. She had to push him away. "You don't care about me. You never did," she said, brittle, trembling. "It was obvious when you married another woman six months after I left. I haven't been with anyone. I couldn't. But you… I meant nothing."

"That… that was your fault," he shot back, hurt and disbelief mingling with lingering anger.

"My fault? How is it my fault?" she demanded, hands trembling, helpless against the storm raging between them.

"You broke my heart, Pippa," he said, voice raw, thick with grief and fury. "I just wanted the pain to stop. Everything… it was a disaster, and it should never have happened."

Her eyes softened, fleetingly, seeing the vulnerability beneath the storm. "Flynn… I left… because I didn't love you."

"You do. You did," he shot back, sharp, disbelief etched deep even as the longing he had buried for years thrummed like a live wire beneath his skin.

"No, Flynn. I didn't… I didn't… just stop," she cried, desperation and heartbreak bleeding through her words. Her legs carried her almost on instinct as she ran inside, up the stairs, breath ragged, into her bedroom.

She threw herself onto the bed, burying her face in the pillow, tears spilling freely. All the grief, restraint, and love denied herself for years poured out in helpless, wrenching sobs. Her body shook with the force of it, and for a moment, she let herself collapse under the weight of everything—under the ache of Flynn, the memory of what they had lost, under the guilt that had haunted every decision.

Chapter Fifteen

The driveway was silent, the night pressing down like a living thing—cold, heavy, unrelenting. Flynn stood motionless, disbelief coiling through his chest until it burned. Pippa had run from him. Again. The sting of it was sharp, clean, merciless.

"Damn Pippa," he muttered, the words low, bitten off. His jaw flexed hard enough to ache, and for a long moment, he just stood there, his breath visible in the cool air. Then, with a frustrated exhale, he turned, intent on retreating to the house—to drown this ache in Scotch or silence, whichever numbed him faster.

The crunch of footsteps on gravel stopped him cold.

He turned sharply, hope flaring where reason told him not to look. "Pipp—?"

"No, Flynn. It's me."

Chloe's voice broke through the darkness, steady but urgent. She stepped into the spill of light from the cottage porch, her expression serious, almost fierce.

Flynn's features hardened. "Chloe," he said, his tone clipped, the exhaustion and bitterness bleeding through. "What do you want?"

"I heard you and Pippa arguing," she said, coming closer, her steps even and deliberate. "It's time you knew the truth."

Flynn folded his arms across his chest, eyes narrowing. "The truth?" His tone was incredulous, sharp. "What truth? That she left me again. Because I think I've got that part figured out."

"You don't know the whole story," Chloe said firmly, her voice calm but charged. "She left because she thought she was protecting you."

Flynn gave a short, humourless laugh. "Protecting me?" His voice dripped disbelief. "You've got to be joking. She walked out twice, Chloe. Both times without a word. That's not protection—that's abandonment."

"She didn't abandon you," Chloe countered, stepping closer. "She loved you. Enough to walk away rather than see you lose everything. She left because your mother told her you'd be disinherited if you married her."

The silence that followed was thick, almost unreal.

Flynn stared at her, the words refusing to land. Then, slowly, he shook his head, a disbelieving half laugh escaping him. "That's ridiculous," he said, voice sharp with incredulity. "You expect me to believe that? That my mother—"

"Yes," Chloe interrupted quietly but firmly. "Your mother told her. She said you'd lose Oakland Park, the inheritance, everything your father built."

Flynn's pulse pounded in his ears, disbelief hardening into anger. "No. No, that's insane. My mother might be many things, but she wouldn't lie like that. She was devastated when Pippa left."

Chloe's expression hardened, frustration flashing across her face. "Oh, please," she snapped, shaking her head. "Devastated? Flynn, open your eyes. She hated what Pippa represented—a woman who didn't fit her definition of suitable. She thought she was protecting you from her idea of ruin."

Flynn's chest tightened, anger and confusion warring inside him. He wanted to shut her out, to dismiss it as nonsense. And yet—something in Chloe's voice, in the absolute certainty behind her words, struck a nerve he couldn't quite ignore.

He swallowed hard, looking away toward the dark stretch of the drive. "No," he said finally, his voice low and rough. "No, I don't believe it. My mother wouldn't do that."

Chloe's laugh was soft, bitter. "Then you don't know your mother as well as you think." She took a slow step back, her eyes never leaving his. "If you actually believe that Flynn… then maybe you don't deserve Pippa after all."

Her words hit him like a slap—quiet, precise, and impossible to deflect.

Without waiting for his reply, Chloe turned and strode toward the cottage. Her footsteps were sharp against the gravel, decisive, final.

Flynn remained where he was, frozen, watching until she disappeared into the warm glow spilling from the cottage windows. The silence that followed was deafening.

The night air felt colder now, biting against his skin. A hollow ache settled deep in his chest—anger, disbelief, and something darker. Doubt.

He turned at last and began the slow walk back to the main house. Each step crunched against the gravel, steady, mechanical, but his mind was far from steady.

What she'd said—it couldn't be true. It wasn't true. His mother wouldn't have lied. Not about that. Not to Pippa.

And yet…

A memory stirred—his mother's cool, composed voice the morning after Pippa's note. *'It's for the best'*, she'd said, the words as smooth and final as polished glass.

His grip tightened until the tendons in his hand stood out.

No. It couldn't be.

But the seed was planted—small, sharp, and merciless—and as Flynn reached the steps of the main house, a heaviness settled in his chest. For the first time in his life, he wasn't entirely sure he knew the truth.

His mind churned as he crossed the marble foyer, fragments of the past breaking loose and swirling like debris in a storm. Three years ago. The note. Pippa's neat handwriting, trembling but resolute. The words had gutted him, leaving a hollow where certainty used to be. It's better this way. He could still hear her voice in his head, soft but final. And then—his mother's calm reassurance. *'She wasn't right for you, darling. You'll see, in time.'*

Now, that same voice echoed through his skull with a venom he couldn't ignore. *Could Gwen have lied? Manipulated Pippa? Or had he simply been too blind to see it?*

By the time he reached his study, the answer didn't matter—he was shaking. He went straight to the decanter, pouring a generous measure of whiskey. The amber liquid sloshed against the crystal, trembling like his hand. He sank into the leather chair behind his desk, the scent of aged wood and smoke wrapping around him like an old, unwelcome friend.

He stared into the glass, swirling it slowly, watching the light fracture through it. His thoughts spiraled back to that time—how his mother had immediately steered Yasmin into his path after Pippa's departure. How he had been too numb, too angry to question it. How he had swallowed the pain, convinced that Pippa had never loved him enough to stay.

Now, piece by piece, the narrative began to splinter.

The way his mother had spoken of Pippa that night at dinner—too cold, too certain. The faint satisfaction in her tone when she'd said, *'You deserve someone who understands our world.'*

Back then, he'd thought it was grief talking. Now, he wasn't so sure.

Flynn's throat tightened as he took a slow sip of whiskey. The burn did little to settle the storm inside him. Disinherited. The very idea was absurd—ludicrous. He'd never been under threat of losing Oakland Park. His mother had influence, not power absolute. And yet… if she'd convinced Pippa otherwise…

His jaw flexed, fury threading through the disbelief. "Goddamn it," he muttered, the words low, rough. The thought that his mother could have interfered, could have ripped Pippa away under the guise of love and protection—it clawed at him, savage and unbearable.

He leaned forward, elbows braced on his knees, glass dangling loosely from one hand. His reflection in the dark window looked older, harder—a man built on resentment and half-truths. And beneath the anger, something else stirred. Something rawer. *What if Chloe's right? What if she left because she loved me?*

The possibility hit him like a physical blow, sharp and stunning.

If Pippa had walked away not out of indifference, but out of love—if she had sacrificed their future to protect him—then everything he had believed these past three years had been a lie.

His anger, his bitterness, his carefully constructed indifference—it had all been built on sand.

He could see her now as clearly as if she stood before him: her wide, tear-bright eyes, the tremor in her hands when she'd finally faced him again. The truth in her silence.

Flynn swallowed hard, his chest tightening with guilt and longing. The weight of what he might have misjudged pressed like a stone against his ribs.

His gaze drifted to the portrait of his father above the mantel—a man defined by principle, by truth. "Did you know?" he whispered under his breath. "Did you see what she did?" The question hung unanswered in the room, heavy as the ticking of the old clock.

Flynn set the glass down, his decision forming with quiet precision. Enough speculation. Enough ghosts. He needed answers, not shadows.

Tomorrow, he would confront Gwen. He would look his mother in the eye and demand the truth—every word, every motive, every carefully crafted lie. He didn't care how ugly it got. He needed to know whether Pippa had ever truly stopped loving him—or if she had been forced to walk away because of a betrayal closer to home.

He leaned back, the chair creaking under his weight, and closed his eyes briefly. The whiskey burned down his throat, its warmth hollow. Sleep would not come easily tonight. But it didn't matter.

Tomorrow, he would tear the truth from the past—no matter the cost.

Morning light spilled into Pippa's room, casting soft golden streaks across the floor and brushing the edges of her champagne gown draped over the chair. She lay awake, staring at the ceiling, her mind replaying the kiss from the driveway—the sharp heat of his lips, the way his hands had held her so tightly, so possessively. She had wanted, more than anything, to melt into him, to stay in his arms and let the world fall away.

But desire and reason warred fiercely within her. She longed for Flynn with a depth that startled her, a yearning that clawed at her chest. Yet she knew—had always known—that giving in completely could destroy him. He had already been hurt enough, left broken once; she could not be the one to break him again.

Pushing herself upright, she swung her legs over the edge of the bed and took a slow, steadying breath. Her fingers traced the edge of the sheets as though drawing strength from the simple act of touch. Her gaze fell to the suitcase she had left unpacked. She had to leave—she had to return to San Francisco, to the life she had built, the career she loved, and the safe distance she needed to protect both herself and Flynn.

Quietly, carefully, she began to pack, folding gowns and blouses with the precision of someone who had done this a hundred times before, but with her heart far heavier than usual. Her father was out of danger, stable, and content— Henry didn't need her constant presence anymore. But she did. She needed to protect him, protect Flynn, protect herself.

If she stayed, she knew she would confess the truth—the things his mother had told her, everything he would lose, the reason she had left all those years ago. And she couldn't. She would not be the cause of a rift between them, no matter how desperately she ached to reach for him; to tell him she had loved him all along.

Every item she packed was a small step away from the life she longed to have in his arms, a sacrifice sharper than she cared to admit. By the time the first birds began their morning song outside the window, the suitcase was zipped, and Pippa stood, shoulders straight, spine rigid with resolve. Her heart still throbbed with the ache of love withheld, but she forced herself to breathe steadily, to claim control over the only thing she could: her departure. She would leave. For now, it was the only way to keep them both safe.

She paused a moment, running a hand along the polished surface of the dresser, knowing she had to tell Chloe first. Her friend needed to know—they weren't lingering in New York longer than necessary. Then there was her father. Henry would ask questions, and she would have to navigate the delicate truth again, explaining that she had to leave for reasons she couldn't fully disclose, reasons that were tangled with her heart and Flynn's in ways he didn't need to bear.

Taking a deep, steadying breath, Pippa squared her shoulders once more. Today, she would act with the same precision and care she applied to every stitch of fabric she styled—deliberate, measured, and unwavering—even if it meant leaving behind the one man who still made her heart ache in ways she could scarcely name.

The sunlight streamed through the tall windows, gilding the breakfast room in gold, but for Flynn, the morning had dragged on like a lifetime. Hours of pacing, restless and tight-jawed, had left him fraying at the edges. He had tried sitting, tried waiting with forced civility, but his fingers drummed against the polished table, a silent countdown to the moment he could confront her.

It was nearly eleven when the faint echo of footsteps finally stirred him. The door eased open, and Gwen swept in, her usual unhurried elegance intact, posture flawless, face composed as though the world had always waited on her.

"Finally," he muttered under his breath, springing to his feet. The chair scraped sharply against the floor. His storm-blue eyes locked on her, every ounce of impatience and fury radiating in waves.

"Flynn," she greeted, smooth, pleasant, almost indulgent, as if nothing were amiss.

He didn't return the courtesy. No chair was offered, no smile given, no acknowledgment of civility. He stood rigid, his gaze fixed, silence heavy enough to press against the walls.

Then, sharp and lethal as a blade, he broke it.

"Mother," he said, each syllable steel. "Did you tell Pippa that I would be disinherited if we married?"

For a flicker of a moment, Gwen's eyes betrayed her—something sharp, defensive—but the mask snapped back into place. She drew herself up, smoothing an imaginary crease in her sleeve. "Flynn, this is ridiculous. Why would I ever say something so extreme?"

But Flynn didn't flinch. His hand slammed onto the polished table, sending silverware skittering. "Don't lie to me! I saw it in her eyes—the hesitation, the way she carried herself after she left. I know you told her!"

Gwen stiffened, lips pressed thin, but she didn't back down. "You're imagining things. Pippa left for her own reasons—"

"Don't!" he snapped, cutting her off. The storm in his gaze made the room shrink, tighter, suffocating. "I don't care what excuse sounds polite or reasonable. Did you tell her she'd make me lose everything if I married her?"

The carefully constructed mask on Gwen faltered for the first time. Her fingers tightened around her coffee cup, knuckles whitening. She opened her mouth, paused, then admitted, "Yes. I did. But only because—"

"Only because what?" he roared, jaw clenching, veins ticking in his neck. "Because you thought you were protecting me? Or because you didn't want her to be the one?"

Silence fell, thick and suffocating, as years of deceit clawed their way to the surface. Flynn's storm-blue eyes bore into her, coiled with hurt, betrayal, and rage. "Because you thought she wasn't good enough for me?"

Gwen's composure wavered. "Yes," she admitted, voice steady but tinged with defensiveness. "I believed—no, I knew—that she would bring complications. She was talented, yes, but she didn't come from a family of influence, of standing. She… she wasn't suitable."

"Not suitable?" he spat, voice trembling with fury. "You broke her heart! You made her believe she was keeping me from losing everything! Do you even hear yourself?"

"I did what I thought was necessary to protect you," she said, though her voice wavered. "You have to understand, Flynn, I only wanted to shield you from losing what's yours—everything your father and I built."

"Shield me?" he barked. "You lied to her! You made her leave, you kept me in the dark, and for what? Money? Prestige? Was that more important than her heart? Than mine?"

The silence that followed was heavy, oppressive. Gwen's mask flickered, a shadow of regret or defensiveness crossing her features. "I… I thought it was the only way."

"The only way?" he repeated, each word jagged with venom. "You lied to the woman I love. The woman I still love. And for what? Because she wasn't good enough for you? You destroyed something real for a lie that never existed!"

Gwen opened her mouth, then faltered.

"Pack your bags, Mother. You're moving into the penthouse. Oakland Park is no longer your home. If I'm lucky enough to win Pippa back, she's coming here—and you won't stand in her way—or mine—ever again."

The room seemed to shrink under his words. Gwen's carefully maintained authority crumbled, decades of control dissolving under the weight of her son's righteous fury.

"You can't kick me out," she hissed, voice sharp and shaky.

"I can," he said, icy and final. "I inherited everything when Father died—everything. You're lucky I'm not throwing you onto the street. Be gone before I return."

Her lips pressed thin, eyes flicking between fury and disbelief. For the first time, she felt powerless.

Flynn watched her leave, chest constricted, every muscle coiled with lingering fury, yet beneath the storm of anger, a hard pulse of triumph beat steadily. The path to Pippa—his Pippa—suddenly felt sharp, undeniable, and within his grasp. He sank into the chair, shoulders rigid, fingers curling into a white-knuckled fist, each heartbeat hammering in time with the racing of his mind.

The confrontation with Gwen had been brutal, exhausting, a collision of decades of control and deceit—but necessary. Now the air was clear, the way forward stark and unyielding. The next battle—the one that truly mattered—was waiting, and he would face it head-on. No hesitation. No compromise. He would win.

Chapter Sixteen

Flynn left the main house, the grand estate unusually quiet in the late-morning sun. Each step along the gravel driveway felt heavy, the crunch beneath his boots echoing in the stillness. The air was crisp, carrying the faint scent of blooming gardens, yet nothing could lighten the weight pressing on his chest.

Ahead, the cottage grew steadily closer, each step heavier than the last, matching the tight, anxious rhythm of his heart. Anticipation and frustration twisted together inside him, a coil of need and anger he could no longer ignore.

At the small porch, he paused, hand hovering over the door handle. The morning's quiet pressed in, the distant chirp of birds failing to soften the ache inside him. With a sharp inhale, he rapped on the door.

It opened almost immediately, and Henry appeared, his expression falling the instant he saw Flynn. "Flynn…"

"I need to see Pippa," Flynn said, his voice low, tight with urgency.

Henry shook his head, hands tightening at his sides. "You can't, Flynn. She's… gone." His tone was gentle, laden with sorrow.

"Gone?" Flynn's storm-blue eyes narrowed, disbelief sharpening every line of his face. "Where did she go?"

Henry's gaze dropped to the floor, lingering for a long, heavy moment. "Back… to San Francisco. She left early this morning. Packed quietly… didn't want to wake anyone. She thought it was best."

Flynn's chest constricted, a harsh, ragged ache spreading through him. He stepped closer, voice hardening. "Best? Best for whom? She's running again, Henry. Running from me… from everything we should have had. I have to find her."

Henry pressed a hand to his face, a weary sigh escaping before he lifted his eyes to meet Flynn's stormy gaze. "Why is she running? She wouldn't tell me… just like the first time she vanished. I thought maybe… maybe she'd found a reason to stay this time."

Frustration and longing collided in Flynn like crashing waves. He ran a hand through his hair, chest tightening with every heartbeat. "She's leaving because of my mother's lies," he said, voice low but sharp, edged with both anger and desperation. "I can't explain it all right now, Henry. Not here, not like this."

Henry's shoulders slumped, resignation heavy in his posture. "Do you know what time her flight is?"

"One-thirty," Henry replied quietly, the sorrow in his voice nearly audible.

Flynn's eyes snapped to his watch. His pulse surged. The world narrowed to a single point—the chance to catch her, to stop her from disappearing again. "I can make it if I leave now," he muttered, determination hardening every line of his face. He glanced back at Henry, urgency blazing in his gaze. "I'll bring her back, Henry. I promise you that."

Before Henry could respond, Flynn bolted up the driveway, gravel crunching sharply beneath his boots. His mind raced—flight times, traffic, every possible route—but all of it shrank beneath the singular, searing thought of Pippa. He couldn't let her go. Not again. Not after everything.

The morning sun glinted off the manicured lawns as he sprinted toward his car, adrenaline and hope coiling tight in his chest. Every second counted; every mile mattered. The world beyond the driveway blurred. There was only one thing that mattered: finding Pippa and bringing her home.

Flynn slid into the sleek black SUV, the engine roaring to life beneath him. Fingers gripped the wheel, knuckles white, as the car surged down the driveway and onto the winding road. Each red light felt like a cruel reminder that time was slipping through his fingers.

His mind raced faster than the traffic ahead—her last smile, the way her eyes had lingered on him that night, the heat of their kiss on the driveway. He could still feel it, still taste it, and it fuelled the urgency driving him forward.

"San Francisco flight… one-thirty. One-thirty," he muttered under his breath, calculating every mile, every minute. He ignored the horn blaring behind him, the blur of city streets, the ache tightening in his chest. Nothing existed except reaching her in time.

At every intersection, Flynn imagined her running toward the gate—suitcase in hand, glancing over her shoulder, unaware he was coming. Each vision struck like a blade of cold fear. What if he didn't get there in time? What if she left before he could explain—before she could see the truth?

The SUV cut through traffic with precision, his eyes flicking between the road and the clock on the dashboard. The city stretched endlessly before him, every red light and slow-moving car a torment designed to test him. But he refused to relent.

Finally, the airport came into view—sprawling, impersonal, indifferent. Flynn swung into a parking space, barely acknowledging the valet, and bolted toward the terminal. His heart hammered, breath ragged, as he pushed through the tide of travellers and luggage carts, scanning the glowing departure screens.

There. Her flight. Gate thirty-two. One-thirty, just as Henry had said.

He prayed she hadn't checked in yet.

Desperation and adrenaline surged through him, mingling with the raw ache clawing at his chest. He couldn't be too late—not again.

And in that moment, all the anger, all the heartbreak, melted into a single, blinding clarity: he couldn't lose her. Not now. Not ever.

Flynn pushed forward, each step a vow, each heartbeat a promise. He would reach her. He would stop her. And this time, he wouldn't let anything—or anyone—come between them.

His long strides carried him through the terminal, the blur of travellers fading from his awareness. Gate thirty-two loomed ahead, the announcement of final boarding echoing overhead.

And there she was—Pippa. Chloe stood at her side, both poised yet tense, Pippa's eyes flicking repeatedly to the departure board as if memorising every detail, already halfway gone.

Flynn's chest tightened, years of longing and regret winding tighter with every step.

"Pippa," he called, his voice low but cutting through the hum of the terminal like a blade.

She froze. Her shoulders stiffened, and then she turned—slowly, carefully. For a heartbeat, neither of them moved. Time fractured around them—the chatter, the rolling luggage, the announcements—all dissolving beneath the weight of everything left unsaid.

"Flynn…" Her voice was soft, startled, threaded with a vulnerability he hadn't heard in years.

"You can't leave," he said, closing the distance between them in a few long strides, his storm-blue eyes locking on hers. "Not like this. Not without knowing the truth. Pipp… please, listen to me."

Her hand tightened around the handle of her carry-on, knuckles white, as if it were the only thing keeping her from falling apart. "Flynn… you don't understand. I can't stay. I won't—"

Then Chloe's voice cut through the tension—firm, quiet, unyielding. "Pippa, you need to listen to him."

Pippa turned to her, sorrow pooling in her eyes. "I can't," she whispered. "You know I can't."

Chloe stepped closer, slipping the carry-on from Pippa's grasp with quiet authority. "You have to," she said softly, then moved a few steps away to the chairs—close enough to watch, far enough to give them space.

"She's right, Pipp," Flynn said, his voice low, taut with urgency and barely leashed emotion. "You need to know… my mother lied."

Pippa blinked, confusion flickering in her eyes. "What do you mean?"

Flynn's jaw tightened, every muscle coiled with restrained fury. "She told you things that weren't true. Lies about what would happen if we were together— about me losing everything, about you not being good enough. None of it was real."

Disbelief rippled across Pippa's face. "That… that's not possible. She wouldn't—"

"Wouldn't lie?" Flynn's voice cracked, pain cutting through the steady hum of the terminal. "She did. She lied to keep us apart, to control my life… our lives. I—" His storm-blue gaze locked on hers, raw and unrelenting. "I couldn't believe it when I realised what she had done. But I know better now. And I can't let you leave without knowing the truth."

The air between them thickened. The sound of the airport dimmed to a low hum, the world narrowing until there was only him—his voice, his eyes, the truth unraveling between them. Pippa's breath caught as the reality of his words settled deep.

She searched his face, desperate for something solid, something real. In his gaze she found it—unwavering, consuming, the same fire she'd tried to bury for years. "Flynn… I—" Her voice broke.

"Don't run, Pipp," he murmured, stepping closer, the heat of him wrapping around her like a tide. "Not now. Not again. I won't let you."

Her name on his lips was both plea and command. "Flynn…"

"Stop pretending you don't care." His words sliced through the noise, fierce and certain. "I know you do. I've known it since the first day I saw you. You left because of lies—her lies. But you never stopped loving me. I can feel it."

Her throat constricted, the ache rising too fast to fight. "Flynn…" she whispered, but her voice fractured, betraying her.

"No," he said sharply, stepping closer until there was barely an inch of air between them. "You don't get to walk away this time. You made me believe you didn't care. But now I know the truth—and I'm not letting you go. Not again."

His hands hovered near her arms, trembling with restraint. The tension between them was unbearable—charged, magnetic.

"I never wanted to hurt you," she whispered, tears threatening. "But if I stayed, I would have. I can't—" Her voice wavered, heavy with the truth she'd carried alone. "I couldn't be the reason you lose everything."

His breath hitched, his voice breaking under the weight of emotion. "Lose everything? The only thing I ever lost was you." His eyes burned into hers, fierce and unflinching. "And I'm not losing you again."

The loudspeaker chimed: Final call for Flight 228 to San Francisco, Gate 32.

The sound jolted them both. Pippa turned toward the gate, where passengers were boarding, then back to Flynn—his eyes storm-dark, begging, commanding, pleading all at once.

She stood frozen—caught between flight and surrender.

Another announcement crackled overhead, sharp and final. Her hands curled helplessly at her sides. Chloe watched silently from the seats, her expression unreadable, their bags resting at her feet.

Pippa took a half-step back, the instinct to flee rising again—but Flynn moved first. Two strides, and he was there, his hand closing around her arm, firm but gentle, grounding her in place.

"Flynn—"

"No," he said roughly, his voice a low growl edged with desperation. "You're not walking away from me again." His storm-blue gaze locked with hers, fierce and unwavering. "You can get on that plane—but not without knowing what you're leaving behind."

Before she could protest, before her defences could rebuild, his hand slid to her waist and he pulled her hard against him, his mouth crashing onto hers.

The kiss was not soft. It was a collision of years—of longing, anger, heartbreak, and hunger. His lips claimed hers with fierce urgency, pouring every sleepless night and every unspoken regret into that searing contact.

For a single heartbeat, she resisted—her palms pressed to his chest, breath trapped in her throat. But then something inside her broke. The wall she'd built for years crumbled beneath the sheer force of him. With a trembling gasp, she yielded, melting against him, her lips parting beneath his, her fingers fisting in his shirt like she could anchor herself to him.

The terminal disappeared. The chatter, the footsteps, the metallic voice over the PA—all gone. There was only the taste of him—warm, intoxicating, achingly familiar. His hand splayed across her back, drawing her closer, deeper. Her pulse thundered, each beat echoing his. Every breath was shared, stolen, given back.

When she tore her lips from his, gasping for air, her forehead rested against his, their breaths mingling, hearts hammering. "Flynn... stop," she whispered, but her trembling voice betrayed the truth.

"Tell me you don't love me," he rasped, his breath rough against her skin. "Say it, and I'll let you go. But if you can't—then you're not getting on that plane."

Tears welled in her eyes. A few feet away, Chloe sat quietly, hands clasped around the luggage, her expression calm but knowing. The gate was still open. The choice was still hers.

Chloe's voice carried softly but firmly, the gentle push that broke the silence. "Tell him the truth, Pipp."

Pippa's gaze flicked to Chloe, then back to Flynn. His eyes held hers, desperate, relentless. Her throat constricted; her voice trembled. "I can't..." She swallowed hard, her tears falling freely now. "I can't tell you I don't love you."

The words hung between them like a living thing. Flynn froze, breath catching, as the truth tore through the air. Then, with a ragged sound—half sob, half relief—he cupped her face and kissed her again.

This kiss was different. Still fierce, but slower—reverent. Every movement spoke of forgiveness, of love reclaimed after too long lost. She clung to him, her tears mingling with his breath, her heart breaking open in his arms.

When at last he drew back, their foreheads rested together, both trembling, both breathing each other in.

His voice was hoarse, raw with emotion. "You're coming home with me, Pipp. No more lies. No more running. You're mine—and I'm yours. Always."

Her lips quivered, caught between disbelief and fragile hope. "I... I can't, Flynn. Your mother—"

"Is gone," he interrupted, firm but gentle. "She's moving into the penthouse. The moment I learned what she did, I made sure she'd never stand between us again. You belong at Oakland Park. With me."

Her eyes widened, surprise softening into something deeper. "Are you sure that's what you want?"

He cupped her face again, his thumbs tracing her cheekbones with aching tenderness. "Pippa Rockwell," he breathed, his voice breaking, "I have loved you every single day since the moment I met you. Even when you left, even when it hurt to breathe. You're everything I've ever wanted. Don't run from us anymore."

Her chest trembled, tears shimmering in her eyes, and at last, she gave in—to truth, to love, to him. "I love you too, Flynn," she whispered, her words unguarded, true.

He kissed her once more—soft, consuming, and full of promise. Every touch spoke of forgiveness, of homecoming, of everything they had both lost and finally found again.

Around them, the terminal faded to nothing. There was only them. And their future.

Chapter Seventeen

Chloe exhaled softly, a smile tugging at the corners of her lips. "Thank goodness you've come to your senses," she murmured, relief clear in her voice.

Pippa returned a small, grateful smile and gave Chloe a quick hug. "Alright… you were right," she whispered. "Oh—our luggage is on its way to San Francisco."

Chloe laughed lightly. "Don't worry. I'll make sure it gets back to you safely."

Flynn reached for Pippa's carry-on, his other hand finding hers, fingers intertwining naturally, his touch grounding her. "Ready?" he asked, his storm-blue eyes both soft and determined.

Pippa nodded, leaning slightly into him as they walked toward the exit. Chloe trailed just a step behind, carry-on in hand, a small, knowing smile playing on her lips.

Sunlight streamed through the terminal windows, catching the edges of the bustling morning crowd, but Pippa barely noticed. Their focus was on each other and the sleek black SUV waiting outside, its polished surface gleaming in the sun. Flynn opened the front door and offered Pippa his hand, guiding her inside, while Chloe climbed into the back with ease.

Sliding into the driver's seat, Flynn murmured, low and private, "Ready to go home?"

Pippa met his gaze, heart still racing, and whispered, "Yes."

He leaned over, brushing his lips softly against hers in a lingering, tender kiss before she settled into the seat. Chloe gave them a teasing wink as she closed the door behind her. The engine purred to life, and the SUV glided smoothly away, carrying Pippa back to the life—and the man—she had never truly stopped loving.

The ride back to Oakland Park felt both endless and fleeting. Pippa sat close to Flynn, her hand still threaded with his, her heart pounding with every passing mile. Chloe filled the silence now and then with light comments, but even she seemed to sense that words weren't enough for what this moment meant.

As the SUV curved up the familiar drive, the grand façade of Oakland Park came into view, its stone walls bathed in golden afternoon light. Pippa's chest tightened. It had once felt like a fortress keeping her out—now, it felt like a threshold she was about to cross with Flynn by her side.

The car slowed near the cottage. Flynn parked smoothly, then rounded to Pippa's side, opening the door with quiet care. His hand steadied her as she stepped out, the gravel crunching beneath her heels.

The cottage door opened almost at once. Henry stood there, his frame filling the doorway. The moment his eyes landed on Pippa, his face broke into a mix of shock and relief.

"Pippa!" His voice was thick, rough with emotion. He stepped out, arms outstretched, and she rushed into them, the familiar scent and warmth of her father anchoring her in a way nothing else could.

"Oh, Dad," she whispered, clinging to him. "I'm here. I'm not going anywhere."

Henry pulled back, cupping her face in his calloused hands. "Thank God. I thought I'd lost you again." His gaze flicked over her shoulder to Flynn, softening, as though he suddenly understood more than Pippa had managed to say. "You brought her back."

Flynn inclined his head, his voice steady. "I intend to keep her here, Henry. Where she belongs."

Henry's eyes glistened, his voice breaking with quiet gratitude. "Then you've done the one thing I prayed for every day she was gone."

Chloe stepped forward, smiling warmly, and Henry pulled her into a quick hug as well, before turning back to his daughter, refusing to let go of her hand. Relief radiated from him, filling the little cottage with a warmth Pippa hadn't felt in years.

Henry ushered them all inside, unwilling to let Pippa's hand slip from his for even a moment. The cottage smelled faintly of coffee and the lavender soap he always kept by the sink, a homely comfort that wrapped around her like a blanket. They settled at the small wooden table, Chloe perched happily beside her grandfather while Pippa sat close to him, their fingers still entwined.

Henry poured coffee with slightly trembling hands, setting a mug in front of his daughter before finally taking his seat. His eyes never strayed far from her face, as if to reassure himself she was truly there. "I don't need to know everything right now," he said gently, his voice still raw, "but I do need to know this— you're safe? You're staying?"

Pippa's throat tightened, but before she could speak, Flynn leaned forward, his steady hand covering hers. "She's safe. And yes, Henry—she's staying." His gaze flicked to Pippa, warm and unwavering. "If she'll have me, she's staying with me. Where she belongs."

Henry let out a long breath, shoulders sagging as if years of worry had finally begun to lift. He reached across and gave Flynn a slow nod. "Then maybe this family can start to heal."

For a while, they sipped their coffee and spoke of smaller things—the way Oakland Park looked in the autumn light. Laughter slipped in here and there, tentative but real, until the air in the cottage felt lighter than it had in years.

At last, Flynn pushed back his chair, his gaze locking on Pippa's. "We need to talk," he said softly, but the quiet weight in his voice promised no more running, no more hiding. He rose and extended his hand, and though her heart pounded, she took it without hesitation.

Together, they crossed the drive toward the main house. The grand oak doors swung open before they reached them, and Mr. Harcourt, ever the image of quiet dignity, stood waiting.

"Mr. Oakland," the butler said with a respectful dip of his head. "I thought you should know—your mother has departed. She informed me she'll be living at the penthouse for the foreseeable future."

A breath Flynn hadn't realised he was holding escaped, the tension in his chest finally easing. "Thank you, Harcourt. That means more than you know."

Then the butler's gaze shifted. His composure softened when it landed on Pippa. For a heartbeat, his eyes glistened, his voice warming in a way she hadn't heard in years. "Miss Rockwell," he said quietly, "welcome home."

The words struck deep, stirring every buried memory, every thread of longing and love. Standing there with Flynn's hand entwined with hers, the halls of Oakland Park no longer felt cold or distant. For the first time, they truly felt like hers.

Flynn led her into the smaller drawing room off the main hall—the one bathed in afternoon light streaming through tall windows, the air rich with the scent of polished oak and old books. He closed the door behind them, the soft click sounding final, a seal between them and the rest of the world.

For a long moment, neither spoke. The silence wasn't empty; it pulsed with everything unsaid—years of loss, of love withheld. Pippa's gaze drifted over the familiar room: the shelves lined with books, the stone hearth, the worn rug beneath their feet. Each detail whispered of the life she had once dreamed of here. A life she had walked away from. Her arms folded tightly across her chest, as though she could hold herself together before she came apart.

Flynn stepped closer, his movements deliberate, his presence impossible to ignore. His storm-blue eyes were fixed on her, unwavering. "Pippa," he said at last, his voice low, roughened by restraint. "I need you to listen—to all of it."

Her eyes met his, uncertainty flickering, though somewhere beneath it, hope began to stir.

"I thought I'd lost you forever," he continued, his hands curling into fists at his sides, as though it took everything not to reach for her. "And when I found out why—what my mother had done—it broke something inside me. I let you go once because I believed you didn't love me. I won't make that mistake again. Not now. Not ever."

Her breath hitched, tears welling in her eyes. "Flynn… I only left because I thought I was protecting you. I thought if I told you what she said, you would have chosen me and lost everything else. I couldn't let that happen—not when you had so much to lose."

He closed the distance between them, his hands finding her shoulders—firm, grounding, unshakable. "You were everything, Pipp. Do you understand? Everything. Oakland Park, the money, the name—none of it mattered compared to you. The only thing I truly lost was you, and it nearly destroyed me."

Her lips trembled, her heart racing beneath the weight of his words. "I—I couldn't be the reason you lost everything."

"My mother lied, Pipp." His voice cut through hers—sharp, unrelenting, certain. "I could have been with anyone I chose. I never would've lost a thing. And even if I had—I'd have given it all up for you. Gladly. Because you are enough. You always were. You always will be." His gaze burned into hers, every word a vow. "The lies, the years, the distance—they don't change what I feel. They don't change who you are to me."

His hand lifted, cupping her cheek. His thumb brushed away a tear before it could fall. When he spoke again, his voice softened, raw and vulnerable in a way she had never heard before. "I love you, Pippa Rockwell. I loved you from the moment I saw you. I loved you through every night you were gone. And I'll love you until my last breath. But I can't do this without you anymore. I need you—here, at Oakland Park, at my side. Always."

Her knees weakened under the weight of his words. She leaned into his touch, the dam inside her finally shattering. "I can't believe it was all a lie," she whispered, her voice shaking.

"I know," he said quietly, his hand still steady on her cheek. "But it was. My mother lied to both of us."

Relief crashed through her like a breaking wave, leaving her trembling. "Flynn… I never stopped loving you. Not for a single day. I just—" Her voice broke, a sob slipping free. "I was so afraid."

That was all it took for him to draw her into his arms. He held her fiercely, as though reclaiming something that had always been his. His lips pressed to her hair, his voice low and sure, carrying the weight of a vow renewed.

"No more fear, Pipp. No more running. You're home. With me."

And for the first time in years, she let herself believe it.

Flynn's hands remained firm at her waist as he led her from the drawing room, their footsteps soft against the polished floors of Oakland Park. Every hallway they passed felt charged, every familiar painting and gleaming fixture a silent witness to their long-delayed reunion. Pippa stayed close, her fingers brushing his as if the smallest touch could steady the whirlwind inside her.

When they reached the grand staircase, Flynn paused, his storm-blue eyes meeting hers. "Upstairs," he murmured, his tone reverent, almost hushed. "I need to be with you."

She nodded, her chest tightening with anticipation, and let him guide her upward. The staircase—once a symbol of polite distance and impossible dreams—now felt like a bridge back to everything they had lost... and everything they were about to reclaim. As they ascended, his hand brushed hers again, their fingers intertwining naturally, grounding her in the certainty of his presence.

At the top, he stopped before the master suite, giving her a moment to steady herself. "This is ours," he said quietly, pressing his hand to the door. "Everything from now on starts here—together."

Pippa swallowed hard, emotion rising thick in her throat, and stepped inside. The room smelled faintly of cedar and sunlight, familiar yet changed by the gravity of what it now meant. She let her gaze drift—across the bed, the tall windows framing the rolling grounds below, the soft, golden light spilling across the floor. This place, once a dream, now felt achingly real.

Flynn moved behind her, his hands settling around her waist. He leaned down, pressing soft, reverent kisses along the curve of her neck, whispering against her skin, "No more running, Pipp. No more hiding. You're mine. Only mine. And I'm yours."

She turned in his arms, her hands sliding up around his neck, her face tilting toward his. Their lips met in a slow, lingering kiss—a promise, a release, and a beginning all at once. Every ache, every lonely night, every unspoken word poured into that single connection. She clung to him as fiercely as he held her, as though touch alone could erase the years they had lost.

When they finally broke apart, Flynn rested his forehead against hers, breath mingling with hers in the hush of the room. "I've waited too long," he murmured, his voice thick with need and truth. "Every day without you has been a mistake I'll never make again."

Tears spilled freely down Pippa's cheeks. "I love you, Flynn. I never stopped," she whispered, her voice trembling yet fierce with honesty.

He kissed her again—deeper this time, no hesitation, no restraint—claiming her with the kind of reverence that spoke of both love and forgiveness. His hands framed her face, his thumbs brushing away her tears before they could fall.

When he pulled back, his forehead rested against hers once more, his voice husky and unsteady. "I want to make love to you," he breathed, the words sacred in their simplicity.

Her breath caught, eyes glistening as she met his gaze. "I want that too," she murmured, the words trembling from her lips like a vow.

But then he drew back slightly, his expression shifting—still full of longing but now touched with something deeper. "But first..." he said softly, "I have to ask you something."

She blinked, startled by the sudden change in his tone. His hands slipped from her waist as he turned, opening the drawer of the bedside table with quiet care. From within, he drew out a small velvet box—its corners worn, the fabric faded by time and waiting.

Turning back to her, Flynn sank to one knee beside the bed, his storm-blue eyes shimmering with vulnerability she had never seen before. His thumb brushed over the box before he opened it, revealing a single, gleaming ring.

"I bought this," he said, his voice rough with memory, "a week before you left. I've kept it every day since—waiting, hoping for another chance to give it to you."

He drew a steady breath, his gaze never wavering. "Pippa Rockwell," he said, his voice a blend of reverence and promise, "would you do me the honour of being my wife?"

Pippa's breath caught as her eyes fell on the ring. The emerald at its centre was extraordinary—deep, vibrant, alive, catching the sunlight like liquid fire. Around it, a halo of flawless diamonds blazed with brilliance, each facet reflecting the chandelier's soft shimmer, each perfect cut a testament to Flynn's exacting taste and devotion. The platinum band, engraved with delicate filigree, spoke of wealth, power, and timeless sophistication. But it was the emerald— alive with green fire—that stole her attention, and her heart.

It wasn't merely a ring. It was a declaration—a promise of unwavering love, a tangible reminder that he had carried her in his heart through every lonely night, every ache of longing. She felt its weight in her hand and in her chest—

the enormity of what it meant, the luxury of a man who could give her the world but chose instead to give her only himself.

Tears pricked at her eyes as she whispered, voice trembling but sure, "Yes… yes, Flynn. God… yes."

A slow, victorious smile curved his lips as he slid the ring onto her finger. The emerald caught the light and flared brilliantly, echoing the joy that surged between them. Flynn rose, pulling her into his arms, and their lips met in a kiss that was no longer tentative or restrained—it was celebration, possession, and promise all at once.

Pippa rested her head against his chest, the warmth of him seeping through her, her heartbeat syncing to his.

"You're mine," he murmured against her hair.

"And you're mine," she breathed, clutching his shirt as though holding him close could reclaim all the lost years.

The world beyond their sanctuary slipped away. Only they remained—the soft gleam of the emerald on her hand, the steady rhythm of two hearts that had finally found their way home.

Sunlight filtered through the curtains, painting the room in gold, but neither noticed. All that existed was the heat between them, the pull of bodies long denied, and the quiet, reverent urgency of rediscovered love. Flynn's hands traced the curve of her back, drawing her closer, feeling the rise and fall of her breath. Pippa's fingers tangled in his hair, tugging him down to her, as if anchoring herself in this fragile, perfect moment. Every kiss was deliberate, tasting, memorising—a wordless apology for all the years apart.

"I've wanted this… I've wanted you," Flynn murmured against her lips, his voice rough with need and tenderness.

"And I've waited… for you," Pippa whispered, pressing her face into his neck, inhaling the scent that had haunted her dreams.

With careful, aching gentleness that contrasted with the fire beneath it, Flynn guided her toward the bed. Their bodies moved as though rediscovering a familiar rhythm, every brush of skin igniting the quiet storm they'd both carried for so long. Pippa arched instinctively to meet him, surrendering at last to the longing she had spent years trying to suppress.

Clothes fell away in slow, deliberate movements—a ritual of trust, of return. Flynn paused often, cupping her face, capturing her lips, memorising her gaze— making certain she knew this wasn't a fleeting passion but the culmination of everything between them, raw and enduring.

When they finally came together, it was both tender and fierce—a communion of hearts and bodies, a symphony of whispered names, shared breaths, and soft, gasping laughter. Pippa clung to him, and he to her, each motion a vow, each sigh a promise reclaimed.

Time slipped away unnoticed. Every kiss, every caress, every shiver of delight spoke of a love reforged in fire and forgiveness. And when at last they lay tangled together, skin to skin, hearts steadying in the quiet aftermath, Flynn pressed a lingering kiss to her temple.

"You're mine," he murmured, voice husky with emotion, "and I'm yours. Always."

Pippa smiled sleepily, her fingers tracing the line of his jaw. "I never stopped loving you," she whispered.

"Never," he agreed softly, holding her closer, letting the silence say what words could not.

Outside, the world went on—but within their room, time bent around them, yielding to the only truth that mattered: they had found their way back, and for the first time in years, everything was exactly as it should be.

Epilogue

Two Years Later…

The Children's Hope Foundation Gala shimmered with laughter, candlelight, and the soft clink of champagne flutes. The dinner had been served, the speeches applauded, and now the orchestra played a lilting waltz that carried effortlessly across the ballroom.

Flynn stood near the edge of the dance floor, watching his wife glide across the polished parquet in the arms of one of the Foundation's major donors.

Pippa looked breathtaking. Her gown—deep crimson silk that hugged her curves before spilling into a cascade of satin folds—caught the light like living fire. The colour made her skin glow, her eyes sparkle, and her dark hair, swept into an elegant chignon, shimmer with warm chestnut undertones. A delicate diamond pendant rested at her throat, the emerald engagement ring gleaming as she moved. She looked poised, radiant, and almost as heartbreakingly beautiful as she had on their wedding day.

That day had been everything he'd wanted it to be—grand, joyful, unforgettable. Pippa had insisted a simple registry ceremony would have been enough, but Flynn had refused. After everything they had endured, he wanted the world to know they belonged to each other, that nothing and no one would ever come between them again.

"Hello, Flynn."

He turned at the familiar voice. His mother stood beside him, composed as ever, her silver hair swept elegantly back, her gown understated but flawless.

"Mother," he said evenly.

It had been Pippa who urged him to mend things with her, to let go of old bitterness for the sake of peace. And though Flynn had tried—had even accepted Gwen's tentative gestures of reconciliation—he doubted he would ever trust her entirely. Pippa had been gracious, warm, always polite, but Flynn's watchfulness where his mother was concerned had never truly waned.

"Pippa looks radiant tonight," Gwen said quietly. For once, there was no edge in her tone—only something that might have been sincerity.

"She always is," he replied, glancing toward the dance floor. "But thank you."

"I'm glad you're happy," Gwen said after a pause. "I can see she makes you happy."

"She does." His gaze softened as he watched Pippa laugh at something her dance partner said, her joy lighting up the room. "More than I ever thought possible."

They spoke a few moments longer—pleasant, careful conversation. And when the music began to fade, Flynn offered his mother a polite nod and excused himself.

He crossed the room just as the orchestra shifted into a slower melody. The donor released Pippa's hand with a smile, and before she could turn, Flynn stepped forward, his hand already outstretched.

"May I?" he asked, his voice low, familiar, and filled with warmth.

Her smile when she saw him could have stopped time. "Always," she said.

He drew her into his arms, their bodies fitting together as naturally as breath. The rest of the world blurred—the glittering chandeliers, the swirl of gowns and tuxedos—until it was only them, moving in perfect rhythm.

Flynn bent his head, his lips brushing her ear. "You're still the most beautiful woman in any room."

Pippa's laugh was soft, her eyes bright with affection. "You're biased, Mr. Oakland."

"Completely," he murmured, his hand settling at the small of her back. "And I intend to stay that way for the rest of my life."

She tilted her head up, meeting his gaze. "Then it's a good thing, Mr. Oakland, that I happen to love you exactly as you are."

He smiled, slow and certain. "And I love you, Mrs. Oakland. Always."

As the music swelled and the crowd around them faded into soft motion, Flynn lowered his head and kissed her—lightly, reverently, as if sealing a promise that needed no words. The orchestra played on, the chandelier light shimmered, and somewhere nearby, Gwen watched them with quiet reflection.

Flynn didn't see anyone else. He saw only Pippa—the woman who had been his past, his salvation, and now, his forever.

Holding her close beneath the golden lights of the gala, he felt a quiet certainty. For all the years lost, they had found everything that truly mattered.

The night slowly drew to a close. In the limousine heading back to Oakland Park, Pippa rested her head against Flynn's shoulder, the soft hum of the engine a gentle rhythm beneath their quiet contentment.

"When is your father coming back from his cruise?" Flynn asked softly, his voice low, almost reluctant to disturb the fragile peace.

She lifted her head, eyes shining with warmth, a smile lighting her face. "Next Monday. He said he's having a wonderful time. I'm so glad he met Susan—she's lovely."

"Do you think he'll pop the question?" Flynn's grin softened as he watched the sparkle in her eyes.

"I wouldn't be surprised if they're engaged by the time they return. Chloe is convinced it will happen on the cruise."

"Hmm. I think she might be right," Flynn chuckled, a soft warmth in his voice. "That's how David proposed to her—on their holiday."

"Yes, he did, didn't he?" she murmured, leaning back against him, letting the comfort of his presence settle around her.

When they arrived home, the estate lay bathed in gentle shadows, the glow from the windows reflecting softly on the polished floors. In their bedroom, Pippa stood before the mirror, serene and radiant in a silk negligee, brushing her hair with calm grace. The reflection of her beauty stole his breath.

Flynn moved behind her, sliding his arms around her waist, pulling her flush against him. "Do you know how beautiful you are?" he whispered, lips brushing the curve of her temple.

She met his gaze in the mirror, eyes soft, luminous. "You make me feel beautiful," she replied, her voice tender and full of trust.

She laid the brush down, guiding his hands gently over her flat stomach, and then looked up at him through the mirror, holding his eyes with steady warmth.

He frowned, following her gaze, and then realisation dawned. A slow smile spread across his face, light and incredulous.

"Pipp...?" he breathed, voice barely audible, reverent in the stillness of the room.

She returned his gaze, radiant and secretive, a smile that held both joy and wonder. Then, softly, he asked, awed, "Are you...?"

She nodded, quiet and shy, sending a jolt of disbelief and joy through him.

Flynn's storm-blue eyes widened, and a laugh, half-disbelief, half-pure delight, escaped him. "You mean…"

"Yes," she whispered, a soft blush rising, her hands instinctively resting over his on her stomach, grounding the reality of it. "We're… we're going to have a baby."

The words hung between them, fragile yet electrifying. For a heartbeat, he could do nothing but stare, mind spinning with the magnitude of the revelation. Then he turned her in his arms, cupping her face, his thumbs brushing along her cheekbones, anchoring her gaze.

"This… this is real?" he murmured, voice thick with awe and disbelief, mixed with something deeper, something he had buried for years.

"It's real," she said softly, eyes shimmering with tears that mirrored his own. "The doctor confirmed it this morning."

He pulled her into a fierce embrace, pressing his lips to her temple, laughter mingling with quiet sobs of joy. "I can't believe it… a baby… our family," he whispered, as if speaking it aloud made it tangible, more alive.

She rested her head against his shoulder, trembling with relief and wonder. "I'm so happy," she murmured, a small, radiant smile breaking through her tears.

Flynn pressed gentle kisses to the crown of her head, then to her temple, each touch a silent vow. "You've made me happier than I ever thought possible. You're going to be an incredible mother. You already are the best wife a man could dream of. I'm the luckiest man alive."

"I'm the lucky one," she replied, lifting her face to meet his. "You've given me everything I could ever want."

"You deserve more than I could ever give," he said softly, voice full of tenderness. "I'm just grateful you love me."

"I do. I love you more than anything."

Her fingers threaded into his hair, holding him as tightly as he held her, and in that quiet, golden-lit room, they let themselves dream—of laughter, little footsteps, their excitement, and the life they would build together. Nothing could touch them; nothing could shake them. This was their moment, their family, the beginning of everything.

The End

Before You Go…

If you fell for these characters and want more love stories filled with emotion, passion, and second chances, my newsletter is where I share them first.

You'll receive:

💕 Early access to new releases

💕 Exclusive reader-only content and extras

👉 **Join my reader list here:** https://alisonreidauthor.com

I'd love to welcome you.

Alison Reid

Thank you for reading Lies & Hearts!

If you enjoyed this collection of emotionally charged romances, keep an eye out for more upcoming romance collections by Alison Reid, including:

Accidental Heirs - *A Billionaire Legacy Romance Collection*

Alpha Kings - *A Billionaire Alpha Male Romance Collection*

Cautious Hearts - *A Trust-After-Heartbreak Romance Collection*

Dark & Dangerous - *Brooding Heroes Romance Collection*

Final Surrender - *Alpha Heroes Yielding to Love Collection*

Forbidden Hearts - *A Forbidden Love Romance Collection*

Forever Mine - *A Longing-for-Love Romance Collection*

Guarded Hearts - *A Surrender to Love Romance Collection*

Hearts & Secrets - *Small Town Romance Collection*

Hearts in Peril - *A Suspenseful Romance Collection*

Hidden Truths - *A Secret Identity Romance Collection*

Love After Regret - *A Second-Chance Redemption Romance Collection*

Misjudged Hearts - *A Love After Judgement Romance Collection*

Torn Between Hearts - *A Love Triangle Romance Collection*

All of Alison Reid's books feature standalone stories, swoon-worthy heroes, and guaranteed happily-ever-afters.

Books by Alison Reid

A Billionaire for Christmas

A Heart in Florence

After The Storm

Always You

Before I Fell

Before the Thaw

Beneath the Lies

Billionaire Bodyguard

Billionaire Rancher

Blueprints of the Heart

Branlow

Collide

Echoes of Deception

Falling for the Billionaire

Forever Yours

Heart of the Outback

Hearts on the Line

Hidden Gem

Kept Promises

Mended Hearts

Mistaken Hearts

New Year's Eve Kiss

Quiet Danger

Reckless Hearts

Find all my books on Amazon:

https://www.amazon.com/author/alisonreid1970

About the Author

Alison Reid writes contemporary and small-town romance filled with heart, passion, and second-chance love stories. Her novels feature strong heroines, irresistible heroes, and the happily-ever-afters readers adore.

Before turning her love of storytelling into a publishing career, Alison spent thirty-five years working as an engineer—proof that happily-ever-afters can be built as carefully as any blueprint. She began writing as a hobby during the COVID lockdowns and quickly discovered a passion she couldn't ignore.

Alison is happily married, has two grown children, and shares her home with two beautiful dogs who are convinced they deserve to be her main characters. When she's not writing, she enjoys reading, spending time with her family, and imagining new love stories. She hopes her books give readers a few hours of escape, joy, and swoon-worthy romance they won't soon forget.